THREE-ACT SPECIAL

3 Complete Mystery
Novels
in
One Volume

NGAIO MARSH

Three-Act Special

3 COMPLETE MYSTERY NOVELS

A WREATH FOR RIVERA
SPINSTERS IN JEOPARDY
NIGHT AT THE VULCAN

Little, Brown and Company
Boston   **Toronto**

A WREATH FOR RIVERA

SPINSTERS IN JEOPARDY

NIGHT AT THE VULCAN

CONTENTS

A
WREATH
FOR
RIVERA

For Bet
Who asked for it and
now gets it
with my love

Contents

Cast of Characters

LORD PASTERN AND BAGOTT
LADY PASTERN AND BAGOTT
FÉLICITÉ DE SUZE, her daughter
THE HONOURABLE EDWARD MANX, Lord Pastern's second cousin
CARLISLE WAYNE, Lord Pastern's niece
MISS HENDERSON, companion-secretary to Lady Pastern
SPENCE ⎫
MISS PARKER ⎪
WILLIAM ⎪
MARY ⎬ domestic staff at Duke's Gate
MYRTLE ⎪
HORTENSE ⎭
BREEZY BELLAIRS ⎫
HAPPY HART, pianist ⎪
SYDNEY SKELTON, tympanist ⎬ of Breezy Bellairs's Boys
CARLOS RIVERA, piano-accordionist ⎭
CAESAR BONN, *maître de café* at the Metronome
DAVID HAHN, his secretary
NIGEL BATHGATE, of the *Evening Chronicle*
DR. ALLINGTON
MRS. RODERICK ALLEYN
RODERICK ALLEYN, CHIEF DETECTIVE-
    INSPECTOR ⎫
DETECTIVE-INSPECTOR FOX ⎪
DR. CURTIS ⎪
DETECTIVE-SERGEANT BAILEY, finger-print ⎪ of the Criminal
    expert ⎬ Investigation
DETECTIVE-SERGEANT THOMPSON, ⎪ Department,
    photographer ⎪ New Scotland Yard
DETECTIVE-SERGEANTS GIBSON, MARKS, ⎪
    SCOTT AND SALLIS ⎪
Sundry policemen, waiters, bandsmen and ⎭
    so on

Letters

From Lady Pastern and Bagott to her niece by marriage, Miss Carlisle Wayne:

3, DUKE'S GATE
EATON PLACE
LONDON, S.W.1

MY DEAREST CARLISLE,

I am informed with that air of inconsequence which characterizes all your uncle's utterances, of your arrival in England. Welcome Home. You may be interested to learn that I have rejoined your uncle. My motive is that of expediency. Your uncle proposed to give Clochemere to the Nation and has returned to Duke's Gate, where, as you may have heard, I have been living for the last five years. During the immediate post-war period I shared its dubious amenities with members of an esoteric Central European sect. Your uncle granted them what I believe colonials would call squatters' rights, hoping no doubt to force me back upon the Cromwell Road or the society of my sister Désirée, with whom I have quarrelled since we were first able to comprehend each other's motives.

Other aliens were repatriated, but the sect remained. It will be a sufficient indication of their activities if I tell you that they caused a number of boulders to be set up in the principal reception room, that their ceremonies began at midnight and were conducted in antiphonal screams, that their dogma appeared to prohibit the use of soap and water and that they were forbidden to cut their hair. Six months ago they returned to Central Europe (I have never inquired the precise habitat) and I was left mistress of this house. I had it cleaned and prepared myself for tranquillity. Judge of my dismay! I found tranquillity intolerable. I had, it seems, acclimatized myself to nightly pandemonium. I had become accustomed to frequent encounters with persons who resembled the minor and dirtier prophets. I was unable to endure silence, and the unremarkable presence of servants. In fine, I was lonely. When one is lonely one thinks of one's mistakes. I thought of your uncle. Is one ever entirely bored by the incomprehensible? I doubt it. When I married your uncle (you will recollect that he was an attaché at your embassy in Paris and a frequent caller at my parents' house) I was already a widow. I was not, therefore, *jeune fille*. I did not demand Elysium. Equally I did not anticipate the ridiculous. It is understood that after a certain time one should not expect the impossible of one's husband. If he is tactful one remains ignorant. So much the better. One is reconciled. But your uncle is not tactful. On the contrary, had there been liaisons of the sort which I trust I have indicated, I should have immediately become aware of them. Instead of second or possibly third establishments I found myself confronted in turn by Salvation Army Citadels, by retreats for Indian yogis, by apartments devoted to the study of Voodoo; by a hundred and one ephemeral and ludicrous obsessions. Your uncle has turned with appalling virtuosity from the tenets of Christadelphians to the practice of nudism. He has perpetrated antics which, with his increasing years, have become the more intolerable. Had he been content to play the pantaloon by himself and leave me to deplore, I should have perhaps been reconciled. On the contrary he demanded my collaboration.

For example in the matter of nudism. Imagine me, a de Fouteaux, suffering a proposal that I should promenade, without costume, behind laurel hedges in The Weald of Kent. It was at this juncture and upon this provocation that I first left your uncle. I have returned at intervals only to be driven away again by further imbecilities. I have said nothing of his temper, of his passion for scenes, of his minor but distressing idiosyncrasies. These failings have, alas, become public property.

Yet, my dearest Carlisle, as I have indicated, we are together again at Duke's Gate. I decided that silence had become intolerable and that I should be forced to seek a flat. Upon this decision came a letter from your uncle. He is now interested in music and has associated himself with a band in which he performs upon the percussion instruments. He wished to use the largest of the reception rooms for practice; in short he proposed to rejoin me at Duke's Gate. I am attached to this house. Where your uncle is, there also is noise and noise has become a necessity for me. I consented.

Félicité, also, has rejoined me. I regret to say I am deeply perturbed on account of Félicité. If your uncle realized, in the smallest degree, his duty as a stepfather, he might exert some influence. On the contrary he ignores, or regards with complacency, an attachment so undesirable that I, her mother, cannot bring myself to write more explicitly of it. I can only beg, my dearest Carlisle, that you make time to visit us. Félicité has always respected your judgment. I hope most earnestly that you will come to us for the last weekend in the month. Your uncle, I believe, intends to write to you himself. I join my request to his. It will be delightful to see you again, my dearest Carlisle, and I long to talk to you.

Your affectionate aunt,

CÉCILE DE FOUTEAUX PASTERN AND BAGOTT

From Lord Pastern and Bagott to his niece Miss Carlisle Wayne:

> 3, DUKE'S GATE
> EATON PLACE
> LONDON, S.W.1

DEAR LISLE,

I hear you've come back. Your aunt tells me she's asked you to visit us. Come on the twenty-sixth and we'll give you some music.

Your aunt's living with me again.

> Your affectionate uncle
> GEORGE

From "The Helping Hand," G.P.F.'s page in *Harmony*:

DEAR G.P.F.

I am eighteen and unofficially engaged to be married. My fiancé is madly jealous and behaves in a manner that I consider more than queer and terribly alarming. I enclose details under separate cover because after all he might read this and then we *should* be in the soup. Also five shillings for a special Personal Chat letter. Please help me.

> "TOOTS"

Poor Child in Distress, let me help you if I can. Remember I shall speak as a man and that is perhaps well, for the masculine mind is able to understand this strange self-torture that is clouding your fiancé's love for you and making you so unhappy. Believe me, there is only *one* way. You must be patient. You must prove your love by your candour. Do not tire of reassuring him that his suspicions are groundless. Remain tranquil. *Go on loving him.* Try a little gentle laughter but if it is unsuccessful *do not continue.* Never let him think you impatient. A thought. *There are some natures so delicate and sensitive that they must be handled like flowers. They need sun. They must be tended. Otherwise their spiritual growth is checked.* Your Personal Chat letter will reach you to-morrow.

Footnote to G.P.F.'s page. G.P.F. will write you a very special Personal Chat if you send a stamped and addressed envelope and five-shilling postal order to "Personal Chat. *Harmony.* 5 Materfamilias Lane, E.C.2."

From Miss Carlisle Wayne to Miss Félicité de Suze:

> FRIARS PARDON
> BENHAM
> BUCKS.

DEAR FÉE,

I've had rather a queer letter from Aunt Cile, who wants me to come on the twenty-sixth. What have you been up to? Love,

> LISLE

From the Honourable Edward Manx to Miss Carlisle Wayne:

HARROW FLATS
SLOANE SQUARE
LONDON, S.W.I

DEAREST LISLE,

Cousin Cécile says you are invited to Duke's Gate for the week-end on Saturday the 26th. I shall come down to Benham in order to drive you back. Did you know she wants to marry me to Félicité? I'm really not at all keen and neither, luckily, is Fée. She's fallen in a big way for an extremely dubious number who plays a piano-accordion in Cousin George's band. I imagine there's a full-dress row in the offing *à cause*, as Cousin Cécile would say, *de* the band and particularly *de* the dubious number whose name is Carlos something. They aren't 'alf cups of tea are they? Why do you go away to foreign parts? I shall arrive at about 5 P.M. on the Saturday.

Love,

NED

From the *Monogram* gossip column:

Rumour hath it that Lord Pastern and Bagott, who is a keen exponent of boogie-woogie, will soon be heard at a certain restaurant "not a hundred miles from Piccadilly." Lord Pastern and Bagott, who, of course, married Madame de Suze, (née de Fouteaux) plays the tympani with enormous zest. His band includes such well-known exponents as Carlos Rivera and is conducted by none other than the inimitable Breezy Bellairs, both of the Metronome. By the way, I saw lovely Miss Félicité (Fée) de Suze, Lady Pastern and Bagott's daughter by her first marriage, lunching the other day at the Tarmac *à deux* with the Hon. Edward Manx, who is, of course, her second cousin on the distaff side.

From Mr. Carlos Rivera to Miss Félicité de Suze:

102 BEDFORD MANSIONS
AUSTERLY SQUARE
LONDON, S.W.I

LISTEN GLAMOROUS,

You cannot do this thing to me. I am not an English Honourable This or Lord That to sit complacent while my woman makes a fool of me. No. With me it is all or nothing. I am a scion of an ancient house. I do not permit trespassers and I am tired, I am very tired indeed, of waiting. I wait no longer. You announce immediately our engagement or—finish! It is understood? *Adios*

CARLOS DE RIVERA

Telegram from Miss Félicité de Suze to Miss Carlisle Wayne:

DARLING FOR PITY'S SAKE COME EVERYTHING TOO TRICKY AND PECULIAR HONESTLY DO COME GENUINE CRI DE COEUR TONS OF LOVE DARLING FEE.

Telegram from Miss Carlisle Wayne to Lady Pastern and Bagott:

THANK YOU SO MUCH LOVE TO COME ARRIVING ABOUT SIX SATURDAY 26TH. CARLISLE.

CHAPTER II

The Persons Assemble

At precisely eleven o'clock in the morning G.P.F. walked in at a side door of the *Harmony* offices in 5 Materfamilias Lane, E.C.2. He went at once to his own room. PRIVATE G.P.F. was written in white letters on the door. He unwound the scarf with which he was careful to protect his nose and mouth from the fog, and hung it, together with his felt hat and overcoat, on a peg behind his desk. He then assumed a green eye-shade, and shot a bolt in his door. By so doing he caused a notice, ENGAGED, to appear on the outside.

His gas fire was burning brightly and the tin saucer of water set before it to humidify the air sent up a little drift of steam. The window was blanketed outside by fog. It was as if a yellow curtain had been hung on the wrong side of the glass. The footsteps of passers-by sounded close and dead and one could hear the muffled coughs and shut-in voices of people in a narrow street on a foggy morning. G.P.F. rubbed his hands together, hummed a lively air, seated himself at his desk and switched on his green-shaded lamp. "Cosy," he thought. The light glinted on his dark glasses, which he took off and replaced with reading spectacles.

"One, two. Button your boot," sang G.P.F. in a shrill falsetto and pulled a wire basket of unopened letters towards him. "Three, four, knock on the gate," he sang facetiously and slit open the top letter. A postal order for five shillings fell out on the desk.

DEAR G.P.F. [he read],

I feel I simply must write and thank you for your *lush* Private Chat letter—which I may as well confess has rocked me to my foundations. You couldn't be more right to call yourself Guide, Philosopher and Friend, honestly you couldn't. I've thought so much about what you've told me and I can't help wondering what you're *like*. To look at and listen to, I mean. I think your voice must be rather deep ["Oh Crumbs!" G.P.F. murmured] and I'm sure you are tall. I wish—

He skipped restlessly through the next two pages and arrived at the peroration:

I've tried madly to follow your advice but my young man really is! I can't help thinking that it would be immensely energizing to talk to you. I mean really *talk*. But I suppose that's hopelessly out of bounds, so I'm having another five bob's worth of Private Chat.

G.P.F. followed the large flamboyant script and dropped the pages, one by one, in a second wire basket. Here, at last, was the end.

I suppose he would be madly jealous if he knew I had written to you like this but I just felt I had to. Your grateful

"TOOTS"

G.P.F. reached for his pad of copy, gazed for a moment in a benign absent manner at the fog-lined window and then fell to. He wrote with great fluency, sighing and muttering under his breath.

"Of course I am happy," he began, "to think that I have helped." The phrases ran out from his pencil ". . . you must still be patient . . . sure you will understand . . . anonymity . . . just think of G.P.F. as a friendly ghost . . . write again if you will . . . more than usually interested . . . best of luck and my blessing . . ." When it was finished he pinned the postal note to the top sheet and dropped the whole in a further basket which bore the legend "Personal Chat."

The next letter was written in a firm hand on good notepaper. G.P.F. contemplated it with his head on one side, whistling between his teeth.

The writer [it said] is fifty years old and has recently consented to rejoin her husband who is fifty-five. He is eccentric to the verge of lunacy but, it is understood, not actually certifiable. A domestic crisis has arisen in which he refuses to take the one course compatible with his responsibilities as a stepfather. In a word, my daughter contemplates a marriage that from every point of view but that of unbridled infatuation is disastrous. If further details are required I am prepared to supply them, but the enclosed cuttings from newspapers covering a period of sixteen years will, I believe, speak for themselves. I do not wish this communication to be published, but enclose a five-shilling postal order which I understand will cover a letter of personal advice.

I am etc.,

CÉCILE DE FOUTEAUX PASTERN AND BAGOTT

G.P.F. dropped the letter delicately and turned over the sheaf of paper clippings. "Peer Sued for Kidnapping Stepdaughter," he read; "Peer Practices Nudism"; "Scene in Mayfair Courtroom"; "Lord Pastern Again"; "Lady Pastern and Bagott Seeks Divorce"; "Peer Preaches Free Love"; "Rebuke from Judge"; "Lord Pastern Now Goes Yogi"; "Boogie-Woogie Peer"; "Infinite Variety."

G.P.F. glanced through the letterpress beneath these headlines, made a small impatient sound and began to write very rapidly indeed. He was still at this employment when, glancing up at the blinded window, he saw, as if on a half-developed negative, a shoulder emerge through the fog. A face peered, a hand was pressed against the glass and then closed to tap twice. G.P.F. unlocked his door and returned to his desk. A moment later the visitor came coughing down the passage. "*Entrez!*" called G.P.F. modishly and his visitor walked into the room.

"Sorry to harry you," he said. "I thought you'd be in, this morning. It's the monthly subscription to that relief fund. Your signature to the cheque."

G.P.F. swivelled round in his chair and held out Lady Pastern's letter. His visitor took it, whistled, read it through and burst out laughing. "Well!" he said. "Well, *honestly.*"

"Press cuttings," said G.P.F. and handed them to him.

"She *must* be in a fizz! That it should come to this!"

"Damned if I know why you say that."

"I'm sorry. Of course there's no reason, but— How have you replied?"

"A stinger."

"May I see it?"

"By all means. There it is. Give me the cheque."

The visitor leant over the desk, at the same time reading the copy sheets and groping in his breast pocket for his wallet. He found a cheque and, still reading, laid it on the desk. Once he looked up quickly as if to speak but G.P.F. was bent over the cheque so he finished the letter.

"Strong," he said.

"Here's the cheque," said G.P.F.

"Thank you." He glanced at it. The signature was written in a small, fat and incredibly neat calligraphy: "G. P. Friend."

"Don't you ever sicken of all this?" the visitor asked abruptly with a gesture towards the wire basket.

"Plenty of interest. Plenty of variety."

"You might land yourself in a hell of a complication one of these days. This letter, for instance—"

"Oh, fiddle," said G.P.F. crisply.

ii

"Listen," said Mr. Breezy Bellairs, surveying his band. "Listen, boys, I know he's dire but he's improving. And listen, it doesn't matter if he's dire. What matters is this, like I've told you: he's George Settinger, Marquis of Pastern and Bagott, and he's Noise Number One for publicity. From the angle of news value, not to mention snob value, he's got all the rest of the big shots fighting to buy him a drink."

"So what?" asked the tympanist morosely.

" 'So what'! Ask yourself, what. Look, Syd, I'm keeping you on with the Boys, first, last and all the while. I'm paying you full-time, same as if you played full-time."

"That's not the point," said the tympanist. "The point is I look silly, stepping down half-way through the bill on a gala night. No! I tell you straight, I don't like it."

"Now, listen, Syd. Listen boy. You're featured, aren't you? What am I going to do for you? I'm going to give you a special feature appearance. I'm going to fetch you out on the floor by me and take a star call, aren't I? That's more than I've ever done, boy. It's good, isn't it? With that coming to you, you should worry if the old bee likes to tear himself to shreds in your corner for half an hour, on Saturday night."

"I remind you," said Mr. Carlos Rivera, "that you speak of a gentleman who shall be my father-in-law."

"O.K., O.K., O.K. Take it easy, Carlos, take it easy, boy! That's fine," Mr. Bellairs gabbled, flashing his celebrated smile. "That's all hunky-dory by us. This is in committee, Carlos. And didn't I say he was improving? He'll be good, pretty soon. Not as good as Syd. That'd be a laughable notion. But good."

"As you say," said the pianist. "But what's all this about his own number?"

Mr. Bellairs spread his hands. "Well, now, it's this way, boys. Lord Pastern's got a little idea. It's a little idea that came to him about this new number he's written."

" 'Hot Guy Hot Gunner'?" said the pianist, and plugged out a phrase in the treble. "What a number!" he said without expression.

"Take it easy now, Happy. This little number his lordship's written will be quite a little hit when we've hotted it up."

"As you say."

"That's right. I've orchestrated it and it's snappy. Now, listen. This little idea he's got about putting it across is quite a notion, boys—in its way. It seems Lord Pastern's got round to thinking he might go places as a soloist with this number. You know. A spot of hot drumming and loosing off a six-shooter."

"For crisake!" the tympanist said idly.

"The idea is that Carlos steps out in a spot light and gives. Hot and crazy, Carlos. Burning the air. Sky the limit."

Mr. Rivera passed the palm of his hand over his hair. "Very well. And then?"

"Lord Pastern's idea is that you get right on your scooter and take it away. And when you've got to your craziest, another spot picks him out and he's sitting in tin-can corner wearing a cowboy hat and he gets up and yells 'Yippy-yi-dee' and shoots off a gun at you and you do a trick fall—"

"I am not an acrobat—"

"Well, anyway you fall and his lordship goes to market and then we switch to a cod funeral march and swing it to the limit. And some of the Boys carry Carlos off and I lay a funny wreath on his breast. Well," said Mr. Bellairs after a silence, "I'm not saying it's dynamic, but it might get by. It's crazy and it might be kind of good, at that."

"Did you say," asked the tympanist, "that we finish up with a funeral march? Was that what you said?"

"Played in the Breezy Bellairs Manner, Syd."

"It was what he said, boys," said the pianist. "We sign ourselves off with a corpse and muffled drums. Come to the Metronome for a gay evening."

"I disagree entirely," Mr. Rivera interposed. He rose gracefully. His suit was dove-grey with a widish pink stripe. Its shoulders seemed actually to curve upwards. He was bronzed. His hair was swept back from his forehead and ears in thick brilliant waves. He had flawless teeth, a slight moustache and large eyes, and he was tall. "I like the idea," he said. "It appeals to me. A little macabre, a little odd, perhaps, but it has something. I suggest, however, a slight alteration. It will be an improvement if, on the conclusion of Lord Pastern's solo, I draw the rod and shoot *him*. He is then carried out and I go into my hot number. It will be a great improvement."

"Listen, Carlos—"

"I repeat, a great improvement."

The pianist laughed pointedly and the others grinned.

"You make the suggestion to Lord Pastern," said the tympanist. "He's going to be your ruddy father-in-law. Make it and see how it goes."

"I think we better do it like he says, Carlos," said Mr. Bellairs. "I think we better."

The two men faced each other. Mr. Bellairs's expression of geniality had become habitual. He might have been a cleverly made ventriloquist's doll with a pale rubber face that was constantly and arbitrarily creased in a roguish grimace. His expressionless eyes with their large pale irises and enormous pupils might have been painted. Wherever he went, whenever he spoke, his lips parted and disclosed his teeth. Two dimples grooved his full cheeks, the flesh creased at the corners of his eyes. Thus, hour after hour, he smiled at the couples who danced slowly past his stand; smiled and bowed and beat the air and undulated and smiled. He sweated profusely from these exertions and at times would mop his face with a snowy handkerchief. And behind him every night his Boys, dressed in soft shirts and sculptured dinner-jackets, with steel pointed buttons and silver revers, flexed their muscles and inflated their lungs in obedience to the pulse of his celebrated miniature baton of chromium-tipped ebony, presented to him by a lady of title. Great use was made of chromium at the Metronome by Breezy's Boys. Their instruments glittered with it, they wore wrist-watches on chromium bracelets, the band title appeared in chromium letters on the piano, which was painted in aluminum to resemble chromium. Above the Boys, a giant metronome, outlined in coloured lights, swung its chromium-tipped pendulum in the same measure. "Hi-dee-ho-dee-oh," Mr. Bellairs would moan. "Gloomp-gloomp, giddy-iddy, hody-or-do." For this and for the way he smiled and conducted his band he was paid three hundred pounds a week by the management of the Metronome, and out of that he paid his Boys. He was engaged with an augmented band for charity balls, and sometimes for private dances. "It was a grand party," people would say, "they had Breezy Bellairs and everything." In his world he was a big noise.

His Boys were big noises. They were all specialists. He had selected them with infinite pains. They were chosen for their ability to make the hideous and extremely difficult rumpus known as the Breezy Bellairs Manner and for the way they looked while they made it. They were chosen because of their sex appeal and their endurance. Breezy said: "The better they like you the more you got to give." Some of his players he could replace fairly easily; the second and third saxophonists and the double-bass, for instance, but Happy Hart the pianist and Syd Skelton the tympanist and Carlos Rivera the piano-accordionist were, he said and believed, the Tops. It was a constant nagging anxiety to Breezy that some day, before his public had *had* Happy or Syd or Carlos, one or all of them might get hostile or fed up or something, and leave him for the Royal Flush Swingsters or Bones Flannagan and His Merry Mixers or the Percy Personalities. So he was always careful how he handled these three.

He was being careful, now, with Carlos Rivera. Carlos was good. His piano-accordion talked in the Big Way. When his engagement to Félicité de Suze was announced it'd be a Big Build-up for Breezy and the Boys. Carlos was as good as they come.

"Listen, Carlos," Breezy urged feverishly, "I got an idea. Listen, how about we work it this way? How about letting his lordship fire at you like what he wants and miss you? See? He looks surprised and goes right ahead pulling the trigger and firing and you go right ahead in your hot number and every time he fires, one of the other boys acts like *he's* been hit and plays a queer note and how about these boys playing a note each down the scale? And you just smile and sign off and bow kind of sardonically and leave him flat? How about that, boys?"

"We-el," said the Boys judicially.

"It is a possibility," Mr. Rivera conceded.

"He might even wind up by shooting himself and getting carried off with the wreath on his breast."

"If somebody else doesn't get in first," grunted the tympanist.

"Or he might hand the gun to me and I might fire it at him and it might be empty, and he might go into his act and end up with a funny faint and get carried out."

"I repeat," Rivera said, "it is a possibility. We shall not quarrel in this matter. Perhaps I may speak to Lord Pastern myself."

"Fine!" Breezy cried, and raised his tiny baton. "That's fine. Come on, boys. What are we waiting for? Is this a practice or is it a practice? Where's this new number? Fine! On your marks. Everybody happy? Swell. Let's go."

iii

"Carlisle Wayne," said Edward Manx, "was thirty years old, but she retained something of the air of adolescence, not in her speech, for that was tranquil and assured, but in her looks and manner. Her movements were fluid; boyish perhaps. She had long legs, slim hands and a thin beautiful face. Her clothes were wisely chosen and gallantly worn but she took no great trouble with them and seemed to be well-dressed rather by accident than design. She liked travel but dreaded sight-seeing and would retain memories as sharp as pencil drawings of unimportant details—a waiter, a group of sailors, a woman in a bookstall. The names of the streets or even the towns where these persons had been encountered would often be lost to her; it was people in whom she was really interested. For people she had an eye as sharp as a needle and she was extremely tolerant."

"Her remote cousin, the Honourable Edward Manx," Carlisle interrupted, "was a dramatic critic. He was thirty-seven years old and of romantic appearance but not oppressively so. His professional reputation for rudeness was cultivated with some pains for, although cursed with a violent temper, he was by instinct of a courteous disposition!"

"Gatcha!" said Edward Manx, turning the car into the Uxbridge Road. "He was something of a snob but sufficiently adroit to disguise this circumstance under a show of social indiscrimination. He was unmarried—"

"—having a profound mistrust of those women who obviously admired him—"

"—and a dread of being rebuffed by those of whom he was not quite sure."

"You *are* as sharp as a needle, you know," said Manx, uncomfortably.

"Which is probably why I, too, have remained unmarried."

"I wouldn't be surprised. All the same I've often wondered—"

"I invariably click with such frightful men."

"Lisle, how old were we when we invented this game?"

"Novelettes? Wasn't it the train when we came back from our first school holidays with Uncle George? He wasn't married then so it must have been over sixteen years ago. Félicité was only two when Aunt Cécile married him and she's eighteen now."

"It was then. I remember you began by saying: 'There was once a very conceited bad-tempered boy called Edward Manx. His elderly cousin, a peculiar peer—'"

"Even in those days, Uncle George was prime material, wasn't he?"

"Lord, yes! Do you remember—"

They told each other anecdotes, familiar to both, of Lord Pastern and Bagott. They recalled his first formidable row with his wife, a distinguished Frenchwoman of great composure, who came to him as a widow with a baby daughter. Lord Pastern, three years after their marriage, became an adherent of a sect that practised baptism by total immersion. He wished his stepdaughter to be rechristened by this method in a sluggish and eel-infested stream that ran through his country estate. Upon his wife's refusal he sulked for a month and then, without warning, took ship to India, where he immediately succumbed to the more painful austerities of the yogi. He returned to England loudly proclaiming that almost everything was an illusion and, going by stealth to his stepdaughter's nursery, attempted to fold her infant limbs into esoteric postures, exhorting her, at the same time, to bend her gaze upon her navel and say "Om." Her nurse objected, was given notice by Lord Pastern and reinstated by his wife. A formidable scene ensued.

"My mama was there, you know," said Carlisle. "She was supposed to be Uncle George's favourite sister but she made no headway at all. She and Aunt Cécile held an indignation meeting with the nanny in the boudoir, and Uncle George sneaked down the servants' stairs with Félicité and drove her thirty miles in his car to some sort of yogi boarding-house. They had to get the police to find them. Aunt Cile laid a charge of kidnapping."

"That was the first time Cousin George became banner headlines in the press," Edward observed.

"The second time was the nudist colony."

"True. And the third was the near-divorce."

"I was away for that," Carlisle observed.

"You're always going away. Here I am, a hard-working pressman who ought to be in constant transit to foreign parts, and you're the one to go away. He was taken with the doctrine of free love, you remember, and asked a number of rather odd women down to Clochemere. Cousin Cécile at once removed with Félicité, who was by now twelve years old, to Duke's Gate, and began divorce proceedings. But it turned out that Cousin George's love was only free in the sense that he delivered innumerable lectures without charge to his guests and then told them to go away and get on with it. So the divorce fell through, but not before counsel and bench had enjoyed an orgy of wisecracks and the press had exhausted itself."

"Ned," Carlisle asked, "do you imagine that it's at all hereditary?"

"His dottiness? No, all the other Settingers seem to be tolerably sane. No, I fancy Cousin George is a sport. A sort of monster, in the nicest sense of the word."

"That's a comfort. After all I'm his blood niece, if that's the way to put it. You're only a collateral on the distaff side."

"Is that a cheap sneer, darling?"

"I wish you'd put me wise to the current set-up. I've had some very queer letters and telegrams. What's Félicité up to? Are you going to marry her?"

"I'll be damned if I do," said Edward with some heat. "It's Cousin Cécile who thought that one up. She offered to house me at Duke's Gate when my flat was wrested from me. I was there for three weeks before I found a new one and naturally I took Fée out a bit and so on. It now appears that the invitation was all part of a deep-laid plot of Cousin Cécile's. She really is excessively French, you know. It seems that she went into a sort of state-huddle with my mama and talked about Félicité's *dot* and the desirability of the old families standing firm. It was all terrifically Proustian. My mama, who was born in the colonies and doesn't like Félicité anyway, kept her head and preserved an air of impenetrable grandeur until the last second when she suddenly remarked that she never interfered in my affairs and wouldn't mind betting I'd marry an organizing secretary in the Society for Closer Relations with Soviet Russia."

"Was Aunt Cile at all rocked?"

"She let it pass as a joke in poor taste."

"What about Fée herself?"

"She's in a great to-do about her young man. He, I don't mind telling you, is easily the nastiest job of work in an unreal sort of way that you are ever likely to encounter. He glistens from head to foot and is called Carlos Rivera."

"One mustn't be insular."

"No doubt, but wait till you see him. He goes in for jealousy in a big way and he says he's the scion of a noble Spanish-American family. I don't believe a word of it and I think Félicité has her doubts."

"Didn't you say in your letter that he played the piano-accordion?"

"At the Metronome, in Breezy Bellairs's Band. He walks out in a spot light, and undulates. Cousin George is going to pay Breezy some fabulous sum to let him, Cousin George, play the tympani. That's how Félicité met Carlos."

"Is she really in love with him?"

"Madly, she says, but she's beginning to take a poor view of his jealousy. He can't go dancing with her himself, because of his work. If she goes to the Metronome with anyone else he looks daggers over his piano-accordion and comes across and sneers at them during the solo number. If she goes to other places he finds out from other bandsmen. They appear to be a very close corporation. Of course, being Cousin George's stepdaughter, she's used to scenes, but she's getting a bit rattled nevertheless. It seems that Cousin Cécile, after her interview with my mama, asked Félicité if she thought she could love me. Fée telephoned at once to know if I was up to any nonsense and asked me to lunch with her. So we did and some fool put it in the paper. Carlos read it and went into his act with unparalleled vigour. He talked about knives and what his family do with their women when they are flighty."

"Fée *is* a donkey," said Carlisle after a pause.

"You, my dearest Lisle, are telling me."

iv

Three, Duke's Gate, Eaton Place, was a pleasant Georgian house of elegant though discreet proportions. Its front had an air of reticence which was modified by a fanlight, a couple of depressed arches and beautifully designed doors. One might have hazarded a guess that this was the town house of some tranquil wealthy family who in pre-war days had occupied it at appropriate times and punctually left it in the charge of caretakers during the late summer and the shooting seasons. A house for orderly, leisured and unremarkable people, one might have ventured.

Edward Manx dropped his cousin there, handing her luggage over to a mild elderly man-servant and reminding her that they would meet again at dinner. She entered the hall and noticed with pleasure that it was unchanged.

"Her ladyship is in the drawing-room, miss," said the butler. "Would you prefer—?"

"I'll go straight in, Spence."

"Thank you, miss. You are in the yellow room, miss. I'll have your luggage taken up."

Carlisle followed him to the drawing-room on the first floor. As they reached the landing, a terrific rumpus broke out beyond a doorway on their left.

A saxophone climbed through a series of lewd dissonances into a prolonged shriek; a whistle was blown and cymbals clashed. "A wireless, at last, Spence?" Carlisle ejaculated. "I thought they were forbidden."

"That is his lordship's band, miss. They practise in the ballroom."

"The band," Carlisle muttered. "I'd forgotten. Good heavens!"

"Miss Wayne, my lady," said Spence, in the doorway.

Lady Pastern and Bagott advanced from the far end of a long room. She was fifty and tall for a Frenchwoman. Her figure was impressive, her hair rigidly groomed, her dress admirable. She had the air of being encased in a transparent, closely fitting film that covered her head as well as her clothes and permitted no disturbance of her surface. Her voice had edge. She used the faultless diction and balanced phraseology of the foreigner who has perfect command but no love of the English language.

"My dearest Carlisle," she said crisply, and kissed her niece with precision, on both cheeks.

"Dear Aunt Cile, how nice to see you."

"It is charming of you to come."

Carlisle thought that they uttered these greetings like characters in a somewhat dated comedy, but their pleasure, nevertheless, was real. They had an affection for each other, an unexacting enjoyment of each other's company. "What I like about Aunt Cécile," she had said to Edward, "is her refusal to be rattled about anything." He had reminded her of Lady Pastern's occasional rages and Carlisle retorted that these outbursts acted like safety-valves and had probably saved her aunt many times from committing some act of physical violence upon Lord Pastern.

They sat together by the large window. Carlisle, responding punctually to the interchange of inquiries and observations which Lady Pastern introduced, allowed her gaze to dwell with pleasure on the modest cornices and well-proportioned panels; on chairs, tables and cabinets which, while they had no rigid correspondence of period, achieved an agreeable harmony born of long association. "I've always liked this room," she said presently. "I'm glad you don't change it."

"I have defended it," Lady Pastern said, "in the teeth of your uncle's most determined assaults."

"Ah," thought Carlisle, "the preliminaries are concluded. Now, we're off."

"Your uncle," Lady Pastern continued, "has, during the last sixteen years, made periodic attempts to introduce prayer-wheels, brass Buddhas, a totem-pole, and the worst excesses of the surrealists. I have withstood them all. On one occasion I reduced to molten silver an image of some Aztec deity. Your uncle purchased it in Mexico City. Apart from its repellent appearance I had every reason to believe it spurious."

"He doesn't change," Carlisle murmured.

"It would be more correct, my dear child, to say that he is constant in inconstancy." Lady Pastern made a sudden and vigorous gesture with both her hands. "He is ridiculous to contemplate," she said strongly, "and entirely impossible to live with. A madman, except in a few unimportant technicalities. He is not, alas, certifiable. If he were, I should know what to do."

"Oh, come!"

"I repeat, Carlisle, I should know what to do. Do not misunderstand me. For myself, I am resigned. I have acquired armour. I can suffer perpetual humiliation. I can shrug my shoulders at unparalleled buffooneries. But when my daughter is involved," said Lady Pastern with uplifted bust, "complaisance is out of the question. I assert myself. I give battle."

"What's Uncle George up to, exactly?"

"He is conniving, where Félicité is concerned, at disaster. I cannot hope that you are unaware of her attachment."

"Well—"

"Evidently, you are aware of it. A professional bandsman who, as no doubt you heard on your arrival, is here, now, at your uncle's invitation, in the ballroom. It is almost certain that Félicité is listening to him. An utterly impossible young man of a vulgarity—" Lady Pastern paused and her lips trembled. "I have seen them together at the theatre," she said. "He is beyond everything. One cannot begin to describe. I am desperate."

"I'm so sorry, Aunt Cile," Carlisle said uneasily.

"I knew I should have your sympathy, dearest child. I hope I shall enlist your help. Félicité admires and loves you. She will naturally make you her confidante."

"Yes, but, Aunt Cile—"

A clamour of voices broke out in some distant part of the house. "They are going," said Lady Pastern hurriedly. "It is the end of the *répétition*. In a moment your uncle and Félicité will appear. Carlisle, may I implore you—"

"I don't suppose—" Carlisle began dubiously, and at that juncture, hearing her uncle's voice on the landing, rose nervously to her feet. Lady Pastern, with a grimace of profound significance, laid her hand on her niece's arm. Carlisle felt a hysterical giggle rise in her throat. The door opened and Lord Pastern and Bagott came trippingly into the room.

CHAPTER III

Preprandial

He was short, not more than five foot seven, but so compactly built that he did not give the impression of low stature. Everything about him was dapper, though not obtrusively so; his clothes, the flower in his coat, his well-brushed hair and moustache. His eyes, light grey with pinkish rims, had a hot impertinent look, his underlip jutted out and there were clearly defined spots of local colour over his cheekbones. He came briskly into the room, bestowed a restless kiss upon his niece and confronted his wife.

"Who's dinin'?" he said.

"Ourselves, Félicité, Carlisle, of course, and Edward Manx. And I have asked Miss Henderson to join us to-night."

"Two more," said Lord Pastern. "I've asked Bellairs and Rivera."

"That is quite impossible, George," said Lady Pastern, calmly.

"Why?"

"Apart from other unanswerable considerations, there is not enough food for two extra guests."

"Tell 'em to open a tin."

"I cannot receive these persons for dinner."

Lord Pastern grinned savagely. "All right. Rivera can take Félicité to a restaurant and Bellairs can come here. Same number as before. How are you, Lisle?"

"I'm very well, Uncle George."

"Félicité will not dine out with this individual, George. I shall not permit it."

"You can't stop 'em."

"Félicité will respect my wishes."

"Don't be an ass," said Lord Pastern. "You're thirty years behind the times, m'dear. Give a gel her head and she'll find her feet." He paused, evidently delighted with this aphorism. "Way you're goin', you'll have an elopement on your hands. Comes to that, I don't see the objection."

"Are you demented, George?"

"Half the women in London'd give anything to be in Fée's boots."

"A Mexican bandsman."

"Fine, well-set-up young feller. Inoculate your old stock. That's Shakespeare, ain't it Lisle? I understand he comes of a perfectly good Spanish family. *Hidalgo*, or whatever it is," he added vaguely. "A feller of good family happens to be an artist and you go and condemn him. Sort of thing that makes you sick." He turned to his niece: "I've been thinkin' seriously of givin' up the title, Lisle."

"*George!*"

"About dinner, can you find something for them to eat or can't you? Speak up."

Lady Pastern's shoulders rose with a shudder. She glanced at Carlisle, who thought she detected a glint of cunning in her aunt's eye. "Very well, George," Lady Pastern said. "I shall speak to the servants. I shall speak to Dupont. Very well."

Lord Pastern darted an extremely suspicious glance at his wife and sat down. "Nice to see you, Lisle," he said. "What have you been doin' with yourself?"

"I've been in Greece, Famine Relief."

"If people understood dietetics there wouldn't be all this starvation," said Lord Pastern darkly. "Are you keen on music?"

Carlisle returned a guarded answer. Her aunt, she realized, was attempting to convey by means of a fixed stare and raised eyebrows some message of significance.

"I've taken it up, seriously," Lord Pastern continued. "Swing. Boogie-woogie. Jive. Find it keeps me up to the mark." He thumped with his heel on the carpet, beat his hands together and in a strange nasal voice intoned: "'Shoo-shoo-shoo, baby, Bye-bye, bye Baby.'"

The door opened and Félicité de Suze came in. She was a striking young woman with large black eyes, a wide mouth and an air of being equal to anything. She cried, "Darling—you're heaven its very self," and kissed Carlisle with enthusiasm. Lord Pastern was still clapping and chanting. His step-daughter took up the burden of his song, raised a finger and jerked rhythmically before him. They grinned at each other. "You're coming along very prettily indeed, George," she said.

Carlisle wondered what her impression would have been if she were a complete stranger. Would she, like Lady Pastern, have decided that her uncle was eccentric to the point of derangement? "No," she thought, "probably not. There's really a kind of terrifying sanity about him. He's overloaded with energy, he says exactly what he thinks and he does exactly what he wants to do. But he's an oversimplification of type, and he's got no perspective. He's never mildly interested in anything. But which of us," Carlisle reflected, "has not, at some time, longed to play the big drum?"

Félicité, with an abandon that Carlisle found unconvincing, flung herself into the sofa beside her mother. "Angel," she said richly, "don't be so *grande dame!* George and I are having fun!"

Lady Pastern disengaged herself and rose. "I must see Dupont."

"Ring for Spence," said her husband. "Why d'you want to go burrowin' about in the servants' quarters?"

Lady Pastern pointed out, with great coldness, that in the present food shortage one did not, if one wished to retain the services of one's cook, send a message at seven in the evening to the effect that there would be two extra for dinner. In any case, she added, however great her tact, Dupont would almost certainly give notice.

"He'll give us the same dinner as usual," her husband rejoined. "The Three Courses of Monsieur Dupont!"

"Extremely witty," said Lady Pastern coldly. She then withdrew.

"George!" said Félicité. "Have you won?"

"I should damn' well think so. Never heard anything so preposterous in me life. Ask a couple of people to dine and your mother behaves like Lady Macbeth. I'm going to have a bath."

When he had gone, Félicité turned to Carlisle, and made a wide helpless gesture. "Darling, *what* a life! Honestly! One prances about from moment to moment on the edge of a volcano, *never* knowing when there'll be a major eruption. I suppose you've heard all about ME."

"A certain amount."

"He's madly attractive."

"In what sort of way?"

Félicité smiled and shook her head. "My dear Lisle, he just does things for me."

"He's not by any chance a bounder?"

"He can bound like a ping-pong ball and I won't bat an eyelid. To me he's heaven; *but* just plain heaven."

"Come off it, Fée," said Carlisle. "I've heard all this before. What's the catch in it?"

Félicité looked sideways at her. "How do you mean, the catch?"

"There's always a catch in your young men, darling, when you rave like this about them."

Félicité began to walk showily about the room. She had lit a cigarette and wafted it to and fro between two fingers, nursing her right elbow in the palm of the left hand. Her manner became remote. "When English people talk about a bounder," she said, "they invariably refer to someone who has more charm and less *gaucherie* than the average Englishman."

"I couldn't disagree more; but go on."

Félicité said loftily: "Of course I knew from the first Mama would kick like the devil. *C'la va sans dire.* And I don't deny Carlos is a bit tricky. In fact, 'It's hell but it's worth it' is a fairly accurate summing-up of the situation at the moment. I'm adoring it, really—I think."

"I don't think."

"Yes, I am," said Félicité violently. "I adore a situation. I've been brought up on situations. Think of George. You know, I honestly believe I've got more in common with George than I would have had with my own father. From all accounts, Papa was excessively *rangé.*"

"You'd do with a bit more orderliness yourself, old girl. In what way is Carlos tricky?"

"Well, he's just *so* jealous he's like a Spanish novel."

"I've never read a Spanish novel unless you count *Don Quixote* and I'm certain you haven't. What's he do?"

"My dear, everything. Rages and despairs and sends frightful letters by special messenger. I got a stinker this morning, *à cause de*—well, *à cause de* something that really is a bit daffy."

She halted and inhaled deeply. Carlisle remembered the confidences that Félicité had poured out in her convent days, concerning what she called her "raves." There had been the music master who had fortunately snubbed Félicité and the medical student who hadn't. There had been the brothers of the other girls and an actor whom she attempted to waylay at a charity matinée. There had been a male medium, engaged by Lord Pastern during his spiritualistic period, and a dietician—Carlisle pulled herself together and listened to the present recital. It appeared that there was a crisis: A *crise* as Félicité called it. She used far more occasional French than her mother and was fond of laying her major calamities at the door of Gallic temperament.

"—and as a matter of fact," Félicité was saying, "I hadn't so much as smirked at another *soul,* and there he was seizing me by the wrists and giving me that shattering sort of look that begins at your boots and travels up to your face and then makes the return trip. And breathing loudly, don't you know, through the nose. I don't deny that the first time was rather fun. But after he got wind of old Edward it really was, and I may say still is, beyond a joke. And now to crown everything, there's the *crise.*"

"But what crisis? You haven't said—"

For the first time Félicité looked faintly embarrassed.

"He found a letter," she said. "In my bag. Yesterday."

"You aren't going to tell me he goes fossicking in your bag? And what letter, for pity's sake? Honestly, Fée!"

"I don't expect you to understand," Félicité said grandly. "We were lunching and he hadn't got a cigarette. I was doing my face at the time and I told him to help himself to my case. The letter came out of the bag with the case."

"And he—well, never mind. W*hat* letter?"

"I know you're going to say I'm mad. It was a sort of rough draft of a letter I sent to somebody. It had a bit in it about Carlos. When I saw it in his hand I was pretty violently rocked. I said something like 'Hi-hi you can't read that,' and of course with Carlos that tore everything wide open. He said 'So.'"

"So what?"

"So, all by itself. He does that. He's Latin-American."

"I thought that sort of 'so' was German."

"Whatever it is I find it terrifying. I began to fluff and puff and tried to pass it off with a jolly laugh but he said that either he could trust me or he couldn't and if he could, how come I wouldn't let him read a letter? I completely lost my head and grabbed it and he began to hiss. We were in a restaurant."

"Good Lord!"

"Well, I know. Obviously he was going to react in a really big way. So in the end the only thing seemed to be to let him have the letter. So I gave it to him on condition he wouldn't read it till we got back to the car. The drive home was hideous. But hideous."

"But what was in the letter, if one may ask, and who was it written to? You are confusing, Fée."

There followed a long uneasy silence. Félicité lit another cigarette. "Come on," said Carlisle at last.

"It happened," said Félicité haughtily, "to be written to a man whom I don't actually know, asking for advice about Carlos and me. Professional advice."

"What can you mean! A clergyman? Or a lawyer?"

"I don't think so. He'd written me rather a marvellous letter and this was thanking him. Carlos, of course, thought it was for Edward. The worst bit, from Carlos's point of view, was where I said: 'I suppose he'd be madly jealous if he knew I'd written to you like this.' Carlos really got weaving after he read that. He—"

Félicité's lips trembled. She turned away and began to speak rapidly, in a high voice. "He roared and stormed and wouldn't listen to anything. It was devastating. You can't conceive what it was like. He said I was to announce our engagement at once. He said if I didn't he'd—he said he'd go off and just simply end it all— He's given me a week. I've got till next Tuesday. That's all. I've got to announce it before next Tuesday."

"And you don't want to?" Carlisle asked gently. She saw Félicité's shoulders quiver and went to her. "Is that it, Fée?"

The voice quavered and broke. Félicité drove her hands through her hair. "I don't know *what* I want," she sobbed. "Lisle, I'm in such a muddle. I'm terrified, Lisle. It's so damned awful, Lisle. I'm terrified."

ii

Lady Pastern had preserved throughout the war and its exhausted aftermath an unbroken formality. Her rare dinner parties had, for this reason, acquired the air of period pieces. The more so since, by feat of superb domestic strategy, she had contrived to retain at Duke's Gate a staff of trained servants, though a depleted one. As she climbed into a long dress, six years old, Carlisle reflected that if the food shortage persisted, her aunt would soon qualify for the same class as that legendary Russian nobleman who presided with perfect equanimity at an interminable banquet of dry bread and water.

She had parted with Félicité, who was still shaking and incoherent, on the landing. "You'll see him at dinner," Félicité had said. "You'll see what I mean." And with a spurt of defiance: "And anyway, I don't care what anyone thinks. If I'm in a mess, it's a thrilling mess. And if I want to get out of it, it's not for other people's reasons. It's only because— Oh, God, what's it matter!"

Félicité had then gone into her own room and slammed the door. It was perfectly obvious, Carlisle reflected, as she finished her face and lit a cigarette, that the wretched girl was terrified and that she herself would, during the week-end, be a sort of buffer-state between Félicité, her mother and her stepfather. "And the worst of it is," Carlisle thought crossly, "I'm fond of them and will probably end by involving myself in a major row with all three at once."

She went down to the drawing-room. Finding nobody there, she wandered disconsolately across the landing and, opening a pair of magnificent double doors, looked into the ballroom.

Gilt chairs and music stands stood in a semicircle like an island in the vast bare floor. A grand piano stood in their midst. On its closed lid, with surrealistic inconsequence, were scattered a number of umbrellas and parasols. She looked more closely at them and recognized a black and white, exceedingly Parisian, affair, which ten years ago or more her aunt had flourished at Ascot. It had been an outstanding phenomenon, she remembered, in the Royal Enclosure and had been photographed. Lady Pastern had been presented with it by some Indian plenipotentiary on the occasion of her first marriage and had clung to it ever since. Its handle represented a bird and had ruby eyes. Its shaft was preposterously thin and was jointed and bound with platinum. The spring catch and the dark bronze section that held it were uncomfortably encrusted with jewels and had ruined many a pair of gloves. As a child, Félicité had occasionally been permitted to unscrew the head and the end section of the shaft, and this, for some reason, had always afforded her extreme pleasure. Carlisle picked it up, opened it, and jeering at herself for being superstitious, hurriedly shut it again. There was a pile of band parts on the piano seat and on the top of this a scribbled programme.

"Floor Show," she read. "(1) A New Way with Old Tunes. (2) Skelton. (3) Sandra. (4) Hot Guy."

At the extreme end of the group of chairs, and a little isolated, was the paraphernalia of a dance-band tympanist—drums, rattles, a tambourine, cymbals, a wire whisk and coconut shells. Carlisle gingerly touched a pedal with her foot and jumped nervously when a pair of cymbals clashed. "It would be fun," she thought, "to sit down and have a whack at everything. What can Uncle George be like in action!"

She looked round. Her coming-out ball had been here; her parents had borrowed the house for it. Utterly remote those years before the war! Carlisle repeopled the hollow room and felt again the curious fresh gaiety of that night. She felt the cord of her programme grow flossy under the nervous pressure of her gloved fingers. She saw the names written there and read them again in the choked print of casualty lists. The cross against the supper dances had been for Edward. "I don't approve," he had said, guiding her with precision, and speaking so lightly that, as usual, she doubted his intention. "We've no business to do ourselves as well as all this." "Well, if you're not having fun—" "But I am. I am." And he had started one of their novelettes: "In the magnificent ballroom at Duke's Gate, the London house of Lord Pastern and Bagott, amid the strains of music and the scent of hot-house blooms—" And she had cut in: "Young Edward Manx swept his cousin into the vortex of the dance." "Lovely," she thought. Lovely it had been. They had had the last dance together and she had been tired yet buoyant, moving without conscious volition; *really* floating, she thought. "Good night, good night, it's been perfect." Later, as the clocks struck four, up the stairs to bed, light-headed with fatigue, drugged with gratitude to all the world for her complete happiness.

"How young," thought Carlisle, looking at the walls and floor of the ballroom, "and how remote. The Spectre of the Rose," she thought, and a phrase of music ended her recollections on a sigh.

There had been no real sequel. More balls, with the dances planned beforehand, an affair or two and letters from Edward, who was doing special articles in Russia. And then the war.

She turned away and recrossed the landing to the drawing-room.

It was still unoccupied. "If I don't talk to somebody soon," Carlisle thought, "I shall get a black dog on my back." She found a collection of illustrated papers and turned them over, thinking how strange it was that photographs of people eating, dancing, or looking at something that did not appear in the picture should command attention.

"Lady Dartmoor and Mr. Jeremy Thringle enjoyed a joke at the opening night of *Fewer and Dearer*." "Miss Penelope Santon-Clarke takes a serious view of the situation at Sandown. With her, intent on his racing card, is Captain Anthony Barr-Barr." "At the Tarmac: Miss Félicité de Suze in earnest conversation with Mr. Edward Manx." "I don't wonder," thought Carlisle, "that Aunt Cécile thinks it would be a good match," and put the paper away from her. Another magazine lay in her lap: a glossy publication with a cover illustration depicting a hilltop liberally endowed with flowers and a young man and woman of remarkable physique gazing with every expression of delight and well-being at something indistinguishable in an extremely blue sky. The title *Harmony* was streamlined across the top of the cover.

Carlisle turned the pages. Here was Edward's monthly review of the shows. Much too good, it was, mordant and penetrating, for a freak publication like this. He had told her they paid very well. Here, an article on genetics by "The Harmony Consultant," here something a bit overemotional about Famine Relief, which Carlisle, an expert in her way, skimmed through with disapproval. Next an article, "Radiant Living," which she passed by with a shudder. Then a two-page article headed "Crime Pays," which proved to be a highly flavoured but extremely outspoken and well-informed article on the drug racket. Two Latin-American business firms with extensive connections in Great Britain were boldly named. An editorial note truculently courted information backed by full protection. It also invited a libel action and promised a further article. Next came a serial by a Big Name and then, on the centre double-page with a banner headline:

THE HELPING HAND
Ask G.P.F. About It
(Guide, Philosopher, Friend)

Carlisle glanced through it. Here were letters from young women asking for advice on the conduct of their engagements and from young men seeking guidance in their choice of wives and jobs. Here was a married woman prepared, it seemed, to follow the instructions of an unknown pundit in matters of the strictest personal concern, and here a widower who requested an expert report on remarriage with someone twenty years his junior. Carlisle was about to turn the page when a sentence caught her eye:

I am eighteen and unofficially engaged to be married. My fiancé is madly jealous and behaves . . .

She read it through to the end. The style was vividly familiar. The magazine had the look of having been frequently opened here. There was cigarette ash in the groove between the pages. Was it possible that Félicité–? But the signature: "Toots"! Could Félicité adopt a nom de plume like Toots? Could her unknown correspondent–? Carlisle lost herself in a maze of speculation from which she was aroused by some faint noise–a metallic click. She looked up. Nobody had entered the room. The sound was repeated and she realized it had come from her uncle's study, a small room that opened off the far end of the drawing-room. She saw that the door was ajar and that the lights were on in the study. She remembered that it was Lord Pastern's unalterable habit to sit in this room for half an hour before dinner, meditating upon whatever obsession at the moment enthralled him, and that he had always liked her to join him there.

She walked down the long deep carpet to the door and looked in.

Lord Pastern sat before the fire. He had a revolver in his hands and appeared to be loading it.

iii

For a few moments Carlisle hesitated. Then, in a voice that struck her as being pitched too high, she said: "What *are* you up to, Uncle George?"

He started and the revolver slipped in his hands and almost fell.

"Hullo," he said. "Thought you'd forgotten me."

She crossed the room and sat opposite him. "Are you preparing for burglars?" she said.

"No." He gave her what Edward had once called one of his leery looks and added: "Although you might put it that way. I'm gettin' ready for my big moment." He jerked his hand towards a small table that stood at his elbow. Carlisle saw that a number of cartridges lay there. "Just goin' to draw the bullets," said Lord Pastern, "to make them into blanks, you know. I like to attend to things myself."

"But what is your big moment?"

"You'll see, to-night. You and Fée are to come. It ought to be a party. Who's your best young man?"

"I haven't got one."

"Why not?"

"Arst yourself."

"You're too damn' stand-offish, me gel. Wouldn't be surprised if you had one of those things—Oedipus and all that. I looked into psychology when I was interested in companionate marriage."

Lord Pastern inserted his eyeglass, went to his desk and rummaged in one of the drawers.

"What's happening to-night?"

"Special extension night at the Metronome. I'm playin'. Floor show at eleven o'clock. My first appearance in public. Breezy engaged me. Nice of him, wasn't it? You'll enjoy yourself, Lisle."

He returned with a drawer filled with a strange collection of objects—pieces of wire, a fret-saw, razor blades, candle-ends, wood-carving knives, old photographs, electrical gear, plastic wood, a number of tools and quantities of putty in greasy paper. How well Carlisle remembered that drawer. It had been a wet-day solace of her childhood visits. From its contents, Lord Pastern, who was dextrous in such matters, had concocted manikins, fly-traps and tiny ships.

"I believe," she said, "I recognize almost everything in the collection."

"Y' father gave me that revolver," Lord Pastern remarked. "It's one of a pair. He had 'em made by his gunsmith to take special target ammunition. Couldn't be bored having to reload with every shot like you do with target pistols, y'know. Cost him a packet, these did. We were always at it, he and I. He scratched his initials one day on the butt of this one. We'd had a bit of a row about differences in performance in the two guns, and shot it out. Have a look."

She picked up the revolver gingerly. "I can't see anything."

"There's a magnifying glass somewhere. Look underneath near the trigger guard."

Carlisle rummaged in the drawer and found a lens. "Yes," she said. "I can make them out now. C.D.W."

"We were crack shots. He left me the pair. The other's in the case, somewhere in that drawer."

Lord Pastern took out a pair of pliers and picked up one of the cartridges. "Well, if you haven't got a young man," he said, "we'll have Ned Manx. That'll please your aunt. No good asking anyone else for Fée. Carlos cuts up rough."

"Uncle George," Carlisle ventured as he busied himself over his task, "do you approve of Carlos? Really?"

He muttered and grunted. She caught disjointed phrases: "—take their course—own destiny—goin' the wrong way to work. He's a damn' fine piano-accordionist," he said loudly and added, more obscurely: "They'd much better leave things to me."

"What's he like?"

"You'll see him in a minute. I know what I'm about," said Lord Pastern, crimping the end of a cartridge from which he had extracted the bullet.

"Nobody else seems to. Is he jealous?"

"She's had things too much her own way. Make her sit up a bit and a good job, too."

"Aren't you making a great number of blank cartridges?" Carlisle asked idly.

"I rather like making them. You never know. I shall probably be asked to repeat my number lots of times. I like to be prepared."

He glanced up and saw the journal which Carlisle still held in her lap. "Thought you had a mind above that sort of stuff," said Lord Pastern, grinning.

"Are you a subscriber, darling?"

"Y' aunt is. It's got a lot of sound stuff in it. They're not afraid to speak their minds, b'God. See that thing on drug-runnin'? Names and everything and if they don't like it they can damn' well lump it. The police," Lord Pastern said obscurely, "are no good; pompous incompetent lot. Hidebound. Ned," he added, "does the reviews."

"Perhaps," Carlisle said lightly, "he's G.P.F., too."

"Chap's got brains," Lord Pastern grunted bewilderingly. "Hog sense in that feller."

"Uncle George," Carlisle demanded suddenly, "you don't know by any chance if Fée's ever consulted G.P.F.?"

"Wouldn't let on if I did, m'dear. Naturally."

Carlisle reddened. "No, of course you wouldn't if she'd told you in confidence. Only usually Fée can't keep anything to herself."

"Well, ask her. She might do a damn' sight worse."

Lord Pastern dropped the bullets he had extracted into the waste-paper basket and returned to his desk. "I've been doin' a bit of writin' myself," he said. "Look at this, Lisle."

He handed his niece a sheet of music manuscript. An air had been set down, with many rubbings out, it seemed, and words had been written under the appropriate notes. "This Hot Guy," Carlisle read, "does he get mean? This Hot Gunner with his accord-een. Shoots like he plays an' he tops the bill. Plays like he shoots an' he shoots to kill. Hi-de oh hi. Ho de oh do. Yip. Shoot buddy, shoot and we'll sure come clean. Hot Guy, Hot Gunner on your accord-een Bo. Bo. Bo."

"Neat," said Lord Pastern complacently. "Ain't it?"

"It's astonishing," Carlisle murmured and was spared the necessity of further comment by the sound of voices in the drawing-room.

"That's the Boys," said Lord Pastern briskly. "Come on."

The Boys were dressed in their professional dinner suits. These were distinctive garments, the jackets being double-breasted with the famous steel pointed buttons and silver revers. The sleeves were extremely narrow and displayed a great deal of cuff. The taller of the two, a man whose rotundity was emphasized by his pallor, advanced, beaming upon his host.

"Well, well, well," he said. "Look who's here."

It was upon his companion that Carlisle fixed her attention. Memories of tango experts, of cinema near-stars with cigarette holders and parti-coloured shoes, of armoured women moving doggedly round dance floors in the grasp of younger men—all these memories jostled together in her brain.

"—and Mr. Rivera—" her uncle was saying. Carlisle withdrew her hand from Mr. Bellairs's encompassing grasp and it was at once bowed over by Mr. Rivera.

"Miss Wayne," said Félicité's Carlos.

He rose from his bow with grace and gave her a look of automatic homage. "So we meet, at last," he said. "I have heard so much." He had, she noticed, a very slight lisp.

Lord Pastern gave them all sherry. The two visitors made loud conversation. "That's very fine," Mr. Breezy Bellairs pronounced and pointed to a small Fragonard above the fireplace. "My God, that's beautiful, you know, Carlos. Exquisite."

"In my father's *hacienda*," said Mr. Rivera, "there is a picture of which I am vividly reminded. This picture to which I refer is a portrait of one of my paternal ancestors. It is an original Goya." And while she was still wondering how a Fragonard could remind Mr. Rivera of a Goya, he turned to Carlisle. "You have visited the Argentine, Miss Wayne, of course?"

"No," said Carlisle.

"But you must. It would appeal to you enormously. It is a little difficult, by the way, for a visitor to see us, as it were, from the inside. The Spanish families are very exclusive."

"Oh."

"Oh, yes. An aunt of mine, Doña Isabella de Manuelos-Rivera, used to say ours was the only remaining aristocracy." He inclined towards Lord Pastern and laughed musically. "But, of course, she had not visited a certain charming house in Duke's Gate, London."

"What? I wasn't listening," said Lord Pastern. "Look here, Bellairs, about to-night—"

"To-night," Mr. Bellairs interrupted, smiling from ear to ear, "is in the bag. We'll rock them, Lord Pastern. Now, don't you worry about to-night. It's going to be wonderful. You'll be there, of course, Miss Wayne?"

"I wouldn't miss it," Carlisle murmured, wishing they were not so zealous in their attentions.

"I've got the gun fixed up," her uncle said eagerly. "Five rounds of blanks, you know. What about those umbrellas, now—"

"You are fond of music, Miss Wayne? But of course you are. You would be enchanted by the music of my own country."

"Tangos and rhumbas?" Carlisle ventured. Mr. Rivera inclined towards her. "At night," he said, "with the scent of magnolias in the air—those wonderful nights of music. You will think it strange, of course, that I should be—" he shrugged up his shoulders and lowered his voice—"performing in a dance band. Wearing these appalling clothes! Here, in London. It is terrible, isn't it?"

"I don't see why."

"I suppose," Mr. Rivera sighed, "I am what you call a snob. There are times when I find it almost unendurable. But I must not say so." He glanced at Mr. Bellairs, who was deep in conversation with his host. "A heart of gold," he whispered. "One of nature's gentlemen. I should not complain. How serious we have become," he added gaily. "We meet and in two minutes I confide in you. You are *simpática*, Miss Wayne. But of course you have been told that before."

"Never," said Carlisle firmly and was glad to see Edward Manx come in.

"Evenin', Ned," said Lord Pastern, blinking at him. "Glad to see you. Have you met—"

Carlisle heard Mr. Rivera draw in his breath with a formidable hiss. Manx, having saluted Mr. Bellairs, advanced with a pleasant smile and extended hand. "We haven't met, Rivera," he said, "but at least I'm one of your devotees at the Metronome. If anything could teach me how to dance I'm persuaded it would be your piano-accordion."

"How do you do," said Mr. Rivera, and turned his back. "As I was saying, Miss Wayne," he continued, "I believe entirely in first impressions. As soon as we were introduced—"

Carlisle looked past him at Manx, who had remained perfectly still. At the first opportunity, she walked round Mr. Rivera and joined him. Mr. Rivera moved to the fireplace, before which he stood with an air of detachment, humming under his breath. Lord Pastern instantly button-holed him. Mr. Bellairs joined them with every manifestation of uneasy geniality. "About my number, Carlos," said Lord Pastern, "I've been tellin' Breezy—"

"Of all the filthy rude—" Manx began to mutter. Carlisle linked her arm in his and walked him away. "He's just plain frightful, Ned. Félicité must be out of her mind," she whispered hastily.

"If Cousin George thinks I'm going to stand round letting a bloody fancy-dress dago insult me—"

"For *pity's* sake don't fly into one of your rages. Laugh it off."

"Heh-heh-heh."

"That's better."

"He'll probably throw his sherry in my face. Why the devil was I asked, if he was coming. What's Cousin Cécile thinking of?"

"It's Uncle George—shut up. Here come the girls."

Lady Pastern, encased in black, entered with Félicité at her heels. She suffered the introductions with terrifying courtesy. Mr. Bellairs redoubled his geniality. Mr. Rivera had the air of a man who never blossoms but in the presence of the great.

"I am so pleased to have the honour, at last, of being presented," he said. "From Félicité I have heard so much of her mother. I feel, too, that we may have friends in common. Perhaps, Lady Pastern, you will remember an uncle of mine who had, I think, some post at our embassy in Paris, many years ago. Señor Alonso de Manuelos-Rivera."

Lady Pastern contemplated him without any change of expression. "I do not remember," she said.

"After all it was much too long ago," he rejoined gallantly. Lady Pastern glanced at him with cold astonishment and advanced upon Manx. "Dearest Edward," she said, offering her cheek, "we see you far too seldom. This is delightful."

"Thank you, Cousin Cécile. For me, too."

"I want to consult you— You will forgive us, George. I am determined to have Edward's opinion on my petit point."

"Let me alone," Manx boasted, "with petit point."

Lady Pastern put her arm through his and led him apart. Carlisle saw Félicité go to Rivera. Evidently she had herself well in hand: her greeting was prettily formal. She turned with an air of comradeship from Rivera to Bellairs and her stepfather. "Will anyone bet me," she said, "that I can't guess what you chaps have been talking about?" Mr. Bellairs was immediately very gay. "Now, Miss de Suze, that's making it just a little tough. I'm afraid you know much too much about us. Isn't that the case, Lord Pastern?" "I'm worried about those umbrellas," said Lord Pastern moodily and Bellairs and Félicité began to talk at once.

Carlisle was trying to make up her mind about Rivera and failing to do so. Was he in love with Félicité? If so was his jealousy of Ned Manx a genuine and therefore an alarming passion? Was he on the other hand a complete adventurer? Could any human being be as patently bogus as Mr. Rivera or was it within the bounds of possibility that the scions of noble Spanish-American families behaved in a manner altogether too faithful to their Hollywood opposites? Was it her fancy or had his olive-coloured cheeks

turned paler as he stood and watched Félicité? Was the slight tic under his
left eye, that smallest possible muscular twitch, really involuntary or, as
everything else about him seemed to be, part of an impersonation along
stereotyped lines? And as these speculations chased each other through her
mind, Rivera himself came up to her.

"But you are so serious," he said. "I wonder why. In my country we have a
proverb: a woman is serious for one of two reasons—she is about to fall in
love or already she loves without success. The alternative being unthinkable,
I ask myself—to whom is this lovely lady about to lose her heart?"

Carlisle thought: "I wonder if this is the line of chat that Félicité has
fallen for." She said: "I'm afraid your proverb doesn't apply out of South
America."

He laughed as if she had uttered some brilliant equivocation and began to
protest that he knew better, indeed he did. Carlisle saw Félicité stare blankly
at them and, turning quickly, surprised just such another expression on Edward Manx's face. She began to feel acutely uncomfortable. There was no
getting away from Mr. Rivera. His raillery and archness mounted with indecent emphasis. He admired Carlisle's dress, her modest jewel, her hair.
His lightest remark was pronounced with such a killing air that it immediately
assumed the character of an impropriety. Her embarrassment at these excesses quickly gave way to irritation when she saw that while Mr. Rivera
bent upon her any number of melting glances he also kept a sharp watch
upon Félicité. "And I'll be damned," thought Carlisle, "if I let him get
away with that little game." She chose her moment and joined her aunt,
who had withdrawn Edward Manx to the other end of the room and, while
she exhibited her embroidery, muttered anathemas upon her other guests.
As Carlisle came up, Edward was in the middle of some kind of uneasy
protestation: "—but, Cousin Cécile, I don't honestly think I can do much
about it. I mean—oh, hullo Lisle. Enjoyed your Latin-American petting
party?"

"Not enormously," said Carlisle, and bent over her aunt's embroidery.
"It's lovely, darling," she said. "How do you do it?"

"You shall have it for an evening bag. I have been telling Edward that I
fling myself on his charity, and," Lady Pastern added in a stormy undertone,
"and on yours, my dearest child." She raised her needlework as if to examine
it and they saw her fingers fumble aimlessly across its surface. "You see,
both of you, this atrocious person. I implore you—" Her voice faltered. "Look,"
she whispered, "look now. Look at him."

Carlisle and Edward glanced furtively at Mr. Rivera, who was in the act
of introducing a cigarette into a jade holder. He caught Carlisle's eye. He did
not smile but glossed himself over with appraisement. His eyes widened.
"Somewhere or other," she thought, "he has read about gentlemen who undress ladies with a glance." She heard Manx swear under his breath and
noted with surprise her own gratification at this circumstance. Mr. Rivera
advanced upon her.

"Oh, Lord!" Edward muttered.

"Here," said Lady Pastern loudly, "is Hendy. She is dining with us. I had forgotten."

The door at the far end of the drawing-room had opened and a woman plainly dressed came quietly in.

"Hendy!" Carlisle echoed. "I had forgotten Hendy," and went swiftly to-wards her.

CHAPTER IV

They Dine

Miss Henderson had been Félicité's governess and had remained with the family after she grew up, occupying a post that was half-way between that of companion and secretary to both Félicité and her mother. Carlisle called her controller-of-the-household and knew that many a time she had literally performed the impossible task this title implied. She was a greyish-haired woman of forty-five; her appearance was tranquil but unremarkable, her voice pleasant. Carlisle, who liked her, had often wondered at her faithfulness to this turbulent household. To Lady Pastern, who regarded all persons as neatly graded types, Miss Henderson was no doubt an employee of good address and perfect manners whose presence at Duke's Gate was essential to her own peace of mind. Miss Henderson had her private room where usually she ate in solitude. Sometimes, however, she was asked to lunch or dine with the family; either because a woman guest had slipped them up, or because her employer felt it was suitable that her position should be defined by such occasional invitations. She seldom left the house and if she had any outside ties, Carlisle had never heard of them. She was perfectly adjusted to her isolation and if she was ever lonely gave no evidence of being so. Carlisle believed Miss Henderson to have more influence than anyone else with Félicité, and it struck her now as odd that Lady Pastern should not have mentioned Hendy as a possible check to Mr. Rivera. But then the family did not often remember Hendy until they actually wanted her for something. "And I myself," Carlisle thought guiltily, "although I like her so much, had forgotten to ask after her." And she made her greeting the warmer because of this omission.

"Hendy," she said, "how lovely to see you. How long is it? Four years?"

"A little over three, I think." That was like her. She was always quietly accurate.

"You look just the same," said Carlisle, nervously aware of Mr. Rivera close behind her.

Lady Pastern icily performed the introductions. Mr. Bellairs bowed and smiled expansively from the hearth-rug. Mr. Rivera, standing beside Carlisle, said: "Ah, yes, of course. Miss Henderson." And might as well have added: "The governess, I believe." Miss Henderson bowed composedly and Spence announced dinner.

They sat at a round table, a pool of candlelight in the shadowed dining-room. Carlisle found herself between her uncle and Rivera. Opposite her, between Edward and Bellairs, sat Félicité. Lady Pastern, on Rivera's right, at first suffered his conversation with awful courtesy, presumably, thought Carlisle, in order to give Edward Manx, her other neighbour, a clear run with Félicité. But as Mr. Bellairs completely ignored Miss Henderson, who was on his right, and lavished all his attention on Félicité herself, this manoeuvre was unproductive. After a few minutes Lady Pastern engaged Edward in what Carlisle felt to be an extremely ominous conversation. She caught only fragments of it as Rivera had resumed his crash tactics with herself. His was a simple technique. He merely turned his shoulder on Lady Pastern, leant so close to Carlisle that she could see the pores of his skin, looked into her eyes and, with rich insinuation, contradicted everything she said. Lord Pastern was no refuge as he had sunk into a reverie from which he roused himself from time to time only to throw disjointed remarks at no one in particular, and to attack his food with a primitive gusto which dated from his Back-to-Nature period. His table manners were defiantly and deliberately atrocious. He chewed with parted lips, glaring about him like a threatened carnivore, and as he chewed he talked. To Spence and the man who assisted him and to Miss Henderson, who accepted her isolation with her usual composure, the conversation must have come through like the dialogue in a boldly surrealistic broadcast.

". . . such a good photograph, we thought, Edward, of you and Félicité at the Tarmac. She so much enjoyed her party with you . . ."

". . . but I'm not at all musical . . ."

". . . you must not say so. You are musical. There is music in your eyes—your voice . . ."

". . . now that's quite a nifty little idea, Miss de Suze. We'll have to pull you in with the Boys . . ."

". . . so it is arranged, my dear Edward."

". . . thank you, Cousin Cécile, but . . ."

". . . you and Félicité have always done things together, haven't you? We were laughing yesterday over some old photographs. Do you remember at Clochemere . . . ?"

". . . Gee, where's my sombrero?"

". . . with this dress you should wear flowers. A cascade of orchids. Just here. Let me show you . . ."

". . . I beg your pardon, Cousin Cécile, I'm afraid I didn't hear what you said . . ."

"Uncle George, it's time you talked to me . . ."

"Eh? Sorry, Lisle, I'm wondering where my sombrero . . ."

"Lord Pastern is very kind in letting me keep you to myself. Don't turn away. Look, your handkerchief is falling."

"*Damn!*"

"Edward!"

"I beg your pardon, Cousin Cécile, I don't know what I'm thinking of."

"Carlos."

". . . in my country, Miss Wayne . . . no, I cannot call you Miss Wayne. Car-r-r-lisle! What a strange name . . . Strange and captivating."

"Carlos!"

"Forgive me. You spoke?"

"About those umbrellas, Breezy."

"Yes, I did speak."

"A thousand pardons, I was talking to Carrlisle."

"I've engaged a table for three, Fée. You and Carlisle and Ned. Don't be late."

"My music to-night shall be for you."

"I am coming also, George."

"*What!*"

"Kindly see that it is a table for four."

"*Maman!* But I thought . . ."

"You won't like it, C."

"I propose to come."

"Damn it, you'll sit and glare at me and make me nervous."

"Nonsense, George," Lady Pastern said crisply. "Be good enough to order the table."

Her husband glowered at her, seemed to contemplate giving further battle, appeared suddenly to change his mind and launched an unexpected attack at Rivera.

"About your being carried out, Carlos," he said importantly. "It seems a pity I can't be carried out too. Why can't the stretcher party come back for me?"

"Now, now, now," Mr. Bellairs interrupted in a great hurry. "We've got everything fixed, Lord Pastern, now, haven't we? The first routine. You shoot Carlos. Carlos falls. Carlos is carried out. You take the show away. Big climax. Finish. Now don't you get me bustled," he added playfully. "It's good and it's fixed. Fine. That's right, isn't it?"

"It is what has been decided," Mr. Rivera conceded grandly. "For myself, I am perhaps a little dubious. Under other circumstances I would undoubtedly insist upon the second routine. I am shot at but I do not fall. Lord Pastern misses me. The others fall. Breezy fires at Lord Pastern and nothing happens. Lord Pastern plays, faints, is removed. I finish the number. Upon this routine under other circumstances, I should insist." He executed a sort of comprehensive bow, taking in Lord Pastern, Félicité, Carlisle and Lady Pastern. "But under these exclusive and most charming circumstances, I yield. I am shot. I fall. Possibly I hurt myself. No matter."

Bellairs eyed him. "Good old Carlos," he said uneasily.

"I still don't see why I can't be carried out too," said Lord Pastern fretfully.

Carlisle heard Mr. Bellairs whisper under his breath: "For the love of Pete!" Rivera said loudly: "No, no, no, no. Unless we adopt completely the second routine, we perform the first as we rehearse. It is settled."

"Carlisle," said Lady Pastern, rising, "shall we . . . ?"

She swept her ladies into the drawing-room.

ii

Félicité was puzzled, resentful and uneasy. She moved restlessly about the room, eyeing her mother and Carlisle. Lady Pastern paid no attention to her daughter. She questioned Carlisle about her experiences in Greece and received her somewhat distracted answers with perfect equanimity. Miss Henderson, who had taken up Lady Pastern's box of embroidery threads, sorted them with quiet movements of her hands and seemed to listen with interest.

Suddenly Félicité said: "I don't see much future in us all behaving as if we'd had the Archbishop of Canterbury to dinner. If you've got anything to say about Carlos, all of you, I'd be very much obliged if you'd say it."

Miss Henderson, her hands still for a moment, glanced up at Félicité and then bent again over her task. Lady Pastern, having crossed her ankles and wrists, slightly moved her shoulders and said: "I do not consider this a suitable occasion, my dear child, for any such discussion."

"Why?" Félicité demanded.

"It would make a scene, and under the circumstances," said Lady Pastern with an air of reasonableness, "there's no time for a scene."

"If you think the men are coming in, *Maman*, they are not. George has arranged to go over the programme again in the ballroom."

A servant came in and collected the coffee cups. Lady Pastern made conversation with Carlisle until the door had closed behind him.

"So I repeat," Félicité said loudly, "I want to hear, *Maman*, what you've got to say against Carlos."

Lady Pastern slightly raised her eyes and lifted her shoulders. Her daughter stamped. "Blast and hell!" she said.

"Félicité!" said Miss Henderson. It was neither a remonstrance nor a warning. The name fell like an unstressed comment. Miss Henderson held an embroidery stiletto firmly between finger and thumb and examined it placidly. Félicité made an impatient movement. "If you think," she said violently, "anybody's going to be at their best in a strange house with a hostess who looks at them as if they smelt!"

"If it comes to that, dearest child, he does smell. Of a particularly heavy kind of scent, I fancy," Lady Pastern added thoughtfully.

From the ballroom came a distant syncopated roll of drums ending in a crash of cymbals and a loud report. Carlisle jumped nervously. The stiletto fell from Miss Henderson's fingers to the carpet. Félicité, bearing witness in her agitation to the efficacy of her governess's long training, stooped and picked it up.

"It is your uncle, merely," said Lady Pastern.

"I ought to go straight out and apologize to Carlos for the hideous way he's been treated," Félicité stormed, but her voice held an overtone of uncertainty and she looked resentfully at Carlisle.

"If there are to be apologies," her mother rejoined, "it is Carlisle who should receive them. I am so sorry, Carlisle, that you should have been subjected to these—" she made a fastidious gesture—"these really insufferable attentions."

"Good Lord, Aunt C," Carlisle began in acute embarrassment and was rescued by Félicité, who burst into tears and rushed out of the room.

"I think perhaps . . . ?" said Miss Henderson, rising.

"Yes, please go to her."

But before Miss Henderson reached the door, which Félicité had left open, Rivera's voice sounded in the hall. "What is the matter?" it said distinctly and Félicité, breathless, answered, "I've got to talk to you." "But certainly, if you wish it." "In here, then." The voices faded, were heard again, indistinctly, in the study. The connecting door between the study and the drawing-room was slammed to from the far side.

"You had better leave them, I think," said Lady Pastern.

"If I go to my sitting-room, she may come to me when this is over."

"Then go," said Lady Pastern, drearily. "Thank you, Miss Henderson."

"Aunt," said Carlisle when Miss Henderson had left them, "what are you up to?"

Lady Pastern, shielding her face from the fire, said: "I have made a decision. I believe that my policy in this affair has been a mistaken one. Anticipating my inevitable opposition, Félicité has met this person in his own setting and has, as I think you would say, lost her eye. I cannot believe that when she has seen him here, and has observed his atrocious antics, his immense vulgarity, she will not come to her senses. Already, one can see, she is shaken. After all, I remind myself, she is a de Fouteaux and a de Suze. Am I not right?"

"It's an old trick, darling, you know. It doesn't always work."

"It is working, however," said Lady Pastern, setting her mouth. "She sees him, for example, beside dear Edward, to whom she has always been devoted. Of your uncle as a desirable contrast, I say nothing, but at least his clothes are unexceptionable. And though I deeply resent, dearest child, that you should have been forced, in my house, to suffer the attentions of this animal, they have assuredly impressed themselves disagreeably upon Félicité."

"Disagreeably—yes," said Carlisle, turning pink. "But look here, Aunt Cécile, he's shooting this nauseating little line with me to—well, to make Fée sit up and take notice." Lady Pastern momentarily closed her eyes. This, Carlisle remembered, was her habitual reaction to slang. "And, I'm not sure," Carlisle added, "that she hasn't fallen for it."

"She cannot be anything but disgusted."

"I wouldn't be astonished if she refuses to come to the Metronome to-night."

"That is what I hope. But I am afraid she will come. She will not give way so readily, I think." Lady Pastern rose. "Whatever happens," she said, "I shall break this affair. Do you hear me, Carlisle? I shall break it."

Beyond the door at the far end of the room, Félicité's voice rose, in a sharp crescendo, but the words were indistinguishable.

"They are quarrelling," said Lady Pastern with satisfaction.

iii

As Edward Manx sat silent in his chair, glass of port and a cup of coffee before him, his thoughts moved out in widening circles from the candle-lit table. Removed from him, Bellairs and Rivera had drawn close to Lord Pastern. Bellairs's voice, loud but edgeless, uttered phrase after phrase. "Sure, that's right. Don't worry, it's in the bag. It's going to be a world-breaker. O.K., we'll run it through. Fine." Pastern fidgeted, stuttered, chuckled, complained. Rivera, leaning back in his chair, smiled, said nothing and turned his glass. Manx, who had noticed how frequently it had been refilled, wondered if he was tight.

There they sat, wreathed in cigar smoke, candle-lit, an unreal group. He saw them as three dissonant figures at the centre of an intolerable design. "Bellairs," he told himself, "is a gaiety merchant. Gaiety!" How fashionable, he reflected, the word had been before the war. Let's be gay, they had all said, and glumly embracing each other had tramped and shuffled, while men like Breezy Bellairs made their noise and did their smiling for them. They christened their children "Gay," they used the word in their drawing-room comedies and in their dismal, dismal songs. "Gaiety!" muttered the disgruntled and angry Edward. "A lovely word, but the thing itself, when enjoyed, is unnamed. There's Cousin George, who is undoubtedly a little mad, sitting, like a mouth-piece for his kind, between a jive merchant and a cad. And here's Fée anticking inside the unholy circle while Cousin Cécile solemnly gyrates against the beat. In an outer ring, I hope unwillingly, is Lisle, and here I sit, as sore as hell, on the perimeter." He glanced up and found that Rivera was looking at him, not directly but out of the corners of his eyes. "Sneering," thought Edward, "like an infernal caricature of himself."

"Buck up, Ned," Lord Pastern said, grinning at him. "We haven't had a word from you. You want takin' out of yourself. Bit of gaiety, what?"

"By all means, sir," said Edward. A white carnation had fallen out of the vase in the middle of the table. He took it up and put it in his coat. "The blameless life," he said.

Lord Pastern cackled and turned to Bellairs. "Well, Breezy, if you think it's all right, we'll order the taxis for a quarter past ten. Think you can amuse yourselves till then?" He pushed the decanter towards Bellairs.

"Sure, sure," Bellairs said. "No, thanks a lot, no more. A lovely wine, mind you, but I've got to be a good boy."

Edward slid the port on to Rivera, who, smiling a little more broadly, refilled his glass.

"I'll show you the blanks and the revolver, when we move," said Lord Pastern. "They're in the study." He glanced fretfully at Rivera, who slowly pulled his glass towards him. Lord Pastern hated to be kept waiting. "Ned, you look after Carlos, will you? D'you mind, Carlos? I want to show Breezy the blanks. Come on, Breezy."

Manx opened the door for his uncle and returned to the table. He sat down and waited for Rivera to make the first move. Spence came in, lingered for a moment and withdrew. There followed a long silence.

At last Rivera stretched out his legs and held his port to the light. "I am a man," he said, "who likes to come to the point. You are Félicité's cousin, yes?"

"No."

"No?"

"I'm related to her stepfather."

"She has spoken of you as her cousin."

"A courtesy title," said Edward.

"You are attached to her, I believe."

Edward paused for three seconds and then said, "Why not?"

"It is not at all surprising," Rivera said and drank half his port. "Carlisle also speaks of you as her cousin. Is that too a courtesy title?"

Edward pushed back his chair. "I'm afraid I don't see the point of all this," he said.

"The point? Certainly. I am a man," Rivera repeated, "who likes to come to the point. I am also a man who does not care to be cold-shouldered or to be—what is the expression?—taken down a garden path. I find my reception in this house unsympathetic. This is displeasing to me. I meet, at the same time, a lady who is not displeasing to me. Quite on the contrary. I am interested. I make a tactful inquiry. I ask, for example, what is the relationship of this lady to my host. Why not?"

"Because it's a singularly offensive question," Edward said and thought: "My God, I'm going to lose my temper."

Rivera made a convulsive movement of his hand and knocked his glass to the floor. They rose simultaneously.

"In my country," Rivera said thickly, "one does not use such expressions without a sequel."

"Be damned to your country."

Rivera gripped the back of his chair and moistened his lips. He emitted a shrill belch. Edward laughed. Rivera walked towards him, paused, and raised his hand with the tips of the thumb and middle finger daintily pressed together. He advanced his hand until it was close to Edward's nose and, without marked success, attempted to snap his fingers. "Bastard," he said cautiously. From the distant ballroom came a syncopated roll of drums ending in a crash of cymbals and deafening report.

Edward said: "Don't be a fool, Rivera."

"I laugh at you till I make myself vomit."

"Laugh yourself into a coma if you like."

Rivera laid the palm of his hand against his waist. "In my country this affair would answer itself with a knife," he said.

"Make yourself scarce or it'll answer itself with a kick in the pants," said Edward. "And if you worry Miss Wayne again I'll give you a damn' sound hiding."

"Aha!" cried Rivera. "So it is not Félicité but the cousin. It is the enchanting little Carlisle. And I am to be warned off, ha? No, no, my friend." He backed away to the door. "No, no, no, no."

"*Get out.*"

Rivera laughed with great virtuosity and made an effective exit into the hall. He left the door open. Edward heard his voice on the next landing. "What is the matter?" and after a pause, "But certainly, if you wish it." A door slammed.

Edward walked once round the table in an irresolute manner. He then wandered to the sideboard and drove his hands through his hair. "This is incredible," he muttered. "It's extraordinary. I never dreamt of it." He noticed that his hand was shaking and poured himself a stiff jorum of whiskey. "I suppose," he thought, "it's been there all the time and I simply didn't recognize it."

Spence and his assistant came in. "I beg your pardon, sir," said Spence. "I thought the gentlemen had left."

"It's all right, Spence. Clear, if you want to. Pay no attention to me."

"Are you not feeling well, Mr. Edward?"

"I'm all right, I think. I've had a great surprise."

"Indeed, sir? Pleasant, I trust."

"In its way, wonderful, Spence. Wonderful."

iv

"There y'are," said Lord Pastern complacently. "Five rounds and five extras. Neat, aren't they?"

"Look good to me," said Bellairs, returning him the blank cartridges.

"But I wouldn't know." Lord Pastern broke open his revolver and began to fill the chamber. "We'll try 'em," he said.

"Not in here, for Pete's sake, Lord Pastern."

"In the ballroom."

"It'll rock the ladies a bit, won't it?"

"What of it?" said Lord Pastern simply. He snapped the revolver shut and gave the drawer a shove back on the desk. "I can't be bothered puttin' that thing away," he said. "You go to the ballroom. I've a job to do. I'll join you in a minute."

Obediently, Breezy left him and went into the ballroom, where he wandered about restlessly, sighing and yawning and glancing towards the door.

Presently his host came in looking preoccupied.

"Where's Carlos?" Lord Pastern demanded.

"Still in the dining-room, I think," said Bellairs with his loud laugh. "Wonderful port you've turned on for us, you know, Lord Pastern."

"Hope he can hold it. We don't want him playin' the fool with the show."

"He can hold it."

Lord Pastern clapped his revolver down on the floor near the tympani. Bellairs eyed it uneasily.

"I wanted to ask you," said Lord Pastern, sitting behind the drums. "Have you spoken to Sydney Skelton?"

Bellairs smiled extensively. "Well, I just haven't got round . . ." he began. Lord Pastern cut him short. "If you don't want to tell him," he said, "I will."

"No, no!" cried Bellairs, in a hurry. "No. I don't think that'd be quite desirable, Lord Pastern, if you can understand." He looked anxiously at his host, who had turned away to the piano and with an air of restless preoccupation examined the black and white parasol. Breezy continued: "I mean to say, Syd's funny. He's very temperamental if you know what I mean. He's quite a tough guy to handle, Syd. You have to pick your moment with Syd, if you can understand."

"Don't keep on asking if I can understand things that are as simple as falling off a log," Lord Pastern rejoined irritably. "You think I'm good on the drums, you've said so."

"Sure, sure."

"You said if I'd made it my profession I'd have been as good as they come. You said any band'd be proud to have me. Right. I am going to make it my profession and I'm prepared to be your full-time tympanist. Good. Tell Skelton and let him go. Perfectly simple."

"Yes, but—"

"He'll get a job elsewhere fast enough, won't he?"

"Yes. Sure. Easy. But . . ."

"Very well, then," said Lord Pastern conclusively. He had unscrewed the handle from the parasol and was now busy with the top end of the shaft. "This comes to bits," he said. "Rather clever, what? French."

"Look!" said Bellairs winningly. He laid his soft white hand on Lord Pastern's coat. "I'm going to speak very frankly, Lord Pastern. You know. It's a hard old world in our game, if you under—I mean, I have to think all round a proposition like this, don't I?"

"You've said you wished you had me permanently," Lord Pastern reminded him. He spoke with a certain amount of truculence but rather absent-mindedly. He had unscrewed a small section from the top end of the parasol shaft. Breezy watched him mesmerized as he took up his revolver and, with the restless concentration of a small boy in mischief, poked this section on a short way up the muzzle, at the same time holding down with his thumb the spring catch that served to keep the parasol closed. "This," he said, "would fit."

"Hi!" Breezy said. "Is that gun loaded?"

"Of course," Lord Pastern muttered. He put down the piece of shaft and glanced up. "You said it to me and Rivera," he added. He had Hotspur's trick of reverting to the last remark but four.

"I know, I know," Bellairs gabbled, smiling to the full extent of his mouth, "but listen. I'm going to put this very crudely . . ."

"Why the hell shouldn't you!"

"Well, then. You're very keen and you're good. Sure, you're good! But, excuse my frankness, will you stay keen? That's my point, Lord Pastern. Suppose, to put it crudely, you died on it."

"I'm fifty-five and as fit as a flea."

"I mean suppose you kind of lost interest. Where," asked Mr. Bellairs passionately, "would I be then?"

"I've told you perfectly plainly . . ."

"Yes, but . . ."

"Do you call me a liar, you bloody fellow?" shouted Lord Pastern, two brilliant patches of scarlet flaming over his cheekbones. He clapped the dismembered parts of the parasol on the piano and turned on his conductor, who began to stammer.

"Now, listen, Lord Pastern . . . I—I'm nervy to-night. I'm all upset. Don't get me flustered, now."

Lord Pastern bared his teeth at him. "You're a fool," he said. "I've been watchin' you." He appeared to cogitate and come to a decision. "Ever read a magazine called *Harmony*?" he demanded.

Breezy shied violently. "Why, yes. Why—I don't know what your idea is, Lord Pastern, bringing that up."

"I've half a mind," Lord Pastern said darkly, "to write to that paper. I know a chap on the staff." He brooded for a moment, whistling between his teeth, and then barked abruptly: "If you don't speak to Skelton to-night, I'll talk to him myself."

"O.K., O.K. I'll have a wee chat with Syd. O.K."

Lord Pastern looked fixedly at him. "You'd better pull y'self together," he said. He took up his drumsticks and without more ado beat out a deafening crescendo, crashed his cymbals, and snatching up his revolver, pointed it at Bellairs and fired. The report echoed madly in the empty ballroom. The piano, the cymbals and the double-bass zoomed in protest and Bellairs, white to the lips, danced sideways.

"For crisake!" he said violently and broke into a profuse sweat.

Lord Pastern laughed delightedly and laid his revolver on the piano. "Good, isn't it?" he said. "Let's just run through the programme. First, there's 'A New Way with Old Tunes,' 'Any Ice To-day?' 'I Got Everythin',' 'The Peanut Vendor' and 'The Umbrella Man.' That's a damn' good idea of mine about the umbrellas."

Bellairs eyed the collection on the piano and nodded.

"The black and white parasol's m'wife's. She doesn't know I've taken it. You might put it together and hide it under the others, will you? We'll smuggle 'em out when she's not lookin'."

Bellairs fumbled with the umbrellas and Lord Pastern continued: "Then Skelton does his thing. I find it a bit dull, that number. And then the Sandra woman does her songs. And then," he said with an affectation of carelessness, "then you say somethin' to introduce me, don't you?"

"That's right."

"Yes. Somethin' to the effect that I happened to show you a thing I'd written, you know, and you were taken with it and that I've decided that my *métier* lies in this direction and all that. What?"

"Quite."

"I come out and we play it once through and then we swing it, and then there's the shootin', and then, by God, I go into my solo. Yes."

Lord Pastern took up his drumsticks, held them poised for a moment and appeared to go into a brief trance. "I'm still not so sure the other routine wasn't the best after all," he said.

"Listen! Listen!" Breezy began in a panic.

Lord Pastern said absently: "Now, you keep your hair on. I'm thinkin'." He appeared to think for some moments and then—ejaculating "Sombrero!" —darted out of the room.

Breezy Bellairs wiped his face with his handkerchief, sank on to the piano stool and held his head in his hands.

After a considerable interval the ballroom doors were opened and Rivera came in. Bellairs eyed him. "How's tricks, Carlos?" he asked dolefully.

"Not good." Rivera, stroking his moustache with his forefinger, walked stiffly to the piano. "I have quarrelled with Félicité."

"You asked for it, didn't you? Your little line with Miss Wayne . . ."

"It is well to show women that they are not irreplaceable. They become anxious and, in a little while, they are docile."

"Has it worked out that way?"

"Not yet, perhaps. I am angry with her." He made a florid and violent gesture. "With them all! I have been treated like a dog, I, Carlos de . . ."

"Listen," said Breezy, "I can't face a temperament from you, old boy.

I'm nearly crazy with worry myself. I just can't face it. God, I wish I'd never taken the old fool on! God, I'm in a mess! Give me a cigarette, Carlos."

"I am sorry. I have none."

"I asked you to get me cigarettes," said Breezy and his voice rose shrilly.

"It was not convenient. You smoke too much."

"Go to hell."

"Everywhere," Rivera shouted, "I am treated with impertinence. Everywhere I am insulted." He advanced upon Bellairs, his head thrust forward. "I am sick of it all," he said. "I have humbled myself too much. I am a man of quick decisions. No longer shall I cheapen myself by playing in a common dance band . . ."

"Here, here, here!"

"I give you, now, my notice."

"You're under contract. Listen, old man . . ."

"I spit on your contract. No longer shall I be your little errand boy. 'Get me some cigarettes.' Bah!"

"Carlos!"

"I shall return to my own country."

"Listen old boy . . . I . . . I'll raise your screw . . ." His voice faltered.

Rivera looked at him and smiled. "Indeed? By how much? It would be by perhaps five pounds?"

"Have a heart, Carlos."

"Or if, for instance, you would care to advance me five hundred . . ."

"You're crazy! Carlos, for Pete's sake . . . Honestly, I haven't got it."

"Then," said Rivera magnificently, "you may look for another to bring you your cigarettes. For me it is . . . finish."

Breezy wailed loudly: "And where will I be? What about me?"

Rivera smiled and moved away. With an elaborate display of nonchalance, he surveyed himself in a wall-glass, fingering his tie. "You will be in a position of great discomfort, my friend," he said. "You will be unable to replace me. I am quite irreplaceable." He examined his moustache closely in the glass and caught sight of Breezy's reflection. "Don't look like that," he said, "you are extremely ugly when you look like that. Quite revolting."

"It's a breach of contract. I can . . ." Breezy wetted his lips. "There's the law," he mumbled. "I suppose . . ."

Rivera turned and faced him.

"The law?" he said. "I am obliged to you. Of course one can call upon the law, can one not? That is a wise step for a band leader to take, no doubt. I find the suggestion amusing. I shall enjoy repeating it to the ladies who smile at you so kindly, and ask you so anxiously for their favourite numbers. When I no longer play in your band their smiles will become infrequent and they will go elsewhere for their favourite numbers."

"You wouldn't do that, Carlos."

"Let me tell you, my good Breezy, that if the law is to be invoked it is I who invoke it."

"Damn and blast you," Breezy shouted in a frenzy.

"What the devil's all the row about?" asked Lord Pastern. He had entered unobserved. A wide-brimmed sombrero decorated his head, its strap supporting his double chin. "I thought I'd wear this," he said. "It goes with the shootin' don't you think? Yipee!"

v

When Rivera left her, Félicité had sat on in the study, her hands clenched between her knees, trying to bury quickly and forever the memory of the scene they had just ended. She looked aimlessly about her, at the litter of tools in the open drawer at her elbow, at the typewriter, at familiar prints, ornaments and books. Her throat was dry. She was filled with nausea and an arid hatred. She wished ardently to rid herself of all memory of Rivera and in doing so to humiliate and injure him. She was still for so long that when at last she moved, her right leg was numb and her foot pricked and tingled. As she rose stiffly and cautiously, she heard someone cross to the landing, pass the study and go into the drawing-room next door.

"I'll go up to Hendy," she thought. "I'll ask Hendy to tell them I'm not coming to the Metronome."

She went out on the landing. Somewhere on the second floor her stepfather's voice shouted: "My sombrero, you silly chap— Somebody's taken it. That's all. Somebody's collared it." Spence came through the drawing-room door, carrying an envelope on a salver.

"It's for you, miss," he said. "It was left on the hall table. I'm sure I'm very sorry it was not noticed before."

She took it. It was addressed in typescript. Across the top was printed a large "Urgent" with "by District Messenger" underneath. Félicité returned to the study and tore it open.

Three minutes later Miss Henderson's door was flung open and she, lifting her gaze from her book, saw Félicité, glowing before her.

"Hendy—Hendy, come and help me dress. Hendy, come and make me lovely. Something marvellous has happened. Hendy, darling, it's going to be a wonderful party."

CHAPTER V

A Wreath for Rivera

Against a deep blue background the arm of a giant metronome kept up its inane and constant gesture. It was outlined in miniature lights, and to those patrons who had drunk enough, it left in its wake a formal ghost pattern of itself in colour. It was mounted on part of the wall overhanging the band alcove. The ingenious young man responsible for the *décor* had so designed this alcove that the band platform itself appeared as a projection from the skeleton tower of the metronome. The tip of the arm swept to and fro above the bandsmen's heads in a maddening reiterative arc, pointing them out, insisting on their noise. An inverted metronome had been considered "great fun" by the ingenious young man but it had been found advisable to switch off the mechanism from time to time and when this was done the indicator pointed downwards. Either Breezy Bellairs or a favoured soloist was careful to place himself directly beneath the light-studded pointer at its tip.

On their semicircular rostrum the seven performers of the dance band crouched, blowing, scraping and hitting at their instruments. This was the band that worked on extension nights, from dinner time to eleven o'clock, at the Metronome. It was known as the Jivesters, and was not as highly paid or as securely established as Breezy Bellairs and His Boys. But of course it was a good band, carefully selected by Caesar Bonn, the manager and *maître de café*, who was also a big shareholder in the Metronome.

Caesar himself, glossy, immeasurably smart, in full control of his accurately graded cordiality, moved, with a light waggle of his hips, from the vestibule into the restaurant and surveyed his guests. He bowed roguishly as his head-waiter, with raised hand, preceded a party of five to their table. "Hullo, Caesar. Evenin'," said Lord Pastern. "Brought my family, you see."

Caesar flourished his hands. "It is a great evening for the Metronome, my lady. A gala of galas."

"No doubt," said her ladyship.

She seated her guests. She herself, with erect bust, faced the dance floor, her back to the wall. She raised her lorgnette. Caesar and the headwaiter hovered. Lord Pastern ordered hock.

"We are much too close, George," Lady Pastern shouted above the Jivesters, who had just broken out in a frenzy. And indeed their table had been crammed in alongside the band dais and hard by the tympanist. Félicité could have touched his foot. "I had it put here specially," Lord Pastern yelled. "I knew you'd want to watch me."

Carlisle, sitting between her uncle and Edward Manx, nervously clutched her evening bag and wondered if they were all perhaps a little mad. What, for instance, had come over Félicité? Why, whenever she looked at Edward, did she blush? Why did she look so often and so queerly at him, like a bewildered and—yes—a besotted schoolgirl? And why, on the landing at Duke's Gate, after a certain atrocious scene with Rivera (Carlisle closed her memory on the scent), had Ned behaved with such ferocity? And why, after all, was she, in the middle of a complicated and disagreeable crisis, so happy?

Edward Manx, seated between Félicité and Carlisle, was also bewildered. A great many things had happend to him that evening. He had had a row with Rivera in the dining-room. He had made an astonishing discovery. Later (and, unlike Carlisle, he found this recollection entirely agreeable) he had come on to the landing at the precise moment when Rivera was making a determined effort to embrace Carlisle and had hit Rivera very hard on the left ear. While they were still, all three of them, staring at each other, Félicité had appeared with a letter in her hands. She had taken one look at Edward and, going first white under her make-up and then scarlet, had fled upstairs. From that moment she had behaved in the most singular manner imaginable. She kept catching his eye and as often as this happened she smiled and blushed. Once she gave a mad little laugh. Edward shook his head and asked Lady Pastern to dance. She consented. He rose, and placing his right hand behind her iron waist walked her cautiously down the dance floor. It was formidable, dancing with Cousin Cécile.

"If anything," she said when they had reached the spot farthest away from the band, "could compensate for my humiliation in appearing at this lamentable affair, my dearest boy, it is the change your presence has wrought in Félicité."

"Really?" said Edward nervously.

"Indeed, yes. From her childhood, you have exerted a profound influence."

"Look here, Cousin Cécile—" Edward began in extreme discomfort, but at that moment the dance band, which had for some time contented itself with the emission of syncopated grunts and pants, suddenly flared up into an elaborate rumpus. Edward was silenced.

Lord Pastern put his head on one side and contemplated the band with an air of critical patronage. "They're not bad, you know," he said, "but they haven't got enough guts. Wait till you hear us, Lisle. What?"

"I know," Carlisle said encouragingly. At the moment his naïveté touched her. She was inclined to praise him as one would a child. Her eyes followed Edward, who now guided Lady Pastern gingerly past the band dais. Carlisle watched them go by and in so doing caught the eye of a man who sat at the next table. He was a monkish-looking person with a fastidious mouth and well-shaped head. A woman with short dark hair was with him. They had an air of comradeship. "They look nice," Carlisle thought. She felt suddenly uplifted and kindly disposed to all the world, and, on this impulse, turned to Félicité. She found that Félicité, also, was watching Edward and still with that doting and inexplicable attention.

"Fée," she said softly, "what's up? What's happened?" Félicité, without changing the direction of her gaze, said: "Something too shattering,
darling. I'm all *bouleversée* but I'm in heaven."

Edward and Lady Pastern, after two gyrations, came to a halt by their
table. She disengaged herself and resumed her seat. Edward slipped in between Carlisle and Félicité. Félicité leant towards him and drew the white
carnation from his coat. "There's nobody else here with a white flower,"
she said softly.

"I'm very *vieux jeu* in my ways," Edward rejoined.

"Let's dance, shall we?"

"Yes, of course."

"Want to dance, C?" asked Lord Pastern.

"No thank you, George."

"Mind if Lisle and I trip a measure? It's a quarter to eleven, I'll have
to go round and join the Boys in five minutes. Come on, Lisle."

You had, thought Carlisle, to keep your wits about you when you danced
with Uncle George. He had a fine sense of rhythm and tremendous vigour.
No stickler for the conventions, he improvised steps as the spirit moved him,
merely tightening his grip upon her as an indication of further variations
and eccentricities. She noticed other couples glancing at them with more animation than usually appears on the faces of British revellers.

"D'you jitter-bug?" he asked.

"No, darling."

"Pity. They think 'emselves too grand for it in this place. Sickenin' lot
of snobs people are, by and large, Lisle. Did I tell you I'm seriously con-
siderin' givin' up the title?"

He swung her round with some violence. At the far end of the room she
caught a glimpse of her cousin and his partner. Ned's back was towards
her. Félicité gazed into his eyes. Her hand moved farther across his shoulders.
He stooped his head.

"Let's rejoin Aunt C, shall we?" said Carlisle in a flat voice.

ii

Breezy Bellairs hung up his overcoat on the wall and sat down, without
much show of enthusiasm, at a small table in the inner room behind the
office. The tympanist, Syd Skelton, threw a pack of cards on the table and
glanced at his watch. "Quarter to," he said. "Time for a brief gamble."

He dealt two poker hands. Breezy and Skelton played show poker on most
nights at about this time. They would leave the Boys in their room behind
the band dais and wander across to the office. They would exchange a word
with Caesar or David Hahn, the secretary, in the main office, and then repair
to the inner room for their game. It was an agreeable prelude to the long
night's business.

"Hear you've been dining in exalted places," said Skelton acidly.

Breezy smiled automatically and with trembling hands picked up his cards. They played in a scarcely broken silence. Once or twice Skelton invited conversation, but without success.

At last he said irritably: "What's the trouble? Why the great big silence?"

Breezy fiddled with his cards and said: "I'm licked to hell, Syd."

"For the love of Mike! What's the tragedy this time?"

"Everything. I'll crack if it goes on. Honest, I'm shot to pieces."

"It's your own show. I've warned you. You look terrible."

"And how do I feel! Listen, Syd, it's this stunt to-night. It's his lordship. It's been a big mistake."

"I could have told you that, too. I did tell you."

"I know. I know. But we're booked to capacity, Syd."

"It's cheap publicity. Nothing more nor less and you know it. Pandering to a silly dope, just because he's got a title."

"He's not all that bad. As an artist."

"He's terrible," said Skelton briefly.

"I know the number's crazy and full of corn but it'll get by. It's not that, old boy, it's him. Honest, Syd, I think he's crackers." Breezy threw his cards face down on the table. "He's got me that *nervy*," he said. "Listen, Syd, he's—he hasn't said anything to you, has he?"

"What about?"

"So he hasn't. All right. Fine. Don't take any notice if he does, old man."

Skelton leant back in his chair. "What the hell are you trying to tell me?" he demanded.

"Now don't make me nervous," Breezy implored him. "You know how nervy I get. It's just a crazy notion he's got. I'll stall him off, you bet." He paused. Skelton said ominously, "It wouldn't be anything about wanting to repeat this fiasco, would it?"

"In a way, it would, Syd. Mind, it's laughable."

"Now, you get this," Skelton said and leant across the table. "I've stood down once, to-night, to oblige you, and I don't like it and I won't do it again. What's more it's given me a kind of unpleasant feeling that I'm doing myself no good, working with an outfit that goes in for cheap sensationalism. You know me. I'm quick-tempered and I make quick decisions. There's other bands."

"Now, Syd, Syd, Syd! Take it easy," Breezy gabbled. "Forget it, old boy. I wouldn't have mentioned anything only he talked about chatting to you himself."

"By God," Skelton said, staring at him, "are you trying to tell me, by any chance, that this old so-and-so thinks he'd like my job? Have you got the flaming nerve to . . ."

"For crisake, Syd! Listen, Syd, I said it was crazy. Listen, it's going to be all right. It's not my fault, Syd. Be fair, now, it's not my fault."

"Whose fault is it then?"

"Carlos," said Breezy, lowering his voice to a whisper. "Take it easy, now. He's next door, having a drink with Caesar. It's Carlos. He's put the idea in the old bee's head. He wants to keep in with him on account the girl can't make up her mind and him wanting the old bee to encourage her. It's all Carlos, Syd. He told him he was wonderful."

Skelton said briefly what he thought of Rivera. Breezy looked nervously towards the door. "This settles it," Skelton said and rose. "I'll talk to Carlos, by God." Breezy clawed at him. "No, Syd, not now. Not before the show. Keep your voice down, Syd, there's a pal. He's in there. You know how he is. He's thrown a temperament once to-night. Geeze," cried Breezy, springing to his feet, "I nearly forgot! He wants us to use the other routine in the new number, after all. Can you beat it? First it's this way and then it's what-have-you. He's got me so's I'm liable to give an imitation of a maestro doing two numbers at once. Gawd knows how his lordship'll take it. I got to tell the Boys. I as near as damn it forgot, I'm that nervy. Listen, you haven't heard what's really got me so worried. You know what I am. It's that gun. It's such a hell of a thing, Syd, and his lordship's made those blanks himself and, by God, I'm nervous. He's dopey enough to mix the real things up with the phony ones. They were all mucked up together in a bloody drawer, Syd, and there you are. And he really points the thing at Carlos, old boy, and fires it. Doesn't he now?"

"I wouldn't lose any sleep if he plugged him," said Skelton with violence.

"Don't talk that way, Syd," Breezy whispered irritably. "It's a hell of a situation. I hoped you'd help me, Syd."

"Why don't you have a look at the gun?"

"Me? I wouldn't know. He wouldn't let me near it. I tell you straight, I'm scared to go near him for fear I start him up bawling me out."

After a long pause, Skelton said: "Are you serious about this gun?"

"Do I look as if I was kidding?"

"It's eight minutes to eleven. We'd better go across. If I get a chance I'll ask him to show me the ammunition."

"Fine, Syd. That'd be swell," said Breezy, mopping his forehead. "It'd be marvellous. You're a pal, Syd. Come on. Let's go."

"Mind," Skelton said, "I'm not passing up the other business. I've just about had Mr. Carlos Rivera. He's going to find something out before he's much older. Come on."

They passed through the office. Rivera, who was sitting there with Caesar Bonn, disregarded them. Breezy looked timidly at him. "I'm just going to fix it with the Boys, old man," he said. "You'll enter by the end door, won't you?"

"Why not?" Rivera said acidly. "It is my usual entrance. I perform as I rehearse. Naturally."

"That's right. Naturally. Excuse my fussiness. Let's go, Syd."

Caesar rose. "It is time? Then I must felicitate our new artist."

He preceded them across the vestibule where crowds of late arrivals still streamed in. Here they encountered Félicité, Carlisle and Edward. "We're going in to wish George luck," said Félicité. "Hullo, Syd. Nice of you to let him have his fling. Come on, chaps."

They all entered the band-room, which was immediately behind the dais end of the restaurant and led into the band alcove. Here they found the Boys assembled with their instruments. Breezy held up his hand and, sweating copiously, beamed at them. "Listen, boys. Get this. We'll use the other routine, if it's all the same with the composer. Carlos doesn't feel happy about the fall. He's afraid he may hurt himself on account he's holding his instrument."

"Here!" said Lord Pastern.

"It's the way you wanted it, Lord Pastern, isn't it?" Breezy gabbled. "That's fine, isn't it? Better egzzit altogether."

"I faint and get carried out?"

"That's right. The other routine. I persuaded Carlos. Everybody happy? Swell."

The Boys began to warm up their instruments. The room was filled with slight anticipatory noises. The double-bass muttered and zoomed.

Skelton strolled over to Lord Pastern. "I had to come in and wish the new sensation all the best," he said, looking hard at him.

"Thank yer."

"A great night," Caesar Bonn murmured. "It will be long remembered."

"Would this be a loaded gun?" Skelton asked and laughed unpleasantly.

The revolver lay, together with the sombrero, near the drums. Lord Pastern took it up. Skelton raised his hands above his head. "I confess everything," he said. "*Is* it loaded?"

"With blanks."

"By cripes," said Skelton with a loud laugh, "I hope they *are* blanks."

"George made them himself," said Félicité.

Skelton lowered his right hand and held it out towards Lord Pastern, who put the revolver into it.

Breezy, at a distance, sighed heavily. Skelton broke the revolver, slipped a finger-nail behind the rim of a cartridge and drew it out.

"Very nice work, Lord Pastern," he said. He spun the cylinder, drawing out and replacing one blank after the other. "Very nice work indeed," he said.

Lord Pastern, obviously gratified, embarked on a history of the revolver, of his own prowess as a marksman, and of the circumstances under which his brother-in-law had presented the revolver to him. He pointed out the initials scratched under the butt. Skelton made a show of squinting down the barrel, snapped the revolver shut and returned the weapon to Lord Pastern. He turned away and glanced at Breezy. "O.K.," he said. "What are we waiting for?" He began to heighten the tension of his drums. "Good luck to the new act," he said and the drum throbbed.

"Thanks, Syd," said Breezy.

His fingers were in his waistcoat pocket. He looked anxiously at Skelton.

He felt in one pocket after another. Sweat hung in fine beads over his eyebrows.

"What's up, boy?" said Happy Hart.

"I can't find my tablet."

He began pulling his pocket linings out. "I'm all to pieces, without it," he said. "God, I know I've got one somewhere!"

The door leading to the restaurant opened and the Jivesters came through with their instruments. They grinned at Breezy's Boys and looked sideways at Lord Pastern. The room was full of oiled heads, black figures and the strange shapes of saxophones, double-basses, piano-accordions and drums.

"We'd better make ourselves scarce, Fée," Edward said. "Come on, Lisle. Good luck, Cousin George."

"Good luck."

"Good luck."

They went out. Breezy still searched his pockets. The others watched him nervously.

"You shouldn't let yourself get this way," said Skelton. Lord Pastern pointed an accusing finger at Breezy. "Now perhaps you'll see the value of what I was tellin' you," he admonished. Breezy shot a venomous glance at him.

"For heaven's sake, boy," said Happy Hart. "We're *on!*"

"I've got to have it. I'm all shaky. I can't look. One of you . . ."

"What *is* all this!" Lord Pastern cried with extreme irritation. He darted at Breezy.

"It's only a tablet," Breezy said. "I always take one. For my nerves."

Lord Pastern said accusingly, "Tablet be damned!"

"For crisake, I *got* to have it, blast you."

"Put your hands up."

Lord Pastern began with ruthless efficiency to search Breezy. He hit him all over and turned out his pockets, allowing various objects to fall about his feet. He opened his cigarette case and wallet and explored their contents. He patted and prodded. Breezy giggled. "I'm ticklish," he said foolishly. Finally Lord Pastern jerked a handkerchief out of Breezy's breast pocket. A small white object fell from it. Breezy swooped on it, clapped his hand to his mouth and swallowed. "Thanks a lot. All set, boys? Let's go."

They went out ahead of him. The lights on the walls had been switched off. Only the pink table lamps glowed. A flood-light, hidden in the alcove ceiling, drove down its pool of amber on the gleaming dais; the restaurant was a swimming cave filled with dim faces, occasional jewels, many colours. The waiters flickered about inside it. Little drifts of cigarette smoke hung above the tables. From the restaurant, the band dais glowed romantically in its alcove. The players and their instruments looked hard and glossy. Above them the arm of the giant metronome pointed motionless at the floor. The Boys, smiling as if in great delight, seated themselves. The umbrellas, the sombrero and the tympani were carried in by waiters.

In the band-room Lord Pastern, standing beside Breezy, fiddled with his revolver, whistled under his breath and peered sideways through the door. Beyond the tympani, he could see the dimly glowing faces of his wife, his stepdaughter, his niece and his cousin. Félicité's face was inclined up to Ned Manx's. Lord Pastern suddenly gave a shrill cackle of laughter.

Breezy Bellairs glanced at him in dismay, passed his hand over his head, pulled down his waistcoat, assumed his ventriloquist's doll smile and made his entrance. The Boys played him on with their signature tune. A patter of clapping filled the restaurant like a mild shower. Breezy smiled, bowed, turned and, using finicking sharp gestures that were expressly his own, conducted.

Syd Skelton bounced slightly in his seat. His foot moved against the floor, not tapping but flexing and relaxing in a constant beat against the syncopated, precise illogic of the noises he made. The four saxophonists swayed together, their faces all looking alike, expressionless because of their lips and puffed cheeks. When they had passages of rest they at once smiled. The band was playing tunes that Carlisle knew; very old tunes. They were recognizable at first and then a bedevilment known as the Breezy Bellairs Manner sent them screeching and thudding into a jungle of obscurity. "All swing bandsmen," Carlisle thought, "ought to be Negroes. There's something wrong about their not being Negroes."

Now three of them were singing. They had walked forward with long easy steps and stood with their heads close together, rocking in unison. They made ineffable grimaces. "Peea-nuts," they wailed. But they didn't let the song about peanuts, which Carlisle rather liked, speak for itself. They bedevilled and twisted and screwed it and then went beaming back to their instruments. There was another old song—"The Umbrella Man." She had a simple taste and its quiet monotony pleased her. They did it once, quietly and monotonously. The flood-light dimmed and a brilliant spot light found the pianist. He was playing by himself and singing. That was all right, thought Carlisle. She could mildly enjoy it. But a piercing shriek cut across the naïve tune. The spot light switched to a doorway at the far end of the restaurant. Carlos Rivera stood there, his hands crawling over the keys of his piano-accordion. He advanced between the tables and mounted the dais. Breezy turned to Rivera. He hardly moved his baton. His flesh seemed to jump about on his submerged skeleton. This was his Manner. Rivera, without accompaniment, squeezed trickles, blasts and moans from his piano-accordion. He was a master of his medium. He looked straight at Carlisle, widening his eyes and bowing himself towards her. The sounds he made were frankly lewd, thought Edward Manx. It was monstrous and ridiculous that people in evening clothes should sit idly in a restaurant, mildly diverted, while Rivera directed his lascivious virtuosity at Carlisle.

Now the spot light was in the centre of the dais and only the tympanist played, while the double-bass slapped his instrument. The others moved one by one through the spot light, holding opened umbrellas and turning them like wheels. It was an old trick and they did it, Carlisle thought, sillily. They underdid it. Lady Pastern during a quieter passage said clearly: "Félicité, that is my Ascot parasol."

"Well, *Maman*, I believe it is."

"Your stepfather had no right whatsoever. It was a wedding present of great value. The handle is jewelled."

"Never mind."

"I object categorically and emphatically."

"He's having difficulty with it. Look, they've stopped turning their parasols."

The players were all back in their seats. The noise broadened and then faded out in an unanticipated wail and they were silent.

Breezy bowed and smiled and bowed. Rivera looked at Carlisle.

A young woman in a beautiful dress and with hair like blond seaweed came out of a side door and stood in the spot light, twisting a length of scarlet chiffon in her hands. She contemplated her audience as if she were a sort of willing sacrifice and began to moo very earnestly: "Yeoo knee-oo it was onlee summer lightning." Carlisle and Edward both detested her.

Next Syd Skelton and a saxophonist played a duet which was a *tour de force* of acrobatics and earned a solid round of applause.

When it was over Skelton bowed and with an expression of huffy condescension walked into the band-room.

In the ensuing pause, Breezy advanced to the edge of the dais. His smile was broad and winning. He said in a weak voice that he wanted to thank them all very very much for the wonderful reception his Boys had been given and that he had a little announcement to make. He felt sure that when he told them what was in store for them, they would agree with him that this was a very very special occasion. (Lady Pastern hissed under her breath.) Some weeks ago, Breezy said, he had been privileged to hear a wonderful little performance on the tympani by a distinguished—well, he wouldn't say amateur. He had prevailed upon this remarkable performer to join with the Boys to-night and as an additional attraction the number given would be this performer's own composition. Breezy stepped back, pronounced Lord Pastern's names and title with emphasis and looked expectantly towards the door at the rear of the alcove.

Carlisle, as all other relations, distant or close, of Lord Pastern, had often suffered acute embarrassment at his hands. To-night she had fully expected to endure again that all too familiar wave of discomfort. When, however, he came through the door and stood before them with pink cheeks and a nervous smile, she was suddenly filled with compassion. It was silly, futile and immensely touching that he should make a fool of himself in this particular way. Her heart went out to him.

He walked to the tympani, made a polite little bow and, with an anxious expression, took his seat. They saw him, with a furtive air, lay his revolver on the dais close to Félicité's chair and place his sombrero over it. Breezy pointed his baton at him and said: "Ladies and gentlemen: 'Hot Guy Hot Gunner.'" He gave the initial down-beat and they were off.

It sounded, really, much like all the other numbers they had heard that night, Carlisle thought. Lord Pastern banged, and rattled, and zinged much in the same way as Syd Skelton. The words, when the three singers came out, were no sillier than those of the other songs. The tune was rather catchy. But, "Oh," she thought, "how vulnerable he is among his tympani!"

Edward thought: "There he sits, cat's meat to any satirist who feels as I do about the social set-up. You might make a cartoon of this or a parable. A cartoon certainly. Cousin George, thumping and banging away under Breezy's baton, and in the background a stream of displaced persons. The metronome is Time . . . finger of scorn . . . making its inane gesture to society. A bit too obvious, of course," he thought, dismissing it, "false, because of its partial truth." And he turned his head to watch Carlisle.

Félicité thought: "There goes George. He has fun, anyway." Her glance strayed to Lord Pastern's sombrero. She touched Edward's knee. He bent towards her and she said in his ear: "Shall I pinch George's gun? I could. Look!" She reached out towards the edge of the dais and slipped her hand under the sombrero.

"Fée, don't!" he ejaculated.

"Do you dare me?"

He shook his head violently.

"Poor George," said Félicité, "what *would* he do?" She withdrew her hand and leant back in her chair, turning the white carnation in her fingers. "Shall I put it in my hair?" she wondered. "It would probably look silly and fall out but it might be a good idea. I wish he'd say something—just one thing— to show we understand each other. After this we can't just go on for ever, pretending."

Lady Pastern thought: "There is no end to one's capacity for humiliation. He discredits me and he discredits his class. It's the same story. There will be the same gossip, the same impertinences in the paper, the same mortification. Nevertheless," she thought, "I did well to come. I did well to suffer this torment to-night. My instinct was correct." She looked steadily at Rivera, who was advancing into the centre of the stage. "I have disposed of you," she thought triumphantly.

Lord Pastern thought: "No mistakes so far. And one, bang and two bang and one crash bang zing. One two and three with his accord-een and wait for it. This is perfectly splendid. I *am* this noise. Look out. Here he comes. Hi-de oh hi. Yip. Here he comes. It's going to work. Hot Gunner with his accord-een."

He crashed his cymbal, silenced it and leant back in his seat.

Rivera had advanced in the spot light. The rest of the band was tacit. The great motionless arm of the metronome stabbed its pointer down at his head. He seemed rapt—at once tormented and exalted. He swayed and jerked and ogled. Although he was not by any means ridiculous, he was the puppet of his own music. The performance was a protracted crescendo, and as it rocketed up to its climax he swayed backwards at a preposterous angle, his instrument raised, the pointer menacing it as it undulated across his chest. A screaming dissonance tore loose from the general din, the spot light switched abruptly to the tympani. Lord Pastern, wearing his sombrero, had risen. Advancing to within five feet of Rivera he pointed his revolver at him and fired.

The accordion blared grotesquely down a scale. Rivera sagged at the knees and fell. The accordion crashed a final chord and was silent. At the same moment as the shot was fired the tenor saxophonist played a single shrill note and sat down. Lord Pastern, apparently bewildered, looked from the recumbent Rivera to the saxophonist, paused for a second and then fired three more blanks. The pianist, the trombone, and finally the double-bass each played a note in a descending scale and each imitated a collapse.

There was a further second's pause. Lord Pastern, looking very much taken-aback, suddenly handed the revolver to Bellairs, who pointed it at him and pulled the trigger. The hammer clicked but there was no discharge. Bellairs aped disgust, shrugged his shoulders, looked at the revolver and broke it open. It discharged its shells in a little spurt. Breezy scratched his head, dropped the revolver in his pocket and made a crisp gesture with his baton hand.

"Yipes," Lord Pastern shouted. The band launched itself into a welter of noise. He darted back and flung himself at his tympani. The spot light concentrated upon him. The metronome, which had been motionless until now, suddenly swung its long arm. Tick-tack, tick-tack, it clacked. A kaleidoscopic welter of coloured lights winked and flickered along its surface and frame. Lord Pastern went madly to work on the drums.

"Hell!" Edward ejaculated. "At this pace he'll kill himself."

Breezy Bellairs had got a large artificial wreath. Dabbing his eyes with his handkerchief he knelt by Rivera, placed the wreath on his chest and felt his heart. He bent his head, groped frantically inside the wreath and then looked up with a startled expression in the direction of the tympani, where the spot light revealed Lord Pastern in an ecstatic fury, wading into his drums. His solo lasted about eighty seconds. During this time four waiters had come in with a stretcher. Bellairs spoke to them excitedly. Rivera was carried off while the saxophones made a grotesque lugubrious sobbing and Lord Pastern, by hitting his big drum and immediately releasing the tension, produced a series of muffled groans.

The metronome clacked to a standstill, the restaurant lights went up and the audience applauded generously. Breezy, white to the lips and trembling, indicated Lord Pastern, who joined him, glistening with sweat, and bowed. Breezy said something inaudible to him and to the pianist and went out, followed by Lord Pastern. The pianist, the double-bass and the three saxophonists began to play a dance tune.

"Good old George!" cried Félicité. "I think he was superb, *Maman* darling, don't you? Ned, wasn't he heaven?"

Edward smiled at her. "He's astonishing," he said, and added: "Cousin C, do you mind if Lisle and I dance? You will, won't you, Lisle?"

Carlisle put her hand on his shoulder and they moved away. The headwaiter slid past them and stooped for a moment over a man at a table further down the room. The man rose, let his eyeglass fall and, with a preoccupied look, passed Carlisle and Edward on his way to the vestibule.

They danced in silence, companionably. At last Edward said: "What will he do next, do you suppose? Is there anything left?"

"I thought it dreadfully pathetic."

"Quintessence of foolery. Lisle, I haven't had a chance to talk to you about that business before we left. I suppose I oughtn't to have hit the fellow, considering the set-up with Fée, but really it was a bit too much. I'm sorry if I made an unnecessary scene, but I must say I enjoyed it." When she didn't answer, he said uncertainly: "Are you seriously annoyed? Lisle, you didn't by any chance . . ."

"No," she said. "No, I didn't. I may as well confess I was extremely gratified." His hand tightened on hers. "I stood," she added, "in the door of my cave and preened myself."

"Did you notice his ear? Not a cauliflower, but distinctly puffy, and a little trickle of blood. And then the unspeakable creature had the infernal nerve to goggle at you over his hurdy-gurdy."

"It's all just meant to be one in the eye for Fée."

"I'm not so sure."

"If it is, he's not having much success."

"How do you mean?" Edward asked sharply.

"Arst yerself, dearie."

"You mean Fée . . ." He stopped short and turned very red. "Lisle," he said, "about Fée . . . Something very odd has occurred. It's astonishing and, well, it's damned awkward. I can't explain but I'd like to think you understood."

Carlisle looked up at him. "You're not very lucid," she said.

"Lisle, my dear . . . Lisle, see here . . ."

They had danced round to the band dais. Carlisle said: "Our waiter's standing over there, watching us. I think he's trying to catch your eye."

"Be blowed to him."

"Yes, he is. Here he comes."

"It'll be some blasted paper on my tracks. Yes, do you want me?"

The waiter had touched Edward's arm. "Excuse me, sir. An urgent call."

"Thank you. Come with me, Lisle. Where's the telephone?"

The waiter hesitated, glanced at Carlisle and said: "If madam will excuse me, sir . . ." His voice sank to a murmur.

"Good Lord!" Edward said and took Carlisle by the elbow. "There's been some sort of trouble. Cousin George wants me to go in. I'll drop you at the table, Lisle."

"What's he up to now, for pity's sake?"

"I'll come as soon as I can. Make my excuses."

As he went out Carlisle saw, with astonishment, that he was very pale.

In the vestibule, which was almost deserted, Edward stopped the waiter. "How bad is it?" he asked. "Is he badly hurt?"

The man raised his clasped hands in front of his mouth. "They say he's dead," said the waiter.

iii

Breezy Bellairs sat at the little table in the inner office where he had played poker. When Edward came through the outer office he had heard scuffling and expostulations and he had opened the door upon a violent struggle. Breezy was being lugged to his feet from a squatting position on the floor and hustled across the room. He was slack, now, and unresisting. His soft hands scratched at the surface of the table. He was dishevelled and breathless; tears ran out of his eyes, and his mouth was open. David Hahn, the secretary, stood behind him and patted his shoulder. "You shouldn't have done it, old boy," he said. "Honest. You shouldn't have done a thing like that."

"Keep off me," Breezy whispered. Caesar Bonn, wringing his hands in the conventional gesture of distress, looked past Edward into the main office. The man with the eyeglass sat at the desk there, speaking inaudibly into the telephone.

"How did it happen?" Edward asked.

"Look," Lord Pastern said.

Edward crossed the room. "You must not touch him," Caesar Bonn gabbled. "Excuse me, sir, forgive me. Dr. Allington has said at once, he must not be touched."

"I'm not going to touch him."

He bent down. Rivera lay on the floor. His long figure was stretched out tidily against the far wall. Near the feet lay the comic wreath of flowers and a little farther off, his piano-accordion. Rivera's eyes were open. His upper lip was retracted and the teeth showed. His coat was thrown open and the surface of his soft shirt was blotted with red. Near the top of the blot a short dark object stuck out ridiculously from his chest.

"What is it? It looks like a dart."

"Shut that door," Bonn whispered angrily. Hahn darted to the communicating door and shut it. Just before he did so, Edward heard the man at the telephone say: "In the office. I'll wait for you, of course."

"This will ruin us. We are ruined," said Bonn.

"They will think it an after-hours investigation, that is all," said Hahn. "If we keep our heads."

"It will all come out. I insist we are ruined."

In a voice that rose to a weak falsetto, Breezy said: "Listen boys. Listen Caesar, I didn't know it was that bad. I couldn't see. I wasn't sure. I can't be blamed for that, can I? I passed the word something was wrong to the Boys. It wouldn't have made any difference if I'd acted different, would it, Dave? They can't say anything to me, can they?"

"Take it easy, old man."

"You did right," Bonn said, vigorously. "If you had done otherwise—what a scene! What a debacle! And to no purpose. No, no, it was correct."

"Yes, but look, Caesar, it's terrible, the way we carried on. A cod funeral march and everything. I knew it was unlucky. I said so when he told me he wanted the other routine. All the Boys said so!" He pointed a quivering finger at Lord Pastern. "It was your big idea. You wished it on us. Look where it's landed us. What a notion, a cod funeral march!"

His mouth sagged and he began to laugh, fetching his breath in gasps and beating on the table.

"Shut up," said Lord Pastern, irritably. "You're a fool."

The door opened and the man with the eyeglass came in. "What's all this noise?" he asked. He stood over Breezy. "If you can't pull yourself together, Mr. Bellairs," he said, "we shall have to take drastic steps to make you." He glanced at Bonn. "He'd better have brandy. Can you beat up some aspirin?"

Hahn went out. Breezy sobbed and whispered.

"The police," said the man, "will be here in a moment. I shall, of course, be required to make a statement." He looked hard at Edward. "Who is this?"

"I sent for him," said Lord Pastern. "He's with my party. My cousin, Ned Manx, Dr. Allington."

"I see."

"I thought I'd like to have Ned," Lord Pastern added wistfully.

Dr. Allington turned back to Breezy and picked up his wrist. He looked sharply at him. "You're in a bit of a mess, my friend," he remarked.

"It's not my fault. Don't look at me like that. I can't be held responsible, my God."

"I don't suggest anything of the sort. Is brandy any good to you? Ah, here it is."

Hahn brought it in. "Here's the aspirin," he said. "How many?" He shook out two tablets. Breezy snatched the bottle and spilt half a dozen on the table. Dr. Allington intervened and gave him three. He gulped them down with the brandy, wiped his face over with his handkerchief, yawned and shivered.

Voices sounded in the outer office. Bonn and Hahn moved towards Breezy. Lord Pastern planted his feet apart and lightly flexed his arms. This posture was familiar to Edward. It usually meant trouble. Dr. Allington put his glass in his eye. Breezy made a faint whispering.

Somebody tapped on the door. It opened and a thick-set man with grizzled hair came in. He wore a dark overcoat, neat, hard and unsmart, and carried a bowler hat. His eyes were bright and he looked longer and more fixedly than is the common habit at those he newly encountered. His sharp impersonal glance dwelt in turn upon the men in the room and upon the body of Rivera, from which they had stepped aside. Dr. Allington moved out from the group.

"Trouble here?" said the newcomer. "Are you Dr. Allington, sir? My chaps are outside. Inspector Fox."

He walked over to the body. The doctor followed him and they stood together, looking down at it. Fox gave a slight grunt and turned back to the others. "And these gentlemen?" he said. Caesar Bonn made a dart at him and began to talk very rapidly.

"If I could just have the names," said Fox and took out his notebook. He wrote down their names, his glance resting longer on Breezy than upon the others. Breezy lay back in his chair and gaped at Fox. His dinner-jacket with its steel buttons sagged on one side. The pocket was dragged down.

"Excuse me, sir," Fox said, "are you feeling unwell?" He stooped over Breezy.

"I'm shot all to hell," Breezy whimpered.

"Well, now, if you'll just allow me . . ." He made a neat unobtrusive movement and stood up with the revolver in his large gloved hand.

Breezy gaped at it and then pointed a quivering hand at Lord Pastern.

"That's not my gun," he chattered. "Don't you think it. It's his. It's his lordship's. He fired it at poor old Carlos and poor old Carlos fell down like he wasn't meant to. That's right, isn't it, chaps? Isn't it, Caesar? God, won't somebody speak up for me and tell the Inspector? His lordship handed me that gun."

"Don't you fret," Fox said comfortably. "We'll have a chat about it presently." He dropped the revolver in his pocket. His sharp glance travelled again over the group of men. "Well, thank you, gentlemen," he said and opened the door. "We'll need to trouble you a little further, Doctor, but I'll ask the others to wait in here, if you please."

They filed into the main office. Four men already waited there. Fox nodded and three of them joined him in the inner room. They carried black canes and a tripod.

"This is Dr. Curtis, Dr. Allington," said Fox. He unbuttoned his overcoat and laid his bowler on the table. "Will you two gentlemen take a look? We'll get some shots when you're ready, Thompson."

One of the men set up a tripod and camera. The doctors behaved like simultaneous comedians. They hitched up their trousers, knelt on their right knees and rested their forearms on their left thighs.

"I was supping here," said Dr. Allington. "He was dead when I got to him, which must have been about three to five minutes after this—" he jabbed a forefinger at the blotch on Rivera's shirt—"had happened. When I got here they had him where he is now. I made a superficial examination and rang the Yard."

"Nobody tried to withdraw the weapon?" said Dr. Curtis and added: "Unusual, that."

"It seems that one of them, Lord Pastern it was, said it shouldn't be touched. Some vague idea of an effusion of blood following the withdrawal. They realized almost at once that he was dead. At a guess, would you say there'd been considerable penetration of the right ventricle? I haven't touched the thing, by the way. Can't make out what it is."

"We'll take a look in a minute," said Dr. Curtis. "All right, Fox."

"All right, Thompson," said Fox.

They moved away. Their shadows momentarily blotted the wall as Thompson's lamp flashed. Whistling under his breath he manoeuvred his camera, flashed and clicked.

"O.K., Mr. Fox," he said at last.

"Dabs," said Fox. "Do what you can about the weapon, Bailey."

The finger-print expert, a thin dark man, squatted by the body.

Fox said: "I'd like to get a statement about the actual event. You can help us, there, Dr. Allington? What exactly was the set-up? I understand a gun was used against the deceased in the course of the entertainment."

He had folded his overcoat neatly over the back of his chair. He now sat down, his knees apart, his spectacles adjusted, his notebook flattened out on the table. "If I may trouble you, Doctor," he said. "In your own words, as we say."

Dr. Allington fitted his glass in position and looked apologetic. "I'm afraid I'm not going to be a success," he said. "To be quite frank, Inspector, I was more interested in my guest than in the entertainment. And, by the way, I'd like to make my apologies to her as soon as possible. She must be wondering where the devil I've got to."

"If you care to write a note, sir, we'll give it to one of the waiters."

"What? Oh, all right," said Dr. Allington fretfully. A note was taken out by Thompson. Through the opened door they caught a glimpse of a dejected group in the main office. Lord Pastern's voice, caught midway in a sentence, said shrilly: ". . . entirely the wrong way about it. Making a mess, as usual . . ." and was shut off by the door.

"Yes, Doctor?" said Fox placidly.

"Oh God, they were doing some kind of idiotic turn. We were talking and I didn't pay much attention except to say it was a pretty poor show, old Pastern making an ass of himself. This chap, here"—he looked distastefully at the body—"came out from the far end of the restaurant and made a hell of a noise on his concertina or whatever it is, and there was a terrific bang. I looked up and saw old Pastern with a gun of some sort in his hand. This chap did a fall, the conductor dropped a wreath on him and then he was carried out. About three minutes later they sent for me."

"I'll just get that down, if you please," said Fox. With raised eyebrows and breathing through his mouth, he wrote at a steady pace. "Yes," he said comfortably, "and how far, Doctor, would you say his lordship was from the deceased when he fired?"

"Quite close. I don't know. Between five and seven feet. I don't know."

"Did you notice the deceased's behaviour, sir, immediately after the shot was fired? I mean, did it strike you there was anything wrong?"

Dr. Allington looked impatiently at the door. "Strike me!" he repeated. "I wasn't struck by anything in particular. I looked up when the gun went off. I think it occurred to me that he did a very clever fall. He was a pretty ghastly-looking job of work, all hair oil and teeth."

"Would you say . . ." Fox began and was interrupted.

"I really wouldn't say anything, Inspector. I've given you my opinion from the time I examined the poor devil . . . To go any further would be unprofessional and stupid. I simply wasn't watching and therefore don't remember. You'd better find somebody who did watch and does remember."

Fox had raised his head and now looked beyond Dr. Allington to the door. His hand was poised motionless over his notebook. His jaw had dropped. Dr. Allington slewed round and was confronted with a very tall dark man in evening dress.

"I was watching," said this person, "and I think I remember. Shall I try, Inspector?"

iv

"Good Lor'!" Fox said heavily and rose. "Well, thank you, Dr. Allington," he said. "I'll have a typed statement sent round to you to-morrow. Would you be good enough to read it through and sign it if it's in order? We'll want you for the inquest, if you please."

"All right. Thanks," said Dr. Allington, making for the door, which the newcomer opened. "Thanks," he repeated. "Hope you make a better fist of it than I did, what?"

"Most unlikely, I'm afraid," the other rejoined pleasantly and closed the door after him. "You're in for a party, Fox," he said, and walked over to the body. Bailey, the finger-print expert, said, "Good evening, sir," and moved away, grinning.

"If I may ask, sir," said Fox, "how do you come to be in on it?"

"May I not take mine ease in mine restaurant with mine wife? Shall there be no more cakes and ale? None for you, at all events, you poor chap," he said, bending over Rivera. "You haven't got the thing out yet, I see, Fox."

"It's been dabbed and photographed. It can come out."

Fox knelt down. His hand wrapped in his handkerchief closed round the object that protruded from Rivera's chest. It turned with difficulty. "Tight," he said.

"Let me look, may I?"

Fox drew back. The other knelt beside him. "But what is it?" he said. "Not an orthodox dart. There's thread at the top. It's been unscrewed from something. Black. Silver-mounted. Ebony, I fancy. Or a dark bronze. What the devil is it? Try again, Fox."

Fox tried again. He twisted. Under the wet silk the wound opened slightly. He pulled steadily. With a jerk and a slight but horrible sound, the weapon was released. Fox laid it on the floor and opened out the hand-kerchief. Bailey clicked his tongue.

Fox said: "Will you look at that. Good Lord, what a set-up! It's a bit of an umbrella shaft, turned into a dart or bolt."

"A black and white parasol," said his companion. Fox looked up quickly but said nothing. "Yes. There's the spring clip, you see. That's why it wouldn't come out readily. An elaborate affair, almost a museum piece. The clip's got tiny jewels in it. And, look, Fox."

He pointed a long finger. Protruding from one end was a steel, about two inches long, wide at the base and tapering sharply to a point. "It looks like some awl or a stiletto. Probably it was originally sunk in a short handle. It's been driven into one end of this bit of parasol shaft and sealed up somehow. Plastic wood, I fancy. The end of the piece of shaft, you see, was hollow. Probably the longer section of the parasol screwed into it and a knob or handle of some kind, in turn, was screwed on the opposite end." He took out his notebook and made a rapid sketch which he showed to Fox. "Like this," he said. "It'll be a freak of a parasol. French, I should think. I remember seeing them in the enclosure at Longchamps when I was a boy. The shaft's so thin that they have to put a separate section in to take the slip and groove. This is the section. But why in the name of high fantasy use a bit of parasol shaft as a sort of dagger?"

"We'll have another shot of this, Thompson." Fox rose stiffly and after a long pause said: "Where were you sitting, Mr. Alleyn?"

"Next door to the Pastern party. A few yards off the dais."

"What a bit of luck," said Fox simply.

"Don't be too sure," rejoined Chief Inspector Alleyn. He sat on the table and lit a cigarette. "This is no doubt a delicate situation, Br'er Fox. I mustn't butt in on your job, you know."

Fox made a short derisive noise. "You'll take over, sir, of course."

"I can at least make my report. I'd better warn you at the outset, I was watching that extraordinary chap Pastern most of the time. What a queer cup of tea it is, to be sure."

"I suppose," said Fox stolidly, "you'll be telling me, sir, that you were his fag at Eton."

Alleyn grinned at this jibe. "If I had been I should probably have spent the rest of my life in a lunatic asylum. No, I was going to say that I watched him to the exclusion of the others. I noticed, for instance, that he really pointed his gun—a revolver of some sort—at this man and that he stood not more than seven feet off him when he did it."

"This is more like it," Fox said and reopened his book. "You don't mind, Mr. Alleyn?" he added primly.

Alleyn said: "You're gloating over this, aren't you? Very well. They did a damn' silly turn, revolving umbrellas and parasols like a bunch of superannuated chorus girls, and I noticed that one parasol, a very pansy Frenchified affair of black and white lace, seemed to be giving trouble. The chap had to shove his hand up to hold it."

"Is that so?" Fox looked at Thompson. "You might get hold of the umbrella." Thompson went out. Bailey moved forward with an insufflator and bent over the weapon.

"I'd better describe the final turn, I suppose," said Alleyn and did so. His voice moved on quietly and slowly. Thompson returned with the black and white parasol. "This is it, sure enough, sir," he said. "A section of the shaft's gone. Look here! No clip anywhere to keep it shut." He laid it beside the dart.

"Good enough," Fox said. "Get your shots, will you."

Thompson, having taken three further photographs of the weapon, folded it in the handkerchief and put it in Fox's case. "I'll fix it up with proper protection when we're finished, Mr. Fox," he said. On a nod from Fox, he and Bailey went out with their gear.

". . . when the shot was fired," Alleyn was saying, "he had swung round, facing Lord Pastern, with his back half turned to the audience and fully turned to the conductor. He was inclined backwards at a grotesque angle, with the instrument raised. He was directly under the point of the metronome, which was motionless. After the report he swung round still further and straightened up a bit. The piano-accordion, if that's what it is, ran down the scale and let out an infernal bleat. His knees doubled and he went down on them, sat on his heels and then rolled over, fetching up on his back with his instrument between himself and the audience. At the same time one of the bandsmen aped being hit. I couldn't see Rivera clearly because the spot light had switched to old Pastern, who, after a moment's hesitation, loosed off the other rounds. Three more of the band chaps did comic staggers as if he'd hit them. Something seemed a bit out of joint here. They all looked as if they weren't sure what came next. However, Pastern gave his gun to Bellairs, who pointed it at him and pulled the trigger. The last round had been used, so there was only a click. Bellairs registered disgust, broke the revolver, pocketed it and gestured as much as to say: 'I've had it. Carry on,' and Lord Pastern then went to market in a big way and generally raised hell. He looked extraordinary. Glazed eyes, sweating, half-smiling and jerking about over his drums. An unnerving exhibition from a middle-aged peer but of course he's as mad as a March hare. Troy and I were snobbishly horrified. It was then that the metronome went into action in a blaze of winking lights. It'd been pointing straight down at Rivera before. A waiter chucked a wreath to the conductor, who knelt down by this chap Rivera and dumped it on his chest. He felt his heart and then looked closely at Rivera and bent over his body, groping inside the wreath. He turned in a startled sort of way to old Pastern. He said something to the blokes with the stretcher. The

wreath hid the face and the accordion was half across the stomach. Bellairs
spoke to the pianist and then to Lord Pastern, who went out with him when
they finished their infernal din. I smelt trouble, saw a waiter speak to Allington and stop a chap in Lady Pastern's party. I had a long argument with
myself, lost it and came out here. That's all. Have you looked at the revolver?"

"I've taken it off Bellairs. It's in my pocket." Fox put his glove on, produced the revolver and laid it on the table. "No known make," he said.

"Probably been used for target-shooting," Alleyn muttered. He laid the
dart beside it. "It'd fit, Fox. Look. Had you noticed?"

"We haven't got very far."

"Of course not."

"I don't know quite what line to take about all the folk in there." Fox
jerked his head in the direction of the restaurant.

"Better get names and addresses. The waiters can do it. They'll know a
lot of them already. They can say it's a new police procedure on extension
nights. It's our good fortune, Br'er Fox, that the public will believe any
foolishness if they are told we are the authors of it. The Pastern party had
better be held."

"I'll fix it," Fox said. He went out, revealing for a moment the assembly
in the outer office ". . . hang about kickin' my heels all night . . ." Lord
Pastern's voice protested and was shut off abruptly.

Alleyn knelt by the body and began to search it. The coat was turned back
and the breast pocket had been pulled out. Four letters and a gold cigarette
case had slipped down between the body and the coat. The case was half-
filled and bore an inscription: "From Félicité." He searched the other pockets. A jade holder. Two handkerchiefs. A wallet with three pound-notes. He
laid these objects out in a row and turned to the piano-accordion. It was a
large, heavily ornamental affair. He remembered how it had glittered as
Rivera swung it across his chest in that last cacophony before he fell. As
Alleyn lifted it, it raised a metallic wail. He put it down hastily on the
table and returned to his contemplation of the body. Fox came back. "That's
all fixed up," he said.

"Good."

Alleyn stood up. "He was a startling fellow to look at," he said. "One felt
one had seen him in innumerable Hollywood band features, ogling the camera man against an exotic background. We might cover him up, don't you
think? The management can produce a clean table-cloth."

"The mortuary man will be outside now, Mr. Alleyn," said Fox. He
glanced down at the little collection on the floor. "Much obliged, sir," he
said. "Anything useful?"

"The letters are written in Spanish. Postmark. He'll have to be dusted, of
course."

"I rang the Yard, Mr. Alleyn. The A.S.M.'s compliments and he'll be
glad if you'll take over."

"That's a thumping great lie," said Alleyn mildly. "He's in Godalming."

"He's come back, sir, and happened to be in the office. Quite a coincidence."

"You go to hell, Fox. Damn it, I'm out with my wife."

"I sent a message in to Mrs. Alleyn. The waiter brought back a note."

Alleyn opened the folded paper and disclosed a lively drawing of a lady asleep in bed. Above her, encircled by a balloon, Alleyn and Fox crawled on all fours inspecting, through a huge lens, a nest from which protruded the head of a foal, broadly winking.

"A very stupid woman, I'm afraid, poor thing," Alleyn muttered, grinning, and showed it to Fox. "Come on," he said. "We'll take another look at the revolver and then get down to statements."

CHAPTER VI

Dope

Above the door leading from the foyer of the Metronome to the office was a clock with chromium hands and figures. As the night wore on, the attention of those persons who were congregated there became increasingly drawn to this clock, so that when at one in the morning the long hand jumped to the hour, everyone observed it. A faint sigh, and a dreary restlessness, stirred them momentarily.

The members of the band who were assembled at the end of the foyer sat in dejected attitudes on gilded chairs that had been brought in from the restaurant. Syd Skelton's hands dangled between his knees, tapping each other flaccidly. Happy Hart was stretched back with his legs extended. The light found out patches on his trousers worn shiny by the pressure of his thighs against the under-surface of his piano. The four saxophonists sat with their heads together, but they had not spoken for some time and inertia, not interest, held them in these postures of intimacy. The double-bass, a thin man, rested his elbows on his knees and his head on his hands. Breezy Bellairs, in the centre of his Boys, fidgeted, yawned, wiped his hands over his face and bit feverishly at his nails. Near the band stood four waiters and the spot-light operator, whose interrogation had just ended, quite fruitlessly.

At the opposite end of the foyer, in a muster of easier chairs, sat Lady Pastern and her guests. Alone of the whole assembly, she held an upright posture. The muscles of her face sagged a little; its lines were clogged with powder and there were greyish marks under her eyes, but her wrists and ankles were crossed composedly, her hair was rigidly in order. On her right and left the two girls drooped in their chairs. Félicité, chain-smoking, gave her attention fitfully to the matter in hand and often took a glass from her bag and looked resentfully at herself, repainting her lips with irritable gestures.

Carlisle, absorbed as usual with detail, watched the mannerisms of her companions through an increasing haze of sleepiness and was only half aware of what they said. Ned Manx listened sharply as if he tried to memorize all that he heard. Lord Pastern was never still. He would throw himself into a chair with an air of abandon and in a moment spring from it and walk aimlessly about the room. He looked with distaste at the speaker of the moment. He grimaced and interjected. At one side, removed from the two main groups, stood Caesar Bonn and the secretary, David Hahn. These two were watchful and pallid. Out of sight, in the main office, Dr. Curtis, having seen to the removal of Rivera's body, jotted down notes for his report.

In the centre of the foyer, Inspector Fox sat at a small table with his notebook open before him and his spectacles on his nose. His feet rested side by side on the carpet and his large knees were pressed together. He contemplated his notes with raised eyebrows.

Behind Fox stood Chief Detective-Inspector Alleyn, and to him the attention of the company, in some cases fitfully, in others constantly, was drawn. He had been speaking for about a minute. Carlisle, though she tried to listen to the sense of his words, caught herself thinking how deep his voice was and how free from mannerisms his habit of speech. "A pleasant chap," she thought, and knew by the small affirmative noise Ned Manx made when Alleyn paused that he agreed with her.

". . . so you see," Alleyn was saying now, "that a certain amount of ground must be covered here and that we must ask you to stay until it *has* been covered. That can't be helped."

"Damned if I see . . ." Lord Pastern began and fetched up short. "What's your name?" he said. Alleyn told him. "I thought so," said Lord Pastern with an air of having found him out in something. "Point is: are you suggestin' I dug a dart in the chap or aren't you? Come on."

"It doesn't, at the moment, seem to be a question, as far as you are concerned, sir, of digging."

"Well, shootin' then. Don't split straws."

"One may as well," Alleyn said mildly, "be accurate."

He turned aside to Fox's case, which lay on a table. From it he took an open box containing the weapon that had killed Rivera. He held the box up, tilting it towards them.

"Will you look at this?" They looked at it. "Do any of you recognize it? Lady Pastern?"

She had made an inarticulate sound, but now she said indifferently: "It looks like part of a parasol handle."

"A black and white parasol?" Alleyn suggested and one of the saxophonists looked up quickly.

"Possibly," said Lady Pastern. "I don't know."

"Don't be an ass, C," said her husband. "Obviously it's off that French thing of yours. We borrowed it."

"You had no right whatever, George . . ."

Alleyn interrupted. "We've found that one of the parasols used in the Umbrella Man number is minus a few inches of its shaft." He glanced at the second saxophonist. "I think you had some difficulty in managing it?"

"That's right," the second saxophonist said. "You couldn't shut it properly, I noticed. There wasn't a clip or anything."

"This is it: five inches of the shaft containing the clip. Notice that spring catch. It is jewelled. Originally, of course, it kept the parasol closed. The actual handle or knob on its own piece of shaft has been engaged with the main shaft of the parasol. Can you describe it?" He looked at Lady Pastern, who said nothing. Lord Pastern said: "Of course you can, C. A damn-fool thing like a bird with emeralds for eyes. French."

"You're sure of that, sir?"

"Of course I'm sure. Damn it, I took the thing to bits when I was in the ballroom."

Fox raised his head and stared at Lord Pastern with a sort of incredulous satisfaction. Edward Manx swore under his breath, the women were rigidly horrified.

"I see," Alleyn said. "When was this?"

"After dinner. Breezy was with me. Weren't you, Breezy?"

Breezy shied violently and then nodded.

"Where did you leave the bits, sir?"

"On the piano. Last I saw of 'em."

"Why," Alleyn asked, "did you dismember the parasol?"

"For fun."

"*Mon dieu, mon dieu,*" Lady Pastern moaned.

"I knew it'd unscrew and I unscrewed it."

"Thank you," Alleyn said. "For the benefit of those of you who haven't examined the parasol closely, I'd better describe it a little more fully. Both ends of this piece of shaft are threaded, one on the outer surface to engage with the top section, the other on the inner surface to receive the main shaft of the parasol. It has been removed and the outer sections screwed together. Now look again at this weapon made from the section that has been removed. You will see that a steel tool has been introduced into this end and sunk in plastic wood. Do any of you recognize this tool? I'll hold it a little closer. It's encrusted with blood and a little difficult to see."

He saw Carlisle's fingers move on the arms of her chair. He saw Breezy rub the back of his hand across his mouth and Lord Pastern blow out his cheeks. "Rather unusual," he said, "isn't it? Wide at the base and tapering. Keen pointed. It might be an embroidery stiletto. I don't know. Do you recognize it, Lady Pastern?"

"No."

"Anybody?" Lord Pastern opened his mouth and shut it again. "Well,"

Alleyn murmured after a pause. He replaced the box containing the weapon and took up Lord Pastern's revolver. He turned it over in his hands.

"If that's the way you chaps go to work," said Lord Pastern, "I don't think much of it. That thing may be smothered with finger-prints, for all you know, and you go pawin' it about."

"It's been printed," Alleyn said without emphasis. He produced a pocket lens and squinted through it down the barrel. "You seem to have given it some rough usage," he said.

"No, I haven't," Lord Pastern countered instantly. "Perfect condition. Always has been."

"When did you last look down the barrel, sir?"

"Before we came here. In my study, and again in the ballroom. Why?"

"George," said Lady Pastern. "I suggest for the last time that you send for your solicitor and refuse to answer any questions until he is here."

"Yes, Cousin George," Edward murmured. "I honestly think . . ."

"My solicitor," Lord Pastern rejoined, "is a snufflin' old ass. I'm perfectly well able to look after myself, C. What's all this about my gun?"

"The barrel," Alleyn said, "is, of course, fouled. That's from the blank rounds. But under the stain left by the discharges there are some curious marks. Irregular scratches, they seem to be. We'll have it photographed but I wonder if in the meantime you can offer an explanation?"

"Here," Lord Pastern ejaculated. "Let me see."

Alleyn gave him the revolver and lens. Grimacing hideously he pointed the barrel to the light and squinted down it. He made angry noises and little puffing sounds through his lips. He examined the butt through the lens and muttered indistinguishable anathemas. Most unexpectedly, he giggled. Finally he dumped it on the table and blew loudly. "Hanky-panky," he said briefly and returned to his chair.

"I beg your pardon?"

"When I examined the gun in my study," Lord Pastern said forcibly, "it was as clean as a whistle. As clean, I repeat, as a whistle. I fired one blank from it in my own house and looked down the barrel afterwards. It was a bit fouled and that was all. All right. There y'are!"

Carlisle, Félicité, Manx and Lady Pastern stirred uneasily. "Uncle George," Carlisle said. "Please."

Lord Pastern glared at her. "Therefore," he said, "I repeat, hanky-panky. The barrel was unmarked when I brought the thing here. I ought to know. It was unmarked when I took it into the restaurant."

Lady Pastern looked steadily at her husband. "You *fool*, George," she said.

"George."

"Cousin George."

"Uncle George . . ."

The shocked voices overlapped and faded out.

Alleyn began again. "Obviously you realize the significance of all this.

When I tell you that the weapon—it is, in effect, a dart or bolt, isn't it?—
is half an inch shorter than the barrel of the revolver and somewhat less in
diameter . . ."

"All right, all right," Lord Pastern interjected.

"I think," said Alleyn, "I should point out . . ."

"You needn't point anything out. And you," Lord Pastern added, turning
on his relatives, "can all shut up. I know what you're gettin' at. The barrel
was unscratched. By God, I ought to know. And what's more, I noticed
when Breezy and I were in the ballroom that this bit of shaft would fit in
the barrel. I pointed it out to him."

"Here, here, here!" Breezy expostulated. "I don't like the way this is going.
Look here—"

"Did anyone else examine the revolver?" Alleyn interposed adroitly.

Lord Pastern pointed at Skelton. "He did," he said. "Ask him."

Skelton moved forward, wetting his lips.

"Did you look down the barrel?" Alleyn asked.

"Glanced," said Skelton reluctantly.

"Did you notice anything unusual?"

"No."

"Was the barrel quite unscarred?"

There was a long silence. "Yes," said Skelton at last.

"There y'are," said Lord Pastern.

"It would be," Skelton added brutally, "seeing his lordship hadn't put his
funny weapon in it yet."

Lord Pastern uttered a short, rude and incredulous word. "Thanks," said
Skelton and turned to Alleyn.

Edward Manx said: "May I butt in, Alleyn?"

"Of course."

"It's obvious that you think this thing was fired from the revolver. It's
obvious, in my opinion, that you are right. How else could he have been
killed? But isn't it equally obvious that the person who used the revolver
could have known nothing about it? If he had wanted to shoot Rivera he
could have used a bullet. If, for some extraordinary reason, he preferred a
sort of rifle grenade or dart or what-not, he would surely have used something less fantastic than the affair you have just shown us. The only object
in using the piece of parasol shaft, if it has in fact been so used, would have
been this: the spring catch—which is jewelled, by the way—would keep the
weapon fixed in the barrel and it wouldn't fall out if the revolver was pointed
downwards, and the person who fired the revolver would therefore be unaware of the weapon in the barrel. You wouldn't," Edward said with great
energy, "fix up an elaborate sort of thing like this unless there was a reason
for it and there would be no reason if you yourself had full control of the
revolver and could load it at the last moment. Only an abnormally eccentric . . ." He stopped short, floundered for a moment and then said:
"That's the point I wanted to make."

"It's well taken," Alleyn said. "Thank you."

"Hi!" said Lord Pastern.

Alleyn turned to him.

"Look here," he said. "You think these scratches were made by the jewels on that spring thing. Skelton says they weren't there when he looked at the gun. If anyone was fool enough to try and shoot a feller with a thing like this, he'd fire it off first of all to see how it worked. In private. Follow me?"

"I think so, sir."

"All right, then," said Lord Pastern with a shrill cackle, "why waste time jabberin' about scratches?"

He flung himself into his chair.

"Did any of you who were there," Alleyn said, "take particular notice when Mr. Skelton examined the revolver?"

Nobody spoke. Skelton's face was very white. "Breezy watched," he said and added quickly: "I was close to Lord Pastern. I couldn't have . . . I mean . . ."

Alleyn said, "Why did you examine it, Mr. Skelton?"

Skelton wetted his lips. His eyes shifted their gaze from Lord Pastern to Breezy Bellairs. "I—was sort of interested. Lord Pastern had fixed up the blanks himself and I thought I'd like to take a look. I'd gone in to wish him luck. I mean . . ."

"*Why don't you tell him!*"

Breezy was on his feet. He had been yawning and fidgeting in his chair. His face was stained with tears. He had seemed to pay little attention to what was said but rather to be in the grip of some intolerable restlessness. His interruption shocked them all by its unexpectedness. He came forward with a shambling movement and grinned at Alleyn.

"I'll tell you," he said rapidly. "Syd did it because I asked him to. He's a pal. I told him. I told him I didn't trust his lordship. I'm a nervous man where firearms are concerned. I'm a nervous man altogether if you can understand." His fingers plucked at his smiling lips. "Don't look at me like that," he said and his voice broke into a shrill falsetto. "Everybody's staring as if I'd done something. Eyes. Eyes. Eyes. O God, give me a smoke!"

Alleyn held out his cigarette case. Breezy struck it out of his hand and began to sob. "Bloody sadist," he said.

"I know what's wrong with you, you silly chap," Lord Pastern said accusingly. Breezy shook a finger at him. "You *know!*" he said. "You started it. You're as good as a murderer. You *are* a murderer, by God!"

"Say that again, my good Bellairs," Lord Pastern rejoined with relish, "and I'll have you in the libel court. Action for slander, b' George."

Breezy looked wildly round the assembly. His light eyes with their enormous pupils fixed their gaze on Félicité. He pointed a trembling hand at her. "Look at that girl," he said, "doing her face and sitting up like Jackie with the man she was supposed to love lying stiff and bloody in the morgue. It's disgusting."

Caesar Bonn came forward, wringing his hands. "I can keep silent no longer," he said. "If I am ruined, I am ruined. If I do not speak, there are others who will." He looked at Lord Pastern, at Edward Manx and at Hahn.

Edward said: "It's got to come out, certainly. In common fairness."

"Certainly. Certainly."

"What," Alleyn asked, "has got to come out?"

"Please, Mr. Manx. You will speak."

"All right, Caesar. I think," Edward said slowly, turning to Alleyn, "that you should know what happened before any of you arrived. I myself had only just walked into the room. The body was where you saw it." He paused for a moment. Breezy watched him, but Manx did not look at Breezy. "There was a sort of struggle going on," he said. "Bellairs was on the floor by Rivera and the others were pulling him off."

"Damned indecent thing," said Lord Pastern virtuously, "trying to go through the poor devil's pockets."

Breezy whimpered.

"I'd like a closer account of this, if you can give it to me. When exactly did this happen?" Alleyn asked.

Caesar and Hahn began talking at once. Alleyn stopped them. "Suppose," he said, "we trace events through the point where Mr. Rivera was carried out of the restaurant!" He began to question the four waiters who had carried Rivera. The waiters hadn't noticed anything was wrong with him. They were a bit flustered anyway because of the confusion about which routine was to be followed. There had been so many contradictory orders that in the end they just watched to see who fell down and then picked up the stretcher and carried him out. The wreath covered his chest. As they lifted him on to the stretcher, Breezy had said quickly: "He's hurt. Get him out." They had carried him straight to the office. As they put the stretcher down they heard him make a noise, a harsh rattling noise, it had been. When they looked closer they found he was dead. They fetched Caesar Bonn and Hahn and then carried the body into the inner room. Then Caesar ordered them back to the restaurant and told one of them to fetch Dr. Allington.

Lord Pastern, taking up the tale, said that while they were still on the dais, after the removal of Rivera, Breezy had gone to him and muttered urgently: "For God's sake come out. Something's happened to Carlos." The pianist, Happy Hart, said that Breezy had stopped at the piano on his way out and had told him in an aside to keep going.

Caesar took up the story. Breezy and Lord Pastern came to the inner office. Breezy was in a fearful state, saying he'd seen blood on Rivera when he put the wreath on his chest. They were still gathered round Rivera's body, laying him out tidily on the floor. Breezy kept gibbering about the blood and then he caught sight of the body and turned away to the wall, retching and scrabbling in his overcoat pockets for one of his tablets and complaining because he had none. Nobody did anything for him and he went into the lavatory off the inner office and was heard vomiting in there. When he came back he looked terrible and stood gabbling about how he felt. At this point Breezy interrupted Caesar. "I told them," he said shrilly. "I told them. It was a terrible shock to me when he fell. It was a shock to all of us, wasn't it, boys?"

The Boys stirred themselves and muttered in unison that it had been a great shock.

"When he fell?" Alleyn said quickly. "Then, definitely, he wasn't supposed to fall?"

They all began to explain at once with great eagerness. Two routines had been rehearsed. There had been a lot of argument about which should be followed. Right up to the last neither Lord Pastern nor Rivera could make up his mind which he preferred. In the one routine Lord Pastern was to have fired the revolver four times at Rivera, who should have smiled and gone on playing. At each of the shots a member of the band was to have played a note in a descending scale and aped having been hit. Then Rivera was to have made his exit and the whole turn continued as they had seen it done, except that it would have ended with Lord Pastern doing a comic fall. Breezy would have then placed the wreath on him and he would have been carried out. In the alternative routine, Rivera was to do the fall. Carlos, the Boys explained, hadn't liked the idea of falling with his instrument so the first of these two plans had been decided on at the last moment.

"When I saw him drop," Breezy chattered, "I was rocked all to hell. I thought he'd done it to put one across us. He was like that, poor old Carlos. He was a bit that way. He didn't fancy the idea of falling, yet he didn't fancy his lordship getting the big exit. He was funny that way. It was a shock to all of us."

"So the end was an improvisation?"

"Not exactly," Lord Pastern said. "I kept my head, of course, and followed the correct routine. It was a bit of a facer but there you were, what? The waiters saw Carlos fall and luckily had the sense to bring the stretcher. It would've been awkward if they hadn't as things turned out. Damn' awkward. I emptied the magazine as we'd arranged and these other fellers did their staggers. Then I handed the gun to Breezy and he snapped it and then broke it open. I always thought my original idea of Carlos getting shot was best. Though of course I did rather see that it ought to be me who was carried out."

"And I thought," Breezy said, "I'd better drop that ruddy wreath on Carlos, like we first said. So I did." His voice jumped into falsetto. "When I saw the blood I thought at first he'd coughed it up. I thought he'd had one of those things—you know—a hemorrhage. At first. And then the wreath stuck on something. You'd scarcely credit it, would you, but I thought: for crisake I'm hanging it on a peg. And then I saw. I told you that, all of you. You can't say I didn't."

"Certainly you told us," Caesar agreed, eyeing him nervously. "In the office." Breezy made a petulant sound and crouched back in his chair. Caesar went on quickly to relate that just before they heard Dr. Allington's voice in the main office, Breezy had darted over to the body and had crouched down beside it, throwing back the coat and thrusting his hand into the breast pocket. He had said: "I've got to get it. He's got it on him," or something like that. They had been greatly shocked by this behaviour. He and Caesar and Hahn had pulled Breezy off and he had collapsed. It was during this scene that Edward Manx had arrived.

"Do you agree that this is a fair account of what happened, Mr. Bellairs?" Alleyn asked after a pause.

For a moment or two it seemed as if he would get some kind of answer. Breezy looked at him with extraordinary concentration. Then he turned his head as if his neck were stiff. After a moment he nodded.

"What did you hope to find in the deceased's pockets?" Alleyn said.

Breezy's mouth stretched in his manikin grin. His eyes were blank. He raised his hands and the fingers trembled.

"Come," Alleyn said, "what did you hope to find?"

"Oh God!" said Lord Pastern fretfully. "Now he's goin' to blub again."

This was an understatement. Hysteria took possession of Breezy. He screamed out some unintelligible protest or appeal, broke into a storm of sobbing laughter and stumbled to the entrance. A uniformed policeman came through the door and held him. "Now, now," said the policeman. "Easy does it, sir, easy does it."

Dr. Curtis came out of the office and stood looking at Breezy thoughtfully. Alleyn nodded to him and he went to Breezy.

Breezy sobbed: "Doctor! Doctor! Listen!" He put his heavy arm about Dr. Curtis's shoulders and with an air of mystery whispered in his ear. "I think, Alleyn . . . ?" said Dr. Curtis. "Yes," Alleyn said, "in the office, will you?"

When the door had shut behind them, Alleyn looked at Breezy's Boys. "Can any of you tell me," he said, "how long he's been taking drugs?"

ii

Lord Pastern, bunching his cheeks, said to nobody in particular, "Six months."

"You knew about it, my lord, did you?" Fox demanded and Lord Pastern grinned savagely at him. "Not bein' a detective-inspector," he said, "I don't have to wait until a dope-fiend throws fits and passes out before I know what's wrong with him."

He balanced complacently, toe and heel, and stroked the back of his head. "I've been lookin' into the dope racket," he volunteered. "Disgraceful show. Runnin' sore in the body politic and nobody with the guts to tackle it." He glared upon Breezy's Boys. "You chaps!" he said, jabbing a finger at them. "What did you do about it! Damn' all."

Breezy's Boys were embarrassed and shocked. They fidgeted, cleared their throats and eyed one another.

"Surely," Alleyn said, "you must have guessed. He's in a bad way, you know."

They hadn't been sure, it appeared. Happy Hart said they knew Breezy took some kind of stuff for his nerves. It was some special kind of dope. Breezy used to get people to buy it for him in Paris. He said it was some kind of bromide, Hart added vaguely. The double-bass said Breezy was a very nervous type. The first saxophone muttered something about hitting the high spots and corpse revivers. Lord Pastern loudly pronounced a succinct but unprintable comment and they eyed him resentfully. "I told him what it'd come to," he announced. "I threatened the chap. Only way. 'If you don't take a pull, by God,' I said, 'I'll give the whole story to the papers. *Harmony*, f'r instance.' I told him so, to-night."

Edward Manx uttered a sharp ejaculation and looked as if he wished he'd held his tongue.

"Who searched him for his bloody tablet?" Skelton demanded, glaring at Lord Pastern.

"The show," Lord Pastern countered virtuously, "had to go on, didn't it? Don't split straws, my good ass."

Alleyn intervened. The incident of the lost tablet was related. Lord Pastern described how he went through Breezy's pockets and boasted of his efficiency. "You fellers call it fannin' a chap," he explained kindly, to Alleyn.

"This was immediately after Mr. Skelton had inspected the revolver and handed it back to Lord Pastern?" Alleyn asked.

"That's right," said one or two of the Boys.

"Lord Pastern, did you at any time after he'd done this lose sight of the revolver or put it down?"

"Certainly not. I kept it in my hip pocket from the time Skelton gave it to me until I went on the stage."

"Did you look down the barrel after Mr. Skelton returned it to you?"
"No."

"I won't have this," said Skelton loudly.

Alleyn glanced thoughtfully at him and returned to Lord Pastern. "Did you, by the way," he said, "find anything in Mr. Bellairs's pockets?"

"A wallet, a cigarette case and his handkerchief," Lord Pastern rejoined importantly. "The pill was in the handkerchief."

Alleyn asked for a closer description of this scene and Lord Pastern related with gusto how Breezy had stood with his hands up, holding his baton as if he were about to give his first down-beat, and how he himself had explored every pocket with the utmost dispatch and thoroughness. "If," he added, "you're thinkin' that he might have had the dart on him, you're wrong. He hadn't. And he couldn't have got at the gun if he had, what's more. And he didn't pick anything up afterwards. I'll swear to that."

Ned Manx said with some violence: "For God's sake, Cousin George, think what you're saying."

"It is useless, Edward," said Lady Pastern. "He will destroy himself out of sheer complacency." She addressed herself to Alleyn. "I must inform you that in my opinion and that of many of his acquaintances, my husband's eccentricity is of a degree that renders his statements completely unreliable."

"That be damned!" shouted Lord Pastern. "I'm the most truthful man I know. You're an ass."

"So be it," said Lady Pastern in her deepest voice, and folded her hands.

"When you came out on the dais," Alleyn went on, disregarding this interlude, "you brought the revolver with you and put it on the floor under a hat. It was near your right foot, I think, and behind the drums. Quite near the edge of the dais."

Félicité had opened her bag and for the fourth time had taken out her lipstick and mirror. She made an involuntary movement of her hands, jerking the lipstick away as if she threw it. The mirror fell at her feet. She half rose. Her open bag dropped to the floor, and the glass splintered under her heel. The carpet was littered with the contents of her bag and blotted with powder. Alleyn moved forward quickly. He picked up the lipstick and a folded paper with typewriting on it. Félicité snatched the paper from his hand. "Thank you. Don't bother. What a fool I am," she said breathlessly.

She crushed the paper in her hand and held it while, with the other hand, she gathered up the contents of her bag. One of the waiters came forward, like an automaton, to help her.

"Quite near the edge of the dais," Alleyn repeated. "So that, for the sake of argument, you, Miss de Suze, or Miss Wayne, or Mr. Manx, could have reached out to the sombrero. In fact, while some of your party were dancing, anyone who was left at the table could also have done this. Do you all agree?"

Carlisle was acutely aware of the muscles of her face. She was conscious of Alleyn's gaze, impersonal and deliberate, resting on her eyes and her mouth and her hands. She remembered noticing him—how many hours ago?—when he sat at the next table. "I mustn't look at Fée or at Ned," she thought. She heard Edward move stealthily in his chair. The paper in Félicité's hand rustled. There was a sharp click and Carlisle jumped galvanically. Lady Pastern had flicked open her lorgnette and was now staring through it at Alleyn.

Manx said: "You were next to our table, I think, weren't you, Alleyn?"

"By an odd coincidence," Alleyn rejoined pleasantly.

"I think it better for us to postpone our answers."

"Do you?" Alleyn said lightly. "Why?"

"Obviously, the question about whether we could have touched this hat, or whatever it was . . ."

"You know perfectly well what it was, Ned," Lord Pastern interjected. "It was my sombrero, and the gun was under it. We've had all that."

". . . this sombrero," Edward amended, "is a question that has dangerous implications for all of us. I'd like to say that quite apart from the possibility, which we have not admitted, of any of us touching it, there is surely no possibility at all that any of us could have taken a revolver from underneath it, shoved a bit of a parasol up the barrel and replaced the gun, without anything being noticed. If you don't mind my saying so, the suggestion of any such manoeuvre is obviously ridiculous."

"Oh, I don't know," said Lord Pastern with an air of judicial impartiality. "All that switchin' about of the light and the metronome waggin' and everybody naturally watchin' me, you know. I should say, in point of fact, it was quite possible. I wouldn't have noticed, I promise you."

"George," Félicité whispered fiercely, "do you *want* to do us in?"

"I want the truth," her stepfather shouted crossly. "I was a Theosophist, once," he added.

"You are and have been and always will be an imbecile," said his wife, shutting her lorgnette.

"Well," Alleyn said and, the attention of the band, the employees of the restaurant and its guests having been diverted to this domestic interchange, swung back to him, "ridiculous or not, I shall put the question. You are, of course, under no compulsion to answer it. Did any of you handle Lord Pastern's sombrero?"

They were silent. The waiter, who had gathered up the pieces of broken mirror, faced Alleyn with an anxious smile. "Excuse me, sir," he said.

"Yes?"

"The young lady," said the waiter, bowing towards Félicité, "did put her hand under the hat. I was the waiter for that table, sir, and I happened to notice. I hope you will excuse me, miss, but I did happen to notice."

Fox's pencil whispered over the paper.

"Thank you," said Alleyn.

Félicité cried out: "This is the absolute *end*. Suppose I said it's not true."

"I shouldn't," Alleyn said. "As Mr. Manx has pointed out, I was sitting next to your table."

"Then why ask?"

"To see if you would frankly admit that you did, in fact, put your hand under the sombrero."

"People," said Carlisle suddenly, "think twice about making frank statements all over the place when a capital crime is involved."

She looked up at Alleyn and found him smiling at her. "How right you are," he said. "That's what makes homicide cases so tiresome."

"Are we to hang about all night," Lord Pastern demanded, "while you sit gossipin'? Never saw such a damned amateur set-up in all m' life. Makes you sick."

"Let us get on by all means, sir. We haven't very much more ground to cover here. It will be necessary, I'm afraid, for us to search you before we can let you off."

"All of us?" Félicité said quickly.

They looked, with something like awe, at Lady Pastern.

"There is a wardress in the ladies' cloak-room," Alleyn said, "and a detective-sergeant in the men's. We shall also need your finger-prints, if you please. Sergeant Bailey will attend to that. Shall we set about it? Perhaps you, Lady Pastern, will go in first?"

Lady Pastern rose. Her figure, tightly encased, seemed to enlarge itself. Everybody stole uneasy glances at it. She faced her husband. "Of the many indignities you have forced upon me," she said, "this is the most intolerable. For this I shall never forgive you."

"Good Lord, C," he rejoined, "what's the matter with bein' searched? Trouble with you is you've got a dirty mind. If you'd listened to my talks on the Body Beautiful that time in Kent . . ."

"Silence!" she said (in French) and swept into the ladies' cloak-room. Félicité giggled nervously.

"Anybody may search me," Lord Pastern said generously. "Come on."

He led the way to the men's cloak-room.

Alleyn said: "Perhaps, Miss de Suze, you would like to go with your mother. It's perfectly in order, if you think she'd prefer it."

Félicité was sitting in her chair with her left hand clutching her bag and her right hand out of sight. "I expect she'd rather have a private martyrdom, Mr. Alleyn," she said.

"Suppose you go and ask her? You can get your part of the programme over when she is free."

He stood close to Félicité, smiling down at her. She said, "Oh, all right. If you like." Without enthusiasm, and with a backward glance at Manx, she followed her mother. Alleyn immediately took her chair and addressed himself to Manx and Carlisle.

"I wonder," he said, "if you can help me with one or two routine jobs that will have to be tidied up. I believe you were both at the dinner party at Lord Pastern's house—it's in Duke's Gate, isn't it?—before this show tonight."

"Yes," Edward said. "We were there."

"And the rest of the party? Bellairs and Rivera and of course Lord and Lady Pastern. Anyone else?"

"No," Carlisle said and immediately corrected herself. "I'd forgotten. Miss Henderson."

"Miss Henderson?"

"She used to be Félicité's governess and stayed on as a sort of general prop and stay to everybody."

"What is her full name?"

"I—I really don't know. Ned, have you ever heard Hendy's Christian name?"

"No," Edward said. "Never. She's simply Hendy. I should think it might be Edith. Wait a moment though," he added, "I do know. Fée told me years ago. She saw it on an electoral roll or something. It's Petronella Xantippe."

"I don't believe you."

"People so seldom have the names you expect," Alleyn murmured vaguely. "Can you give me a detailed description of your evening at Duke's Gate? You see, as Rivera was there, the dinner party assumes a kind of importance."

Carlisle thought: "We're waiting too long. One of us ought to have replied at once."

"I want," Alleyn said at last, "if you can give it to me, an account of the whole thing. When everybody arrived. What you talked about. Whether you were all together most of the time or whether you split up, for instance, after dinner, and were in different rooms. That kind of thing."

They began to speak together and stopped short. They laughed uncomfortably, apologized and invited each other to proceed. At last Carlisle embarked alone on a colourless narrative. She had arrived at Duke's Gate at about five and had seen her aunt and uncle and Félicité. Naturally there had been a good deal of talk about the evening performance. Her uncle had been in very good spirits.

"And Lady Pastern and Miss de Suze?" Alleyn said. Carlisle replied carefully that they were in much their usual form. "And how is that?" he asked. "Cheerful? Happy family atmosphere, would you say?"

Manx said lightly: "My dear Alleyn, like most families they rub along together without—without—"

"Were you going to say 'without actually busting up'?"

"Well—well—"

"Ned," Carlisle interjected, "it's no good pretending Uncle George and Aunt Cécile represent the dead norm of British family life. Presumably, Mr. Alleyn reads the papers. If I say they were much as usual it means they were much as usual on their own lines." She turned to Alleyn. "On their own lines, Mr. Alleyn, they were perfectly normal."

"If you'll allow me to say so, Miss Wayne," Alleyn rejoined warmly, "you are evidently an extremely sensible person. May I implore you to keep it up."

"Not to the extent of letting you think a routine argument to them is matter for suspicion to you."

"They argue," Manx added, "perpetually and vehemently. It means nothing. Well, you've heard them."

"And did they, for example, argue about Lord Pastern's performance in the band?"

"Oh, yes," they said together.

"And about Bellairs or Rivera?"

"A bit," said Carlisle after a pause.

"Boogie-woogie merchants," Manx said, "are not, in the nature of things, my cousin Cécile's cups of tea. She is, as you may have noticed, a little in the *grande dame* line of business."

Alleyn leant forward in his chair and rubbed his nose. He looked, Carlisle thought, like a bookish man considering some point that had been raised in an interminable argument.

"Yes," he said at last. "That's all right, of course. One can see the obvious and rather eccentric *mise en scène*. Everything you've told me is no doubt quite true. But the devil of it is, you know, that you're going to use the palpable eccentricities as a sort of smoke screen for the more profound disturbances."

They were astonished and disconcerted. Carlisle said tentatively that she didn't understand. "Don't you?" Alleyn murmured. "Oh, well! Shall we get on with it? Bellairs has suggested an engagement between Rivera and Miss de Suze. Was there an engagement, if you please?"

"No, I don't think so. Was there, Lisle?"

Carlisle said that she didn't think so either. Nothing had been announced.

"An understanding?"

"He wanted her to marry him, I think. I mean," Carlisle amended with heightened colour, "I know he did. I don't think she was going to. I'm sure she wasn't."

"How did Lord Pastern feel about it?

"Who can tell?" Edward muttered.

"I don't think it bothered him much one way or the other," Carlisle said. "He was too busy planning his début."

But into her memory came the figure of Lord Pastern, bent over his task of drawing bullets from cartridges, and she heard again his grunted: "much better leave things to me."

Alleyn began to lead them step by step through the evening at Duke's Gate. What had they talked about before dinner? How had the party been divided, and into which rooms? What had they themselves done and said? Carlisle found herself charged with an account of her arrival. It was easy to say that her aunt and uncle had argued about whether there should be extra guests for dinner. It was not so easy when he led her back to the likelihood of an engagement between Rivera and Félicité, asking if it had been discussed and by whom, and whether Félicité had confided in her.

"These seem impertinent questions," Alleyn said, and anticipated her attempt to suggest as much. "But, believe me, they are entirely impersonal. Irrelevant matters will be most thankfully rejected and forgotten. We want to tidy up the field of inquiry, that's all." And then it seemed to Carlisle that evasions would be silly and wrong and she said that Félicité had been worried and unhappy about Rivera. She sensed Edward's uneasiness and added that there had been nothing in the Félicité-Rivera situation, nothing at all. "Félicité makes emotional mountains out of sentimental mole-hills," she said. "I think she enjoys it." But she knew while she said this that Félicité's outburst had been more serious than she suggested and she heard her voice lose its integrity and guessed that Alleyn heard this too. She began to be oppressed by his quiet insistence and yet her taste for detail made her a little pleased with her own accuracy, and she felt something like an artist's reluctance to slur or distort. It was easy again to recall her solitary time before dinner in the ballroom. As soon as she began to speak of it the sensation of nostalgia flashed up in her memory and she found herself telling Alleyn that her coming-out ball had been there, that the room had a host of associations for her and that she had stood there, recollecting them.

"Did you notice if the umbrellas and parasols were there?"

"Yes," she said quickly. "I did. They were there on the piano. I remembered the French parasol. It was Aunt Cile's. I remembered Félicité playing with it as a child. It takes to pieces." She caught her breath. "But you know it does that," she said.

"And it was intact then, when you saw it? No bits gone out of the shaft?"

"No, no."

"Sure?"

"Yes. I picked it up and opened it. That's supposed to be unlucky, isn't it? It was all right then."

"Good. And after this you went into the drawing-room. I know this sounds aimlessly exacting but what happened next, do you remember?"

Before she knew where she was she had told him about the magazine, *Harmony*, and there seemed no harm in repeating her notion that Félicité had written one of the letters on G.P.F.'s page. Alleyn gave no sign that this was of interest. It was Edward who, unaccountably, made a stifled ejaculation. Carlisle thought, "Have I blundered?" and hurried on to an account of her visit to her uncle's study when he drew the bullets from the cartridges. Alleyn asked casually how he had set about this and seemed to be diverted from the matter in hand, amused at Lord Pastern's neatness and dexterity.

Carlisle was accustomed to being questioned about Lord Pastern's eccentricities. She considered him fair game and normally enjoyed trying to make sharp, not unkindly little word-sketches of him for her friends. His notoriety was so gross that she had always felt it would be ridiculous to hesitate. She slipped into this habit now.

Then, the picture of the drawer, pulled out and laid on the desk at his elbow, suddenly presented itself. She felt a kind of shrinking in her midriff and stopped short.

But Alleyn had turned to Ned Manx and Ned, dryly and slowly, answered questions about his own arrival in the drawing-room. What impression did he get of Bellairs and Rivera? He hadn't spoken to them very much. Lady Pastern had taken him apart to show him her embroidery.

"*Gros point?*" Alleyn asked.

"And petit point. Like most Frenchwomen of her period, she's pretty good. I really didn't notice the others much."

The dinner party itself came next. The conversation, Ned was saying, had been fragmentary, about all sorts of things. He couldn't remember in detail.

"Miss Wayne has an observer's eye and ear," Alleyn said, turning to her. "Perhaps you can remember, can you? What did you talk about? You sat, where?"

"On Uncle George's right."

"And on your other hand?"

"Mr. Rivera."

"Can you remember what he spoke about, Miss Wayne?" Alleyn offered his cigarette case to her. As he lit her cigarette Carlisle looked past him at Ned, who shook his head very slightly.

"I thought him rather awful, I'm afraid," she said. "He really was a bit too thick. All flowery compliments and too Spanish-grandee for anyone to swallow."

"Do you agree, Mr. Manx?"

"Oh, yes. He was quite unreal and rather ridiculous I thought."

"Offensively so, would you say?"

They did not look at each other. Edward said: "He just bounded sky-high, if you call that offensive."

"Did they speak of the performance to-night?"

"Oh, yes," Edward said. "And I must say I'm not surprised that the waiters were muddled about who they were to carry out. It struck me that both Uncle George and Rivera wanted all the fat and that neither of them could make up his mind to letting the other have the stretcher. Bellairs was clearly at the end of his professional tether about it."

Alleyn asked how long the men had stayed behind in the dining-room. Reluctantly—too reluctantly Carlisle thought, with a rising sense of danger —Ned told them that Lord Pastern had taken Breezy away to show him the blank cartridges. "So you and Rivera were left with the port?" Alleyn said.

"Yes. Not for long."

"Can you recall the conversation?"

"There was nothing that would be any help to you."

"You never know."

"I didn't encourage conversation. He asked all sorts of questions about our various relationships to each other and I snubbed him."

"How did he take that?"

"Nobody enjoys being snubbed, I suppose, but I fancy he had a tolerably thick hide on him."

"Was there actually a quarrel?"

Edward stood up. "Look here, Alleyn," he said, "if I was in the slightest degree implicated in this business I should have followed my own advice and refused to answer any of your questions. I am not implicated. I did not monkey with the revolver. I did not bring about Rivera's death."

"And now," Carlisle thought in despair, "Ned's going to give him a sample of the family temper. O God," she thought, "please don't let him."

"Good," Alleyn said and waited.

"Very well then," Edward said grandly and sat down.

"So there was a quarrel."

"I merely," Edward shouted, "showed the man I thought he was impertinent and he walked out of the room."

"Did you speak to him again after this incident?"

Carlisle remembered a scene in the hall, the two men facing each other, Rivera with his hand clapped to his ear. What was it Ned had said to him? Something ridiculous, like a perky schoolboy. "Put that in your hurdy-gurdy and squeeze it," he had shouted with evident relish.

"I merely ask these questions," Alleyn said, "because the bloke had a thick ear, and I wondered who gave it to him. The skin's broken and I notice you wear a signet ring."

iii

In the main office, Dr. Curtis contemplated Breezy Bellairs with the air of wary satisfaction. "He'll do," he said, and, stepping neatly behind Breezy's chair, he winked at Alleyn. "He must have got hold of something over and above the shot I gave him. But he'll do."

Breezy looked up at Alleyn and gave him the celebrated smile. He was pallid and sweating lightly. His expression was one of relief, of well-being. Dr. Curtis washed his syringe in a tumbler of water on the desk and then returned it to his case.

Alleyn opened the door into the foyer and nodded to Fox, who rose and joined him. Together they returned to the contemplation of Breezy.

Fox cleared his throat. "*Alors*," he said cautiously and stopped.

"*Évidemment*," he said, "*il y a un avancement, n'est-ce pas?*"

He paused, slightly flushed, and looked out of the corners of his eyes at Alleyn.

"*Pas grand'chose*," Alleyn muttered. "But as Curtis says, he'll do for our purpose. You go, by the way, Br'er Fox, from strength to strength. The accent improves."

"I still don't get the practice though," Fox complained. Breezy, who was looking with complete tranquillity at the opposite wall, laughed comfortably. "I feel lovely, now," he volunteered.

"He's had a pretty solid shot," Dr. Curtis said. "I don't know what he'd been up to before but it seems to have packed him up a bit. But he's all right. He can answer questions, can't you, Bellairs?"

"I'm fine," Breezy rejoined dreamily. "Box of birds."

"Well . . ." Alleyn said dubiously. Fox added in a sepulchral undertone: "*Faute de mieux*." "Exactly," Alleyn said and, drawing up a chair, placed himself in front of Breezy.

"I'd like you to tell me something," he said. Breezy lazily withdrew his gaze from the opposite wall and Alleyn found himself staring into eyes that,

because of the enormous size of their pupils, seemed mere structures and
devoid of intelligence.

"Do you remember," he said, "what you did at Lord Pastern's house?"

He had to wait a long time for an answer. At last Breezy's voice, detached
and remote, said: "Don't let's talk. It's nicer not talking."

"Talking's nice too, though."

Dr. Curtis walked away from Breezy and murmured to no one in particular, "Get him started and he may go on."

"It must have been fun at the dinner party," Alleyn suggested. "Did Carlos
enjoy himself?"

Breezy's arm lay curved along the desk. With a luxurious sigh, he slumped
further into the chair and rested his cheek on his sleeve. In a moment or
two his voice began again, independently, it seemed, with no conscious volition on his part. It trailed through his scarcely moving lips in a monotone.

"I told him it was silly but that made no difference at all. 'Look,' I said,
'you're crazy!' Well, of course I was sore on account of he held back on me,
not bringing me my cigarettes."

"What cigarettes?"

"He never did anything I asked him. I was so good to him. I was as good
as gold. I told him. I said, 'Look,' I said, 'she won't take it from you, boy.
She's as sore as hell,' I said, 'and so's he, and the other girl isn't falling so
what's the point?' I knew there'd be trouble. 'And the old bastard doesn't
like it,' I said. 'He pretends it doesn't mean a thing to him but that's all
hooey because he just naturally wouldn't like it.' No good. No notice taken."

"When was this?" Alleyn asked.

"Off and on. Most of the time you might say. And when we were in the
taxi and he said how the guy had hit him, I said: 'There you are, what was I
telling you?'"

"Who hit him?"

There was a longer pause. Breezy turned his head languidly.

"Who hit Carlos, Breezy?"

"I heard you the first time. What a gang, though! The Honourable Edward Manx in serious mood while lunching at the Tarmac with Miss Félicité
de Suze who is of course connected with him on the distaff side. Her stepfather is Lord Pastern and Bagott, but if you ask me it's a punctured romance. *Cherchez la femme.*"

Fox glanced up from his notes with an air of bland interest.

"The woman in this case," Alleyn said, "being . . ."

"Funny name for a girl."

"Carlisle?"

"Sounds dopey to me, but what of that? But that's the sort of thing they
do. Imagine having two names. Pastern and Bagott. And I can look after both
of them, don't you worry. Trying to swing one across me. What a chance!
Bawling me out. Saying he'll write to this bloody paper. Him and his hot-
gunning and where is he now?"

"Swing one across you?" Alleyn repeated quietly. He had pitched his voice on Breezy's level. Their voices ran into and away from each other. They seemed to the two onlookers to speak as persons in a dream, with tranquillity and secret understanding.

"He might have known," Breezy was saying, "that I wouldn't come at it but you've got to admit it was awkward. A permanent engagement. Thanks a lot. How does the chorus go?"

He laughed faintly, yawned, whispered, "Pardon me," and closed his eyes.

"He's going," Dr. Curtis said.

"Breezy," Alleyn said loudly. "*Breezy.*"

"What?"

"Did Lord Pastern want you to keep him on permanently?"

"I told you. Him and his blankety-blankety blank cartridges."

"Did he want you to sack Skelton?"

"It was all Carlos's fault," Breezy said quite loudly and on a plaintive note. "He thought it up. God, was he angry!"

"Was who angry?"

With a suggestion of cunning the voice murmured: "That's telling."

"Was it Lord Pastern?"

"Him? Don't make me laugh!"

"Syd Skelton?"

"When I told him," Breezy whispered faintly, "he looked like murder. Honest, I *was* nervy."

He rolled his face over on his arm and fell into a profound sleep. "He won't come out of that for eight hours," said Dr. Curtis.

iv

At two o'clock the cleaners came in, five middle-aged women who were admitted by the police and who walked through the foyer into the restaurant with the tools of their trade. Caesar Bonn was greatly distressed by their arrival and complained that the pressmen, who had been sent away with a meager statement that Rivera had collapsed and died, would lie in wait for these women and question them. He sent the secretary, David Hahn, after the cleaners. "They are to be silenced at all costs. At all costs, you understand." Presently the drone of vacuum-cleaners arose in the restaurant. Two of Alleyn's men had been there for some time. They now returned to the foyer and, joining the policemen on duty there, glanced impassively at its inhabitants.

Most of the Boys were asleep. They were sprawled in ungainly postures on their small chairs. Trails of ash lay on their clothes. They had crushed out their cigarette butts on empty packets, on the soles of their shoes, on match boxes, or had pitched them at the floor containers. The smell of dead butts seemed to hang over the entire room.

Lady Pastern appeared to sleep. She was inclined backwards in her arm-chair and her eyes were closed. Purplish shadows had appeared on her face and deep grooves ran from her nostrils to the corners of her mouth. Her cheeks sagged. She scarcely stirred when her husband, who had been silent for a considerable time, said: "Hi, Ned!"

"Yes, Cousin George?" Manx responded guardedly.

"I've got to the bottom of this."

"Indeed?"

"I know who did it."

"Really? Who?"

"I disagree entirely and emphatically with capital punishment," Lord Pastern said, puffing out his cheeks at the group of police officials. "I shall therefore keep my knowledge to myself. Let 'em muddle on. Murder's a matter for the psychiatrist, not the hangman. As for judges, they're a pack of conceited old sadists. Let 'em get on with it. They'll have no help from me. For God's sake, Fée, stop fidgetin'."

Félicité was curled up in the chair she had used earlier in the evening. From time to time she thrust her hands out of sight, exploring, it seemed, the space between the upholstered arms and seat. She did this furtively with sidelong glances at the others. Carlisle said: "What *is* it, Fée? What have you lost?" "My hanky." "Here, take mine, for pity's sake," said Lord Pastern and threw it at her.

The searching had gone forward steadily. Carlisle, who liked her privacy, had found the experience galling and unpleasant. The wardress was a straw-coloured woman with large artificial teeth and firm pale hands. She had been extremely polite and uncompromising.

Now the last man to be searched, Syd Skelton, returned from the men's cloak-room and at the same time Alleyn and Fox came out of the office. The Boys woke up. Lady Pastern opened her eyes.

Alleyn said: "As the result of these preliminary inquiries . . ." ("Preliminary!" Lord Pastern snorted.) . . . "I think we have got together enough information and may allow you to go home. I'm extremely sorry to have kept you here so long."

They were all on their feet. Alleyn raised a hand. "There's one restriction, I'm afraid. I think you'll all understand and, I hope, respect it. Those of you who were in immediate communication with Rivera or who had access to the revolver used by Lord Pastern, or who seem to us, for sufficient reasons, to be in any way concerned in the circumstances leading to Rivera's death, will be seen home by police officers. We shall provide ourselves with search-warrants. If such action seems necessary, we shall use them."

"Of all the footlin', pettifoggin' . . ." Lord Pastern began, and was interrupted.

"Those of you who come under this heading," Alleyn said, "are Lord Pastern and the members of his party, Mr. Bellairs and Mr. Skelton. That's all, I think. Thank you, ladies and gentlemen."

"I'm damned if I'll put up with this. Look here, Alleyn . . ."

"I'm sorry, sir. I must insist, I'm afraid."

"George," said Lady Pastern. "You have tried conclusions with the law on more than one occasion and as often as you have done so you have made a fool of yourself. Come home."

Lord Pastern studied his wife with an air of detachment. "Your hair-net's loose," he pointed out, "and you're bulgin' above your waist. Comes of wearin' stays. I've always said . . ."

"I, at least," Lady Pastern said directly to Alleyn, "am prepared to accept your conditions. So, I am sure, are my daughter and my niece. Félicité! Carlisle!"

"Fox," said Alleyn.

She walked with perfect composure to the door and waited there. Fox spoke to one of the plain-clothes men, who detached himself from the group near the entrance. Félicité held out a hand towards Edward Manx. "Ned, you'll come, won't you? You'll stay with us?"

After a moment's hesitation he took her hand.

"Dearest Edward," said Lady Pastern from the door. "We should be so grateful."

"Certainly, Cousin Cécile. Of course."

Félicité still held his hand. He looked at Carlisle. "Coming?" he asked.

"Yes, of course. Good night, Mr. Alleyn," said Carlisle.

"Good night, Miss Wayne."

They went out, followed by the plain-clothes man.

"I should like to have a word with you, Mr. Skelton," Alleyn said. "The rest of you"—he turned to the Boys, the waiters and the spot-light man—"may go. You will be given notice of the inquest. Sorry to have kept you up so late. Good night."

The waiters and the electrician went at once. The band moved forward in a group. Happy Hart said: "What about Breezy?"

"He's sound asleep and will need a bit of rousing. I shall see he's taken home."

Hart shuffled his feet and looked at his hands. "I don't know what you're thinking," he said, "but he's all right. Breezy's O.K. really. I mean he's just been making the pace a bit too hot for himself as you might say. He's a very nervy type, Breezy. He suffers from insomnia. He took the stuff for his nerves. But he's all right."

"He and Rivera got on well, did they?"

Several of the Boys said quickly: "That's right. Sure. They were all right." Hart added that Breezy was very good to Carlos and gave him his big chance in London.

All the Boys agreed fervently with this statement except Skelton. He stood apart from his associates. They avoided looking at him. He was a tall darkish fellow with narrow eyes and a sharp nose. His mouth was small and thin-lipped. He stooped slightly.

"Well, if that's all," Happy Hart said uneasily, "we'll say good night."

"We've got their addresses, haven't we, Fox? Good. Thank you. Good night."

They filed out, carrying their instruments. In the old days when places like the Metronome and Quags and the Hungaria kept going up to two in the morning the Boys had worked through, sometimes going on to parties in private houses. They were Londoners who turned homewards with pale faces and blue jaws at the time when fans of water from giant hose pipes strike across Piccadilly and Whitehall. They had been among the tag-ends of the night in those times, going soberly to their beds as the first milk carts jangled. In summer-time they had undressed in the dawn to the thin stir of sparrows. They shared with taxi drivers, cloak-room attendants, waiters and commissionaires a specialized disillusionment.

Alleyn watched them go and then nodded to Fox. Fox approached Caesar Bonn and David Hahn, who lounged gloomily near the office door. "Perhaps you gentlemen wouldn't mind coming into the office," he suggested. They followed him in. Alleyn turned to Skelton. "Now, Mr. Skelton."

"What's the idea," Skelton said, "keeping me back? I've got a home, same as everybody else. Though how the hell I'm going to get there's nobody's business."

"I'm sorry. It's a nuisance for you, I know, but it can't be helped."

"I don't see why."

The office door was opened from inside. Two constables came out with Breezy Bellairs hanging between them like a cumbersome puppet. His face was lividly pale, his eyes half open. He breathed stertorously and made a complaining noise like a wretched child. Dr. Curtis followed. Bonn and Hahn watched from inside the office.

"All right?" Alleyn said.

"He'll do. We'll just get him into his coat."

They held Breezy up while Curtis, with difficulty, crammed him into his tight-fitting overcoat. During this struggle Breezy's baton fell to the floor. Hahn came forward and picked it up. "You wouldn't think," Hahn said, contemplating it sadly, "how good he was. Not to look at him now."

Dr. Curtis yawned. "These chaps'll see him into his bed," he said. "I'll be off, if you don't want me, Rory."

"Right." The dragging procession disappeared. Fox returned to the office and shut the door.

"That's a nice way," Skelton said angrily, "for a first-class band leader to be seen going home. Between a couple of flatties."

"They'll be very tactful," Alleyn rejoined. "Shall we sit down?"

Skelton said he'd sat down for so long that his bottom was numb. "Let's get cracking for God's sake. I've had it. What's the idea?"

Alleyn took out his notebook.

"The idea," he said, "is further information. I think you can give it to us. By all means let's get cracking."

"Why pick on me? I know no more than the others."

"Don't you?" Alleyn said vaguely. He glanced up. "What's your opinion of Lord Pastern as a tympanist?"

"Dire. What of it?"

"Did the others hold this opinion?"

"They knew. Naturally. It was a cheap stunt. Playing up the snob value." He thrust his hands down in his pockets and began to walk to and fro, impelled, it seemed, by resentment. Alleyn waited.

"It's when something like this turns up," Skelton announced loudly, "that you see how rotten the whole set-up really is. I'm not ashamed of my work. Why the hell should I be? It interests me. It's not easy. It takes doing and anybody that tells you there's nothing to the best type of our kind of music talks through his hat. It's got something. It's clever and there's a lot of hard thinking behind it."

"I don't know about music," Alleyn said, "but I can imagine that from the technical point of view your sort can be almost purely intellectual. Or is that nonsense?"

Skelton glowered at him. "You're not far out. A lot of the stuff we have to play is wet and corny, of course. They," he jerked his head at the empty restaurant, "like it that way. But there's other stuff that's different. If I could pick my work I'd be in an outfit that went for the real McCoy. In a country where things were run decently I'd be able to do that. I'd be able to say: 'This is what I can do and it's the best I can do,' and I'd be directed into the right channels. I'm a communist," he said loudly.

Alleyn was suddenly and vividly reminded of Lord Pastern. He said nothing and after a pause Skelton went on.

"I realize I'm working for the rottenest section of a crazy society but what can I do? It's my job and I have to take it. But this affair! Walking out and letting a dopey old dead beat of a lord make a fool of himself with my instruments, and a lot of dead beat effects added to them! Looking as if I like it! Where's my self-respect?"

"How," Alleyn asked, "did it come about?"

"Breezy worked it because . . ."

He stopped short and advanced on Alleyn. "Here!" he demanded. "What's all this in aid of? What do you want?"

"Like Lord Pastern," Alleyn said lightly, "I want the truth. Bellairs, you were saying, worked it because—of what?"

"I've told you. Snob value."

"And the others agreed?"

"They haven't any principles. Oh, yes. They took it."

"Rivera, for instance, didn't oppose the idea?"

Skelton flushed deeply. "No," he said. Alleyn saw his pockets bulge as the hidden hands clenched. "Why not?" he asked.

"Rivera was hanging his hat up to the girl. Pastern's stepdaughter. He was all out to make himself a hero with the old man."

"That made you very angry, didn't it?"

"Who says it made me angry?"

"Bellairs said so."

"Him! Another product of our so-called civilization. Look at him."

Alleyn asked him if he knew anything about Breezy's use of drugs. Skelton, caught, as it seemed, between the desire of a zealot to speak his mind and an undefined wariness, said that Breezy was the child of his age and circumstances. He was a by-product, Skelton said, of a cynical and disillusioned social set-up. The phrases fell from his lips with the precision of slogans. Alleyn listened and watched and felt his interest stirring. "We all knew," Skelton said, "that he was taking some kind of dope to keep him going. Even *he* knew—old Pastern. He'd nosed it out all right and I reckon he knew where it came from. You could tell. Breezy's changed a hell of a lot. He used to be a nice sort of joker in a way. Bit of a wag. Always having us on. He got off-side with the Dago for that."

"Rivera?"

"That's right. Breezy used to be crazy on practical jokes. He'd fix a silly squeaker in one of the saxes or sneak a wee bell inside the piano. Childish. He got hold of Rivera's p-a and fixed it with little bits of paper between the keys so's it wouldn't go. Only for rehearsal, of course. Rivera came out all glamour and hair oil and swung his p-a. Nothing happened. There was Breezy grinning like he'd split his face and the Boys all sniggering. You had to laugh. Rivera tore the place up: he went mad and howled out he'd quit. Breezy had a hell of a job fixing him. It was quite a party."

"Practical jokes," Alleyn said. "A curious obsession, I always think."

Skelton looked sharply at him. "Here!" he said. "You don't want to get ideas. Breezy's all right. Breezy wouldn't come at anything like this." He laughed shortly, and added with an air of disgust: "Breezy fix Rivera! Not likely."

"About this drug habit—" Alleyn began. Skelton said impatiently: "Well, there you are! It's just one of those things. I told you—we all knew. He used to go to parties on Sundays with some gang."

"Any idea who they were?"

"No, I never asked. I'm not interested. I tried to tell him he was heading for a crash. Once. He didn't like it. He's my boss and I shut up. I'd have turned it up and gone over to another band but I'm used to working with these boys and they do better stuff than most."

"You never heard where he got his drug, whatever it is?"

Skelton muttered, "I never *heard*. Naturally."

"But you formed an opinion, perhaps?"

"Perhaps."

"Going to tell me about it?"

"I want to know what you're getting at. I've got to protect myself, haven't I? I like to get things straight. You've got some notion that because I looked at Pastern's gun I might have shoved this silly umbrella what-have-you up the muzzle. Why don't you come to the point?"

"I shall do so," Alleyn said. "I've kept you behind because of this circumstance and because you were alone with Lord Pastern for a short time after you left the platform and before he made his entrance. So far as I can see at the moment there is no connection between your possible complicity and the fact that Bellairs takes drugs. As a police officer I'm concerned with drug addicts and their source of supply. If you can help me with any information I'll be grateful. Do you know, then, where Bellairs got whatever he took?"

Skelton deliberated, his brows drawn together, his lower lip thrust out. Alleyn found himself speculating about his background. What accumulation of circumstances, ill-adjustments or misfortunes had resulted in this particular case? What would Skelton have been if his history had been otherwise? Were his views, his truculence, his suspicions, rooted in honesty or in some indefinable sense of victimization? To what lengths would they impel him? And finally Alleyn asked himself the inevitable question: could this be a killer?

Skelton wetted his lips. "The drug racket," he said, "is like any other racket in a capitalistic government. The real criminals are the bosses, the barons, the high-ups. They don't get pulled in. It's the little blokes that get caught. You have to think it out. Silly sentiment and big talk won't work. I've got no tickets on the police department in this country. A fairly efficient machine working for the wrong ideas. But drug-taking's no good from any point of view. All right. I'll co-operate this far. I'll tell you where Breezy got his dope."

"And where," said Alleyn patiently, "did Breezy get his dope?"

"From Rivera," said Skelton. "Now! From Rivera."

CHAPTER VII

Dawn

Skelton had gone home, and Caesar Bonn and David Hahn. The cleaners had retired into some remote part of the building. Only the police remained: Alleyn and Fox, Bailey, Thompson, the three men who had searched the restaurant and band-room and the uniformed constable who would remain on duty until he was relieved after daybreak. The time was now twenty minutes to three.

"Well, Foxkin," said Alleyn, "where are we? You've been very mousy and discreet. Let's have your theory. Come on."

Fox cleared his throat and placed the palms of his hands on his knees. "A very peculiar case," he said disapprovingly. "Freakish, you might say. Silly. Except for the corpse. Corpses," Mr. Fox observed with severity, "are never silly."

Detective-Sergeants Bailey and Thompson exchanged winks.

"In the first place, Mr. Alleyn," Fox continued, "I ask myself: Why do it that way? Why fire a bit of an umbrella handle from a revolver when you might fire a bullet? This applies in particular to his lordship. And yet it seems it must have been done. You can't get away from it. Nobody had a chance of stabbing the chap while he was performing, did they now?"

"Nobody."

"All right then. Now, if anybody pushed this silly weapon up the gun after Skelton examined it, they had the thing concealed about their person. Not much bigger than a fountain pen but sharp as hell. Which brings us to Bellairs, for one. If you consider Bellairs, you have to remember that his lordship seems to have searched him very thoroughly before he went out to perform."

"Moreover his lordship in the full tide of his own alleged innocence declares that the wretched Breezy didn't get a chance to pocket anything after he had been searched, or to get at the gun."

"Does he really?" said Fox. "Fancy!"

"In fact his lordship, who, I submit, is no fool, has been at peculiar pains to clear everybody but himself."

"No fool, perhaps," Fox grunted, "but would you say a bit off the plumb mentally?"

"Everybody else says so, at all events. In any case, Fox, I'll give sworn evidence that nobody stabbed Rivera before or at the time he was shot at. He was a good six feet away from everybody except Lord Pastern, who was busy with his blasted gun."

"There you are! And it wasn't planted among the music stands because they were used by the other band. And anyway none of the musicians went near his lordship's funny hat where the gun was. And being like that, I asked myself, isn't his lordship the most likely to use a silly fanciful method if he'd made up his mind to do a man in? It all points to his lordship. You can't get away from it. And yet he seems so pleased with himself and kind of unruffled. Of course you do find that attitude in homicidal mania."

"You do. What about motive?"

"Do we know what he thought of his stepdaughter keeping company with the deceased? The other young lady suggested that he didn't seem to care one way or the other but you never know. Something else may turn up. Personally, as things stand at the moment, I favor his lordship. What about you, Mr. Alleyn?"

Alleyn shook his head. "I'm stumped," he said. "Perhaps Skelton could have got the thing into the revolver when he examined it but Lord Pastern, who undoubtedly is as sharp as a needle, swears he didn't. They were alone together for a minute while Breezy made his announcement but Skelton says he didn't go near Lord Pastern, who had the gun in his hip pocket. It's not likely to be a lie because Pastern could deny it. You didn't hear Skelton. He's an odd chap—a truculent communist. Australian, I should say. A hard, determined thinker. Nobody's fool and completely sincere. One-track minded. There's no doubt he detested Rivera, both on general principles and because Rivera backed up Lord Pastern's appearance to-night. Skelton bitterly resented this and says so. He felt he was prostituting what he is pleased to regard as his art and conniving at something entirely against his social principles. I believe him to be fanatically sincere in this. He looked on Rivera and Lord Pastern as parasites. Rivera, by the way, supplied Breezy Bellairs with his dope, whatever it is. Curtis says cocaine, and it looks as if he found himself something to go on when he searched the body. We'll have to follow that one up, Fox."

"Dope," said Fox profoundly. "There you are! When we do get a windfall it's a dead man. Still, there may be something in his rooms to give us a lead. South America, now. That may link up with the Snowy Santos gang. They operate through South America. It'd be nice," said Mr. Fox, whose talents for some time had been concerned with the sale of illicit drugs, "it'd be lovely, in fact, to get the tabs on Snowy Santos."

"Lovely, wouldn't it?" Alleyn agreed absently. "Get on with your argument, Fox."

"Well, now, sir. Seeing Rivera wasn't meant to fall down and did, you can say he was struck at that moment. I know that sounds like a glimpse of the obvious, but it cuts out any idea that there was some kind of jiggery-pokery after he fell because nobody knew he was going to fall. And unless you feel like saying somebody threw the weapon like a dart at the same time as his lordship fired the first shot— Well," said Fox disgustedly, "that would be a fat-headed sort of notion wouldn't it? So we come back to the idea it was fired from the revolver. Which is supported by the scratches in the barrel. Mind, we'll have to get the experts going there."

"We shall, indeed."

"But saying, for the moment, that the little jewelled clip, acting as a sort of stop, did mark the barrel, we come to Skelton's statement that the scratches were not there when he examined it. And that looks like his lordship again. Look at it how you will, you get back to his lordship, you know."

"Miss de Suze," Alleyn said, rubbing his nose in vexation, "did grope under the damned sombrero. I saw her and so did Manx and so did the waiter. Manx seemed to remonstrate and she laughed and withdrew her hand. She couldn't have got the weapon in then but it shows that it was possible for anyone sitting on her chair to get at the gun. Lady Pastern was left alone at their table while the others danced."

Fox raised his eyebrows and looked puffy. "Very icy," he said. "A haughty

sort of lady and with a will and temper of her own. Look how she's stood
up to his lordship in the past. Very masterful."

Alleyn glanced at his old colleague and smiled. He turned to the group
of waiting men. "Well, Bailey," he said, "we've about got to you. Have you
found anything new?"

Bailey said morosely: "Nothing to write home about, Mr. Alleyn. No
prints on this dart affair. I've packed it up with protection and can have
another go at it."

"The revolver?"

"Very plain sailing, there, Mr. Alleyn. Not a chance for latents."

"That's why I risked letting him handle it."

"Yes, sir. Well now," said Bailey with a certain professional relish, "the
revolver. Lord Pastern's prints on the revolver. And this band leader's. Breezy
Bellairs or whatever he calls himself."

"Yes. Lord Pastern handed the gun to Breezy."

"That's right, sir. So I understand."

"Thompson," said Alleyn suddenly, "did you get a good look at Mr. Manx's
left hand when you dabbed him?"

"Yes, sir. Knuckles a bit grazed. Very slight. Wears a signet ring."

"How about the band platform, Bailey?"

Bailey looked at his boots and said he'd been over the floor space round
the tympani and percussion stand. There were traces of four finger tips
identifiable as Miss de Suze's. No others.

"And Rivera? On the body?"

"Not much there," Bailey said, but they would probably bring up latent
prints where Bellairs and the doctor had handled him. That was all, so far.

"Thank you. What about you other chaps in the restaurant and band-
room? Find anything? Gibson?"

One of the plain-clothes men came forward. "Not much, sir. Nothing out
of the ordinary. Cigarette butts and so on. We picked up the wads and
shells and Bellairs's handkerchief, marked, on the platform."

"He mopped his unpleasant eyes with it when he did his stuff with the
wreath," Alleyn muttered. "Anything else?"

"There was a cork," said Detective-Sergeant Gibson apologetically, "on the
band platform. Might have been dropped by a waiter, sir."

"Not up there. Let's see it."

Gibson produced an envelope from which he shook out a smallish cork
on to the table. Alleyn looked at it without touching it. "When was the band
platform cleaned?"

"Polished in the early morning, Mr. Alleyn, and mopped over before the
evening clients came in."

"Where exactly did you find this thing?"

"Half-way back and six feet to left of centre. I've marked the place."

"Good. Not that it'll help much." Alleyn used his lens. "It's got a black
mark on it." He stopped and sniffed. "Boot polish, I think. It was probably

kicked about the place by bandsmen. But there's another smell. Not wine or spirit and anyway it's not that sort of cork. It's smaller and made with a narrow end and a wide top. No trade-mark. What *is* this smell? Try, Fox."

Fox's sniff was stentorian. He rose, meditated and said: "Now, what am I reminded of?" They waited. "Citronella," Fox pronounced gravely. "Or something like it."

"How about gun oil?" said Alleyn.

Fox turned and contemplated his superior with something like indignation. "Gun oil? You're not going to tell me, Mr. Alleyn, that in addition to stuffing jewelled parasol handles up a revolver somebody stopped it with a cork like a ruddy popgun?"

Alleyn grinned. "The case is taking liberties with your credulity, Br'er Fox." He used his lens again. "The bottom surface has been broken, I fancy. It's a forlorn hope, Bailey, but we might try for dabs."

Bailey put the cork away. Alleyn turned to the others. "I think you can pack up," he said. "I'm afraid I'll have to keep you, Thompson, and you, Bailey, with us. It's a non-stop show. Gibson, you'll pick up a search-warrant and go on to Rivera's rooms. Take someone with you. I want a complete search there. Scott and Watson are attending to Bellairs's rooms and Sallis has gone with Skelton. You'll all report back to me at the Yard at ten. Get people to relieve you when you've finished. Bellairs and Skelton will both have to be kept under observation, damn it, though I fancy that for the next eight hours Breezy won't give anybody a headache except himself. Inspector Fox and I will get extra men and attend to Duke's Gate. All right. We'll move."

In the office a telephone bell rang. Fox went in to answer it and was heard uttering words of reproach. He came out looking scandalized.

"It's that new chap we sent back with his lordship's party. Marks. And what do you suppose he's done?" Fox glared round upon his audience and slapped the palm of his hand on the table. "Silly young chump! When they get in they say they're all going to the drawing-room. 'Oh,' says Marks, 'then it's my duty, if you please, to accompany you.' The gentlemen say they want to retire first, and they go off to the downstairs cloak-room. The ladies have the same idea and they go upstairs and Sergeant Expeditious Marks tries to tear himself in halves which is nothing to what I'll do for him. And while he's exhausting himself running up and down keeping observation, what happens? One of the young ladies slips down the servants' stairs and lets herself out by the back door."

"Which one?" Alleyn asked quickly.

"Don't," said Mr. Fox with bitter scorn, "ask too much of Detective-Sergeant Marks, sir. Don't make it too tough. He wouldn't know which one. Oh, no. He comes bleating to the phone while I daresay the rest of 'em are lighting off wherever the fancy takes 'em. Sergeant ruddy Police-College Marks! What is it?"

A uniformed constable had come in from the front entrance. "I thought I'd better report, sir," he said. "I'm on duty outside. There's an incident."

"All right," said Alleyn. "What incident?"

"A taxi's pulled up some distance away, sir, and a lady got out."

"A lady?" Fox demanded so peremptorily that the constable glanced nervously at him.

"Yes, Mr. Fox. A young lady. She spoke to the driver. He's waiting. She looked round and hesitated. I was in the entrance, sir, well in the shadow, and I don't think she saw me."

"Recognize her?" Alleyn asked.

"I wouldn't be sure, sir. The clothes are different but I reckon it's one of the ladies in Lord Pastern's party."

"Have you locked the doors behind you?"

"Yes, sir."

"Unlock them and make yourself scarce. Clear out, all of you. Scatter. Step lively."

The foyer was emptied in five seconds. The doors into the office and the band-room closed noiselessly. Alleyn darted to the light switches. A single lamp was left to glow pinkly against the wall. The foyer was filled with shadow. He slipped to his knees behind a chair in the corner farthest from the light.

The clock ticked discreetly. Somewhere in a distant basement a pail clanked and a door slammed. Innumerable tiny sounds closer at hand became evident: the tap of a blind cord somewhere in the restaurant, a stealthy movement and scuffle behind the walls, an indefinable humming from the main switchboard. Alleyn smelt carpet, upholstery, disinfectant, and stale tobacco. Entrance into the foyer from outside must be effected through two sets of doors—those giving on the street and those inside made of plate glass and normally open but now swung-to. Through these he could see only a vague greyness crossed by reflections in the glass itself. The image of the one pink lamp floated midway up the right-hand pane. He fixed his gaze on this. Now, beyond the glass doors, there came a paleness. The street door had been opened.

The face appeared quite suddenly against the plate glass, obscuring the reflected lamp and distorted by pressure. One door squeaked faintly as it opened.

She stood for a moment, holding her head scarf half across her face. Then she moved forward swiftly and was down on her knees before an armchair. Her finger-nails scrabbled on its tapestry. So intent was she upon her search that she did not hear him cross the thick carpet behind her, but when he drew the envelope from his pocket it made a slight crackle. Still kneeling, she swung round, saw him and cried out sharply.

"Is this what you are hunting for, Miss Wayne?" Alleyn asked.

ii

He crossed over to the wall and switched up the lights. Without moving, Carlisle watched him. When he returned he still held the envelope. She put her hand to her burning face and said unsteadily: "You think I'm up to no good, I suppose. I suppose you want an explanation."

"I should be glad of an answer to my question. Is this what you want?"

He held the envelope up, but did not give it to her. She looked at it doubtfully. "I don't know—I don't think—"

"The envelope is mine. I'll tell you what it contains. A letter that had been thrust down between the seat and the arm of the chair you have been exploring."

"Yes," Carlisle said. "Yes. That's it. May I have it, please?"

"Do sit down," Alleyn rejoined. "We'd better clear this up, don't you think?"

He waited while she rose. After a moment's hesitation, she sat in the chair.

"You won't believe me, of course," she said, "but that letter—I suppose you have read it, haven't you—has nothing whatever to do with this awful business to-night. Nothing in the wide world. It's entirely personal and rather important."

"Have you even read it?" he asked. "Can you repeat the contents? I should like you to do that, if you will."

"But—not absolutely correctly—I mean—"

"Approximately."

"It—it's got an important message. It concerns someone—I can't tell you in so many words—"

"And yet it's so important that you return here at three o'clock in the morning to try and find it." He paused but Carlisle said nothing. "Why," he said, "didn't Miss de Suze come and collect her own correspondence?"

"Oh dear!" she said. "This is difficult."

"Well, for pity's sake keep up your reputation and be honest about it."

"I am being honest, damn you!" said Carlisle with spirit. "The letter's a private affair and—and—extremely confidential. Félicité doesn't want anyone to see it. I don't know exactly what's in it."

"She funked coming back herself?"

"She's a bit shattered. Everyone is."

"I'd like you to see what the letter's about," said Alleyn after a pause. She began to protest. Very patiently he repeated his usual argument. When someone had been killed the nicer points of behaviour had to be disregarded. He had to prove to his own satisfaction that the letter was immaterial and then he would forget it. "You remember," he said, "this letter dropped out of her bag. Did you notice how she snatched it away from me? I see you did.

Did you notice what she did after I said you would all be searched? She shoved her hand down between the seat and arm of the chair. Then she went off to be searched and I sat in the chair. When she came back she spent a miserable half-hour fishing for the letter and trying to look as if she wasn't. All right."

He drew the letter from the envelope and spread it out before her. "It's been finger-printed," he said, "but without any marked success. Too much rubbing against good solid chair-cover. Will you read it or—"

"Oh, all right," Carlisle said angrily.

The letter was typed on a sheet of plain notepaper. There was no address and no date.

MY DEAR [Carlisle read]: Your loveliness is my undoing. Because of it I break my deepest promise to myself and to others. We are closer than you have ever dreamed. I wear a white flower in my coat to-night. It is yours. But as you value our future happiness, make not the slightest sign—even to me. Destroy this note, my love, but keep my love. G.P.F.

Carlisle raised her head, met Alleyn's gaze and avoided it quickly. "A white flower," she whispered. "G.P.F.? G.P.F.? I don't believe it."

"Mr. Edward Manx had a white carnation in his coat, I think."

"I won't discuss this letter with you," she said strongly. "I should never have read it. I won't discuss it. Let me take it back to her. It's nothing to do with this other thing. Nothing. Give it to me."

Alleyn said, "You must know I can't do that. Think for a moment. There was some attachment, a strong attachment of one kind or another, between Rivera and your cousin—your step-cousin. After Rivera is murdered, she is at elaborate pains to conceal this letter, loses it, and is so anxious to retrieve it that she persuades you to return here in an attempt to recover it. How can I disregard such a sequence of events?"

"But you don't know Fée! She's always in and out of tight corners over her young men. It's nothing. You don't understand."

"Well," he said, looking good-humouredly at her, "help me to understand. I'll drive you home. You can tell me on the way. Fox."

Fox came out of the office. Carlisle listened to Alleyn giving his instructions. The other men appeared from the cloak-room, held a brief indistinguishable conversation with Fox and went out through the main entrance. Alleyn and Fox collected their belongings and put on their coats. Carlisle stood up. Alleyn returned the letter to its envelope and put it in his pocket. She felt tears stinging under her eyelids. She tried to speak and produced only an indeterminate sound.

"What is it?" he said, glancing at her.

"It can't be true," she stammered. "I won't believe it. I won't."

"What? That Edward Manx wrote this letter?"

"He couldn't. He couldn't write like that to her."

"No?" Alleyn said casually. "You think not? But she's quite good-looking, isn't she? Quite attractive, don't you think?"

"It's not that. It's not that at all. It's the letter itself. He couldn't write like that. It's so bogus."

"Have you ever noticed love-letters that are read out in court and published in the papers? Don't they sound pretty bogus? Yet some of them have been written by extremely intelligent people. Shall we go?"

It was cold out in the street. A motionless pallor stood behind the rigid silhouette of roofs. "Dawn's left hand," Alleyn said to nobody in particular and shivered. Carlisle's taxi had gone but a large police car waited. A second man sat beside the driver. Fox opened the door and Carlisle got in. The two men followed. "We'll call at the Yard," Alleyn said.

She felt boxed-up in the corner of the seat and was conscious of the impersonal pressure of Alleyn's arm and shoulder. Mr. Fox, on the farther side, was a bulky man. She turned and saw Alleyn's head silhouetted against the bluish window. An odd notion came into her head. "If Fée happens to calm down and take a good look at him," she thought, "it'll be all up with G.P.F. and the memory of Carlos and everybody." And with that her heart gave a leaden thump or two. "Oh, Ned," she thought, "how you *could!*" She tried to face the full implication of the letter but almost at once shied away from it. "I'm miserable," she thought, "I'm unhappier than I've been for years and years."

"What," Alleyn's voice said close beside her, "I wonder, is the precise interpretation of the initials 'G.P.F.'? They seem to ring some bell in my atrocious memory but I haven't got there yet. Why, do you imagine, G.P.F.?" She didn't answer and after a moment he went on. "Wait a bit, though. Didn't you say something about a magazine you were reading before you visited Lord Pastern in his study? *Harmony?* Was that it?" He turned his head to look at her and she nodded. "And the editor of the tell-it-all-to-auntie page calls himself Guide, Philosopher and Friend? How does he sign his recipes for radiant living?"

Carlisle mumbled: "Like that."

"And you had wondered if Miss de Suze had written to him," Alleyn said tranquilly. "Yes. Now, does this get us anywhere, do you imagine?"

She made a non-committal sound. Unhappy recollections forced themselves upon her. Recollections of Félicité's story about a correspondence with someone she had never met who had written her a "marvellous" letter. Of Rivera reading her answer to this letter and making a scene about it. Of Ned Manx's article in *Harmony*. Of Félicité's behaviour after they all met to go to the Metronome. Of her taking the flower from Ned's coat. And of his stooping his head to listen to her as they danced together.

"Was Mr. Manx," Alleyn's voice asked, close beside her, "wearing his white carnation when he arrived for dinner?"

"No," she said, too loudly. "No. Not till afterwards. There were white carnations on the table at dinner."

"Perhaps it was one of them."

"Then," she said quickly, "it doesn't fit. The letter must have been written before he ever saw the carnation. It doesn't fit. She said the letter came by district messenger. Ned wouldn't have known."

"By district messenger, did she? We'll have to check that. Perhaps we'll find the envelope. Would you say," Alleyn continued, "that he seemed to be very much attached to her?"

(Edward had said: "About Fée. Something very odd has occurred. I can't explain but I'd like to think you understand.")

"Strongly attracted, would you think?" Alleyn said.

"I don't know. I don't know what to think."

"Do they see much of each other?"

"I don't know. He—he stayed at Duke's Gate while he was flat hunting."

"Perhaps an attachment developed then. What do you think?"

She shook her head. Alleyn waited. Carlisle now found his unstressed persistence intolerable. She felt her moorings go and was adrift in the darkness. A wretchedness of spirit that she was unable to control or understand took possession of her. "I won't talk about it," she stammered, "it's none of my business. I can't go on like this. Let me go, please. Please let me go."

"Of course," Alleyn said. "I'll take you home."

iii

When they arrived at Duke's Gate, dawn was so far established that the houses with their blind windows and locked doors were clearly distinguishable in a wan half-light.

The familiar street, emerging from night, had an air of emaciation and secrecy, Carlisle thought, and she was vaguely relieved when milk bottles jingled up a side alley breaking across the blank emptiness. "Have you got a key?" Alleyn said. He and Fox and the man from the front seat waited while she groped in her bag. As she opened the door a second car drew up and four men got out. The men from the front seat joined them. She thought: "This makes us all seem very important. This is an important case. A case of murder."

In the old days she had come back from parties once or twice with Ned Manx at this hour. The indefinable house-smell made itself felt as they entered. She turned on a lamp and it was light in the silent hall. She saw herself reflected in the inner glass doors, her face stained with tears. Alleyn came in first. Standing there, in evening dress, with his hat in his hand, he might have been seeing her home, about to wish her good-bye. The other men followed quickly. "What happens now?" she wondered. "Will he let me go now? What are they going to do?"

Alleyn had drawn a paper from his pocket. "This is a search-warrant," he said. "I don't want to hunt Lord Pastern out of his bed. It will do I think, if—"

He broke off, moved quickly to the shadowed staircase and up half-a-dozen steps. Fox and the other men stood quiet inside the doors. A little French clock in the stair well ticked flurriedly. Upstairs on the first floor a door was flung open. A faint reflected light shone on Alleyn's face. A voice, unmistakably Lord Pastern's, said loudly: "I don't give a damn how upset you are. You can have kittens if you like but you don't go to bed till I've got my time-table worked out. Sit down."

With a faint grin Alleyn moved upstairs and Carlisle, after a moment's hesitation, followed him.

They were all in the drawing-room. Lady Pastern, still in evening dress and now very grey about the eyes and mouth, sat in a chair near the door. Félicité, who had changed into a housecoat and reduced her make-up, looked frail and lovely. Edward had evidently been sitting near her and had risen on Alleyn's entrance. Lord Pastern, with his coat off and his sleeves turned up, sat at a table in the middle of the room. Sheets of paper lay before him and he had a pencil between his teeth. A little removed from this group, her hands folded in the lap of her woollen dressing gown and her grey hair neatly braided down her back, sat Miss Henderson. A plain-clothes officer stood inside the door. Carlisle knew all about him. He was the man who had escorted them home: hours ago, it seemed, in another age. She had given him the slip when she returned to the Metronome and now wondered, for the first time, how dim a view the police would take of this manoeuvre. The man looked awkwardly at Alleyn, who seemed about to speak to him as Carlisle entered, but stood aside to let her pass. Edward came quickly towards her. "Where have you been?" he said angrily. "What's the matter? I—" He looked into her face. "Lisle," he said. "What is it?"

Lord Pastern glanced up. "Hello," he said. "Where the devil did you get to, Lisle? I want you. Sit down."

"It's like a scene from a play," she thought. "All of them sitting about exhausted, in a grand drawing-room. The third act of a thriller." She caught the eye of the plain-clothes officer, who was looking at her with distaste.

"I'm sorry," she said. "I'm afraid I just walked out by the back door."

"I realize that, miss," he said.

"We can't be in two places at once, can we?" Carlisle added brightly. She was trying to avoid Félicité. Félicité was looking at her anxiously, obviously, with inquiring eyebrows.

Lord Pastern said briskly: "Glad you've come, Alleyn, though I must say you've taken your time about it. I've been doin' your job for you. Sit down."

Lady Pastern's voice, sepulchral with fatigue, said: "May I suggest, George, that as in all probability this gentleman is about to arrest you, your choice of phrase is inappropriate."

"That's a damn tiresome sort of thing to say, C," her husband rejoined. "Gets you nowhere. What you want," he continued, darting his pencil at

Alleyn, "is a time-table. You want to know what we were all doin' with ourselves before we went to the Metronome. System. All right. I've worked it
out for you." He slapped the paper before him. "It's incomplete without
Breezy's evidence, of course, but we can get that to-morrow. Lisle, there are
one or two things I want from you. Come here."

Carlisle stood behind him and looked at Alleyn. His face was politely attentive, his eyes were on Lord Pastern's notes. In her turn and in response to
an impatient tattoo of the pencil, she too looked at them.

She saw a sort of table, drawn up with ruled lines. Across the top, one
each at the head of nine columns, she read their names: her own, Lady Pastern's, Félicité's, Edward's, Lord Pastern's, Bellairs's, Rivera's, Miss Henderson's, and Spence's. Down the left-hand side, Lord Pastern had written
a series of times, beginning at 8:45 and ending at 10:30. These were ruled
off horizontally and in the spaces thus formed, under each name, were notes
as to the owner's whereabouts. Thus, at "9:15 approx" it appeared that she
and Lady Pastern had been in the drawing-room, Miss Henderson on her way
upstairs, Félicité in the study, Rivera in the hall, Lord Pastern and Breezy
Bellairs in the ballroom, and Spence in the servants' quarters.

"The times," Lord Pastern explained importantly, "are mostly only approx-
imate. We know some of them for certain but not all. Thing is, it shows you
the groupin'. Who was with who and who was alone. Method. Here y'are,
Lisle. Go over it carefully and check up your entries."

He flung himself back in his chair and ruffled his hair. He reeked of complacency. Carlisle took up the pencil and found that her hand trembled.
Exhaustion had suddenly overwhelmed her. She was nauseated and fuddled
with fatigue. Lord Pastern's time-table swam before her. She heard her voice
saying, "I think you've got it right," and felt a hand under her arm. It was
Alleyn's. "Sit down," he said from an enormous distance. She was sitting
down and Ned, close beside her, was making some sort of angry protest.
She leant forward, propping her head on her hands. Presently it cleared and
she listened, with an extraordinary sense of detachment, to what Alleyn was
now saying.

". . . very helpful, thank you. And now, I'm sure, you'll all be glad to get
to bed. We shall be here during what's left of the night—hardly anything,
I'm afraid, but we shan't disturb you."

They were on their feet. Carlisle, feeling very sick, wondered what would
happen if she got to hers. She looked at the others through her fingers and
thought that there was something a little wrong, a little misshapen, about
all of them. Her aunt, for instance. Why had she not seen before that Lady
Pastern's body was too long and her head too big? It was so. And surely
Félicité was fantastically narrow. Her skeleton must be all wrong: a tiny
pelvis with the hip-bones jutting out from it like rocks. Carlisle's eyes, behind their sheltering fingers, turned to Lord Pastern and she thought how
monstrous it was that his forehead should overhang the rest of his face—a
blind over a shop window; that his monkey's cheeks should bunch themselves

up when he was angry. Even Hendy: Hendy's throat was like some bird's and now that her hair was braided one saw that it was thin on top. Her scalp showed. They were caricatures, really, all of them. Subtly off-pitch: instruments very slightly out of tune. And Ned? He was behind her, but if she turned to look at him, what, in the perceptiveness born of nervous exhaustion, would she see? Were not his eyes black and small? Didn't his mouth, when it smiled, twist and show canine teeth a little too long? But she would not look at Ned.

And now, thought the bemused Carlisle, here was Uncle George at it again. "I've no intention of goin' to bed. People sleep too much. No need for it: look at the mystics. Workin' from this time-table I can show you . . ."

"That's extremely kind of you, sir." Alleyn's voice was clear and pleasant. "But I think not. We have to get through our routine jobs. They're dreary beyond words and we're best left to ourselves while we do them."

"Routine," shouted Lord Pastern. "Official synonym for inefficiency. Things are straightened out for you by someone who takes the trouble to use his head and what do you do? Tell him to go to bed while you gallop about his house makin' lists like a bumbailiff. Be damned if I'll go to bed. Now!"

"Oh, God!" Carlisle thought desperately. "How's he going to cope with this?" She felt the pressure of a hand on her shoulder and heard Ned's voice.

"May I suggest that whatever Cousin George decides to do there's no reason why the rest of us should keep a watch of supererogation."

"None at all," Alleyn said.

"Carlisle, my dear," Lady Pastern murmured as if she were giving the signal to rise from a dinner party. "Shall we?"

Carlisle stood up. Edward was close by and it seemed to her that he still looked angry. "Are you all right?" he asked.

"Perfectly," she said. "I don't know what possessed me. I got a bit rundown in Greece and I suppose—" Her voice died. She was thinking of the long flight of stairs up to her room.

"My dearest child," her aunt said, "I shall never forgive myself that you have been subjected to this ordeal."

"But she's wondering," Carlisle thought, "what I've been up to. They're all wondering."

"Perhaps some wine," her aunt continued, "or whiskey. It is useless to suggest, George, that you . . ."

"I'll get it," Edward said quickly.

But Miss Henderson had already gone and now returned with a glass in her hand. As she took it from her, Carlisle smelt Hendy's particular smell of soap and talcum powder. "Like a baby," she thought and drank. The almost neat whiskey made her shudder convulsively. "Hendy!" she gasped. "You do pack a punch. I'm all right. Really. It's you, Aunt Cécile, who should be given corpse revivers."

Lady Pastern closed her eyes momentarily upon this vulgarism. Félicité, who had been perfectly silent ever since Alleyn and Carlisle came in, said: "I'd like a drink, Ned. Let's have a pub crawl in the dining-room, shall we?"

"The decanter's here if you want it, dear." Miss Henderson also spoke for the first time.

"In that case," Edward said, "if it's all right by you, Alleyn, I'll take myself off."

"We've got your address, haven't we? Right."

"Good-bye, Cousin Cile. If there's anything I can do . . ." Ned stood in the doorway. Carlisle did not look at him. "Good-bye, Lisle," he said. "Good-bye, Fée."

Félicité moved swiftly to him and with an abrupt compulsive movement put her arm round his neck and kissed him. He stood for a moment with his head stooped and his hand on her arm. Then he was gone.

Beneath the heavy mask of exhaustion that her aunt wore, Carlisle saw a faint glimmer of gratification. "Come, my children," Lady Pastern said, almost briskly. "Bed." She swept them past Alleyn, who opened the door for them. As Carlisle turned, with the others, to mount the stairs, she heard Lord Pastern.

"Here I am," he shouted, "and here I stick. You don't turf me off to bed or anywhere else, short of arresting me."

"I'm not, at the moment, proposing to do that," Alleyn said distinctly, "though I think, sir, I should warn you . . ."

The door shut off the remainder of his sentence.

iv

Alleyn shut the door on the retiring ladies and looked thoughtfully at Lord Pastern. "I think," he repeated, "I should warn you that if you do decide, against my advice, to stay with us, what you do and say will be noted and the notes may be used. . . ."

"Oh, fiddle-faddle!" Lord Pastern interrupted shrilly. "All this rigmarole. I didn't do it and you can't prove I did. Get on with your precious routine and don't twaddle so."

Alleyn looked at him with a sort of astonishment. "You bloody little old fellow," he thought. Lord Pastern blinked and smirked and bunched up his cheeks.

"All right, sir," Alleyn said. "But you're going to be given the customary warning, twaddle or not, and what's more I'll have a witness to it."

He crossed the landing, opened the ballroom door, said: "Fox, can you give me a moment?" and returned to the drawing-room, where he waited in silence until Inspector Fox came in. He then said: "Fox, I've asked Lord Pastern to go to bed and he refuses. I want you to witness this. I warn him that from now onwards his words and behaviour will be noted and that the notes may later on be used in evidence. It's a nuisance, of course, but short of taking a much more drastic step, I don't see what else can be done about it. Have the extra men turned up?"

Fox, looking with marked disapproval at Lord Pastern, said that they had.

"Tell them to keep observation, will you? Thank you, Fox, I'll carry on here."

"Thank you, Mr. Alleyn," said Fox. "I'll get on with it in the study then." He turned to the door. Lord Pastern said: "Hi! Where're you goin'? What're you up to?"

"If you'll excuse me for passing the remark, my lord," said Fox severely, "you're acting very foolishly. Very ill-advised and foolish, what you're doing, if I may say so." He went out.

"Great ham-fisted ass of a chap," Lord Pastern remarked.

"On the contrary, sir," Alleyn rejoined with perfect politeness, "an extremely efficient officer and should have had his promotion long ago."

He left Lord Pastern, walked to the center of the long drawing-room and surveyed it for some minutes with his hands in his pockets. A clock on the landing struck five. Alleyn began a closer inspection of the room. He traversed it slowly, moving across and across it and examining any object that lay in his path. Lord Pastern watched him and sighed and groaned audibly. Presently Alleyn came to a chair beside which stood an occasional table. On the table was an embroidery frame, and a work-box of elaborate and elegant design. He opened the lid delicately and stooped to examine the contents. Here, neatly disposed, were innumerable skeins of embroidery silks. The box was fitted with every kind of tool, each in its appointed slot: needle-cases, scissors, bodkins, a thimble, an ivory measure, a tape in a cloisonné case, stilettoes held in their places by silken sheaths. One slot was untenanted. Alleyn sat down and began, with scrupulous care, to explore the box.

"Pity you didn't bring your sewin'," said Lord Pastern, "isn't it?"

Alleyn took out his notebook, glanced at his watch and wrote briefly.

"I'd thank you," Lord Pastern added, "to keep your hands out of m' wife's property." He attempted to repress a yawn, shed a tear over the effort and barked suddenly: "Where's your search-warrant, b' God?"

Alleyn completed another note, rose and exhibited his warrant. "Tscha!" said Lord Pastern.

Alleyn had turned to examine Lady Pastern's embroidery. It was stretched over a frame and was almost completed. A riot of cupids in postures of extreme insouciance circled about a fabulous nosegay. The work was exquisite. He gave a slight appreciative chuckle which Lord Pastern instantly parodied. Alleyn resumed his search. He moved steadily on at a snail's pace. Half an hour crawled by. Presently an odd little noise disturbed him. He glanced up. Lord Pastern, still on his feet, was swaying dangerously. His eyes were glazed and horrible and his mouth was open. He had snored.

Alleyn tiptoed to the door at the far end of the room, opened it and slipped into the study. He heard a sort of roaring noise behind him, shut the door and, finding a key in the lock, turned it.

Inspector Fox, in his shirt-sleeves, was examining the contents of an open drawer on the top of the desk. Laid out in front of him were a tube of plastic wood, an empty bottle marked "gun oil," with no cork in it, and a white ivory handle into which some tool had once fitted.

v

Fox laid a broad finger on the desk beside these exhibits, not so much for an index as to establish their presence and significance. Alleyn nodded and crossed quickly to the door that gave on the landing. He locked it and waited near it with his head cocked. "Here he comes," he said.

There was a patter of feet outside. The handle of the door was turned and then rattled angrily. A distant voice said: "I'm sorry, my lord, but I'm afraid that room's under inspection just now."

"Who the hell d'you think you are?"

"Sergeant Marks, my lord."

"Then let me tell you . . ."

The voices faded out.

"He won't get into the ballroom either," said Fox, "unless he tries a knock-up with Sergeant Whitelaw."

"How about the dining-room?"

"They've finished there, Mr. Alleyn."

"Anything?"

"Wine had been spilt on the carpet. Port, I'd say. And there's a bit of a mark on the table near the centre flower bowl as if a drop or two of water had laid there. White carnations in the bowl. Nothing else. The tables had been cleared, of course."

Alleyn looked at the collection on the desk. "Where did you beat this lot up, Foxkin?"

"In this drawer which was pulled out and left on top of the desk like it is now. Half a junk shop in it, isn't there, sir? These articles were lying on the surface of the other mess."

"Bailey had a go at it?"

"Yes. No prints on any of 'em," said Fox. "Which is funny."

"How about the typewriter?"

"We've printed it. Only his lordship's dabs and they're very fresh."

"No cap on the plastic wood tube."

"It was on the floor."

Alleyn examined the tube. "It's set hard, of course, at the open end but not very deep. Tube's three-quarters full."

"There are crumbs of plastic wood in the drawer and on the desk and the carpet."

Alleyn said absently, "Are there, by Gum!" and turned his attention to the small white handle. "Exhibit B," he said. "Know what it is, Fox?"

"I can make a healthy guess, I fancy, Mr. Alleyn."

"It's the fellow of a number of gadgets in a very elegant French work-box in the drawing-room. Crochet hooks, scissors and so on. They're fixed inside the lid, in slots. One slot's empty."

"This is just a handle, you'll notice, sir."

"Yes. Do you think it ought to have an embroidery stiletto fitted in the hollow end?"

"It's what I reckoned."

"I think you're right."

Fox opened his bag and took out a narrow cardboard box. In this, secured and protected by strings, was the dart. The jewels in the spring clip, tiny emeralds and brilliants, glittered cheerfully. Only a narrow platinum band near the top and the stiletto itself were dulled with Rivera's blood.

"Bailey'll have a go for latent prints," Fox said.

"Yes, of course. We can't disturb it. Later on it can be dismembered, but on looks, Fox, we've got something."

Alleyn held the ivory handle beside the stiletto. "I'll swear they belong," he said, and put it down. "Here's exhibit C. An empty gun-oil bottle. Where's that cork?"

Fox produced it. "It fits," he said, "I've tried. It fits and it has the same stink. Though why the hell it should turn up on the bandstand . . ."

"Ah me," Alleyn said. "Why the hell indeed. Well, look what turns up in your particular fancy's very own drawer in his very own study! Could anything be more helpful?"

Fox shifted bulkily in his chair and contemplated his superior officer for some moments. "I know it seems funny," he said at last. "Leaving evidence all over the place: making no attempt to clear himself, piling up a case against himself, you might say. But then he *is* funny. Would you say he was not responsible within the meaning of the act?"

"I'm never sure what is the precise meaning of the infernal act. Responsible. Not responsible. Who's to mark a crucial division in the stream of human behaviour running down from something we are pleased to call sanity into raving lunacy? Where's the point at which a human being ceases to be a responsible being? Oh, I know the definitions, and I know we do our best with them, but it seems to me it's here, over this business of the pathology of behaviour, that any system of corrective and coercive law shows at its dimmest. Is this decidedly rum peer so far south in the latitude of behaviour that he would publicly murder a man by a ridiculously elaborate method that points directly to himself, and then, in effect, do everything in his power to get himself arrested? There have been cases of the sort, but is this going to be one of them?"

"Well, sir," said Fox stolidly, "I must say I think it is. It's early days yet, but as far as we've got I think it looks like it. This gentleman's previous record and his general run of behaviour point to a mental set-up that, without going beyond the ordinary view, is eccentric. Everyone knows he's funny."

"Yes. Everyone. Everyone knows," Alleyn agreed. "Everyone would say: 'It's in character. It's just like him!'"

With as near an approach to exasperation as Alleyn had ever heard from him, Fox said: "All right, Mr. Alleyn, then. I know what you're getting at. But who could have planted it on him? Tell me that. Do you believe any of the party at the table could have got at the revolver when it was under the sombrero and shoved this silly dart or bolt or what-have-you up it? Do you think Bellairs could have planted the bolt and picked it up after his lordship searched him? Where could he have planted it? In a bare band-room with nothing in it but musical instruments and other men? And how could he have got it into the revolver when his lordship had the revolver on his person and swears to it that it never left him? Skelton. Skelton handled the gun while a roomful of people watched him do it. Could Skelton have palmed this thing up the barrel? The idea's laughable. Well, then."

"All right, old thing," Alleyn said. "Let's get on with it. The servants will be about soon. How far have you got in here?"

"Not much further than what you've seen, sir. The drawer was a daisy. The bullets he extracted when he made his dummies are in the waste-paper basket there."

"Carlisle Wayne watched him at that. How about the ballroom?"

"Bailey and Thompson are in there."

"Oh, well. Let's have another look at Lord Pastern's revolver, Fox."

Fox lifted it from his bag and laid it on the desk. Alleyn sat down and produced his lens.

"There's a very nice lens here, in his lordship's drawer," Fox remarked. Alleyn grunted. He was looking into the mouth of the barrel.

"We'll get a photomicrograph of this," he muttered. "Two longish scratches and some scrabbles." He gave the revolver to Fox, who was sitting in the chair which, nine hours earlier, Carlisle had occupied. Like Carlisle, Fox used Lord Pastern's lens.

"Did you notice," Alleyn said, "that when I gave the thing to that old freak to look at, it was the underside of the butt near the trigger guard that seemed to interest him. I can't find anything there. The maker's plate's on the heel. What was he up to, do you suppose?"

"God knows," Fox grunted crossly. He was sniffing at the muzzle.

"You look like an old maid with smelling salts," Alleyn observed.

"So I may, sir, but I don't smell anything except gun oil."

"I know. That's another thing. Listen."

In some distant part of the house there was movement. A door slammed, shutters were thrown back and a window opened.

"The servants are stirring," Alleyn said. "We'll seal this room, leave a man to watch it and come back to it later on. Let's collect everything we've picked up, find out what the others have got and catch three hours' sleep. Yard at ten o'clock, don't forget. Come on."

But he himself did not move. Fox looked dubiously at him and began to pack away the revolver, the plastic wood, the empty bottle and the ivory handle.

"No, blast it," Alleyn said, "I'll work through. Take those things, Fox, and dispatch them off to the experts. Fix up adequate relief for surveillance here, and away you go. I'll see you at ten. What's the matter?"

"I'd as soon stay, Mr. Alleyn."

"I know all about that. Zealous young officer. Away you go."

Fox passed his hand over his short grizzled hair and said: "I keep very fit, really. Make a point of never thinking about the retiring age. Well, thank you very much, Mr. Alleyn."

"I might have another dig at the witnesses."

"The party upstairs won't wake before ten."

"I'll stir 'em up if I need 'em. Why should they have all the fun? I want to ring up my wife. Good morning to you, Mr. Fox."

Fox unlocked the door on to the landing and turned the handle. The door flew inwards, striking his shoulder. He stepped back with an oath and Lord Pastern's body fell across his feet.

v i

It remained there for perhaps three seconds. Its eyes were open and glared furiously. Fox bent over it and the mouth also opened.

"What the hell d'you think you're doin'?" Lord Pastern demanded.

He rolled over neatly and got to his feet. His jaw and cheeks glistened with a sort of hoar-frost, his eyes were bloodshot and his evening dress disordered. A window on the landing shed the cruel light of early morning upon him and he looked ghastly in it. His manner, however, had lost little of its native aggressiveness. "What are you starin' at?" he added.

"We might fairly ask you," Alleyn rejoined, "what you were up to, sitting, it appears, on the landing with your back to the door."

"I dozed off. Pretty state of affairs when a man's kept out of his own rooms at five o'clock in the morning."

"All right, Fox," Alleyn said wearily, "you get along."

"Very well, sir," said Fox. "Good morning, my lord." He side-stepped Lord Pastern and went out, leaving the door ajar. Alleyn heard him admonishing Sergeant Marks on the landing: "What sort of surveillance do you call this?" "I was only told to keep observation, Mr. Fox. His lordship fell asleep as soon as he touched the floor. I thought he might as well be there as anywhere." Fox growled majestically and passed out of hearing.

Alleyn shut the study door and went to the window. "We haven't finished in this room," he said, "but I think I may disturb it so far."

He drew back the curtains and opened the window. It was now quite light outside. A fresh breeze came in through the window, emphasizing, before it dismissed them, the dense enclosed odors of carpet, leather and stale smoke. The study looked inhospitable and unkempt. The desk lamp still shed a raffish yellowness on the litter that surrounded it. Alleyn turned from the window to face Lord Pastern and found him rummaging with quick inquisitive fingers in the open drawer on the desk.

"I wonder if I can show you what you're hunting for," Alleyn said. He opened Fox's bag and then took out his notebook. "Don't touch anything please, but will you look in that case?"

He did look, but impatiently, and, as far as Alleyn could see, without any particular surprise.

"Where'd you find that?" Lord Pastern demanded, pointing a not very steady finger at the ivory handle.

"In the drawer. Can you identify it?"

"I might be able to," he muttered.

Alleyn pointed to the weapon. "The stiletto that's been sunk in the end with plastic wood might have belonged to this ivory handle. We shall try it. If it fits, it came originally from Lady Pastern's work-box in the drawing-room."

"So you say," said Lord Pastern insultingly. Alleyn made a note.

"Can you tell me if this stiletto was in your drawer here, sir? Before last night?"

Lord Pastern was eyeing the revolver. He thrust out his underlip, shot a glance at Alleyn, and darted his hand towards it.

"All right," Alleyn said, "you may touch it, but please answer my question about the stiletto."

"How should I know?" he said indifferently. "I don't know." Without removing it from the case, he tipped the revolver over and, snatching up his lens, peered at the underside of the butt. He gave a shrill cackle of laughter.

"What did you expect to see?" Alleyn asked casually.

"Hoity-toity," Lord Pastern rejoined. "*Wouldn't* you like to know!"

He stared at Alleyn. His bloodshot eyes twinkled insolently. "It's devilish amusin'," he said. "Look at it whatever way you like, it's damn funny."

He dropped into an armchair, and with an air of gloating relish rubbed his hands together.

Alleyn shut down the lid of Fox's case and succeeded in snatching back his temper. He stood in front of Lord Pastern and deliberately looked into his eyes. Lord Pastern immediately shut them very tight and bunched up his cheeks.

"I'm sleepy," he said.

"Listen to me," Alleyn said. "Have you any idea at all of the personal danger you are in? Do you know the consequences of withholding or refusing crucial information when a capital crime has been committed? It's my duty to tell you that you are under grave suspicion. You've had the formal warning. Confronted with the body of a man whom, one assumes, you were supposed to hold in some sort of regard, you've conducted yourself appallingly. I must tell you, sir, that if you continue in this silly affectation of frivolity,

I shall ask you to come to Scotland Yard where you will be questioned and, if necessary, detained."

He waited. Lord Pastern's face had gradually relaxed during this speech. His mouth now pouted and expelled a puff of air that blew his moustache out. He was, apparently, asleep again.

Alleyn contemplated him for some moments. He then seated himself at the desk in a position that enabled him to keep Lord Pastern in sight. After a moment's cogitation, he pulled the typewriter towards him, took Félicité's letter from his pocket, found a sheet of paper and began to make a copy.

At the first rattle of the keys Lord Pastern's eyes opened, met Alleyn's gaze and shut again. He mumbled something indistinguishable and snored with greater emphasis. Alleyn completed his copy and laid it beside the original. They had been typed on the same machine.

On the floor, beside the chair Carlisle had used on the previous night, lay the magazine *Harmony*. He took it up and ruffled the pages. A dozen or more flopped over and then the binding opened a little. He was confronted with G.P.F.'s page and noticed, as Carlisle had noticed, the cigarette ash in the groove. He read the letter signed "Toots," turned a few more pages and came upon the anti-drug-racket article and a dramatic review signed by Edward Manx. He once more confronted that preposterous figure in the armchair.

"Lord Pastern," he said loudly, "wake up. Wake up."

Lord Pastern jerked galvanically, made a tasting noise with his tongue and lips and uttered a nightmarish sound.

"A-a-ah?"

"Come now, you're awake. Answer me this," said Alleyn and thrust the copy of *Harmony* under his nose. "How long have you known that Edward Manx was G.P.F.?"

CHAPTER VIII

Morning

Lord Pastern blinked owlishly at the paper, swung round in his chair and eyed the desk. The letter and the copy lay conspicuously beside the typewriter.

"Yes," Alleyn said, "that's how I know. Will you give me an explanation of all this?"

Lord Pastern leant forward and, resting his forearm on his knees, seemed to stare at his clasped hands. When he spoke his voice was subdued and muffled.

"No," he said, "I'll be damned if I do. I'll answer no questions. Find out for yourself. I'm for bed."

He pulled himself out of the chair and squared his shoulders. The air of truculence was still there but Alleyn thought it overlaid a kind of indecision. With the nearest approach to civility that he had yet exhibited he added: "I'm within my rights, aren't I?"

"Certainly," Alleyn said at once. "Your refusal will be noted. That's all. If you change your mind about sending for your solicitor, we shall be glad to call him in. In the meantime, I'm afraid, sir, I shall have to place you under very close observation."

"D'you mean some damn bobby's goin' to follow me about like a bulkin' great poodle?"

"If you care to put it that way. It's no use, I imagine, for me to repeat any warnings about your own most equivocal position."

"None whatever." He went to the door and stood with his back to Alleyn, holding the knob and leaning heavily on it. "Get them to give you breakfast," he said without looking round and went slowly out and up the stairs. Alleyn called his thanks after him and nodded to Marks, who was on the landing. Marks followed Lord Pastern upstairs.

Alleyn returned to the study, shut the window, had a last look round, packed Fox's bag, removed it to the landing and finally locked and sealed the door. Marks had been replaced on the landing by another plain-clothes man. "Hullo, Jimson," Alleyn said. "Just come on?"

"Yes, sir. Relieving."

"Have you seen any of the staff?"

"A maid came upstairs just now, Mr. Alleyn. Mr. Fox left instructions they were to be kept off this floor so I sent her down again. She seemed very much put about."

"She would," Alleyn said. "All right. Tactful as you can, you know, but don't miss anything."

"Very good, sir."

He crossed the landing and entered the ballroom where he found Thompson and Bailey packing up. Alleyn looked at the group of chairs round the grand piano and at a sheet of notepaper Bailey had collected. On it was pencilled the band programme for the previous night. Bailey pointed out the light coating of dust on the piano top and showed Alleyn where they had found clear traces of the revolver and the parasol and umbrellas. It was odd, Bailey and Thompson thought, but it appeared that quantities of dust had fallen after these objects had rested in this place. Not so very odd, Alleyn suggested, as Lord Pastern had, on his own statement, fired off a blank round in the ballroom that would probably have brought down quite a lot of dust from the charming but ornately moulded ceiling. "Happy hunting ground," he muttered. "Whose are the prints round these traces of the parasol section and knob? Don't tell me," he added wearily. "His lordship's?"

"That's right," Thompson and Bailey said together. "His lordship's and Breezy's." Alleyn saw them go and then came out and sealed the ballroom doors.

He returned to the drawing-room, collected Lady Pastern's work-box, debated with himself about locking this room up too and decided against it. He then left all his gear under the eye of the officer on the landing and went down to the ground floor. It was now six o'clock.

The dining-room was already prepared for breakfast. The bowl of white carnations, he noticed, had been removed to a side table. As he halted before a portrait of some former Settinger who bore a mild resemblance to Lord Pastern, he heard a distant mingling of voices beyond the service door. The servants, he thought, having their first snack. He pushed open the door, found himself in a servery with a further door which led, it appeared, into the servants' hall. The best of all early morning smells, that of freshly brewed coffee, was clearly discernible. He was about to go forward when a voice, loud, dogged and perceptibly anxious, said very slowly:

"*Parlez, monsieur, je vous en prie, plus lentement, et peut-être je vous er-er—comprendrerai—* No, blast it, as you were, *je vous pouverai—*"

Alleyn pushed open the door and discovered Mr. Fox, seated cosily before a steaming cup of coffee, flanked by Spence and a bevy of attentive ladies and *vis-à-vis* a dark imposing personage in full chef's regalia.

There was only a fractional pause while Alleyn surveyed this tableau. Fox then rose.

"Perhaps you'd like a cup of coffee, Mr. Alleyn," he suggested and, addressing the chef, added carefully: "*C'est, Monsieur—er—le chef-inspecteur Alleyn, monsieur.* Mr. Alleyn, this is Miss Parker, the housekeeper, and Mademoiselle Hortense. And these girls are Mary and Myrtle. This is Mr. Spence and this is Monsieur Dupont and the young chap over there is William. Well!" concluded Fox, beaming upon the company, "this is what I call cosy."

Alleyn took the chair placed for him by William and stared fixedly at his subordinate. Fox responded with a bland smile. "I was just leaving, sir," he said, "when I happened to run into Mr. Spence. I knew you'd want to inform these good people of our little contretemps so here, in point of fact, I am."

"Fancy," said Alleyn.

Fox's technique on the working side of the green baize doors was legendary at the Yard. This was the first time Alleyn had witnessed it in action. But even now, he realzied, the fine bloom of the exotic was rubbed off and it was his own entrance which had destroyed it. The atmosphere of conviviality had stiffened. Spence had risen, the maids hovered uneasily on the edges of their chairs. He did his best and it was a good best, but evidently Fox, who was an innocent snob, had been bragging about him and they all called him "sir."

"Well," he said cheerfully, "if Mr. Fox has been on this job there'll be no need for me to bother any of you. This is the best coffee I've drunk for years."

"I am gratified," said Monsieur Dupont in fluent English. "At present, of course, one cannot obtain the fresh bean as readily as one desires."

Mademoiselle Hortense said, "Naturally," and the others made small affirmative noises.

"I suppose," Fox said genially, "his lordship's very particular about his coffee. Particular about everything, I daresay?" he added, invitingly.

William, the footman, laughed sardonically and was checked by a glance from Spence. Fox prattled on. It would be her ladyship, of course, who was particular about coffee, being of Mademoiselle Hortense's and Monsieur Dupont's delightful nationality. He attempted this compliment in French, got bogged down and told Alleyn that Monsieur Dupont had been giving him a lesson. Mr. Alleyn, he informed the company, spoke French like a native. Looking up, Alleyn found Spence gazing at him with an expression of anxiety.

"I'm afraid this is a great nuisance for all of you," Alleyn said.

"It's not that, sir," Spence rejoined slowly, "it does put us all about very much, I can't deny. Not being able to get things done in the usual way—"

"I'm sure," Miss Parker intervened, "I don't know what her ladyship's going to say about the first floor. Leaving everything. It's very awkward."

"Exactly. But the worrying thing," Spence went on, "is not knowing what it's all about. Having the police in, sir, and everything. Just because the party from this house happens to be present when this Mr. Rivera passes away in a restaurant."

"Quite so," said Miss Parker.

"The circumstances," Alleyn said carefully, "are extraordinary. I don't know if Inspector Fox has told you—"

Fox said that he had been anxious not to distress the ladies. Alleyn, who thought that the ladies looked as if they were half-dead with curiosity, agreed that Fox had shown great delicacy but added that it would have to come out sometime. "Mr. Rivera," he said, "was killed."

They stirred attentively. Myrtle, the younger of the maids, ejaculated, "Murdered?" clapped her hands over her mouth and suppressed a nervous giggle. Alleyn said it looked very much like it and added that he hoped they would all co-operate as far as they were able in helping to clear the ground. He had known, before he met it, what their response would be. People were all very much alike when it came to homicide cases. They wanted to be removed to a comfortable distance where curiosity could be assuaged, prestige maintained and personal responsibility dissolved. With working people this wish was deepened by a heritage of insecurity and the necessity to maintain caste. They were filled with a kind of generic anxiety: at once disturbed by an indefinite threat and stimulated by a crude and potent assault on their imagination.

"It's a matter," he said, "of clearing innocent people, of tidying them up. I'm sure you will be glad to help us in this, if you can."

He produced Lord Pastern's time-table, spread it out before Spence and told them who had compiled it.

"If you can help us check these times, any of you, we shall be very grateful," he said.

Spence put on his spectacles and with an air of slight embarrassment began to read the time-table. The others, at Alleyn's suggestion, collected round him, not altogether unwillingly.

"It's a bit elaborate, isn't it?" Alleyn said. "Let's see if it can be simplified at all. You see that between half-past eight and nine the ladies left the dining-room and went to the drawing-room. So we get the two groups in the two rooms. Can any of you add to or confirm that?"

Spence could. It was a quarter to nine when the ladies went to the drawing-room. When he came away from serving their coffee he passed Lord Pastern and Mr. Bellairs on the landing. They went into his lordship's study. Spence continued on through the dining-room, paused there to see that William had served coffee to the gentlemen and noticed that Mr. Manx and Mr. Rivera were still sitting over their wine. He then went into the servants' hall where a few minutes later he heard the nine o'clock news on the wireless.

"So now," Alleyn said, "we have three groups. The ladies in the drawing-room, his lordship and Mr. Bellairs in the study, and Mr. Manx and Mr. Rivera in the dining-room. Can anyone tell us when the next move came and who made it?"

Spence remembered coming back into the dining-room and finding Mr. Manx there alone. His reticence at this point became more marked, but Alleyn got from him the news that Edward Manx had helped himself to a stiff whiskey. He asked casually if there was anything about his manner which was at all remarkable, and got the surprising answer that Mr. Edward seemed to be very pleased and said he'd had a wonderful surprise.

"And now," Alleyn said, "Mr. Rivera has broken away from the other groups. Where has he gone? Mr. Manx is in the dining-room, his lordship and Mr. Bellairs in the study, the ladies in the drawing-room, and where is Mr. Rivera?"

He looked round the group of faces with their guarded unwilling expressions until he saw William, and in William's eye he caught a zealous glint. William, he thought, with any luck read detective magazines and spent his day-dreams sleuthing. "Got an idea?" he asked.

"Well, sir," William said, glancing at Spence, "if you'll excuse me, I think his lordship and Mr. Bellairs have parted company where you've got to. I was tidying the hall, sir, and I heard the other gentleman, Mr. Bellairs, come out of the study. I glanced up at the landing, like. And I heard his lordship call out he'd join him in a minute and I saw the gentleman go into the ballroom. I went and got the coffee tray from the drawing-room, sir. The ladies were all there. I put it down on the landing and was going to set the study to rights, when I heard the typewriter in there. His lordship doesn't like being disturbed when he's typing, sir, so I took the tray by the staff stairs to the kitchen and after a few minutes came back. And his lordship must have gone into the ballroom while I was downstairs because I could hear him talking very loud to Mr. Bellairs, sir."

"What about, do you remember?"

William glanced again at Spence and said: "Well, sir, it was something about his lordship telling somebody something if Mr. Bellairs didn't want to. And then there was a terrible loud noise. Drums. And a report like a gun. They all heard it down here in the hall, sir."

Alleyn looked at the listening staff. Miss Parker said coldly that his lordship was no doubt practising, as if Lord Pastern were in the habit of loosing firearms indoors and there were nothing at all remarkable in the circumstances. Alleyn felt that both she and Spence were on the edge of giving William a piece of their minds and he hurried on.

"What did you do next?" he asked William.

He had been, it appeared, somewhat shattered by the report, but had remembered his duties. "I crossed the landing, sir, thinking I'd get on with the study, but Miss de Suze came out of the drawing-room. And then—well, the murdered gentleman, he came from the dining-room and they met and she said she wanted to speak to him alone and they went into the study."

"Sure of that?"

Yes, it appeared that William was perfectly certain. He had lingered, evidently, at the end of the landing. He even remembered that Miss de Suze had something in her hand. He wasn't sure what it was. Something bright, it might have been, he said doubtfully. After she and the gentleman had gone into the study and shut the door, Miss Henderson had come out of the drawing-room and gone upstairs.

Alleyn said: "Now, that's a great help. You see it corresponds exactly so far with his lordship's time-table. I'll just check it over, Fox, if you . . ."

Fox took the tip neatly and while Alleyn affected to study Lord Pastern's notes continued what he liked to call the painless extraction method with William. It must, he said, have been awkward for William. You couldn't go barging in on a tête-à-tête, could you, and yet a chap liked to get his job done. Life, said Fox, was funny when you came to think of it. Here was this poor young lady happily engaged in conversation with—well, he supposed he wasn't giving any secrets away if he said with her fiancé, and little did she think that in a couple of hours or so he would be lying dead. Miss Parker and the maids were visibly moved by this. William turned extremely red in the face and shuffled his feet. "She'll treasure every word of that last talk, I'll be bound," said Fox. "Every word of it." He looked inquiringly at William, who, after a longish pause, blurted out very loudly: "I wouldn't go so far as to say that, Mr. Fox."

"That'll do, Will," said Spence quietly but Fox's voice overrode him. "Is that so?" Fox inquired blandly. "You wouldn't? Why not?"

"Because," William announced boldly, "they was at it hammer-and-tongs."

"*Will!*"

William turned on his superior. "I ought to tell the truth, didn't I, Mr. Spence? To the police?"

"You ought to mind your own business," said Miss Parker with some emphasis and Spence murmured his agreement.

"All right then," William said, huffily. "I'm sure I don't want to push myself in where I'm not welcome."

Fox was extremely genial and complimented William on his natural powers of observation and Miss Parker and Spence upon their loyalty and discretion. He suggested, without exactly stating as much and keeping well on the safe side of police procedure, that any statements anybody offered would, by some mysterious alchemy, free all concerned of any breath of suspicion. In a minute or two he had discovered that sharp-eared William, still hovering on the landing, had seen Rivera go into the ballroom and had overheard most of his quarrel with Breezy Bellairs. To this account Spence and Miss Parker raised no objections and it was tolerably obvious that they had already heard it. It became clear that Mademoiselle Hortense was stifling with repressed information. But she had her eye on Alleyn and it was to him that she addressed herself. She had that particular knack, that peculiar talent commanded by so many of her countrywomen, of making evident, without the slightest emphasis, her awareness of her own attractions and those of the man to whom she was speaking. Alleyn, she seemed to assume, would understand perfectly that she was the confidante of Mademoiselle. Monsieur Dupont, who had remained aloof, now assumed an air of gloomy acquiescence. It was understood, he said, that the relationship between a personal maid and her mistress was one of delicacy and confidence.

"About *l'affaire Rivera* . . ." suggested Fox, doggedly Gallic.

Hortense lifted her shoulders and rocked her head slightly. She addressed herself to Alleyn. Undoubtedly this Monsieur Rivera had been passionately attached. That was evident. And Mademoiselle had responded, being extremely impressionable. But an engagement? Not precisely. He had urged it. There had been scenes. Reconciliations. Further scenes. But last night! She suddenly executed a complicated and vivid gesture with her right hand as if she wrote something off on the air. And against the unuttered but almost tangible disapproval of the English servants, Hortense, with a darting incisiveness, said: "Last night everything was ended. But irrevocably *ended.*"

ii

It appeared that at twenty to ten Hortense was summoned to Lady Pastern's bedroom, where she prepared her for the road, putting her into a cloak, and adding, Alleyn supposed, some kind of super-gloss to that already immaculate surface. Hortense kept an eye on the time as the car was ordered for ten-thirty and Lady Pastern liked to have leisure. About ten minutes later Miss Henderson had come in with the news that Félicité was extremely excited and wished to make an elaborate change in her *toilette*. She herself was sent to Félicité's room.

"And conceive the scene, monsieur!" said Hortense, breaking into her native tongue. "The room in complete disarray and Mademoiselle in *déshabillé*. There must be a completely new *toilette*, you understand. Everything, from the foundation, is it not? And while I dress her she relates the whole story. With Monsieur Rivera it is as if it had never been. There has been a formidable quarrel. She had dismissed him forever and in the meantime a letter has arrived in romantic circumstances. It is a letter from a journalistic gentleman she has never seen but with whom she has corresponded frequently. He is about to reveal himself. He declares his passionate attachment. Yet secrecy must be observed. And for myself," Hortense added with conscious rectitude, "I would never, never have allowed myself to repeat one syllable of this matter if it had not become my duty to assure Monsieur that as far as Mademoiselle is concerned, she had no further interest in Monsieur Rivera and was happily released from him and that this is not therefore a *crime passionel*."

"I see," Alleyn said. "Yes, perfectly. It is understood."

Hortense gave him a soubrettish glance and a hard smile.

"And do you know," he said, "who this person was? The letter-writer?"

Félicité, it appeared, had shown her the letter. And as the party was leaving for the Metronome, Hortense had run downstairs with Lady Pastern's vinaigrette and had seen (with what emotion!) Monsieur Edward Manx wearing a white flower in his coat. All was revealed! And how great, Hortense had reflected as Spence closed the front door on their departure, how overwhelming would be the joy of her ladyship, who had always desired this union! Hortense had been quite unable to conceal her own gratification and had sung for pure joy as she rejoined her colleagues in the servants' hall. Her colleagues, with the exception of Monsieur Dupont, now cast black glances at her and refrained from comment.

Alleyn checked over the events related by Hortense and found that they corresponded as nearly as necessary with the group movements suggested by Lord Pastern's notes. From the nucleus of persons, further individuals had broken away. Manx had been alone in the drawing-room. Lady Pastern had been alone in her room until Hortense arrived. Hortense herself, and William, had cruised about the house and so had Spence. Alleyn was about to lay down his pencil when he remembered Miss Henderson. She had gone to her room earlyish in the evening and had presumably stayed there until, after being visited by Félicité, she herself reported this incident to Lady Pastern. It was odd, he thought, that he should have forgotten Miss Henderson.

But there were still a good many threads to be caught up and introduced into the texture. He referred again to Lord Pastern's notes. At 9:26, the notes declared specifically, Lord Pastern, then in the ballroom, had suddenly recollected the sombrero which he desired to wear in his own number. He had glanced at his watch, perhaps, and taken alarm. The note merely said: "9:26. Self. Ballroom. Sombrero. Search for. All over house. William. Spence. Etc."

Questioned on this matter the servants willingly recalled the characteristic hullabaloo that had been raised in this search. It set in immediately after the last event related by William. Félicité and Rivera were in the study, Miss Henderson was on her way upstairs and William himself was hovering on the landing, when Lord Pastern shot out of the ballroom, shouting: "Where's my sombrero?" In no time the hunt was in full cry. Spence, William and Lord Pastern scattered in various directions. The sombrero was finally discovered by Miss Henderson (she was no doubt the "Etc." of the notes) in a cupboard on the top landing. Lord Pastern appeared with the thing on his head and re-entered the ballroom in triumph. During this uproar, Spence, questing in the hall, had found a letter on the table addressed to Miss de Suze.

Here the narrative was interrupted by a dignified passage-of-arms between Spence, William and the parlour-maid, Mary. Mr. Spence, William said resentfully, had torn a strip off him for not taking the letter in to Miss Félicité as soon as it came. William had denied knowledge of the letter and had not opened the door to any district messenger. Nor had Mary. Nor had anyone else. Spence obviously considered that someone was lying. Alleyn asked if any of them had seen the envelope. Hortense, needlessly dramatic, cried out that she had tidied an envelope up from the floor of Mademoiselle's bedroom. Fox held a smothered colloquy about rubbish bins with William, who made an excited exit and returned, flushed with modest triumph, to lay a crushed and stained envelope on the table before Alleyn. Alleyn recognized the eccentricities of Lord Pastern's typewriter and pocketed the envelope.

"It's my belief, Mr. Spence," William announced boldly, "that there never was a district messenger."

Leaving them no time to digest this theory, Alleyn continued with the business of checking Lord Pastern's time-table. Spence, still very anxious, said that having discovered the letter on the hall table he had come upstairs and taken it into the drawing-room, where he found only his mistress, Miss Wayne, and Mr. Manx, who, he thought, had not long arrived there from the dining-room. On returning to the landing Spence encountered Miss de Suze, coming out of the study, and gave her the letter. Sounds of the sombrero hunt reached him from upstairs. He was about to join it when a cry of triumph from Lord Pastern reassured him, and he returned to the servants' quarters. He had noticed the time: 9:45.

"And at that time," Alleyn said, "Lady Pastern and Miss Wayne are about to leave Mr. Manx alone in the drawing-room and go upstairs. Miss de Suze and Miss Henderson are already in their rooms and Lord Pastern is about to descend, wearing his sombrero. Mr. Bellairs and Mr. Rivera are in the ball-

room. We have forty-five minutes to go before the party leaves for the Metronome. What happens next?"

But he had struck a blank. Apart from Hortense's previous account of her
visits to the ladies upstairs there was little to be learned from the servants.
They had kept to their own quarters until, a few minutes before the departure for the Metronome, Spence and William had gone into the hall,
assisted the gentlemen into their overcoats, given them their hats and gloves
and seen them into their cars.

"Who," Alleyn asked, "helped Mr. Rivera into his coat?"

William had done this.

"Did you notice anything about him? Anything at all out of the ordinary,
however slight?"

William said sharply: "The gentleman had a—well, a funny ear, sir. Red
and bleeding a bit. A cauliflower ear, as you might say."

"Had you noticed this earlier in the evening? When you leant over his
chair, serving him, at dinner, for instance?"

"No, sir. It was all right then, sir."

"Sure?"

"Swear to it," said William crisply.

"You think carefully, Will, before you make statements," Spence said
uneasily.

"I know I'm right, Mr. Spence."

"How do you imagine he came by this injury?" Alleyn asked. William
grinned, pure Cockney. "Well, sir, if you'll excuse the expression, I'd say
somebody had handed the gentleman a fourpenny one."

"Who, at a guess?"

William rejoined promptly: "Seeing he was holding his right hand, tender-
like, in his left and seeing the way the murdered gentleman looked at him
so fierce, I'd say it was Mr. Edward Manx, sir."

Hortense broke into a spate of excited and gratified comment. Monsieur
Dupont made a wide, conclusive gesture and exclaimed: "Perfectly! It ex-
plains itself!" Mary and Myrtle ejaculated incoherently while Spence and
Miss Parker, on a single impulse, rose and shouted awfully: "That WILL
DO, William."

Alleyn and Fox left them, still greatly excited, and retraced their steps
to the downstairs hall.

"What have we got out of that little party," Alleyn grunted, "beyond
confirmation of old Pastern's time-table up to half an hour before they all
left the house?"

"Damn all, sir. And what does that teach us?" Fox grumbled. "Only that
every man Jack of them was alone at some time or other and might have got
hold of the parasol handle, taken it to the study, fixed this silly little stiletto
affair in the end with plastic wood and then done Gawd-knows-what. Every
man Jack of 'em."

"And every woman Jill?"

"I suppose so. Wait a bit, though."

Alleyn gave him the time-table and his own notes. They had moved into the entrance lobby, closing the inner glass doors behind them. "Mull it over in the car," Alleyn said, "I think there's a bit more to be got out of it, Fox. Come on."

But as Alleyn was about to open the front door Fox gave a sort of grunt and he turned back to see Félicité de Suze on the stairs. She was dressed for the day and in the dim light of the hall looked pale and exhausted. For a moment they stared at each other through the glass panel and then tentatively, uncertainly, she made an incomplete gesture with one hand. Alleyn swore under his breath and re-entered the hall.

"Do you want to speak to me?" he said. "You're up very early."

"I couldn't sleep."

"I'm sorry," he said formally.

"I think I do want to speak to you."

Alleyn nodded to Fox, who re-entered the hall.

"Alone," said Félicité.

"Inspector Fox is acting with me in this case."

She glanced discontentedly at Fox. "All the same . . ." she said, and then as Alleyn made no answer: "Oh, well!"

She was on the third step from the foot of the stairs, standing there boldly, aware of the picture she made. "Lisle told me," she said, "about you and the letter. Getting it from her, I mean. I suppose you take rather a dim view of my sending Lisle to do my dirty work, don't you?"

"It doesn't matter."

"I was all *bouleversée*. I know it was rather awful letting her go, but I think in a way she quite enjoyed it." He noticed that her upper lip was fuller than the under one and that when she smiled it curved richly. "Darling Lisle," she said, "doesn't have much fun and she's so madly interested always in other people's little flutters." She watched Alleyn out of the corners of her eyes and added: "We're all devoted to her."

"What do you want to ask me, Miss de Suze?"

"Please may I have the letter back? Please!"

"In due course," he said. "Certainly."

"Not now?"

"I'm afraid not now."

"That's rather a bore," said Félicité. "I suppose I'd better come clean in a big way."

"If it's relevant to the matter in hand," Alleyn agreed. "I am only concerned with the death of Mr. Carlos Rivera."

She leant back against the bannister, stretching her arms along it and looking downwards, arranging herself for him to look at. "I'd suggest we went somewhere where we could sit down," she said, "but here seems to be the only place where there's no lurking minor detective."

"Let it be here, then."

"You are not," Félicité said, "making this very easy."

"I'm sorry. I shall be glad to hear what you have to say but to tell the truth, there's a heavy day's work in front of us."

They stood there, disliking each other. Alleyn thought: "She's going to be one of the tricky ones. She may have nothing to say; I know the signs but I can't be sure of them." And Félicité thought: "I didn't really notice him last night. If he'd known what Carlos was like he'd have despised me. He's taller than Ned. I'd like him to be on my side thinking how courageous and young and attractive I am. Younger than Lisle, for instance, with two men in love with me. I wonder what sort of women he likes. I suppose I'm frightened."

She slid down into a sitting position on the stairs and clasped her hands about her knees; young and a bit boyish, a touch of the *gamine*.

"It's about this wretched letter. Well, not wretched at all, really, because it's from a chap I'm very fond of. You've read it, of course."

"I'm afraid so."

"My dear, I don't *mind*. Only, as you've seen, it's by way of being number one secrecy and I'll feel a bit low if it all comes popping out, particularly as it's got utterly *no* connection with your little game. It just couldn't be less relevant."

"Good."

"But I suppose I've got to prove that, haven't I?"

"It would be an excellent move if you can."

"Here we go, then," said Félicité.

Alleyn listened wearily, pinning his attention down to the recital, shutting out the thought of time sliding away, and of his wife, who would soon wake and look to see if he was there. Félicité told him that she had corresponded with G.P.F. of *Harmony* and that his advice had been too marvellously understanding and that she had felt an urge like the kick of a mule to meet him, but that although his replies had grown more and more come-to-ish he had insisted that his identity must remain hidden. "All Cupid-and-Psyche-ish only definitely less rewarding," she said. And then the letter had arrived and Edward Manx had appeared with a white flower in his coat and suddenly, after never having gone much for old Ned, she had felt astronomically up-lifted. Because, after all, it was rather bracing, wasn't it, to think that all the time Ned was G.P.F. and writing these really gorgeous things and falling for one like a dray-load of bricks? Here Félicité paused and then added rather hurriedly and with an air of hauteur: "You'll understand that by this time poor Carlos had, from my point of view, become comparatively a dim figure. I mean, to be as bald as an egg about it, he just faded out. I mean it couldn't have mattered less about Carlos because clearly I wasn't his cup of tea and we'd both gone tepid on it and I knew he wouldn't mind. You do see what I mean about that, don't you?"

"Are you trying to tell me that you and Rivera had parted as friends?"

Félicité shook her head vaguely and raised her eyebrows. "Even that makes it sound too important," she said. "It all just came peacefully unstuck."

"And there was no quarrel, for instance when you and he were in the study between a quarter and half-past nine? Or later, between Mr. Manx and Mr. Rivera?"

There was a long pause. Félicité bent forward and jerked at the strap of her shoe. "What in the world," she said indistinctly, "put these quaint little notions into your head?"

"Are they completely false?"

"I know," she said loudly and cheerfully. She looked up into his face. "You've been gossiping with the servants." She appealed to Fox. "Hasn't he?" she demanded playfully.

"I'm sure I couldn't say, Miss de Suze," said Fox blandly.

"How you could!" she accused Alleyn. "Which of them was it? Was it Hortense? My poor Mr. Alleyn, you don't know Hortense. She's the world's most accomplished liar! She just can't help herself, poor thing. It's pathological."

"So there was no quarrel?" Alleyn said. "Between any of you?"

"My dear, haven't I told you!"

"Then why," he asked, "did Mr. Manx punch Mr. Rivera over the ear?"

Félicité's eyes and mouth opened. Then she hunched her shoulders and caught the tip of her tongue between her teeth. He could have sworn she was astonished and in a moment it was evident that she was gratified.

"No!" she said. "Honestly? Ned did? Well, I must say I call that a handsome tribute. When did it happen? Before we went down to the Met? After dinner? When?"

Alleyn looked steadily at her. "I thought," he said, "that perhaps you could tell me that."

"I? But I promise you . . ."

"Had he got a trickle of blood on his ear when you talked to him in the study? On the occasion, you know, when you say there was no quarrel?"

"Let me think," said Félicité, and rested her head on her crossed arms. But the movement was not swift enough. He had seen the blank look of panic in her eyes. "No," her voice, muffled by her arms, said slowly, "no, I'm sure . . ."

There was some change of light above, where the stairs ran up to the first landing. He looked up. Carlisle Wayne stood there in the shadow. Her figure and posture still retained the effect of movement, as if while she came downstairs she had suddenly been held in suspension as the action of a motion picture may be suspended to give emphasis to a specific moment. Over Félicité's bent head, Alleyn with a slight movement of his hand arrested Carlisle's descent. Félicité had begun to speak again.

"After all," she was saying, "one is a bit uplifted. It's not every day in the week that people give other people cauliflower ears for love of one's bright eyes." She raised her face and looked at him. "How naughty of Ned, but how sweet of him. Darling Ned!"

"No, really!" said Carlisle strongly. "This is too much!"

Félicité, with a stifled cry, was on her feet.

Alleyn said: "Hullo, Miss Wayne. Good morning to you. Have you any theory about why Mr. Manx gave Rivera a clip over the ear? He did give him a clip, you know. Why?"

"If you must know," Carlisle said in a high voice, "it was because Rivera kissed me when we met on the landing."

"Good Lord!" Alleyn ejaculated. "Why didn't you say so before? Kissed *you*, did he? Did you like it?"

"Don't be a *bloody* fool!" Carlisle shouted and bolted upstairs.

"I must say," Félicité said, "I call that rather poor of darling Lisle."

"If you'll excuse us," Alleyn said. He and Fox left her staring thoughtfully at her finger-nails.

iii

"A shave," Alleyn said in the car, "a bath and, with luck, two hours' sleep. I'll take it out at home. We'll send the stuff on to the experts. What about you, Fox? Troy will be delighted to fix you up."

"Thank you very much, sir, but I wouldn't think of troubling Mrs. Alleyn. There's a little place—"

"Be damned to your little place. I've had enough insubordination from you, my lad. To hell with you. You're coming to us."

Fox accepted this singular invitation in the spirit in which it was made. He took out his spectacles, Alleyn's notebook and Lord Pastern's time-table. Alleyn dragged his palm across his jaw, shuddered, yawned and closed his eyes. "A hideous curse on this case," he murmured and appeared to sleep. Fox began to whisper to himself. The car slipped down Cliveden Place, into Grosvenor Place, into Hyde Park Corner. "'T, 't, 't," Fox whispered over the time-table.

"You sound," Alleyn said without opening his eyes, "like Dr. Johnson on his way to Streatham. Can you crack your joints, Foxkin?"

"I see what you mean about this ruddy time-table."

"What *did* I mean? Split me and sink me if I know what I meant."

"Well, sir, our customer, whoever he or she may be—and you know my views on the point—had to be in the ballroom to pick up the bit of umbrella shaft, in the drawing-room to collect the stiletto and alone in the study to fix the stiletto in the bit of umbrella shaft with plastic wood."

"You'll be coming round the mountain when you come."

"It *is* a bit of a mountain and that's a fact. According to what the young lady, Miss Wayne, I mean, told you, sir, this perishing parasol was all right before dinner when she was in the ballroom and handled it, and according to her, his lordship was in the study drawing the bullets out of the cartridges. If that's correct he didn't get a chance to play the fool with the parasol before dinner. What's more it fits in with his lordship's own statement, which

Bellairs can speak to if he ever wakes up, that he took the parasol to bits on the piano *after* dinner. For fun."

"Quite."

"All right. Now where does this get us? If the time-table's correct, his lordship was never alone in the study after that."

"And the only time he was alone at all, moreover, he was up and down the house, bellowing like a bull for his sombrero."

"Doesn't that look like establishing an alibi?" Fox demanded.

"It looks a bit like the original alibi itself, Br'er Fox."

"He might have carried the tube of plastic wood round in his pocket."

"So he might. Together with the bit of parasol and the stiletto, pausing in mid-bellow to fix the job."

"Gah! How about him just taking the stuff in his pocket to the Metronome and fixing everything there?"

"Oh Lord! When? How?"

"Lavatory?" Fox suggested hopefully.

"And when did he put the weapon in the gun? Skelton looked down the barrel just before they started playing, don't forget."

The car had stopped in a traffic jam in Piccadilly. Fox contemplated the Green Park with disapproval, Alleyn still kept his eyes shut. Big Ben struck seven.

"By Gum!" Fox said, bringing his palm down on his knee. "By Gum, how about this? How about his lordship in his damn-your-eyes fashion fitting the weapon into the gun while he sat there behind his drums? In front of everybody, while one of the other turns was on? It's amazing what you can do when you brazen it out. What's that yarn they're always quoting, sir? I've got it. *The Purloined Letter.* Proving that if you make a thing obvious enough nobody notices it?"

Alleyn opened one eye. "*The Purloined Letter*," he said. He opened the other eye. "Fox, my cabbage, my rare edition, my *objet d'art*, my own especial bit of *bijouterie*, be damned if I don't think you've caught an idea. Come on. Let's further think of this."

They talked intensively until the car pulled up, in a *cul-de-sac* off Coventry Street, before Alleyn's flat.

Early sunlight streamed into the little entrance hall. Beneath a Benozzo Gozzoli, a company of dahlias, paper-white in a blue bowl, cast translucent shadows on a white parchment wall. Alleyn looked about him contentedly.

"Troy's under orders not to get up till eight," he said. "You take first whack at the bath, Fox, while I have a word with her. Use my razor. Wait a bit." He disappeared and returned with towels. "There'll be something to eat at half-past nine," he said. "The visitors' room's all yours, Fox. Sleep well."

"Very kind, I'm sure," said Fox. "May I send my compliments to Mrs. Alleyn, sir?"

"She'll be delighted to receive them. See you later."

Troy was awake in her white room, sitting up with her head aureoled in short locks of hair. "Like a faun," Alleyn said, "or a bronze dahlia. Are you well this morning?"

"Bouncing, thanks. And you?"

"As you see. Unhousel'd, unanel'd and un-everything that's civilized."

"A poor state of affairs," said Troy. "You look like the gentleman in that twenty-foot canvas in the Luxembourg. Boiled shirt in dents and gazing out over Paris through lush curtains. I think it's called 'The Hopeless Dawn'! His floozy is still asleep on an elephantine bed, you remember."

"I don't remember. Talking of floozies, oughtn't you to be asleep yourself?"

"God bless my soul!" Troy complained. "I haven't been bitten by the tsetse fly. It's getting on for nine hours since I went to bed, damn it."

"O.K. O.K."

"What's happened, Rory?"

"One of the kind we don't fancy."

"Oh, no."

"You'll hear about it anyway, so I may as well tell you. It's that florid number we saw playing the piano-accordion, the one with the teeth and hair."

"You don't mean—"

"Somebody pinked him with a sort of dagger made out of a bit of a parasol and a needlework stiletto."

"Catch!"

He explained at some length.

"Well but . . ." Troy stared at her husband. "When have you got to be at the Yard?"

"Ten."

"All right. You've got two hours and time for breakfast. Good morning, darling."

"Fox is in the bathroom. I know I'm not fit for a lady's bed chamber."

"Who said?"

"If you didn't, nobody." He put his arm across her and stooped his head. "Troy," he said, "may I ask Fox this morning?"

"If you want to, my dearest."

"I think I might. How much, at a rough guess, would you say I loved you?"

"*Words* fail me," said Troy, imitating the late Harry Tate.

"And me."

"There's Mr. Fox coming out of the bathroom. Away with you."

"I suppose so. Good morning, Mrs. Quiverful."

On his way to the bathroom Alleyn looked in upon Fox. He found him lying on the visitors' room bed, without his jacket but incredibly neat; his hair damp, his jaw gleaming, his shirt stretched tight over his thick pectoral muscles. His eyes were closed but he opened them as Alleyn looked in.

"I'll call you at half-past nine," Alleyn said. "Did you know you were going to be a godfather, Br'er Fox?" And as Fox's eyes widened he shut the door and went whistling to the bathroom.

CHAPTER IX

The Yard

At ten-thirty in the Chief-Inspector's room at New Scotland Yard, routine procedure following a case of homicide was efficiently established.

Alleyn sat at his desk taking reports from Detective-Sergeants Gibson, Watson, Scott and Sallis. Mr. Fox, with that air of good-humour crossed with severity which was his habitual reaction to reports following observation, listened critically to his juniors, each of whom held his official notebook. Six men going soberly about their day's work. Earlier that morning, in other parts of London, Captain Entwhistle, an expert on ballistics, had fitted a dart made from a piece of a parasol into a revolver and had fired it into a bag of sand; Mr. Carrick, a government analyst, had submitted a small cork to various tests for certain oils; and Sir Grantly Morton, the famous pathologist, assisted by Curtis, had opened Carlos Rivera's thorax, and, with the greatest delicacy, removed his heart.

"All right," Alleyn said. "Get yourselves chairs and smoke if you want to. This is liable to be a session."

When they were settled, he pointed the stem of his pipe at a heavy-jawed, straw-coloured detective-sergeant with a habitually startled expression. "You searched the deceased's rooms, didn't you, Gibson? Let's take you first."

Gibson thumbed his notebook open, contemplating it in apparent astonishment, and embarked on a high-pitched recital.

"The deceased man, Carlos Rivera," he said, "lived at 102 Bedford Mansions, Austerly Square S.W.1. Service flats. Rental £500 a year."

"Why don't we all play piano-accordions?" Fox asked of nobody in particular.

"At 3 A.M. on the morning of June 1st," Gibson continued in a shrillish voice, "having obtained a search-warrant, I effected entrance to above premises by means of a key on a ring removed from the body of the deceased. The flat consists of an entrance lobby, six-by-eight feet, a sitting-room, twelve-by-fourteen feet, and a bedroom nine-by-eleven feet. Furnishings. Sitting-room: Carpet, purple, thick. Curtains, full length, purple satin."

"Stay me with flagons!" Alleyn muttered. "Purple."

"You might call it morve, Mr. Alleyn."

"Well, go on."

"Couch, upholstered green velvet, three armchairs ditto, dining table, six dining chairs, open fireplace. Walls painted fawn. Cushions: Seven. Green and purple satin." He glanced at Alleyn. "I beg pardon, Mr. Alleyn? Anything wrong?"

"Nothing. Nothing. Go on."

"*Bookcase. Fourteen books. Foreign. Recognized four as on police lists. Pictures: four.*"

"What were *they* like?" Fox asked.

"Never you mind, you dirty old man," said Alleyn.

"Two were nude studies, Mr. Fox, what you might call heavy pin-ups. The others were a bit more so. *Cigarette boxes: four. Cigarettes, commercial product. Have taken one from each box. Wall safe. Combination lock but found note of number in deceased's pocket-book. Contents—*"

"Half a minute," Alleyn said. "Have all the flats got these safes?"

"I ascertained from inquiries, sir, that deceased had his installed."

"Right. Go on."

"*Contents. I removed a number of papers, two ledgers or account-books and a locked cash-box containing three hundred pounds in notes of low denomination, and thirteen shillings in silver.*" Here Gibson paused of his own accord.

"There now!" said Fox. "Now we *may* be on to something."

"*I left a note of the contents of the safe in the safe and I locked the safe,*" said Gibson, on a note of uncertainty, induced perhaps by misgivings about his prose style. "Shall I produce the contents now, sir, or go on to the bedroom?"

"I doubt if I can take the bedroom," Alleyn said. "But go on."

"It was done up in black, sir. Black satin."

"Do you put all this in your notes?" Fox demanded suddenly. "All this about colours and satin?"

"They tell us to be thorough, Mr. Fox."

"There's a medium to all things," Fox pronounced somberly. "I beg pardon, Mr. Alleyn."

"Not at all, Br'er Fox. The bedroom, Gibson."

But there wasn't anything much to the purpose in Gibson's meticulous account of Rivera's bedroom unless the revelation that he wore black satin pyjamas with embroidered initials could be called, as Alleyn suggested, damning and conclusive evidence as to character. Gibson produced the spoil of the wall safe and they examined it. Alleyn took the ledgers and Fox the bundle of correspondence. For some time there was silence, broken only by the whisper of papers.

Presently, however, Fox brought his palm down on his knee and Alleyn, without looking up, said: "Hullo?"

"Peculiar," Fox grunted. "Listen to this, sir."

"Go ahead."

How tender [Mr. Fox began] is the first burgeoning of love! How delicate the tiny bud, how easily cut with frost! Touch it with gentle fingers, dear lad, lest its fragrance be lost to you forever.

"Cor'!" whispered Detective-Sergeant Scott.

You say [Mr. Fox continued] that she is changeable. So is a day in spring. Be patient. Wait for the wee petals to unfold. If you would care for a very special, etc.

Fox removed his spectacles and contemplated his superior.

"What do you mean by your 'etc.,' Fox? Why don't you go on?"

"That's what it says. Etc. Then it stops. Look."

He flattened a piece of creased blue letter paper out on the desk before Alleyn. It was covered with typing, closely spaced. The Duke's Gate address was stamped on the top.

Alleyn said, "What's that you're holding back?"

Fox laid his second exhibit before him. It was a press-cutting and printed on paper of the kind used in the more exotic magazines. Alleyn read aloud:

DEAR G.P.F.: I am engaged to a young lady who at times is very affectionate and then again goes cold on me. It's not halitosis because I asked her and she said it wasn't and wished I wouldn't harp on about it. I am twenty-two, five-foot-eleven in my socks and well built. I drag down £550 per annum. I am an A grade motor-mechanic and I have prospects of a rise. She reckons she loves me and yet she acts like this. What should be my attitude? Spark-plug.

"I should advise a damn' good hiding," Alleyn said. "Poor old Spark-plug."

"Go on, sir. Read the answer."

Alleyn continued:

DEAR SPARK-PLUG: Yours is not as unusual a problem as perhaps you, in your distress of mind, incline to believe. How tender is the first burgeoning—!

"Yes, here we go again. Yes. All right, Fox. You've found, apparently, a bit of the rough draft and the finished article. The draft, typed on Duke's Gate letter-paper, looks as if it had been crumpled up in somebody's pocket, doesn't it? Half a minute."

He opened his own file and in a moment the letter Félicité had dropped from her bag at the Metronome had been placed beside the other. Alleyn bent over them. "It's a pot-shot, of course," he said, "but I'm ready to bet it's the same machine. The s out of alignment. All the usual indications."

"Where does this lead us?" Fox asked. Gibson, looking gratified, cleared his throat. Alleyn said: "It leads us into a bit of a tangle. The letter to Miss de Suze was typed on the machine in Lord Pastern's study on the paper he uses for that purpose. The machine carried his dabs only. I took a chance and asked him, point-blank, how long he'd known that Edward Manx was G.P.F. He wouldn't answer but I'll swear I rocked him. I'll undertake he typed the letter after he saw Manx put a white carnation in his coat, marked the envelope, 'By District Messenger' and put it on the hall table where it was discovered by the butler. All right. Now, not so long ago, Manx stayed at Duke's Gate for three weeks and I suppose it's reasonable to assume that he may have used the typewriter and the blue letter-paper in the study when he was jotting down notes for his nauseating little G.P.F. numbers in *Harmony*. So this draft may have been typed by Manx. But, as far as we know, Manx met Rivera for the first time last night and incidentally dotted him what William pleasingly called a fourpenny one, because Rivera kissed, *not* Miss de Suze but Miss Wayne. Now, if we're right so far, how and when the hell did Rivera get hold of Manx's rough draft of this sickening G.P.F. stuff? Not last night because we've got it from Rivera's safe, and he didn't go back to his rooms. Answer me that, Fox."

"Gawd knows."

"We don't, at all events. And if we find out, is it going to tie up with Rivera's murder? Well, press on, chaps, press on."

He returned to the ledger and Fox to the bundle of papers. Presently Alleyn said: "Isn't it extraordinary how business-like they are?"

"Who's that, Mr. Alleyn?"

"Why, blackmailers to be sure. Mr. Rivera was a man of parts, Fox. Piano-accordions, drug-running, blackmail. Almost a pity we've got to nab his murderer. He was ripe for bumping off, was Mr. Rivera. This is a neatly kept record of moneys and goods received and disbursed. On the third of February, for instance, we have an entry. 'Cash. £150, 3rd installment. S.F.F.' A week later, a cryptic note on the debit side: '6 doz. per S.S., £360,' followed by a series of credits: 'J.C.M. £10,' 'B.B. £100,' and so on. These entries are in a group by themselves. He's totted them up and balanced the whole thing, showing a profit of £200 on the original outlay of £360."

"That'll be his dope racket, by Gum. 'S.S.' did you say, Mr. Alleyn? By Gum, I wonder if he *is* in with the Snowy Santos bunch."

"And B.B. on the paying side. B.B. is quite a profitable number on the paying side."

"Breezy Bellairs?"

"I shouldn't wonder. It looks to me, Fox, as if Rivera was a medium high-up in the drug racket. He was one of the boys we don't catch easily. It's long odds he never passed the stuff out direct to the small consumer. With the exception, no doubt, of the wretched Bellairs. No, I fancy Rivera's business was confined to his purple satin parlour. At the smallest sign of our getting anywhere near him, he'd have burnt his books and, if necessary, returned to his native *hacienda* or what-have-you."

"Or got in first by laying information against the small man. That's the line they take as often as not."

"Yes, indeed. As often as not. What else have you got in your lucky dip, Br'er Fox?"

"Letters," said Fox. "A sealed package. And the cash."

"Anything that chimes in with his bookkeeping, I wonder?"

"Wait a bit, sir. I wouldn't be surprised. Wait a bit."

They hadn't long to wait. The too familiar raw material of the black-mailer's trade was soon laid out on Alleyn's desk: the dingy, colourless letters, paid for again and again yet never redeemed, the discoloured clippings from dead newspapers, one or two desperate appeals for mercy, the inexorable entries on the credit side. Alleyn's fingers seemed to tarnish as he handled them but Fox rubbed his hands.

"This is something like," Fox said, and after a minute or two: "Look at this, Mr. Alleyn."

It was a letter signed "Félicité" and was some four months old. Alleyn read it through and handed it back to Fox, who said: "It establishes the relationship."

"Apparently."

"Funny," said Fox. "You'd have thought from the look of him, even when he was dead, that any girl in her senses would have picked him for what he was. There are two other letters. Much the same kind of thing."

"Yes."

"Yes. Well now," said Fox slowly. "Leaving the young lady aside for the moment, where, if anywhere, does this get us with his lordship?"

"Not very far, I fancy. Unless you find something revealing a hitherto unsuspected irregularity in his lordship's past, and he doesn't strike me as one to hide his riotings."

"All the same, sir, there may be something. What about his lordship encouraging this affair with his stepdaughter? Doesn't that look as if Rivera had a hold on him?"

"It might," Alleyn agreed, "if his lordship was anybody but his lordship. But it might. So last night, having decided to liquidate Rivera, he types this letter purporting to come from G.P.F. with the idea of throwing the all-too-impressionable Miss de Suze in Edward Manx's arms!"

"There you are!"

"How does Lord Pastern know Manx is G.P.F.? And if Rivera used this G.P.F. copy to blackmail Manx it wasn't a very hot instrument for his purpose, being typed. Anybody at Duke's Gate might have typed it. He would have to find it on Manx and try a bluff. And he hadn't met Manx. All right. For purposes of your argument we needn't pursue that one at the moment. All right. It fits. In a way. Only . . . only . . . " He rubbed his nose. "I'm sorry, Fox, but I can't reconcile the flavour of Pastern and Manx with all this. A most untenable argument, I know. I won't try to justify it. What's in that box?"

Fox had already opened it and shoved it across the desk. "It'll be the stuff itself," he said. "A nice little haul, Gibson."

The box contained neat small packages, securely sealed, and, in a separate carton, a number of cigarettes.

"That'll be it," Alleyn agreed. "He wasn't the direct receiver, evidently. This will have come in by the usual damned labyrinth." He glanced up at Detective-Sergeant Scott, a young officer. "You haven't worked on any of these cases, I think, Scott. This is probably cocaine or heroin, and has no doubt travelled long distances in bogus false teeth, fat men's navels, dummy hearing aids, phony bayonet fitments for electric light bulbs and God knows what else. As Mr. Fox says, Gibson, it's a nice little haul. We'll leave Rivera for the moment, I think." He turned to Scott and Watson. "Let's hear how you got on with Breezy Bellairs."

Breezy, it appeared, lived in a furnished flat in Pikestaff Row, off Ebury Street. To this address Scott and Watson had conveyed him, and with some difficulty put him to bed. Once there, he had slept stertorously through the rest of the night. They had combed out the flat, which, unlike Rivera's, was slovenly and disordered. It looked, they said, as if Breezy had had a frantic search for something. The pockets of his suits had been pulled out, the drawers of his furniture disembowelled and the contents left where they lay. The only thing in the flat that was at all orderly was Breezy's pile of band parts. Scott and Watson had sorted out a bundle of correspondence consisting of bills, dunning reminders, and his fan mail, which turned out to be largish. At the back of a small bedside cupboard they had found a hypodermic syringe which they produced and a number of torn and empty packages which were of the same sort as those found in Rivera's safe. "Almost too easy," said Mr. Fox with the liveliest satisfaction. "We knew it already, of course, through Skelton, but here's positive proof Rivera supplied Bellairs with his dope. By Gum," he added deeply, "I'd like to get this line on the dope-racket followed in to one of the high-ups. Now, I wonder. Breezy'll be looking for his stuff and won't know where to find it. He'll be very upset. I ask myself if Breezy won't be in the mood to talk."

"You'd better remind yourself of your police code, old boy."

"It'll be the same story," Fox muttered. "Breezy won't know how Rivera got it. He won't know."

"He hasn't been long on the injection method," Alleyn said. "Curtis had a look for needle marks and didn't find so very many."

"He'll be fretting for it, though," said Fox, and after a moment's pondering, "Oh, well. It's a homicide we're after."

Nothing more of interest had been found in Breezy's flat and Alleyn turned to the last of the men. "How did you get on with Skelton, Sallis?"

"Well, sir," said Sallis, in a loud public-school voice, "he didn't like me much to begin with. I picked up a search-warrant on the way and he took a very poor view of that. However, we talked sociology for the rest of the journey and I offered to lend him *The Yogi and the Commissar*, which bent the barriers a little. He's Australian by birth, and I've been out there so that helped to establish a more matey attitude."

"Get on with your report now," Fox said austerely. "Don't meander. Mr. Alleyn isn't concerned to know how much Syd Skelton loves you."

"I'm sorry, sir."

"Use your notes and get on with it," Fox counselled.

Sallis opened his notebook and got on with it. Beyond a quantity of communistic literature there was little out of the ordinary to be found in Skelton's rooms, which were in the Pimlico Road. Alleyn gathered that Sallis had conducted his search during a lively exchange of ideas and could imagine Skelton's guarded response to Sallis's pinkish, facile and consciously ironical observations. Finally, Skelton, in spite of himself, had gone to sleep in his chair and Sallis then turned his attention stealthily to a table which was used as a desk.

"I'd noticed that he seemed rather uneasy about this table, sir. He stood by it when we first came in and shuffled the papers about. I had the feeling there was something there that he wanted to destroy. When he was safely off, I went through the stuff on the table and I found this. I don't know if it's much cop, really, sir, but here it is."

He gave a sheet of paper to Alleyn, who opened it up. It was an unfinished letter to Rivera, threatening him with exposure if he continued to supply Breezy Bellairs with drugs.

ii

The other men had gone and Alleyn invited Fox to embark upon what he was in the habit of calling "a hag." This involved the ruthless taking-to-pieces of the case and a fresh attempt to put the bits together in their true pattern. They had been engaged upon this business for about half an hour when the telephone rang. Fox answered it and announced with a tolerant smile that Mr. Nigel Bathgate would like to speak to Mr. Alleyn.

"I was expecting this," Alleyn said. "Tell him that for once in a blue moon I want to see him. Where is he?"

"Down below."

"Hail him up."

Fox said sedately: "The Chief would like to see you, Mr. Bathgate," and in a few moments Nigel Bathgate of the *Evening Chronicle* appeared, looking mildly astonished.

"I must say," he said, shaking hands, "that this is uncommonly civil of you, Alleyn. Have you run out of invectives or do you at last realize where the brains lie?"

"If you think I asked you up with the idea of feeding you with banner headlines you're woefully mistaken. Sit down."

"Willingly. How are you, Mr. Fox?"

"Nicely, thank you, sir. And you?"

Alleyn said: "Now, you attend to me. Can you tell me anything about a monthly called *Harmony?*"

"What sort of things? Have you been confiding in G.P.F., Alleyn?"

"I want to know who he is."

"Has this got anything to do with the Rivera case?"

"Yes, it has."

"I'll make a bargain with you. I want a nice meaty bit of stuff straight from the Yard's mouth. All about old Pastern and how you happened to be there and the shattered romance . . ."

"Who've you been talking to?"

"Charwomen, night porters, chaps in the band. And I ran into Ned Manx, a quarter of an hour ago."

"What had he got to say for himself?"

"He hung out on me, blast him. Wouldn't utter. And he's not on a daily, either. Unco-operative twerp."

"You might remember he's the chief suspect's cousin."

"Then there's no doubt about it being old Pastern?"

"I didn't say so and you won't suggest it."

"Well, hell, give me a story."

"About this paper. *Do* you know G.P.F.? Come on?"

Nigel lit a cigarette and settled down. "I don't know him," he said. "And I don't know anyone who does. He's a chap called G. P. Friend, I'm told, and he's supposed to own the show. If he does, he's on to a damn useful thing. It's a mystery, that paper. It breaks all the rules and rings the bell. It first came out about two years ago with a great fanfare of trumpets. They bought out the old *Triple Mirror*, you know, and took over the plant and the paper and in less than no time trebled the sales. God knows why. The thing's a freak. It mixes sound criticism with girly-girly chat and runs top-price serials alongside shorts that would bring a blush to the cheeks of *Peg's Weekly*. They tell me it's G.P.F.'s page that does the trick. And look at it! That particular racket blew out before the war and yet he gets by with it. I'm told the personal letters at five bob a time are a gold mine in themselves. He's said to have an uncanny knack of hitting on the things all these women want him to say. The types that write in are amazing. All the smarties. Nobody ever sees him. He doesn't get about with the boys and the chaps who free-lance for the rag never get past a sub who's always very bland and entirely uncommunicative. There you are. That's all I can tell you about G.P.F."

"Ever heard what he looks like?"

"No. There's a legend he wears old clothes and dark glasses. They say he's got a lock on his office door and never sees anybody on account he doesn't want to be recognized. It's all part of an act. Publicity. They play it up in the paper itself—'Nobody knows who G.P.F. is.'"

"What would you think if I told you he was Edward Manx?"

"Manx! You're not serious."

"Is it so incredible?"

Nigel raised his eyebrows. "On the face of it, yes. Manx is a reputable and very able specialist. He's done some pretty solid stuff. Leftish and fairly authoritative. He's a coming man. He'd turn sick in his stomach at the sight of G.P.F., I'd have thought."

"He does their dramatic reviews."

"Yes, I know, but that's where they're freakish. Manx has got a sort of damn-your-eyes view about theatre. It's one of his things. He wants state ownership and he'll scoop up any chance to plug it. And I imagine their anti-vice parties wouldn't be unpleasing to Manx. He wouldn't go much for the style, which is tough and coloured, but he'd like the policy. They give battle in a big way, you know. Names all over the place and a general invitation to come on and sue us for libel and see how you like it. Quite his cup of tea. Yes, I imagine *Harmony* runs Manx to give the paper *cachet* and Manx writes for *Harmony* to get at their public. They pay. Top prices."

Nigel paused and then said sharply: "But Manx as G.P.F.! That's different. Have you actually good reason to suspect it? Are you on to something?"

"The case is fluffy with doubts at the moment."

"The Rivera case? It ties up with that?"

"Off the record, it does."

"By God," said Nigel profoundly, "if Ned Manx spews up that page it explains the secrecy! By God, it does."

"We'll have to ask him," Alleyn said. "But I'd have liked to have a little more to go on. Still, we can muscle in. Where's the *Harmony* office?"

"Five Materfamilias Lane. The old *Triple Mirror* place."

"When does this blasted rag make its appearance? It's a monthly, isn't it?"

"Let's see. It's the twenty-seventh to-day. It comes out in the first week of the month. They'll be going to press any time now."

"So G.P.F.'s likely to be on tap at the office?"

"You'd think so. Are you going to burst in on Manx with a brace of manacles?"

"Never you mind."

"Come on," Nigel said. "What do I get for all this?"

Alleyn gave him a brief account of Rivera's death and a lively description of Lord Pastern's performance in the band.

"As far as it goes, it's good," Nigel said, "but I could get as much from the waiters."

"Not if Caesar Bonn knows anything about it."

"Are you going to pull old Pastern in?"

"Not just yet. You write your stuff and send it along to me."

"It's pretty!" Nigel said. "It's as pretty as paint. Pastern's good at any time but like this he's marvellous. May I use your typewriter?"

"For ten minutes."

Nigel retired with the machine to a table at the far end of the room. "I can say you were there, of course," he said hurriedly.

"I'll be damned if you can."

"Come, come, Alleyn, be big about this thing."

"I know you. If we don't ring the bell you'll print some revolting photograph of me looking like a half-wit. Caption: 'Chief Inspector who watched crime but doesn't know whodunit.'"

Nigel grinned. "And would that be a story, and won't that be the day!

Still, as it stands, it's pretty hot. Here we go, chaps." He began to rattle the keys.

Alleyn said: "There's one thing, Fox, that's sticking out of this mess like a road sign and I can't read it. Why did that perishing old mountebank look at the gun and then laugh himself sick? Here! Wait a moment. Who was in the study with him when he concocted his dummies and loaded his gun? It's a thin chance but it might yield something." He pulled the telephone towards him. "We'll talk once more to Miss Carlisle Wayne."

iii

Carlisle was in her room when the call came through and she took it there, sitting on her bed and staring aimlessly at a flower print on the wall. A hammer knocked at her ribs and her throat constricted. In some remote part of her mind she thought: "As if I was in love, instead of frightened sick."

The unusually deep and clear voice said: "Is that you, Miss Wayne? I'm sorry to bother you again so soon but I'd like to have another word with you."

"Yes," said Carlisle. "Would you? Yes."

"I can come to Duke's Gate or, if you would rather, can see you here at the Yard." Carlisle didn't answer at once and he said: "Which would suit you best?"

"I—I think—I'll come to your office."

"It might be easier. Thank you so much. Can you come at once?"

"Yes. Yes, I can, of course."

"Splendid." He gave her explicit instructions about which entrance to use and where to ask for him. "Is that clear? I shall see you in about twenty minutes then."

"In about twenty minutes," she repeated and her voice cracked into an absurd cheerful note as if she were gaily making a date with him. "Right-ho," she said and thought with horror: "But I never say 'right-ho.' He'll think I'm demented."

"Mr. Alleyn," she said loudly.

"Yes? Hullo?"

"I'm sorry I made such an ass of myself this morning. I don't know what happened. I seem to have gone extremely peculiar."

"Never mind," said the deep voice easily.

"Well—all right. Thank you. I'll come straight away."

He gave a small, polite, not unfriendly sound and she hung up the receiver.

"Booking a date with the attractive Inspector, darling?" said Félicité from the door.

At the first sound of her voice Carlisle's body had jerked and she had cried out sharply.

"You *are* jumpy," Félicité said, coming nearer.

"I didn't know you were there."

"Obviously."

Carlisle opened her wardrobe. "He wants to see me. Lord knows why."

"So you're popping off to the Yard. Exciting for you."

"Marvellous, isn't it," Carlisle said, trying to make her voice ironical. Félicité watched her change into a suit. "Your face wants a little attention," she said.

"I know." She went to the dressing-table. "Not that it matters."

When she looked in the glass she saw Félicité's face behind her shoulder. "Stupidly unfriendly," she thought, dabbing at her nose.

"You know, darling," Félicité said, "I'm drawn to the conclusion you're a dark horse."

"Oh Fée!" she said impatiently.

"Well, you appear to have done quite a little act with my late best young man, last night, and here you are having a sly assignation with the dynamic Inspector."

"He probably wants to know what kind of toothpaste we all use."

"Personally," said Félicité, "I always considered you were potty about Ned."

Carlisle's hand shook as she pressed powder into the tear stains under her eyes.

"You *are* in a state, aren't you," said Félicité.

Carlisle turned on her. "Fée, for pity's sake come off it. As if things weren't bad enough without your starting these monstrous hares. You *must* have seen that I couldn't endure your poor wretched incredibly phony young man. You *must* see that Mr. Alleyn's summons to Scotland Yard has merely frightened seven bells out of me. How you *can!*"

"What about Ned?"

Carlisle picked up her bag and gloves. "If Ned writes the monstrous bilge you've fallen for in *Harmony* I never want to speak to him again," she said violently. "For the love of Mike pipe down and let me go and be grilled."

But she was not to leave without further incident. On the first floor landing she encountered Miss Henderson. After her early morning scene with Alleyn on the stairs, Carlisle had returned to her room and remained there, fighting down the storm of illogical weeping that had so suddenly overtaken her. So she had not met Miss Henderson until now.

"Hendy!" she cried out. "What's the matter?"

"Good morning, Carlisle. The matter, dear?"

"I thought you looked—I'm sorry. I expect we all look a bit odd. Are you hunting for something?"

"I've dropped my little silver pencil somewhere. It can't be here," she said as Carlisle began vaguely to look. "Are you going out?"

"Mr. Alleyn wants me to call and see him."

"Why?" Miss Henderson asked sharply.

"I don't know. Hendy, isn't this awful, this business? And to make matters worse I've had a sort of row with Fée."

The light on the first landing was always rather strange, Carlisle told herself, a cold reflected light coming from a distant window making people look greenish. It must be that because Miss Henderson answered her quite tranquilly and with her usual lack of emphasis. "Why, of all mornings, did you two want to have a row?"

"I suppose we're both scratchy. I told her I thought the unfortunate Rivera was ghastly and she thinks I'm shaking my curls at Mr. Alleyn. It was too stupid for words."

"I should think so, indeed."

"I'd better go!"

Carlisle touched her lightly on the arm and crossed to the stairs. She hesitated there, without turning to face Miss Henderson, who had not moved. "What is it?" Miss Henderson said. "Have you forgotten something?"

"No. Hendy, you know, don't you, about the fantastic thing they say killed him? The piece of parasol with an embroidery stiletto in the end?"

"Yes."

"Do you remember—I know this is ridiculous—but do you remember, last night, when there was that devastating bang from the ballroom? Do you remember you and Aunt Cile and Fée and I were in the drawing-room and you were sorting Aunt Cile's work-box?"

"Was I?"

"Yes. And you jumped at the bang and dropped something?"

"Did I?"

"And Fée picked it up."

"Did she?"

"Hendy, was it an embroidery stiletto?"

"I remember nothing about it. Nothing at all."

"I didn't notice where she put it. I wondered if you had noticed."

"If it was something from the work-box, I expect she put it back. Won't you be late, Carlisle?"

"Yes," Carlisle said without turning. "Yes, I'll go."

She heard Miss Henderson walk away into the drawing-room. The door closed gently and Carlisle went downstairs. There was a man in a dark suit in the hall. He got up when he saw her and said: "Excuse me, miss, but are you Miss Wayne?"

"Yes, I am."

"Thank you, Miss Wayne."

He opened the glass doors for her and then the front door. Carlisle went quickly past him and out into the sunshine. She was quite unaware of the man who stepped out from the corner a little way down Duke's Gate and who, glancing impatiently at his watch, waited at the bus stop and journeyed with her to Scotland Yard. "Keep observation on the whole damn boiling," Alleyn had said irritably at six o'clock that morning. "We don't know *what* we want."

She followed a constable, who looked oddly domesticated without his helmet, down a linoleumed corridor to the Chief Inspector's room. She thought: "They invite people to come and make statements. It means something. Suppose they suspect me. Suppose they've found out some little thing that makes them think I've done it." Her imagination galloped wildly. Suppose, when she went into the room, Alleyn said: "I'm afraid this is serious. Carlisle Loveday Wayne, I arrest you for the murder of Carlos Rivera and I warn you . . ." They would telephone for any clothes she wanted. Hendy, perhaps, would pack a suitcase. Perhaps, secretly, they would all be a little lightened, almost pleasurably worried, because they would no longer be in fear for themselves. Perhaps Ned would come to see her.

"In here, if you please, miss," the constable was saying with his hand on the door-knob.

Alleyn rose quickly from his desk and came towards her. "Punctilious," she thought. "He's got nice manners. Are his manners like this when he's going to arrest people?"

"I'm so sorry," he was saying. "This must be a nuisance for you."

The solid grizzled detective was behind him. Fox. That was Inspector Fox. He had pulled up a chair for her and she sat in it, facing Alleyn. "With the light on my face," she thought, "that's what they do."

Fox moved away and sat behind a second desk. She could see his head and shoulders but his hands were hidden from her.

"You'll think my object in asking you to come very aimless, I expect," Alleyn said, "and my first question will no doubt strike you as being completely potty. However, here it is. You told us last night that you were with Lord Pastern when he made the dummies and loaded the revolver."

"Yes."

"Well, now, did anything happen, particularly in respect of the revolver, that struck you both as being at all comic?"

Carlisle gaped at him. "Comic!"

"I told you it was a potty question," he said.

"If you mean did we take one look at the revolver and then shake with uncontrollable laughter, we didn't."

"No," he said. "I was afraid not."

"The mood was sentimental if anything. The revolver was one of a pair given to Uncle George by my father and he told me so."

"You were familiar with it then?"

"Not in the least. My father died ten years ago and when he lived was not in the habit of showing me his armoury. He and Uncle George were both crack shots, I believe. Uncle George told me my father had the revolvers made for target shooting."

"You looked at the gun last night? Closely?"

"Yes—because—" Beset by nervous and unreasoned caution, she hesitated.

"Because?"

"My father's initials are scratched on it. Uncle George told me to look for them."

There was a long pause. "Yes, I see," Alleyn said.

She found she had twisted her gloves tightly together and doubled them over. She felt a kind of impatience with herself and abruptly smoothed them out.

"It was one of a pair," Alleyn said. "Did you look at both of them?"

"No. The other was in a case in the drawer on his desk. I just saw it there. I noticed it because the drawer was under my nose, almost, and Uncle George kept putting the extra dummies, if that's what you call them, into it."

"Ah, yes. I saw them there."

"He made a lot more than he wanted in case," her voice faltered, "in case he was asked to do his turn again sometime."

"I see."

"Is that all?" she said.

"As you've been kind enough to come," Alleyn said with a smile, "perhaps we should think up something more."

"You needn't bother, thank you."

He smiled more broadly. "Fée was doing her stuff for him on the stairs this morning," Carlisle thought. "Was she actually showing the go-ahead signal or was she merely trying to stall him off?"

"It's about the steel end in this eccentric weapon. The bolt or dart," Alleyn said, and her attention snapped taut again. "We are almost certain that it's the business end of an embroidery stiletto from the work-box in the drawing-room. We found the discarded handle. I wonder if by any chance you remember when you last noticed the stiletto. If, of course, you happen to have noticed it."

"So this is it," she thought. "The revolver was nothing, it was a red herring. He's really got me here to talk about the stiletto."

She said: "I don't think the work-box was open when I was in the drawing-room before dinner. At any rate I didn't notice it."

"I remember you told me that Lady Pastern showed you and Manx her petit point. That *was* when you were all in the drawing-room before dinner, wasn't it? We found the petit point, by the way, beside the work-box."

"Therefore," she thought, "Aunt Cile or Ned or I might have taken the stiletto." She repeated: "I'm sure the box wasn't open."

She had tried not to think beyond that one time, that one safe time about which she could quickly speak the truth.

"And after dinner?" Alleyn said casually.

She saw again the small gleaming tool drop from Miss Henderson's fingers when the report sounded in the ballroom. She saw Félicité automatically stoop and pick it up and a second later burst into tears and run furiously from the room. She heard her loud voice on the landing: "I've got to speak to you," and Rivera's: "But certainly, if you wish it."

"After dinner?" she repeated flatly.

"You were in the drawing-room then. Before the men came in. Perhaps

Lady Pastern took up her work. Did you, at any time, see the box open or notice the stiletto?"

How quick was thought? As quick as people said? Was her hesitation fatally long? Here she moved, on the brink of speech. She could hear the irrevocable denial, and yet she had not made it. And suppose he had already spoken to Félicité about the stiletto? "What am I looking like?" she thought in a panic. "I'm looking like a liar already."

"Can you remember?" he asked. So she had waited too long.

"I—don't think I can." Now, she had said it. Somehow it wasn't quite as shaming to lie about remembering as about the fact itself. If things went wrong she could say afterwards: "Yes, I remember, now, but I had forgotten. It had no significance for me at the time."

"You don't *think* you can." She had nothing to say but he went on almost at once: "Miss Wayne, will you please try to look squarely at this business. Will you try to pretend that it's an affair that you have read about and in which you have no personal concern. Not easy. But try. Suppose, then, a group of complete strangers was concerned in Rivera's death and suppose one of them, not knowing much about it, unable to see the factual wood for the emotional trees, was asked a question to which she knew the answer. Perhaps the answer seems to implicate her. Perhaps it seems to implicate someone she is fond of. She doesn't in the least know, it may be, what the implications are but she refuses to take the responsibility of telling the truth about one detail that may fit in with the whole truth. She won't, in fact, speak the truth if by doing so she's remotely responsible for bringing an extraordinarily callous murderer to book. So she lies. At once she finds that it doesn't end there. She must get other people to tell corroborative lies. She finds herself, in effect, whizzing down a dangerous slope with her car out of control, steering round some obstacles, crashing into others, doing irreparable damage and landing herself and possibly other innocent people in disaster. You think I'm overstating her case perhaps. Believe me, I've seen it happen very often."

"Why do you say all this to me?"

"I'll tell you why. You said just now that you didn't remember noticing the stiletto at any time after dinner. Before you made this statement you hesitated. Your hands closed on your gloves and suddenly twisted them. Your hands behaved with violence and yet they trembled. After you had spoken they continued to have a sort of independent life of their own. Your left hand kneaded the gloves and your right hand moved rather aimlessly across your neck and over your face. You blushed deeply and stared very fixedly at the top of my head. You presented me, in fact, with Example A from any handbook on behaviour of the lying witness. You were a glowing demonstration of the bad liar. And now, if all this is nonsense, you can tell counsel for the defence how I bullied you and he will treat me to as nasty a time as his talents suggest when I'm called to give evidence. Now I come to think of it, he'll be very unpleasant indeed. So, however, will prosecuting counsel if you stick to your lapse of memory."

Carlisle said angrily: "My hands feel like feet. I'm going to sit on them. You don't play fair."

"My God," Alleyn said, "this isn't a game! It's murder."

"He was atrocious. He was much nastier than anyone else in the house."

"He may have been the nastiest job of work in Christendom. He was murdered and you're dealing with the police. This is not a threat but it's a warning. We've only just started—a great deal more evidence may come our way. You were not alone in the drawing-room after dinner."

She thought: "But Hendy won't tell and neither will Aunt Cile." But William came in sometime, about then. Suppose he saw Fée on the landing? Suppose he noticed the stiletto in her hand? And then she remembered the next time she had seen Félicité. Félicité had been on the top of the world, in ecstasy because of the letter from G.P.F. She had changed into her most gala dress and her eyes were shining. She had already discarded Rivera as easily as she had discarded all her previous young men. It was fantastic to tell lies for Félicité. There was something futile about this scene with Alleyn. She had made a fool of herself for nothing.

He had taken an envelope from a drawer of his desk and now opened it and shook its contents out before her. She saw a small shining object with a sharp end.

"Do you recognize it?" he asked.

"The stiletto."

"You say that because we've been talking about the stiletto. It's not a bit like it really. Look again."

She leant over it. "Why," she said, "it's a—a pencil."

"Do you know whose pencil?"

She hesitated. "I think it's Hendy's. She wears it on a chain like an old-fashioned charm. She always wears it. She was hunting for it on the landing this morning."

"This is it. Here are her initials. P.X.H. Very tiny. You almost need a magnifying glass. Like the initials you saw on the revolver. The ring at the end was probably softish silver and the gap in it may have opened with the weight of the pencil. I found the pencil in the work-box. Does Miss Henderson ever use Lady Pastern's work-box?"

This at least was plain sailing. "Yes. She tidies it very often for Aunt Cile." And immediately Carlisle thought: "I'm no good at this. Here it comes again."

"Was she tidying the box last night? After dinner?"

"Yes," Carlisle said flatly. "Oh, yes. Yes."

"Did you notice, particularly? When exactly was it?"

"Before the men came in. Well, only Ned came in actually. Uncle George and the other two were in the ballroom."

"Lord Pastern and Bellairs were at this time in the ballroom, and Rivera and Manx in the dining-room. According to the time-table." He opened a file on his desk.

"I only know that Fée had gone when Ned came in."

"She had joined Rivera in the study by then. But to return to this incident in the drawing-room. Can you describe the scene with the work-box? What were you talking about?"

Félicité had been defending Rivera. She had been on edge, in one of her moods. Carlisle had thought: "She's *had* Rivera but she won't own up." And Hendy, listening, had moved her fingers about inside the work-box. There was the stiletto in Hendy's fingers and, dangling from her neck, the pencil on its chain.

"They were talking about Rivera. Félicité considered he'd been snubbed a bit and was cross about it."

"At about this time Lord Pastern must have fired off his gun in the ball-room," Alleyn muttered. He had spread the time-table out on his desk. He glanced up at her. His glance, she noticed, was never vague or indirect, as other people's might be. It had the effect of immediately collecting your attention. "Do you remember that?" he said.

"Oh, yes."

"It must have startled you, surely?"

What were her hands doing now? She was holding the side of her neck again.

"How did you all react to what must have been an infernal racket? What for instance did Miss Henderson do? Do you remember?"

Her lips parted dryly. She closed them again, pressing them together.

"I think you do remember," he said. "What did she do?"

Carlisle said loudly, "She let the lid of the box drop. Perhaps the pencil was caught and pulled off the chain."

"Was anything in her hands?"

"The stiletto," she said, feeling the words grind out.

"Good. And then?"

"She dropped it."

Perhaps that would satisfy him. It fell to the carpet. Anyone might have picked it up. Anyone, she thought desperately. Perhaps he will think a serv-ant might have picked it up. Or even Breezy Bellairs, much later.

"Did Miss Henderson pick it up?"

"No."

"Did anyone?"

She said nothing.

"You? Lady Pastern? No. Miss de Suze?"

She said nothing.

"And a little while afterwards, a very little while, she went out of the room. Because it was immediately after the report that William saw her go into the study with Rivera. He noticed that she had something shiny in her hand."

"She didn't even know she had it. She picked it up automatically. I expect she just put it down in the study and forgot all about it."

"We found the ivory handle there," Alleyn said, and Fox made a slight gratified sound in his throat.

"But you mustn't think there was any significance in all this."

"We're glad to know how and when the stiletto got into the study, at least."

"Yes," she said, "I suppose so. Yes."

Someone tapped on the door. The bare-headed constable came in with a package and an envelope. He laid them on the desk. "From Captain Entwhistle, sir. You asked to have them as soon as they came in."

He went out without looking at Carlisle.

"Oh, yes," Alleyn said. "The report on the revolver, Fox. Good. Miss Wayne, before you go, I'll ask you to have a look at the revolver. It'll be one more identification check."

She waited while Inspector Fox came out from behind his desk and unwrapped the parcel. It contained two separate packages. She knew the smaller one must be the dart and wondered if Rivera's blood was still encrusted on the stiletto. Fox opened the larger package and came to her with the revolver.

"Will you look at it?" Alleyn said. "You may handle it. I would like your formal identification."

Carlisle turned the heavy revolver in her hands. There was a strong light in the room. She bent her head and they waited. She looked up, bewildered. Alleyn gave her his pocket lens. There was a long silence.

"Well, Miss Wayne?"

"But . . . But it's extraordinary. I can't identify it. There are no initials. This isn't the same revolver."

CHAPTER X

The Stiletto,
the Revolver
and His Lordship

"And what," Alleyn asked when Carlisle had left them, "is the betting on the favourite now, Br'er Fox?"

"By Gum," Fox said, "you always tell us that when a homicide case is full of fancy touches it's not going to give much trouble. Do you stick to that, sir?"

"I'll be surprised if this turns out to be the exception but I must say it looks like it at the moment. However, the latest development does at least cast another ray of light on your playmate. Do you remember how the old devil turned the gun over when we first let him see it at the Metronome? D'you remember how he took another look at it in the study and then had an attack of the dry grins and when I asked him what he expected to see had the infernal nerve to come back at me with: 'Hoity-toity'—yes, 'Hoity-toity—wouldn't you like to know?' "

"Ugh!"

"He'd realized all along, of course, that this wasn't the weapon he loaded in the study and took down to the Metronome. Yes," Alleyn added as Fox opened his mouth, "and don't forget he showed Skelton the gun a few minutes before it was fired. Miss Wayne says he pointed out the initials to Skelton."

"*That* looks suspicious in itself," Fox said instantly. "Why go to the trouble of pointing out initials to two people? He was getting something fixed up for himself. So's he could turn round and say: 'That's not the gun I fired.' "

"Then why didn't he say so at once?"

"Gawd knows."

"If you ask me he was sitting pretty, watching us make fools of ourselves."

Fox jabbed his finger at the revolver. "If this isn't the original weapon," he demanded, "what the hell is it? It's the one this projectile-dart-bolt or what-have-you was fired from because it's got the scratches in the barrel. That means someone had this second gun all ready loaded with the dart and ammunition and substituted it for the original weapon. Here! What's the report say, Mr. Alleyn?"

Alleyn was reading the report. "Entwhistle," he said, "has had a ballistic orgy over the thing. The scratches could have been made by the brilliants in the parasol clip. In his opinion they were so made. He's sending photomicrographs to prove it. He's fired the bolt—let's stick to calling this hybrid a bolt, shall we?—from another gun with an identical bore and it is 'somewhat similarly scratched,' which is a vile phrase. He pointed out that wavering, irregular scars were made when the bolt was shoved up the barrel. The spring clip was pressed back with the thumb while it was being inserted and then sprang out once it was inside the barrel, thus preventing the bolt from falling out if the weapon was pointed downwards. The bolt was turned slightly as it was shoved home. The second scar was made by the ejection of the bolt, the clip retaining its pressure while being expelled. He says that the scars in the revolver we submitted don't extend quite as deep up the barrel as those made by the bolt which he fired from his own gun, but he considers that they were made by the same kind of procedure and the same bolt. At a distance of four feet, the projectile shoots true. Over long distances there are 'progressive divergences' caused by the weight of the clip on one side or by air resistance. Entwhistle says he's very puzzled by the fouling from the bore which is quite unlike anything in his experience. He removed it and sent it along for analysis. The analyst finds that the fouling consists of particles of carbon and of various hydrocarbons including members of the paraffin series, apparently condensed from vapour."

"Funny."

"That's all."

"All right," Fox said heavily. "All right. That looks fair enough. The bolt that plugged Rivera *was* shot out of this weapon. This weapon is not the one his lordship showed Miss Wayne and Syd Skelton. But unless you entertain the idea of somebody shooting off another gun at the same instant, this is the one that killed Rivera. You accept that, sir?"

"I'll take it as a working premise. With reservations and remembering our conversation in the car."

"All right. Well, after Skelton examined the gun with the initials, did his lordship get a chance to substitute this one and fire it off? Could he have had this one on him all the time?"

"Hob-nobbing, cheek by jowl, with a dozen or so people at close quarters? I should say definitely not. And, he didn't know Skelton would ask to see the gun. And what did he do with the first gun afterwards? We searched him, remember."

"Planted it? Anyway, where is it?"

"Somewhere at the Metronome if we're on the right track and we've searched the Metronome. But go on."

"Well, sir, if his lordship didn't change the gun who did?"

"His stepdaughter could have done it. Or any other member of his party. They were close to the sombrero, remember. They got up to dance and moved round between the table and the edge of the dais. Lady Pastern was alone at the table for some time. I didn't see her move but I wasn't watching her, of course. All the ladies had largish evening bags. The catch in that theory, Br'er Fox, is that they wouldn't have known they were going to be within reach of the sombrero and it's odds on they didn't know he was going to put his perishing gun under his sombrero, anyway."

Fox bit at his short grizzled moustache, planted the palms of his hands on his knees and appeared to go into a short trance. He interrupted it to mutter: "Skelton, now. Syd Skelton. Could Syd Skelton have worked the substitution? You're going to remind me they were all watching him, but were they watching all that closely? Syd Skelton."

"Go on, Fox."

"Syd Skelton's on his own, in a manner of speaking. He left the band platform before his lordship came on for his turn. Syd walked out. Suppose he had substituted this gun for the other with the initials. Suppose he walked right out and dropped the other one down the first grating he came to? Syd knew he was going to get the chance, didn't he?"

"How, when and where did he convert the bit of parasol shaft and stiletto into the bolt and put it up the barrel of the second revolver? Where did he get his ammunition? And when did he get the gun? *He* wasn't at Duke's Gate."

"Yes," Fox said heavily, "that's awkward. I wonder if you could get round that one. Well, leave it for the time being. Who else have we got? Breezy. From the substitution angle, can we do anything about Breezy?"

"He didn't get alongside Pastern, on either of their statements, from the time Skelton looked at the gun until after Rivera was killed. They were alone together in the band-room before Breezy made his entrance but Pastern, with his usual passionate industry in clearing other people, says Breezy didn't go near him. And Pastern had his gun in his hip pocket, remember."

Fox returned to his trance.

"I think," Alleyn said, "it's going to be one of those affairs where the whittling away of impossibilities leaves one face to face with a mere improbability which, as you would say, *faute de mieux*, one is forced to accept. And I think, so far, Fox, we haven't found my improbable notion an impossibility. At least it has the virtue of putting the fancy touches in a more credible light."

"We'll never make a case of it, I reckon, if it does turn out to be the answer."

"And we'll never make a case of it if we pull in his lordship and base the charge on the assumption that he substituted this gun for the one he loaded and says he fired. Skelton's put up by the defence and swears he examined the thing at his own request and saw the initials and that this is not the same weapon. Counsel points out that three minutes later Lord Pastern goes on for his turn."

Fox snarled quietly to himself and presently broke out: "We call this blasted thing a bolt. Be damned if I don't think we'll get round to calling it a dart. Be damned if I'm not beginning to wonder if it was used like one. Thrown at the chap from close by. After all it's not impossible."

"Who by? Breezy?"

"No," Fox said slowly. "No. Not Breezy. His lordship cleared Breezy in advance by searching him. Would you swear Breezy didn't pick anything up from anywhere after he came out to conduct?"

"I believe I would. He walked rapidly through the open door and down an alleyway between the musicians. He stood in a spot light a good six feet or more away from anything, conducting like a great jerking jelly-fish. They all say he couldn't have picked anything up after Pastern searched him, and in any case I would certainly swear he didn't put his hands near his pockets and that up to the time Rivera fell he was conducting with both hands and that none of his extraordinary antics in the least resembled dart-throwing. I was watching him. They rather fascinated me, those antics. And if you want any more, Br'er Fox, Rivera had his back turned to Breezy when he fell."

"All right. His lordship then. His lordship was facing Rivera. Close to him. *Blast*. Unless he's ambidextrous, how'd he fire off a gun and throw a dart all in a split second? This is getting me nowhere. Who else, then?"

"Do you fancy Lady Pastern as a dart queen?"

Fox chuckled. "That *would* be the day, sir, wouldn't it? But how about

Mr. Manx? We've got a motive for Manx. Rivera had proof that Manx wrote these sissy articles in *Harmony*. Manx doesn't want that known. Blackmail," said Fox without much conviction.

"Foxkin," Alleyn said, "let there be a truce to these barren speculations. May I remind you that up to the time he fell Rivera was raising hell with a piano-accordion?"

Fox said, after another long pause: "You know I like this case. It's got something. Yes. And may I remind *you*, sir, that he wasn't meant to fall? None of them expected him to fall. Therefore he fell because somebody planted a bloody little steel embroidery gadget on a parasol handle in his heart before he fell. So where, if you don't object to the inquiry, Mr. Alleyn, do we go from here?"

"I think," Alleyn said, "that you institute a search for the missing gun and I pay a call on Miss Petronella Xantippe Henderson." He got up and fetched his hat. "And I think, moreover," he added, "that we've been making a couple of perishing fools of ourselves."

"About the dart?" Fox demanded. "Or the gun?"

"About *Harmony*. Think this one over while I call on Miss Henderson and then tell me what you make of it."

Five minutes later he went out, leaving Fox in a concentrated trance.

ii

Miss Henderson received him in her room. It had the curiously separate, not quite congenial air that seems to be the characteristic of sitting-rooms that are permanently occupied by solitary women in other people's houses. There were photographs: of Félicité, as a child, as a schoolgirl and in her presentation dress; one intimidating portrait of Lady Pastern and one, enlarged, it would seem, from a snapshot, of Lord Pastern in knickerbockers and shooting boots, with a gun under his arm, a spaniel at his heels, a large house at his back and an expression of impertinence on his face. Above the desk hung a group of women undergraduates clad in the tube-like brevity of the nineteen-twenties. A portion of Lady Margaret Hall loomed in the background.

Miss Henderson was dressed with scrupulous neatness, in a dark suit that faintly resembled a uniform or habit. She received Alleyn with perfect composure. He looked at her hair, greyish, quietly fashionable in its controlled grooming, at her eyes, which were pale, and at her mouth, which was unexpectedly full.

"Well, Miss Henderson," he said, "I wonder if you will be able to throw any light on this very obscure business."

"I'm afraid it's most unlikely," she said tranquilly.

"You never know. There's one point, at least, where I hope you will help us. You were present at last night's party in this house, both before and after dinner, and you were in the drawing-room when Lord Pastern, with the help of all the people concerned, worked out and wrote down the time-table which he afterwards gave to me."

"Yes," she agreed after he had waited for a second or two.

"Would you say that as far as your personal observations and recollections cover them, the movements set down in the time-table are accurate?"

"Oh yes," she said at once, "I think so. But of course they don't go very far —my recollections. I was the last to arrive in the drawing-room, you know, before dinner and the first to leave after dinner."

"Not quite the first, according to the time-table, surely?"

She drew her brows together as if perturbed at the suggestion of inaccuracy. "Not?" she said.

"The time-table puts Miss de Suze's exit from the drawing-room a second or two before yours."

"How stupid of me. Félicité did go out first but I followed almost at once. I forgot for the moment."

"You were all agreed on this point last night, when Lord Pastern compiled his time-table?"

"Yes. Perfectly."

"Do you remember that just before this there was a great rumpus in the ballroom? It startled you and you dropped a little stiletto on the carpet. You were tidying Lady Pastern's work-box at the time. Do you remember?"

He had thought at first that she used no more make-up than a little powder but he saw now that the faint warmth of her cheeks was artificial. The colour became isolated as the skin beneath and about it bleached. Her voice was quite even and clear.

"It was certainly rather an alarming noise," she said.

"Do you remember, too, that Miss de Suze picked up the stiletto? I expect she meant to return it to you or to the box but she was rather put out just then. She was annoyed, wasn't she, by the, as she considered, uncordial reception given to her fiancé?"

"He was not her fiancé. They were not engaged."

"Not officially, I know."

"Not officially. There was no engagement."

"I see. In any case, do you remember that instead of replacing the stiletto, she still had it in her hand when, a moment later, she left the room?"

"I'm afraid I didn't notice."

"What did you do?"

"Do?"

"At that moment. You had been tidying the box. It was exquisitely neat when we found it this morning. Was it on your knees? The table was a little too far from your chair for you to have used it, I think."

"Then," she said, with her first hint of impatience, "the box was on my knees."

"So that was how the miniature silver pencil you wear on a chain came to be in the box?"

Her hands went to the bosom of her suit, fingering it. "Yes. I suppose so. Yes. I didn't realize . . . Was that where it was?"

"Perhaps you dropped the lid and caught the pencil, dragging it off the chain."

"Yes," she repeated. "Yes. I suppose so. Yes, I remember I did do that."

"Then why did you hunt for it this morning on the landing?"

"I had forgotten about catching it in the box," she said rapidly.

"Not," Alleyn murmured apologetically, "a frightfully good memory."

"These are trivial things that you ask me to remember. In this house we are none of us, at the moment, concerned with trivial things."

"Are you not? Then, I suggest that you searched the landing, not for your trinket, which you say was a trivial thing, but for something that you knew could not be in the work-box because you had seen Miss de Suze take it out with her when she left the drawing-room in a rage. The needlework stiletto."

"But, Inspector Alleyn, I told you I didn't notice anything of the sort."

"Then what were you looking for?"

"You have apparently been told. My pencil."

"A trivial thing but your own? Here it is."

He opened his hand, showing her the pencil. She made no movement and he dropped it in her lap. "You don't seem to me," he remarked casually, "to be an unobservant woman."

"If that's a compliment," she said, "thank you."

"Did you see Miss de Suze again, after she left the drawing-room with the stiletto in her hand and after she had quarrelled with Rivera when they were alone together in the study?"

"Why do you say they quarrelled?"

"I have it on pretty good authority."

"Carlisle?" she said sharply.

"No. But if you cross-examine a policeman about this sort of job, you know, he's not likely to be very communicative."

"One of the servants, I suppose," she said, dismissing it and him without emphasis. He asked her again if she had seen Félicité later that evening and after watching him for a moment she said that she had. Félicité had come to this room and had been in the happiest possible mood. "Excited?" he suggested and she replied that Félicité had been pleasurably excited. She was glad to be going out with her cousin, Edward Manx, to whom she was attached and was looking forward to the performance at the Metronome.

"After this encounter you went to Lady Pastern's room, didn't you? Lady Pastern's maid was with her. She was dismissed, but not before she had heard you say that Miss de Suze was very much excited and that you wanted to have a word with her mother about this."

"Again, the servants."

"Anybody," Alleyn said, "who is prepared to speak the truth. A man has been murdered."

"I have spoken nothing but the truth." Her lips trembled and she pressed them together.

"Good. Let's go on with it then, shall we?"

"There's nothing at all that I can tell you. Nothing at all."

"But at least you can tell me about the family. You understand, don't you, that my job, at the moment, is not so much finding the guilty person as clearing persons who may have been associated with Rivera but are innocent of his murder. That may, indeed it does, take in certain members of the household, the detailed as well as the general set-up. Now, in your position . . ."

"My position!" she muttered, with a sort of repressed contempt. Almost inaudibly she added: "What do you know of my position!"

Alleyn said pleasantly: "I've heard you're called the Controller of the Household." She didn't answer and he went on: "In any case it has been a long association and I suppose, in many ways, an intimate one. With Miss de Suze, for instance. You have brought her up, really, haven't you?"

"Why do you keep speaking about Félicité? This has nothing to do with Félicité." She got up, and stood with her back towards him, changing the position of an ornament on the mantelpiece. He could see her carefully kept and very white hand steady itself on the edge of the shelf. "I'm afraid I'm not behaving very well, am I?" she murmured. "But I find your insistence rather trying."

"Is that because, at the moment, it's directed at Miss de Suze and the stiletto?"

"Naturally, I'm uneasy. It's disturbing to feel that she will be in the smallest degree involved." She leant her head against her hand. From where he stood, behind her, she looked like a woman who had come to rest for a moment and fallen into an idle speculation. Her voice came to him remotely from beyond her stooped shoulders as if her mouth were against her hand. "I suppose she simply left it in the study. She didn't even realize she had it in her hand. It was not in her hand when she came upstairs. It had no importance for her at all." She turned and faced him. "I shall tell you something," she said. "I don't want to. I'd made up my mind I'd have no hand in this. It's distasteful to me. But I see now that I must tell you."

"Right."

"It's this. Before dinner last night and during dinner, I had opportunity to watch those—those two men."

"Rivera and Bellairs?"

"Yes. They were extraordinary creatures and I suppose in a sort of way I was interested."

"Naturally. In Rivera at all events."

"I don't know what servants' gossip you have been listening to, Inspector Alleyn."

"Miss Henderson, I've heard enough from Miss de Suze herself to tell me that there was an understanding between them."

"I watched those two men," she said exactly as if he hadn't spoken. "And I saw at once there was bad blood between them. They looked at each other —I can't describe it—with enmity. They were both, of course, incredibly common and blatant. They scarcely spoke to each other but during dinner, over and over again, I saw the other one, the conductor, eyeing him. He talked a great deal to Félicité and to Lord Pastern but he listened to . . ."

"To Rivera?" Alleyn prompted. She seemed to be incapable of pronouncing his name.

"Yes. He listened to him as if he resented every word he spoke. That would have been natural enough from any of us."

"Was Rivera so offensive?"

An expression of eagerness appeared on her face. Here was something, at last, about which she was ready to speak.

"Offensive?" she said. "He was beyond everything. He sat next to Carlisle and even she was nonplussed. Evidently she attracted him. It was perfectly revolting."

Alleyn thought distastefully: "Now what's behind all this? Resentment? At Carlisle rather than Félicité attracting the atrocious Rivera? Or righteous indignation? Or what?"

She had raised her head. Her arm still rested on the mantelpiece and she had stretched out her hand to a framed photograph of Félicité in presentation dress. He moved slightly and saw that her eyes were fixed on the photograph. Félicité's eyes, under her triple plumage, stared back with the glazed distaste (so suggestive of the unwitting influence of Mr. John Gielgud) that characterizes the modish photograph. Miss Henderson began to speak again and it was as if she addressed herself to the photograph. "Of course, Félicité didn't mind in the least. It was nothing to her. A relief, no doubt. Anything rather than suffer his odious attentions. But it was clear to me that the other creature and he had quarrelled. It was quite obvious."

"But if they hardly spoke to each other how could . . . ?"

"I've told you. It was the way the other person, Bellairs, looked at him. He watched him perpetually."

Alleyn now stood before her. They made a formal conversation piece with the length of the mantelpiece between them. He said: "Miss Henderson, who was beside you at the dinner table?"

"I sat next to Lord Pastern. On his left."

"And on your left?"

She made a fastidious movement with her shoulders. "Mr. Bellairs."

"Do you remember what he talked to you about?"

Her mouth twisted. "I don't remember that he spoke to me at all," she said. "He had evidently realized that I was a person of no importance. He devoted himself to Félicité, who was on his other side. He gave me his shoulder."

Her voice faded out almost before she had uttered the last word as if, too late, she had tried to stop herself.

"If he gave you his shoulder," Alleyn said, "how did it come about that you could see this inimical fixed stare of his?"

The photograph of Félicité crashed on the hearth. Miss Henderson cried out and knelt. "How clumsy of me," she whispered.

"Let me do it. You may cut your fingers."

"No," she said sharply, "don't touch it."

She began to pick the slivers of glass from the frame and drop them in the grate. "There's a looking-glass on the wall of the dining-room," she said. "I could see him in that." And in a flat voice that had lost all its urgency she repeated: "He watched him perpetually."

"Yes," Alleyn said, "I remember the looking-glass. I accept that."

"Thank you," she said ironically.

"One more question. Did you go into the ballroom at any time after dinner?"

She looked up at him warily and after a moment said: "I believe I did. Yes. I did."

"When?"

"Félicité had lost her cigarette case. It was when they were changing and she called out from her room. She had been in the ballroom during the afternoon and thought she might have left it there."

"Had she done so?"

"Yes. It was on the piano. Under some music."

"What else was on the piano?"

"A bundle of parasols."

"Anything else?"

"No," she said. "Nothing."

"Or on the chairs or floor?"

"Nothing."

"Are you sure?"

"Perfectly sure," she said and dropped a piece of glass with a little tinkle in the grate.

"Well," Alleyn said, "if I can't help you, perhaps I'd better take myself off."

She seemed to examine the photograph. She peered at it as if to make certain there were no flaws or scratches on Félicité's image. "Very well," she said and stood up, holding the face of the photograph against her flattish chest. "I'm sorry if I haven't told you the kind of things you want to be told. The truth is so seldom what one really wants to hear, is it? But perhaps you don't think I have told you the truth."

"I think I am nearer to it than I was before I visited you."

He left her, with the broken photograph still pressed against the bosom of her dark suit. On the landing he encountered Hortense. Her ladyship, Hortense said, smiling knowledgeably at him, would be glad to see him before he left. She was in her boudoir.

It was a small, delicately appointed room on the same floor. Lady Pastern rose from her desk, a pretty Empire affair, as he came in. She was firmly encased in her morning dress. Her hair was rigid, her hands ringed. A thin film of make-up had been carefully spread over the folds and shadows of her face. She looked ghastly but completely in order.

"It is so good of you to spare me a moment," she said and held out her hand. This was unexpected. Evidently she considered that her change of manner required an explanation and, without wasting time, she let him have it.

"I did not realize last night," she said concisely, "that you must be the younger son of an old friend of my father's. You are Sir George Alleyn's son, are you not?"

Alleyn bowed. This, he thought, is going to be tiresome.

"Your father," she said, "was a frequent visitor at my parents' house in the Faubourg St.-Germain. He was, in those days, an attaché, I think, at your embassy in Paris." Her voice faded and an extraordinary look came over her face. He was unable to interpret it.

"What is it, Lady Pastern?" he asked.

"Nothing. I was reminded, for a moment, of a former conversation. We were speaking of your father. I remember that he and your mother called upon one occasion, bringing their two boys with them. Perhaps you do not recollect the visit."

"It is extremely kind of you to do so."

"I had understood that you were to be entered in the British Diplomatic Service."

"I was entirely unsuited for it, I'm afraid."

"Of course," she said with a sort of creaking graciousness, "young men after the first war began to find their vocation in unconventional fields. One understands and accepts these changes, doesn't one?"

"Since I am here as a policeman," Alleyn said politely, "I hope so."

Lady Pastern examined him with that complete lack of reticence which is often the characteristic of royal personages. It occurred to him that she herself would also have shaped up well, in an intimidating way, as a policewoman.

"It is a relief to me," she announced, after a pause, "that we are in your hands. You will appreciate my difficulties. It will make an enormous difference."

Alleyn was familiar enough with this point of view, and detested it. He thought it advisable, however, to say nothing. Lady Pastern, erecting her bust and settling her shoulders, continued:

"I need not remind you of my husband's eccentricities. They are public property. You have seen for yourself to what lengths of imbecility he will go.

I can only assure you that though he may be, and indeed is, criminally stupid, he is perfectly incapable of crime as the word is understood in the profession you have elected to follow. He is not, in a word, a potential murderer. Or," she added, apparently as an afterthought, "an actual one. Of that you may be assured." She looked affably at Alleyn. Evidently, he thought, she had been a dark woman. There was a tinge of sable in her hair. Her skin was sallow and he thought she probably used something to deal with a darkness of the upper lip. It was odd that she should have such pale eyes. "I cannot blame you," she said, as he was still silent, "if you suspect my husband. He has done everything to invite suspicion. In this instance, however, I am perfectly satisfied that he is guiltless."

"We shall be glad to find proof of his innocence," Alleyn said.

Lady Pastern closed one hand over the other. "Usually," she said, "I comprehend entirely his motives. But entirely. On this occasion, however, I find myself somewhat at a loss. It is obvious to me that he develops some scheme. But what? Yes: I confess myself at a loss. I merely warn you, Mr. Alleyn, that to suspect my husband of this crime is to court acute embarrassment. You will gratify his unquenchable passion for self-dramatization. He prepares a *dénouement*."

Alleyn took a quick decision. "It's possible," he said, "that we've anticipated him there."

"Indeed?" she said quickly. "I am glad to hear it."

"It appears that the revolver produced last night was not the one Lord Pastern loaded and took to the platform. I think he knows this. Apparently it amuses him to say nothing."

"Ah!" She breathed out a sound of immense satisfaction. "As I thought. It amuses him. Perfectly! And his innocence is established, no doubt?"

Alleyn said carefully: "If the revolver produced is the one he fired, and the scars in the barrel suggest that it is, then a very good case could be made out on the lines of substitution."

"I'm afraid I do not understand. A good case?"

"To the effect that Lord Pastern's revolver was replaced by this other one which was loaded with the bolt that killed Rivera. That Lord Pastern fired it in ignorance of the substitution."

She had a habit of immobility but her stillness now declared itself as if until this moment she had been restless. The creased lids came down like hoods over her eyes. She seemed to look at her hands. "Naturally," she said, "I make no attempt to understand these assuredly very difficult complexities. It is enough, little as he deserves to escape, that my husband clears himself."

"Nevertheless," Alleyn said, "it remains necessary to discover the guilty person." And he thought: "Damn it, I'm beginning to talk like a French phrase book, myself!"

"No doubt," she said.

"And the guilty person, it seems obvious, was one of the party who dined here last night."

Lady Pastern now closed her eyes completely. "A most distressing possibility," she murmured.

"Hands," Alleyn thought. "Carlisle Wayne's hand fingering her neck. Miss Henderson's hand jerking the photograph off the mantelpiece. Lady Pastern's hands closing upon each other like vices. Hands."

"Furthermore," he said, "if the substitution theory is right, the time field is narrowed considerably. Lord Pastern put his revolver under his sombrero on the edge of the band dais, you remember."

"I made a point of disregarding him," his wife said instantly. "The whole affair was entirely distasteful to me. I did not notice and therefore I do *not* remember."

"That's what he did, however. The possibilities, as far as substitution goes, are therefore limited to the people who were within easy reach of his sombrero."

"No doubt you will question the waiters. The man was of the type which makes itself insufferable to servants."

"By Gum," Alleyn thought, "you're almost one up on me there, old girl!" But he said: "We must remember that the substituted weapon was charged with a bolt and blank cartridges. The bolt was made out of a section of your parasol handle and its point of a stiletto from your work-box." He paused. Her fingers were more closely interlocked but she didn't move or speak. "And the blanks," he added, "were, it is almost certain, made by Lord Pastern and left in his study. The waiters are ruled out, I think."

Her lips parted and closed again. She said: "Am I, perhaps, being stupid? It seems to me that this theory of substitution may embrace a wider field. Why could the change of weapons not have been effected before my husband appeared? He was later than the others in appearing. So, for example, was Mr. Bellairs. I believe that is the conductor's name."

"Lord Pastern insists that neither Bellairs nor anyone else had an opportunity to get at his revolver, which he says he carried in his hip pocket until he put it under the sombrero. I am persuaded that the change-over was effected after Lord Pastern made his entrance on the band dais and it's obvious that the substituted revolver must have been prepared by someone who had access to your parasol . . ."

"In the restaurant," she interrupted quickly. "Before the performance. The parasols must have been within reach of all of them."

". . . and also access to the study in this house."

"Why?"

"To get the stiletto which was carried there."

She drew in her breath sharply. "It may have been an entirely different stiletto, I imagine."

"Then why has this particular one disappeared from the study? Your daughter took it away from the drawing-room when she left for her interview in the study with Rivera. Do you remember that?"

He could have sworn that she did if only because she made no sign whatsoever. She couldn't conceal the start of astonishment or dismay which this statement should have produced if she hadn't been prepared for it.

"I remember nothing of the sort," she said.

"That is what happened however," Alleyn said, "and it appears that the steel was removed in the study, since we found the ivory handle there."

After a moment she lifted her chin and looked directly at him. "It is with the greatest reluctance that I remind you of the presence of Mr. Bellairs in this house last night. I believe he was in the study with my husband after dinner. He had ample opportunity to return there."

"According to Lord Pastern's time-table, to which you have all subscribed, he had from about a quarter to ten until half past when, with the exception of Rivera and Mr. Edward Manx, the rest of the party was upstairs. Mr. Manx, I remember, said he was in the drawing-room during this period. He had, by the way, punched Rivera on the ear shortly beforehand."

"Ah!" Lady Pastern breathed out her small ejaculation. She took a moment or two over digesting this information and Alleyn thought she was very well pleased with it. She said, "Dear Edward is immensely impulsive."

"He was annoyed, I gather, because Rivera had taken it upon himself to kiss Miss Wayne."

Alleyn would have given a lot to have Lady Pastern's thoughts floating above her head in clear letters, encased by a balloon as in one of Troy's little drawings, or to have heard them through spectral ear-phones. Were there four elements? Desire that Manx should be concerned only with Félicité? Gratification that Manx should have gone for Rivera? Resentment that Carlisle and not Félicité had been the cause? And fear—fear that Manx should be more gravely involved? Or some deeper fear?

"Unfortunately," she said, "he was a totally impossible person. It is, I feel certain, an affair of no significance. Dear Edward."

Alleyn said abruptly, "Do you ever see a magazine called *Harmony?*" and was startled by her response. Her eyes widened. She looked at him as if he had uttered some startling impropriety.

"Never!" she said loudly. "Certainly not. Never."

"There is a copy in the house. I thought perhaps . . ."

"The servants may take it. I believe it is the kind of thing they read."

"The copy I saw was in the study. It has a correspondence page, conducted by someone who calls himself G.P.F."

"I have not seen it. I do not concern myself with this journal."

"Then," Alleyn said, "there's not much point in my asking if you suspected that Edward Manx was G.P.F."

It was not possible for Lady Pastern to leap to her feet: her corsets alone prevented such an exercise. But, with formidable energy and comparative speed, she achieved a standing position. He saw with astonishment that her bosom heaved and that her neck and face were suffused with a brickish red.

"*Impossible!*" she panted. "Never! I shall never believe it. An insufferable suggestion."

"I don't quite see . . ." Alleyn began but she shouted him down. "Outrageous! He is utterly incapable." She shot a fusillade of adjectives at him. "I cannot discuss such a fantasy. Incredible! Monstrous! Libellous. Libel of the grossest kind. Never!"

"But why do you say that? On account of the literary style?"

Lady Pastern's mouth twice opened and shut. She stared at him with an air of furious indecision. "You may say so," she said at last. "You may put it in that way. Certainly. On account of style."

"And yet you have never read the magazine?"

"Obviously it is a vulgar publication. I have seen the cover."

"Let me tell you," Alleyn suggested, "how the theory has arisen. I really should like you to understand that it's not based on guesswork. May we sit down?"

She sat down abruptly. He saw, and was bewildered to see, that she was trembling. He told her about the letter Félicité had received and showed her the copy he had made. He reminded her of the white flower in Manx's coat and of Félicité's change of manner after she had seen it. He said that Félicité believed Manx to be G.P.F. and had admitted as much. He said they had discovered original drafts of articles that had subsequently appeared on G.P.F.'s page and that these drafts had been typed on the machine in the study. He reminded her that Manx had stayed at Duke's Gate for three weeks. Throughout this recital she sat bolt upright, pressing her lips together and staring, inexplicably, at the top right-hand drawer of her desk. In some incomprehensible fashion he was dealing her blow after shrewd blow, but he kept on and finished the whole story. "So you see, don't you," he ended, "that, at least, it's a probability?"

"Have you asked him?" she said pallidly. "What does he say?"

"I have not asked him yet. I shall do so. Of course, the whole question of his identity with G.P.F. may be irrelevant as far as this case is concerned."

"Irrelevant!" she ejaculated as if the suggestion were wildly insane. She was looking again at her desk. Every muscle of her face was controlled but tears now began to form in her eyes and trickle over her cheeks.

"I'm sorry," Alleyn said, "that you find this distressing."

"It distresses me," she said, "because I find it is true. I am in some confusion of mind. If there is nothing more . . ."

He got up at once. "There's nothing more," he said. "Good-bye, Lady Pastern."

She recalled him before he reached the door. "One moment."

"Yes?"

"Let me assure you, Mr. Alleyn," she said, pressing her handkerchief against her cheek, "that my foolishness is entirely unimportant. It is a personal matter. What you have told me is quite irrelevant to this affair. It is of no consequence whatever, in fact." She drew in her breath with a sound that quivered between a sigh and a sob. "As for the identity of the person who has perpetrated this outrage—I mean the murder, not the journalism—I am persuaded it was one of his own kind. Yes, certainly," she said more vigorously, "one of his own kind. You may rest assured of that." And finding himself dismissed, he left her.

iv

As Alleyn approached the first landing on his way down he was surprised to hear the ballroom piano. It was being played somewhat unhandily and the strains were those of hotly syncopated music taken at a funeral pace. Detective-Sergeant Jimson was on duty on the landing. Alleyn jerked his head at the ballroom doors, which were ajar. "Who's that playing?" he asked. "Is it Lord Pastern? Who the devil opened that room?"

Jimson, looking embarrassed and scandalized, replied that he thought it must be Lord Pastern. His manner was so odd that Alleyn walked past him and pushed open the double doors. Inspector Fox was discovered seated at the piano with his spectacles on his nose. He was inclined forward tensely, and followed with concentration a sheet of music in manuscript. Facing him, across the piano, was Lord Pastern, who, as Alleyn entered, beat angrily, but rhythmically, upon the lid and shouted: "No, no, my good ass, not a bit like it. N'yah—*yo*. Bo bo bo. Again." He looked up and saw Alleyn. "Here!" he said. "Can you play?"

Fox rose, without embarrassment, and removed his spectacles.

"Where have you come from?" Alleyn demanded.

"I had a little matter to report, sir, and as you were engaged for the moment I've been waiting in here. His lordship was looking for someone to try over a piece he's composing but I'm afraid . . ."

"I'll have to get one of these women," Lord Pastern cut in impatiently. "Where's Fée? This chap's no good."

"I haven't sat down to the piano since I was a lad," said Fox mildly.

Lord Pastern made for the door but Alleyn intercepted him. "One moment, sir," he said.

"It's no good worryin' me with any more questions," Lord Pastern snapped at him. "I'm busy."

"Unless you'd prefer to come to the Yard, you'll answer this one, if you please. When did you first realize that the revolver we produced after Rivera was killed was not the one you loaded in the study and carried on to the band platform?"

Lord Pastern smirked at him. "Nosed that out for yourselves, have you?" he remarked. "Fascinatin', the way our police work."

"I still want to know when you made this discovery."

"About eight hours before you did."

"As soon as you were shown the substitute and noticed there were no initials?"

"Who told you about initials? Here!" Lord Pastern said with some excitement. "Have you found my other gun?"

"Where do you suggest we look for it?"

"If I knew where it was, my good fathead, I'd have got it for meself. I value that gun, by God!"

"You handed over the weapon you fired at Rivera to Breezy Bellairs," Fox said suddenly. "Was it that one, my lord? The one with the initials? The one you loaded in this house? The one that's missing?"

Lord Pastern swore loudly. "What d'you think I am?" he shouted. "A bloody juggler? Of course it was."

"And Bellairs walked straight into the office with you and I took it off him a few minutes later and it *wasn't* the same gun. That won't wash, my lord," said Fox, "if you'll excuse my saying so. It won't wash."

"In that case," Lord Pastern said rudely, "you can put up with it dirty." Alleyn made a slight, irritated sound and Lord Pastern instantly turned on him. "What are *you* snufflin' about?" he demanded and before Alleyn could answer he renewed his attack on Fox. "Why don't you ask Breezy about it?" he said. "I should have thought even *you'd* have got at Breezy."

"Are you suggesting, my lord, that Bellairs might have worked the substitution after the murder was committed?"

"I'm not suggestin' anything."

"In which case," Fox continued imperturbably, "perhaps you'll tell me how Rivera was killed?"

Lord Pastern gave a short bark of laughter. "No, really," he said, "it's beyond belief how bone-headed you are."

Fox said: "May I press this point a little further, Mr. Alleyn?"

From behind Lord Pastern, Alleyn returned Fox's inquiring glance with a dubious one. "Certainly, Fox," he said.

"I'd like to ask his lordship if he'd be prepared to swear an oath that the weapon he handed Bellairs after the fatality was the one that is missing."

"Well, Lord Pastern," Alleyn said, "will you answer Mr. Fox?"

"How many times am I to tell you I won't answer any of your tom-fool questions? I gave you a time-table, and that's all the help you get from me."

For a moment the three men were silent: Fox by the piano, Alleyn near the door and Lord Pastern midway between them like a truculent Pekinese —an animal, it occurred to Alleyn, he closely resembled.

"Don't forget, my lord," Fox said, "that last night you stated yourself that anybody could have got at the revolver while it was under the sombrero. Anybody, you remarked, for all you'd have noticed."

"What of it?" he said, bunching his cheeks.

"There's this about it, my lord. It's a tenable theory that one of the party at your own table could have substituted the second gun, loaded with the bolt, and that you could have fired it at Rivera without knowing anything about the substitution."

"That cat won't jump," Lord Pastern said, "and you know it. I didn't tell anybody I was going to put the gun under my sombrero. Not a soul."

"Well, my lord," Fox said, "we can make inquiries about that."

"You can inquire till you're blue in the face and much good may it do you."

"Look here, my lord," Fox burst out, "do you *want* us to arrest you?"

"Not sure I don't. It'd be enough to make a cat laugh." He thrust his hands in his trouser pockets, walked round Fox, eyeing him, and fetched up in front of Alleyn. "Skelton," he said, "saw the gun. He handled it just before he went on, and when he came out while I waited for my entrance he handled it again. While Breezy did the speech about me, it was."

"Why did he handle it this second time?" Alleyn asked.

"I was a bit excited. Nervy work, hangin' about for your entrance. I was takin' a last look at it and I dropped it and he picked it up and squinted down the barrel in a damn-your-eyes supercilious sort of way. Professional jealousy."

"Why didn't you mention this before, my lord?" Fox demanded and was ignored. Lord Pastern grinned savagely at Alleyn. "Well," he said with gloating relish, "what about this arrest? I'll come quietly."

Alleyn said: "You know, I do wish that for once in a blue moon you'd behave yourself."

For the first time, he thought, Lord Pastern was giving him his full attention. He was suddenly quiet and wary. He eyed Alleyn with something of the air of a small boy who is not sure if he can bluff his way out of a misdemeanour.

"You really are making the most infernal nuisance of yourself, sir," Alleyn went on, "and, if you will allow me, the most appalling ass of yourself into the bargain."

"See here, Alleyn," Lord Pastern said with a not entirely convincing return to his former truculence, "I'm damned if I'll take this. I know what I'm up to."

"Then have the grace to suppose we know what we're up to, too. After all, sir, you're not the only one to remember that Rivera played the piano-accordion."

For a moment, Lord Pastern stood quite still with his jaw dropped and his eyebrows half-way up his forehead. He then said rapidly: "I'm late. Goin' to m'club," and incontinently bolted from the room.

CHAPTER XI

Episodes in Two Flats
and an Office

"Well, Mr. Alleyn," said Fox, "that settles it, in my mind. It's going to turn out the way you said. Cut loose the trimmings and you come to the—well, the *corpus delicti* as you might say."

They were sitting in a police car outside the house in Duke's Gate. Both of them looked past the driver, and through the wind-screen, at a jaunty and briskly moving figure, its hat a little to one side and swinging its walking stick.

"There he goes," Fox said, "as cock-sure and perky as you please, and there goes our chap after him. Say what you like, Mr. Alleyn, the art of tailing your man isn't what it was in the service. These young fellows think they signed on for the sole purpose of tearing about the place with the Flying Squad." And having delivered himself of his customary grumble, Fox, still contemplating the diminishing figure of Lord Pastern, added: "Where do we go from here, sir?"

"Before we go anywhere you'll be good enough to explain why your duties led you back to Duke's Gate and, more particularly, to playing that old antic's boogie-woogie on the piano."

Fox smiled in a stately manner. "Well, sir," he said, "as to what brought me, it was a bit of stale information, and another bit that's not so stale. Skelton rang up after you left, to say he had inspected his lordship's revolver the second time and was sorry he hadn't mentioned it last night. He said that he and our Mr. Eton-and-Oxford Detective-Sergeant Sallis got into a discussion about the *petite bourgeoisie* or something and it went out of his head. I thought it better not to ring you at Duke's Gate. Extension wires all over the shop in that house. So, as it seemed to settle the question about which gun his lordship took on the platform with him, I thought I'd pop along and tell you."

"And Pastern saved you the trouble."

"Quite so. And as to the piano, there was his lordship saying he'd been inspired, so to speak, with a new composition and wanted someone to try it over. He was making a great to-do over the ballroom being sealed. Our chaps have finished in there so there seemed no harm in obliging him. I thought it might establish friendly relations," Fox added sadly, "but I can't say it did in the end. Shall we tell this chap where we're going, sir?"

Alleyn said: "We'll call at the Metronome, then we'll have a look at

Breezy and see how the poor swine's shaping up this morning. Then we'll have a very brief snack, Br'er Fox, and when that's over it'll be time to visit G.P.F. in his den. If he's there, blast him."

"Ah, by the way," Fox said, as they moved off, "that's the other bit of information. Mr. Bathgate rang the Yard and said he'd got hold of someone who writes regularly for this paper *Harmony* and it seems that Mr. Friend is generally supposed to be in the office on the afternoon and evening of the last Sunday in the month, on account of the paper going to press the following week. This gentleman told Mr. Bathgate that nobody on the regular staff except the editor ever sees Mr. Friend. The story is he deals direct with the proprietors of the paper but popular opinion in Fleet Street reckons he owns the show himself. They reckon the secrecy business is nothing but a build-up."

"Silly enough to be incredible," Alleyn muttered. "But we're knee-deep in imbecility. I suppose we can take it. All the same, I fancy we'll turn up a better reason for Mr. Friend's elaborate incognito before this interminable Sunday is out."

Fox said, with an air of quiet satisfaction: "I fancy we shall, sir. Mr. Bathgate's done quite a nice little job for us. It seems he pressed this friend of his a bit further and got him on to the subject of Mr. Manx's special articles for the paper and it came out that Mr. Manx is often in their office."

"Discussing his special articles. Picking up his galley sheets or whatever they do."

"Better than that, Mr. Alleyn. This gentleman told Mr. Bathgate that Mr. Manx has been noticed coming out of G.P.F.'s room on several occasions, one of them being a Sunday afternoon."

"Oh."

"Fits, doesn't it?"

"Like a glove. Good for Bathgate. We'll ask him to meet us at the *Harmony* offices. This being the last Sunday in the month, Br'er Fox, we'll see what we can see. But first—the Metronome."

ii

When Carlisle left the Yard, it was with a feeling of astonishment and aimless boredom. So it wasn't Uncle George's revolver after all. So there had been an intricate muddle that someone would have to unravel. Alleyn would unravel it and then someone else would be arrested and she ought to be alarmed and agitated because of this. Perhaps, in the hinterland of her emotions, alarm and agitation were already established and waited to pounce, but in the meantime she was only drearily miserable and tired. She was pestered by all sorts of minor considerations. The thought of returning to Duke's Gate and trying to cope with the situation there was intolerable.

It wasn't so much the idea that Uncle George or Aunt Cile or Fée might have murdered Carlos Rivera that Carlisle found appalling: it was the prospect of their several personalities forcing themselves upon her own; their demands upon her attention and courtesy. She had a private misery, a galling unhappiness, and she wanted to be alone with it.

While she walked irresolutely towards the nearest bus stop, she remembered that not far from here, in a *cul-de-sac* called Coster's Row, was Edward Manx's flat. If she walked to Duke's Gate she would pass the entry into this blind street. She was persuaded that she did not want to see Edward, that an encounter would, indeed, be unbearable; yet, aimlessly, she began to walk on. Church-going people returning home with an air of circumspection made a pattering sound in the empty streets. Groups of sparrows flustered and pecked. The day was mildly sunny. The Yard man, detailed to keep observation on Carlisle, threaded his way through a trickle of pedestrians and recalled the Sunday dinners of his boyhood. Beef, he thought, Yorkshire pudding, gravy, and afterwards a heavy hour or so in the front room. Carlisle gave him no trouble at all but he was hungry.

He saw her hesitate at the corner of Coster's Row and himself halted to light a cigarette. She glanced along the file of house fronts and then, at a more rapid pace, crossed the end of the row and continued on her way. At the same time a dark young man came out of a house six doors down Coster's Row and descended the steps in time to catch a glimpse of her. He shouted, "Lisle!" and waved his arm. She hurried on, and once past the corner, out of his sight, broke into a run. "Hi, Lisle!" he shouted. "Lisle!" and loped after her. The Yard man watched him go by, turn the corner and overtake her. She spun round at the touch of his hand on her arm and they stood face to face.

A third man who had come out from some doorway further up the *cul-de-sac* walked briskly down the path on the same side as the Yard man. They greeted each other like old friends and shook hands. The Yard man offered cigarettes and lit a match. "How's it going, Bob?" he said softly. "That your bird?"

"That's him. Who's the lady?"

"Mine," said the first, whose back was turned to Carlisle.

"Not bad," his colleague muttered, glancing at her.

"I'd just as soon it was my dinner, though."

"Argument?"

"Looks like it."

"Keeping their voices down."

Their movements were slight and casual: acquaintances pausing for a rather aimless chat.

"What's the betting?" said the first.

"They'll separate. I never have the luck."

"You're wrong, though."

"Going back to his place?"

"Looks like it."

"I'll toss you for it."

"O.K." The other pulled his clenched hand out of his pocket. "Your squeak," he said.

"Heads."

"It's tails."

"I never get the luck."

"I'll ring in then and get something to eat. Relieve you in half an hour, Bob."

They shook hands again heartily as Carlisle and Edward Manx, walking glumly towards them, turned into Coster's Row.

Carlisle had seen Edward Manx out of the corner of her eye as she crossed the end of the *cul-de-sac*. Unreasoned panic took hold of her. She lengthened her stride, made a show of looking at her watch and, when he called her name, broke into a run. Her heart pounded and her mouth was dry. She had the sensation of a fugitive in a dream. She was the pursued and, since even in her sudden alarm she was confusedly aware of something in herself that frightened her, she was also the pursuer. This nightmarish conviction was intensified by the sound of his feet clattering after her and of his voice, completely familiar but angry, calling her to stop.

Her feet were leaden, he was overtaking her quite easily. Her anticipation of his seizing her from behind was so vivid that when his hand actually closed on her arm it was something of a relief. He jerked her round to face him and she was glad to feel angry.

"What the hell do you think you're doing?" he said breathlessly.

"That's my business," she panted, and added defiantly, "I'm late. I'll be late for lunch. Aunt Cile will be furious."

"Don't be an ass, Lisle. You ran when you saw me. You heard me call out and you kept on running. What the devil d'you mean by it?"

His heavy eyebrows were drawn together and his lower lip jutted out.

"Please let me go, Ned," she said. "I really am late."

"That's utterly childish and you know it. I'm getting to the bottom of this. Come back to the flat. I want to talk to you."

"Aunt Cile . . ."

"Oh for God's sake! I'll ring Duke's Gate and say you're lunching here."

"No."

For a moment he looked furious. He still held her arm and his fingers bit into it, hurting her. Then he said more gently: "You can't expect me to let a thing like this pass—it's a monstrous state of affairs. I must know what's gone wrong. Last night, after we got back from the Metronome, I could tell there was something. Please, Lisle. Don't let's stand here snarling at each other. Come back to the flat."

"I'd rather not. Honestly. I know I'm behaving queerly."

He had slipped the palm of his hand inside her arm, pressing it against him. His hand was gentler now but she couldn't escape it. He began to speak persuasively and she remembered how, even when they were children, she had never been able to resist his persuasiveness. "You will, Lisle, won't you? Don't be queer, I can't bear all this peculiarity. Come along."

She looked helplessly at the two men on the opposite corner, thinking vaguely that she had seen one of them before. "I wish I knew him," she thought. "I wish I could stop and speak to him."

They turned into Coster's Row. "There's some food in the flat. It's quite a nice flat. I want you to see it. We'll have lunch together, shan't we? I'm sorry I was churlish, Lisle."

His key clicked in the lock of the blue door. They were in a small lobby. "It's a basement flat," he said, "but not at all bad. There's even a garden. Down those stairs."

"You go first," she said. She actually wondered if that would give her a chance to bolt and if she would have the nerve to do it. He looked fixedly at her.

"I don't believe I trust you," he said lightly. "On you go."

He followed close on her heels down the steep stairs and took her arm again as he reached past her and unlocked the second door. "Here we are," he said, pushing it open. He gave her a little shove forward.

It was a large, low-ceilinged room, whitewashed and oakbeamed. French windows opened on a little yard with potted flowers and plane-trees in tubs. The furniture was modern: steel chairs with rubber-foam upholstery, a carefully planned desk, a divan bed with a scarlet cover. A rigorous still-life hung above the fireplace, the only picture in the room. The bookshelves looked as if they had been stocked completely from a Left Book Shop. It was a scrupulously tidy room.

"The oaken beams are strict stockbroker's Tudor," he was saying. "Completely functionless, of course, and pretty revolting. Otherwise not so bad, do you think? Sit down while I find a drink."

She sat on the divan and only half listened to him. His belated pretense that, after all, this was a pleasant and casual encounter did nothing to reassure her. He was still angry. She took the drink he brought and found her hand was shaking so much she couldn't carry the glass to her lips. The drink spilled. She bent her head down and took a quick gulp at it, hoping this would steady her. She rubbed furtively with her handkerchief at the splashes on the cover and knew, without looking, that he watched her.

"Shall we go in, boots and all, or wait till after lunch?" he said.

"There's nothing to talk about. I'm sorry to be such an ass but after all it was a bit of a night. I suppose murder doesn't suit me."

"Oh, no," he said, "that won't do. You don't bolt like a rabbit at the sight of me because somebody killed a piano-accordionist." And after a long pause, he added smoothly, "Unless, by any chance, you think I killed him. Do you?"

"Don't be a dolt," she said, and by some fortuitous mischance, an accident quite beyond her control and unrelated to any recognizable impulse, her answer sounded unconvincing and too violent. It was the last question she had expected from him.

"Well, at least I'm glad of that," he said. He sat on the table near to her. She did not look up at him but straight before her at his left hand, lying easily across his knee. "Come on," he said, "what have I done? There *is* something I've done. What is it?"

She thought: "I'll have to tell him something—part of it. Not the real thing itself but the other bit that doesn't matter so much." She began to search for an approach, a line to take, some kind of credible presentation, but she was deadly tired and she astonished herself by saying abruptly and loud: "I've found out about G.P.F."

His hand moved swiftly, out of her range of sight. She looked up expecting to be confronted by his anger or astonishment but he had turned aside, skewing round to put his glass down on the table behind him.

"Have you?" he said. "That's awkward, isn't it?" He moved quickly away from her and across the room to a wall cupboard which he opened. With his back turned to her he said: "Who told you? Did Cousin George?"

"No," she said, wearily surprised. "No. I saw the letter."

"Which letter?" he asked, groping in the cupboard.

"The one to Félicité."

"Oh," said Manx slowly. "That one." He turned round. He had a packet of cigarettes in his hands and came towards her holding it out. She shook her head and he lit one himself with steady hands. "How did you come to see it?" he said.

"It was lost. It—I—oh, what *does* it matter! The whole thing was perfectly clear. Need we go on?"

"I still don't see why this discovery should inspire you to sprint like an athlete at the sight of me."

"I don't think I know myself."

"What were you doing last night?" he demanded suddenly. "Where did you go after we got back to Duke's Gate? Why did you turn up again with Alleyn? What were you up to?"

It was impossible to tell him that Félicité had lost the letter. That would lead at once to his discovering that Alleyn had read it: worse than that, it would lead inevitably to the admittance, perhaps the discussion, of his new attitude towards Félicité. "He might," she thought, "tell me, point-blank, that he is in love with Fée and I'm in no shape to jump that hurdle."

So she said: "It doesn't matter what I was up to. I can't tell you. In a way it would be a breach of confidence."

"Was it something to do with this G.P.F. business?" Manx said sharply, and after a pause. "You haven't told anybody about this discovery, have you?"

She hadn't told Alleyn. He had found out for himself. Miserably she shook her head. He stooped over her. "You mustn't tell anybody, Lisle. That's important. You realize how important, don't you?"

Isolated sentences of an indescribable archness flashed up in her memory of that abominable page. "You don't need to tell me that," she said, looking away from his intent and frowning eyes, and suddenly burst out: "It's such ghastly stuff, Ned. That magazine. It's like one of our novelettes gone haywire. How you could!"

"My articles are all right," he said, and after a pause: "So that's it, is it. You *are* a purist, aren't you?"

She clasped her hands together and fixed her gaze on them. "I must tell you," she said, "that if, in some hellish, muddled way, entirely beyond my comprehension, this G.P.F. business has anything to do with Rivera's death . . ."

"Well?"

"I mean, if it's going to—I mean—"

"You mean that if Alleyn asks you point-blank about it, you'll tell him?"

"Yes," she said.

"I see."

Carlisle's head ached. She had been unable to face her breakfast and the drink he had given her had taken effect. Their confused antagonism, the sense of being trapped in this alien room, her personal misery: all these circumstances were joined in a haze of uncertainty. The whole scene had become unreal and unendurable. When he put his hands on her shoulders and said loudly: "There's more to it than this. Come on. What is it?" she seemed to hear him from a great distance. His hands were bearing down hard. "I *will* know," he was saying.

At the far end of the room a telephone bell began to ring. She watched him go to it and take the receiver off. His voice changed its quality and became the easy friendly voice she had known for so long.

"Hullo? Hullo, Fée darling. I'm terribly sorry, I should have rung up. They kept Lisle for hours grilling her at the Yard. Yes; I ran into her and she asked me to telephone and say she was so late she'd try for a meal somewhere at hand, so I asked her to have one with me. Please tell Cousin Cécile it's entirely my fault and not hers. I promised to ring for her." He looked at Carlisle over the telephone. "She's perfectly all right," he said. "I'm looking after her."

iii

If any painter, a surrealist for choice, attempted to set the figure of a working detective officer against an appropriate and composite background, he would turn his attention to rooms overlaid with films of dust, to objects suspended in unaccustomed dinginess, to ash-trays and table-cloths, unemptied waste bins, tables littered with powder, dirty glasses, disordered chairs, stale food, and garments that retained an unfresh smell of disuse.

When Alleyn and Fox entered the Metronome at twelve-thirty on this

Sunday morning, it smelt of Saturday night. The restaurant, serveries and kitchens had been cleaned but the vestibule and offices were untouched and upon them the aftermath of festivity lay like a thin pall of dust. Three men in shirt-sleeves greeted Alleyn with that tinge of gloomy satisfaction which marks an unsuccessful search.

"No luck?" Alleyn said.

"No luck yet, sir."

"There's the passage that runs through from the foyer and behind the offices to the back premises," said Fox. "That's the way the deceased must have gone to make his entrance from the far end of the restaurant."

"We've been along there, Mr. Fox."

"Plumbing?"

"Not yet, Mr. Alleyn."

"I'd try that next." Alleyn pointed through the two open doors of Caesar Bonn's office into the inner room. "Begin there," he said.

He went alone into the restaurant. The table he and Troy had sat at was the second on the right. The chairs were turned up on its surface. He replaced one of them and seated himself. "For twenty years," he thought, "I have trained my memory and trained it rigorously. This is the first time I have been my own witness in a case of this sort. Am I any good or am I rotten?"

Sitting alone there, he re-created his scene, beginning with small things: the white cloth, the objects on the table, Troy's long hand close to his own and just within his orbit of vision. He waited until these details were firm in his memory and then reached out a little further. At the next table, her back towards him, sat Félicité de Suze in a red dress. She turned a white carnation in her fingers and looked sidelong at the man beside her. He was between Alleyn and the lamp on their table. His profile was rimmed with light. His head was turned towards the band dais. On his right, more clearly visible, more brilliantly lit, was Carlisle Wayne. In order to watch the performance she had swung round with her back half-turned to the table. Her hair curved back from her temples. There was a look of compassion and bewilderment in her face. Beyond Carlisle, with her back to the wall, a heavy shape almost obscured by the others, sat Lady Pastern. As they moved he could see in turn her stony coiffure, her important shoulders, the rigid silhouette of her bust; but never her face.

Raised above them, close to them, a figure gestured wildly among the tympani. This was a vivid picture because it was contained by a pool of light. Lord Pastern's baldish head darted and bobbed. Metallic high lights flashed among his instruments. The spot light shifted and there in the centre of the stage was Rivera, bent backwards, hugging his piano-accordion to his chest. Eyes, teeth, and steel and mother-of-pearl ornament glittered. The arm of the metronome pointed fixedly at his chest. Behind, half-shadowed, a plump hand jerked up and down, beating the air with its miniature baton. A wide smile glistened in a moon face. Now Lord Pastern faced Rivera on the perimeter of the light pool. His revolver pointed at the contorted figure, flashed, and Rivera fell. Then the further shots and comic falls and then . . . In the deserted restaurant Alleyn brought his hands down sharply on the table. It had been then, and not until then, that the lights began their infernal blinking. They popped in and out down the length of the metronome and about its frame, in and out, red green, blue, green red. Then, and not until then, had the arm swung away from the prostrate figure and, with the rest of that winking stuttering bedazzlement, gone into action.

Alleyn got up and mounted the bandstand. He stood on the spot where Rivera had fallen. The skeleton tower of the metronome framed him. The reverse side of this structure revealed its electrical equipment. He looked up at the pointer of the giant arm which was suspended directly above his head. It was a hollow steel or plastic casting studded with miniature lights and for a moment reminded him fantastically of the jewelled dart. To the right of the band-room door and hidden from the audience by the piano, a small switchboard was sunk in the wall. Happy Hart, they had told Alleyn, was in charge of the lights. From where he sat at the piano and from where he fell to the floor he could reach out to the switches. Alleyn did so, now, pulling down the one marked "Motor." A hidden whirring sound prefaced the first loud *clack*. The giant downward-pointing arm swept semicircularly across, back, across and back to its own ratchet-like accompaniment. He switched on the lights and stood for a moment, an incongruous figure, motionless at the core of his kaleidoscopic setting. The point of the arm, flashing its lights, swept within four inches of his head and away and back and away again. "If you watched the damn' thing for long enough I believe it'd mesmerize you," he thought and turned off the switches.

Back in the offices he found Mr. Fox in severe control of two plumbers who were removing their jackets in the lavatory.

"If we can't find anything fishing with wires, Mr. Alleyn," Fox said, "it'll be a case of taking down the whole job."

"I don't hold out ecstatic hopes," Alleyn said, "but get on with it."

One of the plumbers pulled the chain and contemplated the ensuing phenomena.

"Well?" said Fox.

"I wouldn't say she was a sweetly running job," the plumber diagnosed, "and yet again she *works* if you can understand me." He raised a finger, and glanced at his mate.

"Trap trouble?" ventured his mate.

"Ar."

"We'll leave you to it," Alleyn said and withdrew Fox into the office. "Fox," he said, "let's remind ourselves of the key pieces in this jig-saw atrocity. What are they?"

Fox said promptly: "The set-up at Duke's Gate. The drug racket. *Harmony.* The substitution. The piano-accordion. The nature of the weapon."

"Add one more. The metronome was motionless when Rivera played. It

started its blasted tick-tack stuff after he fell and after the other rounds had
been fired."

"I get you, sir. Yes," said Fox, placidly, "there's that too. Add the metronome."

"Now, let's mug over the rest of the material and see where we are."

Sitting in Caesar Bonn's stale office, they sorted, discarded, correlated and
dissociated the fragments of the case. Their voices droned on to the intermittent accompaniment of plumbers' aquatics. After twenty minutes Fox
shut his notebook, removed his spectacles and looked steadily at his superior
officer.

"It amounts to this," he said. "Setting aside a handful of insignificant details, we're short of only one piece." He poised his hand, palm down, over
the table. "If we can lay hold of that and if, when we've got it, it fits—well,
our little picture's complete."

"If," Alleyn said, "and when."

The door of the inner office opened and the senior plumber entered. With
an air of false modesty he extended a naked arm and bleached hand. On
the palm of the hand dripped a revolver. "Would this," he asked glumly,
"be what you was wanting?"

iv

Dr. Curtis waited for them outside the main entrance to Breezy's flat.

"Sorry to drag you out, Curtis," Alleyn said, "but we may need your opinion
about his fitness to make a statement. This is Fox's party. He's the drug
baron."

"How do you expect he'll be, Doctor?" Fox asked.

Dr. Curtis stared at his shoes and said guardedly: "Heavy hang-over. Shaky.
Depressed. May be resentful. May be placatory. Can't tell."

"Suppose he decides to talk, is it likely to be truthful?"

"Not very. They usually lie."

Fox said: "What's the line to take? Tough or coaxing?"

"Use your own judgement."

"You might tip us the wink, though, Doctor."

"Well," said Curtis, "let's take a look at him."

The flats were of the more dubious modern kind, and brandished chromium steel almost in the Breezy Bellairs Manner—showily and without
significance. Alleyn, Fox and Curtis approached the flat by way of a rococo
lift and a tunnel-like passage. Fox pressed a bell and a plain-clothes officer
answered the door. When he saw them he snibbed back the lock and closed
the door behind him.

"How is he?" Alleyn asked.

"Awake, sir. Quiet enough, but restless."

"Said anything?" Fox asked. "To make sense, I mean."

"Nothing much, Mr. Fox. Very worried about the deceased, he seems to be. Says he doesn't know what he's going to do without him."

"*That* makes sense at all events," Fox grunted. "Shall we go in, sir?"

It was an expensive and rather characterless flat, only remarkable for its high content of framed and signed photographs and its considerable disorder. Breezy, wearing a dressing gown of unbelievable sumptuousness, sat in a deep chair into which he seemed to shrink a little further as they came in. His face was the colour of an uncooked fowl and as flabby. As soon as he saw Dr. Curtis he raised a lamentable wail.

"Doc," he whined, "I'm all shot to heaps. Doc, for petesake take a look at me and tell them."

Curtis picked up his wrist.

"Listen," Breezy implored him, "you know a sick man when you see one— listen—"

"Don't talk."

Breezy pulled at his lower lip, blinked at Alleyn and with the inconsequence of a ventriloquist's doll flashed his celebrated smile.

"Excuse us," he said.

Curtis tested his reflexes, turned up his eyelid and looked at his tongue.

"You're a bit of a mess," he said, "but there's no reason why you shouldn't answer any questions these gentlemen like to put to you." He glanced at Fox. "He's quite able to take in the usual warning," he said.

Fox administered it and drew up a chair, facing Breezy, who shot out a quavering finger at Alleyn.

"What's the idea," he said, "shooing this chap on to me? What's wrong with talking to me yourself?"

"Inspector Fox," Alleyn said, "is concerned with investigations about the illicit drug trade. He wants some information from you."

He turned away and Fox went into action.

"Well, now, Mr. Bellairs," Fox said, "I think it's only fair to tell you what we've ascertained so far. Save quite a bit of time, won't it?"

"I can't tell you a thing. I don't know a thing."

"We're aware that you're in the unfortunate position," Fox said, "of having formed the taste for one of these drugs. Gets a real hold on you, doesn't it, that sort of thing?"

Breezy said: "It's only because I'm overworked. Give me a break and I'll cut it out. I swear I will. But gradually. You have to make it gradual. That's right, isn't it, Doc?"

"I believe," Fox said comfortably, "that's the case. That's what I understand. Now, about the supply. We've learnt on good authority that the deceased, in this instance, was the source of supply. Would you care to add anything to that statement, Mr. Bellairs?"

"Was it the old bee told you?" Breezy demanded. "I bet it was the old bee. Or Syd. Syd knew. Syd's had it in for me. Dirty bolshevik! Was it Syd Skelton?"

Fox said that the information had come from more than one source and asked how Lord Pastern knew Rivera had provided the drugs. Breezy replied that Lord Pastern nosed out all sorts of things. He refused to be drawn further.

"I understand," Fox went on, "that his lordship tackled you in the matter last evening."

Breezy at once became hysterical. "He'd ruin me! That's what he'd do. Look! Whatever happens don't let him do it. He's crazy enough to do it. Honest. Honest he is."

"Do what?"

"Like what he said. Write to that bloody paper about me."

"*Harmony?*" Fox asked, at a venture. "Would that be the paper?"

"That's right. He said he knew someone— God, he's got a thing about it. You know—the stuff. Damn and blast him," Breezy screamed out, "he'll kill me. He killed Carlos and now what'll *I* do, where'll I get it? Everybody watching and spying and I don't *know*. Carlos never told me. I don't *know*."

"Never told you?" Fox said peacefully. "Fancy that now! Never let on how he got it! And I bet he made it pretty hot when it came to paying up. Um?"

"God, you're telling *me!*"

"And no reduction made, for instance, if you helped him out?"

Breezy shrank back in his chair. "I don't know anything about that. I don't get you at all."

"Well, I mean to say," Fox explained, "there'd be opportunities, wouldn't there? Ladies, or it might be their partners, asking the band leader for a special number. A note changes hands and it might be a tip or it might be payment in advance, and the goods delivered next time. We've come across instances. I wondered if he got you to oblige him. You don't have to say anything if you don't want to, mind. We've the names and addresses of all the guests last night and we've got our records. People that are known to like it, you know. So I won't press it. Don't let it worry you. But I thought that he might have had some arrangement with you. Out of gratitude as you might put it—"

"Gratitude!" Breezy laughed shrilly. "You think you know too much," he said profoundly, and drew in his breath. He was short of breath and had broken into a sallow profuse sweat. "I don't know what I'll do without Carlos," he whispered. "Someone'll have to help me. It's all the old bee's fault. Him and the girl. If I could just have a smoke—" He appealed to Dr. Curtis. "Not a prick. I know you won't give me a prick. Just one little smoke. I don't usually in the mornings but this is exceptional, Doc. Doc, couldn't you—"

"You'll have to hang on a bit longer," Dr. Curtis said, not unkindly. "Wait a bit. We won't let it go longer than you can manage. Hang on."

Suddenly and inanely Breezy yawned, a face-splitting yawn that bared his gums and showed his coated tongue. He rubbed his arms and neck. "I keep feeling as if there's something under my skin. Worms or something," he said fretfully.

"About the weapon," Fox began. Breezy leant forward, his hands on his knees, aping Fox. "About the weapon?" he mimicked savagely. "You mind your business about the weapon. Coming here tormenting a chap. Whose gun was it? Whose bloody sunshade was it? Whose bloody stepdaughter was it? Whose bloody business is it? Get out!" He threw himself back in the chair, panting. "Get out. I'm within my rights. Get out."

"Why not?" Fox agreed. "We'll leave you to yourself. Unless Mr. Alleyn . . . ?"

"No," Alleyn said.

Dr. Curtis turned at the door. "Who's your doctor, Breezy?" he asked.

"I haven't got a doctor," Breezy whispered. "Nothing ever used to be wrong with me. Not a thing."

"We'll find someone to look after you."

"Can't *you*? Can't you look after me, Doc?"

"Well," Dr. Curtis said. "I might."

"Come on," said Alleyn and they went out.

v

One end of Materfamilias Lane had suffered a bomb and virtually disappeared but the other stood intact, a narrow City street with ancient buildings, a watery smell, dark entries and impenitent charm.

The *Harmony* offices were in a tall building at a corner where Materfamilias Lane dived downhill and a *cul-de-sac* called Journeyman's Steps led off to the right. Both were deserted on this Sunday afternoon. Alleyn's and Fox's feet rang loudly on the pavement as they walked down Materfamilias Lane. Before they reached the corner they came upon Nigel Bathgate standing in the arched entry to a brewer's yard.

"In me," Nigel said, "you see the detective's ready-reckoner and pocket guide to the City."

"I hope you're right. What have you got for us?"

"His room's on the ground floor with the window on this street. The nearest entrance is round the corner. If he's there the door to his office'll be latched on the inside with an 'Engaged' notice displayed. He locks himself in."

"He's there," Alleyn said.

"How d'you know?"

"He's been tailed. Our man rang through from a call box and he should be back on the job by now."

"Up the side street if he's got the gumption," Fox muttered. "Look out, sir!"

"Softly does it," Alleyn murmured.

Nigel found himself neatly removed to the far end of the archway, engulfed in Fox's embrace and withdrawn into a recess. Alleyn seemed to arrive there at the same time.

"'You cry mum and I'll cry budget'l" Alleyn whispered. Someone was walking briskly down Materfamilias Lane. The approaching footsteps echoed in the archway as Edward Manx went by in the sunlight.

They leant motionless against the dark stone and clearly heard the bang of a door.

"Your sleuth-hound," Nigel pointed out with some relish, "would appear to be at fault. Whom, do you suppose, he's been shadowing? Obviously, not Manx."

"Obviously," Alleyn said, and Fox mumbled obscurely.

"Why are we waiting?" Nigel asked fretfully.

"Give him five minutes," Alleyn said. "Let him settle down."

"Am I coming in with you?"

"Do you want to?"

"Certainly. One merely," Nigel said, "rather wishes that one hadn't met him before."

"May be a bit of trouble, you know," Fox speculated.

"Extremely probable," Alleyn agreed.

A bevy of sparrows flustered and squabbled out in the sunny street, an eddy of dust rose inconsequently and somewhere, out of sight, halliards rattled against an untenanted flagpole.

"Dull," Fox said, "doing your beat in the City of a Sunday afternoon. I had six months of it as a young chap. Catch yourself wondering why the blazes you were there and so on."

"Hideous," Alleyn said.

"I used to carry my *Police Code and Procedure* on me and try to memorize six pages a day. I was," Fox said simply, "an ambitious young chap in those days."

Nigel glanced at his watch and lit a cigarette.

The minutes dragged by. A clock struck three and was followed by an untidy conclave of other clocks, overlapping each other. Alleyn walked to the end of the archway and looked up and down Materfamilias Lane.

"We may as well get under way," he said. He glanced again up the street and made a sign with his hand. Fox and Nigel followed him. A man in a dark suit came down the foot-path. Alleyn spoke to him briefly and then led the way to the corner. The man remained in the archway.

They walked quickly by the window, which was uncurtained and had the legend HARMONY painted across it, and turned into the *cul-de-sac*. There was a side door with a brass plate beside it. Alleyn turned the handle and the door opened. Fox and Nigel followed him into a dingy passage which evidently led back into a main corridor. On their right, scarcely discernible in the sudden twilight, was a door. The word ENGAGED, painted in white, showed clearly. From beyond it they heard the rattle of a typewriter.

Alleyn knocked. The rattle stopped short and a chair scraped on boards.

Someone walked towards the door and a voice, Edward Manx's, said: "Hullo? Who is it?"

"Police," Alleyn said.

In the stillness they looked speculatively at each other. Alleyn poised his knuckles at the door, waited, and said: "May we have a word with you, Mr. Manx?"

After a second's silence the voice said: "One moment. I'll come out."

Alleyn glanced at Fox who moved in beside him. The word ENGAGED shot out of sight noisily and was replaced by PRIVATE G.P.F. A latch clicked and the door opened inwards. Manx stood there with one hand on the jamb and the other on the door. There was a wooden screen behind him.

Fox's boot moved over the threshold.

"I'll come out," Manx repeated.

"On the contrary, we'll come in, if you please," Alleyn said.

Without any particular display of force or even brusqueness, but with great efficiency, they went past him and round the screen. He looked for a second at Nigel and seemed not to recognize him. Then he followed them and Nigel unobtrusively followed him.

There was a green-shaded lamp on a desk at which a figure was seated with its back towards them. As Nigel entered, the swivel-chair creaked and spun around. Dingily dressed and wearing a green eye-shade, Lord Pastern faced them with bunched cheeks.

CHAPTER XII

G.P.F.

He made a high-pitched snarling noise as they closed round him and reached out his hand towards an inkpot on the desk.

Fox said: "Now, my lord, don't you do anything you'll be sorry for," and moved the inkpot.

Lord Pastern sunk his head with a rapid movement between his shoulders. From behind them, Edward Manx said: "I don't know why you've done this, Alleyn. It'll get you no further."

Lord Pastern said: "Shut up, Ned," and glared at Alleyn. "I'll have you kicked out of the force," he said. "Kicked out, by God!" And after a silence: "You don't get a word from me. Not a syllable."

Alleyn pulled up a chair and sat down, facing him. "That will suit us very well," he said. "You are going to listen, and I advise you to do so with as good a grace as you can muster. When you've heard what I've got to say you may read the statement I've brought with me. You can sign it, alter it, dictate another or refuse to do any of these things. But in the meantime, Lord Pastern, you are going to listen."

Lord Pastern folded his arms tightly across his chest, rested his chin on his tie and screwed up his eyes. Alleyn took a folded typescript from his breast pocket, opened it and crossed his knees.

"This statement was prepared," he said, "on the assumption that you are the man who calls himself G. P. Friend and writes the articles signed G.P.F. in *Harmony*. It is a statement of what we believe to be fact and doesn't concern itself overmuch with motive. I, however, will deal rather more fully with motive. In launching this paper and in writing these articles, you found it necessary to observe complete anonymity. Your reputation as probably the most quarrelsome man in England, your loudly publicized domestic rows, and your notorious eccentricities would make an appearance in the role of Guide, Philosopher and Friend a fantastically bad joke. We presume, therefore, that through a reliable agent, you deposited adequate security in a convenient bank with the specimen signature of G. P. Friend as the negotiating instrument. You then set up the legend of your own anonymity and launched yourself in the rôle of oracle. With huge success."

Lord Pastern did not stir but a film of complacency overspread his face.

"This success," Alleyn went on, "it must always be remembered, depends entirely upon the preservation of your anonymity. Once let *Harmony's* devotees learn that G.P.F. is none other than the notoriously unharmonious peer whose public quarrels have been the punctual refuge of the penny-press during the silly season—once let that be known and G.P.F. is sunk, and Lord Pastern loses a fortune. All right. Everything goes along swimmingly. You do a lot of your journalism at Duke's Gate, no doubt, but you also make regular visits to this office wearing dark glasses, the rather shabby hat and scarf which are hanging on the wall there, and the old jacket you have on at this moment. You work behind locked doors and Mr. Edward Manx is possibly your only confidant. You enjoy yourself enormously and make a great deal of money. So, perhaps, in his degree, does Mr. Manx."

Manx said: "I've no shares in the paper if that's what you mean. My articles are paid for at the usual rate."

"Shut up, Ned," said his cousin automatically.

"The paper," Alleyn continued, "is run on eccentric but profitable lines. It explodes bombs. It exposes rackets. It mingles soft-soap and cyanide. In particular it features an extremely efficient and daringly personal attack on the drug racket. It employs experts, it makes accusations, it defies and invites prosecution. Its information is accurate and if it occasionally frustrates its own professed aims by warning criminals before the police are in a position to arrest them, it is far too much inflated with crusader's zeal and rising sales to worry its head about *that*."

"Look here, Alleyn . . ." Manx began angrily, and simultaneously Lord Pastern shouted: "What the hell do you think you're getting at!"

"One moment," Alleyn said. Manx thrust his hands in his pockets and began to move about the room. "Better to hear this out, after all," he muttered.

"Much better," Alleyn agreed. "I'll go on. Everything prospered in the *Harmony* set-up until you, Lord Pastern, discovered an urge to exploit your talents as a tympanist and allied yourself with Breezy Bellairs and His Boys. Almost immediately there were difficulties. First: your stepdaughter, for whom I think you have a great affection, became attracted by Carlos Rivera, the piano-accordionist in the band. You are an observant man; for a supreme egoist, surprisingly so. At some time of your association with the Boys, I don't know precisely when, you became aware that Breezy Bellairs was taking drugs and, more important, that Carlos Rivera was supplying them. Through your association with *Harmony*, you are well up in the methods of drug distribution and you are far too sharp not to realize that the usual pattern was being followed. Bellairs was in a position to act as a minor distributing agent. He was introduced to the drug, acquired a habit for it, was forced to hand it out to clients at the Metronome and as a reward was given as much as Rivera thought was good for him at the usual exorbitant rate."

Alleyn looked curiously at Lord Pastern, who, at that moment, met his eye and blinked twice.

"It's an odd situation," Alleyn said, "isn't it? Here we have a man of eclectic, violent and short-lived enthusiasms suddenly confronted with a situation where his two reigning passions and his one enduring attachment are brought into violent opposition."

He turned to Manx, who had stopped still and was looking fixedly at him.

"A situation of great possibilities from your professional point of view, I should imagine," Alleyn said. "The stepdaughter whom Lord Pastern loves falls for Rivera who is engaged in an infamous trade which Lord Pastern is zealous in fighting. At the same time Rivera's dupe is the conductor of the band in which Lord Pastern burns to perform. As a final twist in an already tricky situation, Rivera has discovered, perhaps amongst Lord Pastern's music during a band rehearsal, some rough drafts for G.P.F.'s page, typed on Duke's Gate letter-paper. He is using them, no doubt, to force on his engagement to Miss de Suze. 'Either support my suit or—' For Rivera, in addition to running a drug racket, is an accomplished blackmailer. How is Lord Pastern to play the drums, break the engagement, preserve his anonymity as G.P.F. and explode the drug racket?"

"You can't possibly," Manx said, "have proof of a quarter of this. It's the most brazen guesswork."

"A certain amount is guesswork. But we have enough information and hard fact to carry us some way. I think that between you, you are going to fill out the rest."

Manx laughed shortly. "What a hope!" he said.

"Well," Alleyn murmured, "let us go on and see. Lord Pastern's inspiration comes out of a clear sky while he is working on his copy for G.P.F.'s page in *Harmony*. Among the letters in his basket seeking guidance, philosophy and friendship is one from his stepdaughter." He stopped short. "I wonder," he said, "if at some time or other there is also one from his wife? Asking perhaps for advice in her marital problems."

Manx looked quickly at Lord Pastern and away again.

"It might explain," Alleyn said thoughtfully, "why Lady Pastern is so vehement in her disapproval of *Harmony*. If she *did* write to G.P.F., I imagine the answer was one of the five-shilling Private Chat letters and extremely displeasing to her."

Lord Pastern gave a short bark of laughter and shot a glance at his cousin.

"However," Alleyn went on, "we are concerned, at this point, with the fact that Miss de Suze does write for guidance. Out of this coincidence, an idea is born. He answers the letter. She replies. The correspondence goes on, becoming, as Miss de Suze put it to me, more and more come-to-ish. Lord Pastern is an adept. He stages (again I quote Miss de Suze) a sort of Cupid-and-Psyche act at one remove. She asks if they may meet. He replies ardently but refuses. He has all the fun of watching her throughout in his own character. Meanwhile he appears to Rivera to be supporting his suit. But the ice gets thinner and thinner and his figure-skating increasingly hazardous. Moreover, here he is with a golden opportunity for a major journalistic scoop. He could expose Bellairs, represent himself as a brilliant investigator who has worked on his own in the band and now hands the whole story over to *Harmony*. And yet—and yet—there are those captivating drums, those entrancing cymbals, those stimulating wire whisks. There is his own composition. There is his début. He skates on precariously but with exhilaration. He fiddles with the idea of weaning Bellairs from his vice and frightens him into fits by threatening to supplant Syd Skelton. He—"

"Did you," Lord Pastern interrupted, "go to that police school or whatever it is? Hendon?"

"No," Alleyn said. "I didn't."

"Well, get on, get on," he snapped.

"We come to the night of the début and of the great inspiration. Lady Pastern quite obviously desires a marriage between her daughter and Mr. Edward Manx."

Manx made an expostulatory sound. Alleyn waited for a moment. "Look here, Alleyn," Manx said, "you can at least observe some kind of decency. I object most strongly—" He glared at Nigel Bathgate.

"I'm afraid you'll have to lump it," Alleyn said mildly. Nigel said: "I'm sorry, Manx. I'll clear out if you like, but I'll hear it all, in any case."

Manx turned on his heel, walked over to the window and stood there with his back to them.

"Lord Pastern," Alleyn continued, "seems to have shared this hope. And now, having built up a spurious but ardent mystery round G.P.F., he gets his big idea. Perhaps he notices Mr. Manx's instant dislike of Rivera and perhaps he supposes this dislike to arise from an attachment to his step-

daughter. At all events he sees Mr. Manx put a white carnation in his coat,
he goes off to his study and he types a romantic note to Miss de Suze in
which G.P.F. reveals himself as the wearer of a white carnation. The note
swears her to secrecy. Miss de Suze, coming straight from a violent quarrel
with Rivera, sees the white flower in Mr. Manx's jacket and reacts according
to plan."

Manx said, "Oh, my *God!*" and drummed with his fingers on the window-
pane.

"The one thing that seems to have escaped Lord Pastern's notice," Alleyn
said, "is the fact that Mr. Manx is enormously attracted, not by Miss de
Suze, but by Miss Carlisle Wayne."

"Hell!" said Lord Pastern sharply and slewed round in his swivel-chair.
"Hi!" he shouted. "Ned."

"For pity's sake," Manx said impatiently, "let's forget it. It couldn't
matter less." He caught his breath. "In the context," he added.

Lord Pastern contemplated his cousin's back with extreme severity and
then directed his attention once more upon Alleyn. "Well?" he said.

"Well," Alleyn repeated, "so much for the great inspiration. But your
activity hasn't exhausted itself. There is a scene with Bellairs in the ballroom,
overheard by your footman and in part related to me by the wretched Breezy
himself. During this scene you suggest yourself as a successor to Syd Skelton,
and tick Bellairs off about his drug habit. You go so far, I think, as to talk
about writing to *Harmony.* The idea, at this stage, would appear to be a
comprehensive one. You will frighten Breezy into giving up cocaine, expose
Rivera and keep on with the band. It was during this interview that you
behaved in a rather strange manner. You unscrewed the end section of Lady
Pastern's parasol, removed the knob and absent-mindedly pushed the bit of
shaft a little way up the muzzle of your revolver, holding down the spring
clip as you did so. You found that it fitted like a miniature ram-rod or bolt.
Or, if you like, a rifle grenade."

"I told you that meself."

"Exactly. Your policy throughout has been to pile up evidence against
yourself. A sane man, and we are presuming you sane, doesn't do that sort
of thing unless he believes he has an extra trick or two in hand, some
conclusive bits of evidence that must clear him. It was obvious that you
thought you could produce some such evidence and you took great glee in
exhibiting the devastating frankness of complete innocence. Another form of
figure-skating on thin ice. You would let us blunder about making clowns
of ourselves, and, when the sport palled or the ice began to crack, you would,
if you'll excuse the mixed metaphor, plank down the extra tricks."

A web of thread-like veins started out on Lord Pastern's blanched cheek-
bones. He brushed up his moustache and, finding his hand shook, looked
quickly at it and thrust it inside the breast of his coat.

"It seemed best," Alleyn said, "to let you go your own gait and see how
far it would take you. You wanted us to believe that Mr. Manx was G.P.F.;

there was nothing to be gained, we thought, and there might be something lost in letting you see we recognized the equal possibility of your being G.P.F. yourself. This became a probability when the drafts of copy turned up amongst Rivera's blackmailing material. Because Rivera had never met Manx but was closely associated with you."

Alleyn glanced up at his colleague. "It was Inspector Fox," he said, "who first pointed out that you had every chance, during the performance, while the spot light was on somebody else, to load the revolver with the fantastic bolt. All right. But there remained your first trump card—the substituted weapon; the apparently irrefutable evidence that the gun we recovered from Breezy was not the one you brought down to the Metronome. But when we found the original weapon in the lavatory beyond the inner office that difficulty, too, fell into place in the general design. We had got as far as abundant motive and damning circumstance. Opportunity began to appear."

Alleyn stood up and with him Lord Pastern, who pointed a quivering finger at him.

"You bloody fool!" he said, drawing his lips back from his teeth. "You can't arrest me—you—"

"I believe I could arrest you," Alleyn rejoined, "but not for murder. Your second trump card is unfortunately valid. You didn't kill Rivera because Rivera was not killed by the revolver."

He looked at Manx. "And now," he said, "we come to you."

ii

Edward Manx turned from the window and walked towards Alleyn with his hands in his pockets. "All right," he said. "You come to me. What have you nosed out about me?"

"This and that," Alleyn rejoined. "On the face of it there's the evidence that you quarrelled with Rivera and clipped him over the ear. Nosing, as you would put it, beneath the surface, there's your association with *Harmony*. You, and perhaps you alone, knew that Lord Pastern was G.P.F. If he told you Rivera was blackmailing him—"

"He didn't tell me."

"—and if, in addition, you knew Rivera was a drug merchant—" Alleyn waited for a moment but Manx said nothing—"why then, remembering your expressed loathing of this abominable trade, something very like a motive began to appear."

"Oh, nonsense," Manx said lightly. "I don't go about devising quaint deaths for everyone I happen to think a cad or a bad lot."

"One never knows. There have been cases. And you could have changed the revolvers."

"You've just told us that he wasn't killed by the revolver."

"Nevertheless the substitution was made by his murderer."

Manx laughed acidly. "I give up," he said and threw out his hands. "Get on with it."

"The weapon that killed Rivera couldn't have been fired from the revolver because at the time Lord Pastern pulled the trigger, Rivera had his piano-accordion across his chest and the piano-accordion is uninjured."

"I could have told you that," said Lord Pastern, rallying.

"It was a patently bogus affair, in any case. How, for instance, could Lord Pastern be sure of shooting Rivera with such a footling tool? A stiletto in the end of a bit of stick? If he missed by a fraction of an inch Rivera might not die instantly and might not die at all. No. You have to be sure of getting the right spot and getting it good and proper, with a bare bodkin."

Manx lit a cigarette with unsteady hands. "Then in that case I can't for the life of me see—" he stopped—"whodunit," he said, "and how."

"Since it's obvious Rivera wasn't hurt when he fell," Alleyn said, "he was stabbed after he fell."

"But he wasn't meant to fall. They'd altered the routine. We've had that till we're sick of the sound of it."

"It will be our contention that Rivera did not know that the routine had been altered."

"Bosh!" Lord Pastern shouted so unexpectedly that they all jumped. "He wanted it changed. I didn't. It was Carlos wanted it."

"We'll take that point a bit later," Alleyn said. "We're considering how, and when, he was killed. Do you remember the timing of the giant metronome? It was motionless, wasn't it, right up to the moment when Rivera fell; motionless and pointing straight down at him. As he leant backwards its steel tip was poised rather menacingly, straight at his heart."

"Oh, for pity's sake!" Manx said disgustedly. "Are you going to tell us somebody dropped the bolt out of the metronome?"

"No. I'm trying to dismiss the fancy touches, not add to them. Immediately after Rivera fell, the arm of the metronome went into action. Coloured lights winked and popped in and out along its entire surface and that of the surrounding tower frame. It swung to and fro with a rhythmic clack. The whole effect, of course carefully planned, was dazzling and unexpected. One's attention was drawn away from the prostrate figure and what actually happened during the next ten seconds or so was quite lost on the audience. To distract attention still further from the central figure, a spot light played on the tympani where Lord Pastern could be seen in terrific action. But what seemed to happen during those ten confusing seconds?"

He waited again and then said: "Of course you remember, both of you. A waiter threw Breezy a comic wreath of flowers. He knelt down and, pretending to weep, using his handkerchief, opened Rivera's coat and felt for his heart. He felt for his heart."

iii

Lord Pastern said: "You're wrong, Alleyn, you're wrong. I searched him. I'll swear he had nothing on him then and I'll swear he didn't get a chance to pick anything up. Where the devil was the weapon? You're wrong. I searched him."

"As he intended you to do. Yes. Did you notice his baton while you searched him?"

"I told you, damn it. He held it above his head. Good God!" Lord Pastern added, and again, "Good God!"

"A short black rod. The pointed steel was held in his palm, protected by the cork out of an empty gun-oil bottle in your desk. Fox reminded me this morning of Poe's story *The Purloined Letter*. Show a thing boldly to unsuspecting observers and they will think it's what they expect it to be. Breezy conducted your programme last night with a piece of parasol handle and a stiletto. You saw the steel mounting glinting as usual at the tip of an ebony rod. The stiletto was concealed in his palm. It really was quite like his baton. Probably that gave him the idea when he handled the dismembered parasol in the ballroom. I think you asked him, didn't you, to put it together."

"Why the hell," Lord Pastern demanded, "didn't you tell us this straight away? Tormentin' people. It's a damn' scandal. I'll take you up on this, Alleyn, by God I will."

"Did you," Alleyn asked mildly, "go out of your way to confide in us? Or did you willfully and dangerously play a silly lone hand? I think I may be forgiven, sir, for giving you a taste of your own tactics. I wish I could believe it had shaken you a bit: but that, I'm afraid, is too much to hope for." Lord Pastern swore extensively, but Manx said, with a grin: "You know, Cousin George, I rather think we bought it. We've hindered the police in the execution of their duty."

"Serve 'em damn well right."

"I'm still sceptical," Manx said. "Where's your motive? Why should he kill the man who supplied him with his dope?"

"One of the servants at Duke's Gate overheard a quarrel between Bellairs and Rivera when they were together in the ballroom. Breezy asked Rivera for cigarettes—drugged cigarettes, of course—and Rivera refused to give him any. He intimated that their association was ended and talked about writing to *Harmony*. Fox will tell you that sort of thing's quite a common gambit when these people fall out."

"Oh, yes," Fox said. "They do it, you know. Rivera would have a cast-iron story ready to protect himself and get in first with the information. We'd pick Breezy up and be no further on. We might suspect Rivera but we wouldn't get on to anything. Not a thing."

"Because," Lord Pastern pointed out, "you're too thick-headed to get your man when he's screamin' for arrest under your great noses. That's why. Where's your initiative? Where's your push and drive? Why can't you—" he gestured wildly—"stir things up? Make a dust?"

"Well, my lord," said Fox placidly, "we can safely leave that kind of thing to papers like *Harmony*, can't we?"

Manx muttered: "But to kill him—no, I can't see it. And to think all that nonsense up in an hour—"

"He's a drug addict," Alleyn said. "He's been drawing near the end of his tether for some time, I fancy, with Rivera looming up bigger and bigger as his evil genius. It's a common characteristic for the addict to develop an intense hatred of the purveyor upon whom he is so slavishly dependent. This person becomes a sort of Mephistopheles-symbol for the addict. When the purveyor is also a blackmailer and, for good measure, in a position where he can terrify his victim by threats of withdrawal, you get an excruciating twist to the screw. I fancy the picture of you, Lord Pastern, firing point-blank at Rivera had begun to fascinate Bellairs long before he saw you fit the section into the barrel of the gun. I believe he had already played with the idea of fooling round with the ammunition. You added fuel to his fire."

"That be damned—" Lord Pastern began to shout, but Alleyn went on steadily.

"Breezy," he said, "was in an ugly state. He was frantic for cocaine, nervous about his show, terrified of what Lord Pastern would do. Don't forget, sir, you, too, had threatened him with exposure. He planned for a right-and-left coup. You were to hang, you know, for the murder. He has always had a passion for practical jokes."

Manx gave a snort of nervous laughter. Lord Pastern said nothing.

"But," Alleyn went on, "it was all too technicolour to be credible. His red herrings were more like red whales. The whole set-up has the characteristic unreason and fantastic logic of the addict. A Coleridge creates Kubla Khan but a Breezy Bellairs creates a surrealistic dagger made of a parasol handle and a needlework stiletto. An Edgar Allan Poe writes 'The Pit and the Pendulum' but a Breezy Bellairs steals a revolver and makes little scratches in the muzzle with the stiletto; he smokes it with a candle-end and puts it in his overcoat pocket. Stung to an intolerable activity by his unsatisfied lust for cocaine he plans grotesquely but with frantic precision. He may crack at any moment, lose interest or break down, but for a crucial period he goes to work like a demon. Everything falls into place. He tells the band, but *not* Rivera, that the other routine will be followed. Rivera has gone to the end of the restaurant to make his entrance. He persuades Skelton to look at Lord Pastern's revolver at the last minute. He causes himself to be searched, holding his dagger over his head, trembling with strangled laughter. He conducts. He kills. He finds Rivera's heart, and with his hands protected by a handkerchief and hidden from the audience by a comic wreath, he digs his stiletto in and grinds it round. He shows distress. He goes to the room where the body lies and shows greater distress. He changes the carefully scarred revolver in his overcoat pocket with the one Lord Pastern fired. He goes into the lavatory and makes loud retching noises while he disposes of Lord Pastern's unscarred gun. He returns and, being now at the end of his course, frantically searches the body and probably finds the dope he needs so badly. He collapses. That, as we see it, is the case against Breezy Bellairs."

"Poor dope," Manx said. "If you're right."

"Poor dope. Oh, yes," Alleyn said. "Poor dope."

Nigel Bathgate murmured: "Nobody else could have done it."

Lord Pastern glared at him but said nothing.

"Nobody," Fox said.

"But you'll never get a conviction, Alleyn."

"That," Alleyn said, "may be. It won't ruin our lives if we don't."

"How young," Lord Pastern demanded suddenly, "does a fellar have to be to get into detection?"

"If you'll excuse me, Alleyn," Edward Manx said hurriedly, "I think I'll be off."

"Where are you goin', Ned?"

"To see Lisle, Cousin George. We lunched," he explained, "at cross-purposes. I thought she meant she knew it was you. I thought she meant the letter was the one Fée got from *Harmony*. But I see now: she thought it was me."

"What the hell are you talkin' about?"

"It doesn't matter. Good-bye."

"Hi, wait a minute. I'll come with you." They went out into the deserted sunlight, Lord Pastern locking the door behind him.

"I'll be off too, Alleyn," said Nigel as they stood watching the two figures, one lean and loose-jointed, the other stocky and dapper, walk briskly away up Materfamilias Lane. "Unless—what are you going to do?"

"Have you got the warrant, Fox?"

"Yes, Mr. Alleyn."

"Come on, then."

"The Judges' Rules," Fox said, "may be enlightened but there are times when they give you the pip. I suppose you don't agree with that, Mr. Alleyn."

"They keep you and me in our place, Br'er Fox, and I fancy that's a good thing."

"If we could confront him," Fox burst out. "If we could break him down."

"Under pressure he might make a hysterical confession. It might not be true. That would appear to be the idea behind the Judges' Rules."

Fox muttered unprintably.

Nigel Bathgate said: "Where are we heading?"

"We'll call on him," Alleyn grunted. "And with any luck we'll find he already has a visitor. Caesar Bonn of the Metronome."

"How d'you know?"

"Information received," said Fox. "He made an arrangement over the telephone."

"And so, what do you do about it?"

"We pull Bellairs in, Mr. Bathgate, for receiving and distributing drugs."

"Fox," said Alleyn, "thinks there's a case against him. Through the customers."

"Once he's inside," Fox speculated dismally, "he *may* talk. In spite of the Usual Caution. Judges' Rules!"

"He's a glutton for limelight," Alleyn said unexpectedly.

"So what?" Nigel demanded.

"Nothing. I don't know. He may break out somewhere. Here we go."

It was rather dark in the tunnel-like passage that led to Breezy's flat. Nobody was about but a plain-clothes man on duty at the far end: a black figure against a mean window. Walking silently on the heavy carpet, they came up to him. He made a movement of his head, murmured something that ended with the phrase, "hammer and tongs."

"Good," Alleyn said and nodded. The man stealthily opened the door into Breezy's flat.

They moved into an entrance lobby where they found a second man with a notebook pressed against the wall and a pencil poised over it. The four silent men almost filled the cramped lobby.

In the living-room beyond, Caesar Bonn was quarrelling with Breezy Bellairs.

"Publicity!" Caesar was saying. "But of what a character! No, no! I am sorry. I regret this with all my heart. For me as for you it is a disaster."

"Listen, Caesar, you're all wrong. My public won't let me down. They'd *want* to see me." The voice rose steeply. "They *love* me," Breezy cried out, and after a pause: "You bloody swine, they *love* me."

"I must go."

"All right. You'll see. I'll ring Carmarelli. Carmarelli's been trying to get me for years. Or the Lotus Tree. They'll be fighting for me. And your bloody clientele'll follow me. They'll eat us. I'll ring Stein. There's not a restaurateur in town—"

"One moment." Caesar was closer to the door. "To spare you discomfiture I feel I must warn you. Already I have discussed this matter with these gentlemen. An informal meeting. We are all agreed. It will not be possible for you to appear at any first-class restaurant or club."

They heard a falsetto whining. Caesar's voice intervened. "Believe me," he said, "when I say I mean this kindly. After all, we are old friends. Take my advice. Retire. You can afford to do so, no doubt." He gave a nervous giggle. Breezy had whispered. Evidently they were close together on the other side of the door. "No, no!" Caesar said loudly. "I can do nothing about it. Nothing! Nothing!"

Breezy screamed out abruptly: "I'll ruin you!" and the pencil skidded across the plain-clothes officer's notebook.

"You have ruined yourself," Caesar gabbled. "You will keep silence. Understand me: there must be complete silence. For you there is no more spot light. You are finished. *Keep off!*" There was a scuffle, and a stifled ejaculation. Something thudded heavily against the door and slid down its surface. "There, now!" Caesar panted. He sounded scandalized and breathlessly triumphant. Unexpectedly, after a brief pause, he went on in a reflective voice: "No, truly, you are too stupid. This decides me. I am resolved. I inform the police of your activities. You will make a foolish appearance in court. Everyone will laugh a little and forget you. You will go to gaol or perhaps to a clinic. If you are of good behaviour you may, in a year or so, be permitted to conduct a little band."

"*Christ!* Tell them, then! Tell them!" Beyond the door Breezy stumbled to his feet. His voice broke into falsetto. "But it's me that'll tell the tale, me! If I go to the dock, by God, I'll wipe the grins off all your bloody faces. You haven't heard anything yet. Try any funny business with ME! Finished! By God, I've only just started. You're all going to hear how I slit up a bloody Dago's heart for him."

"This is it," Alleyn said, and opened the door.

SPINSTERS
IN
JEOPARDY

For
Anita and Val Muling
with my thanks

Contents

Cast of Characters

RODERICK ALLEYN, Chief Detective-Inspector, Criminal Investigation Department, New Scotland Yard

AGATHA TROY ALLEYN, his wife

RICKY, their son

MISS TRUEBODY, their fellow-passenger

DR. CLAUDEL, a French physician

RAOUL MILANO, of Roqueville. Owner-driver

DR. ALI BARADI, a surgeon

MAHOMET, his servant

MR. OBERON, of the Château de la Chèvre d'Argent

GINNY TAYLOR
ROBIN HERRINGTON } his guests
CARBURY GLANDE
ANNABELLA WELLS

TERESA, the fiancée of Raoul

M. DUPONT, of the Sûreté. Acting Commissaire at the Préfecture, Roqueville

M. CALLARD, Managing Director of the Compagnie Chimique des Alpes Maritimes

M. AND MADAME MILANO, the parents of Raoul

MARIE, a maker of figurines

M. MALAQUIN, proprietor of the Hôtel Royal

P. E. GARBEL, a chemist

Prologue

Without moving his head, Ricky slewed his eyes round until he was able to look slantways at the back of his mother's easel.

"I'm getting pretty bored, however," he announced.

"Stick it a bit longer, darling, I implore you, and look at Daddy."

"Well, because it's just about as boring a thing as a person can have to do. Isn't it, Daddy?"

"When I did it," said his father, "I was allowed to look at your mama, so I wasn't bored. But as there are degrees of boredom," he continued, "so there are different kinds of bores. You might almost say there are recognizable schools."

"To which school," said his wife, stepping back from her easel, "would you say Mr. Garbel belonged? Ricky, look at Daddy for five minutes more and then I promise we'll stop."

Ricky sighed ostentatiously and contemplated his father.

"Well, as far as we know him," Alleyn said, "to the epistolatory school. There, he's a classic. In person he's undoubtedly the sort of bore that shows you things you don't want to see. Snapshots in envelopes. Barren conservatories. Newspaper cuttings. He's relentless in this. I think he carries things on his person and puts them in front of you without giving you the smallest clue about what you're meant to say. You're moving, Ricky."

"Isn't it five minutes yet?"

"No, and it never will be if you fidget. How long is it, Troy, since you first heard from Mr. Garbel?"

"About eighteen months. He wrote for Christmas. All told I've had six letters and five postcards from Mr. Garbel. This last arrived this morning. That's what put him into my head."

"Daddy, who is Mr. Garbel?"

"One of Mummy's admirers. He lives in the Maritime Alps and writes love letters to her."

"Why?"

"He says it's because he's her third cousin once removed, but I know better."

"What do you know better?"

With a spare paintbrush clenched between her teeth, Troy said indistinctly: "Keep like that, Ricky darling, I *implore* you."

"O.K. Tell me properly, Daddy, about Mr. Garbel."

"Well, he suddenly wrote to Mummy and said Mummy's great-aunt's daughter was his second cousin, and that he thought Mummy would like to know that he lived at a place called Roqueville in the Maritime Alps. He sent a map of Roqueville, marking the place where the road he lived on ought to be shown, but wasn't, and he told Mummy how he didn't go out much or meet many people."

"Pretty dull, however."

"He told her about all the food you can buy there that you can't buy here, and he sent her copies of newspapers with bus timetables marked and messages at the side saying: 'I find this bus convenient and often take it. It leaves the corner by the principal hotel every half-hour.' Do you still want to hear about Mr. Garbel?"

"Unless it's time to stop, I might as well."

"Mummy wrote to Mr. Garbel and said how interesting she found his letter."

"Did you, Mummy?"

"One has to be polite," Troy muttered and laid a thin stroke of rose on the mouth of Ricky's portrait.

"And he wrote back sending her three used bus tickets and a used train ticket."

"Does she collect them?"

"Mr. Garbel thought she would like to know that they were his tickets punched by guards and conductors all for him. He also sends her beautifully coloured postcards of the Maritime Alps."

"What's that? May I have them?"

". . . with arrows pointing to where his house would be if you could see it and to where the road goes to a house he sometimes visits only the house is off the postcard."

"Like a picture puzzle, sort of?"

"Sort of. And he tells Mummy how, when he was young and doing chemistry at Cambridge, he almost met her great-aunt who was his second cousin once removed."

"Did he have a shop?"

"No, he's a special kind of chemist without a shop. When he sends Mummy presents of used tickets and old newspapers he writes on them: 'Sent by P. E. Garbel, 16 Rue des Violettes, Roqueville, to Mrs. Agatha Alleyn (née Troy) daughter of Stephen and Harriet Troy (née Baynton).' "

"That's you, isn't it, Mummy? What else?"

"Is it possible, Ricky," asked his wondering father, "that you find this interesting?"

"Yes," said Ricky. "I like it. Does he mention me?"

"I don't think so."

"Or you?"

"He suggests that Mummy might care to read parts of his letter to me."

"May we go and see him?"

"Yes," said Alleyn. "As a matter of fact I think we may."

Troy turned from her work and gaped at her husband. "What can you mean?" she exclaimed.

"Is it time, Mummy? Because it must be, so may I get down?"

"Yes, thank you, my sweet. You have been terribly good and I must think of some exciting reward."

"Going to see Mr. Garbel frinstance?"

"I'm afraid," Troy said, "that Daddy, poor thing, was being rather silly."

"Well then—ride to Babylon?" Ricky suggested, and looked out of the corners of his eyes at his father.

"All right," Alleyn groaned, parodying despair. "O.K. *All right.* Here we go!"

He swung the excitedly squealing Ricky up to his shoulders and grasped his ankles.

"Good old horse," Ricky shouted and patted his father's cheek. "Non-stop to Babylon. Good old horse."

Troy looked dotingly at him. "Say to Nanny that I said you could ask for an extra high tea."

"Top highest with strawberry jam?"

"If there is any."

"Lavish!" said Ricky and gave a cry of primitive food-lust. "Giddy-up horse," he shouted. The family of Alleyn broke into a chant:

> "How many miles to Babylon?
> Five score and ten.
> Can I get there by candle-light?"

"*Yes! And back again!*" Ricky yelled, and was carried at a canter from the room.

Troy listened to the diminishing rumpus on the stairs and looked at her work.

"How happy we are!" she thought, and then, foolishly, "Touch wood!" And she picked up a brush and dragged a touch of colour from the hair across the brow. "How lucky I am," she thought, more soberly, and her mood persisted when Alleyn came back with his hair tousled like Ricky's and his tie under his ear.

He said: "May I look?"

"All right," Troy agreed, wiping her brushes, "but don't say anything."

He grinned and walked round to the front of the easel. Troy had painted a head that seemed to have light as its substance. Even the locks of dark hair might have been spun from sunshine. It was a work in line rather than in mass, but the line flowed and turned with a subtlety that made any further elaboration unnecessary. "It needs another hour," Troy muttered.

"In that case," Alleyn said, "I can at least touch wood."

She gave him a quick grateful look and said, "What is all this about Mr. Garbel?"

"I saw the A.C. this morning. He was particularly nice, which generally means he's got you pricked down for a particularly nasty job. On the face of it this one doesn't sound so bad. It seems M.I.5 and the Sûreté are having a bit of a party with the Narcotics Bureau, and our people want somebody with fairly fluent French to go over for talks and a bit of field-work. As it is M.I.5 we'd better observe the usual rule of airy tact on your part and phony inscrutability on mine. But it turns out that the field-work lies, to coin a coy phrase, not a hundred miles from Roqueville."

"Never!" Troy ejaculated. "In the Garbel country?"

"Precisely. Now it occurs to me that what with war, Ricky and the atrocious nature of my job, we've never had a holiday abroad together. Nanny is due for a fortnight at Reading. Why shouldn't you and Ricky come with me to Roqueville and call on Mr. Garbel?"

Troy looked delighted, but she said: "You can't go round doing top-secret jobs for M.I.5 trailing your wife and child. It would look so amateurish. Besides, we agreed never to mix business with pleasure, Rory."

"In this case the more amateurish I look, the better. And I should only be based on Roqueville. The job lies outside it, so we wouldn't really be mixing business with pleasure."

He looked at her for a moment. "Do come," he said, "you know you're dying to meet Mr. Garbel."

Troy scraped her palette. "I'm dying to come," she amended, "but not to meet Mr. Garbel. And yet: I don't know. There's a sort of itch, I confess it, to find out just how deadly dull he is. Like a suicidal tendency."

"You must yield to it. Write to him and tell him you're coming. You might enclose a bus ticket from Putney to the Fulham Road. How do you address him: 'Dear Cousin—' But what is his Christian name?"

"I've no idea. He's just P. E. Garbel. To his intimates, he tells me, he is known as Peg. He adds, inevitably, a quip about being square in a round hole."

"Roqueville being the hole?"

"Presumably."

"Has he a job, do you think?"

"For all I know he may be writing a monograph on bicarbonate-of-soda. If he is he'll probably ask us to read the manuscript."

"At all events we must meet him. Put down that damn palette and tell me you're coming."

Troy wiped her hands on her smock. "We're coming," she said.

ii

In his Château outside Roqueville, Mr. Oberon looked across the nighted Mediterranean towards North Africa and then smiled gently upon his assembled guests.

"How fortunate we are," he said. "Not a jarring note. All gathered together with one pure object in mind." He ran over their names as if they composed a sort of celestial roll-call. "Our youngest disciple," he said, beaming on Ginny Taylor. "A wonderful field of experience awaits her. She stands on the threshold of ecstasy. It is not too much to say, of ecstasy. And Robin too." Robin Herrington, who had been watching Ginny Taylor, looked up sharply. "Ah, youth, youth," sighed Mr. Oberon, ambiguously, and turned to the remaining guests, two men and a woman. "Do we envy them?" he asked, and answered himself. "No! No, for ours is the richer tilth. We are the husbandmen, are we not?"

Dr. Baradi lifted his dark, fleshy and intelligent head. He looked at his host. "Yes, indeed," he said. "We are precisely that. And when Annabella arrives—I think you said she was coming?"

"Dear Annabella!" Mr. Oberon exclaimed. "Yes. On Tuesday. Unexpectedly."

"Ah!" said Carbury Glande, looking at his paint-stained finger-nails. "On Tuesday. Then she will be rested and ready for our Thursday rites."

"Dear Annabella!" Dr. Baradi echoed sumptuously.

The sixth guest turned her ravaged face and short-sighted eyes towards Ginny Taylor.

"Is this your first visit?" she asked.

Ginny was looking at Mr. Oberon. She wore an expression that was unbecoming to her youth, a look of uncertainty, excitement and perhaps fear.

"Yes," she said. "My first."

"A neophyte," Baradi murmured richly.

"Soon to be so young a priestess," Mr. Oberon added. "It is very touching." He smiled at Ginny with parted lips.

A tinkling crash broke across the conversation. Robin Herrington had dropped his glass on the tessellated floor. The remains of his cocktail ran into a little pool near Mr. Oberon's feet.

Mr. Oberon cut across his apologies. "No, no," he said. "It is a happy symbol. Perhaps a promise. Let us call it a libation," he said. "Shall we dine?"

CHAPTER I

Journey to the South

Alleyn lifted himself on his elbow and turned his watch to the blue light above his pillow. Twenty minutes past five. In another hour they would be in Roqueville.

The abrupt fall of silence when the train stopped must have woken him. He listened intently but, apart from the hiss of escaping steam and the slam of a door in a distant carriage, everything was quiet and still.

He heard the men in the double sleeper next his own exchange desultory remarks. One of them yawned loudly.

Alleyn thought the station must be Douceville. Sure enough, someone walked past the window and a lonely voice announced to the night: *"Douce-v-i-ll-e."*

The engine hissed again. The same voice, apparently continuing a broken conversation, called out: *"Pas ce soir, par exemple!"* Someone else laughed distantly. The voices receded to be followed by the most characteristic of all stationary train noises, the tap of steel on steel. The taps tinkered away into the distance.

Alleyn manoeuvred himself to the bottom of his bunk, dangled his long legs in space for a moment, and then slithered to the floor. The window was not completely shuttered. He peered through the gap and was confronted by the bottom of a poster for Dubonnet and the lower half of a porter carrying a lamp. The lamp swung to and fro, a bell rang, and the train clanked discreetly. The lamp and poster were replaced by the lower halves of two discharged passengers, a pile of luggage, a stretch of empty platform, and a succession of swiftly moving pools of light. Then there was only the night hurrying past with blurred suggestions of rocks and olive trees.

The train gathered speed and settled down to its perpetual choriambic statement: "What a to-*do*. What a to-*do*."

Alleyn cautiously lowered the window-blind. The train was crossing the seaward end of a valley and the moon in its third quarter was riding the western heavens. Its radiance emphasized the natural pallor of hills and trees and dramatized the shapes of rocks and mountains. With the immediate gesture of a shutter, a high bank obliterated this landscape. The train passed through a village and for two seconds Alleyn looked into a lamplit room where a woman watched a man intent over an early breakfast. What occupation got them up so soon? They were there, sharp in his vision, and were gone.

He turned from the window wondering if Troy, who shared his pleasure in train journeys, was awake in her single berth next door. In twenty minutes he would go and see. In the meantime he hoped that, in the almost complete darkness, he could dress himself without making a disturbance. He began to do so, steadying himself against the lurch and swing of this small, noisy and unstable world.

"Hullo." A treble voice ventured from the blackness of the lower bunk. "Are we getting out soon?"

"Hullo," Alleyn rejoined. "No, go to sleep."

"I couldn't be wakier. Matter of fac' I've been awake pretty well all night."

Alleyn groped for his shirt, staggered, barked his shin on the edge of his suitcase and swore under his breath.

"Because," the treble voice continued, "if we aren't getting out why are you dressing yourself?"

"To be ready for when we are."

"I see," said the voice. "Is Mummy getting ready for getting out, too?"

"Not yet."

"Why?"

"It's not time."

"Is she asleep?"

"I don't know, old boy."

"Then how do you know she's not getting ready?"

"I don't know, really. I just hope she's not."

"Why?"

"I want her to rest, and if you say why again I won't answer."

"I see." There was a pause. The voice chuckled. "Why?" it asked.

Alleyn had found his shirt. He now discovered that he had put it on inside out. He took it off.

"If," the voice pursued, "I said a sensible why, would you answer, Daddy?"

"It would have to be entirely sensible."

"Why are you getting up in the dark?"

"I had hoped," Alleyn said bitterly, "that all little boys were fast asleep and I didn't want to wake them."

"Because now you know they aren't asleep so why—?"

"You're perfectly right," Alleyn said. The train rounded a curve and he ran with some violence against the door. He switched on the light and contemplated his son.

Ricky had the newly made look peculiar to little boys in bed. His dark hair hung sweetly over his forehead, his eyes shone and his cheeks and lips were brilliant. One would have said he was so new that his colours had not yet dried.

"I like being in a train," he said, "more lavishly than anything that's ever happened so far. Do you like being in a train, Daddy?"

"Yes," said Alleyn. He opened the door of the washing-cabinet, which lit itself up. Ricky watched his father shave.

"Where are we now?" he said presently.

"By a sea. It's called the Mediterranean and it's just out there on the other side of the train. We shall see it when it's daytime."

"Are we in the middle of the night?"

"Not quite. We're in the very early morning. Out there everybody is fast asleep," Alleyn suggested, not very hopefully.

"Everybody?"

"Almost everybody. Fast asleep and snoring."

"All except us," Ricky said with rich satisfaction, "because we are lavishly wide awake in the very early morning in a train. Aren't we, Daddy?"

"That's it. Soon we'll pass the house where I'm going tomorrow. The train doesn't stop there, so I have to go on with you to Roqueville and drive back. You and Mummy will stay in Roqueville."

"Where will you be most of the time?"

"Sometimes with you and sometimes at this house. It's called the Château de la Chèvre d'Argent. That means the House of the Silver Goat."

"Pretty funny name, however," said Ricky.

A stream of sparks ran past the window. The light from the carriage flew across the surface of a stone wall. The train had begun to climb steeply. It gradually slowed down until there was time to see nearby objects lamplit, in the world outside: a giant cactus, a flight of steps, part of an olive grove. The engine laboured almost to a standstill. Outside their window, perhaps a hundred yards away, there was a vast house that seemed to grow out of the cliff. It stood full in the moonlight, and shadows, black as ink, were thrown by buttresses across its recessed face. A solitary window, veiled by a patterned blind, glowed dully yellow.

"*Somebody* is awake out there," Ricky observed. " 'Out,' 'in'?" he speculated. "Daddy, what are those people? 'Out' or 'in'?"

"Outside for us, I suppose, and inside for them."

"Outside the train and inside the house," Ricky agreed. "Suppose the train ran through the house, would they be 'in' for us?"

"I hope," his father observed glumly, "that you don't grow up a metaphysician."

"What's that? Look, there they are in their house. We've stopped, haven't we?"

The carriage window was exactly opposite the lighted one in the cliff-like wall of the house. A blurred shape moved in the room on the other side of the blind. It swelled and became a black body pressed against the window.

Alleyn made a sharp ejaculation and a swift movement.

"Because you're standing right in front of the window," Ricky said politely, "and it would be rather nice to see out."

The train jerked galvanically and with a compound racketing noise, slowly entered a tunnel, emerged, and gathering pace, began a descent to sea-level.

The door of the compartment opened and Troy stood there, in a woollen dressing-gown. Her short hair was rumpled and hung over her forehead like her son's. Her face was white and her eyes dark with perturbation. Alleyn turned quickly. Troy looked from him to Ricky. "Have you seen out of the window?" she asked.

"I have," said Alleyn. "And so, by the look of you, have you."

Troy said, "Can you help me with my suitcase?" and to Ricky: "I'll come back and get you up soon, darling."

"Are you both going?"

"We'll be just next door. We shan't be long," Alleyn said.

"It's only because it's in a train."

"We know," Troy reassured him. "But it's all right. Honestly. O.K.?"

"O.K.," Ricky said in a small voice, and Troy touched his cheek.

Alleyn followed into her own compartment. She sat down on her bunk and stared at him. "I can't believe that was true," she said.

"I'm sorry you saw it."

"Then it was true. Ought we to do anything? Rory, ought you to do anything? Oh *dear*, how tiresome."

"Well, I can't do much while moving away at sixty miles an hour. I suppose I'd better ring up the Préfecture when we get to Roqueville."

He sat down beside her. "Never mind, darling," he said, "there may be another explanation."

"I don't see how there can be, unless— Do you mind telling me what you saw?"

Alleyn said carefully, "A lighted window, masked by a spring blind. A woman falling against the blind and releasing it. Beyond the woman, but out of sight to us, there must have been a brilliant lamp and in its light, farther back in the room and on our right, stood a man in a white garment. His face, oddly enough, was in shadow. There was something that looked like a wheel, beyond his right shoulder. His right arm was raised."

"And in his hand—?"

"Yes," Alleyn said, "that's the tricky bit, isn't it?"

"And then the tunnel. It was like one of those sudden breaks in an old-fashioned film, too abrupt to be really dramatic. It was there and then it didn't exist. No," said Troy, "I won't believe it was true. I won't believe something is still going on inside that house. And what a house too! It looked like a Gustave Doré, really bad romantic."

Alleyn said: "Are you all right to get dressed? I'll just have a word with the car attendant. He may have seen it, too. After all, we may not be the only people awake and looking out, though I fancy mine was the only compartment with the light on. Yours was in darkness, by the way?"

"I had the window shutter down, though. I'd been thinking how strange it is to see into other people's lives through a train window."

"I know," Alleyn said. "There's a touch of magic in it."

"And then—to see that! Not so magical."

"Never mind. I'll talk to the attendant and then I'll come back and get Ricky up. He'll be getting train-fever. We should reach Roqueville in about twenty minutes. All right?"

"Oh, I'm right as a bank," said Troy.

"Nothing like the Golden South for a carefree holiday," Alleyn said. He grinned at her, went out into the corridor and opened the door of his own sleeper.

Ricky was still sitting up in his bunk. His hands were clenched and his eyes wide open. "You're being a pretty long time, however," he said.

"Mummy's coming in a minute. I'm just going to have a word with the chap outside. Stick it out, old boy."

"O.K.," said Ricky.

The attendant, a pale man with a dimple in his chin, was dozing on his stool at the forward end of the carriage. Alleyn, who had already discovered that he spoke very little English, addressed him in diplomatic French that had become only slightly hesitant through disuse. Had the attendant, he asked, happened to be awake when the train paused outside a tunnel a few minutes ago? The man seemed to be in some doubt as to whether Alleyn was about to complain because he was asleep or because the train had halted. It took a minute or two to clear up this difficulty and to discover that the attendant had, in point of fact, been asleep for some time.

"I'm sorry to trouble you," Alleyn said, "but can you, by any chance, tell me the name of the large building near the entrance to the tunnel?"

"Ah, yes, yes," the attendant said. "Certainly, Monsieur, since I am a native of these parts. It is known to everybody, this house, on account of its great antiquity. It is the Château de la Chèvre d'Argent."

"I thought it might be," said Alleyn.

i i

Alleyn reminded the sleepy attendant that they were leaving the train at Roqueville and tipped him generously. The man thanked him with that peculiarly Gallic effusiveness that is at once too logical and too adroit to be offensive.

"Do you know," Alleyn said, as if on an afterthought, "who lives in the Château de la Chèvre d'Argent?"

The attendant believed it was leased to an extremely wealthy gentleman, possibly an American, possibly an Englishman, who entertained very exclusively. He believed the ménage to be an excessively distinguished one.

Alleyn waited for a moment and then said, "I think there was a little trouble there tonight. One saw a scene through a lighted window when the train halted."

The attendant's shoulders suggested that all things are possible and that speculation is vain. His eyes were as blank as boot buttons in his pallid face.

Should he not perhaps fetch the baggage of Monsieur and Madame and the little one, in readiness for their descent at Roqueville? He had his hand on the door of Alleyn's compartment when from somewhere towards the rear of the carriage, a woman screamed twice.

They were short screams, ejaculatory in character, as if they had been wrenched out of her, and very shrill. The attendant wagged his head from side to side in exasperation, begged Alleyn to excuse him and went off down the corridor to the rearmost compartment. He tapped. Alleyn guessed at an agitated response. The attendant went in and Troy put her head out of her own door.

"What now, for pity's sake?" she asked.

"Somebody having a nightmare or something. Are you ready?"

"Yes. But what a rum journey we're having!"

The attendant came back at a jog-trot. Was Alleyn perhaps a doctor? An English lady had been taken ill. She was in great pain: the abdomen, the attendant elaborated, clutching his own in pantomime. It was evidently a formidable seizure. If Monsieur, by any chance—

Alleyn said he was not a doctor. Troy said, "I'll go and see the poor thing, shall I? Perhaps there's a doctor somewhere in the train. You get Ricky up, darling."

She made off down the swaying corridor. The attendant began to tap on doors and to enquire fruitlessly of his passengers if they were doctors. "I shall see my comrades of the other *voitures*," he said importantly. "Evidently one must organize."

Alleyn found Ricky sketchily half-dressed and in a child's panic.

"Where have you been, however?" he demanded. "Because I didn't know where everyone was. We're going to be late for getting out. I can't find my pants. Where's Mummy?"

Alleyn calmed him, got him ready and packed their luggage. Ricky, white-faced, sat on the lower bunk with his gaze turned on the door. He liked, when travelling, to have his family under his eye. Alleyn, remembering his own childhood, knew his little son was racked with an illogical and bottomless anxiety, an anxiety that vanished when the door opened and Troy came in.

"Oh golly, Mum!" Ricky said and his lip trembled.

"Hullo, there," Troy said in the especially calm voice she kept for Ricky's panics. She sat down beside him, putting her arm where he could lean back against it, and looked at her husband.

"I think that woman's very ill," she said. "She looks frightful. She had what she thought was some kind of food poisoning this morning and dosed herself with castor-oil. And then, just now she had a violent pain, really awful, she says, in the appendix place and now she hasn't any pain at all and looks ghastly. Wouldn't that be a perforation, perhaps?"

"Your guess is as good as mine, my love."

"Rory, she's about fifty and she comes from the Bermudas and has no relations in the world and wears a string bag on her head and she's never been abroad and we can't just let her be whisked on into the Italian Riviera with a perforated appendix, if that's what it is."

"Oh, damn!"

"Well, can we? I said—" Troy went on, looking sideways at her husband— "that you'd come and talk to her."

"Darling, what the hell can I do?"

"You're calming in a panic, isn't he, Rick?"

"Yes," said Ricky again turning white. "I don't suppose you're both going away, are you, Mummy?"

"You can come with us. You could look through the corridor window at the sea. It's shiny with moonlight and Daddy and I will be just on the other side of the poor thing's door. Her name's Miss Truebody and she knows Daddy's a policeman."

"Well, I must say . . ." Alleyn began indignantly.

"We'd better hurry, hadn't we?" Troy stood up, holding Ricky's hand. He clung to her like a limpet.

At the far end of the corridor their own car attendant stood with two of his colleagues outside Miss Truebody's door. They made dubious grimaces at one another and spoke in voices that were drowned by the racket of the train. When they saw Troy, they all took off their silver-braided caps and bowed to her. A doctor, they said, had been discovered in the *troisième voiture* and was now with the unfortunate lady. Perhaps Madame would join him. Their own attendant tapped on the door and with an ineffable smirk at Troy, opened it. "Madame!" he invited.

Troy went in, and Ricky feverishly transferred his hold to Alleyn's hand. Together, they looked out of the corridor window.

The railway, on this part of the coast, followed an embankment a few feet above sea level and as Troy had said, the moon shone on the Mediterranean. A long cape ran out over the glossy water and near its tip a few points of yellow light showed in early-rising households. The stars were beginning to pale.

"That's Cap St. Gilles," Alleyn said. "Lovely, isn't it, Rick?"

Ricky nodded. He had one ear tuned to his mother's voice which could just be heard beyond Miss Truebody's door.

"Yes," he said, "it is lovely." Alleyn wondered if Ricky was really as pedantically mannered a child as some of their friends seemed to think.

"Aren't we getting a bit near?" Ricky asked. "Bettern't Mummy come now?"

"It's all right. We've ten minutes yet and the train people know we're getting off. I promise it's all right. Here's Mummy now."

She came out followed by a small bald gentleman with waxed moustaches, wearing striped professional trousers, patent-leather boots and a frogged dressing-gown.

"Your French is badly needed. This is the doctor," Troy said, and haltingly introduced her husband.

The doctor was formally enchanted. He said crisply that he had examined the patient, who almost certainly suffered from a perforated appendix and should undoubtedly be operated upon as soon as possible. He regretted extremely that he himself had an urgent professional appointment in St. Céleste and could not, therefore, accept responsibility. Perhaps the best thing to do would be to discharge Miss Truebody at Roqueville and send her back by the evening train to St. Christophe where she could go to a hospital. Of course, if there was a surgeon in Roqueville the operation might be performed there. In any case he would give Miss Truebody an injection of morphine. His shoulders rose. It was a position of extreme difficulty. They must hope, must they not, that there would be a medical man and suitable accommodation available at Roqueville? He believed he had understood Madame to say that she and Monsieur l'Inspecteur-en-Chef would be good enough to assist their compatriot.

Monsieur l'Inspecteur-en-Chef glared at his wife and said they would, of course, be enchanted. Troy said in English that it had obviously comforted Miss Truebody and impressed the doctor to learn of her husband's rank. The doctor bowed, delivered a few definitive compliments and, lurching in a still dignified manner down the swinging corridor, made for his own carriage, followed by his own attendant.

Troy said: "Come and speak to her, Rory. It'll help."

"Daddy?" Ricky said in a small voice.

"We won't be a minute," Troy and Alleyn answered together, and Alleyn added, "We know how it feels, Rick, but one has to get used to these things." Ricky nodded and swallowed.

Alleyn followed Troy into Miss Truebody's compartment. "This is my husband, Miss Truebody," Troy said. "He's had a word with the doctor and he'll tell you all about it."

Miss Truebody lay on her back with her knees a little drawn up and her sick hands closed vise-like over the sheet. She had a rather blunt face that in health probably was rosy, but now was ominously blotched and looked as if it had shrunk away from her nose. This effect was heightened by the circumstance of her having removed her teeth. There were beads of sweat along the margin of her grey hair and her upper lip and the ridges where her eyebrows would have been if she had possessed any; the face was singularly smooth and showed none of the minor blemishes characteristic of her age. Over her head she wore, as Troy had noticed, a sort of net bag made of pink string. She looked terrified. Something in her eyes reminded Alleyn of Ricky in one of his travel-panics.

He told her, as reassuringly as might be, of the doctor's pronouncement. Her expression did not change and he wondered if she had understood him. When he had finished she gave a little gasp and whispered indistinctly: "Too awkward, so inconvenient. Disappointing." And her mottled hands clutched at the sheet.

"Don't worry," Alleyn said, "don't worry about anything. We'll look after you."

Like a sick animal, she gave him a heart-rending look of gratitude and shut her eyes. For a moment Troy and Alleyn watched her being slightly but inexorably jolted by the train, and then stole uneasily from the compartment. They found their son dithering with agitation in the corridor and the attendant bringing out the last of their luggage.

Troy said hurriedly: "This is frightful. We can't take the responsibility. Or must we?"

"I'm afraid we must. There's no time to do anything else. I've got a card of sorts up my sleeve in Roqueville. If it's no good we'll get her back to St. Christophe."

"What's your card? *Not*," Troy ejaculated, "Mr. Garbel?"

"No, no, it's—hi—look! We're there."

The little town of Roqueville, wan in the first thin wash of dawnlight, slid past the windows, and the train drew into the station.

Fortified by a further tip from Troy and in evident relief at the prospect of losing Miss Truebody, the attendant enthusiastically piled the Alleyns' luggage on the platform while the guard plunged into earnest conversation with Alleyn and the Roqueville station-master. The doctor reappeared fully clad and gave Miss Truebody a shot of morphine. He and Troy, in incredible association, got her into a magenta dressing-gown in which she looked like death itself. Troy hurriedly packed Miss Truebody's possessions, uttered a few words of encouragement, and with Ricky and the doctor joined Alleyn on the platform.

Ricky, his parents once deposited on firm ground and fully accessible, forgot his terrors and contemplated the train with the hard-boiled air of an experienced traveller.

The station-master with the guard and three attendants in support was saying to the doctor: "One is perfectly conscious, Monsieur le Docteur, of the extraordinary circumstances. Nevertheless, the schedule of the Chemin de Fer des Alpes Maritimes cannot be indefinitely protracted."

The doctor said: "One may, however, in the few moments that are being squandered in this unproductive conversation, M. le Chef de Gare, consult the telephone directory and ascertain if there is a doctor in Roqueville."

"One may do so undoubtedly, but I can assure M. le Docteur that such a search will be fruitless. Our only doctor is at a conference in St. Christophe. Therefore, since the train is already delayed one minute and forty seconds . . ."

He glanced superbly at the guard, who began to survey the train like a sergeant-major. A whistle was produced. The attendants walked towards their several cars.

"Rory!" Troy cried out. "We can't . . ."

Alleyn said: "All right," and spoke to the station-master. "Perhaps," he said, "M. le Chef de Gare, you are aware of the presence of a surgeon—I believe his name is Dr. Baradi—among the guests of M. Oberon some twenty kilometres back at the Château de la Chèvre d'Argent. He is an Egyptian gentleman. I understand he arrived two weeks ago."

"*Alors*, M. l'Inspecteur-en-Chef . . ." the doctor began but the station-master, after a sharp glance at Alleyn, became alert and neatly deferential. He remembered the arrival of the Egyptian gentleman for whom he had caused a taxi to be produced. If the gentleman should be—he bowed—as M. l'Inspecteur-en-Chef evidently was informed, a surgeon, all their problems were solved, were they not? He began to order the sleeping-car attendants about and was briskly supported by the guard. Troy, to the renewed agitation of her son, and with the assistance of their attendant, returned to the sleeping-car and supported Miss Truebody out of it, down to the platform and into the waiting-room, where she was laid out, horribly corpse-like, on a bench. Her luggage followed. Troy, on an afterthought, darted back and retrieved from a tumbler in the washing cabinet, Miss Truebody's false teeth, dropping them with a shudder into a tartan spongebag. On the platform the doctor held a private conversation with Alleyn. He wrote in his notebook, tore out the page and gave it to Alleyn with his card. Alleyn, in the interests of Franco-British relationships, insisted on paying the doctor's fee and the train finally drew out of Roqueville in an atmosphere of the liveliest cordiality. On the strangely quiet platform Alleyn and Troy looked at each other.

"This," Alleyn said, "is not your holiday as I had planned it."

"What do we do now?"

"Ring up the Chèvre d'Argent and ask for Dr. Baradi, who, I have reason to suppose, is an admirable surgeon and an unmitigated blackguard."

They could hear the dawn cocks crowing in the hills above Roqueville.

iii

In the waiting-room Ricky fell fast asleep on his mother's lap. Troy was glad of this as Miss Truebody had begun to look quite dreadful. She too had drifted into a kind of sleep. She breathed unevenly, puffing out her unsupported lips, and made unearthly noises in her throat. Troy could hear her husband and the station-master talking in the office next door and then Alleyn's voice only, speaking on the telephone and in French! There were longish pauses during which Alleyn said: "*'Allo! 'Allo!*" and "*Ne coupez pas, je vous en prie, mademoiselle,*" which Troy felt rather proud of understanding. A grey light filtered into the waiting-room; Ricky made a touching little sound, rearranged his lips, sighed, and turned his face against her breast in an abandonment of relaxation. Alleyn began to speak at length, first in French, and then in English. Troy heard fragments of sentences.

". . . I wouldn't have roused you up like this if it hadn't been so urgent.

. . . Dr. Claudel said definitely that it was really a matter of the most extreme urgency. . . . He will telephone from St. Céleste. I am merely a fellow-passenger . . . yes, yes, I have a car here. . . . Good. . . . Very well. . . . Yes, I understand. Thank you." A bell tinkled.

There was a further conversation and then Alleyn came into the waiting-room. Troy, with her chin on the top of Ricky's silken head, gave him a nod and an intimate family look: her comment on Ricky's sleep. He said: "It's not fair."

"What?"

"Your talent for turning my heart over."

"I thought," Troy said, "you meant about our holiday. What's happened?"

"Baradi says he'll operate if it's necessary." Alleyn looked at Miss True-body. "Asleep?"

"Yes. So, what are we to do?"

"We've got a car. The Sûreté rang up the local commissioner yesterday and told him I was on my way. He's actually one of their experts who's been sent down here on a special job, superseding the local chap for the time being. He's turned on an elderly Mercedes and a driver. Damn civil of him. I've just been talking to him. Full of apologies for not coming down himself but he thought, very wisely, that we'd better not be seen together. He says our chauffeur is a reliable chap with an admirable record. He and the car are on tap outside the station now and our luggage will be collected by the hotel waggon. Baradi suggests I take Miss Truebody straight to the Chèvre d'Argent. While we're on the way he will make what preparations he can. Luckily he's got his instruments, and Claudel has given me some pipkins of anaesthetic. Baradi asked if I could give the anaesthetic."

"Can you?"

"I did once, in a ship. As long as nothing goes very wrong, it's fairly simple. If Baradi thinks it is safe to wait he'll try to get an anaesthetist from Douce-ville or somewhere. But it seems there's some sort of doctors' jamboree on today at St. Christophe and they've all cleared off to it. It's only ten kilo-metres from here to the Chèvre d'Argent by the inland road. I'll drop you and Ricky at the hotel here, darling, and take Miss Truebody on."

"Are there any women in the house?"

"I don't know." Alleyn stopped short and then said: "Yes. Yes, I do. There are women."

Troy watched him for a moment and then said: "All right. Let's get her aboard. You take Ricky."

Alleyn lifted him from her lap and she went to Miss Truebody. "She's tiny," Troy said under her breath. "Could she be carried?"

"I think so. Wait a moment."

He took Ricky out and was back in a few seconds with the station-master and a man wearing a chauffeur's cap over a mop of glossy curls.

He was a handsome little fellow with an air of readiness. He saluted Troy gallantly, taking off his peaked cap and smiling at her. Then he saw Miss Truebody and made a clucking sound. Troy had put a travelling rug on the bench and they made a sort of stretcher of it and carried Miss Truebody out to a large car in the station yard. Ricky was curled up on the front seat. They managed to fit Miss Truebody into the back one. The driver pulled down a tip-up seat and Troy sat on that. Miss Truebody had opened her eyes. She said in a quiet, clear voice: "Too kind," and Troy took her hand. Alleyn, in the front, held Ricky on his lap and they started off up a steep little street through Roqueville. The thin dawnlight gave promise of a glaring day. It was already very warm.

"To the Hôtel Royal, Monsieur?" asked the driver.

"No," said Troy with Miss Truebody's little claw clutching at her fingers. "No, please, Rory. I'll come with her. Ricky won't wake for hours. We can wait in the car or he can drive us back. I might be some use."

"To the Château de la Chèvre d'Argent," Alleyn said, "and gently."

"Perfectly, Monsieur," said the driver. "Always, always gently."

Roqueville was a very small town. It climbed briefly up the hill and petered out in a string of bleached villas. The road mounted between groves of olive trees and the air was like a benison, soft and clean. The sea extended itself beneath them and enriched itself with a blueness of incredible intensity.

Alleyn turned to look at Troy. They were quite close to each other and spoke over their shoulders like people in a Victorian "Conversation" chair. It was clear that Miss Truebody, even if she could hear them, was not able to concentrate or indeed to listen. "Dr. Claudel," Alleyn said, "thought it was the least risky thing to do. I half expected Baradi would refuse, but he was surprisingly co-operative. He's supposed to be a good man at his job." He made a movement of his head to indicate the driver. "This chap doesn't speak English," he said. "And, by the way, darling, no more chat about my being a policeman."

Troy said: "Have I been a nuisance?"

"It's all right. I asked Claudel to forget it and I don't suppose Miss Truebody will say anything or that anybody will pay much attention if she does. It's just that I don't want to brandish my job at the Chèvre d'Argent." He turned and looked into her troubled face. "Never mind, my darling. We'll buy false beards and hammers in Roqueville and let on we're archeologists. Or load ourselves down with your painting-gear." He paused for a moment. "That, by the way, is not a bad idea at all. Distinguished painter visits Côte d'Azur with obscure husband and child. We'll keep it in reserve."

"But honestly, Rory. How's this débâcle going to affect your job at the Chèvre d'Argent?"

"In a way it's useful entrée. The Sûreté suggested that I call there representing myself either to be an antiquarian captivated by the place itself—it's an old Saracen stronghold—or else I was to be a seeker after esoteric knowledge and offer myself as a disciple. If both failed I could use my own judgment about being a heroin addict in search of fuel. Thanks to Miss Truebody,

however, I shall turn up as a reluctant Good Samaritan. All the same,"
Alleyn said, rubbing his nose, "I wish Dr. Claudel could have risked taking
her on to St. Céleste or else waiting for the evening train back to St.
Christophe. I don't much like this party, and that's a fact. This'll larn the
Alleyn family to try combining business with pleasure, won't it?"

"Ah, well," said Troy, looking compassionately at Miss Truebody, "we're
doing our blasted best and no fool can do more."

They were silent for some time. The driver sang to himself in a light
tenor voice. The road climbed the Maritime Alps into early sunlight. They
traversed a tilted landscape compounded of earth and heat, of opaque clay
colours—ochres and pinks—splashed with magenta, tempered with olive-grey
and severed horizontally at its base by the ultramarine blade of the Mediterranean. They turned inland. Villages emerged as logical growths out of rock
and earth. A monastery safely folded among protective hills spoke of some
tranquil adjustment of man's spirit to the quiet rhythm of soil and sky.

"It's impossible," Troy said, "to think that anything could go very much
amiss in these hills."

A distant valley came into view. Far up it, a strange anachronism in that
landscape, was a long modern building with glittering roofs and a great display of plate glass.

"The factory," the driver told them, "of the Compagnie Chimique des
Alpes Maritimes."

Alleyn made a little affirmative sound as if he saw something that he had
expected and for as long as it remained in sight he looked at the glittering
building.

They drove on in silence. Miss Truebody turned her head from side to
side and Troy bent over her. "Hot," she whispered, "such an oppressive
climate. Oh, dear!"

"One approaches the objective," the driver announced, and changed gears.
The road tipped downwards and turned the flank of a hill. They had crossed
the headland and were high above the sea again. Immediately below them
the railroad emerged from a tunnel. On their right was a cliff that mounted
into a stone face pierced irregularly with windows. This in its turn broke
against the skyline into fabulous turrets and parapets. Troy gave a sharp
ejaculation. "Oh, no!" she said. "It's not that! No, it's too much!"

"Well, darling," Alleyn said, "I'm afraid that's what it is."

"La Chèvre d'Argent," said the driver, and turned up a steep and exceedingly narrow way that ended in a walled platform from which one looked
down at the railway and beyond it sheer down again to the sea. "Here one
stops, Monsieur," said the driver. "That is the entrance."

He pointed to a dark passage between two masses of rock from which walls
emerged as if by some process of evolution. He got out and opened the
doors of the car. "It appears," he said, "that Mademoiselle is unable to
walk."

"Yes," Alleyn said. "I shall go and fetch the doctor. Madame will remain with Mademoiselle and the little boy." He settled the sleeping Ricky into the front seat and got out. "You stay here, Troy," he said. "I shan't be long."

"Rory, we shouldn't have brought her to this place."

"There was no alternative that we could honestly take."

"Look!" said Troy.

A man in white was coming through the passage. He wore a Panama hat. His hands and face were so much the colour of the shadows that he looked like a white suit walking of its own accord towards them. He moved out into the sunlight and they saw that he was olive-coloured with a large nose, full lips and a black moustache. He wore dark glasses. The white suit was made of sharkskin and beautifully cut. His sandals were white suède. His shirt was pink and his tie green. When he saw Troy he took off his hat and the corrugations of his oiled hair shone in the sunlight.

"Dr. Baradi?" Alleyn said.

Dr. Baradi smiled brilliantly, swept off his Panama hat and held out a long dark hand. "So you bring my patient?" he said. "Mr. Allen, is it not?" He turned to Troy. "My wife," Alleyn said, and saw Troy's hand lifted to the full lips. "Here is your patient," he added. "Miss Truebody."

"Ah, yes." Dr. Baradi went to the car and bent over Miss Truebody. Troy, rather pink in the face, moved to the other side. "Miss Truebody," she said, "here is the doctor."

Miss Truebody opened her eyes, looked into the dark face and cried out: "Oh! No! No!"

Dr. Baradi smiled at her. "You must not trouble yourself about anything," they heard him say. He had a padded voice. "We are going to make everything much more comfortable for you, isn't it? You must not be frightened of my dark face. I assure you I am quite a good doctor."

Miss Truebody said: "Please excuse me. Not at all. Thank you."

"Now, without moving you, if I may just—that will do very nicely. You must tell me if I hurt you." A pause. Cicadas had broken out in a chittering so high-pitched that it shrilled almost above the limit of human hearing. The driver moved away tactfully. Miss Truebody moaned a little. Dr. Baradi straightened up, walked to the edge of the platform, and waited there for Troy and Alleyn. "It is a perforated appendix undoubtedly," he said. "She is very ill. I should tell you that I am the guest of Mr. Oberon, who places a room at our disposal. We have an improvised stretcher in readiness." He turned towards the passage-way: "And here it comes!" he said, looking at Troy with an air of joyousness which she felt to be entirely out of place.

Two men walked out of the shadowed way onto the platform carrying between them a gaily striped object, evidently part of a garden seat. Both the men wore aprons. "The gardener," Dr. Baradi explained, "and one of the indoor servants, strong fellows both and accustomed to the exigencies of our entrance. She has been given morphine, I think."

"Yes," Alleyn said. "Dr. Claudel gave it. He has sent you an adequate amount of something called, I think, Pentothal. He was taking a supply of it to a brother-medico, an anaesthetist, in St. Céleste and said that you would probably need some and that the local chemist would not be likely to have it."

"I am obliged to him. I have already telephoned to the pharmacist in Roqueville who can supply ether. Fortunately he lives above his establishment. He is sending it up here by car. It is fortunate also that I have my instruments with me." He beamed and glittered at Troy. "And now, I think . . ."

He spoke in French to the two men, directing them to stand near the car. For the first time apparently he noticed the sleeping Ricky and leaned over the door to look at him.

"Enchanting," he murmured, and his teeth flashed at Troy. "Our household is also still asleep," he said, "but I have Mr. Oberon's warmest invitation that you, Madame, and the small one join us for *petit déjeuner*. As you know, your husband is to assist me. There will be a little delay before we are ready and coffee is prepared."

He stood over Troy. He was really extremely large: his size and his padded voice and his smell, which was compounded of hair-lotion, scent and something that reminded her of the impure land-breeze from an eastern port, all flowed over her.

She moved back and said quickly: "It's very nice of you, but I think Ricky and I must find our hotel."

Alleyn said: "Thank you so much, Dr. Baradi. It's extremely kind of Mr. Oberon and I hope I shall have a chance to thank him for all of us. What with one thing and another, we've had an exhausting journey and I think my wife and Ricky are in rather desperate need of a bath and a rest. The man will drive them down to the hotel and come back for me."

Dr. Baradi bowed, took off his hat, and would have possibly kissed Troy's hand again if Alleyn had not somehow been in the way.

"In that case," Dr. Baradi said, "we must not insist."

He opened the door of the car. "And now, dear lady," he said to Miss Truebody, "we make a little journey, isn't it? Don't move. There is no need."

With great dexterity and no apparent expenditure of energy, he lifted her from the car and laid her on the improvised stretcher. The sun beat down on her glistening face. Her eyes were open, her lips drawn back a little from her gums. She said: "But where is—? You're not taking me away from—? I don't know her name."

Troy went to her. "Here I am, Miss Truebody," she said. "I'll come and see you quite soon. I promise."

"But I don't know where I'm going. It's so unsuitable. . . . Unseemly really. . . . Somehow with another lady . . . English . . . I don't know what they'll do to me. . . . I'm afraid I'm nervous. . . . I had hoped . . ."

Her jaw trembled. She made a thin shrill sound, shocking in its nakedness. "No," she stammered, "no . . . no . . . no." Her arm shot out and her hand closed on Troy's skirt. The two bearers staggered a little and looked agitatedly at Dr. Baradi.

"She should not be upset," he murmured to Troy. "It is most undesirable. Perhaps, for a little while, you'll be so kind . . ."

"But of course," Troy said, and in answer to a look from her husband, "of course, Rory, I must."

And she bent over Miss Truebody and told her she wouldn't go away. She felt as though she herself was trapped in the kind of dream that, without being a positive nightmare, threatens to become one. Baradi released Miss Truebody's hand and as he did so, his own brushed against Troy's skirt.

"You're so kind," he said. "Perhaps Mr. Allen will bring the little boy. It is not well for such tender ones to sleep overlong in the sun on the Côte d'Azur."

Without a word Alleyn lifted Ricky out of the car. Ricky made a small questioning sound, stirred, and slept again.

The men walked off with the stretcher, Dr. Baradi followed them. Troy, Alleyn and Ricky brought up the rear.

In this order the odd little procession moved out of the glare into the shadowed passage that was the entrance to the Château de la Chèvre d'Argent.

The driver watched them go, his lips pursed in a soundless whistle and an expression of concern darkening his eyes. Then he drove the car into the shade of the hill and composed himself for a long wait.

CHAPTER II

Operation Truebody

At first their eyes were sun-dazzled so that they could scarcely see their way. Dr. Baradi paused to guide them. Alleyn, encumbered with Ricky and groping up a number of wide, shallow and irregular steps, was aware of Baradi's hand piloting Troy by the elbow. The blotches of non-existent light that danced across their vision faded and they saw that they were in a sort of hewn passage-way between walls that were incorporated in rock, separated by outcrops of stone and pierced by stairways, windows and occasional doors. At intervals they went through double archways supporting buildings that straddled the passage and darkened it. They passed an open doorway and saw into a cave-like room where an old woman sat among shelves filled with small gaily painted figures. As Troy passed, the woman smiled at her and gestured invitingly, holding up a little clay goat.

Dr. Baradi was telling them about the Chèvre d'Argent.

"It is a fortress built originally by the Saracens. One might almost say it was sculptured out of the mountain, isn't it? The Normans stormed it on several occasions. There are legends of atrocities and so on. The fortress is, in effect, a village since the many caves beneath and around it have been shaped into dwellings and house a number of peasants, some dependent on the Château and some, like the woman you have noticed, upon their own industry. The Château itself is most interesting, indeed unique. But not inconvenient. Mr. Oberon has, with perfect tact, introduced the amenities. We are civilized, as you shall see."

They arrived at a double gate of wrought iron let into the wall on their left. An iron bell hung beside it. A butler appeared beyond the doors and opened them. They passed through a courtyard into a wide hall with deep-set windows through which a cool ineffectual light was admitted.

Without at first taking in any details of this shadowed interior, Troy received an impression of that particular kind of suavity that is associated with costliness. The rug under her feet, the texture and colour of the curtains, the shape of cabinets and chairs and, above all, a smell which she thought must arise from the burning sweet-scented oils, all united to give this immediate reaction. "Mr. Oberon," she thought, "must be immensely rich." Almost at the same time she saw above the great fireplace a famous Brueghel which, she remembered, had been sold privately some years ago. It was called: "Consultation of Sorceresses." An open door showed a stone stairway built inside the thickness of the wall.

"The stairs," Dr. Baradi said, "are a little difficult. Therefore we have prepared rooms on this floor."

He pulled back a leather curtain. The men carried Miss Truebody into a heavily carpeted stone passage hung at intervals with rugs and lit with electric lights fitted into ancient hanging lamps, witnesses, Troy supposed, of Mr. Oberon's tact in modernization. She heard Miss Truebody raise her piping cry of distress.

Dr. Baradi said: "Perhaps you would be so kind as to assist her into bed?"

Troy hurried after the stretcher and followed it into a small bedroom charmingly furnished and provided, she noticed, with an adjoining bathroom. The two bearers waited with an obliging air for further instructions. As Baradi had not accompanied them, Troy supposed that she herself was for the moment in command. She got Miss Truebody off the stretcher and onto the bed. The bearers hovered solicitously. She thanked them in her school-girl French and managed to get them out of the room, but not before they had persuaded her into the passage, opened a further door, and exhibited with evident pride a bare freshly scrubbed room with a bare freshly scrubbed table near its window. A woman rose from her knees as the door opened, a scrubbing brush in her hand and a pail beside her. The room reeked of disinfectant. The indoor servant said something about it being "convenable," and the gardener said something about somebody, she thought himself, being *"bien fatigué, infiniment fatigué."* It dawned upon her that they wanted a tip. Poor Troy scuffled in her bag, produced a 500 franc note and gave it to the indoor servant, indicating that they were to share it. They thanked her and, effulgent with smiles, went back to get the luggage. She hurried to Miss Truebody and found her crying feverishly.

Remembering what she could of hospital routine, Troy washed the patient, found a clean nightdress (Miss Truebody wore white locknit nightdresses, sprigged with posies), and got her into bed. It was difficult to make out how much she understood of her situation. Troy wondered if it was the injection of morphine or her condition or her normal habit of mind or all three, that made her so confused and vague. When she was settled in bed she began to talk with hectic fluency about herself. It was difficult to understand her as she had frantically waved away the offer of her false teeth. Her father, it seemed, had been a doctor, a widower, living in the Bermudas. She was his only child and had spent her life with him until, a year ago, he had died, leaving her, as she put it, quite comfortably though not well off. She had decided that she could just afford a trip to England and the continent. Her father, she muttered distractedly, had "not kept up," had "lost touch." There had been an unhappy break in the past, she believed, and their relations were never mentioned. Of course there were friends in the Bermudas but not, it appeared, very many or very intimate friends. She rambled on for a little while, continually losing the thread of her narrative and frowning incomprehensibly at nothing. The pupils of her eyes were contracted and her vision seemed to be confused. Presently her voice died away and she dozed uneasily.

Troy stole out and returned to the hall. Alleyn, Ricky and Baradi had gone, but the butler was waiting for her and showed her up the steep flight of stairs in the wall. It seemed to turn about a tower and they passed two landings with doors leading off them. Finally the man opened a larger and heavier door and Troy was out in the glare of full morning on a canopied roof-garden hung, as it seemed, in blue space where sky and sea met in a wide crescent. Not till she had advanced some way towards the balustrade did Cap St. Gilles appear, a sliver of earth pointing south.

Alleyn and Baradi rose from a breakfast-table near the balustrade. Ricky lay, fast asleep, on a suspended seat under a gay canopy. The smell of freshly ground coffee and of *brioches* and *croissants* reminded Troy that she was hungry.

They sat at the table. It was long, spread with a white cloth and set for a number of places. Troy was foolishly reminded of the Mad Hatter's Tea-party. She looked over the parapet and saw the railroad about eighty feet below her and perhaps a hundred feet from the base of the Chèvre d'Argent. The walls, buttressed and pierced with windows, fell away beneath her in a sickening perspective. Troy had a hatred of heights and drew back quickly. "Last night," she thought, "I looked into one of those windows."

Dr. Baradi was assiduous in his attentions and plied her with coffee. He gazed upon her remorselessly and she sensed Alleyn's annoyance rising with her own embarrassment. For a moment she felt weakly inclined to giggle.

Alleyn said: "See here, darling, Dr. Baradi thinks that Miss Truebody is extremely ill, dangerously so. He thinks we should let her people know at once."

"She has no people. She's only got acquaintances in the Bermudas; I asked. There seems to be nobody at all."

Baradi said: "In that case . . ." and moved his head from side to side. He turned to Troy and parodied helplessness with his hands. "So, in that direction, we can do nothing."

"The next thing," Alleyn said, speaking directly to his wife, "is the business of giving an anaesthetic. We could telephone to a hospital in St. Christophe and try to get someone, but there's this medical jamboree and in any case it'll mean a delay of some hours. Or Dr. Baradi can try to get his own anaesthetist to fly from Paris to the nearest airport. More delay and considerable expense. The other way is for me to have a shot at it. Should we take the risk?"

"What," Troy asked, making herself look at him, "do you think, Dr. Baradi?"

He sat near and a little behind her on the balustrade. His thighs bulged in their sharkskin trousers. "I think it will be less risky if your husband, who is not unfamiliar with the procedure, gives the anaesthetic. Her condition is not good."

His voice flowed over her shoulder. It was really extraordinary, she thought, how he could invest information about peritonitis and ruptured abscesses with such a gross suggestion of flattery. He might have been paying her the most objectionable compliments imaginable.

"Very well," Alleyn said, "that's decided, then. But you'll need other help, won't you?"

"If possible, two persons. And here we encounter a difficulty." He moved round behind Troy but spoke to Alleyn. His manner was now authoritative. "I doubt," he said, "if there is anyone in the house-party who could assist me. It is not every layman who enjoys a visit to an operating theatre. Surgery is not everybody's cup of tea." The colloquialism came oddly from him. "I have spoken to our host, of course. He is not yet stirring. He offers every possible assistance and all the amenities of the Château with the reservation that he himself shall not be asked to perform an active part. He is," said Dr. Baradi—putting on his sun-glasses—"allergic to blood."

"Indeed," said Alleyn politely.

"The rest of our household—we are seven—" Dr. Baradi explained playfully to Troy, "is not yet awake. Mr. Oberon gave a party here last night. Some friends with a yacht in port. We were immeasurably gay and kept going till five o'clock. Mr. Oberon has a genius for parties and a passion for charades. They were quite wonderful, our charades." Troy was about to give a little ejaculation, which she immediately checked. He beamed at her. "I

was cast for one of King Solomon's concubines. And we had the Queen of
Sheba, you know. She stabbed Solomon's favourite wife. It was all a little
strenuous. I don't think any of my friends will be in good enough form to
help us. Indeed, I doubt if any of them, even at the top of his or her form,
would care to offer for the role. I don't know if you have met any of them.
Grizel Locke, perhaps? The Honourable Grizel Locke?"

The Alleyns said they did not know Miss Locke.

"What about the servants?" Alleyn suggested. Troy was all too easily en-
visaging Dr. Baradi as one of King Solomon's concubines.

"One of the men is a possibility. He is my personal attendant and valet and
is not quite unfamiliar with surgical routine. He will not lose his head. Any
of the others would almost certainly be worse than useless. So we need one
other, you see."

A silence fell upon them, broken at last by Troy.

"I know," she said, "what Dr. Baradi is going to suggest." Alleyn looked
fixedly at her and raised his left eyebrow.

"It's quite out of the question. You well know that you're punctually sick
at the sight of blood, my darling."

Troy, who was nothing of the sort, said: "In that case I've no suggestions.
Unless you'd like to appeal to cousin Garbel."

There was a moment of silence.

"To whom?" said Baradi softly.

"I'm afraid I was being facetious," Troy mumbled.

Alleyn said: "What about our driver? He seems a hardy, intelligent sort
of chap. What would he have to do?"

"Fetch and carry," Dr. Baradi said. He was looking thoughtfully at Troy.
"Count sponges. Hand instruments. Clean up. Possibly, in an emergency,
play a minor role as unqualified assistant."

"I'll speak to him. If he seems at all possible I'll bring him in to see you.
Would you like to stroll back to the car with me, darling?"

"Please don't disturb yourselves," Dr. Baradi begged them. "One of the
servants will fetch your man."

Troy knew that her husband was in two minds about this suggestion and
also about leaving her to cope with Dr. Baradi. She said: "You go, Rory, will
you? I'm longing for my sun-glasses and they're locked away in my dressing-
case."

She gave him her keys and a ferocious smile. "I think, perhaps, I'll have a
look at Miss Truebody," she added.

He grimaced at her and walked out quickly.

Troy went to Ricky. She touched his forehead and found it moist. His
sleep was profound and when she opened the front of his shirt he did not
stir. She stayed, lightly swinging the seat, and watched him, and she thought
with tenderness that he was her defense in a stupid situation which fatigue
and a confusion of spirit, brought about by many untoward events, had perhaps created in her imagination. It was ridiculous, she thought, to feel any-

thing but amused by her embarrassment. She knew that Baradi watched her and she turned and faced him.

"If there is anything I can do before I go," she said and kept her voice down because of Ricky, "I hope you'll tell me."

It was a mistake to speak softly. He at once moved towards her and, with an assumption of intimacy, lowered his own voice. "But how helpful!" he said. "So we shall have you with us for a little longer? That is good: though it should not be to perform these unlovely tasks."

"I hope I'm equal to them." She moved away from Ricky and raised her voice. "What are they?"

"She must be prepared for the operation."

He told her what should be done and explained that she would find everything she needed for her purpose in Miss Truebody's bathroom. In giving these specifically clinical instructions, he reverted to his professional manner, but with an air of amusement that she found distasteful. When he had finished she said: "Then I'll get her fixed up now, shall I?"

"Yes," he agreed, more to himself than to her. "Yes, certainly, we shouldn't delay too long." And seeing a look of preoccupation and responsibility on his face, she left him, disliking him less in that one moment than at any time since they had met. As she went down the stone stairway she thought: "Thank heaven, at least, for the Queen of Sheba."

ii

Alleyn found their driver in his vest and trousers on the running-board of the car. A medallion of St. Christopher dangled from a steel chain above the mat of hair on his chest. He was exchanging improper jokes with a young woman and two small boys, who, when he rose to salute his employer, drifted away without embarrassment. He gave Alleyn a look that implied a common understanding of women, and opened the car door.

Alleyn said: "We're not going yet. What is your name?"

"Raoul, Monsieur. Raoul Milano."

"You've been a soldier, perhaps?"

"Yes, Monsieur. I am thirty-three and therefore I have seen some service."

"So your stomach is not easily outraged, then; by a show of blood, for instance? By a formidable wound, shall we say?"

"I was a medical orderly, Monsieur. My stomach also is an old campaigner."

"Excellent! I have a job for you, Raoul. It is to assist Dr. Baradi, the gentleman you have already seen. He is about to remove Mademoiselle's appendix and since we cannot find a second doctor, we must provide unqualified assistants. If you will help us there may be a little reward and certainly there will be much grace in performing this service. What do you say?"

Raoul looked down at his blunt hands and then up at Alleyn:

"I say yes, M'sieur. As you suggest, it is an act of grace and in any case one may as well do something."

"Good. Come along, then." Alleyn had found Troy's sun-glasses. He and Raoul turned towards the passage, Raoul slinging his coat across his shoulders with the grace of a ballet dancer.

"So you live down in Roqueville?" Alleyn asked.

"In Roqueville, M'sieur. My parents have a little café, not at all smart, but the food is good and I also hire myself out in my car, as you see."

"You've been up to the Château before, of course?"

"Certainly. For little expeditions and also to drive guests and sometimes tourists. As a rule Mr. Oberon sends a car for his guests." He waved a hand at a row of garage-doors, incongruously set in a rocky face at the back of the platform. "His cars are magnificent."

Alleyn said: "The Commissaire at the Préfecture sent you to meet us, I think?"

"That is so, M'sieur."

"Did he give you my name?"

"Yes, M'sieur l'Inspecteur-en-Chef. It is Ahrr-lin. But he said that M'sieur l'Inspecteur-en-Chef would prefer, perhaps, that I did not use his rank."

"I would greatly prefer it, Raoul."

"It is already forgotten, M'sieur."

"Again, good."

They passed the cave-like room, where the woman sat among her figurines. Raoul hailed her in a cheerful manner and she returned his greeting. "You must bring your gentleman in to see my statues," she shouted. He called back over his shoulder: "All in good time, Marie," and added, "She is an artist, that one. Her saints are pretty and of assistance in one's devotions; but then she overcharges ridiculously, which is not so amusing."

He sang a stylish little cadence and tilted up his head. They were walking beneath a part of the Château de la Chèvre d'Argent that straddled the passage-way. "It goes everywhere, this house," he remarked. "One would need a map to find one's way from the kitchen to the best bedroom. Anything might happen."

When they reached the entrance he stood aside and took off his chauffeur's cap. They found Dr. Baradi in the hall. Alleyn told him that Raoul had been a medical orderly and Baradi at once described the duties he would be expected to perform. His manner was cold and uncompromising. Raoul gave him his full attention. He stood easily, his thumbs crooked in his belt. He retained at once his courtesy, his natural grace of posture, and his air of independence.

"Well," Baradi said sharply when he had finished: "Are you capable of this work?"

"I believe so, M'sieur le Docteur."

"If you prove to be satisfactory, you will be given 500 francs. That is extremely generous payment for unskilled work."

"As to payment, M'sieur le Docteur," Raoul said, "I am already employed by this gentleman and consider myself entirely at his disposal. It is at his request that I engage myself in this task."

Baradi raised his eyebrows and looked at Alleyn. "Evidently an original," he said in English. "He seems tolerably intelligent but one never knows. Let us hope that he is at least not too stupid. My man will give him suitable clothes and see that he is clean."

He went to the fireplace and pulled a tapestry bell-rope. "Mrs. Allen," he said, "is most kindly preparing our patient. There is a room at your disposal and I venture to lend you one of my gowns. It will, I'm afraid, be terribly voluminous but perhaps some adjustment can be made. We are involved in compromise, isn't it?"

A man wearing the dress of an Egyptian house-servant came in. Baradi spoke to him in his own language, and then to Raoul in French: "Go with Mahomet and prepare yourself in accordance with his instructions. He speaks French." Raoul acknowledged this direction with something between a bow and a nod. He said to Alleyn: "Monsieur will perhaps excuse me?" and followed the servant, looking about the room with interest as he left it.

Baradi said: "Italian blood there, I think. One comes across these hybrids along the coast. May I show you to my room?"

It was in the same passage as Miss Truebody's, but a little further along it. In Alleyn the trick of quick observation was a professional habit. He saw not only the general sumptuousness of the room but the details also: the Chinese wallpaper, a Wu Tao-tzu scroll, a Ming vase.

"This," Dr. Baradi needlessly explained, "is known as the Chinese room but, as you will observe, Mr. Oberon does not hesitate to introduce modulation. The bureau is by Vernis-Martin."

"A modulation, as you say, but an enchanting one. The cabinet there is a bolder departure. It looks like a Mussonier."

"One of his pupils, I understand. You have a discerning eye. Mr. Oberon will be delighted."

A gown was laid out on the bed. Baradi took it up. "Will you try this? There is an unoccupied room next door with access to a bathroom. You have time for a bath and will, no doubt, be glad to take one. Since morphine has been given there is no immediate urgency, but I should prefer all the same to operate as soon as possible. When you are ready, my own preparations will be complete and we can discuss final arrangements."

Alleyn said: "Dr. Baradi, we haven't said anything about your fee for the operation: indeed, it is neither my business nor my wife's, but I do feel some concern about it. I imagine Miss Truebody will at least be able . . ."

Baradi held up his hand. "Let us not discuss it," he said. "Let us assume that it is of no great moment."

"If you prefer to do so." Alleyn hesitated and then added: "This is an extraordinary situation. You will, I'm sure, realize that we are reluctant to take such a grave responsibility. Miss Truebody is a complete stranger to us.

You yourself must feel it would be much more satisfactory if there was a relation or friend from whom we could get some kind of authority. Especially as her illness is so serious."

"I agree. However, she would undoubtedly die if the operation was not performed and, in my opinion, would be in the gravest danger if it was unduly postponed. As it is, I'm afraid there is a risk, a great risk, that she will not recover. We can," Baradi added, with what Alleyn felt was a genuine, if controlled, anxiety, "only do our best and hope that all may be well."

And on this note Alleyn turned to go. As he was in the doorway Baradi, with a complete change of manner, said: "Your enchanting wife is with her. Third door on the left. Quite enchanting. Delicious, if you will permit me."

Alleyn looked at him and found what he saw offensive.

"Under these unfortunate circumstances," he said politely, "I can't do anything else."

Evidently Dr. Baradi chose to regard this observation as a pleasantry. He laughed richly. "Delicious!" he repeated, but whether in reference to Alleyn's comment or as a reiterated observation upon Troy it was impossible to determine. Alleyn, who had every reason and no inclination for keeping his temper, walked into the next room.

iii

Troy had carried out her instructions and Miss Truebody had slipped again into sleep. The sound of her breathing cut the silence into irregular intervals. Her eyes were not quite closed. Segments of the eyeballs appeared under the pathetic insufficiency of her lashes. Troy was at once unwilling to leave her and anxious to return to Ricky. She heard Alleyn and Dr. Baradi in the passage. Their voices were broken off by a door slam and again there was only Miss Truebody's breathing. Troy waited, hoping that Alleyn knew where she was and would come to her. After what seemed an interminable interval there was a tap at the door. She opened it and he was there in a white gown looking tall, elegant and angry. Troy shut the door behind her and they whispered together in the passage.

"Rum go," he said, "isn't it?"

"Not 'alf. When do you begin?"

"Soon. He's trying to make himself aseptic. A losing battle, I should think."

"Frightful, isn't he?"

"The bottom. I'm so sorry, darling, you have to suffer his atrocious gallantries."

"Well, I daresay they're just elaborate Oriental courtesy, or something."

"Elaborate bloody impertinence."

"Never mind, Rory. I'll skip out of his way."

"I shouldn't have brought you to this damn place."

"Fiddle! In any case he's going to be too busy."

"Is she asleep?"

"Sort of. I don't like to leave her, but suppose Ricky should wake?"

"Go up to him. I'll stay with her. Baradi's going to give her an injection before I get going with the ether. And, Troy—"

"Yes?"

"It's important these people don't get a line on who I am."

"I know."

"I haven't told you anything about them, but I think I'll have to come moderately clean when there's a chance. It's a rum setup. I'll get you out of it as soon as possible."

"I'm not worrying now we know about the charades. Funny! You said there might be an explanation, but we never thought of charades, did we?"

"No," Alleyn said, "we didn't, did we?" and suddenly kissed her. "Now, I suppose I'll have to wash again," he added.

Raoul came down the passage with Baradi's servant. They were carrying the improvised stretcher and were dressed in white overalls.

Raoul said: "Madame!" to Troy, and to Alleyn, "It appears, Monsieur, that M. le Docteur orders Mademoiselle to be taken to the operating room. Is that convenient for Monsieur?"

"Of course. We are under Dr. Baradi's orders."

"Authority," Raoul observed, "comes to roost on strange perches, Monsieur."

"That," Alleyn said, "will do."

Raoul grinned and opened the door. They took the stretcher in and laid it on the floor by the bed. When they lifted her down to it, Miss Truebody opened her eyes and said distinctly: "But I would prefer to stay in bed." Raoul deftly tucked blankets under her. She began to wail dismally.

Troy said: "It's all right, dear. You'll be all right," and thought: "But I never call people dear!"

They carried Miss Truebody into the room across the passage and put her on the table by the window. Troy went with them, holding her hand. The window coverings had been removed and a hard glare beat down on the table. The room still reeked of disinfectant. There was a second table on which a number of objects were now laid out. Troy, after one glance, did not look at them again. She held Miss Truebody's hand and stood between her and the instrument table. A door in the wall facing her opened and Baradi appeared against a background of bathroom. He wore his gown and a white cap. Their austerity of design emphasized the opulence of his nose and eyes and teeth. He had a hypodermic syringe in his left hand.

"So, after all, you are to assist me?" he murmured to Troy. But it was obvious that he didn't entertain any such notion.

Still holding the flaccid hand, she said: "I thought perhaps I should stay with her until . . ."

"But of course! Please remain a little longer." He began to give instructions to Alleyn and the two men. He spoke in French presumably, Troy thought, to spare Miss Truebody's feelings. "I am left-handed," he said. "If I should ask for anything to be handed to me you will please remember that. Now, Mr. Allen, we will show you your equipment, isn't it? Milano!" Raoul brought a china dish from the instrument table. It had a bottle and a hand towel on it. Alleyn looked at it and nodded. "*Parfaitement*," he said.

Baradi took Miss Truebody's other hand and pushed up the long sleeve of her nightgown. She stared at him and her mouth worked soundlessly.

Troy saw the needle slide in. The hand she held flickered momentarily and relaxed.

"It is fortunate," Baradi said as he withdrew the needle, "that this little Dr. Claudel had Pentothal. A happy coincidence."

He raised Miss Truebody's eyelid. The pupil was out of sight. "Admirable," he said. "Now, Mr. Allen, we will, in a moment or two, induce a more profound anaesthesia which you will continue. I shall scrub up and in a few minutes more we begin operations." He smiled at Troy, who was already on the way to the door. "One of our party will join you presently on the roof-garden. Miss Locke; the Honourable Grizel Locke. I believe she has a vogue in England. Quite mad, but utterly charming."

Troy's last impression of the room, a vivid one, was of Baradi, enormous in his white gown and cap, of Alleyn standing near the table and smiling at her, of Raoul and the Egyptian servant waiting near the instruments, and of Miss Truebody's wide-open mouth and of the sound of her breathing. Then the door shut off the picture as abruptly as the tunnel had shut off her earlier glimpse into a room in the Chèvre d'Argent.

"Only *that* time—" Troy told herself, as she made her way back to the roof-garden—"it was only a charade."

CHAPTER III

Morning with Mr. Oberon

The sun shone full on the roof-garden now, but Ricky was shielded from it by the canopy of his swinging couch. He was, as he himself might have said, lavishly asleep. Troy knew he would stay so for a long time.

The breakfast-table had been cleared and moved to one side and several more seats like Ricky's had been set out. Troy took the one nearest to his. When she lifted her feet it swayed gently. Her head sank back into a heap of cushions. She had slept very little in the train.

It was quiet on the roof-garden. A few cicadas chittered far below and once, somewhere a long way away, a car hooted. The sky, as she looked into it, intensified itself in blueness and bemused her drowsy senses. Her eyes closed and she felt again the movement of the train. The sound of the cicadas became a dismal chattering from Miss Truebody and soared up into nothingness. Presently, Troy, too, was fast asleep.

When she awoke, it was to see a strange lady perched, like some fantastic fowl, on the balustrade near Ricky's seat. Her legs, clad in scarlet pedalpushers, were drawn up to her chin which was sunk between her knees. Her hands, jewelled and claw-like, with vermilion talons, clasped her shins, and her toes protruded from her sandals like branched corals. A scarf was wound around her skull and her eyes were hidden by sun-glasses in an enormous frame below which a formidable nose jutted over a mouth whose natural shape could only be conjectured. When she saw Troy was awake and on her feet she unfolded herself, dropped to the floor, and advanced with a hand extended. She was six feet tall and about forty-five to fifty years old.

"How do you do?" she whispered. "I'm Grizel Locke. I like to be called Sati, though. The Queen of Heaven, you will remember. Please call me Sati. Had a good nap, I hope? I've been looking at your son and wondering if I'd like to have one for myself."

"How do you do?" Troy said without whispering and greatly taken aback. "Do you think you would?"

"Won't he wake? I've got *such* a voice as you can hear when I speak up." Her voice was indeed deep and uncertain like an adolescent boy's. "It's hard to say," she went on. "One might go all possessive and peculiar and, on the other hand, one might get bored and off-load him on repressed governesses. I was off-loaded as a child which, I am told, accounts for almost everything. Do lie down again. You must feel like a boiled owl. So do I. Would you like a drink?"

"No, thank you," Troy said, running her fingers through her short hair.

"Nor would I. What a poor way to begin your holiday. Do you know anyone here?"

"Not really. I've got a distant relation somewhere in the offing but we've never met."

"Perhaps we know them. What name?"

"Garbel. Something to do with a rather rarefied kind of chemistry. I don't suppose you—?"

"I'm afraid not," she said quickly. "Has Baradi started on your friend?"

"She's not a friend or even an acquaintance. She's a fellow-traveller."

"How sickening for you," said the lady earnestly.

"I mean, literally," Troy explained. She was indeed feeling like a boiled owl and longed for nothing as much as a bath and solitude.

"Lie down," the lady urged. "Put your boots up. Go to sleep again if you like. I was just going to push ahead with my tanning, only your son distracted my attention."

Troy sat down and as her companion was so insistent she did put her feet up.

"That's right," the lady observed. "I'll blow up my li-low. The servants, alas, have lost the puffer."

She dragged forward a flat rubber mattress. Sitting on the floor she applied her painted mouth to the valve and began to blow. "Uphill work," she gasped a little later, "still, it's an exercise in itself and I daresay will count as such."

When the li-low was inflated she lay face down upon it and untied the painted scarf that was her sole upper garment. It fell away from a back so thin that it presented, Troy thought, an anatomical subject of considerable interest. The margins of the scapulae shone like ploughshares and the spinal vertebrae looked like those of a flayed snake.

"I've given up oil," the submerged voice explained, "since I became a Child of the Sun. Is there any particular bit that seems underdone, do you consider?"

Troy, looking down upon a uniformly dun-coloured expanse, could make no suggestions and said so.

"I'll give it ten minutes for luck and then toss over the bod," said the voice. "I must say I feel ghastly."

"You had a late night, Dr. Baradi tells us," said Troy, who was making a desperate effort to pull herself together.

"Did we?" The voice became more indistinct, and added something like: "I forget."

"Charades and everything, he said."

"Did he? Oh. Was I in them?"

"He didn't say particularly," Troy answered.

"I passed," the voice muttered, "utterly and definitively out." Troy had just thought how unattractive such statements always were when she noticed with astonishment that the shoulder blades were quivering as if their owner was convulsed. "I suppose you might call it charades," the lady was heard to say.

Troy was conscious of a rising sense of uneasiness.

"How do you mean?" she asked.

Her companion rolled over. She had taken off her sun-glasses. Her eyes were green with pale irises and small pupils. They were singularly blank in expression. Clad only in her scarlet pedal-pushers and head-scarf, she was an uncomfortable spectacle.

"The whole thing is," she said rapidly, "I wasn't at the party. I began one of my headaches after luncheon, which was a party in itself, and I passed, as I mentioned a moment ago, out. That must have been at about four o'clock, I should think, which is why I am up so early, you know." She yawned suddenly and with gross exaggeration as if her jaws would crack.

"Oh, God," she said, "here I go again!"

Troy's jaws quivered in imitation. "I hope your headache is better," she said.

"Sweet of you. In point of fact it's hideous."

"I'm so sorry."

"I'll have to find Baradi if it goes on. And it will, of course. How long will he be over your fellow-traveller's appendix? Have you seen Ra?"

"I don't think so. I've only seen Dr. Baradi."

"Yes, yes," she said restlessly, and added, "You wouldn't know, of course. I mean Oberon, our Teacher, you know. That's our name for him—Ra. Are you interested in The Truth?"

Troy was too addled with unseasonable sleep and a surfeit of anxiety to hear the capital letters. "I really don't know," she stammered. "In the truth—?"

"Poor sweet, I'm muddling you." She sat up. Troy had a painter's attitude towards the nude but the aspect of this lady, so wildly and so unpleasingly displayed, was distressing and doubly so because Troy couldn't escape the impression that the lady herself was far from unself-conscious. Indeed she kept making tentative clutches at her scarf and looking at Troy as if she felt she ought to apologize for herself. In her embarrassment Troy turned away and looked vaguely at the tower wall which rose above the roof-garden not far from where she sat. It was pierced at ascending intervals by narrow slits. Troy's eyes, glazed with fatigue, stared in aimless fixation at the third slit from the floor level. She listened to a strange exposition on The Truth as understood and venerated by the guests of Mr. Oberon.

". . . just a tiny group of Seekers . . . Children of the Sun in the Outer . . . Evil exists only in the minds of the earthbound . . . goodness is oneness . . . the great Dark co-exists with the great Light. . . ." The phrases disjointed and eked out by ineloquent and unco-ordinated gestures, tripped each other up by the heels. Clichés and aphorisms were tumbled together from the most unlikely sources. One must live dangerously, it appeared, in order to attain merit. Only by encompassing the gamut of earthly experience could one return to the oneness of universal good. One ascended through countless ages by something which the disciple, corkscrewing an unsteady finger in illustration, called the mystic navel spiral. It all sounded the most dreadful nonsense to poor Troy but she listened politely and, because her companion so clearly expected them, tried to ask one or two intelligent questions. This was a mistake. The lady, squinting earnestly up at her, said abruptly: "You're fey, of course. But you know that, don't you?"

"Indeed, I don't."

"Yes, yes," she persisted, nodding like a mandarin. "Unawakened perhaps, but it's there, oh! so richly. Fey as fey can be."

She yawned again with the same unnatural exaggeration and twisted round to look at the door into the tower.

"He won't be long appearing," she whispered. "It isn't as if he ever touched anything and he's always up for the rites of Ushas. What's the time?"

"Just after ten," said Troy, astonished that it was no later. Ricky, she thought, would sleep for at least another hour, perhaps for two hours. She tried to remember if she had ever heard how long an appendectomy took to perform. She tried to console herself with the thought that there must be a limit to this vigil, that she would not have to listen forever to Grizel Locke's esoteric small-talk, that somewhere down at the Hôtel Royal in Roqueville there was a tiled bathroom and a cool bed, that perhaps Miss Locke would go in search of whoever it was she seemed to await with such impatience, and finally that she herself might, if left alone, sleep away the remainder of this muddled and distressing interlude.

It was at this juncture that something moved behind the slit in the tower wall. Something that tweaked at her attention. She had an impression of hair or fur and thought at first that it was an animal, perhaps a cat. It moved again and was gone, but not before she recognized a human head. She came to the disagreeable conclusion that someone had stood at the slit and listened to their conversation. At that moment she heard steps inside the tower. The door moved.

"Someone's coming!" she cried out in warning. Her companion gave an ejaculation of relief, but made no attempt to resume her garment. "Miss Locke! Do look out!"

"What? Oh! Oh, all right. Only, do call me Sati." She picked up the square of printed silk. Perhaps, Troy thought, there was something in her own face that awakened in Miss Locke a dormant regard for the conventions. Miss Locke blushed and began clumsily to knot the scarf behind her.

But Troy's gaze was upon the man who had come through the tower door onto the roof-garden and was walking towards them. The confusion of spirit that had irked her throughout the morning clarified into one recognizable emotion.

She was frightened.

ii

Troy would have been unable to say at that moment why she was afraid of Mr. Oberon. There was nothing in his appearance, one would have thought, to inspire fear. Rather, he had, at first sight, a look of mildness.

Beards, in general, are not rare nowadays though beards like his are perhaps unusual. It was blonde, sparse and silky and divided at the chin which was almost bare. The moustache was a mere shadow at the corners of his mouth, which was fresh in colour. The nose was straight and delicate and the light eyes abnormally large. His hair was parted in the middle and so long that it overhung the collar of his gown. This, and a sort of fragility in the general structure of his head, gave him an air of effeminacy. What was startling and to Troy quite shocking, was the resemblance to Roman Catholic devotional prints such as the "Sacred Heart." She was to learn that this resemblance was deliberately cultivated. He wore a white dressing-gown to which his extraordinary appearance gave the air of a ceremonial robe.

It seemed incredible that such a being could make normal conversation. Troy would not have been surprised if he had acknowledged the introduction in Sanskrit. However, he gave her his hand, which was small and well-formed, and a conventional greeting. He had a singularly musical voice and spoke without any marked accent, though Troy fancied she heard a faint American inflection. She said something about his kindness in offering harbourage to Miss Truebody. He smiled gently, sank on to an Algerian leather seat, drew his feet up under his gown and placed them, apparently, against his thighs. His hands fell softly to his lap.

"You have brought," he said, "a gift of great price. We are grateful."

From the time that they had confronted each other he had looked fully into Troy's eyes and he continued to do so. It was not the half-unseeing attention of ordinary courtesy but an unswerving fixed regard. He seemed to blink less than most people.

His disciple said: "Dearest Ra, I've got the most monstrous headache."

"It will pass," he said, still looking at Troy. "You know what you should do, dear Sati."

"Yes, I do, don't I! But it's so hard sometimes to feel the light. One gropes and gropes."

"Patience, dear Sati. It will come."

She sat up on her li-low, seized her ankles and with a grunt of discomfort adjusted the soles of her feet to the inside surface of her thighs. "Om," she said discontentedly.

Mr. Oberon said to Troy: "We speak of things that are a little strange to you. Or perhaps they are not altogether strange?"

"Just what *I* thought," the lady began eagerly. "Isn't she *fey?*"

He disregarded her.

"Should I explain that we—my guests here and I—follow what we believe to be the true Way of Life? Perhaps, up here, in this ancient house, we have created an atmosphere that to a visitor is a little overwhelming. Do you feel it so?"

Troy said: "I'm afraid I'm just rather addled with a long journey, not much sleep, and an anxious time with Miss Truebody."

"I have been helping her. And, I hope, our friend Baradi."

"Have you?" Troy exclaimed in great surprise. "I thought . . . ? But how kind of you. . . . Is . . . is the operation going well?"

He smiled, showing perfect teeth. "Again, I do not make myself clear. I have been with them, not in the body but in the spirit."

"Oh," mumbled Troy. "I'm sorry."

"Particularly with your friend. This was easy because when by the will, or, as with her, by the agency of an anaesthetic, the soul is set free of the body, it may be greatly helped. Hers is a pure soul. She should be called Miss Truesoul instead of Miss Truebody." He laughed, a light breathy sound, and showed the pink interior of his mouth. "But we must not despise the body," he said, apparently as an afterthought.

His disciple whispered: "Oh, no! No, indeed! No," and started to breathe deeply, stopping one nostril with a finger and expelling her breath with a hissing sound. Troy began to wonder if Miss Locke was, perhaps, a little mad.

Oberon had shifted his gaze from Troy. His eyes were still very wide open and quite without expression. He had seen the sleeping Ricky.

It was with the greatest difficulty that Troy gave her movement towards Ricky a semblance of casualness. Her instinct, she afterwards told Alleyn, was entirely that of a mother cat. She leaned over her small son and made a pretence of adjusting the cushion behind him. She heard Oberon say: "A beautiful child," and thought that no matter how odd it might look, she would stand between Ricky and his eyes until something else diverted their gaze. But Ricky himself stirred a little, flinging out his arm. She moved him over with his face away from Oberon. He murmured: "Mummy?" and she answered: "Yes," and kept her hand on him until he had fallen back into sleep.

She turned and looked past the ridiculous back of the deep-breathing disciple to the figure seated in the glare of the sun, and, being a painter, she recognized, in the midst of her alarm, a remarkable subject. At the same time it seemed to her that Oberon and she acknowledged each other as enemies.

This engagement, if it was one, was broken off by the appearance of two more of Mr. Oberon's guests: a tall girl and a lame young man who were introduced as Ginny Taylor and Robin Herrington. Both their names were familiar to Troy, the girl's as that of a regular sacrifice on the altars of the glossy weeklies, and the man's as that of the reputably wildish son of a famous brewer who was also an indefatigable patron of the fine arts. To Troy their comparative normality was as a freshening breeze and she was ready to overlook the shadows under their eyes and their air of unease. They greeted her politely, lowered their voices when they saw Ricky and sat together on one seat, screening him from Mr. Oberon. Troy returned to her former place.

Mr. Oberon was talking. It seemed that he had bought a book in Paris, a newly discovered manuscript, one of those assembled by Roger de Gaignières. Troy knew that he must have paid a fabulous sum for it and, in spite of herself, listened eagerly to a description of the illuminations. He went on to speak of other works: of the calendar of Charles d'Angoulême, of Indian art, and finally of the moderns—Rouault, Picasso and André Derain. "But, of course, André is not a modern. He derives quite blatantly from Rubens. Ask Carbury, when he comes, if I am not right."

Troy's nerves jumped. Could he mean Carbury Glande, a painter whom she knew perfectly well and who would certainly, if he appeared, greet her with feverish effusiveness? Mr. Oberon no longer looked at her or at anyone in particular, yet she had the feeling that he talked at her and he was talking very well. Yes, here was a description of one of Glande's works. "He painted it yesterday from the Saracens' Watchtower: the favourite interplay of lemon and lacquer-red with a single note of magenta, and everything arranged about a central point. The esoteric significance was eloquent and the whole thing quite beautiful." It was undoubtedly Carbury Glande. Surely, surely, the operation must be over and if so, why didn't Alleyn come and take them away? She tried to remember if Carbury Glande knew she was married to a policeman.

Ginny Taylor said: "I wish I knew about Carbury. I can't get anything from his works. I can only say awful Philistinish things such as they look as if they were too easy to do." She glanced in a friendly manner at Troy.

"Do *you* know about modern art?" she asked.

"I'm always ready to learn," Troy hedged with a dexterity born of fright.

"I shall never learn however much I try," sighed Ginny Taylor and suddenly yawned.

The jaws of everyone except Mr. Oberon quivered responsively.

"Lord, I'm sorry," said Ginny, and for some unaccountable reason looked frightened. Robin Herrington touched her hand with the tip of his fingers. "I wonder why they're so infectious," he said. "Sneezes, coughs and yawns. Yawns worst of all. To read about them's enough to set one going."

"Perhaps," Mr. Oberon suggested, "it's another piece of evidence, if a homely one, that separateness is an illusion. Our bodies as well as our souls have reflex actions." And while Troy was still wondering what on earth this might mean his Sati gave a little yelp of agreement.

"True! True!" she cried. She dived, stretched out with her right arm and grasped her toes. At the same time she wound her left arm behind her head and seized her right ear. Having achieved this unlikely posture, she gazed devotedly upon Mr. Oberon. "Is it all right, dearest Ra," she asked, "for me to press quietly on with my Prana and Pranayama?"

"It is well at all times, dear Sati, if the spirit also is attuned."

Troy couldn't resist stealing a glance at Ginny Taylor and Robin Herrington. Was it possible that they found nothing to marvel at in these antics? Ginny was looking doubtfully at Sati, and young Herrington was looking at Ginny as if, Troy thought with relief, he invited her to be amused with him.

"Ginny?" Mr. Oberon said quietly.

The beginning of a smile died on Ginny's lips. "I'm sorry," she said quickly. "Yes, Ra?"

"Have you formed a design for today?"

"No. At least . . . this afternoon . . ."

"I thought, if it suited general arrangements," Robin Herrington said, "that I might ask Ginny to come into Douceville this afternoon. I want her to tell me what colour I should have for new awnings on the afterdeck."

But Ginny had got up and walked past Troy to Mr. Oberon. She stood before him white-faced with the dark marks showing under her eyes.

"Are you going, then, to Douceville?" he asked. "You look a little pale, my child. We were so late with our gaieties last night. Should you rest this afternoon?"

He was looking at her as he had looked at Troy.

"I think perhaps I should," she said in a flat voice.

"I, too. The colour of the awnings can wait until the colour of the cheeks is restored. Perhaps Annabella would enjoy a drive to Douceville. Annabella Wells," he explained to Troy, "is with us. Her latest picture is completed and she is to make a film for Durant Frères in the spring."

Troy was not much interested in the presence of a notoriously erratic if brilliant actress. She had been watching young Herrington, whose brows were drawn together in a scowl. He got up and stood behind Ginny, looking at Oberon over the top of her head. His hands closed and he thrust them into his pockets.

"I thought a drive might be a good idea for Ginny," he said.

But Ginny had sunk down on the end of the li-low at Mr. Oberon's feet. She settled herself there quietly, with an air of obedience. Mr. Oberon said to Troy: "Robin has a most wonderful yacht. You must ask him to show it to you." He put his hand on Ginny's head.

"I should be delighted," said Robin and sounded furious. He had turned aside and now added in a loud voice: "Why not this afternoon? I still think Ginny should come to Douceville."

Troy knew that something had happened that was unusual between Mr. Oberon and his guests and that Robin Herrington was frightened as well as angry. She wanted to give him courage. Her heart thumped against her ribs.

In the dead silence they all heard someone come quickly up the stone stairway. When Alleyn opened the door their heads were already turned towards him.

iii

He waited for a moment to accustom his eyes to the glare and during that moment he and the five people whose faces were turned towards him were motionless.

One grows scarcely to see one's lifelong companions and it is more difficult to call up the face of one's beloved than that of a mere acquaintance. Troy had never been able to make a memory-drawing of her husband. Yet, at that moment, it was as if a veil of familiarity was withdrawn and she looked at him with fresh perception.

She thought: "I've never been gladder to see him."

"This is my husband," she said.

Mr. Oberon had risen and come forward. He was five inches shorter than Alleyn. For the first time Troy thought him ridiculous as well as disgusting.

He held out his hand. "We're so glad to meet you at last. The news is good?"

"Dr. Baradi will be able to tell you better than I," Alleyn said. "Her condition was pretty bad. He says she will be very ill."

"We shall all help her," Mr. Oberon said, indicating the antic Sati, the bemused Ginny Taylor and the angry-looking Robin Herrington. "We can do so much."

He put his hand on Alleyn's arm and led him forward. The reek of ether accompanied them. Alleyn was introduced to the guests and offered a seat but he said: "If we may, I think perhaps I should see my wife and Ricky on their way back to Roqueville. Our driver is free now and can take them. He will come back for me. We're expecting a rather urgent telephone call at our hotel."

Troy, who dreaded the appearance of Carbury Glande, knew Alleyn had said "my wife" because he didn't want Oberon to learn her name. He had an air of authority that was in itself, she thought, almost a betrayal. She got up quickly and went to Ricky.

"Perhaps," Alleyn said, "I should stay a little longer in case there's any change in her condition. Baradi is going to telephone to St. Christophe for a nurse and, in the meantime, two of your maids will take turns sitting in the room. I'm sure, sir, that if she were able, Miss Truebody would tell you how grateful she is for your hospitality."

"There is no need. She is with us in a very special sense. She is in safe hands. We must send a car for the nurse. There is no train until the evening."

"I'll go," Robin Herrington said. "I'll be there in an hour."

"Robin," Oberon explained lightly, "has driven in the Monte Carlo rally. We must hope that the nurse has iron nerves."

Alleyn said to Robin: "It sounds an admirable idea. Will you suggest it to Dr. Baradi?"

He went to Ricky and lifted him in his arms. Troy gave her hand to Mr. Oberon. His own wrapped itself round hers, tightened, and was suddenly withdrawn. "You must visit us again," he said. "If you are a voyager of the spirit, and I think you are, it might interest you to come to one of our meditations."

"Yes, do come," urged his Sati, who had abandoned her exercises on Alleyn's entrance. "It's madly wonderful. You must. Where are you staying?"

"At the Royal."

"Couldn't be easier. No need to hire a car. The Douceville bus leaves from the corner. Every half-hour. You'll find it perfectly convenient."

Troy was reminded vividly of Mr. Garbel's letters. She murmured something non-committal, said goodbye and went to the door.

"I'll see you out," Robin Herrington offered and took up his heavy walking stick.

As she groped down the darkened stairway she heard their voices rumbling above her. They came slowly; Alleyn because of Ricky and Herrington because of his stiff leg. The sensation of nightmare that threatened without declaring itself mounted in intensity. The stairs seemed endless, yet when she reached the door into the hall she was half-scared of opening it because Carbury Glande might be on the other side. But the hall was untenanted. She hurried through it and out to the courtyard. The iron gates had an elaborate fastening. Troy fumbled with it, dazzled by the glare of sunlight beyond. She pulled at the heavy latch, bruising her fingers. A voice behind her and at her feet said: "Do let me help you."

Carbury Glande must have come up the stairs from beneath the court-yard. His face, on a level with her knees, peered through the interstices of the wrought-iron banister. Recognition dawned on it.

"Can it be Troy?" he exclaimed hoarsely. "But it *is!* Dear heart, how magical and how peculiar. Where *have* you sprung from? And why are you scrabbling away at doors? Has Oberon alarmed you? I may say he petrifies me. What are you up to?"

He had arrived at her level, a short gnarled man whose hair and beard were red and whose face, at the moment, was a dreadful grey. He blinked up at Troy as if he couldn't get her into focus. He was wearing a pair of floral shorts and a magenta shirt.

"I'm not up to anything," said Troy. "In fact, I'm scarcely here at all. We've brought your host a middle-aged spinster with a perforated appendix and now we're on our way."

"Ah, yes. I heard about the spinster. Ali Baradi woke me at cockcrow, full of professional zeal, and asked me if I'd like to thread needles and count sponges. How he dared! Are you going?"

"I must," Troy said. "Do open this damned door for me."

She could hear Alleyn's and Herrington's voices in the hall and the thump of Herrington's stick.

Glande reached for the latch. His hand, stained round the nails with paint, was tremulous. "I am, as you can see, a wreck," he said. "A Homeric party and only four hours' sottish insensitivity in which to recover. Imagine it! There you are."

He opened the doors and winced at the glare outside. "Oberon will be thrilled you're here," he said. "Did you know he bought a thing of yours at the Rond-Point show? It's in the library. 'Boy with a Kite.' He adores it."

"Look here," Troy said hurriedly, "be a good chap and don't tell him I'm me. I've come here for a holiday and I'd so much rather . . ."

"Well, if you like. Yes, of course. Yes, I understand. And on mature consideration I fancy this ménage is not entirely your cup of tea. You're almost pathologically normal, aren't you? Forgive me if I bolt back to my burrow, the glare is really *more* than I can endure. God, somebody's coming!"

He stumbled away from the door. Alleyn, with Ricky in his arms, came out of the hall followed by Robin Herrington. Glande ejaculated: "Oh, sorry!" and bolted down the stairs. Herrington scowled after him and said: "That's our tame genius. I'll come to the car, if I may."

As they walked in single file down the steps and past the maker of figurines, Troy had the feeling that Robin wanted to say something to them and didn't know how to begin. They had reached the open platform where Raoul waited by the car before he blurted out:

"I do hope you will let me drive you down, to see the yacht. Both of you,

I mean. I mean . . ." he stopped short. Alleyn said: "That's very nice of you. I hadn't heard about a yacht."

"She's quite fun." He stood there, still with an air of hesitancy. Alleyn shifted Ricky and looked at Troy, who held out her hand to Robin.

"Don't come any further," she said. "Goodbye and thank you."

"Goodbye. If we may, Ginny and I will call at the hotel. It's the Royal, I suppose. I mean, it might amuse you to come for a drive. I mean, if you don't know anybody here . . ."

"It'd be lovely," Troy temporized, wondering if Alleyn wanted her to accept.

"As a matter of fact," Alleyn said, "we *have* got someone we ought to look up in Roqueville. Do you know anybody about here with the unlikely name of Garbel?"

Robin's jaw dropped. He stared at them with an expression of extraordinary consternation. "I . . . no. No. We haven't really met any of the local people. No. Well, I mustn't keep you standing in the sun. Goodbye."

And with a precipitancy as marked as his former hesitation, he turned and limped off down the passage-way.

"Now what," Troy asked her husband, "in a crazy world, is the significance of that particular bit of lunacy?"

"I've not the beginning of a notion," he said. "But I suggest that when we've got time to think, we call on Mr. Garbel."

CHAPTER IV

The Elusiveness of Mr. Garbel

Ricky woke up before they could get him to the car and was bewildered to find himself transported. He was hot, hungry, thirsty and uncomfortable, and he required immediate attention.

While Troy and Alleyn looked helplessly about the open platform Raoul advanced from the car, his face brilliant with understanding. He squatted on his heels beside the flushed and urgent Ricky and addressed him in very simple French which he appeared to understand and to which he readily responded. Marie, of the figurines, Raoul explained to the parents, would offer suitable hospitality and he and Ricky went off together, Ricky glancing up at him with admiration.

"It appears," Alleyn said, "that a French nanny and those biweekly conversational tramps with Mademoiselle to the Round Pond have not been unproductive. Our child has the rudiments of the language."

"Mademoiselle," Troy rejoined, "says he's prodigiously quick for his age. An amazing child, she thinks." And she added hotly: "Well, all right, I don't say so to anyone else, do I?"

"My darling, you do not and you shall never say so too often to me. But for the moment let us take our infant phenomenon for granted and look at the situation Chèvre d'Argent. Tell me as quickly as you can, what happened before I cropped up among those cups of tea on the roof-top."

They sat together on the running-board of the car and Troy did her best. "Admirable," he said when she had finished. "I fell in love with you in the first instance because you made such beautiful statements. Now, what do you suppose goes on in that house?"

"Something quite beastly," she said vigorously. "I'm sure of it. Oberon's obviously dishing out to his chums some fantastic hodgepodge of mysticism-cum-religion-cum, I'm very much afraid, eroticism. Grizel Locke attempted a sort of résumé. You never heard such a rigmarole . . . yoga, Nietzsche, black-magic. Voodoo, I wouldn't be surprised. With Lord knows what fancy touches of their own thrown in. It ought to be merely silly but it's not, it's frightening. Grizel Locke, I should say, is potty but the two young ones in any other setting would have struck me as being pleasant children. The boy's obviously in a state about the girl, who seems to be completely in Oberon's toils. It's so fantastic, it isn't true."

"Have you ever heard of the case of Horus and the Swami Vivi Ananda?"

"No."

"They appeared before Curtis Bennett with Edward Carson prosecuting and got swinging sentences for their pains. There's no time to tell you about them now, but you've more or less described their setup and I assure you there's nothing so very unusual about the religio-erotic racket. Oberon's name, by the way, is Albert George Clarkson. He's a millionaire and undoubtedly one of the drug barons. The cult of the Children of the Sun in the Outer is merely a useful sideline and a means, I suspect, of gratifying a particularly nasty personal taste. They suggested as much at the Sûreté though they don't know exactly what goes on among the Sun's Babies. The Sûreté is interested solely in the narcotics side of the show and the Yard's watching it from our end."

"And you?"

"I'm supposed to be the perishing link or something. What about the red-headed gentleman with painty hands and a carry-over who was letting you out?"

"He might be serious, Rory. He's Carbury Glande. He paints those post-surrealist things . . . witches' sabbaths and mystic unions. You must remember. Rather pretty colour and good design, but a bit nasty in feeling. The thing is, he knows me and although I asked him not to, he'll probably talk."

"Does he know about us?"

"I can't tell. He might."

"Damn!"

"I shouldn't have come, should I? If Glande knows who you are, he won't be able to resist telling them and bang goes your job."

"They didn't give me Glande's name at the Sûreté. He must be a later arrival. Never mind, we'll gamble on his not knowing you made a *mésalliance* with a policeman. Now, listen, my darling, I don't know how long I'll be up here. It may be an hour and it may be twenty-four. Will you settle yourself and Ricky at the Royal and forget about the Chèvre d'Argent? If there's any goat on the premises it will probably be your devoted husband. I'll make what hay I can while the sun shines in the Outer and I'll turn up as soon as maybe. One thing more. Will you try, when you've come to your poor senses, to ring up Mr. Garbel? He may not be on the telephone, of course, but if he is . . ."

"Lord, yes! Mr. Garbel! Now why, for pity's sake, did Robin Herrington run like a rabbit at the mention of P. E. Garbel? Can cousin Garbel be a drug baron? Or an addict, if it comes to that? It might account for his quaint literary style."

"Have you by any chance brought his letters?"

"Only the last, for the sake of his address."

"Hang on to it, I implore you. If he is on the telephone and answers, ask him to luncheon tomorrow and I'll be there. If, by any chance, he turns up before then, find out if he knows any of Oberon's chums and is prepared to talk about them. Here come Raoul and Ricky. Forget about this blasted business, my own true love, and enjoy yourself if you can."

"What about Miss Truebody?"

"Baradi is pretty worried, he says. I'm quite certain he's doing all that can be done for her. He's a kingpin at his job, you know, however much he may stink to high heaven as a chap."

"Shouldn't I wait with her?"

"*No.* Any more of that and I'll begin to think you like having your hand kissed by luscious Oriental gentlemen. Hullo, Rick, ready for your drive?"

Ricky advanced with his hands behind his back and with strides designed to match those of his companion. "Is Raoul driving us?" he asked.

"He is. You and Mummy."

"Good. Daddy, look! Look, Mummy!"

He produced from behind his back a little goat, painted silver grey with one foot upraised and mounted on a base that roughly traced the outlines of the Château de la Chèvre d'Argent. "The old lady made it and Raoul gave it to me," Ricky said. "It's a silver goat and when it's nighttime it makes itself shine. Doesn't it, Raoul? *N'est-ce pas, Raoul?*"

"*Oui, oui. Une chèvre d'argent qui s'illumine.*"

"Daddy, isn't Raoul kind?"

Alleyn, a little embarrassed, told Raoul how kind he was and Troy, haltingly, attempted to say that he shouldn't.

Raoul said: "But it is nothing, Madame. If it pleases this young gallant and does not offend Madame, all is well. What are my orders, Monsieur?"

"Will you drive Madame and Ricky to their hotel? Then go to M. le Commissaire at the Préfecture and give him this letter. Tell him that I will call on him as soon as possible. Tell him also about the operation and of course reply to any questions he may ask. Then return here. There is no immediate hurry and you will have time for *déjeuner*. Do not report at the Château but wait here for me. If I haven't turned up by 3:30 you may ask for me at the Château. You will remember that?"

Raoul repeated his instructions. Alleyn looked steadily at him. "Should you be told I am not there, drive to the nearest telephone, ring up the Préfecture and tell M. le Commissaire precisely what has happened. Understood?"

"Well understood, Monsieur."

"Good. One thing more, Raoul. Do you know anyone in Roqueville called Garbel?"

"Garr-bel? No, Monsieur. It will be an English person for whom Monsieur enquires?"

"Yes. The address is 16 Rue des Violettes."

Raoul repeated the address. "It is an apartment house, that one. It is true one finds a few English there, for the most part ladies no longer young and with small incomes who do not often engage taxis."

"Ah, well," Alleyn said. "No matter."

He took off his hat and kissed his wife. "Have a nice holiday," he said, "and give my love to Mr. Garbel."

"What were you telling Raoul?"

"Wouldn't you like to know! Goodbye, Rick. Take care of your mama, she's a good kind creature and means well."

Ricky grinned. He was quick, when he didn't understand his father's remarks, to catch their intention from the colour of his voice. "*Entendu*," he said, imitating Raoul, and climbed into the car beside him.

"I suppose I may sit here?" he said airily.

"He *is* a precocious little perisher and no mistake," Alleyn muttered. "Do you suppose it'll all peter out and he'll be a dullard by the time he's eight?"

"A lot of it's purely imitative. It sounds classier than it is. Move up, Ricky, I'm coming in front, too."

Alleyn watched the car drive down the steep lane to the main road. Then he turned back to the Château de la Chèvre d'Argent.

ii

On the way back to Roqueville Raoul talked nursery French to Ricky and Troy, pointing out the places of interest: the Alpine monastery where, in the cloisters, one might see many lively pictures executed by the persons of the district whose relations had been saved from abrupt destruction by the intervention of Our Lady of Paysdoux; villages that looked as if they had been thrown against the rocks and had stuck to them; distant prospects of little towns. On a lonely stretch of road, Troy offered him a cigarette and while he lit it he allowed Ricky to steer the scarcely moving car. Ricky's dotage on Raoul intensified with every kilometre they travelled together and Troy's understanding of French improved with astonishing rapidity. Altogether they enjoyed each other's company immensely and the journey seemed a short one. They could scarcely believe that the cluster of yellow and pink buildings that presently appeared beneath them was Roqueville.

Raoul turned aside from the steeply descending road and drove down a narrow side-street past an open market where bunches of dyed immortelles hung shrilly above the stalls and the smell of tuberoses was mingled with the pungency of fruit and vegetables. All the world, Raoul said, was abroad at this hour in the market and he flung loud unembarrassed greetings to many persons of his acquaintance. Troy felt her spirits rising and Ricky dropped into the stillness that with him was a sign of extreme pleasure. He sighed deeply and laid one hand on Raoul's knee and one, clasping his silver goat, on Troy's.

They were in a shadowed street where the houses were washed over with faint candy-pink, lemon and powder-blue. Strings of washing hung from one iron balcony to another.

"Rue des Violettes," Raoul said, pointing to the street-sign and presently halted. "Numero seize."

Troy gathered that he offered her an opportunity to call on Mr. Garbel or, if she was not so inclined, to note the whereabouts of his lodging. She could see through the open door into a dim and undistinguished interior. A number of raffish children clustered about the car. They chattered in an incomprehensible patois and stared with an air of hardihood at Ricky, who instantly became stony.

Troy thought Raoul was offering to accompany her into the house, but sensing panic in the breast of her son, she managed to say that she would go in by herself. "I can leave a note," she thought, and said to Ricky: "I won't be a moment. You stay with Raoul, darling."

"O.K.," he agreed, still fully occupied with disregarding the children. He was like a dog who, when addressed by his master, wags his tail but does not lower his heckles. Raoul shouted at the children and made a shooing noise driving them from the car. They retreated a little, skittishly twitting him. He got out and opened the door for Troy, removing his cap as if she were a minor royalty. Impressed by this evidence of prestige, most of the children fell back, though two of the hardier raised a beggar's plaint and were silenced by Raoul.

The door of Number 16 was ajar. Troy pushed it open and crossed a dingy tessellated floor to a lift-well beside which hung a slotted board holding cards, some with printed and some with written names on them. She had begun hunting up and down the board when a voice behind her said: "Madame?"

Troy turned as if she'd been struck. The door of a sort of cubby-hole opposite the lift was held partly open by a grimy and heavily ringed hand. Beyond the hand Troy could see folds of a black satin dress, an iridescence of bead-work and three quarters of a heavy face and piled-up coiffure.

She felt as if she'd been caught doing something shady. Her nursery French deserted her.

"Pardon," she stammered. "*Je désire—je cherche—Monsieur Garbel—le nom de Garbel.*"

The woman said something incomprehensible to Troy, who replied, "*Je ne parle pas français. Malheureusement,*" she added on an afterthought. The woman made a resigned noise and waddled out of her cubby-hole. She was enormously fat and used a walking stick. Her eyes were like black currents sunk in uncooked dough. She prodded with her stick at the top of the board and, strangely familiar in that alien place, a spidery signature in faded ink was exhibited: "P. E. Garbel."

"*Ah, merci,*" Troy cried, but the fat woman shook her head contemptuously and appeared to repeat her former remark. This time Troy caught something like . . . "*Pas chez elle . . . il y a vingt-quatre heures.*"

"Not at home?" shouted Troy in English. The woman shrugged heavily and began to walk away. "May I leave a note?" Troy called to her enormous back. "*Puis-je vous donner un billet pour Monsieur?*"

The woman stared at her as if she were mad. Troy scrambled in her bag and produced a notebook and the stub of a BB pencil. Sketches she had made of Ricky in the train fell to the floor. The woman glanced at them with some appearance of interest. Troy wrote: "Called at 11:15. Sorry to have missed you. Hope you can lunch with us at the Royal tomorrow." She signed the note, folded it over and wrote: "M. P. E. Garbel" on the flap. She gave it to the woman (was she a concierge?) and stooped to recover her sketches, aware as she did so, of a dusty skirt, dubious petticoats and broken shoes. When she straightened up it was to find her note displayed with a grey-rimmed sunken finger-nail jabbing at the inscription. "She can't read my writing," Troy thought and pointed first to the card and then to the note, nodding like a mandarin and smiling constrainedly. "Garbel," said Troy, "Gar-r-bel." She remembered about tipping and pressed a 100 franc note into the padded hand. This had an instantaneous effect. The woman coruscated with black unlovely smiles. "Mademoiselle," she said, gaily waving the note. "Madame," Troy responded. "*Non, non, non, non, Mademoiselle,*" insisted the woman with an ingratiating leer.

Troy supposed this to be a compliment. She tried to look deprecating, made an ungraphic gesture and beat a retreat.

Ricky and Raoul were in close conversation in the car when she rejoined them. Three of the hard-boiled children were seated on the running-board while the others played leap-frog in an exhibitionist manner up and down the street.

"Darling," Troy said as they drove away, "you speak French much better than I do."

Ricky slewed his eyes round at her. They were a brilliant blue and his lashes, like his hair, were black. "*Naturellement!*" he said.

"Don't be a prig, Ricky," said his mother crossly. "You're much too uppity. I think I must be bringing you up very badly."

"Why?"

"Now then!" Troy warned him.

"Did you see Mr. Garbel, Mummy?"

"No, I left a note."

"Is he coming to see us?"

"I hope so," said Troy and after a moment's thought added: "If he's true."

"If he writes letters to you he must be true," Ricky pointed out. "*Naturellement!*"

Raoul drove them into a little square and pulled up in front of the hotel.

At that moment the concierge at 16 Rue des Violettes, after having sat for ten minutes in morose cogitation, dialled the telephone number of the Chèvre d'Argent.

iii

Alleyn and Baradi stood on either side of the bed. The maid, an elderly pinched-looking woman, had withdrawn to the window. The beads of her rosary clicked discreetly through her fingers.

Miss Truebody's face, still without its teeth, seemed to have collapsed about her nose and forehead and to be less than human-sized. Her mouth was a round hole with puckered edges. She was snoring. Each expulsion of her breath blew the margin of the hole outwards and each intake sucked it in so that in a dreadful way her face was busy. Her eyes were incompletely closed and her almost hairless brows drawn together in a meaningless scowl.

"She will be like this for some hours," Baradi said. He drew Miss Truebody's wrist from under the sheet: "I expect no change. She is very ill, but I expect no change for some hours."

"Which sounds," Alleyn said absently, "like a rough sketch for a villanelle."

"You are a poet?"

Alleyn waved a hand: "Shall we say, an undistinguished amateur."

"You underrate yourself, I feel sure," Baradi said, still holding the flaccid wrist. "You publish?"

Alleyn was suddenly tempted to say: "The odd slim vol," but he controlled himself and made a slight modest gesture that was entirely non-committal. Dr. Baradi followed this up with his now familiar comment. "Mr. Oberon," he said, "will be delighted," and added: "He is already greatly moved by your personality and that of your enchanting wife."

"For my part," Alleyn said, "I was enormously impressed with his."

He looked with an air of ardent expectancy into that fleshy mask and could find in it no line or fold that was either stupid or credulous. What was Baradi? Part Egyptian, part French? Wholly Egyptian? Wholly Arab? "Which is the kingpin," Alleyn speculated, "Baradi or Oberon?" Baradi, taking out his watch, looked impassively into Alleyn's face. Then he snapped open his watch and a minute went past, clicked out by the servant's beads.

"Ah, well," Baradi muttered, putting up his watch, "it is as one would expect. Nothing can be done for the time being. This woman will report any change. She is capable and, in the village, has had some experience of sickbed attendance. My man will be able to relieve her. We may have difficulty in securing a trained nurse for tonight, but we shall manage."

He nodded at the woman, who came forward and listened passively to his instructions. They left her, nun-like and watchful, seated by the bed.

"It is eleven o'clock, the hour of meditation," Baradi said as they walked down the passage, "so we must not disturb. There will be something to drink in my room. Will you join me? Your car has not yet returned."

He led the way into the Chinese room where his servant waited behind a table set with Venetian goblets, dishes of olives and sandwiches and something that looked like Turkish Delight. There was also champagne in a silver ice-bucket. Alleyn was almost impervious to irregular hours but the last twenty-four had been exacting, the heat was excessive, and the reek of ether had made him feel squeamish. Lager was his normal choice but champagne would have done very nicely indeed. It was an arid concession to his job that obliged him to say with what he hoped was the right degree of pale complacency: "Will you forgive me if I have water? You see, I've lately become rather interested in a way of life that excludes alcohol."

"But how remarkable. Mr. Oberon will be most interested. Mr. Oberon," Baradi said—signing to the servant that the champagne was to be opened—"is perhaps the greatest living authority on such matters. His design for living transcends many of the ancient cults, drawing from each its purest essence. A remarkable synthesis. But while he himself achieves a perfect balance between austerity and, shall we say, selective enjoyment, he teaches that there is no merit in abstention for the sake of abstention. His disciples are encouraged to experience many pleasures, to choose them with the most exquisite discrimination: 'arrange' them, indeed, as a painter arranges his pictures or a composer traces out the design for a fugue. Only thus, he tells us, may the Ultimate Goal be reached. Only thus may one experience Life to the Full. Believe me, Mr. Allen, he would smile at your rejection of this admirable vintage, thinking it as gross an error, if you will forgive me, as over-indulgence. Let me persuade you to change your mind. Besides, you have had a trying experience. You are a little nauseated, I think, by the fumes of ether. Let me, as a doctor," he ended playfully, "insist on a glass of champagne."

Alleyn had taken up a ruby goblet and was looking into it with admiration. "I must say," he said, "this is all most awfully interesting: what you've been saying about Mr. Oberon's teaching, I mean. You make my own fumbling ideas seem pitifully naïve." He smiled. "I should adore some champagne from this quite lovely goblet."

He held it out and watched the champagne mount and cream. Baradi was looking at him across the rim of his own glass. One could scarcely, Alleyn thought, imagine a more opulent picture: the corrugations of hair glistened, the eyes were lustrous, the nose overhung a bubbling field of amber stained with ruby, one could guess at the wide expectant lips.

"To the fullness of life," said Dr. Baradi.

"Yes, indeed," Alleyn rejoined, and they drank.

The champagne was, in fact, admirable.

Alleyn's head was as strong as the next man's but he had had a light breakfast and therefore helped himself freely to the sandwiches, which were delicious. Baradi, always prepared, Alleyn supposed, to experience life to the full, gobbled up the sweetmeats, popping them one after another into his red mouth and abominably washing them down with champagne.

The atmosphere took on a spurious air of unbuttoning, which Alleyn was careful to encourage. So far, he felt tolerably certain, Baradi knew nothing about him, but was nevertheless concerned to place him accurately. The situation was a delicate one. If Alleyn could establish himself as an eager neophyte to the synthetic mysteries preached by Mr. Oberon, he would have taken a useful step towards the performance of his job. At least he would be able to give an inside report on the domestic setup in the Château de la Chèvre d'Argent. Officers on loan to the Special Branch preserve a strict anonymity and it was unlikely that his name would be known in the drug-racket as a M.I.5 investigator. It might be recognized, however, as that of a detective-officer of the C.I.D. Carbury Glande might respect Troy's request, but if he didn't, it was more than likely that he or one of the others would remember she had married a policeman. Alleyn himself remembered the exuberances of the gossip columnists at the time of their marriage and later, when Troy had held one-man shows or when he had appeared for the police in some much-publicized case. It looked as if he should indeed make what hay he could while the sun shone on the Chèvre d'Argent.

"If Miss Truebody and I get through this party," he thought, "blow me down if I don't take her out and we'll break a bottle of fizz on our own account."

Greatly cheered by this thought, he began to talk about poetry and esoteric writing, speaking of Rabindranath Tagore and the Indian "Tantras," of the "Amanga Ranga" and parts of the Cabala. Baradi listened with every appearance of delight, but Alleyn felt a little as if he were prodding at a particularly resilient mattress. There seemed to be no vulnerable spot and, what was worse, his companion began to exhibit signs of controlled restlessness. It was clear that the champagne was intended for a stirrup cup and that he waited for Alleyn to take his departure. Yet, somewhere, there must be a point of penetration. And remembering with extreme distaste Dr. Baradi's attentions to Troy, Alleyn drivelled hopefully onward, speaking of the secret

rites of Eleusis and the cult of Osiris. Something less impersonal at last
appeared in Baradi as he listened to these confidences. The folds of flesh
running from the corners of his nostrils to those of his mouth became more
apparent and he began to look like an Eastern and more fleshy version of
Charles II. He went to the bureau by Vernis-Martin, unlocked it, and
presently laid before Alleyn a book bound in grey silk on which a design
had been painted in violet, green and repellent pink.

"A rare and early edition," he said. "Carbury Glande designed and executed the cover. Do admire it!"

Alleyn opened the book at the title page. It was a copy of *The Memoirs
of Donatien Alphonse François, Marquis de Sade.*

"A present," said Baradi, "from Mr. Oberon."

It was unnecessary, Alleyn decided, to look any further for the chink in
Dr. Baradi's armour.

From this moment, when he set down his empty goblet on the table in
Dr. Baradi's room, his visit to the Chèvre d'Argent developed into a covert
battle between himself and the doctor. The matter under dispute was Alleyn's
departure. He was determined to stay for as long as the semblance of ordinary
manners could be preserved. Baradi obviously wanted to get rid of him but,
for reasons about which Alleyn could only conjecture, avoided any suggestion
of precipitancy. Alleyn felt that his safest line was to continue in the manner
of a would-be disciple to the cult of the Children of the Sun. Only thus,
he thought, could he avoid planting in Baradi a rising suspicion of his own
motives. He must be a bore, a persistent bore, but no more than a bore.
And he went gassing on, racking his memory for remnants of esoteric
gossip. Baradi spoke of a telephone call. Alleyn talked of telepathic communication. Baradi said that Troy would doubtless be anxious to hear about Miss
Truebody; Alleyn asked if Miss Truebody would not be greatly helped by
the banishment of anxiety from everybody's mind. Baradi mentioned luncheon. Alleyn prattled of the lotus posture. Baradi said he must not waste any
more of Alleyn's time; Alleyn took his stand on the postulate that time, in
the commonly accepted sense of the word, did not exist. A final skirmish
during which an offer to enquire for Alleyn's car was countered by Rosi-
crucianism and the fiery cross of the Gnostics, ended with Baradi saying
that he would have another look at Miss Truebody and must then report to
Mr. Oberon. He said he would be some time and begged Alleyn not to
feel he must wait for his return. At this point Baradi's servant reappeared
to say a telephone call had come through for him. Baradi at once remarked
that no doubt Alleyn's car would arrive before he returned. He regretted
that Mr. Oberon's meditation class would still be in progress and must not
be interrupted, and he suggested that Alleyn might care to wait for his car
in the hall or in the library. Alleyn said that he would very much like to
stay where he was and to examine the de Sade. With a flush of exasperation
mounting on his heavy cheeks, Baradi consented, and went out, followed
by his man.

They had turned to the right and gone down the passage to the hall. The rings on an embossed leather curtain in the entrance clashed as they went through.

Alleyn was already squatting at the Vernis-Martin bureau.

He had the reputation in his department of uncanny accuracy when a quick search was in question. It's doubtful if he ever acted more swiftly than now. Baradi had left the bottom drawer of the bureau open.

It contained half a dozen books, each less notorious if more infamous than the de Sade, and all on the proscribed list at Scotland Yard. He lifted them one by one and replaced them.

The next drawer was locked but yielded to the application of a skeleton-key Alleyn had gleaned from a housebreaker of virtuosity. It contained three office ledgers and two notebooks. The entries in the first ledger were written in a script that Alleyn took to be Egyptian, but occasionally there appeared proper names in English characters. Enormous sums of money were shown in several currencies: piastres, francs, pounds and lire neatly flanked each other in separate columns. He turned the pages rapidly, his hearing fixed on the passage outside, his mind behind his eyes.

Between the first ledger and the second lay a thin quarto volume in violet leather, heavily embossed. The design was tortuous, but Alleyn recognized a pentagram, a triskelion, winged serpents, bulls and a broken cross. Superimposed over the whole was a double-edged sword with formalized flames rising from it in the shape of a raised hand. The covers were mounted with a hasp and lock which he had very little trouble in opening.

Between the covers was a single page of vellum, elaborately illuminated and embellished with a further number of symbolic ornaments. Baradi had been gone three minutes when Alleyn began to read the text:

> Here in the names of Ra and the Sons of Ra and the Daughters of Ra who are also, in the Mystery of the Sun, the Sacred Spouses of Ra, I, about to enter into the Secret Fellowship of Ra, swear before Horus and Osiris, before Annum and Apsis, before the Good and the Evil that are One God, who is both Good and Evil, that I will set a seal upon my lips and eyes and ears and keep forever secret the mysteries and the Sacred Rites of Ra.
>
> I swear that all that passes in this place shall be as if it had never been. If I break this oath in the least degree may my lips be burnt away with the fire that is now set before them. May my eyes be put out with the knife that is now set before them. May my ears be stopped with molten lead. May my entrails rot and my body perish with the disease of the crab. May I desire death before I die and suffer torment for evermore. If I break silence may these things be unto me. I swear by the fire of Ra and the Blade of Ra. So be it.

Alleyn uttered a single violent expletive, relocked the covers and opened the second ledger.

It was inscribed: "Compagnie Chimique des Alpes Maritimes," and contained names, dates and figures in what appeared to be a balance of expenditure and income. Alleyn's attention sharpened. The company seemed to be showing astronomical profits. His fingers, nervous and delicate, leafed through the pages, moving rhythmically.

Then abruptly they were still. Near the bottom of a page, starting out of the unintelligible script and written in a small, rather elaborate handwriting, was a name—P. E. Garbel.

The curtain rings clashed in the passage. He had locked the drawer and with every appearance of avid attention was hanging over the de Sade, when Baradi returned.

iv

Baradi had brought Carbury Glande with him and Alleyn thought he knew why. Glande was introduced and after giving Alleyn a damp runaway handshake, retired into the darker part of the room fingering his beard, and eyed him with an air, half curious, half defensive. Baradi said smoothly that Alleyn had greatly admired the de Sade book-wrapper and would no doubt be delighted to meet the distinguished artist. Alleyn responded with an enthusiasm which he was careful to keep on an amateurish level. He said he wished so much he knew more about the technique of painting. This would do nicely, he thought, if Glande, knowing he was Troy's husband, was still unaware of his job. If, on the other hand, Glande knew he was a detective, Alleyn would have said nothing to suggest that he tried to conceal his occupation. He thought it extremely unlikely that Glande had respected Troy's request for anonymity. No. Almost certainly he had reported that their visitor was Agatha Troy, the distinguished painter of Mr. Oberon's "Boy with a Kite." And then? Either Glande had also told them that her husband was a C.I.D. officer, in which case they would be anxious to find out if his visit was pure coincidence; or else Glande had been able to give little or no information about Alleyn and they merely wondered if he was as ready a subject for skulduggery as he had tried to suggest. A third possibility and one that he couldn't see at all clearly, involved the now highly debatable integrity of P. E. Garbel.

Baradi said that Alleyn's car had not arrived, and with no hint of his former impatience suggested that they show him the library.

It was on the far side of the courtyard. On entering it he was confronted with Troy's "Boy with a Kite." Its vigour and cleanliness struck like a sword-thrust across the airlessness of Mr. Oberon's library. For a second the "Boy" looked with Ricky's eyes at Alleyn.

A sumptuous company of books lined the walls with the emphasis, as was to be expected, upon mysticism, the occult and Orientalism. Alleyn recognized a number of works that a bookseller's catalogue would have described as rare, curious, and collector's items. Of far greater interest to Alleyn, however, was a large framed drawing that hung in a dark corner of that dark room. It was, he saw, a representation, probably medieval, of the Château de la Chèvre d'Argent and it was part elevation and part plan. After one desirous glance he avoided it. He professed himself fascinated with the books and took them down with ejaculations of interest and delight. Baradi and Glande watched him and listened.

"You are a collector, perhaps, Mr. Allen?" Baradi conjectured.

"Only in a very humble way. I'm afraid my job doesn't provide for the more expensive hobbies."

There was a moment's pause. "Indeed?" Baradi said. "One cannot, alas, choose one's profession. I hope yours is at least congenial."

Alleyn thought: "He's fishing. He doesn't know or he isn't sure." And he said absently, as he turned the pages of a superb Book of the Dead, "I suppose everyone becomes a little bored with his job at times. What a wonderful thing this is, this book. Tell me, Dr. Baradi, as a scientific man—"

Baradi answered his questions. Glande glowered and shuffled impatiently. Alleyn reflected that by this time it was possible that Baradi and Robin Herrington had told Oberon of the Alleyns' enquiries for Mr. Garbel. Did this account for the change in Baradi's attitude? Alleyn was now unable to bore Dr. Baradi.

"It would be interesting," Carbury Glande said in his harsh voice, "to hear what Mr. Alleyn's profession might be. I am passionately interested in the employment of other people."

"Ah, yes," Baradi agreed. "Do you ever play the game of guessing at the occupation of strangers and then proving yourself right or wrong by getting to know them? Come!" he cried with a great show of frankness. "Let us confess, Carbury, we are filled with unseemly curiosity about Mr. Allen. Will he allow us to play our game? Indulge us, my dear Allen. Carbury, what is your guess?"

Glande muttered: "Oh, I plump for one of the colder branches of learning. Philosophy."

"Do you think so? A don, perhaps? And yet there is something that to me suggests that Mr. Allen was born under Mars. A soldier. Or, no. I take that back. A diplomat."

"How very perceptive of you," Alleyn exclaimed, looking at him over the Book of the Dead.

"Then I am right?"

"In part, at least. I started in the Diplomatic," said Alleyn truthfully, "but left it at the file-and-corridor stage."

"Really? Then, perhaps, I am allowed another guess. No!" he cried after a pause. "I give up. Carbury, what do you say?"

"I? God knows! Perhaps he left the Diplomatic Service under a cloud and went big-game hunting."

"I begin to think you are all psychic in this house," Alleyn said delightedly. "How on earth do you do it?"

"A mighty hunter!" Baradi ejaculated, clapping his hands softly.

"Not at all mighty, I'm afraid, only pathetically persevering."

"Wonderful," Carbury Glande said, drawing his hand across his eyes and suppressing a yawn. "You live in South Kensington, I feel sure, in some magnificently dark apartment from the walls of which glower the glass eyes of monstrous beasts. Horns, snouts, tusks. Coarse hair. Lolling tongues made of a suitable plastic. Quite wonderful."

"But Mr. Allen is a poet and a hunter of rare books as well as of rare beasts. Perhaps," Baradi speculated, "it was during your travels that you became interested in the esoteric?"

Alleyn suppressed a certain weariness of spirit and renewed his raptures. You saw some rum things, he said with an air of simple credulity, in native countries. He had been told and told on good authority— He rambled on, saying that he greatly desired to learn more about the primitive beliefs of ancient races.

"Does your wife accompany you on safari?" Glande asked. "I should have thought—" He stopped short. Alleyn saw a flash of exasperation in Baradi's eyes.

"My wife," Alleyn said lightly, "couldn't approve less of blood sports. She is a painter."

"I am released," Glande cried, "from bondage!" He pointed to the "Boy with a Kite." "*Ecce!*"

"No!" Really, Alleyn thought, Baradi was a considerable actor. Delight and astonishment were admirably suggested. "Not—? Not Agatha Troy? But, my dear Mr. Allen, this is quite remarkable. Mr. Oberon will be enchanted."

"I can't wait," Carbury Glande said, "to tell him." He showed his teeth through his moustache. "I'm afraid you're in for a scolding, Alleyn. Troy swore me to secrecy. I may say," he added, "that I knew in a vague way, that she was a wedded woman but she has kept the Mighty Hunter from us." His tongue touched his upper lip. "Understandably, perhaps," he added.

Alleyn thought that nothing would give him more pleasure than to seize Dr. Baradi and Mr. Carbury Glande by the scruffs of their respective necks and crash their heads together.

He said apologetically: "Well, you see, we're on holiday."

"Quite," said Baradi and the conversation languished.

"I think you told us," Baradi said casually, "that you have friends in Roqueville and asked if we knew them. I'm afraid that I've forgotten the name."

"Only one. Garbel."

Baradi's smile looked as if it had been left on his face by an oversight. The red hairs of Glande's beard quivered very slightly as if his jaw was clenched.

"A retired chemist of sorts," Alleyn said.

"Ah, yes! Possibly attached to the monstrous establishment which defaces our lovely olive groves. Monstrous," Baradi added, "aesthetically speaking."

"Quite abominable!" said Glande. His voice cracked and he wetted his lips.

"No doubt admirable from an utilitarian point-of-view. I believe they produce artificial manure in great quantities."

"The place," Glande said, "undoubtedly stinks," and he laughed unevenly.

"Aesthetically?" Alleyn asked.

"Always, aesthetically," said Baradi.

"I noticed the factory on our way up. Perhaps we'd better ask there for our friend."

There was a dead silence.

"I can't think what has become of that man of mine," Alleyn said lightly.

Baradi was suddenly effusive. "But how inconsiderate we are! You, of course, are longing to rejoin your wife. And who can blame you? No woman has the right to be at once so talented and so beautiful. But your car? No doubt, a puncture or perhaps merely our Mediterranean *dolce far niente*. You must allow us to send you down. Robin would, I am sure, be enchanted. Or, if he is engaged in meditation, Mr. Oberon would be delighted to provide a car. How thoughtless we have been!"

This, Alleyn realized, was final. "I wouldn't dream of it," he said. "But I do apologize for being such a pestilent visitor. I've let my ruling passion run away with me and kept you hovering interminably. The car will arrive any moment now, I feel sure, and I particularly want to see the man. If I might just wait here among these superb books I shan't feel I'm making a nuisance of myself."

It was a toss-up whether this would work. They wanted, he supposed, to consult together. After a fractional hesitation, Baradi said something about their arrangements for the afternoon. Perhaps, if Mr. Allen would excuse them, they should have a word with Mr. Oberon. There was the business of the nurse—Glande, less adroit, muttered unintelligibly and they went out together.

Alleyn was in front of the plan two seconds after the door had shut behind them.

It was embellished with typical medieval ornaments—a coat of arms, a stylized goat and a great deal of scroll-work. The drawing itself was in two main parts, an elevation, treated as if the entire face of the building had been removed and a multiple plan of great intricacy. It would have taken an hour to follow out the plan in detail. With a refinement of concentration that Mr. Oberon himself might have envied, Alleyn fastened his attention upon the main outlines of the structural design. The great rooms and principal bedrooms were all, more or less, on the library level. Above this level the Château rose irregularly in a system of connected turrets to the battlements. Below it, the main stairway led down by stages through a maze of rooms that grew progressively smaller until, at a level which must have been below that of the railway, they were no bigger than prison cells and had probably served as such for hundreds of years. A vast incoherent maze that

had followed, rather than overcome the contour of the mountain; an archi-
tectural compromise, Alleyn murmured, and sharpened his attention upon
one room and its relation to the rest.

It was below the library and next to a room that had no outside windows.
He marked its position and cast back in his mind to the silhouette of the
Château as he had seen it, moonlit, in the early hours of that morning.
He noticed that it had a window much longer than it was high and he
remembered the shape of the window they had seen.

If it was true that Mr. Oberon and his guests were now occupied, as
Baradi had represented, with some kind of esoteric keep-fit exercises on the
roof-garden, it might be worth taking a risk. He thought of two or three
plausible excuses, took a final look at the plan, slipped out of the library and
ran lightly down a continuation of the winding stair that, in its upper reaches,
led to the roof-garden.

He passed a landing, a closed door and three narrow windows. The stairs
corkscrewed down to a wider landing from which a thickly carpeted passage
ran off to the right. Opposite the stairway was a door and, a few steps away,
another—the door he sought.

He went up to it and knocked.

There was no answer. He turned the handle delicately. The door opened
inwards until there was a wide enough gap for him to look through. He found
himself squinting along a wall hung with silk rugs and garnished about midway along with a big prayer wheel. At the far end there was an alcove occupied
by an extremely exotic-looking divan. He opened the door fully and walked
into the room.

From inside the door his view of Mr. Oberon's room was in part blocked
by the back of an enormous looking-glass screwed to the floor at an angle
of about 45 degrees to the outside wall. For the moment he didn't move
beyond this barrier, but from where he stood, looked at the left-hand end
of the room. It was occupied by a sort of altar hung with a stiffly embroidered
cloth and garnished with a number of objects: a pentacle in silver, a triskelion in bronze and a large crystal affair resembling a sunburst. Beside the
altar was a door, leading, he decided, into the windowless room he had noted
on the plan.

He moved forward with the intention of walking round the looking-glass
into the far part of the room.

"Bring me the prayer wheel," said a voice beyond the glass.

It fetched Alleyn up with the jolt of a punch over the heart. He looked
at the door. If the glass had hidden him on his entrance it would mask his
exit. He moved towards the door.

"I am at the Third Portal of the Outer and must not uncover my eyes.
Do not speak. Bring me the prayer wheel. Put it before me."

Alleyn walked forward.

There, on the other side of the looking-glass facing it and seated on the
floor, was Mr. Oberon, stark naked, with the palms of his hands pressed to

his eyes. Beyond him was a long window masked by a dyed silk blind, almost transparent, with the design of the sun upon it.

Alleyn took the prayer wheel from the wall. It was an elaborate affair, heavily carved, with many cylinders. He set it before Oberon.

He turned and had reached the door when somebody knocked peremptorily on it. Alleyn stepped back as it was flung open. It actually struck his shoulder. He heard someone go swiftly past and into the room.

Baradi's voice said: "Where are you? Oh. Oh, there you are! See here, I've got to talk to you."

He must be behind the glass. Alleyn slipped round the door and darted out. As he ran lightly up the stairs he heard Baradi shut the door.

There was nobody on the top landing. He walked back into the library, having been away from it for five and a half minutes.

He took out his notebook and made a very rough sketch of Mr. Oberon's room, taking particular pains to mark the position of the prayer wheel on the wall. Then he set about memorizing as much of its detail as he had been able to take in. He was still at this employment when the latch turned in the door.

Alleyn pulled out from the nearest shelf a copy of Mr. Montague Summers's major work on witchcraft. He was apparently absorbed in it when a woman came into the library.

He looked up from the book and knew that as far as preserving his anonymity was concerned, he was irrevocably sunk.

"If it's not Roderick Alleyn!" said Annabella Wells.

CHAPTER V

Ricky in Roqueville

It was some years ago, in a transatlantic steamer, that Alleyn had met Annabella Wells: the focal point of shipboard gossip to which she had seemed to be perfectly indifferent. She had watched him with undisguised concentration for four hours and had then sent her secretary with an invitation for drinks. She herself drank pretty heavily and, he thought, was probably a drug addict. He had found her an embarrassment and was glad when she suddenly dropped him. Since then she had turned up from time to time as an onlooker at criminal trials where he appeared for the police. She was, she told him, passionately interested in criminology.

In the English theatre her brilliance had been dimmed by her outrageous eccentricities, but in Paris, particularly in the motion-picture studios, she was still one of the great ones. She retained a ravaged sort of beauty and an individuality which would be arresting when the last of her good looks had been rasped away. A formidable woman, and an enchantress still.

She gave him her hand and the inverted and agonized smile for which she was famous. "They said you were a big-game hunter," she said. "I couldn't wait."

"It was nice of them to get that impression."

"An accurate one, after all. Are you on the prowl down here? After some master-felon?"

"I'm on a holiday with my wife and small boy."

"Ah, yes! The beautiful woman who paints famous pictures. I am told by Baradi and Glande that she is beautiful. There is no need to look angry, is there?"

"Did I look angry?"

"You looked as if you were trying not to show a certain uxorious irritation."

"Did I, indeed?" said Alleyn.

"Baradi *is* a bit lush. I will allow and must admit that he's a bit lush. Have you seen Oberon?"

"For a few moments."

"What did you think of *him?*"

"Isn't he your host?"

"Honestly," she said, "you're not true. Much more fabulous, in your way, than Oberon."

"I'm interested in what I have been told of his philosophy."

"So they said. What sort of interest?"

"Personal and academic."

"My interest is personal and unacademic." She opened her cigarette case. Alleyn glanced at the contents. "I see," he said, "that it would be useless to offer you a Capstan."

"Will you have one of these? They're Egyptian. The red won't come off on your lips."

"Thank you. They would be wasted on me." He lit her cigarette. "I wonder," he said, "if I could persuade you to say nothing about my job."

"Darling," she rejoined—she called everyone "darling"—"you could persuade me to do anything. My trouble was, you wouldn't try. Why do you look at me like that?"

"I was wondering if any dependence could be placed on a heroin addict. Is it heroin?"

"It is. I get it," said Miss Wells, "from America."

"How very tragic."

"Tragic?"

"You weren't taking heroin when you played Hedda Gabler at the Unicorn in '42. Could you give a performance like that now?"

"*Yes,*" she said vehemently.

"But what a pity you don't!"

"My last film is the best thing I've ever done. Everyone says so." She looked at him with hatred. "I can still do it," she said.

"On your good days, perhaps. The studio is less exacting than the theatre. Will the cameras wait when the gallery would boo? I couldn't know less about it."

She walked up to him and struck him across the face with the back of her hand.

"You have deteriorated," said Alleyn.

"Are you mad? What are you up to? Why are you here?"

"I brought a woman who may be dying to your Dr. Baradi. All I want is to go away as I came in—a complete nonentity."

"And you think that by insulting me you'll persuade me to oblige you."

"I think you've already talked to your friends about me and that they've sent you here to find out if you were right."

"You're a very conceited man. Why should I talk about you?"

"Because," Alleyn said, "you're afraid."

"Of you?"

"Specifically. Of me."

"You idiot," she said. "Coming here with a dying spinster and an arty-crafty wife and a dreary little boy! For God's sake, get out and get on with your holiday."

"I should like it above all things."

"Why don't you want them to know who you are?"

"It would quite spoil my holiday."

"Which might mean anything."

"It might."

"Why do you say I'm afraid?"

"You're shaking. That may be a carry-over from alcohol or heroin, or both, but I don't think it is. You're behaving like a frightened woman. You were in a blue funk when you hit me."

"You're saying detestable, unforgivable things to me."

"Have I said anything that is untrue?"

"My life's my own. I've a right to do what I like with it."

"What's happened to your intelligence? You should know perfectly well that this sort of responsibility doesn't end with yourself. What about those two young creatures? The girl?"

"I didn't bring them here."

"No, really," Alleyn said, going to the door, "you're saying such very stupid things. I'll go down to the front and see if my car's come. Goodbye to you."

She followed him and put her hand on his arm. "Look!" she said. "Look at me. I'm terrifying, aren't I? A wreck? But I've still got more than my share of what it takes. Haven't I?"

"For Baradi and his friends?"

"Baradi!" she said contemptuously.

"I really didn't want to insult you with Oberon."

"What do you know about Oberon?"

"I've seen him."

She left her hand on him, but with an air of forgetfulness. A tremor communicated itself to his arm. "You don't know," she said. "You don't know what he's like. It's no good thinking about him in the way you think about other men. There are *hommes fatals,* too, you know. He's terrifying and he's marvellous. You can't understand that, can you?"

"No. To me, if he wasn't disgusting, he'd be ludicrous. A slug of a man."

"Do you believe in hypnotism?"

"Certainly. If the subject is willing."

"Oh," she said hopelessly, "I'm willing enough. Not that it's as simple as hypnotism." She hung her head, looking, with that gesture, like the travesty of a shamed girl. He couldn't hear all she said but caught one phrase: ". . . wonderful degradation. . . ."

"For God's sake," Alleyn said, "what nonsense is this?"

She frowned and looked at him out of her disastrous eyes. "Could you help me?" she said.

"I have no idea. Probably not."

"I'm in a bad way."

"Yes."

"If I were to keep faith? I don't know what you're up to, but if I were to keep faith and not tell them who you are? Even if it ruined me? Would you think you could help me then?"

"Are you asking me if I could help you to cure yourself of drugging? I couldn't. Only an expert could do that. If you've still got enough character and sense of purpose to keep faith, as you put it, perhaps you should have enough guts to go through with a cure. I don't know."

"I suppose you think I'm trying to bribe you?"

"In a sense—yes."

"Do you know," she said discontentedly, "you're the only man I've ever met—" She stopped and seemed to hesitate. "I can't get this right," she said. "With you it's not an act, is it?"

Alleyn smiled for the first time. "I'm not attempting the well-known gambit of rudeness introduced with a view to amorous occasions," he said. "Is that what you mean?"

"I suppose it is."

"You should stick to classical drama. Shakespeare's women don't fall for the insult-and-angry-seduction stuff. Sorry. I'm forgetting Richard III."

"Beatrice and Benedick? Petruchio and Katharina?"

"I was excluding comedy."

"How right you were. There's nothing very funny about my situation."

"No, it seems appalling."

"What can I do? Tell me, what can I do?"

"Leave the Chèvre d'Argent today. Now, if you like. I've got a car outside. Go to a doctor in Paris and offer yourself for a cure. Recognize your responsibility and, before further harm can come of this place, tell me or the local commissary or anyone else in a position of authority everything you know about the people here."

"Betray my friends?"

"A meaningless phrase. In protecting them you betray decency itself. Can you think of that child Ginny Taylor and still question what you should do?"

She stepped back from him as if he was a physical menace.

"You're not here by accident," she said. "You've planned this visit."

"I could hardly plan a perforated appendix in an unknown maiden lady. The place and all of you speak for yourselves. Yawning your heads off because you want your heroin. Pin-point pupils and leathery faces."

She caught her breath in what sounded like a sigh of relief. "Is that all?" she said.

"I really must go. Goodbye."

"I can't do it. I can't do what you ask."

"I'm sorry."

He opened the door. She said: "I won't tell them what you are. But don't come back. Don't come back here. I'm warning you. Don't come back."

"Goodbye," Alleyn said, and without encountering anyone walked out of the house and down the passage-way to the open platform.

Raoul was waiting there with the car.

ii

When she returned to the roof-garden, Annabella Wells found the men of the house party waiting for her. Dr. Baradi closed his hand softly round her arm, leading her forward.

"Don't," she said, "you smell of hospitals."

Carbury Glande said: "Annabella, who is he? I mean we all know he's Agatha Troy's husband but, for God's sake, *who* is he?"

"You know as much as I do."

"But you said you'd crossed the Atlantic with him. You said it was a shipboard affair and one knows they don't leave many stones unturned, especially in your hands, my angel."

"He was one of my rare failures. He talked of nothing but his wife. He spread her over the Atlantic like an overflow from the Gulf Stream. I gave him up as a bad job. A dull chap, I decided."

"I rather liked him," young Herrington said defiantly.

Mr. Oberon spoke for the first time. "A dangerous man," he said. "Whoever he is and whatever he may be. Under the circumstances, a dangerous man."

Baradi said: "I agree. The enquiry for Garbel is inexplicable."

"Unless they are initiates," Glande said, "and have been given the name."

"They are not initiates," Oberon said.

"No," Baradi agreed.

Young Herrington said explosively: "My God, is there no other way out?"

"Ask yourself," said Glande.

Mr. Oberon rose. "There is no other way," he said tranquilly. "And they must not return. That at least is clear. They must not return."

iii

As they drove back to Roqueville, Alleyn said: "You did your job well this morning, Raoul. You are, evidently, a man upon whom one may depend."

"It pleases Monsieur to say so," said Raoul cheerfully. "The Egyptian gentleman is also, it appears, good at his job. In wartime a medical orderly learns to recognize talent, Monsieur. Very often one saw the patients zipped up like a placket-hole. *Paf!* and he's open. *Pan!* and he's shut. But this was different."

"Dr. Baradi is afraid that she may not recover."

"She had not the look of death upon her."

"Can you recognize it?"

"I fancy that I can, Monsieur."

"Did Madame and the small one get safely to their hotel?"

"Safely, Monsieur. On the way we stopped in the Rue des Violettes. Madame inquired for Mr. Garbel."

Alleyn said sharply: "Did she see him?"

"I understand he was not at home, Monsieur."

"Did she leave a message?"

"I believe so, Monsieur. I saw Madame give a note to the concierge."

"I see."

"She is a type, that one," Raoul said thoughtfully.

"The concierge? Do you know her?"

"Yes, Monsieur. In Roqueville all the world knows all the world. She's an original, is old Blanche."

"In what way?"

"*Un article défraîchi.* One imagines she has other interests besides the door-keeping. To be fat is not always to be idle. But the apartments," Raoul added politely, "are perfectly correct." Evidently he felt it would be in bad taste to disparage the address of any friend of the Alleyns.

Alleyn said, choosing his French very carefully: "I am minded to place a great deal of confidence in you, Raoul."

"If Monsieur pleases."

"I think you were more impressed with Dr. Baradi's skill than with his personality."

"That is a fact, Monsieur."

"I also. Have you seen Mr. Oberon?"

"On several occasions."

"What do you think about him?"

"I have no absolute knowledge of his skill, Monsieur, but I think even less of his personality than of the Egyptian's."

"Do you know how he entertains his guests?"

"One hears a little gossip from time to time. Not much, Monsieur. The servants at the Château are for the most part imported and extremely reticent. But there is an under-chambermaid from the Paysdoux, who is not unapproachable. A blonde, which is unusual in the Paysdoux."

"What has the unusual blonde to say about it?"

Raoul did not answer at once and Alleyn turned his head to look at him. He was scowling magnificently.

"I do not approve of what Teresa has to say. Her name, Monsieur, is Teresa. I find what she has to say immensely unpleasing. You see, it's like this, Monsieur. The time has come when I should marry and for one reason or another—one cannot rationalize about these things—my preference is for Teresa. She has got what it takes," Raoul said, using a phrase—*elle a du fond* —which reminded Alleyn of Annabella Wells's desperate claim. "But in a wife," Raoul continued, "one expects certain reticences where other men are in question. I dislike what Teresa tells me of her employer, Monsieur. I particularly dislike her account of a certain incident."

"Am I to hear it?"

"I shall be glad to recount it. It appears, Monsieur, that Teresa's duties are confined to the sweeping of carpets and polishing of floors and that it is not required of her to take *petit déjeuner* to guests or to perform any personal services for them. She is young and inexperienced. And so, one morning, this Egyptian surgeon witnesses Teresa from the rear when she is on her knees polishing. Teresa is as good from behind as she is from in front, Monsieur. And the doctor passes her and pauses to look. Presently he returns with Mr. Oberon and they pause and speak to each other in a foreign language. Next, the *femme de charge* sends for Teresa and she is instructed that she is to serve *petit déjeuner* to this animal Oberon, if Monsieur will overlook the description, in his bedroom and that her wage is to be raised. So Teresa performs this service. On the first morning there is no conversation. On the second he enquires her name. On the third this *vilain coco* asks her if she is not a fine strong girl. On the fourth he talks a lot of *blague* about the spirituality of the body and the non-existence of evil, and on the fifth, when Teresa enters, he is displayed, immodestly clad, before a full-length glass in his salon. I must tell you, Monsieur, that to reach the bedroom, Teresa must first pass through the salon. She is obliged to approach this unseemly animal. He looks at her fixedly and speaks to her in a manner that is irreligious and blasphemous and anathema. Monsieur, Teresa is a good girl. She is frightened, not so much of this animal, she tells me, as of herself because she feels herself to be like a bird when it is held in terror by a snake. I have told her she must leave, but she says that the wages are good and they are a large family with sickness and much in debt. Monsieur, I repeat, she is a good girl and it is true she needs the money, but I cannot escape the thought that she is in a kind of bondage from which she cannot summon enough character to escape. And on some mornings, when she goes in, there is nothing to which one could object, but on others he talks and talks and stares and stares at Teresa. So that when I last saw her we quarrelled and I have told her that unless she leaves her job before she is no longer respectable she may look elsewhere for a husband. So she wept and I was discomforted. She is not unique but, there it is, I have a preference for Teresa."

Alleyn thought: "This is the first bit of luck I've had since we got here." He looked up the valley at the glittering works of the Maritime Alps Chemical Company and said: "I think it well to tell you that I am interested professionally in the ménage at the Chèvre d'Argent. If it had not been for the accident of Mademoiselle's illness I should have tried to gain admittance there. M. le Commissaire is also interested. We are colleagues in this affair. You and I agreed to forget my rank, Raoul, but for the purposes of this discussion perhaps we should recall it."

"Good, M. l'Inspecteur-en-Chef."

"There's no reason on earth why you should put yourself out for an English policeman in an affair which, however much it may also concern the French police, hasn't very much to do with you. Apart from Teresa, for whom you have a preference."

"There is always Teresa."

"Are you a discreet man?"

"I don't chatter like a one-eyed magpie, Monsieur."

"I believe you. It is known to the police here and in London that the Chèvre d'Argent is used as a place of distribution in a particularly ugly trade."

"Women, Monsieur?"

"Drugs. Women, it seems, are a purely personal interest. A side-line. I believe neither Dr. Baradi nor Mr. Oberon is a drug addict. They are engaged in the traffic from a business point-of-view. I think that they have cultivated the habit of drug-taking among their guests and are probably using at least one of them as a distributor. Mr. Oberon has also established a cult."

"A cult, Monsieur?"

"A synthetic religion concocted from scraps of mysticism, witchcraft, mythology, Hindooism, Egyptology, what-have-you, with, I very much suspect, a number of particularly revolting fancy touches invented by Mr. Oberon."

"Anathema," Raoul said, "all this is anathema. What do they do?" he added with undisguised interest.

"I don't know exactly but I must, I'm afraid, find out. There have been other cases of this sort. No doubt there are rites. No doubt the women are willing to be drugged."

Raoul said: "It appears that I must be firm with Teresa."

"I should be very firm, Raoul."

"This morning she is in Roqueville at the market. I am to meet her at my parents' restaurant, where I shall introduce a firm note. I am disturbed for her. All this, Monsieur, that you have related is borne out by Teresa. On Thursday nights the local servants and some of the other permanent staff are dismissed. It is on Thursday, therefore, that I escort Teresa to her home up in the Paysdoux where she sleeps the night. She has heard a little gossip, not much, because the servants are discreet, but a little. It appears that there is a ceremony in a room which is kept locked at other times. And on Fridays nobody appears until late in the afternoon and then with an air of having a formidable *gueule de bois*. The ladies are strangely behaved on Fridays. It is as if they are half-asleep, Teresa says. And last Friday a young English lady, who has recently arrived, seemed as if she was completely *bouleversée*; dazed, Monsieur," Raoul said, making a graphic gesture with one hand. "In a trance. And also as if she had wept."

"Isn't Teresa frightened by what she sees on Fridays?"

"That is what I find strange, Monsieur. Yes: she says she is frightened, but it is clear to me that she is also excited. That is what troubles me in Teresa."

"Did she tell you where the room is? The room that is unlocked on Thursday nights?"

"It is in the lower part of the Château, Monsieur. Beneath the library, Teresa thinks. Two flights beneath."

"And today is Wednesday."

"Well, Monsieur?"

"I am in need of an assistant."

"Yes, Monsieur?"

"If I asked at the Préfecture they would give me the local gendarme, who is doubtless well-known. Or they would send me a clever man from Paris who as a stranger would be conspicuous. But a man of Roqueville who is well-known and yet is accepted as the friend of one of the maids at the Chèvre d'Argent is not conspicuous if he calls. Do you in fact call often to see Teresa?"

"Often, Monsieur."

"Well, Raoul?"

"Well, Monsieur?"

"Do you care, with M. le Commissaire's permission, to come adventuring with me on Thursday night?"

"Enchanted," said Raoul, gracefully.

"It may not be uneventful, you know. They are a formidable lot, up there."

"That is understood, Monsieur. Again, it will be an act of grace."

"Good. Here is Roqueville. Drive to the hotel, if you please. I shall see Madame and have some luncheon and at three o'clock I shall call on M.

le Commissaire. You will be free until then, but leave me a telephone number and your address."

"My parents' restaurant is in the street above that of the hotel. L'Escargot Bienvenu, 20 Rue des Sarrasins. Here is a card, Monsieur, with the telephone number."

"Right."

"My father is a good cook. He has not a great repertoire, but his judgment is sound. Such dishes as he makes he makes well. His *filets mignons* are a speciality of the house, Monsieur, and his sauces are inspired."

"You interest me profoundly. In the days when there was steak in England, one used to dream of *filet mignon* but even then one came to France to eat it."

"Perhaps if Monsieur and Madame find themselves a little weary of the table d'hôte at the Royal they may care to eat cheaply but with satisfaction at L'Escargot Bienvenu."

"An admirable suggestion."

"Of course, we are not at all smart. But good breeding," Raoul said simply, "creates its own background and Monsieur and Madame would not feel out of place. Here is your hotel, Monsieur, and—" His voice changed. "Here is Madame."

Alleyn was out of the car before it stopped. Troy stood in the hotel courtyard with her clasped hands at her lips and a look on her face that he had never seen there before. When he took her arms in his hands he felt her whole body trembling. She tried to speak to him but at first was unable to find her voice. He saw her mouth frame the word "Ricky."

"What is it, darling?" he said. "What's the matter with him?"

"He's gone," she said. "They've taken him. They've taken Ricky."

iv

For the rest of their lives they would remember too vividly the seconds in which they stood on the tessellated courtyard of the hotel, plastered by the mid-day sun. Raoul on the footpath watched them and the blank street glared behind him. The air smelt of petrol. There was a smear of magenta bougainvillea on the opposite wall, and in the centre of the street a neat pile of horse-droppings. It was already siesta time and so quiet that they might have been the only people awake in Roqueville.

"I'll keep my head and be sensible," Troy whispered. "Won't I, Rory?"

"Of course. We'll go indoors and you'll tell me about it."

"I want to get into the car and look somewhere for him, but I know that won't do."

"I'll ask Raoul to wait."

He did so. Raoul listened, motionless. When Alleyn had spoken Raoul said, "Tell Madame it will be all right, Monsieur. Things will come right."

As they turned away he called his reassurance after them and the sound of his words followed them: "*Les affaires s'arrangeront. Tout ira bien, Madame.*"

Inside the hotel it seemed very dark. A porter sat behind a reception desk and an elegantly dressed man stood in the hall wringing his hands.

Troy said: "This is my husband. This is the manager, Rory. He speaks English. I'm sorry, Monsieur, I don't know your name."

"Malaquin, Madame. Mr. Alleyn, I am sure there is some simple explanation— There have been other cases—"

"I'll come and see you, if I may, when I've heard what has happened."

"But of course. *Garçon*—"

The porter, looking ineffably compassionate, took them up in the lift. The stifling journey was interminable.

Troy faced her husband in a large bedroom made less impersonal by the slight but characteristic litter that accompanied her wherever she went. Beyond her was an iron-railed balcony and beyond that the arrogant laundry-blue of the Mediterranean. He pushed a chair up and she took it obediently. He sat on his heels before her and put his hands on the arms of the chair.

"Now, tell me, darling," he said. "I can't do anything until you've told me."

"You were such a lifetime coming."

"I'm here now. Tell me."

"Yes."

She did tell him. She made a great effort to be lucid, frowning when she hesitated or when her voice shook, and always keeping her gaze on him. He had said she was a good witness and now she stuck to the bare bones of her story, but every word was shadowed by a multitude of unspoken terrors.

She said that when they arrived at the hotel Ricky was fretful and white after his interrupted sleep and the excitement of the drive. The manager was attentive and suggested that Ricky could have a tray in their rooms. Troy gave him a bath and put him into pyjamas and dressing-gown and he had his luncheon, falling asleep almost before it was finished. She put him to bed in a dressing-room opening off her own bedroom. She darkened the windows, and seeing him comfortably asleep with his silver goat clutched in his hand, had her bath, changed and lunched in the dining-room of the hotel. When she returned to their rooms Ricky had gone.

At first she thought that he must have wakened and gone in search of a lavatory or that perhaps he had had one of his panics and was looking for her. It was only after a search of their bathroom and the passages, stairs and such rooms as were open that with mounting anxiety she rang for the chambermaid, and then, as the woman didn't understand English, spoke on the telephone to the manager. M. Malaquin was helpful and expeditious. He said he would at once speak to the servants on duty and report to her. As she put down the receiver Troy looked at the chair across which she had laid Ricky's day clothes ready for his awakening—a yellow shirt and brown linen shorts—and she saw that they were gone.

From that moment she had fought against a surge of terror so imperative that it was accompanied by a physical pain. She ran downstairs and told the manager. The porter and two of the waiters and Troy herself had gone out into the deserted and sweltering streets, Troy running uphill and breathlessly calling Ricky's name. She stopped the few people she met, asking them for a *"petit garçon, mon fils."* The men shrugged, one woman said something that sounded sympathetic. They all shook their heads or made negative gestures with their fingers. Troy found herself in a maze of back streets and stone stairways. She thought she was lost, but looking down a steep alleyway, saw one of the waiters walk across at the lower end and she ran down after him. When she reached the cross-alley she was just in time to see his coat-tails disappear round a further corner. Finally she caught him up. They were back in the little square, and there was the hotel. Her heart rammed against her ribs and she suffered a disgusting sense of constriction in her throat. Sweat poured between her shoulder blades and ran down her forehead into her eyes. She was in a nightmare.

The waiter grimaced. He was idiotically polite and deprecating and he couldn't understand a word that she said. He pursed his lips, bowed and went indoors. She remembered the Commissary of Police and was about to ask the manager to telephone the Préfecture when she heard Raoul's car turn into the street.

Alleyn said: "Right. I'll talk to the Préfecture. But before I do, my dearest dear, will you believe one thing?"

"All right. I'll try."

"Ricky isn't in danger. I'm sure of it."

"But it's true. He's been—it's those people up there—they've kidnapped him, haven't they?"

"It's possible that they've taken a hand. If they have it's because they want to keep me busy. It's also possible, isn't it, that something entered into his head and he got himself up and trotted out."

"He'd never do it, Rory. Never. You know he wouldn't."

"All right. Now, I'll ring the Préfecture. Come on."

He sat her beside him on the bed and kept his arm about her. While he waited for the number he said: "Did you lock the door?"

"No. I didn't like the idea of locking him in. The manager's spoken to the servants. They didn't see anybody. Nobody asked for our room numbers."

"The heavy trunk is still in the hall downstairs and the room number's chalked on it. What colour are his clothes?"

"Pale yellow shirt and brown shorts."

"Right. We may as well— *'Allo! 'Allo! . . .'*"

He began to talk into the telephone, keeping his free hand on her shoulder. Troy turned her cheek to it for a moment and then freed herself and went out on the balcony.

The little square—it was called the Place des Sarrasins—was at the top of a hilly street and the greater part of Roqueville lay between it and the sea. The maze of alleys where Troy had lost herself was out of sight behind and above the hotel. As if from a high tower, she looked down into the streets and prayed incoherently that in one of them she would see a tiny figure: Ricky, in his lemon-coloured shirt and brown linen shorts. But all Troy could see was a pattern of stucco and stone, a distant row of carriages whose drivers and horses were snoozing, no doubt, in the shadows, a system of tiled roofs and the paint-like blue of the sea. She looked nearer at hand and there, beneath her, was Raoul Milano's car, seeming like a toy, and Raoul himself, rolling a cigarette. The hotel porter, at that moment, came out and she heard the sound of his voice. Raoul got up and they disappeared beneath her into the hotel.

The tone of Alleyn's voice suggested that he was near the end of his telephone call. She had turned away from her fruitless search of the map-like town and was about to go indoors when out of the tail of her eye she caught a flicker of colour.

It was a flicker of lemon-yellow and brown.

The hot iron of the balcony rail scorched the palms of her hands. She leant far out and stared at a tall building on a higher level than herself, a building that was just in view round the corner of the hotel. It was perhaps a quarter of a mile away and from behind a huddle of intervening roofs, rose up in a series of balconies. It was on the highest of these, behind a blur of iron railings, that she saw her two specks of colour.

"Rory," she cried. "Rory!"

It took several seconds that seemed like as many minutes for Alleyn to find the balcony. "It's Ricky," she said, "isn't it? It must be Ricky." And she ran back into the room, snatched the thin cover from her bed and waved it frantically from the balcony.

"Wait a moment," Alleyn said.

His police case had been brought up to their room and contained a pair of very powerful field glasses. While he focussed them on the distant balcony he said: "Don't be too certain, darling, there may be other small boys in yellow and—no—no, it's Ricky. He's all right. Look."

Troy's eyes were masked with tears of relief. Her hands shook and her fingers were too precipitant with the focussing governors. "I can't do it—I can't see."

"Steady. Wipe your eyes. Here, I will. He's still there. He may have spotted us. Try this way. Kneel down and rest the glasses on the rail. Get each eye right in turn. Quietly does it."

Circles of blurred colour mingled and danced in the two fields of vision. They swam together and clarified. The glasses were in focus now but were trained on some strange blue door, startling in its closeness. She moved them and an ornate gilded steeple was before her with a cross and a clock telling a quarter to two. "I don't know where I am. It's a church. I can't find him."

"You're nearly there. Keep at that level and come round gently."

And suddenly Ricky looked through iron rails with vague, not quite frightened eyes whose gaze, while it was directed at her, yet passed beyond her.

"Wave," she said. "Go on waving."

Ricky's strangely impersonal and puzzled face moved a little so that an iron standard partly hid it. His right arm was raised and his hand moved to and fro above the railing.

"He's seen!" she said. "He's waving back."

The glasses slipped a little. The wall of their hotel, out-of-focus and stupid, blotted out her vision. Someone was tapping on the bedroom door behind them.

"*Entrez!*" Alleyn called, and then sharply, "Hullo! Who's that?"

"What? I've lost him."

"A woman came out and led him away. They've gone indoors."

"A woman?"

"Fat and dressed in black."

"Please let's go quickly."

Raoul had come through the bedroom and stood behind them. Alleyn said in French, "Do you see that tall building, just to the left of our wall and to the right of the church? It's pinkish with blue shutters and there's something red on one of the balconies."

"I see it, Monsieur."

"Do you know what building it is?"

"I think so, Monsieur. It will be Number 16 in the Rue des Violettes where Madame enquired this morning."

"Troy," Alleyn said. "The Lord knows why, but Ricky's gone to call on Mr. Garbel."

Troy stopped short on her way to the door. "Do you mean . . . ?"

"Raoul says that's the house."

"But— No," Troy said vigorously. "No, I don't believe it. He wouldn't just get up and go there. Not of his own accord. Not like that. He wouldn't. Come on, Rory."

They were following her when Alleyn said: "When did these flowers come?"

"What flowers? Oh, that. I hadn't noticed it. I don't know. Dr. Baradi, I should think. Please don't let's wait."

An enormous florist's box garnished with a great bow of ribbon lay on the top of a pile of suitcases.

Watched in an agony of impatience by his wife, Alleyn slid a card from under the ribbon and looked at it.

"So sorry," he read, "that I shall be away during your visit. Welcome to Roqueville. P. E. Garbel."

CHAPTER VI

Consultation

Troy wouldn't wait for the lift. She ran downstairs with Alleyn and Raoul at her heels. Only the porter was there, sitting at the desk in the hall.

Alleyn said: "This will take thirty seconds, darling. I'm in as much of a hurry as you. Please believe it's important. You can get into the car. Raoul can start the engine." And to the porter he said: "Please telephone this number and give the message I have written on the paper to the person who answers. It is the number of the Préfecture and the message is urgent. It is expected. Were you on duty here when flowers came for Madame?"

"I was on duty when the flowers arrived, Monsieur. It was about an hour ago. I did not know they were for Madame. The woman went straight upstairs without enquiry, as one who knows the way."

"And returned?"

The porter lifted his shoulders. "I did not see her return, Monsieur. No doubt she used the service stairs."

"No doubt," Alleyn said and ran out to the car.

On the way to the Rue des Violettes he said, "I'm going to stop the car a little way from the house, Troy, and I'm going to ask you to wait in it while I go indoors."

"Are you? But why? Ricky's there, isn't he? We saw him."

"Yes, we saw him. But I'm not too keen for other people to see us. Cousin Garbel seems to be known, up at the Chèvre d'Argent."

"But Robin Herrington said he didn't know him and anyway, according to the card on the flowers, Cousin Garbel's gone away. That must be what the concierge was trying to tell me. She said he was '*pas chez elle.*'"

"'*Pas chez soi*' surely?"

"All right. Yes, of course. I couldn't really understand her. I don't understand anything," Troy said desperately. "I just want to get Ricky."

"I know, darling. Not more than I do."

"He didn't look as if he was in one of his panics. Did he?"

"No."

"I expect we'll have a reaction and be furiously snappish with him for frightening us, don't you?"

"We must learn to master our ugly tempers," he said, smiling at her.

"Rory, he will be there still? He won't have gone?"

"It's only ten minutes ago that we saw him on a sixth floor balcony."

"Was she a fat shiny woman who led him in?"

"I hadn't got the glasses. I couldn't spot the shine with the naked eye."

"I didn't like the concierge. Ricky would hate her."

"That is the street, Monsieur," said Raoul. "At the intersection."

"Good. Draw up here by the kerb. I don't want to frighten Madame, but I think all may not be well with the small one whom we have seen on the balcony at Number 16. If anyone were to leave by the back or side of the house, Raoul, would they have to come this way from that narrow side-street and pass this way to get out of Roqueville?"

"This way, Monsieur, either to go east or west out of Roqueville. For the rest there are only other alleyways with flights of steps that lead nowhere."

"Then if a car should emerge from behind Number 16 perhaps it may come about that you start your car and your engine stalls and you block the way. In apologizing you would no doubt go up to the other car and look inside. And if the small one were in the car you would not be able to start your own though you would make a great disturbance by leaning on your horn. And by that time, Raoul, it is possible that M. le Commissaire will have arrived in his car. Or that I have come out of Number 16."

"Aren't you going, Rory?"

"At once, darling. All right, Raoul?"

"Perfectly, Monsieur."

Alleyn got out of the car, crossed the intersection, turned right and entered Number 16.

The hall was dark and deserted. He went at once to the lift-well, glanced at the index of names and pressed the call-button.

"Monsieur?" said the concierge, partly opening the door of her cubby-hole.

Alleyn looked beyond the ringed and grimy hand at one beady eye, the flange of a flattened nose and half a grape-coloured mouth.

"Madame," he said politely and turned back to the lift.

"Monsieur desires?"

"The lift, Madame."

"To ascend where, Monsieur?"

"To the sixth floor, Madame."

"To which apartment on the sixth floor?"

"To the principal apartment. With a balcony."

The lift was wheezing its way down.

"Unfortunately," said the concierge, "the tenant is absent on vacation. Monsieur would care to leave a message?"

"It is the small boy for whom I have called. The small boy whom Madame has been kind enough to admit to the apartment."

"Monsieur is mistaken. I have admitted no children. The apartment is locked."

"Can Nature have been so munificent as to lavish upon us a twin-sister of Madame? If so she has undoubtedly admitted a small boy to the principal apartment on the sixth floor."

The lift came into sight and stopped. Alleyn opened the door.

"One moment," said the concierge. He paused. Her hand was withdrawn from the cubby-hole door. She came out, waddling like a duck and bringing a bunch of keys.

"It is not amusing," she said, "to take a fool's trip. However, Monsieur shall see for himself."

They went up in the lift. The concierge quivered slightly and gave out the combined odours of uncleanliness, frangipani, garlic and hot satin. On the sixth floor she opened a door opposite the lift, waddled through it and sat down panting and massively triumphant on a high chair in the middle of a neat and ordered room whose French windows gave on to a balcony.

Alleyn completely disregarded the concierge. He stopped short in the entrance to the room and looked swiftly round it: at the dressing-table, the shelf above the wash-basin, the gown hanging on the bed-rail and at the three pairs of shoes set out against the wall. He moved to the wardrobe and pulled open the door. Inside it were three sober dresses and a couple of modestly trimmed straw hats. An envelope was lying on the floor of the wardrobe. He stooped down to look at it. It was a business envelope and bore the legend "Compagnie Chimique des Alpes Maritimes." He read the superscription:

A Mlle. Penelope E. Garbel,
16 Rue des Violettes,
Roqueville-de-Sud,
Côte d'Azur

He straightened up, shut the wardrobe door with extreme deliberation and contemplated the concierge, still seated like some obscene goddess, in the middle of the room.

"You disgusting old bag of tripes," Alleyn said thoughtfully in English, "you little know what a fool I've been making of myself."

And he went out to the balcony.

ii

He stood where so short a time ago he had seen Ricky stand and looked across the intervening rooftops to one that bore a large sign: HÔTEL ROYAL. Troy had left the bed-cover hanging over the rail of their balcony.

"A few minutes ago," Alleyn said, returning to the immovable concierge, "from the Hôtel Royal over there I saw my son who was here, Madame, on this balcony."

"It would require the eyes of a hawk to recognize a little boy at that distance. Monsieur is mistaken."

"It required the aid of binoculars and those I had."

"Possibly the son of the laundress who was on the premises and has now gone."

"I saw you, Madame, take the hand of my son, who like yourself was clearly recognizable, and lead him indoors."

"Monsieur is mistaken. I have not left my office since this morning. Monsieur will be good enough to take his departure. I do not insist," the concierge said magnificently, "upon an apology."

"Perhaps," Alleyn said, taking a mille franc note from his pocket-book, "you will accept this instead."

He stood well away from her, holding it out. The eyes glistened and the painted lips moved, but she did not rise. For perhaps four seconds they confronted each other. Then she said, "If Monsieur will wait downstairs I shall be pleased to join him. I have another room to visit."

Alleyn bowed, stooped and pounced. His hand shot along the floor and under the hem of the heavy skirt. She made a short angry noise and tried to trample on the hand. One of her heels caught his wrist.

"Calm yourself, Madame. My intentions are entirely honourable."

He stepped back neatly and extended his arm, keeping the hand closed.

"A strange egg, Madame Blanche," Alleyn said, "for a respectable hen to lay."

He opened his hand. Across the palm lay a little clay goat, painted silver.

iii

From that moment the proceedings in Number 16 Rue des Violettes were remarkable for their unorthodoxy.

Alleyn said: "You have one chance. Where is the boy?"

She closed her eyes and hitched her colossal shoulders up to her earrings.

"Very good," Alleyn said and walked out of the room. She had left the key in the lock. He turned it and withdrew the bunch.

It did not take long to go through the rest of the building. For the rooms that were unoccupied he found a master-key. As he crossed each threshold he called once: "Ricky?" and then made a rapid search. In the occupied rooms his visits bore the character of a series of disconnected shots on a cinema screen. He exposed in rapid succession persons of different ages taking their siestas in varying degrees of déshabillé. On being told that there was no small boy within, he uttered a word of apology and under the dumbfounded gaze of spinsters, elderly gentlemen, married or romantic couples and, in one instance, an outraged Negress of uncertain years, walked in, opened cupboards, looked under and into beds and, with a further apology, walked out again.

The concierge had begun to thump on the door of the principal apartment of the sixth floor.

On the ground floor he found a crisp bright-eyed man with a neat moustache, powerful shoulders and an impressive uniform.

"M. l'Inspecteur-en-Chef Alleyn? Allow me to introduce myself. Dupont

of the Sûreté, at present acting as Commissary at the Préfecture, Roqueville."
He spoke fluent English with a marked accent. "So we are already in trouble,"
he said as they shook hands. "I have spoken to Madame Alleyn and to
Milano. And the boy is not yet found?"

Alleyn quickly related what had happened.

"And the woman Blanche? Where is she, my dear Inspecteur-en-Chef?"

"She is locked in the apartment of Miss P. E. Garbel on the sixth floor.
The distant thumping which perhaps you can hear is produced by the woman
Blanche."

The Commissary smiled all over his face. "And we are reminded how
correct is the deportment of Scotland Yard. Let us leave her to her activities
and complete the search. As we do so will you perhaps be good enough to
continue your report."

Alleyn complied and they embarked on an exploration of the unsavoury
private apartments of Madame Blanche. Alleyn checked at a list of telephone
numbers and pointed to the third. "The Château Chèvre d'Argent," he said.

"Indeed? Very suggestive," said M. Dupont; and with a startling and
incredible echo from Baker Street added, "Pray continue your most interesting narrative while we explore the basement."

But Ricky was not in any room on the ground floor nor in the cellars
under the house. "Undoubtedly they have removed him," said Dupont,
"when they saw you wave from your balcony. I shall at once warn my con-
frères in the surrounding districts. There are not many roads out of Roqueville and all cars can be checked. We then proceed with a tactful but
thorough investigation of the town. This affair is not without precedent.
Have no fear for your small son. He will come to no harm. Excuse me.
I shall telephone from the office of the woman Blanche. Will you remain
or would you prefer to rejoin Madame?"

"Thank you. I will have a word with her if I may."

"Implore her," M. Dupont said briskly, "to remain calm. The affair will
arrange itself. The small one is in no danger." He bowed and went into the
cubby-hole. As he went out Alleyn heard the click of a telephone dial.

A police-car was drawn up by the kerb outside Number 16. Alleyn crossed
the road to Raoul's car.

There was no need to calm Troy: she was very quiet indeed, and perfectly collected. She looked ill with anxiety but she smiled at him and said:
"Bad luck, darling. No sign?"

"Some signs," he said, resting his arms on the door beside her. "Dupont
agrees with me that it's an attempt to keep me occupied. He's sure Ricky's
all right."

"He *was* there, wasn't he? We did see him?"

Alleyn said: "We did see him," and after a moment's hesitation he took
the little silver goat from his pocket. "He left it behind him."

Raoul ejaculated: *"La petite chèvre d'argent."*

Troy's lips quivered. She took the goat in her hands and folded it between them. "What do we do now?"

"Dupont is stopping all cars driving out of Roqueville and will order a house-to-house search in the town. He's a good man."

"I'm sure he is," Troy said politely. She looked terrified. "You're not going back to the Chèvre d'Argent, are you? You're not going to call their bluff?"

"We're going to take stock." Alleyn closed his hand over hers. "I know one wants to drive off madly in all directions, yelling for Ricky but honestly, darling, that's not the form for this kind of thing. We've *got* to take stock. So far we've scarcely had time to think, much less reason."

"It's just—when he knows he's lost—it's his nightmare—mislaying us."

Two gendarmes, smart in their uniforms and sun-helmets, rode past on bicycles, turned into the Rue des Violettes, dismounted and went into Number 16.

"Dupont's chaps," said Alleyn. "Now we shan't be long. And I have got one bit of news for you. Cousin Garbel is a spinster."

"What on earth do you mean?"

"His name is Penelope and he wears a straw hat trimmed with parma violets."

Troy said: "Don't muddle me, darling. I'm so desperately addled already."

"I'm terribly sorry. It's true. Your correspondent is a woman who has some connection with the chemical works we saw this morning. For reasons I can only guess at, she's let you address her letters as if to a man. How *did* you address them?"

"To M. P. E. Garbel."

"Perhaps she thought you imagined 'M.' to be the correct abbreviation of Mademoiselle?"

Troy shook her head: "It doesn't seem to matter much now, but it's quite incredible. Look: something's beginning to happen."

The little town was waking up. Shop doors opened and proprietors came out in their shirt sleeves scratching their elbows. At the far end of the Rue des Violettes there was an eruption of children's voices and a clatter of shoes on stone. The driver of the police-car outside Number 16 started up his engine and the Commissary came briskly down the steps. He made a crisp signal to the driver, who turned his car, crossed the intersection and finally pulled up in front of Raoul. M. Dupont walked across, saluted Troy and addressed himself to Alleyn.

"We commence our search of houses in Roqueville, my dear Inspecteur-en-Chef. The road patrols are installed and a general warning is being issued to my colleagues in the surrounding territory. Between 2:15 by the church clock when you saw your son until the moment when you arrived at these apartments, there was an interval of about ten minutes. If he was removed in an auto it was during those minutes. The patrols were instructed at five minutes to three. Again if he was removed in an auto it has had half an hour's advance and can in that time have gone at the most no further

on our roads than fifty kilometres. Outside every town beyond that radius
we have posted a patrol and if they have nothing to report we shall search
exhaustively within the radius. Madame, it is most fortunate that you saw
the small one from your hotel. Thus have you hurled a screwdriver in the
factory."

The distracted Troy puzzled over the Commissary's free use of English
idiom, but Alleyn gave a sharp exclamation. "*The factory!*" he said. "By the
Lord, I wonder."

"Monsieur?"

"My dear Dupont, you have acted with the greatest expedition and judgment. What do you suggest we do now?"

"I am entirely at your disposal, M. l'Inspecteur-en-Chef. May I suggest
that perhaps a fuller understanding of the situation—"

"Yes, indeed. Shall we go to our hotel?"

"Enchanted, Monsieur."

"I think," Alleyn said, "that our driver here is very willing to take an
active part. He's been extremely helpful already."

"He is a good fellow, this Milano," said Dupont and addressed Raoul in
his own language: "See here, my lad, we are making enquiries for the missing
boy in Roqueville. If he is anywhere in the town it will be at the house
of some associate of the woman Blanche at Number 16. Are you prepared
to take a hand?"

Raoul, it appeared, was prepared. "If he is in the town, M. le Commissaire,
I shall know it inside an hour."

"Oh, *là-là!*" M. Dupont remarked, "what a song our cock sings."

He scowled playfully at Raoul and opened the doors of the car. Troy
and Alleyn were ushered ceremoniously into the police-car and the driver
took them back to the hotel.

In their bedroom, which had begun to take on a look of half-real
familiarity, Troy and Alleyn filled in the details of their adventures from
the time of the first incident in the train until Ricky's disappearance. M.
Dupont listened with an air of deference tempered by professional detachment. When they had finished he clapped his knees lightly and made a
neat gesture with his thumb and forefinger pressed together.

"Admirable!" he said. "So we are in possession of our facts and now we
act in concert, but first I must tell you one little fact that I have in my
sleeve. There has been, four weeks ago, a case of child-stealing in the Paysdoux.
It was the familiar story. A wealthy family from Lyons. A small one. A
flightish nurse. During the afternoon promenade a young man draws the
attention of this sexy nurse. The small one gambols in the gardens by our
casino. The nurse and the young man are tête-à-tête upon a seat. Auto-
mobiles pass to and fro, sometimes stopping. In one are the confederates
of the young man. Presently the nurse remembers her duty. The small one
is vanished and remains so. Also vanished is the young man. A message is
thrown through the hotel window. The small one is to be recovered with

five hundred mille francs at a certain time and at a place outside St. Céleste. There are the customary threats in the matter of informing the police. Monsieur Papa, under pressure from Madame Maman, obeys. He is driven to within a short distance of the place. He continues on foot. A car appears. Stops. A man with a handkerchief over his face and a weapon in his hand gets out. Monsieur Papa, again following instructions, places the money under a stone by the road and retires with his hands above his head. The man collects and examines the money and returns to the car. The small one gets out. The car drives away. The small one," said M. Dupont, opening his eyes very wide at Troy, "is not pleased. He wishes to remain with his new acquaintances."

"Oh, *no!*" Troy cried out.

"But yes. He has found them enchanting. Nevertheless he rejoins his family. And now, having facilitated the escape of the cat, Monsieur Papa attempts to close the bag. He informs the police." M. Dupont spread his hands in the classic gesture and waited for his audience-reaction.

"The usual story," Alleyn said.

"M. Dupont," Troy said, "do you think the same men have taken Ricky?"

"No, Madame. I think we are intended to believe it is the same men."

"But why? Why should it not be these people?"

"Because," M. Dupont rejoined, touching his small moustache, "this morning at 7:30 these people were apprehended and are now locked up in the *poste de police* at St. Céleste. Monsieur Papa had the forethought to mark the notes. It was tactfully done. A slight addition to the décor. And the small one gave useful information. The news of the arrest would have appeared in the evening papers but I have forbidden it. The affair was already greatly publicized."

"So our friends," Alleyn suggested, "unaware of the arrest, imitate the performance and hope our reactions will be those of Monsieur Papa and Madame Maman and that you will turn our attention to St. Céleste."

"But can you be so sure—" Troy began desperately. M. Dupont bent at the waist and gazed respectfully at her. "Ah, Madame," he said, "consider. Consider the facts. At the Château de la Chèvre d'Argent there is a group of persons very highly involved in the drug 'raquette.' By a strange accident your husband, already officially interested in these persons, is precipitated into their midst. One, perhaps two of the guests, know who he is. The actress Wells, who is an addict, is sent to make sure. She returns and tells them: 'We entertain, let me inform you, the most distinguished and talented officer of The Scotland Yard. If we do not take some quick steps he will return to enquire for his invalid. It is possible he already suspects.' And it is agreed he must not return. How can he be prevented from doing so? By the apparent kidnapping of his son. This is effected very adroitly. The woman with the bouquet tells the small Ricketts that his mother awaits him at the house she visited this morning. In the meantime a car is on its way from the Château to take them to St. Céleste. He is to be kept in the apartment of Garbel until it comes. The old Blanche takes him there. She omits to lock the doors on to the balcony. He goes out. You see him. He sees you. Blanche observes. He is removed and before you can reach him there the car arrives and he is removed still further."

"Where?"

"If, following the precedent, they go to St. Céleste, they will be halted by our patrols, but I think perhaps they will have thought of that and changed their plans and if so it will not be to St. Céleste."

"I agree," Alleyn said.

"We shall be wiser when their message arrives, as arrive it assuredly will. There is also the matter of this Mademoiselle Garbel whose name is in the books and who has some communication with the Compagnie Chimique des Alpes Maritimes, which may very well be better named the Compagnie pour l'Elaboration de Diacetylmorphine. She is of the 'raquette,' no doubt, and you have enquired for her."

"For him. We thought: 'him.' "

"Darling," Alleyn said, "can you remember the letters pretty clearly?"

"No," said poor Troy, "how should I? I only know they were full of dreary information about buses and roads and houses."

"Have you ever checked the relationship?"

"No. He—she—talked about distant cousins who I knew had existed but were nearly all dead."

"Did she ever write about my job?"

"I don't think, directly. I don't think she ever wrote things like 'how awful' or 'how lovely' to be married to a chief detective-inspector. She said things about my showing her letters to my distinguished husband, who would no doubt be interested in their contents."

"And, unmitigated clod that I am, I wasn't. My dear Dupont," Alleyn said, "I've been remarkably stupid. I think this lady has been trying to warn me about the activities of the drug racket in the Paysdoux."

"But I thought," Troy said, "I thought it was beginning to look as if it was she who had taken Ricky. Weren't the flowers a means of getting into our rooms while I was at luncheon? Wasn't the message about being away a blind? Doesn't it look as if she's one of the gang? She knew we were coming here. If she wanted to tell you about the drug racket why did she go away?"

"Why indeed? We don't know why she went away."

"Rory, I don't want to be a horror, but— No," said Troy, "I won't say it."

"I'll say it for you. Why in Heaven's name can't we do something about Ricky instead of sitting here gossiping about Miss Garbel?"

"But, dear Madame," cried M. Dupont, "we *are* doing things about Ricketts. Only—" M. Dupont continued, fortunately mistaking for an agonized sob the snort of hysteria that had escaped Troy—"only by an assemblage of the known facts can we arrive at a rational solution. Moreover, if the former case is to be imitated we shall certainly receive a message and it is im-

portant that we are here when it arrives. In the meantime all precautions
have been taken. But all!"

"I know," Troy said, "I'm terribly sorry. I know."

"You brought Miss Garbel's last letter, darling. Let's have a look at it."

"I'll get it."

Troy was not very good at keeping things tidy. She had a complicated
rummage in her travelling case and handbag before she unearthed the final
Garbel letter, which she handed with an anxious look to Alleyn. It was in a
crumpled condition and he spread it out on the arm of his chair.

"Here it is," he said, and read aloud.

My DEAR AGATHA TROY,

I wrote to you on December 17th of last year and hope that you
received my letter and that I may have the pleasure of hearing from you
in the not *too* distant future! I pursue my usual round of activities. Most
of my jaunts take me into the district lying *west* of Roqueville, a district known as the Paysdoux (Paysdoux, literally translated, but allowing
for the reversed position of the adjective, means Sweet Country) though
a close acquaintance with some of the inhabitants might suggest that
Pays *Dopes* would be a better title!!! (Forgive the parenthesis and the
indifferent and slangy *pun*. I have never been able to resist an opportunity to play on words.)

"Hell's boots!" Alleyn said. "Under our very noses! *Pays Dopes* indeed,
District of Dopes and Dope pays." He read on:

As the acquaintances I visit most frequently live some thirty kilometres
(about seventeen miles) away on the western reaches of the Route
Maritime I make use of the omnibus, No. 16, leaving the Place des
Sarrasins at five minutes past the hour. The fare at the present rate of
exchange is about 1/– English, single, and 1/9 return. I enclose a ticket
which will no doubt be of interest. It is a pleasant drive and commands
a pretty prospect of the Mediterranean on one's left and on one's right
a number of ancient buildings as well as some evidence of progress, if
progress it can be called, in the presence of a large *chemical* works, in
which, owing to my chosen profession, I have come to take some interest.

"Oh Lord!" Alleyn lamented. "Why didn't I read this before we left?
We have been so bloody superior over this undoubtedly admirable spinster."

"Please?" said M. Dupont.

"Listen to this, Dupont. Suppose this lady, who is a qualified chemist,
was in the hands of the drug racket. Suppose she worked for them. Suppose
she wanted to let someone in authority in England know what goes on
inside the racket. Now. Do you imagine that there is any reason why she
shouldn't write what she knows to this person and put the letter in the
post?"

"There is good reason to suppose she might fear to do so, Mr. Chief," rejoined Dupont, who no doubt considered that the time had come for a more familiar mode of address. "As an Englishwoman she is perhaps not quite trusted in the 'raquette.' Her correspondence may be watched. Someone who can read English at the *bureau-de-poste* may be bribed. Perhaps she merely suspects that this may be so. They are thorough, these blackguards. Their net is fine in the mesh."

"So she writes her boring letters and every time she writes, she drops a veiled hint, hoping I may see the letter. The Chèvre d'Argent is about thirty kilometres west on the Route Maritime. She tells us by means of tedious phrases, ferocious puns, and used bus tickets that she is a visitor there. How did she address her letters, Troy?"

"To 'Agatha Troy.' She said in her first letter that she understood that I would prefer to be addressed by my professional name. Like an actress, she added, though not in other respects. With the usual row of ejaculation marks. I don't think she ever used your name. You were always my brilliant and distinguished husband!"

"And is my face red!" said Alleyn. M. Dupont's was puzzled. Alleyn continued reading the letter.

If ever you and your distinguished husband should visit "these parts"! you may care to take this drive which is full of interesting topographic features that often escape the notice of the *ordinary Tourist*. I fear my own humble account of our local background is a somewhat *Garbelled* (!!!!) version and suggest that first-hand observation would be much more rewarding! With kindest regards . . .

"Really—" Alleyn said, handing the letter back to Troy—"short of cabling: 'Drug barons at work come and catch them' she could scarcely have put it more clearly."

"You didn't read the letters. I only told you about bits of them. I ought to have guessed."

"Well, it's no good blackguarding ourselves. Look here, both of you. Suppose we're on the right track about Miss Garbel. Suppose, for some reason, she's in the racket yet wants to put me wise about it and has hoped to lure me over here. Why, when Troy writes and tells her we're coming, does she go away without explanation?"

"And why," Troy interjected, "does she send flowers by someone who used them as a means of kidnapping Ricky and taking him to her flat?"

"The card on the flowers isn't in her writing."

"She might have telephoned the florist."

"Which can be checked," said M. Dupont, "of course. Will you allow me? This, I assume is the bouquet."

He inspected the box of tuberoses. "Ah, yes. Le Pot des Fleurs. May I telephone, Madame?"

While he did so, Troy went out to the balcony and Alleyn, seeing her there, her fingers against her lips in the classic gesture of the anxious woman, joined her and put his arm about her shoulders.

"I'm looking at that other balcony," she said. "It's silly, isn't it? Suppose he came out again. It's like one of those dreams of frustration."

He touched her cheek and she said: "You mustn't be too nice to me."

"Little perisher," Alleyn muttered, "you may depend upon it he's airing his French and saying 'why' with every second breath he draws. Did you know W. S. Gilbert was pinched by bandits when he was a kid?"

"I think I did. Might they have taken him to the Chèvre d'Argent? As a sort of double bluff?"

"I don't think so, my darling. My bet is he's somewhere nearer than that."

"Nearer to Roqueville? Where, Rory, where?"

"It's a guess and an unblushing guess, but—"

M. Dupont came bustling out to the balcony.

"*Alors!*" he began and checked himself. "My dear Monsieur and Madame, we progress a little. Le Pot des Fleurs tells me the flowers were bought and removed by a woman of the servant class, not of the district, who copied the writing on the card from a piece of paper. They do not remember seeing the woman before. We may find she is a maid at the Château, may we not?"

"May we?" said Troy a little desperately.

"But there are better news than these, Madame. The good Raoul Milano has reported to the hotel. It appears that an acquaintance of his, an idle fellow living in the western suburb, has seen a car, a light blue Citroën, at 2:30 P.M. driving out of Roqueville by the western route. In the car were the driver, a young woman and a small boy dressed in yellow and brown. The man wears a red beret and the woman is bare-headed. The car was impeded for a moment by an omnibus and the acquaintance of Milano heard the small one talking. He spoke in French but childishly and with a little difficulty, using foreign words. He appeared to be making an enquiry. The acquaintance heard him say '*pourquoi*' several times."

"Conclusive," Alleyn said, watching Troy.

She cried out: "Did he seem frightened?"

"Madame, no. It appears that Milano made the same enquiry. The acquaintance said the small one seemed exigent. The actual phrase," M. Dupont said, turning to Alleyn, "was: '*Il semblait être impatient de comprendre quelque chose'!*"

"He was impatient to understand something," Troy ejaculated, "is that it?"

"*Mais oui, Madame,*" said Dupont and added a playful compliment in French to the effect that Troy evidently spoke the language as if she were born to it. Troy failed to understand a word of this and gazed anxiously at him. He continued in English. "Now, between Roqueville and the point where our nearest patrol on the western route is posted there are three deviations: all turning inland. Two are merely rural lanes. The third is a road that leads to a monastery and also—" Here M. Dupont raised his forefinger and looked roguish.

"And also," Alleyn said, "to the Factory of the Maritime Alps Chemical Company."

"*Parfaitement!*" said M. Dupont.

"And you think he's there!" Troy cried out. "But why? Why take him there?"

Alleyn said: "As I see it, and I don't pretend, Lord knows, to see at all clearly, this might be the story. Oberon & Co. have a strong interest in the factory but they don't realize we know it. Baradi and your painting chum Glande were at great pains to deplore the factory: to repudiate the factory as an excrescence in the landscape. But we suspect it probably houses the most impudent manufactory of hyoscine in Europe and we know Oberon's concerned in the traffic. All right. They realize we've seen Ricky on the balcony of Number 16 and have called in the police. If Blanche has succeeded in getting herself out of durance vile she's told them all about it. They've lost their start. They daren't risk taking Ricky to St. Céleste, as they originally planned. What are they to do with him? It would be easy and safe to house him in one of the offices at the factory and have him looked after. You must remember that nobody up at the Château knows that he understands a certain amount of French."

"The people who've got him will have found that out by now."

"And also that his French doesn't go beyond the nursery stage. They may have told him that we've gone back to look after Miss Truebody and have arranged for him to be minded until we are free. I think they may have meant to keep him at Number 16 while we went haring off to St. Céleste. *La Belle Blanche* (damn her eyes) probably rang up and said we'd spotted him on the balcony and they thought up the factory in a hurry."

"Could they depend on our going to St. Céleste? Just on the strength of our probably getting to hear about the other kidnapping?"

"No," said Alleyn and Dupont together.

"Then—I don't understand."

"Madame," said Dupont, "there is no doubt that you shall be directed, if not to a place near St. Céleste, at least to some other place along the eastern route. To some place as far as possible from the true whereabouts of Ricketts."

"Directed?"

"There will be a little note or a little telephone message. Always remember they fashion themselves on the pattern of the former affair, being in ignorance of this morning's arrest."

"It all sounds so terribly like guesswork," Troy said after a moment. "Please, what do we do?"

Alleyn looked at Dupont, whose eyebrows rose portentously. "It is a little difficult," he said. "From the point-of-view of my department, it is a delicate situation. We are not yet ready to bring an accusation against the organization behind the factory. When we are ready, Madame, it will be a very big matter, a matter not only for the department but for the police forces of several nations, for the International Police and for the United Nations Organization itself."

Troy suddenly had a nightmarish vision of Ricky in his lemon shirt and brown shorts abandoned to a labyrinth of departmental corridors.

Watching her, Alleyn said: "So that we mustn't suggest, you see, that we are interested in anything but Ricky."

"Which, God knows, I'm not," said Troy.

"Ah, Madame," Dupont said, "I too am a parent." And to Troy's intense embarrassment he kissed her hand.

"It seems to me," Alleyn said, "that the best way would be for your department, my dear Dupont, to make a great show of watching the eastern route and the country round St. Céleste and for us to make an equally great show of driving in a panic-stricken manner about the countryside. Indeed, it occurs to me that I might very well help matters by ringing up the Château and *registering* panic. What do you think?"

Dupont made a tight purse of his mouth, drew his brows together, looked pretty sharply at Alleyn and then lightly clapped his hands together.

"In effect," he said, "why not?"

Alleyn went to the telephone. "Baradi, I fancy," he said thoughtfully, and after a moment's consideration: "Yes, I think it had better be Baradi."

He dialled the hotel office and gave the number. While he waited he grimaced at Troy: "Celebrated imitation about to begin. You will notice that I have nothing in my mouth."

They could hear the bell ringing, up at the Chèvre d'Argent.

"'*Allo, 'allo!*" Alleyn began in a high voice and broke into a spate of indifferent French. Was that the Chèvre d'Argent? Could he speak to Dr. Baradi? It was extremely urgent. He gave his name. They heard the telephone quack: "*Un moment, Monsieur.*" He grinned at Troy and covered the receiver with his hand. "Let's hope they have to wake him up," he said. "Give me a cigarette, darling."

But before he could light it Baradi had come to the telephone. Alleyn's deep voice was pitched six tones above its normal range and sounded as if it was only just under control. He began speaking in French, corrected himself, apologized and started again in English. "Do forgive me," he said, "for bothering you again. The truth is, we are in trouble here. I know it sounds ridiculous but *has* my small boy by any chance turned up at the Château? Yes. Yes, we've lost him. We thought there might be the chance—there are buses, they say—and we're at our wits' end. No, I was afraid not. It's just that my wife is quite frantic. Yes. Yes, I know. Yes, so we've been told. Yes, I've seen the police but you know what they're like." Alleyn turned towards M. Dupont, who immediately put on a heroic look. "They're the same wherever you go, red-tape and inactivity. Most unsatisfactory." M. Dupont bowed. "Yes, if it's the same blackguards we shall be told what we have to do. No, no, I refuse to take any risks of that sort. Somehow or another I'll raise the money but it won't be easy with the restrictions." Alleyn pressed his lips together. His long fingers blanched as they tightened round the receiver. "Would you really?" he said and the colour of his voice, its diffidence and its hesitancy, so much at variance with the look in his eyes, gave him the uncanny air of a ventriloquist. "Would you really? I say, that's *most* awfully kind of you both. I'll tell my wife. It'll be a great relief to her to know—yes, well I ought to have said something about that, only I'm so damnably worried—I'm afraid we shan't be able to do anything about Miss Truebody until we've found Ricky. I am taking my wife to St. Céleste, if that's where—yes, probably this afternoon if—I don't think we'll feel very like coming back after what's happened, but of course— Is she? Oh, dear! I'm very sorry. That's very good of him. I *am* sorry. Well, if you really don't mind. I'm afraid I'm not much use. Thank you. Yes. Well, goodbye."

He hung up the receiver. His face was white.

"He offers every possible help," he said, "financial and otherwise, and is sure Mr. Oberon will be immeasurably distressed. He has now, no doubt, gone away to enjoy a belly laugh at our expense. It is going to be difficult to keep one's self-control over Messrs. Oberon and Baradi."

"I believe you," said M. Dupont.

"Rory, you're certain now, in your own mind, aren't you?"

"Yes. He didn't utter a word that was inconsistent with genuine concern and helpfulness, but I'm certain in my own mind."

"Why?"

"One gets a sixth sense about that sort of bluff. And I think he made a slip. He said: 'Of course you can do nothing definite until these scoundrels ring you up.' "

M. Dupont cried, "Ahah!"

"But you said to him," Troy objected, "that we would be told what to do."

" 'Would be *told* what to do!' Exactly. In the other case the kidnappers' instructions came by letter. Why should Baradi think that this time they would telephone?"

As if in answer, the bedroom telephone buzzed twice.

"This will be it," said Alleyn and took up the receiver.

CHAPTER VII

Sound of Ricky

Alleyn was used to anonymous calls on the telephone. There was a quality of voice that he had learned to recognize as common to them all. Though this new voice spoke in French it held the familiar tang of artifice. He nodded to Dupont, who at once darted out of the room.

The voice said: "M. Allen?"

"*C'est Allen qui parle.*"

"*Bien. Écoutez. A sept heures demain soir, presentez-vous à pied et tout seul, vis-à-vis du pavillon de chasse en ruines, il y a sept kilomètres vers le midi du village St. Céleste-des-Alpes. Apportez avec vous cent mille francs en billets de cent. N'avertissez-pas la police, ou le petit apprendra bien les consequences. Compris?*"

Alleyn repeated it in stumbling French, as slowly as possible and with as many mistakes as he dared to introduce. He wanted to give Dupont time. The voice grew impatient in correction. Alleyn, however, repeated his instructions for the third time and began to expostulate in English. "*Plus rien à dire,*" said the voice and rang off.

Alleyn turned to Troy. "Did you understand?" he asked.

"I don't know. I think so."

"Well, it's all right, my dearest. It's as we thought. Tomorrow evening outside a village called St. Céleste-des-Alpes with a hundred quid in my hand. The village, no doubt, will be somewhere above St. Céleste."

"You didn't recognize the voice?"

"It wasn't Baradi or Oberon. It wasn't young Herrington. I wouldn't swear it wasn't Carbury Glande, who was croaking with hangover this morning and might have recovered by now. And I would by no means swear that it wasn't Baradi's servant, whom I've only heard utter about six phrases in Egyptian but who certainly understands French. There was a bit of an accent and I didn't think it sounded local."

Dupont tapped and entered. "Any luck?" Alleyn said.

"Of a kind. I rang the *centrale* and was answered by an imbecile but the call has been traced. And to where do you suppose?"

"Number 16, Rue des Violettes?"

"Precisely!"

"Fair enough," Alleyn said. "It must be their town office."

"I also rang the Préfecture. No reports have come in from the patrols. What was the exact telephone message, if you please?"

Alleyn told him in French, wrapping up the threats to Ricky in words
that were outside Troy's vocabulary.

"The same formula," Dupont said, "as in the reported version of the
former affair. My dear Mr. Chief and Madame, it seems that we should
now pursue our hunch."

"To the chemical works?"

"Certainly."

"Thank God!" Troy ejaculated.

"All the same," Alleyn said, "it's tricky. As soon as we get there the gaff
is blown. The Château, having been informed that the telephone message
went through, will wait for us to go to St. Céleste. When we turn up at
the factory, the factory will ring the Château. Tricky! How far away is St.
Céleste?"

"About seventy kilometres."

"Is it possible to start off on the eastern route and come round to the
factory by a detour? Behind Roqueville?"

M. Dupont frowned. "There are some mountain lanes," he said. "Little
more than passages for goats and cattle but of a width that is possible."

"Possible for Raoul who is, I have noticed, a good driver."

"He will tell us, at least. He is beneath."

"Good." Alleyn turned to his wife. "See here, darling. Will you go down
and ask Raoul to fill up his tank—*faire plein d'essence* will be all right—and
ask him to come back as soon as he's done it. Will you then ask for the
manager and tell him we're going to St. Céleste, but would like to leave
our heavy luggage here and keep our rooms. Perhaps you should offer to pay
a week in advance. Here's some money. I'll bring down a couple of suitcases
and join you in the hall. All right?"

"All right. V*oulez-vous*," Troy said anxiously, "*faire plein d'essence et
revenez ici.* O.K.?"

"O.K."

When she had gone Alleyn said, "Dupont, I wanted a word with you.
You can see what a hellish business this is for me, can't you? I know damn
well how important it is not to let our investigation go off like a damp
squib. I realize, nobody better, that a premature enquiry at the factory might
prejudice a very big coup. I'm here on a job and my job is with the police
of your country and my own. In a way it's the most critical assignment I've
ever had."

"And for me, also."

"But the boy's my boy and his mother's my wife. It looked perfectly
safe to bring them here and they gave me admirable cover, but as things
have turned out, I shouldn't have brought them. But for the unfortunate
Miss Truebody, of course, it *would* have been all right."

"And she, too, provided admirable cover. An unquestioned entrée."

"Not for long, however. What I'm trying to say is this: I've fogged out
a scheme of approach. I realize that in suggesting it I'm influenced by an

almost overwhelming anxiety about Ricky. I'll be glad if you tell me at once if you think it impracticable and, from the police angle, unwise."

Dupont said: "M. l'Inspecteur-en-Chef, I understand the difficulty and respect, very much, your delicacy. I shall be honoured to advise."

"Thank you. Here goes, then. It's essential that we arouse no suspicion of our professional interest in the factory. It's highly probable that the key men up there have already been informed from the Château of my real identity. There's a chance, I suppose, that Annabella Wells has kept her promise, but it's a poor chance. After all, if these people don't know who I am why should they kidnap Ricky? All right. We make a show of leaving this hotel and taking the eastern route for St. Céleste. That will satisfy anybody who may be watching us at this end. We take to the hills and double back to the factory. By this time, you, with a suitable complement of officers, are on your way there. I go in and ask for Ricky. I am excitable and agitated. They say he's not there. I insist that I've unimpeachable evidence that he is there. I demand to see the manager. I produce Raoul, who says he took his girl for a drive and saw a car with Ricky in it turn in at the factory gates. They stick to their guns. I make a hell of a row. I tell them I've applied to you. You arrive with a car-load of men. You take the manager aside and tell him I am a V.I.P. on holiday."

"*Comment?* V.I.P.?"

"A very important person. You see it's extremely awkward. That you think the boy's been kidnapped and that it's just possible one of their workmen has been bribed to hide him. You'll say I'll make things very hot for you at the Sûreté if you don't put on a show of searching for Ricky. You produce a *mandat de perquisition*. You are terribly apologetic and very bored with me, but you say that unfortunately you have no alternative. As a matter of form you must search the factory. Now, what does the manager do?"

Dupont's sharp eyebrows were raised to the limit. Beneath them his round eyes stared with glazed impartiality at nothing in particular. His arms were folded. Alleyn waited.

"In effect," Dupont said at last, "he sends his secretary to investigate. The secretary returns with Ricketts and there are a great many apologies. The manager assures me that there will be an exhaustive enquiry and appropriate dismissals."

"What do you say to this?"

"Ah," said Dupont, suddenly lowering his eyebrows and unfolding his arms. "That is more difficult."

"Do I perhaps intervene? Having clasped my son to my bosom and taken him out with his mother to the car, thus giving the manager an opportunity to attempt bribery at a high level, do I not return and take it as a matter of course that you consider this an admirable opportunity to pursue your search for the kidnappers?"

Dupont's smile irradiated his face. "It is possible," he said. "It is conceivable."

"Finally, my dear Dupont, can we act along these lines or any other that suggest themselves without arousing the smallest suspicion that we are interested in anything but the recovery of the child?"

"The word of operation is indeed 'act.' From your performance on the telephone, Mr. Chief, I can have no misgivings about your own performance. And for myself"—here Dupont tapped his chest, touched his moustache and gave Alleyn an indescribably roguish glance—"I believe I shall do well enough."

They stood up. Alleyn put his police bag inside a large suitcase. After looking at the chaos within Troy's partly unpacked luggage, he decided on two cases. He also collected their overcoats and Ricky's.

"Shall we be about it?" he asked.

"*En avant, alors!*" said Dupont.

ii

Mr. Oberon looked down at the figure on the bed. "Quite peaceful," he said. "Isn't it strange?"

"The teeth," Baradi pointed out, "make a great difference."

"There is a certain amount of discolouration."

"Hypostatic staining. The climate."

"Then there is every reason," Mr. Oberon observed with satisfaction, "for an immediate funeral."

"Certainly."

"If they have in fact gone off to St. Céleste they cannot return until the day after tomorrow."

"If, on the other hand, this new man at the Préfecture is intelligent, which Allen says is not the case, they may pick up some information."

"Let us—" Mr. Oberon suggested as he absent-mindedly rearranged the sprigged locknit nightgown which was pinned down by crossed hands to the rigid bosom—"let us suppose the worst. They recover the child," he raised his hand. "Yes, yes, it is unlikely, but suppose it happens. They call to enquire. They ask to see her."

The two men were silent for a time. "Very well," Baradi said. "So they see her. She will not be a pretty sight, but they see her."

Mr. Oberon was suddenly inspired. "There must be flowers," he ejaculated. "Masses and masses of flowers. A nest. A coverlet all of flowers, smelling like incense. Tuberoses," he cried softly clapping his hands together. "They will be entirely appropriate. I shall order them. Tuberoses! And orchids."

iii

The eastern route followed the seaboard for three miles out of Roqueville and then turned slightly inland. At this point a country road branched off it to the left. Raoul took the road which mounted into the hills by a series of hairpin bends. They climbed out of soft coastal air and entered a region of mountain freshness. A light breeze passed like a hand through the olive groves and sent spirals of ruddy dust across the road. The seaboard with its fringe of meretricious architecture had dwindled into an incident, while the sea and sky and warm earth widely enlarged themselves.

The road, turning about the contour of the hills, was littered with rock and scarred by wheel tracks. Sometimes it became a ledge traversing the face of sheer cliffs, and in normal times Troy, who disliked heights, would have feared these passages. Now she dreaded them merely because they had to be taken slowly.

"How long," she asked, "will it be, do you suppose?"

"Roqueville's down there a little ahead of us. We'll pass above it in a few minutes. I gather we now cast back into the mountains for about the same distance as we've travelled already and then work round to a junction with the main road to the factory. Sorry about these corners, darling," Alleyn said as they edged round a bend that looked like a take-off into space. "Are you minding it very much?"

"Only because it's slow. Raoul's a good driver, isn't he?"

"Very good indeed. Could you bear it if I told you about this job? I think perhaps I ought to, but it'll be a bit dreary."

"Yes," Troy said. "I'd like that. The drearier the better because I'll have to concentrate."

"Well, you know it's to do with the illicit drug trade, but I don't suppose you know much about the trade itself. By and large it's probably the worst thing apart from war that's happened to human beings in modern times. Before the 1914 war the nations most troubled by the opium racket had begun to do something about it. There was a Shanghai conference and a Hague Convention. Both were cautious tentative shows. None of the nations came to them with a clean record and all the delegates were embarrassed by murky backgrounds in which production, manufacture and distribution involved the revenue both of states and of highly placed individuals. Dost thou attend me?"

"Sir," said Troy, "most heedfully."

They exchanged the complacent glance of persons who recognize each other's quotations.

"At the Hague Convention they did get round to making one or two conservative decisions but before they were ratified the war came along and the whole thing lapsed. After the peace the traffic was stepped up most murderously. It's really impossible to exaggerate the scandal of those years. At the top end were nations getting a fat revenue out of the sale of opium and its derivatives. An investigator said at one stage that half Europe was being poisoned to bolster up the domestic policy of Bulgaria. The goings-on were fantastic. Chargés d'affaires smuggled heroin in their diplomatic baggage. Drug barons built works all over Europe. Diacetylmorphine, which is heroin to you, was brewed on the Champs Élysées. Highly qualified chemists were offered princely salaries to work in drug factories and a great number of them fell for it. Many of the smartest and most fashionable people in European society lived on the trade: murderers, if the word has any meaning. At the other end of the stick were the street pedlars, at the foot of Nurse Cavell's statue among other places, and the addicts. The addicts were killing themselves in studies, studios, dressing-rooms, brothels, boudoirs and garrets; young intellectuals and young misfits were ruining themselves by the score. Girls were kept going by their *souteneurs* with shots of the stuff. And so on. Thou attendest not."

"Oh, good sir, I do."

"I pray thee, mark me. At the Peace Conference this revolting baby was handed over to the League of Nations, who appointed an Advisory Committee who began the first determined assault on the thing. The international police came in, various bodies were set up and a bit of real progress was made. Only a bit. Factories pulled down in Turkey were rebuilt in Bulgaria. Big centralized industries were busted only to reappear like crops of small ulcers in other places. But something was attempted and a certain amount was achieved by 1939."

"Oh, dear! History at it again?"

"More or less. The difference lies in the fact that this time the preliminary work had been done and the machinery for investigation partly set up. But the Second World War did its stuff and everything lapsed. U.N.O. doesn't start from scratch in the way that the League did. But it faces the old situation and it's still up against the Big Boys. The police still catch the sprats at the customs counter and miss the mackerels in high places. The factories have again moved: from Bulgaria into post-war Italy and from post-war Italy, it appears, into the Paysdoux of Southern France. And the Big Boys have moved with them. Particularly Dr. Baradi and Mr. Oberon."

"Are they really big?"

"Not among the tops, perhaps. There we climb into very rarefied altitudes and by as hazardous a road as this one. But Oberon and Baradi are certainly in the mackerel class. Oberon, I regret to tell you, is a British subject at the moment although he began in the Middle East where he ran a quack religion of a dubious sort and got six months for his pains. He came to us by way of Portugal and Egypt. In Portugal he practiced the same game during the war and made his first connection with the dope trade. In Egypt he was stepped up in the racket and made the acquaintance of his chum Baradi. By that time he'd acquired large sums of money. Two fortunes fell into his lap from rich disciples in Lisbon—middle-aged women, who became Daughters of the Sun or something, remade their wills and died shortly afterwards."

"Oh, Lord!"

"You may well say so. Baradi's a different story. Baradi was a really brilliant medical student who trained in Paris and has become one of the leading surgeons of his time. He had some sort of entrée to court circles in Cairo and, thanks to his skill and charms, any number of useful connections in France. You may not think him very delicious but it appears that a great many women do. He got in with the Boys in Paris and Egypt and is known to be a trafficker in a big way. It's his money and Oberon's that's behind the Chemical Company of the Maritime Alps. That's as much as the combined efforts of the international police, the Sûreté and the Yard have gleaned about Baradi and Oberon, and it's on that information I'm meant to act."

"And is Ricky a spanner in the works?"

"He may be a spanner in their works, my pretty. He gives us an excuse for getting into the factory. They may have played into our hands when they took Ricky into the factory."

"If they took him there," Troy said under her breath.

"If they drove beyond the turn-off to the factory the patrols would have got them. Of course he may be maddening the monks in the monastery further up."

"Mightn't the car have pushed on and come round by this appalling route?"

"The patrols on the eastern route will get it if it did and there are no fresh tyre tracks."

"It's so strange," Troy said, "to hear you doing your stuff."

Raoul humoured the car down a steep incline and past a pink-washed hovel overhanging the cliff. A peasant stood in the doorway. At Alleyn's suggestion Raoul called to him.

"He friend! Any other driver come this way today?"

"*Pas un de si bête!*"

"That was: 'no such fool,' wasn't it?" Troy asked.

"It was."

"I couldn't agree more."

They bumped and sidled on for some time without further conversation. Raoul sang. The sky was a deeper blue and the Mediterranean, now almost purple, made unexpected gestures between the tops of hills. Troy and Alleyn each thought privately how much, in spite of the road, they would have enjoyed themselves if Ricky had been with them.

Presently Raoul, speaking slowly out of politeness to Troy, pointed to a valley they were about to enter.

"The Monastery Road, M'sieur—Madame. We descend."

They did so, precipitately. The roofs of the Monastery of Our Lady of Paysdoux appeared, tranquil and modest, folded in a confluence of olive groves. As they came into the lower valley they looked down on an open place where a few cars were parked and where visitors to the cloisters moved in and out of long shadows. The car dived down behind the monastery, turned and ran out into the head of a good sealed road. "The factory," Raoul said, "is round the next bend. Beyond, Monsieur can see the main road and away to the right is the headland with the tunnel that comes out by the Château de la Chèvre d'Argent."

"Is there a place lower down and out of sight of the factory where we can watch the main road on the Roqueville side?"

"Yes, Monsieur. As one approaches the bend."

"Let us stop there for a moment."

"Good, Monsieur."

Raoul's point of observation turned out to be a pleasant one overlooking the sea and commanding a full view of the main road as it came through the hills from Roqueville. He ran the car to the outer margin of their road and stopped. Alleyn looked at his watch. "A quarter past four. The works shut down at five. I hope Dupont's punctual. We'll have a final check. Raoul first, darling, if you don't mind. See how much you can follow and keep your eye on the main road for the police car. *Alors*, Raoul."

Raoul turned to listen. He had taken off his chauffeur's cap, and his head, seen in profile against the Homeric blue of the Mediterranean, took on a classic air. Its colour was a modulation of the tawny earth. Grape-like curls clustered behind his small ears, his mouth was fresh, reflected light bloomed on his cheekbones and his eyes held a look of untroubled acceptance. It was a beautiful head, and Troy thought: "When we're out of this nightmare I shall want to paint it."

Alleyn was saying: ". . . so you will remain at first in the car. After a time I may fetch or send for you. If I do you will come into the offices and tell a fairy story. It will be to this effect . . ."

Raoul listened impassively, his eyes on the distant road. When Alleyn had done, Raoul made a squaring movement with his shoulders, blew out his cheeks into a mock-truculent grimace and intimated that he was ready for anything.

"Now, darling," Alleyn said, "do you think you can come in with me and keep all thought of our inside information out of your mind? You know only this: Ricky has been kidnapped and Raoul has seen him being driven into the factory. I'm going to have a shot at the general manager, who is called Callard. We don't know much about him. He's a Parisian who worked in the States for a firm that was probably implicated in the racket and he speaks English. Any of the others we may run into may also speak English. We'll assume, whatever we find, that they understand it. So don't say anything to me that they shouldn't hear. On the other hand, you can with advantage keep up an agitated chorus. I shall speak bad French. We don't know what may develop so we'll have to keep our heads and ride the skids as we meet them. How do you feel about it?"

"Should I be a brave little woman biting on the bullet or should I go in, boots and all, and rave?"

"Rave if you feel like it, my treasure. They'll probably expect it."

"I daresay a Spartan mother would seem more British in their eyes or is that a contradiction in terms? Oh, Rory!" Troy said in a low voice. "It's so grotesque. Here we are half-crazy with anxiety and we have to put on a sort of anxiety act. It's—it's a cruel thing, isn't it?"

"It'll be all right," Alleyn said. "It *is* cruel but it'll be all right. I promise. You'll be as right as a bank whatever you do. Hallo, there's Dupont."

A car had appeared on the main road from Roqueville.

"M. le Commissaire," said Raoul, and flicked his headlamps on and off. The police car, tiny in the distance, winked briefly in response.

"We're off," said Alleyn.

iv

The entrance hall of the factory was impressive. The décor was carried out in obscured glass, chromium and plastic and was beautifully lit. In the centre was a sculptured figure, modern in treatment, suggestive of some beneficent though pin-headed being, who drew strength from the earth itself. Two flights of curved stairs led airily to remote galleries. There was an imposing office on the left. Double doors at the centre back and a series of single doors in the right wall all bore legends in chromium letters. The front wall was plate glass and commanded a fine view of the valley and the sea.

Beyond a curved counter in the outer office a girl sat over a ledger. When she saw Alleyn and Troy she rose and stationed herself behind a chromium notice on the counter: *Renseignements.*

"Monsieur?" asked the girl. "Madame?"

Alleyn, without checking his stride, said: "Don't disarrange yourself, Mademoiselle," and made for the central doors.

The girl raised her voice: "One moment, Monsieur, whom does Monsieur wish to see?"

"M. Callard, le Contrôleur."

The girl pushed a bell on her desk. Before Alleyn could reach the double doors they opened and a commissionaire came through. Alleyn turned to the desk.

"Monsieur has an appointment?" asked the girl.

"No," Alleyn said, "but it is a matter of extreme urgency. I must see M. Callard, Mademoiselle."

The girl was afraid that M. Callard saw nobody without an appointment. Troy observed that her husband was making his usual impression on the girl, who touched her hair, settled her shoulders and gave him a look.

Troy said in a high voice: "Darling, what's she saying? Has she seen him?"

The girl just glanced at Troy and then opened her eyes at Alleyn. "Perhaps I can be of assistance to Monsieur?" she suggested.

Alleyn leaned over the counter and haltingly asked her if by any chance she had seen a little boy in brown shorts and a yellow shirt. The question seemed to astonish her. She made an incredulous sound and repeated it to the commissionaire, who merely hitched up his shoulders. They had not seen any little boys, she said. Little boys were not permitted on the premises.

Alleyn stumbled about with his French and asked the girl if she spoke English. She said that unfortunately she did not.

"Mademoiselle," Alleyn said to Troy, "doesn't speak English. I think she says M. Callard won't see us. And she says she doesn't know anything about Ricky."

Troy said: "But we know he's here. We must see the manager. Tell her we must."

This time the girl didn't so much as glance at Troy. With a petunia-tipped finger and thumb she removed a particle of mascara from her lashes and discreetly rearranged her figure for Alleyn to admire. She said it was too bad that she couldn't do anything for him. She thought he had better understand this and said that at any other time she might do a lot. She reacted with a facial expression which corresponded, Troy thought, with the "haughty little *moue*" so much admired by Edwardian novelists.

He said: "Mademoiselle, will you have the kindness of an angel? Will you take a little message to M. Callard?" She hesitated and he added in English: "And do you know that there is a large and I believe poisonous spider on your neck?"

She flashed a smile at him. "Monsieur makes a *grivoiserie* at my expense. He says naughty things in English, I believe, 'to pull a carrot at me.'"

"Doesn't speak English," Alleyn said to Troy without moving his eyes from the girl. He took out his pocket-book, wrote a brief message and slid it across the counter with a five hundred franc note underneath. He playfully lifted the girl's hand and closed it over both.

"Well, I must say!" said Troy, and she thought how strange it was that she could be civilized and amused and perhaps a little annoyed at this incident.

With an air that contrived to suggest that Alleyn as well as being a shameless flirt was also a gentleman, the girl moved back from the counter, glanced through the plate-glass windows of the main office where a number of typists and two clerks looked on with undisguised curiosity, seemed to change her mind, and came out by way of a gate at the top of the counter and walked with short steps to the double doors. The commissionaire opened them for her. They looked impassively at each other. She passed through and he followed her.

Alleyn said: "She's taking my note to the boss. It ought to surprise him. By all the rules he should have been rung up and told we're on the road to St. Céleste."

"Will he see us?"

"I don't see how he can refuse."

While they waited, Troy looked at the spidery stairs, the blind doors and the distant galleries. "If he should appear!" she thought. "If there could be another flash of yellow and brown." She began to imagine how it would be when they found Ricky. Would his face be white with smudges under the eyes? Would he cry in the stifled inarticulate fashion that always gripped her heart in a stricture? Would he shout and run to her? Or, by a merciful chance, would he behave like the other boy and want to stay with his terrible new friends? She thought: "It's unlucky to anticipate. He may not be here at all. It may be a false scent. If we don't find him before tonight I think I shall crack up."

She knew Alleyn's mind followed hers as closely as one mind can follow another, and she knew that as far as one human being can find solace in another she found solace in him, but she suffered, nevertheless, a great loneliness of spirit. She turned to him and saw compassion and anger in his eyes.

"If anything could make me want more to get these gentlemen," he said, "it would be this. We'll get them, Troy."

"Oh, yes," she said. "I expect you will."

"Ricky's here. I know it in my bones. I promise you."

The girl came back through the double doors. She was very formal.

"Monsieur Callard will see Monsieur and Madame," she said. The commissionaire waited on the far side, holding one door open. As Alleyn stood aside for Troy to go through, the girl moved nearer to him. Her back was turned to the commissionaire. Her eyes made a sign of assent.

He murmured: "And I may understand—what, Mademoiselle?"

"What Monsieur pleases," she said, and minced back to the desk.

Alleyn caught Troy up and took her arm in his hand. The commissionaire was several paces ahead. "Either that girl's given me the tip that Ricky's here," Alleyn muttered, "or she's the smartest job off the skids in the Maritime Alps."

"What did she say?"

"Nothing. Just gave the go-ahead signal."

"Good Lord! Or did it mean Ricky?"

"It'd better mean Ricky," Alleyn said grimly.

They were in an inner hall, heavily carpeted and furnished with modern wall-tables and chairs. They passed two doors and were led to a third in the end wall. The commissionaire opened it and went in. They heard a murmur of voices. He returned and asked them to enter.

A woman with blue hair and magnificent poise rose from a typewriter. "*Bon jour, Monsieur et Madame,*" she said. "*Entrez, s'il vous plaît.*" She opened another door. "*Monsieur et Madame Allen,*" she announced.

"Come right in!" invited a voice in hearty American. "C'm on! Come right in."

v

M. Callard was a fat man with black eyebrows and bluish chops. He was not a particularly evil-looking man: rather one would have said that there was something meretricious about him. His mouth looked as if it had been disciplined by meaningless smiles and his eyes seemed to assume rather than possess an air of concentration. He was handsomely dressed and smelt of expensive cigars. His English was fluent and falsely Americanized with occasional phrases and inflections that made it clear he wasn't speaking his native tongue.

"Well, well, well," he said, pulling himself up from his chair and extending his hand. The other held Alleyn's note. "Very pleased to meet you, Mr. —— I just can't quite get the signature."

"Alleyn."

"Mr. Allen."

"This is my wife."

"Mrs. Allen," said M. Callard, bowing. "Now, let's sit down, shall we, and get acquainted. What's all this I hear about Junior?"

Alleyn said: "I wouldn't have bothered you if we hadn't by chance heard that our small boy who went missing early this afternoon, had, Heaven knows how, turned up at your works. In your office they didn't seem to know anything about him and our French doesn't go very far. It's a great help that your English is so good. Isn't it, darling?" he said to Troy.

"Indeed, yes. M. Callard, I can't tell you how anxious we are. He just disappeared from our hotel. He's only six and it's so dreadful—"

To her horror Troy heard her voice tremble. She was silent.

"Now, that's just too bad," M. Callard said. "And what makes you think he's turned up in this part of the world?"

"By an extraordinary chance," Alleyn said, "the man we've engaged to drive us took his car up this road earlier this afternoon and he saw Ricky in another car with a man and woman. They turned in at the entrance to your works. We don't pretend to understand all this, but you can imagine how relieved we are to know he's all right."

M. Callard sat with a half smile on his mouth, looking at Alleyn's left ear. "Well," he said, "I don't pretend to understand it either. Nobody's told me anything. But we'll soon find out."

He bore down with a pale thumb on his desk bell. The blue-haired secretary came in and he spoke to her in French.

"It appears," he said, "that Monsieur and Madame have been given information by their chauffeur that their little boy who has disappeared was seen in an auto somewhere on our premises. Please make full enquiries, Mademoiselle, in all departments."

"At once, Monsieur le Directeur," said the secretary and went out.

M. Callard offered Troy a cigarette and Alleyn a cigar, both of which were refused. He seemed mysteriously to expand. "Maybe," he said, "you folks are not aware there's a gang of kidnappers at work along this territory. Child-kidnappers."

Alleyn at once broke into a not too coherent and angry dissertation on child-kidnappers and the inefficiency of the police. M. Callard listened with an air of indulgence. He had taken a cigar and he rolled it continuously between his thumb and fingers, which were flattish and backed with an unusual amount of hair. This movement was curiously disturbing. But he listened with perfect courtesy to Alleyn and every now and then made sympathetic noises. There was, however, a certain quality in his stillness which Alleyn recognized. M. Callard was listening to him with only part of his attention. With far closer concentration he listened for something outside the room: and for this, Alleyn thought, he listened so far in vain.

The secretary came back alone.

She told M. Callard that in no department of the works nor among the gardens outside had anyone seen a small boy. Troy only understood the tenor of this speech. Alleyn, who had perfectly understood the whole of it, asked to have it translated. M. Callard obliged, the secretary withdrew, and the temper of the interview hardened. Alleyn got up and moved to the desk. His hand rested on the top of a sound system apparatus. Troy found herself looking at the row of switches and the loud-speaker and at the good hand above them.

Alleyn said he was not satisfied with the secretary's report. M. Callard said he was sorry but evidently there had been some mistake. Alleyn said he was certain there was no mistake. Troy, taking her cue from him, let something of her anxiety and anger escape. M. Callard received her outburst with odious compassion and said it was quite understandable that she was not just 100 per cent reasonable. He rose, but before his thumb could reach the bell-push Alleyn said that he must ask him to listen to the account given by their chauffeur.

"I'm sure that when you hear the man you will understand why we are so insistent," Alleyn said. And before Callard could do anything to stop him he went out leaving Troy to hold, as it were, the gate open for his return.

Callard made a fat, wholly Latin gesture, and flopped back into his chair. "My dear lady," he said, "this good man of yours is just a little difficult. Certainly I'll listen to your chauffeur who is, no doubt, one of the local peasants. I know how they are around here. They say what they figure you want them to say and they don't worry about facts: it's not conscious lying, it's just that they come that way. They're just naturally obliging. Now, your husband's French isn't so hot and my guess is, he's got this guy a little bit wrong. We'll soon find out if I'm correct. Pardon me if I make a call. This is a busy time with us and right now I'm snowed under."

Having done his best to make Troy thoroughly uncomfortable he put through a call on his telephone, speaking such rapid French that she scarcely understood a word of what he said. He had just hung up the receiver when something clicked. This sound was followed by a sense of movement and space beyond the office. M. Callard glanced at the switchboard on his desk and said: "Ah?" A disembodied voice spoke in mid-air.

"*Monsieur le Directeur? Le service de transport avise qu'il est incapable d'expédier la marchandise.*"

"*Qu'est-ce qu'il se passe?*"

"*Rue barrée!*"

"*Bien. Prenez garde. Remettez la marchandise à sa place.*"

"*Bien, Monsieur*," said the voice. The box clicked and the outside world was shut off.

"My, oh my," sighed M. Callard, "the troubles I have!" He opened a ledger on his desk and ran his flattened forefinger down the page.

Troy thought distractedly that perhaps he was right about Raoul and then, catching herself up, remembered that Raoul had in fact never seen the car drive in at the factory gates with Ricky and a man and woman in it, that they were bluffing and that perhaps all Alleyn's and Dupont's theories were awry. Perhaps this inhuman building had never contained her little son. Perhaps it was idle to torture herself by thinking of him: near at hand yet hopelessly withheld.

M. Callard looked at a platinum mounted wristwatch and then at Troy, and sighed again. "He's trying to shame me out of his office," she thought and she said boldly: "Please don't let me interrupt your work." He glanced at her with a smile from which he seemed to make no effort to exclude the venom.

"My work requires the closest concentration, Madame," said M. Callard.

"Sickening for you," said Troy.

Alleyn came back with Raoul at his heels. Through the door Troy caught a glimpse of the blue-haired secretary, half-risen from her desk, expostulation frozen on her face. Raoul shut the door.

"This is Milano, M. Callard," Alleyn said. "He will tell you what he saw. If I have misunderstood him you will be able to correct me. He doesn't speak English."

Raoul stood before the desk and looked about him with the same air of interest and ease that had irritated Dr. Baradi. His gaze fell for a moment on the sound system apparatus and then moved to M. Callard's face.

"Well, my friend," said M. Callard in rapid French. "What's the tarradiddle Monsieur thinks you've told him?"

"I think Monsieur understood what I told him," Raoul said cheerfully and even more rapidly. "I spoke slowly and what I said, with all respect, was no tarradiddle. With Monsieur's permission I will repeat it. Early this afternoon, I do not know the exact time, I drove my young lady along the road to the factory. I parked my car and we climbed a little way up the hillside opposite the gates. From here we observed a car come up from the main road. In it were a man and a woman and the small son of Madame and Monsieur who is called Riki. This little Monsieur Riki was removed from the car and taken into the factory. That is all, Monsieur le Directeur."

M. Callard's eyelids were half-closed. His cigar rolled to and fro between his fingers and thumb.

"So. You see a little boy and a man and a woman. Let me tell you that early this afternoon a friend of my works-superintendent visited the factory with his wife and boy and that undoubtedly it was this boy whom you saw."

"With respect, what is the make of the car of the friend of Monsieur's works-superintendent?"

"I do not concern myself with the cars of my employees' acquaintances."

"Or with the age and appearance of their children, Monsieur?"

"Precisely."

"This was a light blue Citroën, 1946, Monsieur, and the boy was Riki, the son of Monsieur and Madame, a young gentleman whom I know well. He was not two hundred yards away and was speaking his bizarre French, the French of an English child. His face was as unmistakable," said Raoul, looking full into M. Callard's face, "as Monsieur's own. It was Riki."

M. Callard turned to Alleyn: "How much of all that did you get?" he asked.

Alleyn said: "Not a great deal. When he talks to us he talks slowly. But I'm sure—"

"Pardon me," M. Callard said, and turned smilingly to Raoul.

"My friend," he said, "you are undoubtedly a conscientious man. But I assure you that you are making a mistake. Mistakes can cost a lot of money. On the other hand, they sometimes yield a profit. As much, for the sake of argument, as five thousand francs. Do you follow me?"

"No, Monsieur."

"Are you sure? Perhaps—" suggested M. Callard thrusting his unoccupied hand casually into his breast pocket—"when we are alone I may have an opportunity to make my meaning plainer and more acceptable."

"I regret. I shall still be unable to follow it," Raoul said.

M. Callard drew a large handkerchief from his breast pocket and dabbed his lips with it. "*Sacré nigaud,*" he said pleasantly and shot a venomous glance at Raoul before turning to Troy and Alleyn.

"My dear good people," he said expansively, "I'm afraid this boy has kidded you along quite a bit. He admits that he did not get a good look at the child. He was up on the hillside with a dame and his attention was— well, now," said M. Callard smirking at Troy, "shall we say, kind of semi-detached. It's what I thought. He's told you what he figures you'd like to be told and if you ask him again he'll roll out the same tale all over."

"I'm afraid I don't believe that," said Alleyn.

"I'm afraid you don't have an alternative," said M. Callard. He turned on Raoul. "*Fichez-moi le camp,*" he said toughly.

"What's that?" Alleyn demanded.

"I've told him to get out."

"*Vous permettez, Madame, Monsieur?*" Raoul asked and placed himself between the two men with his back to M. Callard.

"What?" Alleyn said. He winked at Raoul. Raoul responded with an ineffable grimace. "What? Oh, all right. *All right. Oui. Allez.*"

With a bow to Troy and another that was rather less respectful than a nod to M. Callard, Raoul went out. Alleyn walked up to the desk and took up his former position.

"I'm not satisfied," he said.

"That's too bad."

"I must ask you to let me search this building."

"You!" said M. Callard and laughed. "Pardon my mirth but I guess there'd be two of you gone missing if you tried that one. This is quite a building, Mr.—" he glanced again at Alleyn's note—"Mr. Allen."

"If it's as big as all that your secretary's enquiries were too brief to be effective. I don't believe any enquiries have been made."

"*Look!*" M. Callard said, and smacked the top of his desk with a flat palm. "This sound system operates throughout these works. I can speak to every department or all departments together. We don't have to go round on a hiking trip when we make general enquiries. Now!"

"Thank you," Alleyn said and his hand darted over the switchboard. There was a click. "*Ricky!*" he shouted, and Troy cried out: "*Ricky!* Are you there? *Ricky!*"

And as if they had conjured it from the outer reaches of space a small voice said excitedly: "They've come! *Mummy!*"

A protesting outcry was cut off as M. Callard struck at Alleyn's hand with a heavy paper knife. At the same moment M. Dupont walked into the room.

CHAPTER VIII

Ricky Regained

Troy could scarcely endure the scene that followed and very nearly lost control of herself. She couldn't understand a word of what was said. Alleyn held her by the arm and kept saying: "In a minute, darling. He'll be here in a minute. He's all right. Hold on. He's all right."

Dupont and Callard were behaving like Frenchmen in English farces. Callard, especially, kept giving shrugs that began in his middle and surged up to his ears. His synthetic Americanisms fell away and when he threw a sentence in English at Troy or at Alleyn he spoke it like a Frenchman. He shouted to Alleyn: "If I lose my temper it is natural. I apologize. I knew nothing. It was the fault of my staff. There will be extensive dismissals. I am the victim of circumstances. I regret that I struck you."

He pounded his desk bell and shouted orders into the sound system. Voices from the other places said in mid-air: "*Immédiatement, M. le Directeur.*" "*Tout de suite, Monsieur.*" "*Parfaitement, M. le Directeur.*" The secretary ran in at a high-heeled double and set up a gabble of protest which was cut short by Dupont. She teetered out again and could be heard yelping down her own sound system.

With one part of her mind Troy thought of the door and how it must soon open for Ricky and with another part she thought it was unlucky to anticipate this event and that the door would open for the secretary or a stranger and, so complicated were her thoughts, she also wondered if, when she saw Ricky, he would have a blank look of panic in his eyes, or if he would cry or be casually pleased, or if these speculations too were unlucky and he wouldn't come at all.

Stifled and terrified, she turned on Dupont and Callard and cried out: "Please speak English. You both can. Where is he? Why doesn't he come?"

"Madame," said Dupont gently, "he is here."

He had come in as she turned away from the door.

The secretary was behind him. She gave his shoulder a little push and he made a fastidious movement away from her and into the room. Troy knew that if she spoke her voice would shake. She held out her hand.

"Hallo, Rick," Alleyn said. "Sorry we've muddled you about."

"You have, rather," Ricky said. He saw Dupont and Callard. "How do you do," he said. He looked at Troy and his lip trembled. He ran savagely into her arms and fastened himself upon her. His fierce hard little body was rammed against hers, his arms gripped her neck and his face burrowed into it. His heart thumped piston-like at her breast.

"We'll take him out to the car," Alleyn said.

Troy rose, holding Ricky with his legs locked about her waist. Alleyn steadied her and they went out through the secretary's room and the lobby and the entrance hall to where Raoul waited in the sunshine.

ii

When they approached the car Ricky released his hold on his mother as abruptly as he had imposed it. She put him down and he walked a little distance from her. He acknowledged Raoul's greeting with an uncertain nod and stood with his back turned to them, apparently looking at M. Dupont's car which was occupied by three policemen.

Alleyn murmured: "He'll get over it all right. Don't worry."

"He thinks we've let him down. He's lost his sense of security."

"We can do something about that. He's puzzled. Give him a moment and then I'll try."

He went over to the police car.

"I suppose," Ricky said to nobody in particular, "Daddy's not going away again."

Troy moved close to him. "No, darling, I don't think so. Not far anyway. He's on a job, though, helping the French police."

"Are those French policemen?"

"Yes. And the man you saw in that place is a French detective."

"As good as Daddy?"

"I don't expect quite as good but good all the same. He helped us find you."

Ricky said: "Why did you let me be got lost?"

"Because," Troy explained with a dryness in her throat, "Daddy didn't know about it. As soon as he knew, it was all right, and you weren't lost any more. We came straight up here and got you."

The three policemen were out of the car and listening ceremoniously to Alleyn. Ricky watched them. Raoul, standing by his own car, whistled a lively air and rolled a cigarette.

"Let's go and sit with Raoul, shall we," Troy suggested, "until Daddy's ready to come home with us?"

Ricky looked miserably at Raoul and away again. "He might be cross of me," he muttered.

"*Raoul* cross with you, darling? *No*. Why?"

"Because—because—I—lost—I lost—"

"No, you didn't!" Troy cried. "We found it. Wait a moment." She rooted in her bag. "Look."

She held out the little silver goat. Ricky's face was transfused with a flush of relief. He took the goat carefully into his square hands. "He's the nicest thing I've ever had," he said. "He shines in the night. *Il s'illume*. Raoul and the lady said he does."

"Has he got a name?"

"His name's Goat," Ricky said.

He walked over to the car. Raoul opened the door and Ricky got into the front seat casually displaying the goat.

"*C'est ça*," Raoul said comfortably. He glanced down at Ricky, nodded three times with an air of sagacity, and lit his cigarette. Ricky shoved one hand in the pocket of his shorts and leaned back. "Coming, Mum?" he asked.

Troy got in beside him. Alleyn called Raoul, who swept off his chauffeur's cap to Troy and excused himself.

"What's going to happen?" Ricky asked.

"I think Daddy's got a job for them. He'll come and tell us in a minute."

"Could we keep Raoul?"

"While we are here I think we can."

"I daresay he wouldn't like to live with us always."

"Well, his family lives here. I expect he likes being with them."

"I do think he's nice, however. Do you?"

"Very," Troy said warmly. "Look, there he goes with the policemen."

M. Dupont had appeared in the factory entrance. He made a crisp signal. Raoul and the three policemen walked across and followed him into the factory. Alleyn came to the car and leaned over the door. He pulled Ricky's forelock and said: "How's the new policeman?" Ricky blinked at him.

"Why?" he asked.

"I think you've helped us to catch up with some bad lots."

"Why?"

"Well, because they thought we'd be so busy looking for you we wouldn't have time for them. But, sucks to them, we didn't lose you and do you know why?"

"Why?"

"Because you waved from the balcony and dropped your silver goat and that was a clue and because you called out to us and we knew you were there. Pretty good."

Ricky was silent.

Troy said: "Jolly good, helping Daddy like that."

Ricky was turned away from her. She could see the charming back of his neck and the curve of his cheek. He hunched his shoulders and tucked in his chin.

"Was the fat, black smelly lady a bad lot?" he asked in a casual tone.

"Not much good," Alleyn said.

"Where is she?"

"Oh, I shut her up. She's a silly old thing, really. Better, shut up."

"Was the other one a bad lot?"

"Which one?"

"The Nanny."

Alleyn and Troy looked at each other over his head.

"The one who fetched you from the hotel?" Alleyn asked.

"Yes, the new Nanny."

"Oh, *that* one. Hadn't she got a red hat or something?"

"She hadn't got a hat. She'd got a moustache."

"Really? Was her dress red perhaps?"

"No. Black with kind of whitey blobs."

"Did you like her?"

"Not extra much. Quite, though. She wasn't bad. I didn't think I had to have a Nan over here."

"Well, you needn't. She was a mistake. We won't have her."

"Anyway, she shouldn't have left me there with the fat lady, should she, Daddy?"

"No." Alleyn reached over the door and took the goat. He held it up admiring it. "Nice, isn't it?" he said. "Did she speak English, that Nanny?"

"Not properly. A bit. The man didn't."

"The driver?"

" 'M."

"Was he a chauffeur like Raoul?"

"No. He had funny teeth. Sort of black. Funny sort of driver for a person to have. He didn't have a cap like Raoul or anything. Just a red beret and no coat and he wasn't very clean either. He's Mr. Garbel's driver, only Mr. Garbel's a *Mademoiselle* and not a Mr."

"*Is* he? How d'you know?"

"May I have Goat again, please? Because the Nanny said you were waiting for me in Mademoiselle Garbel's room. Only you weren't. And because Mademoiselle Garbel rang up. The lady in the goat shop has got other people that light themselves at night too. Saints and shepherds and angels and Jesus. Pretty decent."

"I'll have a look next time I'm there. When did Miss Garbel ring up, Rick?"

"When I was in her room. The fat lady told the Nanny. They didn't know about me understanding which was sucks to them."

"What did the fat lady say?"

" '*Mademoiselle Garbel a téléphoné.*' Easy!"

"What did she telephone about, do you know?"

"Me. She said they were to take me away and they told me you would be up here. Only—"

Ricky stopped short and looked wooden. He had turned rather white.

"Only—?" Alleyn said and then after a moment: "Never mind. I think I know. They went away to talk on the telephone and you went out on the balcony. And you saw Mummy and me waving on our balcony and you didn't know quite what was up with everybody. Was it like that?"

"A bit."

"Muddly?"

"A bit," Ricky said tremulously.

"I know. We were muddled too. Then that fat old thing came out and took you away, didn't she?"

Ricky leaned back against his mother. Troy slipped her arm round him and her hand protected his two hands and the silver goat. He looked at his father and his lip trembled.

"It was beastly," he said. "She was beastly." And then in a most desolate voice: "They took me away. I was all by myself for ages in there. They said you'd be up here and you weren't. You weren't here at all." And he burst into a passion of sobs, his tear-drenched face turned in bewilderment to Alleyn. His precosity fell away from him: he was a child who had not long ago been a baby.

"It's all right, old boy," Alleyn said, "it was only a sort of have. They're silly bad lots and we're going to stop their nonsense. We wouldn't have been able to if you hadn't helped."

Troy said: "Daddy *did* come, darling. He'll always come. We both will."

"Well, anyway," Ricky sobbed, "another time you'd jolly well better be a bit quicker."

A whistle at the back of the factory gave three short shrieks. Ricky shuddered, covered his ears and flung himself at Troy.

"I'll have to go in," Alleyn said. He closed his hand on Ricky's shoulder and held it for a moment. "You're safe, Rick," he said, "you're safe as houses."

"O.K.," Ricky said in a stifled voice. He slewed his head round and looked at his father out of the corners of his eyes.

"Do you think in a minute or two you could help us again? Do you think you could come in with me to the hall in there and tell me if you can see that old Nanny and Mr. Garbel's driver?"

"Oh, *no*, Rory," Troy murmured. "Not now!"

"Well, of course, Rick needn't if he'd hate it, but it'd be helping the police quite a lot."

Ricky had stopped crying. A dry sob shook him, but he said: "Would you be there? And Mummy?"

"We'll be there."

Alleyn reached over, picked up Troy's gloves from the floor of the car and put them in his pocket.

"Hi!" Troy said. "What's that for?"

"'To be worn in my beaver and borne in the van,'" he quoted, "or something like that. If Raoul or Dupont or I come out and wave will you and Ricky come in? There'll be a lot of people there, Rick, and I just want you to look at 'em and tell me if you can see that Nanny and the driver. O.K.?"

"O.K.," Ricky said in a small voice.

"Good for you, old boy."

He saw the anxious tenderness in Troy's eyes and added: "Be kind enough, both of you, to look upon me as a tower of dubious strength."

Troy managed to grin at him. "We have every confidence," she said, "in our wonderful police."

"Like hell!" Alleyn said and went back to the factory.

iii

He found a sort of comic-opera scene in full swing in the central hall. Employees of all conditions were swarming down the curved stairs and through the doors: men in working overalls, in the white coat of the laboratory, in the black jacket of bureaucracy; women equally varied in attire and age: all of them looking in veiled annoyance at their watches. A loud-speaker bellowed continually:

"*'Allo, 'allo, Messieurs et Dames, faites attention, s'il vous plaît. Tous les employés, ayez la bonté de vous rendre immédiatement au grand vestibule. 'Allo, 'allo.*"

M. Dupont stood in a commanding position on the base of the statue and M. Callard, looking sulky, stood at a little distance below him. A few paces distant, Raoul, composed and god-like in his simplicity, surveyed the milling chorus. The gendarmes were nowhere to be seen.

Alleyn made his way to Dupont, who was obviously in high fettle and, as actors say, well inside the skin of his part. He addressed Alleyn in English with exactly the right mixture of deference and veiled irritability. Callard listened moodily.

"Ah, Monsieur! You see we make great efforts to clear up this little affair. The entire staff is summoned by Monsieur le Directeur. We question everybody. This fellow of yours is invited to examine the persons. You are invited to bring the little boy, also to examine. Monsieur le Directeur is most anxious to assist. He is immeasurably distressed, is it not, Monsieur le Directeur?"

"That's right," said M. Callard without enthusiasm.

Alleyn said with a show of huffiness that he was glad to hear that they recognized their responsibilities. M. Dupont bent down as if to soothe him and he murmured: "Keep going as long as you can. Spin it out."

"To the last thread."

Alleyn made his way to Raoul and was able to mutter: "Ricky describes the driver as a man with black teeth, a red beret, as your friend observed, and no jacket. The woman has a moustache, is bareheaded and wears a black dress with a whitish pattern. If you see a man and woman answering to that description you may announce that they resemble the persons in the car."

Raoul was silent. Alleyn was surprised to see that his face, usually a ready mirror of his emotions, had gone blank. The loud-speaker kept up its persistent demands. The hall was filling rapidly.

"Well, Raoul?"

"Would Monsieur describe again the young woman and the man?"

Alleyn did so. "If there are any such persons present you may pretend to recognize them, but not with positive determination. The general appearance, you may say, is similar. Then we may be obliged to bring Ricky in to see if he identifies them."

Raoul made a singular little noise in his throat. His lips moved. Alleyn saw rather than heard his response.

"*Bien, Monsieur*," he said.

"M. Dupont will address the staff when they are assembled. He will speak at some length. I shall not be present. He will continue proceedings until I return. Your *soi-disant* identification will then take place. *Au 'voir, Raoul.*"

"'*Voir, Monsieur.*"

Alleyn edged through the crowd and round the wall of the room to the double doors. The commissionaire stood near them and eyed him dubiously. Alleyn looked across the sea of heads and caught the notice of M. Dupont, who at once held up his hand. "*Attention!*" he shouted. "*Approchez-vous davantage, je vous en prie.*" The crowd closed in on him, and Alleyn, left on the margin, slipped through the doors.

He had at the most fifteen minutes in which to work. The secretary's office was open, but the door into M. Callard's room was, as he had anticipated, locked. It responded to his manipulation and he relocked it behind him. He went to the desk and turned on the general inter-communication switch in the sound system releasing the vague rumour of a not quite silent

crowd and the voice of M. Dupont embarked on an elaborate exposé of
child-kidnapping on the Mediterranean coast.

Perhaps, Alleyn thought, at this rate he would have a little longer than
he had hoped. If he could find a single piece of evidence, enough to ensure
the success of a surprise investigation by the French police, he would be
satisfied. He looked at the filing cabinet against the walls. The drawers had
independent key-holes but the first fifteen were unlocked. He tried them
and shoved them back without looking inside. The sixteenth, marked with
the letter P, was locked. He got it open. Inside he found a number of the
usual folders each headed with its appropriate legend: *Produits chimiques
en commande; Peron et Cie; Plastiques,* and so on. He went through the
first of these, memorizing one or two names of drugs he had been told to
look out for. Peron et Cie was on the suspect list at the Sûreté and a glance
at the correspondence showed a close business relationship between the two
firms. He flipped over the next six folders and came to the last which was
headed: *Particulier à M. Callard. Secret et confidentiel.*

It contained rough notes, memoranda and a number of letters, and Alleyn
would have given years of routine plodding for the right to put the least of
them into his pocket. He found letters from distributors in New York, Cairo,
London, Paris and Istanbul, letters that set out modes of conveyance, suggested suitable contacts, gave details of the methods used by other illicit
traders and warnings of leakage. He found a list of the guests at the Chèvre
d'Argent with Robin Herrington's name scored under and a query beside it.

"*Cette pratique abominable,*" boomed the voice of M. Dupont, warming
to its subject, "*cette tache indéracinable sur l'honneur de notre com-
munauté—*"

"Boy," Alleyn muttered in the manner of M. Callard, "you said it."

He laid on the desk a letter from a wholesale firm dealing in cosmetics
in Chicago. It suggested quite blandly that *Crème Veloutée* in tubes might
be a suitable mode of conveyance for diacetylmorphine and complained that
the last consignment of calamine lotion had been tampered with in transit
and had proved on opening to contain nothing but lotion. It suggested that
a certain customs official had set up in business on his own account and had
better be dealt with pretty smartly.

Alleyn unshipped from his breast pocket a minute and immensely expensive camera. Groaning to himself he switched on M. Callard's fluorescent
lights.

"*—et, Messieurs, Dames,*" thundered the voice of M. Dupont, "*parmi vous,
ici, ici, dans cette usine, ce crime dégoûtant a élevé sa tête hideuse.*"

Alleyn took four photographs of the letter, replaced it in the folder and
the folder in its file, relocked the drawer and stowed away his Lilliputian
camera. Then, with an ear to M. Dupont, who had evidently arrived at the
point where he could not prolong the cackle but must come to the 'osses,
Alleyn made notes, lest he should forget them, of points from the other

documents. He returned his notebook to his pocket, switched off the loud-speaker and turned to the door.

He found himself face-to-face with M. Callard.

"And what the hell," M. Callard asked rawly, "do you think you are doing?"

Alleyn took Troy's gloves from his pocket. "My wife left these in your office. I hope you don't mind."

"She did not and I do. I locked this office."

"If you did someone obviously unlocked it. Perhaps your secretary came back for something."

"She did not," said M. Callard punctually. He advanced a step. "Who the hell are you?"

"You know very well who I am. My boy was kidnapped and brought into your premises. You denied it until you were forced to give him up. Your behaviour is extremely suspicious, M. Callard, and I shall take the matter up with the appropriate authorities in Paris. I have never," continued Alleyn, who had decided to lose his temper, "heard such damned impudence in my life! I was prepared to give you the benefit of the doubt but in view of your extraordinary behaviour I am forced to suspect that you are implicated personally in this business. And in the former affair of child-stealing. Undoubtedly in the former affair."

M. Callard began to shout in French, but Alleyn shouted him down. "You are a child-kidnapper, M. Callard. You speak English like an American. No doubt you have been to America where child-kidnapping is a common racket."

"*Sacré nom d'un chien—*"

"It's no use talking jargon to me, I don't understand a bloody word of it. Stand aside and let me out."

M. Callard's face was not an expressive one, but Alleyn thought he read incredulity and perhaps relief in it.

"You broke into my office," M. Callard insisted.

"I did nothing of the sort. Why the hell should I? And pray what have you got in your office," Alleyn asked as if on a sudden inspiration, "to make you so damned touchy about it? Ransom money?"

"*Imbécile! Sale cochon!*"

"Oh, get to hell!" Alleyn said, and advanced upon him. He stood, irresolute, and Alleyn with an expert movement neatly shouldered him aside and went back to the hall.

iv

Dupont saw him come in. Dupont, Alleyn considered, was magnificent. He must have had an appalling job spinning out a short announcement into a fifteen-minute harangue, but he wore the air of an orator in the first flush of his eloquence.

His gaze swept over Alleyn and round his audience.

"Eh bien, Messieurs, Dames, chacun à sa tâche. Defilez, s'il vous plaît, devant cette statue. . . . Rappelez-vous de mes instructions. Milano!"

He signalled magnificently to Raoul, who stationed himself below him, at the base of the statue. Raoul was pale and stood rigid like a man who faces an ordeal. M. Callard appeared through the double doors and watched with a leaden face.

The gendarmes, who had also reappeared, set about the crowd in a business-like manner, herding it to one side and then sending it across in single file in front of Raoul. Alleyn adopted a consequential air and bustled over to Dupont.

"What's all this, Monsieur?" he asked querulously. "Is it an identification parade? Why haven't I been informed of the procedure?"

Dupont bent in a placatory manner towards him and Alleyn muttered: "Enough to justify a search," and then shouted: "I have a right to know what steps are being taken in this affair."

Dupont spread his blunt hands over Alleyn as if he were blessing him.

"Calm yourself, Monsieur. Everything arranges itself," he said magnificently and added in French for the benefit of the crowd: "The gentleman is naturally overwrought. Proceed, if you please."

Black-coated senior executive officers and white-coated chemists advanced, turned and straggled past with dead-pan faces. They were followed by clerks, assistant chemists, stenographers and laboratory assistants. One or two looked at Raoul, but by far the greater number kept on without turning their heads. When they had gone past, the gendarmes directed them to the top of the hall where they formed up into lines.

Alleyn watched the thinning ranks of those who were yet to come. At the back, sticking together, were a number of what he supposed to be the lesser fry: cleaners, van-drivers, workers from the canteen and porters. In a group of women he caught sight of one a little taller than the rest. She stood with her back towards the statue and at first he could see only a mass of bronze hair with straggling tendrils against the opulent curve of a full neck. Presently her neighbor gave her a nudge and for a moment she turned. Alleyn saw the satin skin and liquid eyes of a Murillo peasant. She had a brilliant mouth and had caught her under-lip between her teeth. Above her upper lip was a pencilling of hair.

Her face flashed into sight and was at once turned away again with a movement that thrust up her shoulder. It was clad in a black material spattered with a whitish-grey pattern.

Behind the girls was a group of four or five men in labourer's clothes: boiler-men, perhaps, or outside hands. As the girls hung back, the gendarme in charge of this group sent the men forward. They edged self-consciously past the girls and slouched towards Raoul. The third was a thick-set fellow wearing a tight-fitting short-sleeved vest and carrying a red beret. He walked hard on the heels of the men in front of him and kept his eyes on the ground. He had two long red scratches on the cheek nearest to Raoul. As he passed by, Alleyn looked at Raoul, who swallowed painfully and muttered: *"Voici le type."*

Dupont raised an eyebrow. The gendarme at the top of the room moved out quietly and stationed himself near the men. The girls came forward one by one and Alleyn still watched Raoul. The girl in the black dress with the whitish-grey pattern advanced, turned and went past with averted head. Raoul was silent.

Alleyn moved close to Dupont. "Keep your eye on that girl, Dupont. I think she's our bird."

"Indeed? Milano has not identified her."

"I think Ricky will."

Watched by the completely silent crowd, Alleyn went out of the hall and, standing in the sunshine, waved to Troy. She and Ricky got out of the car and, hand-in-hand, came towards him.

"Come on, Rick," he said, "let's see if you can find the driver and the Nanny. If you do we'll go and call on the goat-shop lady again. What do you say?"

He hoisted his little son across his shoulders and, holding his ankles in either hand, turned him toward the steps.

"Coming, Mum?" Ricky asked.

"Rather! Try and stop me."

"Strike up the band," Alleyn said. "Here comes the Alleyn family on parade."

He heard his son give a doubtful chuckle. A small hand was laid against his cheek. "Good old horse," Ricky said courageously and in an uncertain falsetto: "How many miles to Babylon?"

"Five score and ten," Alleyn and Troy chanted and she linked her arm through his.

They marched up the steps and into the hall.

The crowd was still herded at one end of the great room and had broken into a subdued chattering. One of the gendarmes stood near the man Raoul had identified. Another had moved round behind the crowd to a group of girls. Alleyn saw the back of that startlingly bronze head of hair and the curve of the opulent neck. M. Callard had not moved. M. Dupont had come down from his eminence and Raoul stood by himself behind the statue, looking at his own feet.

"Ah-ha!" cried M. Dupont, advancing with an air of camaraderie, "so here is Ricketts."

He reached up his hand. Ricky stooped uncertainly from his father's shoulders to put his own in it.

"This is Ricky," Alleyn said, "M. Dupont, Ricky, Superintendent of Police in Roqueville. M. Dupont speaks English."

"How do you do, sir," said Ricky in his company voice.

M. Dupont threw a complimentary glance at Troy.

"So we have an assistant," he said. "This is splendid. I leave the formalities to you, M. Alleyn."

"Just have a look at all these people, Rick," Alleyn said, "and tell us if you can find the driver and the Nanny who brought you up here."

Troy and Dupont looked at Ricky. Raoul, behind the statue, continued to look at his boots. Ricky, wearing the blank expression he reserved for strangers, surveyed the crowd. His attention came to halt on the thick-set fellow in the short-sleeved jersey. Dupont and Troy watched him.

"Mum?" said Ricky.

"Hallo?"

Ricky whispered something inaudible and nodded violently.

"Tell Daddy."

Ricky stooped his head and breathed noisily into his father's ear.

"O.K.," Alleyn said. "Sure?"

" 'M."

"Tell M. Dupont."

"*Monsieur, voici le chauffeur.*"

"*Montrez avec le doigt, mon brave,*" said M. Dupont.

"Point him out, Rick," said Alleyn.

Ricky had been instructed by his French Nanny that it was rude to point. He turned pink in the face and made a rapid gesture, shooting out his finger at the man. The man drew back his upper lip and bared a row of blackened teeth. The first gendarme shoved in beside him. The crowd stirred and shifted.

"Bravo," said M. Dupont.

"Now the Nanny," Alleyn said. "Can you see her?"

There was a long pause. Ricky, looking at the group of girls at the back, said: "There's someone that hasn't turned round."

M. Dupont shouted: "*Présentez-vous de face, tout le monde!*"

The second gendarme pushed through the group of girls. They melted away to either side as if an invisible wedge had been driven through them. The impulse communicated itself to their neighbours: the gap widened and stretched, opening out as Alleyn carried Ricky towards it. Finally Ricky, on his father's shoulders, looked up an exaggerated perspective to where the girl stood with her back to them, her hands clasped across the nape of her neck as if to protect it from a blow. The gendarme took her by the arm, turned her, and held down the hands that now struggled to reach her face. She and Ricky looked at each other.

"Hallo, Teresa," said Ricky.

v

Two cars drove down the Roqueville road. In the first was M. Callard and two policemen and in the second, a blue Citroën, were its owner and a third policeman. The staff of the factory had gone. M. Dupont was busy in M. Callard's office and a fourth gendarme stood, lonely and important, in the empty hall. Troy had taken Ricky, who had begun to be very pleased with himself, to Raoul's car. Alleyn, Raoul and Teresa sat on an ornamental garden seat in the factory grounds. Teresa wept and Raoul gave her cause to do so.

"Infamous girl," Raoul said, "to what sink of depravity have you retired? I think of your perfidy," he went on, "and I spit."

He rose, retired a few paces, spat and returned. "I compare your behaviour," he continued, "to its disadvantage with that of Herod, the Anti-Christ who slit the throats of first-born innocents. Ricky is an innocent and also, Monsieur will correct me if I speak in error, a first-born. He is, moreover, the son of Monsieur, my employer, who, as you observe, can find no words to express his loathing of the fallen woman with whom he finds himself in occupation of this contaminated piece of garden furniture."

"Spare me," Teresa sobbed. "I can explain myself."

Raoul bent down in order to place his exquisite but distorted face close to hers. "Female ravisher of infants," he apostrophized. "Trafficker in unmentionable vices. Associate of perverts."

"You insult me," Teresa sobbed. She rallied slightly. "You also lie like a brigand. The Holy Virgin is my witness."

"She blushes to hear you. Answer me," Raoul shouted and made a complicated gesture a few inches from her eyes. "Did you not steal the child? Answer!"

"Where there is no intention, there is no sin," Teresa bawled, taking her stand on dogma. "I am as pure as the child himself. If anything, purer. They told me his papa wished me to call for him."

"Who told you?"

"Monsieur," said Teresa, changing colour.

"Monsieur Goat! Monsieur Filth! In a word, Monsieur Oberon."

"It is a lie," Teresa repeated but rather vaguely. She turned her sumptuous and tear-blubbered face to Alleyn. "I appeal to Monsieur who is an English nobleman and will not spit upon the good name of a virtuous girl. I throw myself at his feet and implore him to hear me."

Raoul also turned to Alleyn and spread his hands out in a gesture of ineffable poignancy.

"If Monsieur pleases," he said, making Alleyn a present of the whole situation.

"Yes," Alleyn said. "Yes. Well now—"

He looked from one grand-opera countenance to the other. Teresa gazed at him with nerveless compliance, Raoul with grandeur and a sort of gloomy sympathy. Alleyn got up and stood over the girl.

"Now, see here, Teresa," he began. Raoul took a respectful step backwards. "It appears that you have behaved very foolishly for a long time and you are a fortunate girl to have come out of it without involving yourself in disaster."

"Undoubtedly," Teresa said with a hint of complacency, "I am under the protection of Our Lady of Paysdoux for whom I have a special devotion."

"Which you atrociously abuse," Raoul remarked to the landscape.

"Be that as it may," Alleyn hurriedly intervened. "It's time you pulled yourself together and tried to make amends for all the harm you have done. I think you must know very well that your employer at the Château is a bad man. In your heart you know it, don't you, Teresa?"

Teresa placed her hand on her classic bosom. "In my heart, Monsieur, I am troubled to suffocation in his presence. It is in my soul that I find him impure."

"Well, wherever it is, you are perfectly correct. He is a criminal who is wanted by the police of several countries. He has made fools of many silly girls before you. You're lucky not to be in gaol, Teresa. M. le Commissaire would undoubtedly have locked you up if I had not asked him to give you a chance to redeem yourself."

Teresa opened her mouth and let out an appropriate wail.

"To such deplorable depths have you reduced yourself," said Raoul, who had apparently assumed the maddening role of chorus. "And me!" he pointed out.

"However," Alleyn went on, "we have decided to give you this chance. On condition, Teresa, that you answer truthfully any questions I ask you."

"The Holy Virgin is my witness—" Teresa began.

"There are also other less distinguished witnesses," said Raoul. "In effect, there is the child-thief Georges Martel with whom you conspired and who is probably your paramour."

"It is a lie."

"How," Alleyn asked, "did it come about that you took Ricky from the hotel?"

"I was in Roqueville. I go to the market for the *femme de charge*. At one o'clock following my custom I visited the restaurant of the parents of Raoul, who is killing me with cruelty," Teresa explained, throwing a poignant glance at her fiancé. "There is a message for me to telephone the Château. I do so. I am told to wait as Monsieur wishes to speak to me. I do so. My heart churns in my bosom because that unfortunately is the effect Monsieur has upon it: it is not a pleasurable sensation."

"Tell that one in another place," Raoul advised.

"I swear it. Monsieur instructs me: there is a little boy at the Hôtel Royal who is the son of his dear friends, Monsieur and Madame All*aine*. He plans with Monsieur All*aine* a little trick upon Madame, a drollery, a *blague*. They have *nounou* for the child and while they are here I am to be presented by Monsieur as a *nounou* and I am to receive extra salary."

"More atrocity," said Raoul. "How much?"

"Monsieur did not specify. He said an increase. And he instructs me to go to Le Pot des Fleurs and purchase tuberoses. He tells me, spelling it out, the message I am to write. I have learned a little English from the servants of English guests at the Château so I understand. The flowers are from Mademoiselle Garbel who is at present at the Château."

"Is she, by Heaven!" Alleyn ejaculated. "Have you seen her?"

"Often, Monsieur. She is often there."

"What does she look like?"

"Like an Englishwoman. All Englishwomen with the exception, no doubt, of Madame, the wife of Monsieur, have teeth like mares and no *poitrine*. So, also, Mademoiselle Garbel."

"Go on, Teresa."

"In order that the drollery shall succeed, I am to go to the hotel while Madame is at *déjeuner*. I shall have the tuberoses and if without enquiry I can ascertain the apartments of Monsieur and Madame I am to go there. If I am questioned I am to say I am the new *nounou* and go up to the *appartements*. I am to remove the little one by the service stairs. Outside Georges Martel, who is nothing to me, waits in his auto. And from that point Georges will command the proceedings!"

"And that's what you did? No doubt you saw the number of the *appartement* on the luggage in the hall."

"Yes, Monsieur."

"And then?"

"Georges drives us to 16 Rue des Violettes where the concierge tells me she will take the little boy to the *appartement* of Mademoiselle Garbel where his father awaits him. I am to stay in the auto in the back-street with Georges. Presently the concierge returns with the little boy. She says to Georges that the affair is in the water as the parents have seen the boy. She says that the orders are to drive at once to the factory. Georges protests: 'Is it not to St. Céleste?' She says: 'No, at once, quickly to the factory.' The little boy is angry and perhaps frightened and he shouts in French and in English that his papa and mama are not in a factory but in their hotel. But Georges uses blasphemous language and drives quickly away. And Monsieur will, I entreat, believe me when I tell him I regretted then very much everything that had happened. I was afraid. Georges would tell me nothing except to keep my mouth sewn up. So I see that I am involved in wickedness and I say several decades of the rosary and try to make amusements for the little boy who is angry and frightened and weeps for the loss of a statue bought from Marie of the Chèvre d'Argent. I think also of Raoul," said Teresa.

"It's easy to see," Raoul observed, "that in the matter of intelligence you have not invented the explosive." But he was visibly affected, nevertheless. "You should have known at once that it was a lot of *blague* about the *nounou*."

"And when you got to the factory?" Alleyn asked.

"Georges took the little boy inside. He then returned alone and we drove round to the garages at the back. I tried to run away and when he grasped my arms I inflicted some formidable scratches on his face. But he threw me a smack on the ear and told me Monsieur Oberon would put me under a malediction."

"When he emerges from gaol," Raoul said thoughtfully, "I shall make a meat *pâté* of Georges. He is already fried."

"And then, Teresa?"

"I was frightened again, Monsieur, not of Georges but of what Monsieur Oberon might do to me. And presently the whistle blew and a loud-speaker summoned everybody to the hall. And Georges said we should clear out. He walked a little way and peeped round the corner and came back saying there were gendarmes at the gates and we must conceal ourselves. But one of the gendarmes came into the garage and said we must go into the hall. And when we arrived Georges left me saying: 'Get out, don't hang round my heels.' So I went to some of the girls I knew and when I heard the announcement of Monsieur le Commissaire and saw Raoul and they said Raoul had seen me: Oh, Monsieur, judge of my feelings! Because, say what you will, Raoul is the friend of my heart and if he no longer loves me I am desolate."

"You are as silly as a foot," said Raoul, greatly moved, "but it is true that I love you."

"Ah!" said Teresa simply. "*Quelle extrase!*"

"And upon that note," said Alleyn, "we may return to Roqueville and make our plans."

CHAPTER IX

Dinner at Roqueville

On the return journey Alleyn and Troy sat in the back seat with Ricky between them. Teresa, who was to be given a lift to the nearest bus stop, sat in the front by Raoul. She leaned against him in a luxury of reconciliation, every now and then twisting herself sideways in order to gaze into his face. Ricky, who suffered from an emotional hangover and was, therefore, inclined to be querulous and in any case considered Raoul his especial property, looked at these manifestations with distaste.

"Why does she do that?" he asked fretfully. "Isn't she silly? Does Raoul like her?"

"Yes," said Troy, hugging him.

"I bet he doesn't really."

"They are engaged to be married," said Troy, "I think."

"You and Mummy are married, aren't you, Daddy?"

"Yes."

"Well, Mummy doesn't do it."

"True," said Alleyn, who was in good spirits, "but I should like it if she did."

"Ooh, Daddy, you would *not*."

Teresa wound her arm round Raoul's neck.

"*Je t'adore!*" she crooned.

"Oh, gosh!" said Ricky and shut his eyes.

"All the same," Alleyn said, "we'll have to call a halt to her raptures." He leaned forward. "Raoul, shall we stop for a moment? If Teresa misses her bus you may drive her back from Roqueville."

"Monsieur, may I suggest that we drive direct to Roqueville where, if Monsieur and Madame please, my parents will be enchanted to invite them to an *apéritif* or, if preferred, a glass of good wine, and perhaps an early but well-considered dinner. The afternoon has been fatiguing. Monsieur has not eaten, I think, since morning and Madame and Monsieur Ricky may be glad to dine early. Teresa is, no doubt, not expected at the house of infamy, being, as they will suppose, engaged in the abduction of Ricky and in any case I do not permit her to return."

Teresa made a complicated noise, partly protesting but mostly acquiescent. She essayed to tuck one of Raoul's curls under his cap.

Ricky, with his eyes still shut, said: "Is Raoul asking us to tea, Daddy? May we go? Just us however," he added pointedly.

"We shall all go," Alleyn said, "including Teresa. Unless, Troy darling, you'd rather take Ricky straight to the hotel."

Ricky opened his eyes. "Please not, Mummy. Please let's go with Raoul."

"All right, my mammet. How kind of Raoul."

So Alleyn thanked Raoul and accepted his invitation, and as they had arrived at the only stretch of straight road on their journey Raoul passed his right arm round Teresa and broke into song.

They drove on through an evening drenched in a sunset that dyed their faces and hands crimson and closely resembled the coloured postcards that are sold on the Mediterranean coast. Two police-cars passed them with a great sounding of horns and Alleyn told Troy that M. Dupont had sent for extra men to effect a search of the factory. "It was too good an opening to miss," he said. "He'll certainly find enough evidence to throw a spanner through the plate glass and thanks for the greater part, let's face it, to young Rick."

"What have I done, Daddy?"

"Well, you mustn't buck too much about it but by being a good boy and not making a fuss when you were a bit frightened you've helped us to shut up that factory back there and stop everybody's nonsense."

"Lavish!" said Ricky.

"Not bad. And now you can pipe down for a bit while I talk to Mummy."

Ricky looked thoughtfully at his father, got down from his seat and placed himself between Alleyn's knees. He then aimed a blow with his fist at Alleyn's chest and followed it up with a tackle. Alleyn picked him up. "Pipe down, now," he said, and Ricky, suddenly quiescent, lay against his father and tried to hide his goat from the light in the hope that it would illuminate itself.

"The next thing," Alleyn said to Troy, "is to tackle our acquaintance of this morning. And from this point onwards, my girl, you fade, graciously but inexorably, *out*. You succour your young, reside in your classy pub, and if your muse grows exigent you go out with Raoul and your young and paint pretty peeps of the bay, glimpsed between sprays of bougainvillea."

"And do we get any pretty peeps of you?"

"I expect to be busyish. Would you rather move on to St. Céleste or back to St. Christophe? Does this place stink for you, after today?"

"I don't think so. We know the real kidnappers are in jug, don't we? And I imagine the last thing Oberon and Co. will try on is another shot at the same game."

"The very last. After tomorrow night," Alleyn said, "I hope they will have no chance of trying anything on except the fruitless contemplation of their past infamies and whatever garments they are allowed to wear in the local lock-up."

"Really? A coup in the offing?"

"With any luck. But see here, Troy, if you're going to feel at all jumpy we'll pack you both off to—well, home, if necessary."

"I don't want to go home," Ricky said from inside Alleyn's jacket. "I think Goat's beginning to illumine himself, Daddy."

"Good. What about Troy?"

"I'd rather stay, Rory. Indeed, if it wasn't for the young, and yet I suppose because of him, I'd rather muck in on the job. I'm getting a first-hand look at the criminal classes and it's surprising how uncivilized it makes one feel."

Alleyn glanced at the now hazardously entwined couple in the front seat. He adjusted Ricky and flung an arm round Troy.

"A fat lot they know about it," he muttered.

As the car slipped down the familiar entry into Roqueville he said: "And how would you muck in, may I ask?"

"I might say I wanted to do a portrait of Oberon in the lotus bud position and thus by easy degrees become a Daughter of the Sun."

"Like hell, you might."

"Anyway, let's stay if only to meet Cousin Garbel."

She felt Alleyn's arm harden. Like Teresa, she turned to look at her man.

"Rory," she said, "did you believe Baradi's story about the charades?"

"Did you?"

"I thought I did. I wanted to. Now, I don't think I do."

"Nor do I," Alleyn said.

"*On arrive*," said Raoul, turning into a narrow street. "*Voici L'Escargot Bienvenu*."

ii

It was, as Raoul had said, an unpretentious restaurant. They entered through a *portière* of wooden beads into a white-washed room with fresh window curtains and nine tables. A serving counter ran along one side and on it stood baskets of fresh fruit, of bread and of *langoustes* bedded in water-cress. Bottles of wine and polished glasses filled the shelves behind the counter and an open door led into an inner room where a voice was announcing the weather forecast in French. There were no customers in the restaurant, and Raoul, having drawn out three chairs and seated his guests, placed his arm about Teresa's waist and led her into the inner room.

"Maman! Papa!" he shouted.

An excited babble broke out in the background.

"Come to think of it," Alleyn said, "I'm damned hungry. Raoul told me his papa was particularly good with steak. *Filet mignon?* What do you think?"

"Are we going to be allowed to pay?"

"No. Which means that good or bad we'll have to come back for more. But my bet is, it'll be good."

The hubbub in the background came closer, and Raoul reappeared accompanied by a magnificent Italian father and a plump French mother, both of whom he introduced with ceremony. Everybody was very polite, Ricky was made much of and a bottle of extremely good sherry was opened. Ricky was given grenadine. Healths were drunk, Teresa giggled modestly in the background. M. Milano made a short but succinct speech in which he said he understood that Monsieur and Madame Ah-laine had been instrumental in saving Teresa from a fate that was worse than death and had thus preserved the honour of both families and made possible an alliance that was the dearest wish of their hearts. It was also, other things being equal, a desirable match from the practical point of view. Teresa and Raoul listened without embarrassment and with the detachment of connoisseurs. M. Milano then begged that he and Madame might be excused as they believed they were to have the great pleasure of serving an early dinner and must therefore make a little preparation with which Teresa would no doubt be pleased to assist. They withdrew. Teresa embraced Raoul with passionate enthusiasm and followed them.

Alleyn said: "Bring a chair, Raoul. We have much to say to each other."

"Monsieur," Raoul said without moving, "no mention has been made of my neglect of duty this afternoon. I mean, Monsieur, my failure, which was deliberate, to identify Teresa."

"I have decided to overlook it. The circumstances were extraordinary."

"That is true, Monsieur. Nevertheless, the incident had the effect of incensing me against Teresa who, foolish as she is, has yet got something which caused me to betray my duty. That is why I spoke a little sharply to Teresa."

With results," he added, "that are, as Monsieur may have noticed, not undesirable."

"I have noticed. Sit down, Raoul."

Raoul bowed and sat down. Madame Milano, beaming and business-like, returned with a book in her hands. It was a shabby large book with a carefully mended binding. She laid it on the table in front of Ricky.

"When my son was no larger than this little Monsieur," she said, "it afforded him much amusement."

"*Merci*, Madame," Ricky said, eyeing it.

Troy and Alleyn also thanked her. She made a deprecating face and bustled away. Ricky opened the book. It was a tale of heroic and fabulous adventures enchantingly illustrated with coloured lithographs. Ricky honoured it with the silence he reserved for special occasions. He removed himself and the book to another table. "Coming, Mum?" he said and Troy joined him. Alleyn looked at the two dark heads bent together over the book and for a moment or two he was lost in abstraction. He heard Raoul catch his breath in a vocal sigh, a sound partly affirmative, partly envious. Alleyn looked at him.

"Monsieur is fortunate," Raoul said simply.

"I believe you," Alleyn muttered. "And now, Raoul, we make a plan. Earlier today, and I must say it feels more like last week, you said you were willing to join in an enterprise that may be a little hazardous: an enterprise that involves an unsolicited visit to the Chèvre d'Argent on Thursday night."

"I remember, Monsieur."

"Are you still of the same mind?"

"If possible, I feel an increase of enthusiasm."

"Good, now, listen. It is evident that there is a close liaison between the persons at the Château and those at the factory. Tonight the commissary will conduct an official search of the factory and he will find documentary evidence of the collaboration. It is also probable that he will find quantities of illicitly manufactured heroin. It is not certain whether he will find direct and conclusive evidence of sufficient weight to warrant an arrest of Mr. Oberon and Dr. Baradi and their associates. Therefore, it would be of great assistance if they could be arrested for some other offense and could be held while further investigations were made."

"There is no doubt, Monsieur, that their sins are not confined to contraband."

"I agree."

"They are capable of all."

"Not only capable but culpable! I think," Alleyn said, "that one of them is a murderer."

Raoul narrowed his eyes. His stained mechanic's hands, lying on the table, flexed and then stretched.

"Monsieur speaks with confidence," he said.

"I ought to," Alleyn said drily, "considering that I saw the crime."

"You—"

"Through a train window." And Alleyn described the circumstances.

"Bizarre," Raoul commented, summing up the incident. "And the criminal, Monsieur?"

"Impossible to say. I had the impression of a man or woman in a white gown with a cowl or hood. The right arm was raised and held a weapon. The face was undistinguishable although there was a strong light thrown from the side. The weapon was a knife of some sort."

"The animal," said Raoul, who had settled upon this form of reference for M. Oberon, "displays himself in a white robe."

"Yes."

"And the victim was a woman, Monsieur?"

"A woman. Also, I should say, wearing some loose-fitting garment. One saw only a shape against a window blind and then for a second, against the window itself. The man, if it was a man, had already struck and had withdrawn the weapon which he held aloft. The impression was melodramatic," he added, almost to himself. "Over-dramatic. One might have believed it was a charade."

"A charade, Monsieur?"

"Dr. Baradi offered the information that there were charades last night. It appears that someone played the part of the Queen of Sheba stabbing King Solomon's principal wife. He himself enacted a concubine."

"Obviously he is not merely a satyr but also a perverted being—a distortion of nature. Only such a being could invent such a disgusting lie."

While he grinned at Raoul's scandalized sophistry Alleyn wondered at the ease with which they talked to each other. And, being a modest man, he found himself ashamed. Why, in Heaven's name, he thought, should he not find it good to talk to Raoul, who had an admirable mind and a simple approach? He thought: "We understand so little of our fellow creatures. Somewhere in Raoul there is a limitation but when it comes to the Oberons and Baradis he, probably by virtue of his limitation, is likely to be a much more useful judge than . . ."

"The Queen of Sheba," Raoul fumed, "is a Biblical personage. She was the *chère amie* of the Lord's anointed. To murder he adds a blasphemy which has not even the merit of being true. Unfortunately he is left-handed," he added in a tone of acute disappointment.

"Exactly! Moreover he offered this information," Alleyn pointed out. "One must remember the circumstances. The scene, real or simulated, reached its climax as the train drew up and stopped. The blind was released as the woman fell against it. And the man, not necessarily Oberon or Baradi, you know, saw other windows—those of the train."

"So knowing Monsieur must have been in the train and awake, since he was to alight at Roqueville, this blasphemer produces his lies."

"It might well be so. M. Dupont and I both incline to think so. Now, you see, don't you, that if murder *was* done in that room in the early hours of this morning, we have great cause to revisit the Château. Not only to arrest a killer but to discover why he killed. Not only to arrest a purveyor of drugs who has caused many deaths but to discover his associates. And not only for these reasons but also to learn, if we can, what happens in the locked room on Thursday nights. For all these reasons, Raoul, it seems imperative that we visit the Château."

"Well, Monsieur."

"Two courses suggest themselves. I may return openly to enquire after the health of Mademoiselle Truebody. If I do this I shall have to admit that Ricky has been found."

"They will have learned as much from the man Callard, Monsieur."

"I am not so sure. This afternoon M. Dupont ordered that all outward calls from the factory should be blocked at central and that the Château should be cut off. At the Château they will be extremely anxious to avoid any sign that they are in touch with the factory. They will, of course, question Teresa, to whom we must give instructions. If I pursue our first course I shall tell the story of the finding of Ricky to Mr. Oberon and his guests and I shall utter many maledictions against Callard as a child-kidnapper. And, having seen Miss Truebody, I must appear to go away and somehow or another remain. I've no idea how this can be done. Perhaps, if one had a colleague within the place one might manage it. The alternative is for me, and you, Raoul, to go secretly to the Château. To do this we would again need a colleague who would admit and conceal us."

Raoul put his head on one side with the air of a collector examining a doubtful treasure. "Monsieur refers, of course, to Teresa," he said.

"I do."

"Teresa," Raoul continued anxiously, "has not displayed herself to advantage this afternoon. She was *bouleversée* and therefore behaved foolishly. Nevertheless, she is normally a girl of spirit. She is also at the present time desirous of re-establishing herself in my heart. Possibly I have been too lenient with her but one inclines to leniency where one's affections are engaged. I have, as Monsieur knows, forbidden her return to this temple of shame. Nevertheless, where the cause is just and with the protection of Our Lady of Paysdoux (about whose patronage Teresa is so unbecomingly cocksure), there can be no sin."

"I take it," Alleyn said, "that you withdraw your objection?"

"Yes, Monsieur. Not without misgivings because Teresa is dear to me and, say what you like, it is no place for one's girl."

"Judging by the lacerations on Georges Martel's face, Teresa is able to defend herself on occasion."

"True," Raoul agreed, cheering up. "She has enterprise."

"Suppose we talk to her about it?"

"I will produce her."

Raoul went out to the kitchen.

"Hallo, you two," Alleyn said.

"Hallo, yourself," Troy said.

"Daddy, this is a lavish book. I can read it better than Mummy."

"Don't buck," Alleyn said automatically.

"Have you sent Raoul to get that nanny-person? Teresa?"

"Yes."

"Why?"

"We've got a job for her."

"*Not* minding me?"

"No, no. Nothing to do with you, old boy."

"Well, good, anyway," said Ricky returning to his book.

Raoul came back with Teresa, who now wore an apron and seemed to be in remarkably high spirits. On Alleyn's invitation she sat down using, however, the very edge of her chair. Alleyn told her briefly what he wanted her to do. Raoul folded his arms and scowled thoughtfully at the tablecloth.

"You see, Teresa," Alleyn said, "these are bad men and also unfortunately extremely clever men. They think they've made a fool of you as they have of a great many other silly girls. The thing is—are you ready to help Raoul and me and the police of your own country to put a stop to their wickedness?"

"Ah, yes, Monsieur," said Teresa cheerfully. "I now perceive my duty and with the help of Raoul and the holy saints, dedicate myself to the cause."

"Good. Do you think you can keep your head and behave sensibly and with address if an emergency should arise?"

Teresa gazed at him and said that she thought she could.

"Very well. Now, tell me: were you on duty last evening?"

"Yes, Monsieur. During the dinner I helped the housemaids go round the bedrooms and then I worked in the kitchen."

"Was there a party?"

"A party? Well, Monsieur, there was the new guest, Mlle. Wells, who is an actress. And after dinner there was a gathering of all the guests in the private apartments of M. Oberon. I know this because I heard the butler say that Monsieur wished it made ready for a special welcome for Mlle. Wells. And this morning," said Teresa, looking prim, "Jeanne Barre, who is an underhousemaid, said that Mlle. Locke, the English noblewoman, must have taken too much wine because her door was locked with a notice not to disturb and this is always a sign she has been indiscreet."

"I see. Tell me, Teresa: have you ever seen into the room that is only opened on Thursday night?"

"Yes, Monsieur. On Thursday morning I dust this room and on Friday it is my duty to clean it."

"Where is it exactly?"

"It is down the stairs, three flights, from the vestibule, and beneath the library. It is next to the private apartments of M. Oberon."

"Has it many windows?"

"It has no windows, Monsieur. It is in a very old part of the Château."

"And M. Oberon's rooms?"

"Oh, yes, Monsieur. The salon has a window which is covered always by a white blind with a painting of the sun because Monsieur dislikes a brilliant light, so it is always closed. But Monsieur has nevertheless a great lamp fashioned like the sun and many strange ornaments and a strange wheel which Monsieur treasures and a magnificent bed and in the salon a rich divan," said Teresa, warming to her subject, "and an enormous mirror where—" There she stopped short and blushed.

"Continue," Raoul ordered, with a face of thunder.

"Where once when I took in *petit déjeuner* I saw Monsieur contemplating himself in a state of nature."

Alleyn, with an eye on Raoul, said hurriedly, "Will you describe the room that you clean?"

Raoul reached across the table and moved his forefinger to and fro in front of his beloved's nose. "Choose your words, my treasure," he urged. "Invent nothing. Accuracy is all."

"Yes, indeed it is," said Alleyn heartily.

Thus warned, Teresa looked self-consciously at her folded hands and with a slightly sanctimonious air began her recital.

"If you please, Monsieur, it is a large room and at first I thought perhaps it was a chapel."

"A *chapel?*" Alleyn exclaimed. Raoul made a composite noise suggestive of angry incredulity.

"Yes, Monsieur. I thought perhaps it was reserved for the private devotions of M. Oberon and his friends. Because at one side is a raised place with a table like the holy altar, covered in a cloth which is woven in a rich pattern with gold and silver and jewels. But although one saw the holy cross, there were other things in the pattern that one does not see in altar cloths."

"The hoof prints of anathema!" Raoul ejaculated.

"Go on, Teresa," said Alleyn.

"And on the table there was something that was also covered with an embroidered cloth."

"What was that, do you suppose?"

Teresa's white eyelids were raised. She gave Alleyn the glance of a cunning child.

"Monsieur must not think badly of me if I tell him I raised the cloth and looked. Because I wanted to see if it was a holy relic."

"And was it?"

"No, Monsieur. At first I thought it was a big monstrance made of glass. Only it was not a monstrance although in shape it resembled a great sun and inside the sun a holy cross broken and a figure like this."

With a sort of disgusted incredulity Alleyn watched her trace with her finger on the table, a pentagram. Raoul groaned heavily.

"And it was, as I saw when I looked more closely, Monsieur, a great lamp because there were many, many electric bulbs behind it and behind the sun at the back was a bigger electric bulb than I have ever seen before. So I dropped the heavy cloth over it and wondered."

"What else did you see?"

"There was nothing else in the room, Monsieur. No chairs or any furniture or anything. The walls were covered with black velvet and there were no pictures."

"Any doors, other than the one leading from Mr. Oberon's room?"

"Yes, Monsieur. There was a door in the wall opposite the table. I didn't notice it the first time I cleaned the room because it is covered like the walls and had no handle. But the second time it was open and I was told to clean the little room beyond."

"What was it like, this room?"

"On the floor there were many black velvet cushions and one large one like the mattress for a divan. And the walls here also were covered in black velvet and there was a black velvet curtain behind which were hanging a great number of white robes such as the robe Monsieur wears and one black velvet robe. And on the table there were many candles in black candlesticks which I had to clean. There was also a door from the passage into this little room."

"Nastier and nastier," Alleyn muttered in English.

"I beg Monsieur's pardon?"

"Nothing. And this was the only other door into the big room?"

"No, Monsieur, there was another, very small like a trap-door behind the table, painted with signs like the signs on the sun lamp and on the floor."

"There were signs on the floor?"

"Yes, Monsieur. I had been told to clean the floor, Monsieur. It is a beautiful floor with a pattern made of many pieces of stone and the pattern is the same as the other." Her finger traced the pentagram again. "And when I came to clean it, Monsieur, I knew the room was not a chapel."

"Why?"

"Because the floor in front of the table was as dirty as a farmyard," said Teresa. "It was like our yard at my home in the Paysdoux. There had been an animal in the room."

"An animal!" Raoul ejaculated. "I believe you! And what sort of animal?"

"That was easy to see," said Teresa simply. "It was a goat."

iii

Alleyn decided finally that the following evening he and Raoul would call at the Chèvre d'Argent. He would arrive after the hour of six when, according to Teresa, the entire household would have retired for something known as private meditation, but which was supposed by Teresa to be a sound sleep. It was unusual at this time for anyone to appear, and indeed again, according to Teresa, a rule of silence and solitude was imposed from six until nine by

Mr. Oberon. On Thursdays there was no dinner, but Teresa understood that there was a very late supper at which the guests were served by the Egyptian servant only. Teresa herself was dismissed with the other servants as soon as their late afternoon and early evening tasks were executed. If they didn't encounter any member of the household on their way through the tunnel Alleyn and Raoul were to go past the main entrance and down a flight of steps to a little-used door through which Teresa would admit them. No attention would be paid to Raoul if he was seen by any other servants who might still be about, and if Alleyn kept in the background it might be possible to suggest that he was a relative from Marseilles. "A distinguished relative," Raoul amended, "seeing that in appearance and in speech Monsieur is clearly of a superior class."

Teresa would then conceal Alleyn and Raoul in her own room where, with any luck, she would have already secreted two of the white robes. She was pretty certain there were many more in the little ante-room than would be needed by M. Oberon's guests. It would be tolerably easy when she cleaned this room to remove them under cover of the laundry it was her duty to collect from the bedrooms.

"Is it not as I have said, Monsieur?" Raoul remarked, indicating his fiancée. "She is not without enterprise, is Teresa?" Teresa looked modestly at Alleyn and passionately at Raoul.

If all went well, up to this point, Teresa would have done as much as could be expected of her. She would take her departure as usual and could either wait in Raoul's car or catch the evening bus to her home in Paysdoux. It should be possible for Alleyn and Raoul to pass through the house without attracting attention. The cowls of their robes would be drawn over their heads and it might be supposed if they were seen that they were belated guests or even early arrivals for the ceremony. Teresa had heard that occasionally there were extra people on Thursday nights, people staying in Roqueville or in St. Christophe.

And then? "Then," Alleyn said, "it will be up to us, Raoul."

The alternative to this plan was tricky. If he was spotted on his way into the Chèvre d'Argent, Alleyn would put a bold face on it and say that he had come to see Miss Truebody. No doubt Baradi would be summoned from his private meditation and Alleyn would have to act upon the situations as they arose. Raoul would still call on Teresa and hide in her room.

"All right," Alleyn said. "That's as far as we need go. Now Teresa, this evening you will return to the Château and Mr. Oberon will no doubt question you about today's proceedings. You will tell him exactly what happened at the factory, up to and after the identification parade. You will tell him that Ricky identified you. Then, you will say, the police made you come back to Roqueville and asked you many questions, accusing you of complicity in the former kidnapping affair and asking who were your colleagues in that business. You will say that you told the police you know nothing: that Georges

Martel offered you a little money to fetch the boy and beyond that you know nothing at all. This is important, Teresa. Repeat it, please."

Teresa folded her hands and repeated it, prompted without necessity by Raoul.

"Excellent," Alleyn said. "And you will, of course, have had no conversation with me. Perhaps it will be well to say, if you are asked, that you returned to Roqueville in Raoul's car. You may have been seen doing so. But you will say that Madame and I were so overjoyed on recovering our son that we had nothing to say except that no doubt the police would deal with you."

"Yes, Monsieur."

"Have courage, my little one," Raoul admonished her. "Lie no more than is necessary, you understand, but when you do lie, lie like a brigand. It is in the cause of the angels."

"Upon whose protection and of that of Our Lady of Paysdoux," Teresa neatly interpolated, "I hurl myself."

"Do so."

Teresa rose and made a convent-child's bob. Raoul also asked to be excused. As they went together to the door, Alleyn said: "By the way, did you hear tomorrow's weather forecast for the district?"

"Yes, Monsieur. It is for thunderstorms. There are electrical disturbances."

"Indeed? How very apropos. Thank you, Raoul."

"Monsieur," said Raoul obligingly and withdrew his beloved into the inner room.

Alleyn rejoined his family. "Did you get much of that?" he asked.

"I've reached exhaustion point for French," Troy said. "I can't even try to listen. And Ricky, as you see, is otherwise engaged."

Ricky looked up from a brilliant picture of two knights engaged in single combat. "I bet there'll be a wallop when they crash," he said. "Whang! I daresay I'd be able to read this pretty soon if we stayed here. I can read a bit, can't I, Mummy?"

"English, you can."

"I know. So don't you daresay I could, French, Daddy?"

"I wouldn't put it past you. Did you know what we were talking about, just now?"

"I wasn't listening much." Ricky lowered his voice to a polite whisper. "If it isn't a rude question," he said, "when's dinner?"

"Soon. Pipe down, now. I want to talk to Mummy."

"O.K. What are you going to do in Teresa's bedroom tomorrow night, Daddy?"

"I must say I should like to be associated with that enquiry," said Troy warmly.

"I am changing there for a party."

"Who's having a party?" Ricky demanded.

"A silver goat. I rather think he lights himself up."

The door opened. Teresa came in with a tray.

iv

The dinner was superb, the *filets mignons* particularly being inspired. When it was finished the Alleyns invited the Milanos to join them for *fines* and M. Milano produced a bottle of distinguished cognac. The atmosphere was gay and *comme il faut*. Presently the regular clientele of the house began to come in: quiet middle-class people who greeted Madame Milano and took down their own table-napkins from hooks above their special places. A game of draughts was begun at the corner table. Troy, who had enjoyed herself enormously but was in a trance of fatigue, said she thought that they should go. Elaborate leave-takings were begun. Ricky, full of vegetables and rich gravy and sticky with grenadine, yawned happily and bestowed a smile of enchanting sweetness upon Madame Milano.

"*Mille remerciements, chère Madame,*" he said, stumbling a little over the long word, "*de mon beau repas,*" and held out his hand. Madame made a complicated, motherly, bustling movement and ejaculated, "*Ah, mon Dieu, quel amour d'enfant!*" There followed a great shaking of hands and interchange of compliments and the Alleyns took their departure on the crest of the wave.

Raoul drove them back to their hotel where, regrettably, a great fuss was again made over Ricky, who began to show infantile signs of vainglory and struck an attitude before M. Malaquin, the proprietor, shouting: "Kidnappers! Huh! Easy!" and was applauded by the hall porter.

Alleyn said: "That's more than enough from you, my friend," picked his son up and bore him into the lift. Troy followed wearily, saying: "Don't be an ass, Ricky darling." When they got upstairs Ricky, who had been making tentative sounds of defiance, became quiet. When he was ready for bed he turned white and said he wouldn't sleep in "that room." His parents exchanged the look that recognizes a dilemma. Troy muttered: "It *is* trying him a bit high, isn't it?" Alleyn locked the outer door of Ricky's room and took him into the passage to show him that it couldn't be opened. They returned, leaving the door between the two rooms open. Ricky hung back. He had shadows under his eyes and looked exhausted and miserable. "Why can't Daddy go in there?" he asked angrily.

Alleyn thought a moment and then said: "I can of course, and you can be with Mummy."

"Please," Ricky said. "Please."

"Well, I must say that's a bit more civil. Look here, old boy, will you lend me your goat to keep me company? I want to see if it really does light itself up."

"Yes, of course he will," said Troy with an attempt at maternal prompting, "which," she thought, "I should find perfectly maddening if I were Ricky."

Ricky said: "I want to be in here with Mummy and I want Goat to be here too. Please," he added.

"All right," Alleyn said. "You won't see him light himself up, of course, because Mummy will want her lamp on for some time, won't you, darling?"

"For ages and ages," Troy, who desired nothing less, agreed.

Ricky said: "Please take him in there and tell me if he illumines." He fished his silver goat out of the bosom of his yellow shirt. Alleyn took it into the next room, put it on the bedside table, shut the door and turned out the lights.

He sat on the bed staring into the dark and thinking of the events of the long day and of Troy and Ricky, and presently a familiar experience revisited him. He seemed to see himself for the first time, a stranger, a being divorced from experience, a chrysalis from which his spirit had escaped and which it now looked upon, he thought, with astonishment as a soul might look after death at its late housing. He thought: "I suppose Oberon imagines he's got all this sort of thing taped. Raoul and Teresa too, after *their* fashion and belief. But I have never found an answer." The illusion, if it were an illusion and he was never certain about this, could be dismissed, but he held to it still and in a little while he found he was looking at a fluorescence, a glimmer of something, no more than a bat-light. It grew into a shape. It was Ricky's little figurine faithfully illuminating itself in the dark. And Ricky's voice, still rather fretful, brought Alleyn back to himself.

"Daddy!" he was shouting. "Is he doing it? *Daddy!*"

"Yes," Alleyn called, rousing himself, "he's doing it. Come and see. But shut the door after you or you'll spoil it."

There was a pause. A blade of light appeared and widened. He saw Ricky come in, a tiny figure in pyjamas. "Shut the door, Ricky," Alleyn repeated, "and wait a moment. If you come to me, you'll see."

The room was dark again.

"If you'd go on talking, however," Ricky's voice said, very small and polite, "I'd find you."

Alleyn went on talking and Ricky found him. He stood between his father's knees and watched the goat shining. "He honestly is silver," he said. "It's all true." He leaned back against his father, smelling of soap, and laid his relaxed hand on Alleyn's. Alleyn lifted him on to his knee. "I'm fizzily and 'motionly zausted," Ricky said in a drawling voice.

"What in the world does that mean?"

"It's what Mademoiselle says I am when I'm overtired." He yawned cosily. "I'll look at Goat a bit more and then I daresay . . ." His voice trailed into silence.

Alleyn could hear Troy moving about quietly in the next room. He waited until Ricky was breathing deeply and then put him to bed. The door opened and Troy stood there listening. Alleyn joined her. "He's off," he said and watched while she went to see for herself. They left the door open.

"I don't know whether that was sound child-psychiatry or a barefaced cheat," Alleyn said, "but it's settled his troubles. I don't think he'll be frightened of his bedroom now."

"Suppose he wakes and gets a panic, poor sweet."

"He won't. He'll see his precious goat and go to sleep again. What about you?"

"I'm practically snoring on my feet."

" 'Fizzily and 'motionly zausted'?"

"Did he say that?"

"Queer little bloke that he is, he did. Shall I stay with you, too, until you go to sleep?"

"But—what about you?"

"I'm going up to the factory. Dupont's still there and Raoul's hiring me his car."

"Rory, you can't. You must be dead."

"Not a bit of it. The night's young and it'll be tactful to show up. Besides I've got to make arrangements for tomorrow."

"I don't know how you do it."

"Of course you don't, my darling. You're not a cop."

She tried to protest but was so bemused with sleepiness that her voice trailed away as Ricky's had done. By the time Alleyn had washed and found himself an overcoat, Troy too was in bed and fast asleep. He turned off the lights and slipped out of the room.

Left to itself, the little silver goat glowed steadfastly through the night.

CHAPTER X

Thunder in the Air

Alleyn left word at the office that he might be late coming in and said that unless he himself rang up no telephone calls were to be put through to Troy. Anybody who rang was to be asked to leave a message. It was nine o'clock.

The porter opened the doors and Alleyn ran down the steps to Raoul's car. There was another car drawn up beside it, a long and stylish racing model with a G.B. plate. The driver leaned out and said cautiously: "Hallo, sir."

It was Robin Herrington.

"Hullo," Alleyn said.

"I'm on my way back actually, from Douceville. As a matter of fact I was just coming in on the chance of having a word with you," Herrington said rapidly, and in a muted voice. "I'm sorry you're going out. I mean, I don't suppose you could give me five minutes. Sorry not to get out, but as a matter of fact I sort of thought— It wouldn't take long. Perhaps I could drive you to wherever you're going and then I wouldn't waste your time. Sort of."

"Thank you, I've got a car but I'll give you five minutes with pleasure. Shall I join you?"

"Frightfully nice of you, sir. Yes, please do."

Alleyn walked round and climbed in.

"It won't take five minutes," Herrington said nervously and was then silent.

"How," Alleyn asked after waiting for some moments, "is Miss Truebody?"

Robin shuffled his feet. "Pretty bad," he said. "She was when I left. Pretty bad, actually."

Alleyn waited again and was suddenly offered a drink. His companion opened a door and a miniature cocktail cabinet lit itself up.

"No, thank you," Alleyn said. "What's up?"

"I will, if you don't mind. A very small one." He gave himself a tot of neat brandy and swallowed half of it. "It's about Ginny," he said.

"Oh!"

"As a matter of fact, I'm rather worried about her, which may sound a bit funny."

"Not very."

"Oh. Well, you see, she's so terrifyingly young, Ginny. She's only nineteen. And, as a matter of fact, I don't think this is a madly appropriate setting for her." Alleyn was silent and after a further pause Robin went on, "I don't know if you've any idea what sort of background Ginny's got. Her people were killed when she was a kid. In the blitz. She was trapped with them and hauled out somehow, which rocked her a good deal at the time and actually hasn't exactly worn off even now. She's rather been nobody's baby. Her guardian's a pretty odd old number. More interested in marmosets and miniatures than children, really. He's her great uncle."

"You don't mean Mr. Penderby Locke?" Alleyn said, recognizing this unusual combination of hobbies.

"Yes, that's right. He's quite famous on his own pitch, I understand, but he couldn't have been less interested in Ginny."

"Then—Miss Taylor is related to Miss Grizel Locke who, I think, is Penderby Locke's sister, isn't she?"

"Is she? I don't know. Yes, I think she must be," Robin said, shooting out the words quickly and hurrying on. "The thing is, Ginny just sort of grew up rather much under her own steam. She was sent to a French family and they weren't much cop, I gather, and then she came back to England and somebody brought her out and she got in with a pretty vivid set and had a miserable love affair with a poor type of chap and felt life wasn't as gay as it's cracked up to be. And this affair busted up when they were staying with some of his chums at Cannes and Ginny felt what was the good of anything anyway, and I must say I know what that's like."

"She arrived at this philosophy in Cannes?"

"Yes. And she met Baradi and Oberon there. And I was there too, as it happened," said Robin with a change of voice. "So we were both asked to come on here. About a fortnight ago."

"I see. And then?"

"Well, it's a dimmish sort of thing to talk about one's hosts, but I don't think it was a particularly good thing, her coming. I mean it's all right for oneself."

"Is it?"

"Well, I don't know. Just to do once and—and perhaps not do again. Quite amusing, really," said Robin miserably. "I mean, I'm not madly zealous about being a Child of the Sun. I just thought it might be fun. Of a sort. I mean, one knows one's way about."

"One would, I should think, need to."

"Ginny doesn't," Robin said.

"No?"

"She thinks she does, poor sweet, but actually she hasn't a clue when it comes to—well, to this sort of party, you know."

"What sort of party?"

Robin pushed his glass back and shut the cupboard with a bang. "You saw, didn't you, sir?"

"I believe Dr. Baradi is a very good surgeon. I only met the others for a few moments, you know."

"Yes, but—well, you know Annabella Wells, don't you? She said so."

"We crossed the Atlantic in the same ship. There were some five hundred other passengers."

"I'd have thought she'd have shown up if there'd been five million," Robin said with feeling. Alleyn glanced at his watch. "I'm sorry, I'm not exactly pressing ahead with this," Robin said.

"Don't you think you'd better tell me what you want me to do?"

"It sounds so odd. Mrs. Allen will think it such cheek."

"Troy? How can it concern her?"

"I—well, I was wondering if Mrs. Allen would ask Ginny to dinner tomorrow night."

"Why tomorrow night, particularly?"

Robin muttered: "There's going to be a sort of party up there. I'd rather Ginny was out of it."

"Would she be rather out of it?"

"Hell!" Robin shouted. "She would if she were herself. My God, she would!"

"And what exactly," Alleyn asked, "do you mean by that?"

Robin hit the wheel of his car with his clenched fist and said almost inaudibly: "He's got hold of her. Oberon. She thinks he's the bottom when she's not—it's just one of those bloody things."

"Well," Alleyn said, "we'd be delighted if Miss Taylor would dine with us but don't you think she'll find the invitation rather odd? After all, we've scarcely met her. She'll probably refuse."

"I'd thought of that," Robin said eagerly. "I know. But I thought if I could get her to come for a run in the car, I'd suggest we called on Mrs. Allen. Ginny liked Mrs. Allen awfully. And you, sir, if I may say so. Ginny's interested in art and all that and she was quite thrilled when she knew Mrs. Allen was Agatha Troy. So I thought if we might we could call about cocktail time and I'd say I'd got to go somewhere to see about something for the yacht or something and then I could ring up from somewhere and say I'd broken down."

"She would then take a taxi back to the Chèvre d'Argent."

Robin gulped. "Yes, I know," he said. "But—well, I thought perhaps by that time Mrs. Allen might have sort of talked to her and got her to see. Sort of."

"But why doesn't Miss Locke talk to her? Surely, as her aunt— What's the matter?"

Robin had made a violent ejaculation. He mumbled incoherently: "Not that sort. I've told you. They didn't care about Ginny."

Alleyn was silent for a minute.

"I know it's a hell of a lot to ask," Robin said desperately.

"I think it is," Alleyn said, "when you are so obviously leaving most of the facts out of your story."

"I don't know what you mean."

"You are asking us to behave in a difficult and extremely odd manner. You want us, in effect, to kidnap Miss Taylor. We have had," Alleyn said, "our bellyful of kidnapping, this afternoon. I suppose you heard about Ricky."

Robin made an inarticulate noise that sounded rather like a groan. "I know. Yes. We did hear. I'm awfully sorry. It must be terribly worrying."

"And how," Alleyn asked, "did you hear about it?" and would have given a good deal to have had a clear view of Robin's face.

"Well, I—well, we rang up the hotel this afternoon."

"I thought you said you had been to Douceville all the afternoon."

"Hell!"

"I think you must have known much earlier that Ricky was kidnapped, didn't you?"

"Look here, sir, I don't know what to say."

"I'll tell you. If you want me to help you with this child, Ginny, and I believe you do, you will answer, fully and truthfully, specific questions that I shall put to you. If you don't want to answer, we'll say good night and forget we had this conversation. But don't lie. I shall know," Alleyn said mildly, "if you lie."

Robin waited for a moment and then said: "Please go ahead."

"Right. What precisely do you expect to happen at this party?"

A car came down the square. Its headlights shone momentarily on Robin's face. It looked very young and frightened, like the face of a sixth-form boy in serious trouble with his tutor. The car turned and they were in the dark again.

Robin said: "It's a regular thing. They have it on Thursday nights. It's a sort of cult. They call it the Rites of the Children of the Sun in the Outer and Oberon's the sort of high priest. You have to swear not to talk about it. I've sworn. I can't talk. But it ends pretty hectically. And tomorrow Ginny— I've heard them—Ginny's cast for—the leading part."

"And beforehand?"

"Well—it's different from ordinary nights. There's no dinner. We go to our rooms until the Rites begin at eleven. We're meant not to speak to each other or anything."

"Do you not eat or drink?"

"Oh, there are drinks. And so on."

"What does 'so on' mean?" Robin was silent. "Do you take drugs? Reefers? Snow?"

"What makes you think that?"

"Come on. Which is it?"

"Reefers mostly. There's food when we smoke. There has to be. I don't know if they are the usual kind. Oberon doesn't smoke. I don't think Baradi does."

"Are they traffickers?"

"I don't know much about them."

"Do you know that much?"

"I should think they might be."

"Have they asked you to take a hand?"

"Look," Robin said, "I'm sorry but I've got to say it. I don't know much about you either, sir. I mean, I don't know that you won't—" He had turned his head and Alleyn knew he was peering at him.

"Inform the police?" Alleyn suggested.

"Well—you might."

"Come: you don't, as you say, know me. Yet you've elected to ask me to rescue this wretched child from the clutches of your friends. You can't have it both ways."

"You don't know," Robin said. "You don't know how tricky it all is. If they thought I'd talked to you!"

"What would they do?"

"Nothing!" Robin cried in a hurry. "Nothing! Only I've accepted, as one says, their hospitality."

"You *have* got your values muddled, haven't you?"

"Have I? I daresay I have."

"Tell me this. Has anything happened recently—I mean within the last twenty-four hours—to precipitate the situation?"

Robin said: "Who are you?"

"My dear chap, I don't need to be a thought-reader to see there's a certain urgency behind all this preamble."

"I suppose not. I'm sorry. I'm afraid I can't answer any more questions. Only—only, for God's sake, sir, will you do something about Ginny?"

"I'll make a bargain with you. I gather that you want to remove the child without giving a previous warning to the house party."

"That's it, sir. Yes."

"All right. *Can* you persuade her, in fact, to drive into Roqueville at six o'clock?"

"I don't know. I was gambling on it. If *he's* not about, I might. She—I think she is quite fond of me," Robin said humbly, "when he's not there to bitch it all up."

"Failing a drive, could you get her to walk down to the car park?"

"I might do that. She wants to buy one of old Marie's silver goats."

"Would it help to tell her we had rung up and asked if she would choose a set of the figures for Ricky? Aren't there groups of them for Christmas? Cribs?"

"That might work. She'd like to do that."

"All right. Have your car waiting and get her to walk on to the park. Suggest you drive down to our hotel with the figures."

"You know, sir, I believe that'd do it."

"Good. Having got her in the car it's up to you to keep her away from the Château. Take her to see Troy by all means. But I doubt if you'll get her to stay to dinner. You may have to stage a breakdown on a lonely road. I don't know. Use your initiative. Block up the air vent in your petrol cap. One thing more. Baradi, or someone, said something about a uniform of sorts that you all wear on occasion."

"That's right. It's called the mantle of the sun. We wear them about the house and—and always on Thursday nights."

"Is it the white thing Oberon had on this morning?"

"Yes. A sort of glorified monk's affair with a hood."

"Could you bring two of them with you?"

Robin turned his head and peered at Alleyn in astonishment. "I suppose I could."

"Put them in your car during the day."

"I don't see—"

"I'm sure you don't. Two of your own will do, if you have two. You needn't worry about bringing Miss Taylor's gown specifically."

"Hers!" Robin cried out. "Bring hers! But that's the whole thing! Tomorrow night they'll make Ginny wear the Black Robe."

"Then you must bring a black robe," Alleyn said.

ii

On Thursday evening the Côte d'Azur, inclined always to the theatrical, became melodramatic and, true to the weather report, staged a thunderstorm.

"It's going to rain," a voice croaked from the balustrade of the Chèvre d'Argent. "Listen! Thunder!"

Far to southward the heavens muttered an affirmative.

Carbury Glande looked at the brilliantly-clad figure perched, knees to chin, on the balustrade. It mingled with a hanging swag of bougainvillea. "One sees a voice rather than a person. You look like some fabulous bird, dear Sati," he said. "If I didn't feel so ghastly I'd like to paint you."

"Rumble, mumble, jumble and clatter," said the other, absorbed in de- lighted anticipation. "And then the rains. That's the way it goes." She pursed her lips out and, drawing in air with the smoke, took a long puff at an attenuated cigarette.

Baradi walked over to her and removed the cigarette. "Against the rules," he said. "Everything in its appointed time. You're over-excited." He threw the cigarette away and returned to his chair.

A whiteness flickered above the horizon and was followed after a pause by a tinny rattle.

"We do this sort of thing much better at the Comédie Française," Anna- bella Wells paraphrased, twisting her mouth in self-contempt.

Baradi leaned forward until his nose was placed in surrealistic association with her ear. Beneath the nose his moustache shifted as if it had a life of its own and beneath the moustache his lips pouted and writhed in almost soundless articulation. Annabella Wells's expression did not change. She nodded slightly. His face hung for a moment above her neck and then he leaned back in his chair.

Above the blacked Mediterranean the sky splintered with forked lightning.

"One. Two. Three. Four," the hoarse voice counted to an accompaniment of clapping hands. The other guests ejaculated under a canopy of thunder.

"You always have to count," the voice explained when it could be heard again.

"The thing I really hate," Ginny Taylor said rapidly, "is not the thunder or lightning but the pauses between bouts. Like this one."

"Come indoors," Robin Herrington said. "You don't have to stay out here."

"It's a kind of dare I have with myself."

"Learning to be brave?" Annabella Wells asked with a curious inflexion in her voice.

"Ginny will have the courage of a lioness," said Baradi, "and the fire of a phoenix."

Annabella got up with an abrupt expert movement and walked over to the balustrade. Baradi followed her. Ginny pushed her hair back from her forehead and looked quickly at Robin and away again. He moved nearer to her. She turned away to the far end of the roof-garden. Robin hovered uncertainly. The other four guests had drawn closer together. Carbury Glande half-closed his eyes and peered at the cloud-blocked sky and dismal sea. "Gloriously ominous," he said, "and quite unpaintable. Which is such a good thing."

The pause was not really one of silence. It was dramatized by minor noises, themselves uncannily portentous. Mr. Oberon's canary, for instance, hopped scratchily from cage-floor to perch and back again. A cicada had forgotten to stop chirruping in the motionless cactus slopes that Mr. Oberon called his *jardin exotique*. Down in the servants' quarters a woman laughed, and many kilometres away, towards Douceville, a train shrieked effeminately. Still, beside the threat of thunder, these desultory sounds added up to silence.

Glande, with an eye on Ginny, muttered: "I damned well think we need something. After all—" He swallowed. "After everything. It's nervy work waiting." His voice shot up into falsetto. "I don't pretend to be phlegmatic. I'm a bloody artist, I am."

Baradi said: "Keep your voice down. You certainly have a flair for the appropriate adjective," and laughed softly.

Glande fingered his lips and stared at Baradi. "How you can!" he whispered.

Annabella, looking out to sea, said: "Keep your hand to the plough, Carbury dear. You've put it there. No looking back."

"*I'm* on your side," announced the voice from the balustrade. "Look what I am doing for you all."

From her remote station Ginny said: "I can't stand this."

"Well, don't," Robin said quietly. "Old Marie asked me to tell you there's only one of the big silver goats left. Why not dodge down before the rain and get it? In the passage you won't see if there's lightning. Come on."

Ginny looked at Baradi. He caught her glance and walked across to her. "What is it?" he said.

"I thought I might go to old Marie's shop," Ginny said. "It's away from the storm."

"Why not?" he said. "What a good idea."

"I thought I might," Ginny repeated doubtfully.

For a split second lightning wrote itself across the sky in livid calligraphy. The voice on the balustrade had counted two when the heavens crashed together in a monstrous report. Ginny's mouth was wide open. She ran into the tower and Robin followed her.

The initial clap was succeeded by a prolonged rattle and an ambiguous omnipotent muttering. Above this rumpus Glande could be heard saying: "What I mean to say: do we know we can trust them? After all, they're comparative strangers and I must say I don't like the boy's manner."

Baradi, who was watching Annabella Wells, said: "There's no need to disturb yourself on their account. Robin is much too heavily involved and as for Ginny, can we not leave her safely to Ra? In any case, she knows nothing."

"The boy does. He might blurt out something to those other two—Troy and her bloody high-hat husband."

"If Mr. and Mrs. Allen should arrive there need be no meeting."

"How do you know they don't suspect something already?"

"I have told you. The girl Teresa reports that having recovered the boy, they have retired to their hotel in high glee."

"There was a bungle over the kid. There might be another bungle. Suppose Allen hangs about like he did last time asking damn-fool esoteric questions?"

"They were not as silly as you may think, my dear Carbury. The man is an intelligent man. He behaved intelligently during the operation. He would make a good anaesthetist."

"Well—there you are!"

"Please don't panic. He is both intelligent and inquisitive. That is why we thought it better to remove him, if possible, to St. Céleste, until the Truebody has been disposed of." Baradi's teeth gleamed under his moustache.

"I can see no cause for amusement."

"Can you not? You must cultivate a taste for irony. Annabella," Baradi continued, looking at her motionless figure against the steel-dark sky, "Annabella tells us that Mr. Allen, as far as she knows, is the person he appears to be: a dilettante with a taste for mysticism, curious literature and big-game hunting. The latter, I may add, in the generally accepted sense of the expression."

"Oh, for God's sake!" Glande cried out. The voice from the balustrade broke into undisciplined laughter. "Shut up!" he shouted. "Shut up, Sati! You of all people to laugh. It's so damned undignified. Remember who you are!"

"Yes, Grizel dear," Annabella Wells said, "pray do remember that."

It had grown so dark that the lightning darted white on their faces. They saw one another momentarily as if by a flash-lamp, each wearing a look of fixity. The thunder-clap followed at once. One might have imagined the heavens had burst outward like a gas-filled cylinder.

Mr. Oberon, wearing his hooded gown, stepped out of the tower door and contemplated his followers.

"*Cher maître*," shouted Baradi, waving his hand, "you come most carefully upon your hour. What an entrance! Superb!"

The volley rolled away into silence. Mr. Oberon moved forward and, really as if he had induced it, rain struck down in an abrupt deluge.

"You will get wet, dear Sati," said Mr. Oberon.

Glande said: "What's happened?"

They all drew near to Mr. Oberon. The rain made a frightful din, pelting like bullets on water and earth and stone and on the canvas awning above their heads. Landscape and seascape were alive with its noise. The four guests, with the anxious air of people who are hard-of-hearing, inclined their heads towards their host.

"What's happened?" Glande repeated, but with a subdued and more deferential manner.

"All is well. It is arranged for tomorrow afternoon. An Anglican ceremony," said Oberon, smiling slightly. "I have spoken to the—should I call him priest? I was obliged to call on him. The telephone is still out of order. He is a dull man but very obliging. A private funeral, of course."

"But the other business—the permit or whatever it is?"

"I've already explained," Baradi cut in irritably, "that my authority as a medical man is perfectly adequate. The appropriate official will be happy to receive me tomorrow when the necessary formalities will be completed."

"Poor old Truebody," said Annabella Wells.

"The name is, by the way, to be Halebory. Pronounced Harber. So English."

"They'll want to see the passport," Glande said instantly.

"They shall see it. It has received expert attention."

"Sati," said Mr. Oberon gently, "you have been smoking, I think."

"Dearest Ra, only the least puff."

"Yet, there is our rule. Not until tonight."

"I was upset. It's so difficult. Please forgive me. Please."

Mr. Oberon looked blankly at her. "You will go to your room and make an exercise. The exercise of the Name. You will light your candle and looking at the flame without blinking you will repeat one hundred times: 'I am Sati who am Grizel Locke!' Then you will remain without moving until it is time for the Rites. So."

She touched her forehead and lips and chest with a jerky movement of her hand and went at once.

"Where is Ginny?" Mr. Oberon asked.

"She was nervous," said Baradi. "The storm upset her. She went down to the shop where one buys those rather vulgar figurines."

"And Robin?"

"He went with her," said Annabella loudly.

Mr. Oberon's mouth parted to show his teeth. "She must rest," he said. "You are, of course, all very careful to say nothing of an agitating nature in front of her. She knows the lady has died as the result of a perforated appendix. Unfortunately it was unavoidable that she should be told so much. There must be no further disturbance. When she returns send her to her room. It is the time of meditation. She is to remain in her room until it is time for the Rites. There she will find the gift of enlightenment."

He moved to the tower door. The rain drummed on the awning above their heads but they heard him repeat: "She must rest," before he went indoors.

iii

Old Marie's shop was a cave sunk in the face of the hill and protected at its open end by the Chèvre d'Argent, which at this point straddled the passage. Ginny and Robin were thus hidden from the lightning and even the thunder sounded less formidable in there. The walls of the cave had been hewn out in shelves and on these stood Marie's figurines. She herself sat at a table over an oil lamp and wheezed out praises of her wares.

"She's got lots of goats," Ginny pointed out, speaking English.

"Cunning old cup-of-tea," Robin said. "Thought you needed gingering up, I suppose. By the way," he added, "Miss Troy or Mrs. Allen or whatever she should be called, wanted a set of nativity figures—don't you call it a crib? —for the little boy. Marie wasn't here when they left yesterday. I promised I'd get one and take it down this afternoon. How awful! I entirely forgot."

"Robin! How could you! And they'll want it more than ever after losing him like that."

"She thought perhaps you wouldn't mind choosing one."

"Of course I will," Ginny said, and began to inspect the groups of naïve little figures. Old Marie shouted: "Look, Mademoiselle, the Holy Child illuminates himself. And the beasts! One would say the she-ass almost burst herself with good milk. And the lamb is infinitely touching. And the ridiculous price! I cannot bring myself to charge more. It is an act of piety on my part."

Robin bought a large silver goat and Ginny bought the grandest of the cribs. "Let's take it down now," he said. "The storm's nearly over, I'm sure, and the car's out. It'd save my conscience. Do come, Ginny."

She raised her troubled face and looked at him. "I don't know," she said, "I suppose—I don't know."

"We shan't be half-an-hour. Come on."

He took her by the arm and hurried her into the passage-way. They ran into a world of rain, Ginny protesting and Robin shouting encouragement. With the help of his stick he broke into quite a lively sort of canter. "Do be careful!" Ginny cried. "Your dot-and-go-one leg!"

"Dot-and-go-run, you mean. Come on."

Their faces streamed with cool water and they laughed without cause. "It's better out here," Robin said. "Isn't it, Ginny?"

The car stood out on the platform like a rock in a waterfall. He bundled her into it. "You look like—you look as you're meant to look," he said. "It's better outside. Say it's better, Ginny."

"I don't know what's come over you," Ginny said, pressing her hands to her rain-blinded face.

"I've got out. We've both got out." He scrambled in beside her and peered into the trough behind the driver's seat. "What are you doing?" Ginny asked hysterically. "What's happened? We've gone mad. What are you looking for?"

"Nothing. A parcel for my tailor. It's gone. Who cares! Away we go."

He started up his engine. Water splashed up like wings on either side and cascaded across the windscreen. They roared down the steep incline and turned left above the tunnel and over the high headland, on the road to Roqueville.

High up in the hills on their vantage point in the factory road, Alleyn and Raoul waited in Raoul's car.

"In five minutes," Alleyn said, "it will be dark."

"I shall still know the car, Monsieur."

"And I. The rain's lifting a little."

"It will stop before the light goes, I think."

"How tall are you, Raoul?"

"One mètre, sixty, Monsieur."

"About five foot eight," Alleyn muttered, "and the girl's tall. It ought to be all right. Where was the car exactly?"

"Standing out on the platform, Monsieur. The parcel was in the trough behind the driver's seat."

"He's stuck to his word so far, at least. Where did you put the note?"

"On the driver's seat, Monsieur. He could not fail to see it."

But Robin, driving in a state of strange exhilaration towards Roqueville, sat on the disregarded note and wondered if it was by accident or intention that Ginny leaned a little towards him.

"It will be fine on the other side of the hill," he shouted. "What do you bet?"

"It couldn't be."

"You'll see. You'll see. You'll jolly well see."

"Robin, what *has* come over you?"

"I'll tell you when we get to Roqueville. There you are! What did I say?"

They drove down the mountain-side into a translucent dusk, rain-washed and fragrant.

"There they go," Alleyn said and turned his field glasses on the tiny car. "She's with him. He's brought it off. So far."

"And now, Monsieur?"

Alleyn watched the car diminish. Just before it turned the point of a distant headland, Robin switched on his lamps. Alleyn lowered the glasses. "It is almost lighting-up time, Raoul. We wait a little longer." They turned as if by a shared consent and looked to the west where, above and beyond the tunnelled hill, the turrets of the Chèvre d'Argent stood black against a darkling sky.

Presently, out on Cap St. Gilles pricks of yellow began to appear. The window of a cottage in the valley showed red. Behind them the factory presented a dark front to the dusk, but higher up in its folded hills the monastery of Our Lady of Paysdoux was alive with glowing lights.

"They are late with their lamps at the Chèvre d'Argent," said Raoul.

"Which is not surprising," Alleyn rejoined. "Seeing that Monsieur le Commissaire has arranged that their electrical service is disconnected. The thunderstorm will have lent a happy note of credibility to the occurrence. The telephone also is still disconnected." He used his field glasses. "Yes," he said, "they are lighting candles. Start up your engine, Raoul. It is time to be off."

iv

"You disturb yourself without cause," Baradi said, "she is buying herself a silver goat. Why not? It is a good omen."

"Already she's been away half-an-hour."

"She has gone for a walk, no doubt."

"With him."

"Again, why not? The infatuation is entirely on one side. Let it alone."

"I am unusually interested and therefore nervous," said Mr. Oberon. "It means more to me, this time, than ever before and besides the whole circumstance is extraordinary. The mystic association. The blood-sacrifice and then, while the victim is still here, the other, the living sacrifice. It is unique."

Baradi looked at him with curiosity. "Tell me," he said, "How much of all this"—he made a comprehensive gesture—"means anything to you? I mean I can understand the, what shall I call it, the factual pleasure. That is a great deal. I envy you your flair. But the esoteric window-dressing—is it possible that for you—?" He paused. Mr. Oberon's face was as empty as a mask. He touched his lips with the tip of his tongue.

He said: "Wherein, if not in my belief, do you suppose the secret of my flair is to be found? I am what I am and I go back to beyond the dawn. I was the King of the Wood."

Baradi examined his own shapely hands. "Ah, yes?" he said politely. "A fascinating theory."

"You think me a poseur?"

"No, no. On the contrary. It is only as a practical man I am concerned with the hazards of the situation. You, I gather, though you have every cause, are not at all anxious on that account? The Truebody situation, I mean?"

"I find it immeasurably stimulating."

"Indeed," said Baradi drily.

"Only the absence of the girl disturbs me. It is almost dark. Turn on the light."

Baradi reached out his hand to the switch. There was a click.

"No lights, it seems," he said and opened the door. "No lights anywhere. There must be a fuse."

"How can she be walking in the dark? And with a cripple like Robin? It is preposterous."

"The British do these things."

"I am British. I have my passport. Telephone the bureau in Roqueville."

"The telephone is still out of order."

"We must have light."

"It may be a fault in the house. The servants will attend to it. One moment."

He lifted the receiver from Mr. Oberon's telephone. A voice answered.

"What is the matter with the lights?" Baradi asked.

"We cannot make out, Monsieur. There is no fault here. Perhaps the storm has brought down the lines."

"Nothing but trouble. And the telephone? Can one telephone yet to Roqueville?"

"No, Monsieur. The centrale sent up a man. The fault is not in the Château. They are investigating. They will ring through when the line is clear."

"Since yesterday afternoon we have been without the telephone. Unparalleled incompetence!" Baradi ejaculated. "Have Mr. Herrington and Mlle. Taylor returned?"

"I will enquire, Monsieur."

"Do so, and ring Mr. Oberon's apartments if they are in."

He clapped down the receiver. "I am uneasy," he said. "It has happened at a most tiresome moment. We have only the girl Teresa's account of the affair at the factory. No doubt she is speaking the truth. Having found the boy, they are satisfied. All the same it is not too amusing, having had the police in the factory."

"Callard will have handled them with discretion."

"No doubt. The driver, Georges Martel, however, will be examined by the police."

"Can he be trusted?"

"He has too much at stake to be anything but dependable. We pay him very highly. Also he has his story. He was rung up by an unknown client purporting to be the boy's father. He took the job in good faith and merely asked the girl Teresa to accompany him. They know nothing. The police will at once suspect the former kidnappers. Nevertheless, I wish we had not attempted the affair with the boy."

"One wanted to rid oneself of the parents."

"Exactly. Of the father. If the circumstances were different," Baradi said softly, "I should not be nearly so interested in ridding myself of Mama. Women!" he ejaculated sententiously.

"Women!" Mr. Oberon echoed with an inexplicable laugh and added immediately: "All the same I am getting abominably anxious. I don't trust him. And then, the light! Suppose it doesn't come on again before the Rites. How shall we manage?"

"Something can be done with car batteries, I think, and a soldering iron. Mahomet is ingenious in such matters. I shall speak to him in a moment."

Baradi walked over to the window and pulled back the silk blind. "It is quite dark." The blind shot up with a whirr and click. "It really is much too quick on the trigger," he observed.

Mr. Oberon said loudly: "Don't do that! You exacerbate my nerves. Pull it down. Tie it down." And while Baradi busied himself with the blind he added: "I shall send out. My temper is rising and that is dangerous. I must not become angry. If his car has gone I shall send after it."

"I strongly suggest you do nothing of the sort. It would be an unnecessary and foolish move. She will return. Surely you have not lost your flair."

Mr. Oberon, in the darkness, said: "You are right. She will return. She must."

"As for your rising temper," said Baradi, "you had better subdue it. It is dangerous."

CHAPTER XI

P. E. Garbel

Raoul slowed down at a point above the entrance to the tunnel.

"Where should we leave the car, Monsieur?"

"There's a recess off the road, on the far side, near the tunnel and well under the lee of the hill. Pull in there."

The silhouette of the Chèvre d'Argent showed black above the hills against a clearing but still stormy sky. A wind had risen and cloud-rack scurried across a brilliant display of stars.

"Gothic in spirit," Alleyn muttered, "if not in design."

The road turned the headland. Raoul dropped to a crawl and switched off his lights. Alleyn used a pocket torch. When they came down to the level of the tunnel exit he got out and guided Raoul into a recess hard by the stone facing.

Raoul dragged out a marketing basket from which the intermingled smells of cabbage, garlic and flowers rose incongruously on the rain-sweetened air.

"Have you hidden the cloaks underneath?" Alleyn asked him.

"Yes, Monsieur. It was an excellent notion. It is not unusual for me to present myself with such gear. The aunt of Teresa is a market-gardener."

"Good. We'll smell like two helpings of a particularly exotic soup."

"Monsieur?"

"No matter. Now, Raoul, to make certain we understand each other will you repeat the instructions?"

"Very well, Monsieur. We go together to the servants' entrance. If, by mischance, we encounter anybody on the way who recognizes Monsieur, Monsieur will at once say he has come to enquire for the sick Mademoiselle. I will continue on and will wait for Monsieur at the servants' entrance. If Monsieur, on arriving there, is recognized by one of the servants who may not yet have left, he will say he has been waiting for me and is angry. He will say he wishes to speak to Teresa about the stealing of Riki. If, on the other hand, all goes well and we reach the servants' quarters together and unchallenged, we go at once to Teresa's room. Monsieur is seen but not recognized, he is introduced as the intellectual cousin of Teresa who has been to England, working in a bank, and has greatly improved his social status, and again we retire quickly to Teresa's room before the Egyptian valet or the butler can encounter Monsieur. In either case, Teresa is to give a message saying it has come by a peasant on a bicycle. It is to say that Mr. Herrington's car has broken down but that Miss Taylor and he will arrive in time for the party. Finally, if Monsieur does not come at all, I wait an hour then go to seek for him."

"And if something we have not in the least anticipated turns up?"

Raoul laughed softly in the dark: "One must then use one's wits, Monsieur."

"Good, shall we start?"

They walked together up the steep incline to the platform.

A goods train came puffing up from Douceville. The glow from the engine slid across the lower walls and bastions of the Chèvre d'Argent. Behind the silk blind a dim light burned: a much fainter light than the one they had seen from the window of their own train. Higher up, at odd intervals in that vast façade, other windows glowed or flickered where candles had been placed or were carried from one room to another.

The train tooted and clanked into the tunnel.

It was quite cold on the platform. A mountain breeze cut across it and lent credibility to the turned-up collar of Alleyn's raincoat and the scarf across his mouth. The passage was almost pitch dark but they thought it better not to use a torch. They slipped and stumbled on wet and uneven steps. The glow from old Marie's door was a guide. As they passed by she shouted from behind the oil-lamp: "Hola, there! Is it still raining?"

Raoul said quietly: "The stars are out. Good night, Marie," and they hurried into the shadows. They heard her shouting jovially after them: "Give her something to keep out the cold."

"She speaks of Teresa," Raoul whispered primly. "There is a hint of vulgarity in Marie."

Alleyn stifled a laugh. They groped their way round a bend in the passage, brushing their hands against damp stone. Presently an elegant design of interlaced rosettes appeared against a background of reflected warmth. It was the wrought-iron gate of the Chèvre d'Argent.

"As quick as we dare," Alleyn whispered.

The passage glinted wet before the doorway. The soles of his shoes were like glass. He poised himself and moved lightly forward. As he entered the patch of light he heard a slither and an oath. Raoul hurtled against him, throwing him off his balance. He clung to the gate while Raoul, in a wild attempt to recover himself, clutched at the nearest object.

It was the iron bell-pull.

The bell gave tongue with a violence that was refracted intolerably by the stone walls.

Three cabbages rolled down the steps. Raoul by some desperate effort still clung to the basket with one hand and to the bell-pull with the other.

"Monsieur! Monsieur!" he stammered.

"Go on," Alleyn said. "*Go on!*"

Raoul let go the bell-pull and a single note fell inconsequently across the still-echoing clangour. He plunged forward and was lost in shadow.

Alleyn turned to face the door.

"Why, if it's not Mr. Allen!" said Mr. Oberon.

ii

He stood on the far side of the door with his back to a lighted candelabrum that had been set down on a chest in the entry. Little could be seen of him but his shape, enveloped in his white gown with the hood drawn over his head. He moved towards the door and his hands emerged and grasped two of the iron bars.

Alleyn said: "I'm afraid we made an appalling din. My chauffeur slipped and grabbed your bell-pull."

"Your chauffeur?"

"He's taken himself off. I fancy he knows one of your maids. He had some message for her, it seems."

Mr. Oberon said, as if to explain his presence at the door: "I am waiting for someone. Have you seen—" He paused and shifted his hands on the bars. His voice sounded out of focus. "Perhaps you met Ginny. Ginny Taylor? And Robin Herrington? We are a little anxious about them."

"No," Alleyn said. "I didn't see them. I came to ask about Miss Truebody."

Mr. Oberon didn't move. Alleyn peered at him. "How is she?" he asked.

Mr. Oberon said abruptly: "Our telephone has been out of order since yesterday afternoon. Do forgive me. I am a little anxious, you know."

"How is Miss Truebody?"

"Alas, she is dead," said Mr. Oberon.

They faced each other like actors in some medieval prison scene. The shadow of twisted iron was thrown across Alleyn's face and chest.

"Perhaps," Alleyn said, "I may come in for a moment."

"But, of course. How dreadful of me! We are all so distressed. Mahomet!"

Evidently the Egyptian servant had been waiting in the main hall. He unlocked the door, opened and stood aside. When Alleyn had come in he relocked the door.

With the air of having arrived at a decision, Mr. Oberon led the way into the great hall. Mahomet came behind them bringing the candelabrum, which he set down on a distant table. In that vast interior it served rather to emphasize the dark than relieve it.

"Monsieur," said Mahomet in French, "may I speak?"

"Well?"

"There is a message brought by a peasant from Mr. Herrington. He has had trouble with his auto. He is getting a taxi. He and Mlle. Taylor will arrive in time for the ceremony."

"Ah!" It was a long-drawn-out sigh. "Who took the message?"

"The girl Teresa, who was on her way to catch the omnibus. The peasant would not wait so the girl returned with the message. Miss Taylor also sent

THREE-ACT SPECIAL

a message. It was that Monsieur must not trouble himself. She will not fail the ceremony. She will go immediately to her room."

"Is all prepared?"

"All is prepared, Monsieur."

Mr. Oberon raised his hand in dismissal. Mahomet moved away into the shadows. Alleyn listened for the rattle of curtain rings but there was no other sound than that of Mr. Oberon's uneven breathing. "Forgive me again," he said, coming closer to Alleyn. "As you heard it was news of our young people."

"I'm afraid my French is too rudimentary for anything but the most childish phrases."

"Indeed? It appears they have had a breakdown but all is now well."

Alleyn said: "When did Miss Truebody die?"

"Ah, yes. We are so sorry. Yesterday afternoon. We tried to get you at the hotel, of course, but were told that you had gone to St. Céleste for a few days."

"We changed our plans," Alleyn said. "May I speak to Dr. Baradi?"

"To Ali? I am not sure—I will enquire—Mahomet!"

"Monsieur?" said a voice in the shadows.

"Tell your master that the English visitor is here. Tell him the visitor knows that his compatriot has left us."

"Monsieur."

The curtain rings jangled together.

"He will see if our friend is at home."

"I feel," Alleyn said, "that I should do everything that can be done. In a way she is our responsibility."

"That is quite wonderful of you, Mr. Allen," said Mr. Oberon, who seemed to have made a return to his normal form. "But I already sensed in you a rare and beautiful spirit. Still, you need not distress yourself. We felt it our privilege to speed this soul to its new life. The interment is tomorrow at three o'clock. Anglican. I shall, however, conduct a little valedictory ceremony here."

The curtain rings clashed again. Alleyn saw a large whiteness move towards them.

"Mr. Allen?" said Baradi, looming up on the far side of the candelabrum. He wore a white robe and his face was a blackness within the hood. "I am so glad you've come. We were puzzled what to do when we heard you had gone to St. Céleste."

"Fortunately there was no occasion. We ran Ricky to earth, I'm glad to say."

They both made enthusiastic noises. They were rejoiced. An atrocious affair. Where had he been found?

"In the chemical factory, of all places," Alleyn said. "The police think the kidnappers must have got cold feet and dumped him there." He al-

SPINSTERS IN JEOPARDY

lowed their ejaculations a decent margin and then said: "About poor Miss Truebody—"

"Yes about her," Baradi began crisply. "I'm sorry it happened as it did. I can assure you that it would have made no difference if there had been a hospital with an entire corps of trained nurses and surgeons. And certainly, may I add, she could not have had a more efficient anaesthetist. But, as you know, peritonitis was greatly advanced. Her condition steadily deteriorated. The heart, by the way, was not in good trim. Valvular trouble. She died at 4:28 yesterday afternoon without recovering consciousness. We found her address in her passport. I have made a report which I shall send to the suitable authorities in the Bermudas. Her effects, of course, will be returned to her home there. I understand there are no near relatives. I have completed the necessary formalities here. I should have preferred, under the circumstances, to have asked a brother medico look at her, but it appears they are all in conclave at St. Christophe."

"I expect I should write to—well, to somebody."

"By all means. Enclose a letter with my report. The authorities in the Bermudas will see that it reaches the lawyer or whoever is in charge of her affairs."

"I think perhaps—one has a feeling of responsibility—I think perhaps I should see her."

There was an infinitesimal pause.

"Of course," Baradi said. "If you wish, of course, I must warn you that the climatic conditions and those of her illness and death have considerably accelerated the usual post-mortem changes."

"We have done what we could," Mr. Oberon said. "Tuberoses and orchids."

"How very kind. If it's not troubling you too much."

There was a further slight pause. Baradi said: "Of course," again and clapped his hands. "No electricity," he explained. "So provoking." The servant reappeared, carrying a single candle. Baradi spoke to him in their own language and took the candle from him. "I'll go with you," he said. "We have moved her into a room outside the main part of the Château. It is quite suitable and cooler."

With this grisly little announcement he led Alleyn down the now familiar corridor past the operating room and into a much narrower side-passage that ended in a flight of descending steps and a door. This, in turn, opened on a further reach of the outside passage-way. The night air smelled freshly after the incense-tainted house. They turned left and walked a short distance down the uneven steps. Alleyn thought that they could not be far from the servants' entrance.

Baradi stopped at a deeply recessed doorway and asked Alleyn to hold the candle. Alleyn produced his torch and switched it on. It shone into Baradi's face.

"Ah!" he said, blinking, "that will be better. Thank you." He set down the candle. It flickered and guttered in the draught. He thrust his hand under his gown and produced a heavily furnished key-ring that might have hung from the girdle of a medieval gaoler. Alleyn turned his light on it and Baradi selected a great key with a wrought-iron loop. He stooped to fit it in a key-hole placed low in the door. His wide sleeves drooped from his arms, his hood fell over his face, and his shadow, grotesque and distorted, sprawled down the steps beyond him.

"If you would lend me your torch," he said. "It is a little awkward, this lock."

Alleyn gave him his torch. The shadow darted across the passage and reared itself up the opposite wall. After some fumbling, the key was engaged and noisily turned. Baradi shoved at the door and with a grind of its hinges it opened suddenly inwards and he fell forward with it, dropping the torch, nose first, on the stone threshold. There was a tinkle of glass and they were left with the guttering candle.

"*Ah, sacré nom d'un chien!*" Baradi ejaculated. "My dear Mr. Allen, what have I done!"

Alleyn said: "Be careful of the broken glass."

"I am wearing sandals. But how careless! I am so sorry."

"Never mind. The passage seems to be unlucky for us this evening. Let's hope there's not a third mishap. Don't give it another thought. Shall we go in?" Alleyn laid down his walking stick and took up the candle and the broken torch. They went in, Baradi shutting the door with a heave and a weighty slam.

It seemed to be a small room with white-washed stone walls and a shuttered window. Candlelight wavered over a bank of flowers. A coffin stood in the middle on trestles. The mingled odours of death and tuberoses were horrible.

"I hope you are not over-sensitive," Baradi said. "We have done our best. Mr. Oberon was most particular, but—well—as you see—"

Alleyn saw. The lid of the coffin had been left far enough withdrawn to expose the head of its inhabitant, which was literally bedded in orchids. A white veil of coarse net lay over the face, but it did little to soften the inexorable indignities of death.

"The teeth," said Baradi, "make a difference, don't they?"

Looking at them Alleyn was reminded of Teresa's generality to the effect that all English spinsters have teeth like mares. This lonely spinster's dentist had evidently subscribed to Teresa's opinion and Alleyn saw the other stigmata of her kind: the small mole, the lines and pouches, the pathetic tufts of grey hair from which the skin had receded.

He backed away. "I thought it better to see her," he said, and his voice was constrained and thin. "In case there should be any question of identification."

"Much better. Are you all right? For the layman it is not a pleasant experience."

Alleyn said: "I find it quite appalling. Shall we go? I'm afraid I—" His voice faded. He turned away with a violent movement and at the same time jerked his handkerchief. It flapped across the candle flame and extinguished it.

In the malodorous dark Baradi cursed unintelligibly. Alleyn gabbled: "The door, for God's sake, where is the door? I'm going to be sick." He lurched against Baradi and sent him staggering to the far end of the room. He drop-kicked the candlestick in the opposite direction. His hands were on the coffin. His left hand discovered the edge of the lid, slid under it, explored a soft material, a tight band and the surface beneath. His fingers, inquisitive and thrusting, found what they sought.

"I can't stand this!" he choked out. "The door!"

Baradi was now swearing in French. "Idiot!" he was saying. "*Maladroit, imbécile!*"

Alleyn made retching noises. He found his way unerringly to the door and dragged it open. A pale lessening of the dark was admitted. He staggered out into the passage-way and rested against the stone wall. Baradi came after him and dragged the door shut. Alleyn heard him turn the key in the lock.

"That was not an amusing interlude," Baradi said. "I warned you it would not be pleasant."

Alleyn had his handkerchief pressed to his mouth. He said indistinctly: "I'm sorry. I didn't realize—I'll be all right."

"Of course you will," Baradi snapped at him. "So shall I when my bruises wear off."

"Please don't let me keep you. Fresh air. I'll go back to the car. Thank you: I'm sorry."

Apparently Baradi had regained his temper. He said: "It is undoubtedly the best thing you can do. I recommend a hot bath, a stiff drink, two aspirins and bed. If you're sure you're all right and can find your way back—"

"Yes, yes. It's passing off."

"Then if you will excuse me. I am already late. Good night, Mr. Allen."

Alleyn, over his handkerchief, watched Baradi return up the steps, open the side-door and disappear into the house. He waited for some minutes, accustoming his eyes to the night.

"Somehow," he thought, "I must get a wash," and he wiped his left hand vigorously on his handkerchief which he then threw into the shadows.

But he did not wipe away the memory of a not very large cavity under the left breast of a sprigged locknit nightgown.

iii

He had been right about the nearness of the servants' entrance. The stone passage-way dipped, turned and came to an end by a sort of open pent-house. Alleyn had to grope his way down steps, but the non-darkness that is star-

light had filtered into the purlieus of the Chèvre d'Argent and glistened
faintly on ledges and wet stone. He paused for a moment and looked back
and upwards. The great mass of stone and rock made a black hole in the
spangled heavens. The passage-way had emerged from beneath a bridge-
like extension of the house. This linked the seaward portion with what he
imagined must be the original fortress, deep inside the cliff-face. Alleyn
moved into an inky-dark recess. A light had appeared on the bridge.

It was carried by the Egyptian servant, who appeared to have something
else, possibly a tray, in his hand. He was followed by Baradi. Unmistakably
it was Baradi. The servant turned and his torchlight flickered across the
dark face. The doctor no longer wore his robe. Something that looked like a
smooth cord hung round his neck. They moved on and were lost inside
the house. Alleyn gave a little grunt of satisfaction and continued on his
way.

A lantern with a stub of candle in it hung by a half-open door and threw
a yellow pool on the flat surface beneath.

"Monsieur?" a voice whispered.

"Raoul?"

"Oui, Monsieur. Tout va bien. Allons."

Raoul slid out of the pent-house. Alleyn's wrist was grasped. He moved
into the pool of light. Raoul pushed the door open with his foot. They
entered a stone corridor, passed two closed doors and turned right. Raoul
tapped with his finger-tips on a third door. Teresa opened it and admitted
them.

It was a small neat bedroom, smelling a little fusty. One of old Marie's
Madonnas, neatly inscribed: "Notre Dame de Paysdoux" stood on a corner
shelf with a stool before it. Dusty paper flowers, candles and a photograph
of Teresa in her confirmation dress, with folded hands and upturned eyes,
completed the décor. A sacred print, looking dreadfully like Mr. Oberon,
hung nearby. Across the bed were disposed two white gowns. A washstand
with a jug and basin stood in a further corner.

Teresa, looking both nervous and complacent, pushed forward her only
chair.

Alleyn said: "Is it possible to wash one's hands, Teresa? A little water and
some soap?"

"I will slip out for some warm water, Monsieur. It is quite safe to do so.
Monsieur will forgive me. I had forgotten. The English always wish to wash
themselves."

Alleyn did not correct this aphorism. When she had gone he said: "Well,
Raoul?"

"The servants have gone out, Monsieur, with the exception of the Egyptian, who is occupied downstairs. The guests are in their rooms. It is unlikely that they will emerge before the ceremony." He extended his hands,
palms upwards. "Monsieur, how much mischief have I made by my
imbecility?"

Alleyn said: "Well, Raoul, you certainly rang the bell," and then seeing his companion's bewilderment and distress, added: "It was not so bad after all. It worked out rather well. Dr. Baradi and I have visited the body of a murdered woman."

"Indeed, Monsieur?"

"It lies among orchids in a handsome coffin in a room across the passage of entrance. The coffin, as M. le Commissaire had already ascertained, arrived this morning from an undertaker in Roqueville."

"But Monsieur—"

"There is a wound, covered by a surgical dressing, under the left breast."

"Teresa has told me that the English lady died."

"Here *is* Teresa," Alleyn said and held up his hand.

While he washed he questioned Teresa about Miss Truebody.

"Teresa, in what room of the house did the English lady die? Was it where we put her after the operation?"

"No, Monsieur. She was moved at once from there. The Egyptian and the porter carried her to a room upstairs in the Saracen's watch-tower. It is not often used. She was taken there because it would be quieter, Monsieur."

"I'll be bound she was," Alleyn muttered. He dried his hands and began to outline a further plan of action. "Last night," he said, "I learned from Mr. Herrington a little more than Teresa perhaps may know, of the normal procedure on Thursday nights. At eleven o'clock a bell is rung. The guests then emerge from their rooms wearing their robes which have been laid out for them. They go in silence to the ceremony known as the Rites of the Children of the Sun. First they enter the small ante-room where each takes up a lighted candle. They then go into the main room and stay there until after midnight. Supper is served in Mr. Oberon's salon. The whole affair may go on, after a fashion, until five o'clock in the morning."

Teresa drew in her breath with an excited hiss.

"Now it is my intention to witness this affair. To that end I propose that you, Raoul, and I replace Miss Taylor and Mr. Herrington, who will not be there. Electricity will not be restored in the Château tonight and by candle-light we have at least a chance of remaining unrecognized."

Teresa made a little gesture. "If Monsieur pleases," she said.

"Well, Teresa?"

"The Egyptian has brought in iron boxes from Mr. Oberon's auto and a great deal of electrical cord and a soldering iron; he has arranged that the sun lamp in the room of ceremonies shall be lighted."

"Indeed? How very ingenious of him."

"Monsieur," Raoul said, eyeing the gowns on the bed, "is it your intention that I make myself to pass for a lady?"

Teresa cackled and clapped her hand over her mouth.

"Exactly so," said Alleyn. "You are about the same height as Miss Taylor. In the black gown with the hood drawn over your face and your hands—by the way, you too must wash your hands—hidden in the sleeves, you should, with luck, pass muster. You have small feet. Perhaps you may be able to wear Miss Taylor's slippers."

"*Ah, mon Dieu, quelle blague!*"

"Comport yourself with propriety, Teresa, Monsieur is speaking."

"If you cannot manage this I have bought a pair of black slippers which will have to do instead."

"And my costume, Monsieur?" Raoul asked, indicating with an expressive gesture his stained singlet, his greenish black trousers and his mackintosh hitched over his shoulders.

"I understand that, apart from the gown and slippers there is no costume at all."

"*Ah, mon Dieu, en voilà une affaire!*"

"*Teresa! Attention!*"

"However, the gown is voluminous. For propriety's sake, Raoul, you may retain your vest and underpants. In any case you must be careful to conceal your legs which, no doubt, are unmistakably masculine."

"They are superb," said Teresa. "But undoubtedly masculine."

"It seems to me," continued Alleyn, who had become quite used to the peculiarities of conversation with Raoul and Teresa, "that our first difficulty is the problem of getting from here to the respective rooms of Mr. Herrington and Miss Taylor. Teresa, I see, has brought two white gowns. Mr. Herrington has provided us with a white and a black one. Miss Taylor would have appeared in black tonight. Therefore, you must put on the black, Raoul, and I shall wear the longest of the white. Teresa must tell us where these rooms are. If the Egyptian or any of the guests should see us on our way to them we must hope they will observe the rule of silence which is enforced before the ceremony and pay no attention. It will be best if we can find our way without candles. Once inside our rooms we remain there until we hear the bell. How close, Teresa, are these rooms to the room where the ceremony is held? The room you described to me yesterday."

"The young lady's is nearby, Monsieur. It is therefore close also to the apartment of Mr. Oberon."

"In that case, Raoul, when you hear the bell, go at once to the ante-room. Take a candle and, by the communicating door, go into the ceremonial room. There will be five or six black cushions on the floor and a large black divan. If there are six cushions, yours will be apart from the others. If there are five, your position will be on the divan. I am only guessing at this. One thing I do know—the rule of silence will be observed until the actual ceremony begins. If you are in the wrong position it will be attributed, with luck, to stage-fright and somebody will put you right. Where is Mr. Herrington's room, Teresa?"

"It is off the landing, Monsieur, going down to the lower storey where the ceremonies are held."

"And the other guests'?"

"They are in the higher parts of the Château, Monsieur. Across the outside passage and beyond it."

"Do you know the room of Miss Grizel Locke?"

"Yes, Monsieur."

"Have you seen her today?"

"Not since two days ago, Monsieur, but that is not unusual. As I have informed Monsieur, it is the lady's habit to keep to her room and leave a notice that she must not be disturbed."

"I see. Now, if I leave Mr. Herrington's room on the first stroke of the bell, I should arrive hard on your heels, Raoul, and in advance of the others. I may even go in a little earlier." He looked at his watch. "It is half-past seven. Let us put on our gowns. Then, Teresa, you must go out and, if possible, discover the whereabouts of the Egyptian."

"Monsieur, he was summoned by M. Baradi before you came in. I heard him speaking on the house telephone."

"Let us hope the doctor keeps his man with him for some time. Now then, Raoul. On with the motley!"

The gowns proved to be amply made, wrapping across under their girdles. The hoods would come well forward and, when the head was bent, completely exclude any normal lighting from the face. "But it will be a different story if one holds a lighted candle," Alleyn said. "We must not be seen with our candles in our hands."

He had bought for Raoul a pair of feminine sandals, black and elegant with highish heels. Raoul said he thought they would fit admirably. With a grimace of humorous resignation he washed his small, beautiful and very dirty feet and then fitted them into the sandals. "Oh, là, là!" he said, "one must be an acrobat, it appears." And for the diversion of Teresa he minced to and fro, wagging his hips and making unseemly gestures. Teresa crammed her fists in her mouth and was consumed with merriment. "Ah, mon Dieu," she gasped punctually, "quel drôle de type!"

Alleyn wondered rather desperately if he was dealing with children or merely with the celebrated latin joie de vivre. He called them to order and they were at once as solemn as owls.

"Teresa," he said, "you will go a little ahead of us with your candle. Go straight through the house and down the stairs to the landing beneath the library. If you see anybody, blow your nose loudly."

"Have you a handkerchief, my jewel?"

"No."

"Accept mine," said Raoul, offering her a dubious rag.

"If anybody speaks to you and, perhaps, asks you why you are still on the premises, say that you missed your bus because of the message about Miss Taylor. If it is necessary, you must say you are going to her room to do some little act of service that you had forgotten and that then you will leave to catch the later bus. If it is possible, in this event, Raoul and I will conceal ourselves until the coast is clear. If this is not possible, we will behave as Mr. Herrington and Miss Taylor would behave under the rule of silence. You will continue to Miss Taylor's room, open the door for Raoul and go in for a moment, but only for a moment. Then, Teresa, I have another task for you," continued Alleyn, feeling for the second time in two days that he had become as big a bore as Prospero. Teresa, however, was a complacent Ariel and merely gazed submissively upon him.

"You will find Mr. Oberon and will tell him that Miss Taylor has returned and asks to be allowed her private meditation alone in her room until the ceremony. That is very important."

"Ah, Monsieur, if he were not so troubling to my soul!"

"If you value my esteem, Teresa—" Raoul began.

"Yes, yes, Monsieur," said Teresa in a hurry, "I am resolved! I will face it."

"Good. Having given this message, come and report to me. After that your tasks for the night are finished. You will catch the late bus for your home in the Paysdoux. Heaven will reward you and I shall not forget you. Is all that clear, Teresa?"

Teresa repeated it all.

"Good. Now, Raoul, we may not have a chance to speak to each other again. Do as I have said. You are enacting the role of a frightened yet fascinated girl who is under the rule of silence. What will happen during the ceremony I cannot tell you. Mr. Herrington could not be persuaded to confide more than you already know. You can only try to behave as the others do. If there is a crisis I shall deal with it. You will probably see and hear much that will shock and anger you. However beastly the behaviour of these people, you must control yourself. Have you ever heard of the Augean Stables?"

"No, Monsieur."

"They were filthy and were cleansed. It was a heroic task. Now, when you get to Miss Taylor's room you will find a robe, like the one you are wearing, laid out for her. If there is no difference you need not change. I don't think you need try to wear her shoes but if there is anything else set out for her—gloves perhaps—you must wear whatever it may be. One thing more. There may be cigarettes in Miss Taylor's room. Don't smoke them. If cigarettes are given to us during the ceremony we must pretend to smoke. Like this."

Alleyn pouted his lips as if to whistle, held a cigarette in the gap between them and drew in audibly. "They will be drugged cigarettes. Air and smoke will be inhaled together. Keep your thumb over the end like this and you will be safe. That's all. A great deal depends upon us, Raoul. There have been many girls before Miss Taylor who have become the guests of Mr. Oberon. I think perhaps of all evil-doers, his kind are the worst. Monsieur le Commissaire and I are asking much of you."

Raoul, perched on his high heels and peering out of the black hood, said: "Monsieur l'Inspecteur-en-Chef, in the army one learns to recognize authority. I recognize it in you, Monsieur, and I shall serve it to the best of my ability."

Alleyn was acutely embarrassed and more than a little touched by this speech. He said: "Thank you. Then we must all do our best. Shall we set about it? Now, Teresa, as quietly as you can unless you meet anybody, and then—boldly. Off you go."

"Courage, my beloved. Courage and good sense."

Teresa bestowed a melting glance upon Raoul, opened the door and, after a preliminary look down the passage, took up her candle and went out. Alleyn followed with his walking stick in his hand and Raoul, clicking his high heels and taking small steps, brought up the rear.

Down in Roqueville Troy absent-mindedly arranged little figures round a crib and pondered on the failure of her session with Ginny and Robin. She heard again Ginny's desperate protest: "I don't want to, I don't want to but I must. I've taken the oath. Dreadful things will happen if I don't go back."

"You don't really believe that," Robin had said and she had cried out: "You've sworn and you won't tell. If we don't believe why don't we tell?"

Suddenly, with something of Ricky's abandon, she had flung her arms round Troy. "If you could help," she had stammered, "but you can't; you can't!" And she had run out of the room like a frightened animal. Robin, limping after her, had turned at the door.

"It's all right," he had said. "Mrs. Allen, it's all right. She won't go back."

There was a tidily arranged pile of illustrated papers in the private sitting-room where they had had their drinks. Troy found herself idly turning the pages of the top one. Photographs of sun-bathers and race-goers flipped over under her abstracted gaze. Dresses by Dior and dresses by Fath, Prince Aly Khan leading in his father's horse, the new ballet at the Marigny—"*Les invités reunis pour quelques jours au Château de la Chèvre d'Argent. De gauche à droite: l'Hôte, M. Oberon; Mlle. Imogen Taylor, M. Carbury Glande, Dr. Baradi, M. Robin Herrington et la Hon. Grizel Locke*—" Troy's attention was arrested and then transfixed. It was a clear photograph taken on the roof-garden. There they were, perfectly recognizable, all except Grizel Locke.

The photograph of Grizel Locke was that of a short, lean woman with the face of a complete stranger.

iv

Robin was driving up a rough lane into the hills with Ginny beside him saying feverishly: "You're sure this is a shorter way? It's a quarter to eight, Robin! Robin, you're sure?"

He thought: "The tank was half-full. How long will it take for half a tank of air to be exhausted?"

"There's tons of time," he said, "and I'm quite sure." As he turned the next corner the engine missed and then stopped. Robin crammed on his brakes.

Looking at Ginny's blank face he thought: "Now, we're for it. It's tonight or nevermore for Ginny and me."

Dupont, waiting under the stars on the platform outside the Chèvre d'Argent, looked at his watch. It was a quarter to eight. He sighed and settled himself inside his coat. He expected a long vigil.

v

Teresa's candle bobbed ahead. Sometimes it vanished round corners, sometimes dipped or ascended as she arrived at steps and sometimes it was stationary for a moment as she stopped and listened. Presently they were on familiar ground. Forward, on their left, was the operating room: opposite this, the room where Miss Truebody had waited. Nearer, on their right, a thin blade of light across the carpet indicated the door into Baradi's room. Teresa's hand, dramatized by candlelight, shielded the flame. Beyond her, the curtain at the end of the passage was faintly defined against some further diffusion of light.

She passed Baradi's door. Alleyn and Raoul approached it. Alleyn held up a warning hand. He halted and then crept forward. His ear was at the door. Beyond it, like erring souls, Baradi and his servant were talking together in their own language.

Alleyn and Raoul moved on. Teresa had come to the curtain. They saw her lift it and a triangle of warmth appeared. Her candle sank to the floor. The foot of the curtain was raised and the candle, followed by the doubled-up shape of Teresa, disappeared beneath it.

"Good girl," Alleyn thought, "she's remembered the rings."

He followed quickly. He was tall enough to reach the rings and hold the top of the curtain to the rail while he raised the skirt for Raoul to pass through.

Now Raoul was in the great hall where the candelabrum still burned on the central table. Teresa had already passed into the entrance lobby. Alleyn still held the curtain in his hand when Teresa blew her nose.

He slipped back behind the curtain, leaving a peephole for himself. He saw Raoul hesitate and then move forward until his back was to the light and he saw a white-robed figure that might have been himself come in from the lobby. Looking beyond the six burning candles he watched the two figures confront each other. The white hood was thrust back and Carbury Glande's red beard jutted out. Alleyn heard him mutter:

"Well, thank God for you, anyway. You *have* put him in a tizzy! What happened?"

The black cowl moved slightly from side to side. The head was bent.

"Oh, *all* right!" Glande said pettishly. "What a stickler you are, to be sure!"

The white figure crossed the end of the hall and disappeared up the stairway.

Raoul moved on into the lobby and Alleyn came out of cover and followed him. When he entered the lobby, Alleyn went to the carved chest that stood against the back wall. It was there that the Egyptian servant had put the key of the wrought-iron door. Alleyn found the key and through the grill tossed it out of reach into the outside passage-way.

From the lobby, the staircase wound downwards. Teresa's candle, out of sight and sinking, threw up her own travelling shadow and that of Raoul. Alleyn followed them, but they moved faster than he and he was left to grope his way down in a kind of twilight. He had completed three descending spirals when he arrived at the landing. The door he had noticed on his previous visit was now open and beyond it was a bedroom with a light burning before a looking-glass. This, evidently, was Robin Herrington's room. Alleyn went in. On the inside door-handle hung a notice: "*Heure de Méditation. Ne dérangez pas.*" He hung it outside and shut the door.

The room had the smell and sensation of luxury that were characteristic of the Chèvre d'Argent. A white robe, like his own, was laid out together with silk shorts and shirt and a pair of white sandals. Alleyn changed quickly. On a table near the bed was a silver box, an ashtray, an elaborate lighter and, incongruously, a large covered dish which, on examination, proved to contain a sumptuous assortment of hors d'oeuvres and savouries. In the box were three cigarettes: long, thin and straw-coloured. He took one up, smelt it, broke it across and put the two halves in his case. He held a second to his candle, kept it going by returning it continuously to the flame and, as it was consumed, broke the ash into the tray.

"Three of those," he thought, "and young Herrington's values would be as cockeyed as one of Carbury Glande's abstracts."

There was the lightest of taps on the door. It opened slightly. "Monsieur?" whispered Teresa.

He let her in.

"Monsieur, it is to tell you that I have executed your order. I have spoken to Mr. Oberon. Tonight he was not as formerly he has been. He was not interested in me, but all the same he was excited. One would have thought he was intoxicated, Monsieur, but he does not take wine."

"You gave the message?"

"Yes, Monsieur. He listened eagerly and questioned me, saying: 'Have you seen her?' and I thought best, with the permission of the saints, to say 'yes.' "

"Quite so, Teresa."

"He then asked me if Mademoiselle Taylor was quite well and I said she was and then if she seemed happy and I said: 'Yes, she seemed pleased and excited,' because that is how one is, Monsieur, when one keeps an appointment. And I repeated that Mademoiselle had asked to be alone and he said: 'Of course, of course. It is essential,' as if to himself. And he was staring in a strange manner as if I was not there and so I left him. And al-

though I was frightened, Monsieur, I was not troubled as formerly by M.
Oberon because Raoul is the friend of my bosom and to him I will be
constant."

"I should certainly stick to that, if I were you. You are a good girl, Teresa,
and now you must catch your bus. Tomorrow you shall choose a fine present
against your wedding-day."

"Ah, Monsieur!" Teresa exclaimed and neatly sketching ineffable astonishment and delight, she slipped out of the room.

It was now eight o'clock. Alleyn settled down to his vigil. He thought of
poor Miss Truebody and of the four remaining guests and Mr. Oberon,
each in his or her room, and each, he believed, oppressed by an almost
intolerable sense of approaching climax. He wondered if Robin Herrington
had followed his advice about blocking the vent in the cap on his petrol
tank and he wondered if Troy had had any success in breaking down Ginny's
enthralment.

He turned over in his mind all he had read of that curious expression of
human credulity called magic. As it happened he had been obliged on a
former case to dig up evidence of esoteric ritual and had become fascinated
by its witness to man's industry in the pursuit of a chimera. Hundreds and
hundreds of otherwise intelligent men, he found, had subjected themselves
throughout the centuries to the boredom of memorizing and reciting senseless formulae, to the indignity of unspeakable practices and to the threat of
the most ghastly reprisals. Through age after age men and women had
starved, frightened and exhausted themselves, had got themselves racked,
broken and burned, had delivered themselves up to what they believed to
be the threat of eternal damnation and all without any firsthand evidence of
the smallest success. Age after age the Oberons and Baradis had battened on
this unquenchable credulity, had traced their pentagrams, muttered their
interminable spells, performed their gruelling ceremonies and taken their
toll. And at the same time, he reflected, the Oberons (never the Baradis)
had ended by falling into their own traps. The hysteria they induced was
refracted upon themselves. Beyond the reek of ceremonial smoke they too
began to look for the terrifying reward.

He wondered to what class of adept Oberon belonged. There was a definite hierarchy. There had always been practitioners who, however misguided,
could not be accused of charlatanism. To this day, he believed, such beings
existed, continuing their barren search for a talisman, for a philosopher's
stone, for power and for easy money.

Magical rituals from the dawn of time had taken on the imprint of their
several ages. From the scope and dignity of the Atkadian Inscriptions to the
magnificence of the Graeco-Egyptian Papyri, from the pious Jewish mysteries to the squalors, brutalities and sheer silliness of the German pseudo-
Faustian cults. From the Necromancer of the Coliseum to the surprisingly
fresh folklorishness of the English genre: each had its peculiar character and
its own formula of frustration. And alongside the direct line like a bastard

brother ran the cult of Satanism, the imbecile horrors of the Black Mass, the Amatory Mass and the Mortuary Mass.

If Oberon had read all the books in his own library he had a pretty sound knowledge of these rituals together with a generous helping of Hindooism, Voodoo and Polynesian mythology: a wide field from which to concoct a ceremony for the downfall of Ginny Taylor and her predecessors. Alleyn fancied that the orthodox forms would not be followed. The oath of silence he had read in Baradi's room was certainly original. "If it's the Amatory Mass as practised by Madame de Montespan," he thought, "poor old Raoul's sunk from the word go." And he began to wonder what he should do if this particular crisis arose.

He spent the rest of his vigil eating the savouries that had no doubt been provided to satisfy the hunger of the reefer addict and smoking his own cigarettes. He checked over the possibilities of disaster and found them many and formidable. "All the same," he thought, "it's worth it. And if the worst comes to the worst we can always—"

Somebody was scratching at his door.

He ground out his cigarette, extinguished his candle and seated himself on the floor with his back to the door and his legs folded Oberon-wise under his gown. He was facing the dressing-table with its large tilted looking-glass. The scratching persisted and turned into a feather-light tattoo of finger-tips. He kept his gaze on that part of the darkness where he knew the looking-glass must be. He heard a fumbling and a slight rap and guessed that the notice had been moved from the door-handle. A vertical sliver of light appeared. He watched the reflexion of the opening door and of the white-robed candle-bearer. He caught a glimpse, under the hood, of a long face with a beaked nose. Robed like that she seemed incredibly tall: no longer the figure of fantasy that she had presented yesterday in pedal-pushers and scarf and yet, unmistakably, the same woman. The door was shut. He bent his head and looked from under his brows at the reflexion of the woman, who advanced so close that he could hear her breathing behind him.

"I know it's against the Rule," she whispered, "I've got to speak to you."

He made no sign.

"I don't know what they'll do to me if they find out but I'm actually past caring!" In the glass he saw her put the candle on the table. "Have you smoked?" she said. "If you have I suppose it's no good. I haven't." He heard her sit heavily in the chair. "Well," she whispered almost cosily, "it's about Ginny. You've never seen an initiation, have you? I mean of that sort. You might at least nod or shake your head."

Alleyn shook his head.

"I thought not. You've got to stop her doing it. She's fond of you, you may depend upon it. If it was not for *him* she'd be in love, like any other nice girl, with you. And you're fond of her. I know. I've watched. Well, you've got to stop it. She's a thoroughly nice girl," the prim whisper insisted, "and you're still a splendid young fellow. Tell her she mustn't."

Alleyn's shoulders rose in an exaggerated shrug.

"Oh, *don't!*" The whisper broke into a vocal protest. "If you only knew how I've been watching you both. If you only knew what I'm risking. Why, if you tell on me I don't know what they won't do. Murder me, as likely as not. It wouldn't be the first time unless you believe she killed herself, and I certainly don't."

The voice stopped. Alleyn waited.

"One way or another," the voice said quite loudly, "you've got to give me a sign."

He raised his hand and made the Italian negative sign with his finger.

"You won't! You mean you'll let it happen. To Ginny? In front of everybody? Oh, dear me!" The voice sighed out most lamentably. "Oh, dear, dear me, it's enough to break one's heart!" There was a further silence. Alleyn thought: "The time's going by: we haven't much longer. If she'd just say one thing!"

The voice said strongly, as if its owner had taken fresh courage: "Very well. I shall speak to her. It won't do any good. I look at you and I ask myself what sort of creature you are. I look—"

She broke off. She had moved her candle so that its reflexion in the glass was thrown back upon Alleyn. He sat frozen.

"*Who are you?*" the voice demanded strongly. "You're not Robin Herrington."

She was behind him. She jerked the hood back from his head and they stared at each other in the looking-glass.

"And you're not Grizel Locke," Alleyn said. He got up, faced her and held out his hand. "Miss P. E. Garbel, I presume," he said gently.

CHAPTER XII

Eclipse of the Sun

"Then you guessed!" said Miss Garbel, clinging to his hand and shaking it up and down as if it were a sort of talisman. "How did you guess? How did you get here? What's happening?"

Alleyn said: "We've got twenty-five minutes before that damn bell goes. Don't let's squander them. I wasn't sure. Yesterday morning, when you talked like one of your letters, I wondered."

"I couldn't let either of you know who I was. Oberon was watching. They all were. I thought the remark about the Douceville bus might catch your attention."

"I didn't dare ask outright, of course. Now, tell me. Grizel Locke's dead, isn't she?"

"Yes; small hours of yesterday morning. We were told an overdose of self-administered heroin. I think—murdered."

"Why was she murdered?"

"I think, because she protested about Ginny. Ginny's her niece. I think she may have threatened them with exposure."

"Who killed her?"

"I haven't an idea. Oh, not a notion!"

"What exactly were you told?"

"That if it was found out we'd all be in trouble. That the whole thing would be discovered: the trade in diacetylmorphine, the connection with the factory—have you discovered about the factory?—everything, they said, would come out and we'd all be arrested and the British subjects would be extradited and tried and imprisoned. Then, it appears, you rang up about Miss Truebody. Baradi saw it as a chance to dispose of poor Grizel Locke. She would be buried, you see, and you would be told it was Miss Truebody. Then later on when you were out of the way and Miss Truebody was well, a made-up name would be put over the grave. Baradi said that if anybody could save Miss Truebody's life, he could. I'm guessing at how much you know. Stop me if I'm not clear. And then you or your wife asked about 'Cousin Garbel.' You can imagine how that shocked them! I was there, you see. I'm their liaison with the factory. I work at the factory. I'll tell you why and how if we've time. Of course I guessed who you were, but I told them I hadn't a notion. I said I supposed you must be some unknown people with an introduction or something. They were terribly suspicious. They said I must see you both and find out what you were doing, and why you'd asked about me. Then Baradi said it would be better if I didn't present myself as me. And then they said I must pretend to be Grizel Locke so that if there was ever an enquiry or trouble, you and Cousin Aggie—"

"Who!" Alleyn ejaculated.

"Your wife, you know. She was called Agatha after my second cousin, once—"

"Yes, yes. Sorry. I call her Troy."

"Really? Quaint! I've formed the habit of thinking of her as Cousin Aggie. Well, the plan was that I'd be introduced to you as Grizel Locke and I should tell them afterwards if I recognized you or knew anything about you. They made me wear Grizel's clothes and paint my face, in case you'd heard about her or would be asked about her afterwards. And then, tomorrow, after the funeral we are meant to meet again and I'm to say I'm leaving for a trip to Budapest. If possible, you are to see me go. So that if a hue-and-cry goes out for Grizel Locke, you will support the story that she's left for Hungary. I'm to go as far as Marseilles and stay there until you're both out of the way. The factory has extensive connections in Marseilles. At the same time we're to give out that I, as myself, you know, have gone on holiday. How much longer have we got?"

"Twenty-one minutes."

"I've time, at least, to tell you quickly that whatever you're planning you mustn't depend too much upon me. You see, I'm one of them."

"You mean," Alleyn said, "you've formed the habit—?"

"I'm fifty. Sixteen years ago I was a good analytical chemist but terribly poor. They offered me a job on a wonderful salary. Research. They started me off in New York, and after the war they brought me over here. At first I thought it was all right and then gradually I discovered what was happening. They handled me on orthodox lines. A man, very attractive, and parties. I was always plain and he was experienced and charming. He started me on marihuana—reefers, you know—and I've never been able to break off. They see to it I get just enough to keep me going. They get me up here and make me nervous and then give me cigarettes. I'm very useful to them. When I smoke I get very silly. I hear myself saying things that fill me with bitter shame. But when I've got the craving to smoke and when *he's* given me cigarettes, I—well, you've seen. It wasn't all play-acting when I pretended to be Grizel Locke. We all get like that with Oberon. He has a genius for defilement."

"Why did you write as you did to Troy? I must tell you that we didn't realize what you were up to until yesterday."

"I was afraid you wouldn't. But I daren't be explicit. Their surveillance is terribly thorough and my letters might have been opened. They weren't, as it turned out, otherwise you would have been recognized as my correspondent. I wrote—"

The voice, half vocal, half whispering, faltered. She pushed back her hood and tilted her tragi-comic face towards Alleyn's. "I began to write because of the girls like Ginny. You've seen me and you've seen Annabella Wells—frightful, aren't we? Grizel Locke was the same. Drug-soaked old horrors. We're what happens to the Ginnys. And there are lots and lots of Ginnys: bomb-children I call 'em. No moral stamina and no nervous reserve. Parents killed within the child's memory and experience. Sense of insecurity and impending disaster. The poor ones with jobs have the best chance. But the others—the rich Ginnys—if they run into our sort of set—whoof! And once they're made Daughters of the Sun it's the end of them. Too ashamed to look back or up or anywhere but at him. So when I saw in the English papers that my clever kinswoman had married *you*, I thought: 'I'll do it. I haven't the nerve or self-control to fight on my own but I'll try and hint.' So I did. I was a little surprised when Cousin Aggie replied as if to a man, but I did not correct her. Her mistake gave me a foolish sense of security. How long, now?"

"Just over seventeen minutes. Listen! Herrington and Ginny won't come back tonight. My chauffeur and I are replacing them. Can we get away with it? What happens in the ceremony?"

She had been talking eagerly and quickly, watching him with a bird-like attentiveness. Now it was as if his question touched her with acid. She actually threw up her hands in a self-protective movement and shrank away from him.

"I can't tell you. I've taken an oath of silence."

"All that dagger and fire and molten lead nonsense?"

"You can't know! How do you know? Who's broken faith?"

"Nobody. I hoped you might."

"Never!"

"A silly gimcrack rigmarole. Based on infamy."

"It's no good. I told you. I'm no good."

"My man's about Ginny's height and he's wearing the black robe. Has he a chance of getting by?"

"Not to the end. Of course not." She caught her breath in something that might have been a sob or a wretched giggle. "How can you dream of it?"

"Will anybody be asked to take this oath—alone?"

"No—I can tell you nothing—but—he—no. Why are you doing this?"

"We think the ceremony may give us an opportunity for an arrest on a minor charge. Not only that—" Alleyn hesitated. "I feel as you do," he said hurriedly, "about this wretched child. For one thing she's English and there's a double sense of responsibility. At the same time I'm not here to do rescue work, particularly if it prejudices the success of my job. What's more, if Oberon and Baradi suspect that this child and young Herrington have done a bolt, they'll also suspect a betrayal. They'll have the machinery for meeting such a crisis. All evidence of their interest in the racket will be destroyed and they'll shoot the moon. Whereas, if, by good luck, we can diddle them into thinking Ginny Taylor and Robin Herrington have returned to their unspeakable fold we may learn enough, here, tonight to warrant an arrest. We can then hold the principals, question the smaller fry and search the whole place."

"I'm small fry. How do you know I won't warn them?"

"I've heard you plead for Ginny."

"You've told me she's safe," whimpered Miss Garbel. She bit her fingertips and looked at him out of the corner of her pale eyes. "That's all I wanted. You ask me to bring ruin on myself. I've warned you. I'm no good. I've no integrity left. In a minute I must smoke and then I'll be hopeless. You ask too much."

Alleyn said: "You're a braver woman than you admit. You've tried for months to get me here, knowing that if I succeed your job will be gone and you will have to break yourself of your drug. You risked trying to tip me off yesterday morning and you risked coming to plead with young Herrington here tonight. You're a woman of science with judgment and curiosity and a proper scepticism. You know, positively, that this silly oath of silence was taken under the influence of your drug, that the threats it carries are meaningless, that it's your clear duty to abandon it. I think you will believe me when I say that if you keep faith with us tonight you will have our full protection afterwards."

"You can't protect me," she said, "from myself."

"We can try. Come! Having gone so far, why not all the way?"

"I'm so frightened," said Miss Garbel. "You can't think. So dreadfully frightened."

She clasped her claw-like hands together. Alleyn covered them with his own. "All right," he said. "Never mind. You've done a lot. I won't ask you to tell me about the rites. Don't go to the ceremony. Can you send a message?"

"I must go. There must be seven."

"One for each point of the pentagram, with Oberon and the Black Robe in the middle?"

"Did *they* tell you? Ginny and Robin? They wouldn't dare."

"Call it a guess. Before we separate I'm going to ask you to make one promise tonight. Shall we say for Grizel Locke's sake? Don't smoke so much marihuana that you may lose control of yourself and perhaps betray us."

"I shan't betray you. I *can* promise that. I don't promise not to smoke and I implore you to depend on me for nothing more than this. I won't give you away."

"Thank you a thousand times, my dear cousin-by-marriage. Before the night is over I shall ask if I may call you Penelope."

"Naturally you may. In my bad moments," said poor Miss Garbel, "I have often cheered myself up by thinking of you both as Cousins Roddy and Aggie."

"Have you really?" Alleyn murmured and was saved from the necessity of further comment by the sound of a cascade of bells.

Miss Garbel was thrown into a great state of perturbation by the bells which, to Alleyn, were reminiscent of the dinner chimes that tinkle through the corridors of ocean liners.

"There!" she ejaculated with a sort of wretched triumph. "The Temple bells! And here we are in somebody else's room and goodness *knows* what will become of us."

"I'll see if the coast's clear," Alleyn said. He took up his stick and then opened the door. The smell of incense hung thick on the air. Evidently candles had been lit on the lower landing. The stairwell sank into reflected light through which there rose whorls and spirals of scented smoke. As he watched, a shadow came up from below and the sound of bells grew louder. It was the Egyptian servant. Alleyn watched the distorted image of his tarboosh travel up the curved wall followed by that of his body and of his hands bearing the chime of bells. Alleyn stood firm, leaning on his stick with his hood over his face. The Egyptian followed his own shadow upstairs, ringing his little carillon. He crossed the landing, made a salutation as he passed Alleyn and continued on his way upstairs.

Alleyn looked back into the room. Miss Garbel stood there, biting her knuckles. He went to her.

"It's all right," he said. "You can go down. If you feel *very* brave and venturesome keep as close as you dare to the Black Robe and if he looks like he's making a mistake try and stop him. He only speaks French. Now, you'd better go."

She shook her head two or three times. Then, with an incredible suggestion of conventional leave-taking she began to settle herself inside her robe. She actually held out her hand.

"Goodbye. I'm sorry I'm not a braver woman," she said.

"You've been very brave for a long time and I'm exceedingly grateful," Alleyn said.

He watched her go and after giving her about thirty seconds, blew out the candle and followed her.

ii

The stairs turned three times about the tower before he came limping to the bottom landing. Here a lighted candelabrum stood near a door: the door he had noticed yesterday morning. Now it was open. The air was dense with the reek of incense so that each candle flame blossomed in a nimbus. His feet sank into the deep carpet and dimly he could make out the door into Oberon's room and the vista of wall-tapestries, receding into a passage.

Through the open door he saw four separate candlesticks, each with a lighted black candle. This, then, was the ante-room. Alleyn went in. The black velvet walls absorbed light and an incense burner hanging from the ceiling further obscured it. He could make out a partly opened curtain and behind this a rack of hanging robes. He could not be sure he was alone. Limping carefully, he made for the candles and took one up.

Remembering what Teresa had told him, he turned to the right and with his free hand explored the wall. The velvet surface was disagreeable to his touch. He moved along still pressing it and in a moment it yielded. He had found the swing-door into the temple.

There was an unwholesomeness about the silent obedience of the velvet door. It was as if everyday objects had begun to change their values. He followed his hand and walked, as it seemed, through the retreating wall into the temple.

At first he was aware only of two candle flames below the level of his knees and some distance ahead, six glowing braziers. Then he saw a white robe, squatting not far from a candle and then a black robe, near a second flame. He felt the tessellated floor under his feet and, using his stick, tapped his way across. "All the same," he thought, "young Herrington's stick is rubber-shod."

By the light of his own candle he made out the shape of the giant pentagram in the mosaic of the floor. It had been let into the pavement and was traced in some substance that acted as a reflector. The five-pointed star was enclosed in a double circle and he saw that at each of the points there was a smaller circle and in this a black cushion and a brazier filled with glowing embers. It was on one of these cushions that the white robe squatted. He drew close to it. A recognizable hand crept out from under the sleeve. It was Miss Garbel's. He turned to the centre of the pentagram. Raoul was holding his candle under his own face. His hands and arms were gloved in black. He was seated, cross-legged on a black divan and in front of him was a brazier.

Alleyn murmured: "The lady behind you and to your right is not un-friendly. She knows who you are."

Raoul signalled an assent.

"Depend on me for nothing—nothing," admonished a ghost-whisper in French and then added in a sort of frenzy, "Not there! Not in the middle. Not yet. Like me. *There!*"

"Quick, Raoul. *There!*"

Raoul darted into the point of the pentagram in front of Miss Garbel's. He put down his candle on the floor and pulled forward his hood.

Alleyn moved to the encircled point opposite Miss Garbel's. He had seated himself on the cushion before his brazier and had laid down his stick and candle when a light danced across the facets of the pentagram. He sensed, rather than heard, the entrance of a new figure. It passed so close that he recognized Annabella Wells's scent. She moved into the encircled point on his right and seated herself facing outwards as he did. At the same time there was a new glint of candlelight and the sound of a subsidence behind and to the left of Alleyn. In a moment or two a figure, unmistakably Baradi's, swept round the pentagram and entered it between Annabella and Raoul. Alleyn guessed he had taken up his position at the centre. At the same time the bells cascaded close at hand. "Here we go," he thought.

The five candles and six braziers furnished light enough for him to get a fitful impression of the preposterous scene. By turning his head slightly and slewing round his eyes, he could see the neighbouring points of the great pentagonal star, each protected by its circle and each containing its solitary figure, seated before a brazier and facing outward. Outside the pentagram and facing the points occupied by Annabella and Raoul was the altar. Alleyn could see the glint of metal in the embroidered cloth and quite distinctly, could make out the shape of the great crystal sun-burst standing in the middle.

The sound of bells came close and then stopped. A door opened in the wall beside the altar and the Egyptian servant walked through. He wore only a loin cloth and the squarish head-dress of antiquity. Before each of the initiates he set down a little box. "More reefers," thought Alleyn, keeping his head down. "Damned awkward if he wants to light them for us."

But the Egyptian made no attempt to do so. He moved away and out of the tail of his eye, Alleyn saw Annabella Wells reach out to her brazier, take a pair of tongs and light her cigarette with a piece of charcoal. Alleyn found that his brazier, too, was provided with tongs.

Because of the form of the pentagram the occupants of the five points all had their backs turned to Baradi and their shoulders to each other. If Baradi was on his feet he would have a sort of aerial survey of their backs. If he was seated on the divan he would have a still less rewarding view. Alleyn reached out for a cigarette, hid it inside his robe and produced one of his own. This he lit with a coal from the brazier. He wondered if it had occurred to Raoul to employ the same ruse.

Little spires of smoke began to rise from the five points of the star. The Egyptian had retired to a dark corner beyond the altar and presently began to strike a drum and play a meandering air on some reed instrument. To Alleyn the scene was preposterous and phony. He remembered Troy's comment on the incident of the train window: hadn't she compared it to bad cinematography? Even the ritual, for what it was worth, was bogus: a vamped-up synthesis, he thought, of several magic formulae. The reedy phrase trickled on like a tourist-class advertisement for Cairo, the drum throbbed and presently he sensed a stir of excitement among the initiates. The Egyptian began to chant and to increase the pace and volume of his drumming. Drum and voice achieved a sort of crescendo at the peak of which a second voice entered with a long vibrant call, startling in its unexpectedness. It was Baradi's.

From that moment it was impossible altogether to dismiss the Rites of the Sun as cheap or ridiculous. No doubt they were both but they were also alarming.

Alleyn supposed that Baradi spoke Egyptian and that his chant was one of the set invocations of ritual magic. He thought he recognized the characteristic repetition of names: "O Oualbpaga! O Kammara! O Kamalo! O Karhenmou! O Amagaa! O Thoth! O Anubis!" The drum thumped imperatively. Small feral noises came from the points of the pentagram. Behind Alleyn, Carbury Glande began to beat with his palm on the floor. The other initiates followed, Alleyn with them. The Egyptian left his drum and running about the pentagram, threw incense on the braziers. Columns of heavily scented smoke arose amid sharp cries from the initiates. A gong crashed and there was immediate silence.

It was startling, after the long exhortations in an incomprehensible tongue to hear Baradi cry in a loud voice: "Children of the Sun in the Outer, turn inward, now turn in. Silence, silence, silence, symbol of the imperishable god protect us, silence. Turn inward now, turn in."

This injunction was taken literally by the initiates who reversed their positions on the cushions and thus faced Baradi and the centre of the pentagram. Looking across, diagonally, to the Black Robe, Alleyn saw that Raoul had not moved. The exhortations, being in English, had meant nothing to him. Alleyn dared not look up at Baradi. He could see his feet and his white robe, up to the knees. Between drifts of incense he caught sight of the other initiates, all waiting. It seemed as if an age went by before the Black Robe rose, turned and reseated itself. He saw Baradi's feet shift and his robe swing as he faced the altar.

Baradi intoned in a loud voice: "Here in the Names of Ra and the Sons of Ra—"

It was the oath Alleyn had read. Baradi gave it out phrase by phrase and the initiates repeated it after him. Alleyn spoke on the top register of his very deep voice. Raoul, of course, said nothing. Miss Garbel's thin pipe was unmistakable. Annabella's trained and vibrant voice rang out loudly. Carbury Glande's sounded unco-ordinated and hysterical.

"If I break this oath in the least degree," Baradi dictated and was echoed, "may my lips be burned with the fire that is now set before them." He gestured over his brazier. A tongue of flame darted up from it.

"May my eyes be put out by the knife that is now set before them."

With a suddenness that was extraordinarily unnerving, five daggers dropped from the ceiling and checked with a jerk before the five initiates' faces. A sixth, bigger, fell in front of Baradi, who seized and flourished it. The others hung glittering in the flamelight of the brazier. The women gave little whimpering febrile cries.

The oath of silence was taken through to its abominable conclusion. The flame subsided, the smaller daggers were drawn up to the ceiling, presumably by the Egyptian. The initiates turned outward again and Baradi settled down to a further exhortation, this time in English.

It was the blackest possible kind of affair, quite short and entirely infamous. Baradi demanded darkness and the initiates put out their candles. Alleyn dared not look at Raoul, but knew by the delayed flicker of light that he was a little slow with this. Then Baradi urged first of all the necessity of experiencing something called "the caress of the left hand of perfection" and went on to particularize in terms that would have appalled anyone who was not an alienist or a member of Mr. Oberon's chosen circle. The Egyptian had returned to his reed and drum and the merciless repetition of a single phrase had its own effect. Baradi began to pour out a stream of names: Greek, Jewish, Egyptian: Pan, Enlil, Elohim, Ra, Anubis, Seti, Adonis, Ra, Silenus, Ereschigal, Tetragramaton, Ra. The recurrent "Ra" was presently taken up by the initiates, who began to bark it out with an enthusiasm, Alleyn thought, only to be equalled by the organized cheers of an American ball game.

"There are two signs," Baradi intoned. "There is the Sign of the Sun, Ra" ("Ra," barked the initiates), "and there is the sign of the Goat, Pan. And between the Sun and the Goat runs the endless cycle of the senses. Ra."

"Ra!"

"We demand a sign."

"We demand a sign."

"What shall the sign be?"

"The sign of the goat which is also the sign of the Sun which is also the sign of Ra."

"Let the goat come forth which is the Sun which is Ra."

"Ra!"

The drumming was increased to a frenzy. The initiates beat on the floor and clapped. Baradi must have thrown more incense on his brazier: the air was thick with billowing fumes. Alleyn could scarcely make out the shape of the altar. Now Baradi must be striking cymbals together.

The din was intolerable. The initiates, antic figures, half-masked by whorls of smoke, seemed to have gone down on all fours and to be flinging their hands high as they slapped the floor and cried out. Baradi broke into a chant, possibly in his own language, interspersed with further strings of names—Pan, Hylaesos, Lupercus, Silenus, Faunus—names that were caught up and shouted in a fury of abandon by the other voices. Alleyn, shouting with the rest, edged round on his knees, until he could look across the pentagram to Raoul. In the glow of the braziers he could just make out the black crouching figure and the black gloved hands rising and falling like drumsticks.

"A Sign, a Sign, let there be a Sign!"

"*It comes.*"

"It comes."

"*It is here.*"

Again the well-staged crescendo that ended, this time, in a deafening crash of cymbals followed by a dead silence.

And across that silence: bathetic, ridiculous and disturbing, broke the unmistakable bleat of a billy goat.

The smoke eddied and swirled, and there, on the altar for all the world like one of old Marie's statuettes, it appeared, horned and shining, a silver goat whose hide glittered through the smoke. It opened its mouth sideways and superciliously bleated. Its pale eyes stared and it stamped and tossed its head.

"It's been shoved up there from the back," Alleyn thought. "They've treated it with fluorescent paint. *Ça s'illumine.*"

Baradi was speaking again.

"Prepare, prepare," he chanted. "The Sign is the Shadow of the Substance. The Goat-god is the precursor of the Man-god. The Man-god is the Bridegroom. He is the Spouse. He is Life. He is the Sun. Ra!"

There was a blare of light, for perhaps a second literally blinding in its intensity. "Flash-powder," thought Alleyn. "The Egyptian must be remarkably busy." When his eyes had adjusted themselves, the goat had disappeared and in its place the sun-burst blazed on the altar. "Car batteries," thought Alleyn, "perhaps. Flex soldered at the terminals. Well done, Mahomet or somebody."

"Ra! Ra! Ra!" the initiates ejaculated with Baradi as their cheerleader.

The door to the left of the altar had opened. It admitted a naked man.

He advanced through wreaths of incense and stood before the blazing sun-burst. It was, of course, Mr. Oberon.

iii

Of the remainder of the ceremony, as far as he witnessed it, Alleyn afterwards prepared an official report. Neither this, nor a manual called *The Book
of Ra*, which contained the text of the ritual, has ever been made public.
Indeed, they have been stowed away in the archives of Scotland Yard where
they occupy a place of infamy rivalling that of the *Book of Horus and the
Swami Viva Ananda*. There are duplicates at the Sûreté. In the trial they
were not put in as primary evidence, and the judge, after a distasteful glance,
said that he saw no reason why the jury should be troubled to look at them.

For purposes of this narrative it need only be said that with the appearance
of Oberon, naked, in the role of Ra or Horus, or both, the Rites took on the
character of unbridled Phallicism. He stood on some raised place before the
blazing sun-burst, holding a dagger in both hands. More incense burners
were set reeking at his feet, and there he was, the nearest approach, Alleyn
afterwards maintained, that he had ever seen, to a purely evil being.

His entry stung the initiates into their last pitch of frenzy. Incredible
phrases were chanted, indescribable gestures were performed. The final crescendo of that scandalous affair rocketed up to its point of climax. For the
last time the Egyptian's drum rolled and Baradi clashed his cymbals. For
the last time pandemonium gave place to silence.

Oberon came down from his eminence and walked towards the encircled
pentagram. His feet slapped the tessellated pavement. His hair, lit from
behind, was a nimbus about his head. He entered the pentagram and the
initiates turned inwards, crouching beastily at the points. Oberon placed
himself at the centre. Baradi spoke.

"Horus who is Savitar who is Baldur who is Ra. The Light, The Beginning
and The End, The Life, The Source and The Fulfilment. Choose, now,
Lord, O choose."

Oberon extended his arm and pointed his dagger at Raoul.

Baradi went to Raoul. He held out his hand. In the capricious glare from
the sun-burst Alleyn could see Raoul on his knees, his shadow thrown before
him towards Oberon's feet. His face was deeply hidden in his hood. Alleyn
saw the gloved hand and arm reach out. Baradi took the hand. He passed
Raoul across him with a dancer's gesture.

Raoul now faced Oberon.

Somewhere in the shadows the Egyptian servant cried out shrilly.

Baradi's dark hands, themselves seeming gloved, closed on the shoulders
of Raoul's robe. Suddenly, with a flourish, and to a roll of the drum, he
swept it free of its wearer. "Behold!" he shouted: "The Bride!"

And then, in the glare from the sun-burst, where, like an illustration from
La Vie Parisienne, Mr. Oberon's victim should have been discovered; there
stood Raoul in his underpants, black slippers and Ginny Taylor's gloves.

A complete surprise is often something of an anti-climax and so, for a moment or two, was this. It is possible that Annabella Wells and Carbury Glande were too fuddled with marihuana to get an immediate reaction. Miss Garbel, of course, had been prepared. As for Oberon and Baradi, they faced each other across the preposterous Thing they had unveiled and their respective jaws dropped like those of a pair of simultaneous comedians. Raoul himself merely cast a scandalized glance at Oberon and uttered in a loud apocalyptic voice the single word: "*Anathema!*"

It was then that Miss Garbel erupted in a single hoot of hysteria. It escaped from her and was at once cut off by her own hand clapped across her mouth. She squatted, heaving, in the corner of the pentacle, her terrified eyes staring over her knuckles at Baradi.

Baradi, in an unrecognizable voice and an unconscious quotation, said: "Which of you has done this?"

Oberon gave a bubbling cry: "I am betrayed!"

Raoul, hearing his voice, repeated: "Anathema!" and made the sign of the cross.

Oberon dragged Miss Garbel to her feet. He held her with his right hand; in his left was the dagger. She chattered in his face: "You can't! You can't! I'm protected. You can't!"

Alleyn advanced until he was quite close to them. Glande and Annabella Wells were on their feet.

"Is this your doing?" Oberon demanded, lowering his face to Miss Garbel's.

"Not mine!" she chattered. "Not this time. Not mine!"

He flung her off. Baradi turned on Raoul.

"Well!" Baradi said in French, "so I know you, now. Where's your master?"

"Occupy yourself with your own affairs, Monsieur."

"We are lost!" Oberon cried out in English.

His hand moved. The knife glinted.

"*Alors, Raoul!*" said Alleyn.

Raoul stooped and ran. He ran out of the pentacle and across the floor. The Egyptian darted out and was knocked sideways. His head struck the corner of the altar and he lay still. Raoul sped through the open door into Oberon's room. Oberon followed him. Alleyn followed Oberon and caught him up on the far side of the great looking-glass. He seized his right hand as it was raised. "Not this time," Alleyn grunted and jerked his arm. The dagger flew from Oberon's hand and splintered the great glass. At the same moment Raoul kicked. Oberon gave a scream of pain, staggered across the room and lurched against the window. With a whirr and a clatter the blind flew up and Oberon sank on the floor moaning. Alleyn turned to find Baradi facing him with the knife in his left hand.

"You," Baradi said. "I might have guessed. *You!*"

iv

From the moment that the affair began, as it were, to wind itself up in Oberon's room, it became a straight-out conflict between Alleyn and Baradi. Alleyn had guessed that it would be so. Even while he sweated to remember his police training in unarmed combat he found time to consider that Oberon, naked and despicable, had at last become a negligible element. Alleyn was even aware of Carbury Glande and Annabella Wells teetering uncertainly in the doorway, and of Miss Garbel, who hovered like a spinsterly half-back on the edge of the scrimmage.

But chiefly he was aware of Baradi's dark infuriated body, smelling of sandalwood and sweat, and of the knowledge that he himself was the fitter man. They struggled together ridiculously and ominously, looking, in their white robes, like a couple of frenzied monks. There was, for Alleyn, a sort of pleasure in this fight. "I needn't worry. For once, I needn't worry," he thought. "For once the final arbitrament is as simple as this. I'm fitter than he is."

And when Raoul, absurd in his underpants and long gloves, suddenly hurled himself at Baradi and brought him down with a crash, Alleyn was conscious of a sort of irritation. He looked across the floor and saw that Raoul's foot, in its ridiculous sandal, had pinned down Baradi's left wrist. He saw Baradi's fingers uncurl from the knife-handle. He shoved free, landed a short-arm jab on the point of Baradi's jaw and felt him go soft. They had brought down the prayer wheel in their struggle. Alleyn reached for it and flung it at the window. It crashed through and he heard it fall with the broken glass on the railway line below. Oberon screamed out an oath. Alleyn fetched his breath and blew with all the wind he had on M. Dupont's police whistle. It trilled shrilly, like a toy, and was answered and echoed and answered again outside.

"The house is surrounded," Alleyn said, looking at Glande and Oberon. "I have a police authority. Anyone trying violence or flight will be dealt with out-of-hand. Stay where you are, all of you."

The glare from the sun-burst streamed through the doorway on clouds of incense. Alleyn bound Baradi's arms behind his back with the cord of his gown. Raoul tied his ankles together with the long gloves. Baradi's head lolled drunkenly and he made uncouth noises.

"I want to make a statement," Oberon said shrilly. "I am a British subject. I have my passport. I offer myself for Queen's evidence. I have my passport."

Annabella Wells, standing in the doorway, began to laugh. Carbury Glande said: "Shut up, for God's sake. This is IT."

Abruptly the room was lit. Wall-lamps, a bedside lamp and a standard lamp all came to life. By normal standards it was not a brilliant illumination, but it had the effect of reducing that unlikely interior to an embarrassing state of anti-climax. Glande, Annabella Wells and poor Miss Garbel, huddled in their robes, looked dishevelled and ineffectual. Baradi had a trickle of blood running from his nose into his moustache. The Egyptian servant staggered into the doorway, holding his head in his hands and wearing the foolish expression of a punch-happy pugilist. Oberon, standing before the cracked looking-glass as no doubt he had often done before: Oberon, naked, untactfully lit, was so repellent a sight that Alleyn threw the cover of the divan at him.

"You unspeakable monstrosity," he said, "get behind that."

"I offer a full statement. I am the victim of Dr. Baradi. I claim protection."

Baradi opened his eyes and shook the blood from his moustache.

"I challenge your authority," he said, blinking at Alleyn.

"Alleyn. Chief Detective-Inspector, C.I.D., New Scotland Yard. On loan to the Sûreté. My card and my authority are in my coat-pocket and my coat's in young Herrington's room."

Baradi twisted his head to look at Annabella. "Did you know this?" he demanded.

"Yes, darling," she said.

"You little—"

"Is that Gyppo for what, darling?"

"In a moment," Alleyn said, "the Commissioner of Police will be here and you will be formally arrested and charged. I don't know that I'm obliged to give you the customary warning but the habit's irresistible. Anything you say—"

Baradi and Annabella entirely disregarded him.

"*Why* didn't you tell me who he was?" Baradi said. "*Why?*"

"He asked me not to. He's got something. I didn't know he was here tonight. I didn't think he'd come back."

"Liar!"

"As you choose, my sweet."

"—may be used in evidence."

"You can't charge *me* with anything," Carbury Glande said. "I am an artist. I've formed the habit of smoking and I come to France to do it. I'm not mixed up in anything. If I hadn't had my smokes tonight I'd bloody well fight you."

"Nonsense," said Alleyn.

"I desire to make a statement," said Oberon, who was now wrapped in crimson satin and sitting on the divan.

"I wish to speak to you alone, Mr. Alleyn," said Baradi.

"All in good time."

"Garbel!" Baradi ejaculated.

"Shall I answer him, Roddy dear?"

"If you want to, Cousin Penelope."

"*Cousin!*" Mr. Oberon shouted.

"Only by marriage. I informed you," Miss Garbel reminded him, "of the relationship. And I think it only right to tell you that if it hadn't been for all the Ginnys—"

"My God," Carbury Glande shouted, "where are Ginny and Robin?"

"Ginny!" Oberon cried out. "Where is Ginny?"

"I hope," rejoined Miss Garbel, " 'in no place so unsanctified where such as thou mayst find her.' The quotation, cousin, is from *Macbeth*."

"And couldn't be more appropriate," murmured Alleyn, bowing to her. He sat down at Mr. Oberon's desk and drew a sheet of paper towards him.

"This woman," Baradi said to Alleyn, "is not in her right mind. I tell you this professionally. She has been under my observation for some time. In my considered opinion she is unable to distinguish between fact and fantasy. If you base your preposterous behaviour on any statement of hers—"

"Which I don't, you know."

"I am an Egyptian subject. I claim privilege. And I warn you, that if you hold me, you'll precipitate a political incident."

"My dear M. l'Inspecteur-en-Chef," said M. Dupont, coming in from the passage, "do forgive me if I am a little unpunctual."

"On the contrary, my dear M. le Commissaire, you come most punctually upon your cue."

M. Dupont shook hands with Alleyn. He was in tremendous form, shining with leather and wax and metal: gloved, holstered and batoned. Three lesser officers appeared inside the door.

"And these," said M. Dupont, touching his moustache and glancing round the room, "are the personages. You charge them?"

"For the moment, with conspiracy."

"I am a naturalized British subject. I offer myself as Queen's evidence. I charge Dr. Ali Baradi with murder."

Baradi turned his head and in his own language shot a stream of very raw-sounding phrases at his late partner.

"All these matters," said M. Dupont, "will be dealt with in an appropriate manner. In the meantime, *Messieurs et Dames*, it is required that you accompany my officers to the *Poste de Police* in Roqueville where an accusation will be formally laid." He nodded to his men, who advanced with a play of handcuffs.

Annabella Wells held her robe about her with one practiced hand and swept back her hair with the other. She addressed herself in French to Dupont.

"M. le Commissaire, do you recognize me?"

"Perfectly, Madame. Madame is the actress Annabella Wells."

"Monsieur, you are a man of the world. You will understand that I find myself in a predicament."

"It is not necessary to be a man of the world to discover your predicament, Madame. It is enough to be a policeman. If Madame would care to make some adjustment to her toilette—a walking costume, perhaps—I shall be delighted to arrange the facilities. There is a *femme-agent de police* in attendance."

She looked at him for a moment, seemed to hesitate, and then turned on Alleyn.

"What are you going to do with me?" she said. "You've trapped me finely, haven't you? What a fool I was! Yesterday morning I might have guessed. And I kept faith! I didn't tell them what you were. God, *what* a fool!"

"It's probably the only really sensible thing you've done since you came here. Don't regret it."

"Is it wishful thinking or do I seem to catch the suggestion that I may be given a chance?"

"Give yourself a chance, why not?"

"Ah," she said, shaking her head. "That'll be the day, won't it?"

She grinned at him and moved over to the door where Raoul waited. Raoul stared at her with a kind of incredulity. He had kicked off his sandals and wore only his pants and his St. Christopher medal and, thus arrayed, contrived to look god-like.

"What a charmer!" she said in English. "Aren't you?"

"*Madame?*"

"*Quel charmeur vous êtes!*"

"*Madame!*"

She asked him how old he was and if he had seen many of her films. He said he believed he had seen them all. Was he a cinephile, then? "*Madame,*" Raoul said, "*Je suis un fervent—de vous!*"

"When they let me out of gaol," Annabella promised, "I shall send you a photograph."

The wreckage of her beauty spoke through the ruin of her make-up. She made a good exit.

"Ah, Monsieur," said Raoul. "What a tragedy! And yet it is the art that counts and she is still an artist."

This observation went unregarded. They could hear Annabella in conversation with the *femme-agent* in the passage outside.

"My dear Dupont," Alleyn murmured, "may I suggest that in respect of this woman we make no arrest. I feel certain that she will be of much greater value as a free informant. Keep her under observation, of course, but for the moment, at least—"

"But, of course, my dear Alleyn," M. Dupont rejoined, taking the final plunge into intimacy. "I understand perfectly, but perfectly."

Alleyn was not quite sure what Dupont understood so perfectly but thought it better merely to thank him. He said: "There is a great deal to be explained. May we get rid of the men first?"

Dupont's policemen had taken charge of the four men. Oberon, still wrapped in crimson satin, was huddled on his bed. His floss-like hair hung in strands over his face. Above the silky divided beard the naked mouth was partly open. The eyes stared, apparently without curiosity, at Alleyn.

Dupont's men had lifted Baradi from the floor, seated him on the divan and pulled his white robe about him. His legs had been unbound, but he was now handcuffed. He, too, watched Alleyn, but sombrely, with attentiveness and speculation.

Carbury Glande stood nearby, biting his nails. The Egyptian servant flashed winning smiles at anybody who happened to look at him. Miss Garbel sat at the desk with an air of readiness, like an eccentrically uniformed secretary.

Dupont glanced at the men. "You will proceed under detention to the *Commissariat de Police* at Roqueville. M. l'Inspecteur-en-Chef and I will later conduct an interrogation. The matter of your nationalities and the possibility of extradition will be considered. And now—forward."

Oberon said: "A robe. I demand a robe."

"Look here, Alleyn," Glande said, "what's going to be done about me? I'm harmless, I tell you. For God's sake tell him to let me get some clothes on."

"Your clothes'll be sent after you and you'll get no more and no less than was coming to you," Alleyn said. "In the interest of decency, my dear Dupont, Mr. Oberon should, perhaps, be given a garment of some sort."

Dupont spoke to one of his men, who opened a cupboard-door and brought out a white robe.

"If," Miss Garbel said delicately, "I might be excused. Of course, I don't know—?" She looked enquiringly from Alleyn to Dupont.

"This is Miss Garbel, Dupont, of whom I have told you."

"Truly? Not, as I supposed, the Honourable Locke?"

"Miss Locke has been murdered. She was stabbed through the heart at five thirty-eight yesterday morning in this room. Her body is in a coffin in a room on the other side of the passage-of-entry. Dr. Baradi was good enough to show it to me."

Baradi clasped his manacled hands together and brought them down savagely on his knees. The steel must have cut and bruised him, but he gave no sign.

Glande cried out: "Murdered! My God, they told us she'd given herself an overdose."

"Then the—pardon me, Mademoiselle, if I express it a little crudely—the third English spinster, my dear Inspecteur-en-Chef? The Miss Truebody?"

"Is to the best of my belief recovering from her operation in a room beyond a bridge across the passage-of-entry."

Baradi got clumsily to his feet. He faced the great cheval-glass. He said something in his own language. As he spoke, through the broken window, came the effeminate shriek of a train whistle followed by the labouring uphill clank of the train itself. Alleyn held up his hand and they were all still and looked through the broken window. Alleyn himself stood beside Baradi, facing the looking-glass, which was at an angle to the window. Baradi made to move but Alleyn put his hand on him and he stood still, as if transfixed. In the great glass they both saw the reflection of the engine pass by and then the carriages, some of them lit and some in darkness. The train dragged to a standstill. In the last carriage a lighted window, which was opposite their own window, was unshuttered. They could see two men playing cards. The men looked up. Their faces were startled.

Alleyn said: "Look, Baradi. Look in the glass. The angle of incidence is always equal to the angle of refraction, isn't it? We see their reflexion and they see ours. They see you in your white robe. They see your handcuffs. Look, Baradi!"

He had taken a paper-knife from the desk. He raised it in his left hand as if to stab Baradi.

The men in the carriage were agitated. Their images in the glass talked excitedly and gestured. Then, suddenly, they were jerked sideways and in the glass was only the reflexion of the wall and the broken window and the night outside.

"Yesterday morning, at five thirty-eight, I was in a railway carriage out there," Alleyn said. "I saw Grizel Locke fall against the blind and when the blind shot up I saw a man with a dark face and a knife in his right hand. He stood in such a position that the prayer wheel showed over his shoulder and I now know that I saw, not a man, but his reflexion in that glass and I know he stood where you stand and that he was a left-handed man. I know that he was you, Baradi."

"And really, my dear Dupont—" Alleyn said a little later, when the police-car had removed the four men and the two ladies had gone away to change —"really, this is all one has to say about the case. When I saw the room yesterday morning I realized what had happened. There was this enormous cheval-glass screwed into the floor at an angle of about forty-five degrees to the window. To anybody looking in from outside it must completely exclude the right-hand section of the room. And yet, I saw a man, apparently *in* the right-hand section of the room. He must, therefore, have been an image in the glass of a man in the left-hand section of the room. To clinch it, I saw part of the prayer wheel near the right shoulder of the image. Now, if you sit in a railway-carriage outside that window, you will, I think, see part of the prayer wheel, or rather, since I chucked the prayer wheel through the window, you will see part of its trace on the faded wall, just to your left of the glass. The stabber, it was clear, must be a left-handed man and Baradi is the only left-handed man we have. I was puzzled that his face was more shadowed than the direction of the light seemed to warrant. It is, of course, a dark face."

"It is perfectly clear," Dupont said, "though the verdict is not to be decided in advance. The motive was fear, of course."

"Fear of exposure. Miss Garbel believes that Grizel Locke was horrified when her young niece turned up at the Chèvre d'Argent. It became obvious that Ginny Taylor was destined to play the major role, opposite Oberon, in these unspeakable Rites. The day before yesterday it was announced that she would wear the Black Robe tonight. My guess is that Grizel Locke, herself the victim of the extremes of mood that agonize all drug-addicts, brooded on the affair and became frantic with—with what emotion? Remorse? Anxiety? Shame?"

"But jealousy? She is, after all, about to become the supplanted mistress, is she not? Always an unpopular assignment."

"Perhaps she was moved by all of these emotions. Perhaps, after a sleepless night or—God knows—a night of pleading, she threatened to expose the drug racket if Oberon persisted with Ginny Taylor. Oberon, finding her intractable, summoned Baradi. She threatened both of them. The scene rose to a climax. Perhaps—is it too wild a guess?—she hears the train coming and threatens to scream out their infamy from the window. Baradi reverts to type and uses a knife, probably one of the symbolic knives with which they frighten the initiates. She falls against the blind and it flies up. There, outside, is the train with a dimly lighted compartment opposite their own window. And, between the light and the window of the compartment is the shape of a man—myself."

Dupont lightly struck his hands together. "A pretty situation, in effect!"

"He no sooner takes it in than it is over. The train enters the tunnel and Baradi and Oberon are left with Grizel Locke's body on their hands. And within an hour I ring up about Miss Truebody. And by the way, I suggest we visit Miss Truebody. Here comes Miss Garbel who, I daresay, will show us to her room."

Miss Garbel appeared, scarcely recognizable, wearing an unsmart coat and skirt and no make-up. It was impossible to believe this was the woman who, an hour ago, had lent herself to the Rites of the Children of the Sun and who, yesterday morning, had appeared in pedal-pushers and a scarf on the roof-garden. Dupont looked at her with astonishment. She was very tremulous and obviously distressed. She went to the point, however, with the odd directness that Alleyn was learning to expect from her.

"You are yourself again, I see," he said.

"Alas, yes! Or not, of course altogether, alas. It is nice not having to pretend to be poor Grizel any more but, as you noticed, I found it only too easy, at certain times, to let myself go. I sometimes think it is a peculiar property of marihuana to reduce all its victims to a common denominator. When we are 'high,' as poor Grizel used to call it, we all behave rather in her manner. I am badly in need of a smoke now, after all the upset, which is why I'm so shaky, you know."

"I expect you'd like to go back to your own room in the Rue des Violettes. We'll take you there."

"I would like it of all things, but I think I should stay to look after our patient, I've been doing quite a bit of the nursing—Mahomet and I took it in turns with one of the maids. Under the doctor's instructions, of course. Would you like to see her?"

"Indeed, we should. It's going to be difficult to cope with Miss Truebody. Of course, they never sent for a nurse?"

"No, no! Too dangerous, by far. But I assure you every care has been taken of the poor thing."

"I'll bet it has. They didn't want two bodies on their hands. M. le Commissaire has arranged for a doctor and a nurse to come up by the night train from St. Christophe. In the meantime, shall we visit her?"

Miss Garbel led the way up to the front landing. M. Dupont indicated the wrought-iron door. "We discovered the key, my dear Alleyn," he said gaily. "An excellent move!" They climbed to the roof-garden and thence through a labyrinth of rooms to one of the bridge-like extensions that straddled the outside passage-way.

They were half-way across this bridge when their attention was caught by the sound of voices and of boots on the cobblestones below.

From the balustrade they looked down into a scene that might have been devised by a film director. The sides of the house fell away from moon-patched shadow into a deep blackness. At one point a pool of light from an open door lay across the passage-way. Into this light moved an incongruous company of foreshortened figures: the Egyptian servant, Baradi and Oberon in their white robes, Carbury Glande bareheaded and in shorts, and six gendarmes in uniform. They shifted in and out of the light, a curious pattern of heads and shoulders.

"*Alors*," said Dupont, looking down at them: "*Bon débarras!*"

His voice echoed stonily in the passage. One of the white hoods was tilted backwards. The face inside it was thus exposed to the light but, being itself dark, seemed still to be in shadow. Alleyn and Baradi looked at each other. With a peck of his head Baradi spat into the night.

"*Pas de ça!*" said one of the gendarmes and turned Baradi about. It was then seen that he was handcuffed to his companion.

"Mr. Oberon," Alleyn said, "will be delighted."

The procession moved off with a hollow clatter down the passage. Raoul appeared in the doorway, rolling a cigarette, and watched them go.

Miss Garbel made a curious and desolate sound but immediately afterwards said brightly: "Shall we—?" and led them indoors.

"Here we are!" she said and tapped. A door was opened by the woman Alleyn had already seen at Miss Truebody's bedside.

"These are the friends of Mademoiselle," said Miss Garbel. "Is she awake?"

"She is awake but M. le Docteur left orders, Mademoiselle, that no one—" She saw Dupont's uniform and her voice faded.

"M. le Docteur," said Miss Garbel, "has reconsidered his order."

The woman stood aside and they went into the room. Dupont stayed by the door but Alleyn walked over to the bed. There, on the pillow, was the smooth, blunt and singularly hairless face he had remembered. She looked at him and smiled and this time she was wearing her teeth. They made a great difference.

"Why, it's Mr. Alleyn," she murmured in a thread-like voice. "How kind!"

"You're getting along splendidly," Alleyn said. "I won't tire you now, but if there is anything you want you'll let us know."

"Nothing. Much better. The doctor—too kind."

"There will be another doctor tomorrow and a new nurse to help these."

"Not—? But—Dr. Baradi—?"

"He has been obliged to go away," Alleyn said, "on a case of some urgency."

"Oh." She closed her eyes.

Alleyn and Dupont went outside. Miss Garbel came to the door.

"If you don't want me," she said, "I'll stay and take my turn. I'm all right, you know. Quite reliable until morning."

"And always," he rejoined warmly.

"Ah," she said, shaking her head. "That's another story."

She showed them where a stairway ran down to ground level and she peered after them, smiling and nodding over the banister.

"We must pay one more visit," Alleyn said.

"The third English spinster," Dupont agreed. He seemed to have a sort of relish for this phrase.

But when they stood in the white-washed room and the raw light from an unshaded lamp now shone dreadfully on what was left of Grizel Locke, he looked thoughtful and said: "All three, each after her own fashion, may be said to have served the cause of justice."

"This one," Alleyn said drily, "may be said to have died for it."

v

It was a quarter past two when Grizel Locke was carried in her coffin down to a mortuary van that shone glossily in the moonlight. Two hours later Alleyn and Dupont walked out of the Château de la Chèvre d'Argent. They left two men on guard and with Raoul went down the passage-way to the open platform. It was flooded in moonlight. The Mediterranean glittered down below and the hills reared themselves up fabulously against the stars. Robin Herrington's rakish car was parked at the edge of the platform.

Alleyn said: "These are our chickens come home to roost."

"Ah!" said M. Dupont cosily. "It is a night for love."

"Nevertheless, if you will excuse me—"

"But, of course!"

Alleyn, whistling tunelessly and tactfully, went over to the car. Robin was in the driver's seat with Ginny beside him. Her head was on his shoulder. He showed no particular surprise at seeing Alleyn.

"Good morning," Alleyn said. "So you had a breakdown."

"We did, sir, but we think we're under our own steam again."

"I'm glad to hear it. You will find the Chèvre d'Argent rather empty. Here's my card. The gendarme at the door will let you in. If you'd rather

ollect your possessions and come back to Roqueville, I expect we could get
ooms for you both at the Royal."

He waited for an answer but it was perfectly clear to him that although
hey smiled and nodded brightly they had not taken in a word of his little
peech.

Robin said: "Ginny's going to marry me."

"I hope you will both be *very* happy."

"We think of beginning again in one of the Dominions."

"The Dominions are, on the whole, both tolerant and helpful."

Ginny, speaking for the first time, said: "Will you please thank Mrs.
lleyn? She sort of did the trick."

"I shall. She'll be delighted to hear it." He looked at them for a moment
nd they beamed back at him. "You'll be all right," he said. "Get a tough
ob and forget you've had bad dreams. I'm sure it will work out."

They smiled and nodded.

"I'll have to ask you to come and see me later in the morning. At the
réfecture at eleven?"

"Thank you," they said vaguely. Ginny said: "You can't think how happy
e are, all of a sudden. And just imagine, I was furious when the car broke
own! And yet, if it hadn't, we might never have found out."

"Strange coincidence," said Alleyn, looking at Robin. And seeing that they
ere incapable of coming out of the moonlight he said: "Good morning and
ood luck to you both," and left them to themselves.

On the way down to Roqueville he and Dupont discussed the probable
evelopment of the case. "Oberon," Alleyn said, "has gone to pieces, as you
ee. He will try and buy his way out with information."

"Callard also is prepared to upset the peas. But thanks to your admirable
andling of the case we shall be able to dispense with such aids, and Oberon,
trust, will be tried with Baradi."

"Of the pair, Oberon is undoubtedly the more revolting," Alleyn said
houghtfully. "I wonder how many deaths could be laid at the door of those
wo. I don't know how you feel about it, Dupont, but I put their sort at the
op of the criminal list. If they hadn't directly killed poor Grizel, by God,
hey'd still be mass murderers."

"Undoubtedly," said Dupont, stifling a yawn. "I imagine we take state-
ents from the painter, the actress Wells and the two young ones and let it
o at that. They may be more useful running free. Particularly if they return
o the habit."

"The young ones won't. I'm sure of that. As for the others: there are cures."

In the front seat, Raoul, influenced no doubt by the moonlight and by his
limpse of Ginny and Robin, began to sing:

"*La nuit est faite pour l'amour.*"

"Raoul," Alleyn said in French for his benefit, "did a good job of work
onight, didn't he?"

"Not so bad, not so bad. We shall have you in the service yet, my friend," said Dupont. He leaned forward and struck Raoul lightly on the shoulder.

"No, M. le Commissaire, it is not my *métier*. I am about to settle with Teresa. And yet, if M. l'Inspecteur-en-Chef Alleyn should come back one day, who knows?"

They drove through the sleeping town to the little Square des Sarrasins and put Alleyn down at the hotel.

Troy was fast asleep, with Ricky curled in beside her. The little silver goat illuminated himself on the bedside table. The French windows were wide open and Alleyn went out for a moment on the balcony. To the east the stars had turned pale and the first dawn cock was crowing in the hills above Roqueville.

NIGHT
AT
THE
VULCAN

Contents

Cast of Characters

MARTYN TARNE
BOB GRANTLEY, business manager
FRED BADGER, night-watchman
CLEM SMITH, stage-manager
BOB CRINGLE, dresser to Adam Poole
ADAM POOLE, actor-manager
HELENA HAMILTON, leading lady
CLARK BENNINGTON, her husband
GAY GAINSFORD, his niece
J. G. DARCEY, character actor
PARRY PERCIVAL, juvenile
JACQUES DORÉ, designer and assistant to Adam Poole
DR. JOHN JAMES RUTHERFORD, playwright

of the
Vulcan
Theatre

CHIEF DETECTIVE-INSPECTOR ALLEYN
DETECTIVE-INSPECTOR FOX
DETECTIVE-SERGEANT GIBSON
DETECTIVE-SERGEANT BAILEY, finger-print expert
DETECTIVE-SERGEANT THOMPSON, photographer
P. C. LORD MICHAEL LAMPREY
DR. CURTIS

of the
Criminal
Investigation
Department,
New Scotland
Yard

CHAPTER I

The Vulcan

As she turned into Carpet Street the girl wondered at her own obstinacy. To what a pass it had brought her, she thought. She lifted first one foot and then the other, determined not to drag them. They felt now as if their texture had changed: their bones, it seemed, were covered by sponge and burning wires.

A clock in a jeweller's window gave the time as twenty-three minutes to five. She knew by the consequential scurry of its second-hand that it was alive. It was surrounded by other clocks that made mad dead statements of divergent times as if, she thought, to set before her the stages of that day's fruitless pilgrimage. Nine o'clock, the first agent. Nine thirty-six, the beginning of the wait for auditions at the Unicorn; five minutes past twelve, the first dismissal. "Thank you, Miss—ah— Thank you, dear. Leave your name and address. Next, please." No record of her flight from the smell of restaurants, but it must have been about ten to two, a time registered by a gilt carriage-clock in the corner, that she had climbed the stairs to Garnet Marks's Agency on the third floor. Three o'clock exactly at the Achilles where the auditions had already closed, and the next hour in and out of film agencies. "Leave your picture if you like, dear. Let you know if there's anything." Always the same. As punctual as time itself. The clocks receded, wobbled, enlarged themselves and at the same time spread before their dials a tenuous veil. Beneath the arm of a bronze nude that brandished an active swinging dial, she caught sight of a face: her own. She groped in her bag, and presently in front of the mirrored face a hand appeared and made a gesture at its own mouth with the stub of a lipstick. There was a coolness on her forehead, something pressed heavily against it. She discovered that this was the shop-window.

Behind the looking-glass was a man who peered at her from the shop's interior. She steadied herself with her hand against the window, lifted her suitcase and turned away.

The Vulcan Theatre was near the bottom of the street. Although she did not at first see its name above the entry, she had, during the past fortnight, discovered a sensitivity to theatres. She was aware of them at a distance. The way was downhill: her knees trembled and she resisted with difficulty an impulse to break into a shamble. Among the stream of faces that approached and sailed past there were now some that, on seeing hers, sharpened into awareness and speculation. She attracted notice.

The stage-door was at the end of an alleyway. Puddles of water obstructed her passage and she did not altogether avoid them. The surface of the wall was crenellated and damp.

"She knows," a rather shrill uncertain voice announced inside the theatre, "but she *mustn't* be told." A second voice spoke unintelligibly. The first voice repeated its statement with a change of emphasis: "She *knows* but she mustn't be *told*," and after a further interruption added dismally: "Thank you very much."

Five young women came out of the stage-door and it was shut behind them. She leant against the wall as they passed her. The first two muttered together and moved their shoulders petulantly, the third stared at her and at once she bent her head. The fourth passed by quickly with compressed lips. She kept her head averted and heard, but did not see, the last girl halt beside her.

"Well, for God's sake!" She looked up and saw, for the second time that day, a too-large face, over-painted, with lips that twisted downwards, tinted lids, and thickly mascaraed lashes.

She said: "I'm late, aren't I?"

"You've had it, dear. I gave you the wrong tip at Marks's. The show here, with the part I told you about, goes on this week. They were auditioning for a tour— 'That'll be all for to-day, ladies, thank you. What's the hurry, here's your hat!' For what it's worth, it's all over."

"I lost my way," she said faintly.

"Too bad." The large face swam nearer. "Are you all right?" it demanded. She made a slight movement of her head. "A bit tired. All right, really." "You look shocking. Here: wait a sec. Try this."

"No, no. Really. Thank you so much but—"

"It's O.K. A chap who travels for a French firm gave it to me. It's marvellous stuff: cognac. Go *on*."

A hand steadied her head. The cold mouth of the flask opened her lips and pressed against her teeth. She tried to say: "I've had nothing to eat," and at once was forced to gulp down a burning stream. The voice encouraged her: "Do you a power of good. Have the other half."

She shuddered, gasped and pushed the flask away. "No, please!"

"Is it doing the trick?"

"This is wonderfully kind of you. I am so grateful. Yes, I think it must be doing the trick."

"Gra-a-a-nd. Well, if you're sure you'll be O.K. . . ."

"Yes, indeed. I don't even know your name."

"Trixie O'Sullivan."

"I'm Martyn Tarne."

"Look nice in the programme, wouldn't it? If there's nothing else I can do . . ."

"Honestly. I'll be fine."

"You look better," Miss O'Sullivan said doubtfully. "We may run into each other again. The bloody round, the common task." She began to move away. "I've got a date, actually, and I'm running late."

"Yes, of course. Good-bye, and thank you."

"It's open in front. There's a seat in the foyer. Nobody'll say anything. Why not sit there for a bit?" She was half-way down the alley. "Hope you get fixed up," she said. "God, it's going to rain. What a life!"

"What a life," Martyn Tarne echoed, and tried to sound gay and ironic. "I hope you'll be all right. 'Bye."

"Good-bye and thank you."

The alley was quiet now. Without moving she took stock of herself. Something thrummed inside her head and the tips of her fingers tingled but she no longer felt as if she were going to faint. The brandy glowed at the core of her being, sending out ripples of comfort. She tried to think what she should do. There was a church, back in the Strand: she ought to know its name. One could sleep there, she had been told, and perhaps there would be soup. That would leave two and fourpence for to-morrow: all she had. She lifted her suitcase—it was heavier than she had remembered—and walked to the end of the alleyway. Half a dozen raindrops plopped into a puddle. People hurried along the footpath with upward glances and opened their umbrellas. As she hesitated, the rain came down suddenly and decisively. She turned towards the front of the theatre and at first thought it was shut. Then she noticed that one of the plate-glass doors was ajar.

She pushed it open and went in.

The Vulcan was a new theatre, fashioned from the shell of an old one. Its foyer was an affair of geranium-red leather, chromium steel and double glass walls housing cacti. The central box-office, marked RESERVED TICKETS ONLY, was flanked by doors and beyond them, in the corners, were tubular steel and rubber-foam seats. She crossed the heavily carpeted floor and sat in one of these. Her feet and legs, released from the torment of supporting and moving her body, throbbed ardently.

Facing Martyn, on a huge easel, was a frame of photographs under a printed legend:

Opening at this theatre
on
THURSDAY, MAY 11TH
THUS TO REVISIT
A *New Play*
by
JOHN JAMES RUTHERFORD

She stared at two large familiar faces and four strange smaller ones. Adam Poole and Helena Hamilton: those were famous faces. Monstrously enlarged, they had looked out at the New Zealand and Australian public from hoardings and from above cinema entrances. She had stood in queues many times to see them, separately and together. They were in the centre, and surrounding them were Clark Bennington with a pipe and stick and a look of faded romanticism in his eyes, J. G. Darcey with pince-nez and hair *en brosse*, Gay Gainsford, young and intense, and Parry Percival, youngish and dashing. The faces swam together and grew dim.

It was very quiet in the foyer and beginning to get dark. On the other side of the entrance doors the rain drove down slantways, half-blinding her vision of homeward-bound pedestrians and the traffic of the street beyond them. She saw the lights go on in the top of a bus, illuminating the passive and remote faces of its passengers. The glare of headlamps shone pale across the rain. A wave of loneliness, excruciating in its intensity, engulfed Martyn and she closed her eyes. For the first time since her ordeal began, panic rose in her throat and sickened her. Phrases drifted with an aimless rhythm on the tide of her desolation: "You're sunk, you're sunk, you're utterly sunk, you asked for it, and you've got it. What'll happen to you now?"

She was drowning at night in a very lonely sea. She saw lights shine on some unattainable shore. Pieces of flotsam bobbed indifferently against her hands. At the climax of despair, metallic noises, stupid and commonplace, set up a clatter in her head.

Martyn jerked galvanically and opened her eyes. The whirr and click of her fantasy had been repeated behind an obscured-glass wall on her left. Light glowed beyond the wall and she was confronted by the image of a god, sand-blasted across the surface of the glass and beating at a forge under the surprising supervision, it appeared, of Melpomene and Thalia. Further along, a notice in red light, Dress Circle and Stalls, jutted out from an opening. Beyond the hammer-blows of her heart a muffled voice spoke peevishly.

". . . not much use to *me*. What? Yes, I know, old boy, but that's not the point."

The voice seemed to listen. Martyn thought: "This is it. In a minute I'll be turned out."

". . . something pretty bad," the voice said irritably. "She's gone to hospital. . . . They *said* so but nobody's turned up. . . . Well, you know what she's like, old boy, don't you? We've been snowed under all day and I haven't been able to do anything about it . . . auditions for the northern tour of the old piece . . . yes, yes, that's all fixed but . . . Look, another thing: the *Onlooker* wants a story and pictures for this week . . . yes, on stage. In costume. Nine-thirty in the morning and everything still in the boxes. . . . Well, can't you think of *anyone*? . . . Who? . . . Oh, God, I'll give it a pop. All right, old boy, thanks."

To Martyn, dazed with brandy and sleep, it was a distortion of a daydream. Very often had she dreamt herself into a theatre where all was confusion because the leading actress had laryngitis and the understudy was useless. She would present herself modestly: "I happen to know the lines.

I could perhaps . . ." The sudden attentiveness, when she began to speak the lines . . . the opening night . . . the grateful tears streaming down the boiled shirts of the management . . . the critics . . . no image had been too gross for her.

"Eileen?" said the voice. "Thank God! Listen, darling, it's Bob Grantley here. Listen, Eileen, I want you to do something terribly kind. I know it's asking a hell of a lot but I'm in trouble and you're my last hope. Helena's dresser's ill. Yes, indeed, poor old Tansley. Yes, I'm afraid so. Just this afternoon, and we haven't been able to raise anybody. First dress rehearsal to-morrow night and a photograph call in the morning and nothing unpacked or anything. I know what a good soul you are and I wondered . . . Oh, God! I see. Yes, I see. No, of course. Oh, well, never mind. I know you would. Yes. 'Bye."

Silence. Precariously alone in the foyer, she meditated an advance upon the man beyond the glass wall and suppressed a dreadful impulse in herself towards hysteria. This was her day-dream in terms of reality. She must have slept longer than she had thought. Her feet were sleeping still. She began to test them, tingling and pricking, against the floor. She could see her reflection in the front doors, a dingy figure with a pallid face and cavernous shadows for eyes.

The light behind the glass wall went out. There was, however, still a yellow glow coming through the box-office door. As she got to her feet and steadied herself, the door opened.

"I believe," she said, "you are looking for a dresser."

ii

As he had stopped dead in the lighted doorway she couldn't see the man clearly but his silhouette was stocky and trim.

He said with what seemed to be a mixture of irritation and relief: "Good Lord, how long have you been here?"

"Not long. You were on the telephone. I didn't like to interrupt."

"Interrupt!" he ejaculated as if she talked nonsense. He looked at his watch, groaned, and said rapidly: "You've come about this job? From Mrs. Greenacres, aren't you?"

She wondered who Mrs. Greenacres could be? An employment agent? She hunted desperately for the right phrase, the authentic language.

"I understood you required a dresser and I would be pleased to apply." Should she have added "sir"?

"It's for Miss Helena Hamilton," he said rapidly. "Her own dresser who's been with her for years—for a long time—has been taken ill. I explained to Mrs. Greenacres. Photograph call for nine in the morning and first dress rehearsal to-morrow night. We open on Thursday. The dressing's heavy. Two quick changes and so on. I suppose you've got references?"

Her mouth was dry. She said: "I haven't brought—" and was saved by the telephone bell. He plunged back into the office and she heard him shout "Vulcan!" as he picked up the receiver. "Grantley, here," he said. "Oh, hullo, darling. Look, I'm desperately sorry, but I've been held up or I'd have rung you before. For God's sake apologize for me. Try and keep them going till I get there. I know, I know. Not a smell of one until—" The voice became suddenly muffled: she caught isolated words. "I think so . . . yes, I'll ask . . . yes . . . Right. 'Bye, darling."

He darted out, now wearing a hat and struggling into a raincoat. "Look," he said, "Miss—"

"Tarne."

"Miss Tarne. Can you start right away? Miss Hamilton's things are in her dressing-room. They need to be unpacked and hung out to-night. There'll be a lot of pressing. The cleaners have been in but the room's not ready. You can finish in the morning but she wants the things that can't be ironed— I wouldn't know—hung out. Here are the keys. We'll see how you get on and fix up something definite to-morrow if you suit. The night-watchman's there. He'll open the room for you. Say I sent you. Here!"

He fished out a wallet, found a card and scribbled on it. "He's a bit of a stickler: you'd better take this."

She took the card and the keys. "To-night?" she said. "Now?"

"Well, can you?"

"I—yes. But—"

"Not worrying about after-hours are you?"

"No."

For the first time he seemed, in the darkish foyer, to be looking closely at her. "I suppose," he muttered, "it's a bit—" and stopped short.

Martyn said in a voice that to herself sounded half-choked: "I'm perfectly trustworthy. You spoke of references. I have—"

"Oh, yes, yes," he said. "Good. That'll be O.K. then. I'm late. Will you be all right? You can go through the house. It's raining outside. Through there, will you? Thank you. Good night."

Taking up her suitcase, she went through the door he swung open and found herself in the theatre.

She was at the back of the stalls, standing on thick carpet at the top of the ramp and facing the centre aisle. It was not absolutely dark. The curtain was half-raised and a bluish light filtered in from off-stage through some opening—a faintly discerned window—in the scenery. This light was dimly reflected on the shrouded boxes. The dome was invisible, lost in shadow, and so far above that the rain, hammering on the roof beyond it, sounded much as a rumour of drums to Martyn. The deadened air smelt of naphthalene and plush.

She started off cautiously down the aisle. "I forgot," said Mr. Grantley's voice behind her. She managed to choke back a yelp. "You'd better get some flowers for the dressing-room. She likes roses. Here's another card."

"I don't think I've—"

"Florian's at the corner," he shouted. "Show them the card."

The door swung to behind him and a moment later she heard a more remote slam. She waited for a little while longer, to accustom herself to the dark. The shadows melted and the shape of the auditorium filtered through them like an image on a film in the darkroom. She thought it beautiful: the curve of the circle, the fan-like shell that enclosed it, the elegance of the proscenium and modesty of the ornament—all these seemed good to Martyn, and her growing sight of them refreshed her. Though this encouragement had an unreal, rather dream-like character, yet it did actually dispel something of her physical exhaustion so that it was with renewed heart that she climbed a little curved flight of steps on the Prompt side of the proscenium, pushed open the pass-door at the top and arrived back-stage.

She was on her own ground. A single blue working-light, thick with dust, revealed a baize letter-rack and hinted at the batten-and-canvas backs of scenery fading upwards into yawning blackness. At her feet a litter of flex ran down into holes in the stage. There were vague, scarcely discernible shapes that she recognized as stacked flats, light bunches, the underside of perches, a wind machine and rain box. She smelt paint and glue size. As she received the assurance of these familiar signs she heard a faint scuffling noise—a rattle of paper, she thought. She moved forward.

In the darkness ahead of her a door opened on an oblong of light which widened to admit the figure of a man in an overcoat. He stood with bent head, fumbled in his pocket and produced a torch. The beam shot out, hunted briefly about the set and walls and found her. She blinked into a dazzling white disc and said: "Mr. Grantley sent me round. I'm the dresser."

"Dresser?" the man said hoarsely. He kept his torchlight on her face and moved towards her. "I wasn't told about no dresser," he said.

She held Mr. Grantley's card out. He came closer and flashed his light on it without touching it. "Ah," he said with a sort of grudging cheerfulness, "that's different. Now I know where I am, don't I?"

"I hope so," she said, trying to make her voice friendly. "I'm sorry to bother you. Miss Hamilton's dresser has been taken ill and I've got the job."

"*Aren't* you lucky," he said with obvious relish and added, "Not but what she isn't a lady when she takes the fit for it."

He was eating something. The movement of his jaws, the succulent noises he made and the faint odour of food were an outrage. She could have screamed her hunger at him. Her mouth filled with saliva.

"'E says to open the star room," he said. "Come on froo while I get the keys. I was 'avin' me bit er supper."

She followed him into a tiny room choked with junk. A kettle stuttered on a gas ring by a sink clotted with dregs of calcimine and tea leaves. His supper was laid out on a newspaper—bread and an open tin of jam. He explained that he was about to make a cup of tea and suggested she should wait while he did so. She leant against the door and watched him. The fragrance of freshly brewed tea rose above the reek of stale size and dust. She thought, "If he drinks it now I'll have to go out."

"Like a drop of char?" he said. His back was turned to her.

"Very much."

He rinsed out a stained cup under the tap.

Martyn said loudly: "I've got a tin of meat in my suitcase. I was saving it. If you'd like to share it and could spare some of your bread . . ."

He swung round and for the first time she saw his face. He was dark and thin and his eyes were brightly impertinent. Their expression changed as he stared at her.

"'Ullo, 'ullo!" he said. "Who give *you* a tanner and borrowed 'alf-a-crahn? What's up?"

"I'm all right."

"*Are* you? Your looks don't flatter you, then."

"I'm a bit tired and—" Her voice broke and she thought in terror that she was going to cry. "It's nothing," she said.

"'Ere!" He dragged a box out from under the sink and not ungently pushed her down on it. "Where's this remarkable tin of very pertikler meat? Give us a shine at it."

He shoved her suitcase over and while she fumbled at the lock busied himself with pouring out tea. "Nothin' to touch a drop of the old char when you're browned off," he said. He put the reeking cup of dark fluid beside her and turned away.

"With any luck," Martyn thought, folding back the garments in her case, "I won't have to sell these now."

She found the tin and gave it to him. "Coo!" he said. "Looks lovely, don't it? Tongue and veal and a pitcher of sheep to show there's no deception. Very tempting."

"Can you open it?"

"Can I open it? Oh, dear."

She drank her scalding tea and watched him open the tin and turn its contents out on a more than dubious plate. Using his clasp knife he perched chunks of meat on a slab of bread and held it out to her. "You're in luck," he said. "Eat it slow."

She urged him to join her but he said he would set his share aside for later. They could both, he suggested, take another cut at it to-morrow. He examined the tin with interest while Martyn consumed her portion. She had never before given such intense concentration to a physical act. She would never have believed that eating could bring so fierce a satisfaction.

"Comes from Australia, don't it?" her companion said, still contemplating the tin.

"New Zealand."

"Same thing."

Martyn said: "Not really. There's quite a big sea in between."

"Do you come from there?"

"Where?"

"Australia."

"No. I'm a New Zealander."

"Same thing."

She looked up and found him grinning at her. He made the gesture of wiping the smile off his face. "Oh, dear," he said.

Martyn finished her tea and stood up. "I must start my job," she said.

"Feel better?"

"Much, much better."

"Would it be quite a spell since you ate anything?"

"Yesterday."

"I never fancy drinkin' on an empty stomach, myself."

Her face burnt against the palms of her hands. "But I don't . . . I mean, I know. I mean I was a bit faint and somebody . . . a girl . . . she was terribly kind . . ."

"Does yer mother know yer aht?" he asked ironically, and took a key from a collection hung on nails behind the door. "If you *must* work," he said.

"Please."

"Personally escorted tour abaht to commence. Follow in single file and don't talk to the guide. I thank you."

She followed him to the stage and round the back of the set. He warned her of obstructions by bobbing his torchlight on them and, when she stumbled against a muffled table, took her hand. She was disquieted by the grip of his fingers, calloused and wooden, and by the warmth of his palm, which was unexpectedly soft. She was oppressed with renewed loneliness and fear.

"End of the penny section," he said, releasing her. He unlocked a door, reached inside and switched on a light.

"They call this the Greenroom," he said. "That's what it was in the old days. It's been done up. Guv'nor's idea."

It was a room without a window, newly painted in green. There were a number of armchairs in brown leather, a round table littered with magazines, a set of well-stocked bookshelves and a gas fire. Groups of framed Pollock's prints decorated the walls: "Mr. Dale as Claude Amboine," "Mr. T. Hicks as Richard I," "Mr. S. French as Harlequin." This last enchanted Martyn because the diamonds of Mr. French's costume had been filled in with actual red and green sequins and he glittered in his frame.

Above the fireplace hung a largish sketch—it was little more than that—of a man of about thirty-five in mediaeval dress, with a hood that he was in the act of pushing away from his face. The face was arresting. It had great purity of form, being wide across the eyes and heart-shaped. The mouth, in particular, was of a most subtle character, perfectly masculine but drawn with extreme delicacy. It was well done: it had both strength and refinement. Yet it was not these qualities that disturbed Martyn. Reflected in the glass that covered the picture she saw her own face lying ghost-wise across the other;

their forms intermingled like those in a twice-exposed photograph. It seemed to Martyn that her companion must be looking over her shoulder at this double image and she moved away from him and nearer to the picture. The reflection disappeared. Something was written faintly in one corner of the sketch. She drew closer and saw that it was a single word: *Everyman.*

"Spittin' image of 'im, ain't it?" said the night-watchman behind her.

"I don't know," she said quickly. "Is it?"

"*Is* it! Don't you know the Guv'nor when you see 'im?"

"The Governor?"

"'Strewth you're a caution and no error. Don't you know who owns this show? That's the great Mr. Adam Poole, that is."

"Oh," she murmured after a pause, and added uneasily: "I've seen him in the pictures, of course."

"Go on!" he jeered. "Where would that be? Australia? Fancy!"

He had been very kind to her, but she found his remorseless vein of irony exasperating. It would have been easier and less tedious to have let it go but she found herself embarked on an explanation. Of course she knew all about Mr. Adam Poole, she said. She'd seen his photograph in the foyer. All his pictures had been shown in New Zealand. She knew he was the most distinguished of the younger contemporary actor-managers. She was merely startled by the painting because . . . But it was impossible to explain why the face in the painting disturbed her and the unfinished phrase trailed away into an embarrassed silence.

Her companion listened to this rigmarole with an equivocal grin and when she gave it up merely remarked: "Don't apologize. It's the same with all the ladies. 'E fair rocks 'em. Talk about 'aving what it takes."

"I don't mean that at all," she shouted angrily.

"You should see 'em clawing at each other to get at 'im rahnd the stage-door, first nights. Something savage! Females of the speeches? Disgrace to their sexes more like. There's an ironing board etceterer in the wardrobe-room further along. You can plug in when you're ready. 'Er royal 'ighness is over the way."

He went out, opened a further door, switched on a light and called to her to join him.

iii

As soon as she crossed the threshold of the star dressing-room she smelt greasepaint. The dressing-shelf was bare, the room untenanted, but the smell of cosmetics mingled with the faint reek of gas. There were isolated dabs of colour on the shelves and the looking-glass; the lamp bulbs were smeared with cream and red where sticks of greasepaint had been warmed at them; and on a shelf above the wash-basin somebody had left a miniature frying-pan of congealed mascara in which a hair-pin was embedded.

It was a largish room, windowless and dank, with an air of submerged grandeur about it. The full-length cheval-glass swung from a gilt frame. There was an Empire couch, an armchair and an ornate stool before the dressing-shelf. The floor was carpeted in red with a florid pattern that use had in part obliterated. A number of dress-boxes bearing the legend *Costumes by Pierrot et Cie* were stacked in the middle of the room, and there were two suitcases on the shelf. A gas heater stood against one wall and there was a caged jet above the wash-basin.

"Here we are," said the night-watchman. "All yer own."

She turned to thank him and encountered a speculative stare. "Cosy," he said, "ain't it?" and moved nearer. "Nice little hidey hole, ain't it?"

"You've been very kind," Martyn said. "I'll manage splendidly, now. Thank you very much indeed."

"Don't mention it. Any time." His hand reached out clumsily to her arm. "Been aht in the rain," he said thickly. "Naughty girl."

"It'll soon dry off. I'm quite all right."

She moved behind the pile of dress-boxes and fumbled with the string on the top one. There was a hissing noise. She heard him strike a match and a moment later was horribly jolted by an explosion from the gas heater. It forced an involuntary cry from her.

"'Ullo, *'ullo!*" her companion said. "Ain't superstitious, are we?"

"Superstitious?"

He made an inexplicable gesture towards the gas fire. "*You* know," he said, grinning horridly at her.

"I'm afraid I don't understand?"

"Don't tell me you never 'eard abaht the great Jupiter case! Don't they learn you nothing in them anty-podes?"

The heater reddened and purred.

"Come to think of it," he said, "it'd be before your time. I wasn't 'ere myself when it occurred, a-course, but them that was don't give you a chance to forget it. Not that they mention it direct-like, but it don't get forgotten."

"What was it?" Martyn asked against her will.

"Sure yer not superstitious?"

"No, I'm not."

"You ain't been long in this business, then. Nor more am I. Shake 'ands." He extended his hand so pointedly that she was obliged to put her own in it and had some difficulty in releasing herself.

"It must be five years ago," he said, "all of that. A bloke in Number Four dressing-room did another bloke in, very cunning, by blowing dahn the tube of 'is own gas fire. Like if I went nex' door and blew dahn the tube, this fire'd go aht. And if you was dead drunk, like you might of been if this girl-friend of yours'd been very generous with 'er brandy, you'd be commy-tose and before you knew where you was you'd be dead. Which is what occurred. It made a very nasty impression and the theatre was shut dahn for a long while until they 'ad it all altered and pansied up. The Guv'nor won't 'ave it mentioned. 'E changed the name of the 'ouse when 'e took it on. But call it what you like, the memory, as they say, lingers on. Silly, though, ain't it? You and me don't care. That's right, ain't it? We'd rather be cosy. Wouldn't we?" He gave a kind of significance to the word "cosy." Martyn unlocked the suitcases. Her fingers were unsteady and she turned her back in order to hide them from him. He stood in front of the gas fire and began to give out a smell of hot dirty cloth. She took sheets from a suitcase, hung them under the clothes pegs round the walls, and began to unpack the boxes. Her feet throbbed cruelly and she surreptitiously shuffled them out of her wet shoes.

"That's the ticket," he said. "Dry 'em orf, shall we?"

He advanced upon her and squatted to gather up the shoes. His hand, large and prehensile, with a life of its own, darted out and closed over her foot. " 'Ow abaht yer stockings?"

Martyn felt not only frightened but humiliated and ridiculous—wobbling, dead tired, on one foot. It was as if she were half-caught in some particularly degrading kind of stocks.

She said: "Look here, you're a good chap. You've been terribly kind. Let me get on with the job."

His grip slackened. He looked up at her without embarrassment, his thin London face sharp with curiosity. "O.K.," he said. "No offence meant. Call it a day, eh?"

"Call it a day."

"You're the boss," he said, and got to his feet. He put her shoes down in front of the gas fire and went to the door. "Live far from 'ere?" he asked. A feeling of intense desolation swept through her and left her without the heart to prevaricate.

"I don't know," she said. "I've got to find somewhere. There's a women's hostel near Paddington, I think."

"Broke?"

"I'll be all right, now I've got this job."

His hand was in his pocket. " 'Ere," he said.

"No, no. Please."

"Come orf it. We're pals, ain't we?"

"No, really. I'm terribly grateful but I'd rather not. I'm all right."

"You're the boss," he said again, and after a pause: "I can't get the idea, honest I can't. The way you speak and be'ave and all. What's the story? 'Ard luck or what?"

"There's no story, really."

"Just what you say yourself. No questions asked." He opened the door and moved into the passage. "Mind," he said over his shoulder, "it's against the rules but I won't be rahnd again. My mate relieves me at eight ack emma but I'll tip 'im the wink if it suits you. Them chairs in the Greenroom's not bad for a bit of kip and there's the fire. I'll turn it on. Please yerself, a-course."

"Oh," she said, "could I? Could I?"

"Never know what you can do till you try. Keep it under your titfer, though, or I'll be in trouble. So long. Don't get down'earted. It'll be all the same in a fahsand years."

He had gone. Martyn ran into the passage and saw his torchlight bobbing out on the stage. She called after him: "Thank you—thank you so much! I don't know your name, but thank you and good night."

"Badger's the name," he said, and his voice sounded hollow in the empty darkness. "Call me Fred."

The light bobbed out of sight. She heard him whistling for a moment and then a door slammed and she was alone.

With renewed heart she turned back to her job.

iv

At ten o'clock she had finished. She had traversed with diligence all the hazards of fatigue: the mounting threat of sleep, the clumsiness that makes the simplest action an ordeal, the horror of inertia and the temptation to let go the tortured muscles and give up, finally and indifferently, the awful struggle.

Five carefully ironed dresses hung sheeted against the walls, the make-up was laid out on the covered dressing-shelf. The boxes were stacked away, the framed photographs set out. It only remained to buy roses in the morning for Miss Helena Hamilton. Even the vase was ready and filled with water.

Martyn leant heavily on the back of a chair and stared at two photographs of the same face in a double leather case. They were not theatre photographs but studio portraits, and the face looked younger than the face in the Greenroom: younger and more formidable, with the mouth set truculently and the gaze withdrawn. But it had the same effect on Martyn. Written at the bottom of each of these photographs, in a small incisive hand, was: *Helena from Adam, 1950.* "Perhaps," she thought, "he's married to her."

Hag-ridden by the fear that she had forgotten some important detail, she paused in the doorway and looked round the room. No, she thought, there was nothing more to be done. But as she turned to go she saw herself, cruelly reflected in the long cheval-glass. It was not, of course, the first time she had seen herself that night; she had passed before the looking-glasses a dozen times and had actually polished them, but her attention had been ruthlessly fixed on the job in hand and she had not once focussed her eyes on her own image. Now she did so. She saw a girl in a yellow sweater and dark skirt with black hair that hung in streaks over her forehead. She saw a white, heart-shaped face with smudges under the eyes and a mouth that was normally firm and delicate but now drooped with fatigue. She raised her hand, pushed the hair back from her face and stared for a moment or two longer. Then she switched off the light and blundered across the passage into the Greenroom. Here, collapsed in an armchair with her overcoat across her, she slept heavily until morning.

CHAPTER II

In a Glass Darkly

Martyn slept for ten hours. A wind got up in the night and found its way into the top of the stagehouse at the Vulcan. Up in the grid old back-cloths moved a little and, since the Vulcan was a hemp-house, there was a soughing among the forest of ropes. Flakes of paper, relics of some Victorian snowstorm, were dislodged from the top of a batten and fluttered down to the stage. Rain, driven fitfully against the theatre, ran in cascades down pipes and dripped noisily from ledges into the stage-door entry. The theatre mice came out, explored the contents of paste-pots in the sink-room and scuttled unsuccessfully about a covered plate of tongue and veal. Out in the auditorium there arose at intervals a vague whisper, and in his cubby-hole off the dock Fred Badger dozed and woke uneasily. At one o'clock he went on his rounds. He padded down corridors, flicking his torchlight on framed sketches for décor and costumes, explored the foyer and examined the locked doors of the offices. He climbed the heavily carpeted stairs and, lost in meditation, stood for a long time in the dress circle among shrouded rows of seats and curtained doorways. Sighing dolorously he returned back-stage and made a stealthy entrance onto the set. Finally he creaked to the Greenroom door and, impelled by who knows what impulse, furtively opened it.

Martyn lay across the chair, her knees supported by one of its arms and her head by the other. The glow from the gas fire was reflected in her face. Fred Badger stood for quite a long time eyeing her and scraping his chin with calloused fingers. At last he backed out, softly closed the door and tiptoed to his cubby-hole, where he telephoned the fire-station to make his routine report.

At dawn the rain stopped and cleaning-vans swept the water down Carpet Street with their great brushes. Milk-carts clinked past the Vulcan and the first bus roared by. Martyn heard none of them. She woke to the murmur of the gas fire, and the confused memory of a dream in which someone tapped gently at a door. The windowless room was still dark but she looked at her watch in the fire-glow and found it was eight o'clock. She got up stiffly, crossed the room and opened the door on grey diffused daylight. A cup of tea with a large sandwich balanced on it had been left on the floor of the passage. Underneath it was a torn scrap of paper on which was scrawled: *Keep your pecker up matey see you some more.*

With a feeling of gratitude and timid security she breakfasted in the Greenroom, and afterwards explored the empty passage, finding at the far end an unlocked and unused dressing-room. To this room she brought her own suitcase and here, with a chair propped under the door-handle, she stripped and washed in icy water. In clean clothes, with her toilet complete, and with a feeling of detachment, as if she herself looked on from a distance at these proceedings, she crossed the stage and went out through the side door and up the alleyway into Carpet Street.

It was a clean sunny morning. The air struck sharply at her lips and nostrils and the light dazzled her. A van had drawn up outside the Vulcan and men were lifting furniture from it. There were cleaners at work in the foyer and a telegraph boy came out whistling. Carpet Street was noisy with traffic. Martyn turned left and walked quickly downhill until she came to a corner shop called Florian. In the window a girl in a blue coverall was setting out a large gilt basket of roses. The door was still locked but Martyn, emboldened by fresh air and a sense of freedom and adventure, tapped on the window and when the girl looked up pointed to the roses and held up Mr. Grantley's card. The girl smiled and, leaving the window, came to let her in.

Martyn said: "I'm sorry to bother you, but Mr. Grantley at the Vulcan told me to get some roses for Miss Helena Hamilton. He didn't give me any money and I'm afraid I haven't got any. Is all this very irregular and tiresome?"

"That will be quayte O.K.," the girl said in a friendly manner. "Mr. Grantley has an account."

"Perhaps you know what sort of roses I should get," Martyn suggested. She felt extraordinarily light and rather loquacious. "You see, I'm Miss Hamilton's dresser but I'm new and I don't know what she likes."

"Red would be quayte in order, I think. There are some lovely Bloody Warriors just in." She caught Martyn's eye and giggled. "Well, they do think of the weirdest names, don't they? Look: aren't they lovelies?"

She held up a group of roses with drops of water clinging to their half-opened petals. "Gorgeous," she said, "aren't they? Such a colour."

Martyn, appalled at the price, took a dozen. The girl looked curiously at her and said: "Miss Hamilton's dresser. Fancy! Aren't you lucky?" and she was vividly reminded of Fred Badger.

"I feel terribly lucky this morning," she said and was going away when the girl, turning pink under her make-up, said: "Pardon me asking, but I don't suppose you could get me Miss Hamilton's autograph. I'd be ever so thrilled."

"I haven't even seen her yet but I'll do my best."

"You *are* a duck. Thanks a million. Of course," the girl added, "I'm a real fan. I never miss any of her pictures and I do think Adam Poole—pardon me, Mr. Poole—is simply mawvellous. I mean to say I just think he's mawvellous. They're so mawvellous together. I suppose he's crazy about her in real life, isn't he? I always say they couldn't act together like that—you know, so gorgeously—unless they had a pretty hot clue on the sayde. Don't you agree?"

Martyn said she hadn't had a chance of forming an opinion as yet and left the florist in pensive contemplation of the remaining Bloody Warriors.

When she got back to the theatre its character had completely changed: it

was alive and noisy. The dock-doors were open and sunlight lay in incongruous patches on painted canvas and stacked furniture. Up in the grid there
was a sound of hammering. A back-cloth hung diagonally in mid-air and descended in jerks, while a man in shirt-sleeves shouted: "Down on yer long.
Now yer short. Now bodily. Right-oh! Dead it. Now find yer Number Two."

A chandelier lay in a heap in the middle of the stage, and above it was
suspended a batten of spotlights within reach of an elderly mechanic who
fitted pink and straw-coloured mediums into their frames. Near the stage-
door a group of men stared at a small Empire desk from which a stage-hand
had removed a cloth wrapping. A tall young man in spectacles, wearing a
red pullover and corduroy trousers, said irritably: "It's too bloody chi-chi.
Without a shadow of doubt, he'll hate its guts."

He glanced at Martyn and added: "Put them in her room, dear, will you?"

She hurried to the dressing-room passage and found that here too there was
life and movement. A vacuum-cleaner hummed in the Greenroom, a bald
man in overalls was tacking cards on the doors, somewhere down the passage
an unseen person sang cheerfully and the door next to Miss Hamilton's was
open. These signs of preparation awakened in Martyn a sense of urgency. In
a sudden fluster she unwrapped her roses and thrust them into the vase.
The stalks were too long and she had nothing to cut them with. She ran down
the passage to the empty room, and reflected as she rootled in her suitcase
that she would be expected to have sewing materials at hand. Here was the
housewife an aunt had given her when she left New Zealand but it was
depleted and in a muddle. She ran back with it, sawed at the rose stems with
her nail-scissors and, when someone in the next room tapped on the wall,
inadvertently jammed the points into her hand.

"And how," a disembodied voice inquired, "is La Belle Tansley this
morning?"

Sucking her left hand and arranging roses with her right, Martyn wondered how she should respond to this advance. She called out tentatively:
"I'm afraid it's not Miss Tansley."

"What's that?" the voice said vaguely, and a moment later she heard the
brisk sound of a clothes-brush at work.

The roses were done at last. She stood with the ends of the stalks in her
hand and wondered why she had become so nervous.

"Here we go again," a voice said in the doorway. She spun round to face a
small man in an alpaca coat with a dinner-jacket in his hands. He stared at
her with his jaw dropped. "Pardon me," he said. "I thought you was Miss
Tansley."

Martyn explained. "Well!" he said. "That'll be her heart, that will. She
ought to have given up before this. I warned her. In hospital, too? T'ch,
t'ch, t'ch." He wagged his head and looked, apparently in astonishment, at
Martyn. "So that's the story," he continued, "and you've stepped into the
breach. Fancy that! Better introduce ourselves, hadn't we? The name's

Cringle but Bob'll do as well as anything else. I'm 'is lordship's dresser. How are you?"

Martyn gave him her name and they shook hands. He had a pleasant face covered with a cobweb of fine wrinkles. "Been long at this game?" he asked, and added: "Well, that's a foolish question, isn't it? I should have said: Will this be your first place, or Are you doing it in your school holidays, or something of that sort."

"Do you suppose," Martyn said anxiously, "Miss Hamilton will think I'm too young?"

"Not if you give satisfaction, she won't. She's all right if you give satisfaction. Different from my case. Slave meself dizzy, I can, and if 'is lordship's in one of 'is moods, what do I get for it? Spare me days, I don't know why I put up with it and that's a fact. But *she's* all right if she likes you." He paused and added tentatively: "But you know all about that, I dare say." Martyn was silent and felt his curiosity reach out as if it were something tangible. At last she said desperately: "I'll try. I want to give satisfaction."

He glanced round the room. "Looks nice," he said. "Are you pressed and shook out? Yes, I can see you are. Flowers too. Very nice. Would you be a friend of hers? Doing it to oblige, like?"

"No, no. I've never seen her. Except in the pictures, of course."

"Is that a fact?" His rather bird-like eyes were bright with speculation. "Young ladies," he said, "have to turn their hands to all sorts of work these days, don't they?"

"I suppose so. Yes."

"No offence, I hope, but I was wondering if you come from one of those drama-schools. Hoping to learn a bit, watching from the side, like."

A kind of sheepishness that had hardened into obstinacy prevented her from telling him in a few words why she was there. The impulse of a fortnight ago to rush to somebody—the ship's captain, the High Commissioner for her own country, anyone—and unload her burden of disaster had given place almost at once to a determined silence. This mess was of her own making, she had decided, and she herself would see it out. And throughout the loneliness and panic of her ordeal, to this resolution she had stuck. It had ceased to be a reasoned affair with Martyn: the less she said, the less she wanted to say. She had become crystallized in reticence.

So she met the curiosity of the little dresser with an evasion. "It'd be wonderful," she said, "if I did get the chance."

A deep voice with an unusually vibrant quality called out on the stage. "Bob! Where the devil have you got to? Bob!"

"Cripes!" the little dresser ejaculated. "Here we are *and* in one of our tantrums. *In here, sir! Coming, sir!*"

He darted towards the doorway but before he reached it a man appeared there, a man so tall that for a fraction of a second he looked down over the dresser's head directly into Martyn's eyes.

"This young lady," Bob Cringle explained with an air of discovery, "is the new dresser for Miss Hamilton. I just been showing her the ropes, Mr. Poole, sir."

"You'd much better attend to your work. I want you." He glanced again at Martyn. "Good morning," he said and was gone. "Look at this!" she heard him say angrily in the next room. "Where *are* you!"

Cringle paused in the doorway to turn his thumbs down and his eyes up. "Here we are, sir. What's the little trouble?" he was saying pacifically as he disappeared.

Martyn thought: "The picture in the Greenroom is more like him than the photographs." Preoccupied with this discovery she was only vaguely aware of a fragrance in the air and a new voice in the passage. The next moment her employer came into the dressing-room.

ii

An encounter with a person hitherto only seen and heard on the cinema screen is often disconcerting. It is as if the two-dimensional and enormous image had contracted about a living skeleton and in taking on substance had acquired an embarrassing normality. One is not always glad to change the familiar shadow for the strange reality.

Helena Hamilton was a blonde woman. She had every grace. To set down in detail the perfections of her hair, eyes, mouth and complexion, her shape and the gallantry of her carriage would be to reiterate merely that which everyone had seen in her innumerable pictures. She was, in fact, quite astonishingly beautiful. Even the circumstance of her looking somewhat older than her moving shadow could not modify the shock of finding her its equal in everything but this.

Coupled with her beauty was her charm. This was famous. She could reduce press conferences to a conglomerate of eager, even naïve, males. She could make a curtain-speech that every leading woman in every theatre in the English-speaking world had made before her and persuade the last man in the audience that it was original. She could convince bit-part actresses playing maids in first acts that there, but for the grace of God, went she.

On Martyn, however, taken off her balance and entirely by surprise, it was Miss Hamilton's smell that made the first impression. At ten guineas a moderately sized bottle, she smelt like Master Fenton, all April and May. Martyn was very much shorter than Miss Hamilton but this did not prevent her from feeling cumbersome and out-of-place, as if she had been caught red-handed with her own work in the dressing-room. This awkwardness was in part dispelled by the friendliness of Miss Hamilton's smile and the warmth of her enchanting voice.

"You've come to help me, haven't you?" she said. "Now, that *is* kind. I know all about you from Mr. Grantley and I fully expect we'll get along famously together. The only thing I *don't* know, in fact, is your name."

Martyn wondered if she ought to give only her Christian name or only her surname. She said: "Tarne. Martyn Tarne."

"But what a charming name!" The brilliant eyes looked into Martyn's face and their gaze sharpened. After a fractional pause she repeated: "Really charming," and turned her back.

It took Martyn a moment or two to realize that this was her cue to remove Miss Hamilton's coat. She lifted it from her shoulders—it was made of Persian lamb and smelt delicious—and hung it up. When she turned round she found that her employer was looking at her. She smiled reassuringly at Martyn and said: "You've got everything arranged very nicely. Roses, too. Lovely."

"They're from Mr. Grantley."

"Sweet of him but I bet he sent you to buy them."

"Well—" Martyn began and was saved by the entry of the young man in the red sweater with a dressing-case for which she was given the keys. While she was unpacking it the door opened and a middle-aged, handsome man with a raffish face and an air of boldness came in. She remembered the photographs in the foyer. This was Clark Bennington. He addressed himself to Miss Hamilton.

"Hullo," he said, "I've been talking to John Rutherford."

"What about?" she asked and sounded nervous.

"About that kid. Young Gay. He's been at her again. So's Adam." He glanced at Martyn. "I wanted to talk to you," he added discontentedly.

"Well, so you shall. But I've got to change now, Ben. And look, this is my new dresser, Martyn Tarne."

He eyed Martyn with more attention. "Quite a change from old Tansley," he said. "And a very nice change, too." He turned away. "Is Adam down?" He jerked his head at the wall.

"Yes."

"I'll see you later, then."

"All right, but—yes, all right."

He went out, leaving a faint rumour of alcohol behind him.

She was quite still for a moment after he had gone. Martyn heard her fetch a sigh, a sound half-impatient, half-anxious. "Oh, well," she said, "let's get going, shall we?"

Martyn had been much exercised about the extent of her duties. Did, for instance, a dresser undress her employer? Did she kneel at her feet and roll down her stockings? Did she unhook and unbutton? Or did she stand capably aside while these rites were performed by the principal herself? Miss Hamilton solved the problem by removing her dress, throwing it to Martyn and waiting to be inserted into her dressing-gown. During these operations a rumble of male voices sounded at intervals in the adjoining room. Presently there was a tap at the door. Martyn answered it and found the little dresser with a florist's box in his hands. "Mr. Poole's compliments," he said and winked broadly before retiring.

Miss Hamilton by this time was spreading a yellow film over her face. She asked Martyn to open the box and, on seeing three orchids that lay crisp and fabulous on their mossy bed, sang "Darling!" on two clear notes.

The voice beyond the wall responded. "Hullo?"

"They're quite perfect. Thank you, my sweet."

"Good," the voice said. Martyn laid the box on the dressing-table and saw the card: *Until to-morrow. Adam.*

She got through the next half hour pretty successfully, she hoped. There seemed to be no blunders and Miss Hamilton continued charming and apparently delighted. There were constant visitors. A tap on the door would be followed by a head looking round and always by the invitation to come in. First there was Miss Gay Gainsford, a young and rather intense person with a pretty air of deference, who seemed to be in a state of extreme anxiety.

"Well, darling," Miss Hamilton said, glancing at her in the glass. "Everything under strict control?"

Miss Gainsford said unevenly: "I suppose so. I'm trying to be good and sort of *biddable*, do you know, but underneath I realize that I'm seething like a cauldron. Butterflies the size of *bats* in the stomach."

"Well, of course. But you mustn't be terrified, really, because whatever happens we all know John's written a good play, don't we?"

"I suppose we do."

"We do indeed. And Gay—you're going to make a great personal success in this part. I want you to tell yourself you are. Do you know? *Tell* yourself."

"I wish I could believe it." Miss Gainsford clasped her hands and raised them to her lips. "It's not very easy," she said, "when he—John—Dr. Rutherford—so obviously thinks I'm a misfit. Everybody keeps telling me it's a marvellous part, but for me it's thirteen sides of hopeless hell. Honestly, it is."

"Gay, what *nonsense!* John may seem hard—"

"*Seem!*"

"Well, he may *be* hard, then. He's famous for it, after all. But you'll get your reward, my dear, when the time comes. Remember," said Miss Hamilton with immense gravity, "we all have faith in you."

"Of course," said Miss Gainsford with an increased quaver in her voice, "it's too marvellous your feeling like that about it. You've been so miraculously kind. And Uncle Ben, of course. Both of you. I can't get over it."

"But, my dear, that's utter nonsense. You're going to be one of our rising young actresses."

"You do *really* think so!"

"But yes. We all do." Her voice lost a little colour and then freshened. "We all do," she repeated firmly and turned back to her glass.

Miss Gainsford went to the door and hesitated there. "Adam doesn't," she said loudly.

Miss Hamilton made a quick expressive gesture toward the next dressing-room and put her finger to her lips. "He'll be *really* angry if he hears you say that," she whispered, and added aloud with somewhat forced casualness: "Is John down this morning?"

"He's on-stage. I think he said he'd like to speak to you."

"I want to see him particularly. Will you tell him, darling?"

"Of course, Aunty Helena," Miss Gainsford said rather miserably, and added: "I'm sorry, I forgot. Of course, Helena, darling." With a wan smile she was gone.

"Oh, dear!" Miss Hamilton sighed and catching Martyn's eye in the looking-glass made a rueful face. "If only—" she began and stopped unaccountably, her gaze still fixed on Martyn's image. "Never mind," she said.

There was a noisy footfall in the passage followed by a bang on the door, and, with scarcely a pause for permission, by the entry of a large, florid and angry-looking man wearing a sweater, a leather waistcoat, a muffler and a very old duffel coat.

"Good morning, John darling," said Miss Hamilton gaily and extended her hand. The new-comer planted a smacking kiss on it and fixed Martyn with a china-blue and bulging pair of eyes. Martyn turned away from this embarrassing regard.

"What have we here?" he demanded. His voice was loud and rumbling.

"My new dresser. Dr. Rutherford, Martyn."

"Stay me with flagons!" said Dr. Rutherford. He turned on Miss Hamilton. "That fool of a wench Gainsford said you wanted me," he said. "What's up?"

"John, what have you been saying to that child?"

"I? Nothing. Nothing to what I could, and, mark you, what I ought to say to her. I merely asked her if, for the sake of my sanity, she'd be good enough to play the central scene without a goddam simper on her fat and wholly unsuitable dial."

"You're frightening her."

"She's terrifying me. She may be your niece, Helena—"

"She's not my niece. She's Ben's niece."

"If she was the Pope's niece she'd still be a goddam pain in the neck. I wrote this part for an intelligent actress who could be made to look reasonably like Adam. What do you give me? A moronic amateur who looks like nothing on God's earth."

"She's extremely pretty."

"Lollypops! Adam's too damn easy on her. The only hope lies in shaking her up. Or kicking her out and I'd do that myself if I had my way. It ought to have been done a month back. Even now—"

"Oh, my dear John! We open in two days, you might remember."

"An actress worth her salt'd memorize it in an hour. I told her—"

"I do beg you," she said, "to leave her to Adam. After all he is the producer, John, and he's very wise."

Dr. Rutherford pulled out of some submerged pocket a metal box. From this he extracted a pinch of snuff, which he took with loud and uncouth noises.

"In a moment," he said, "you'll be telling me the author ought to keep out of the theatre."

"That's utter nonsense."

"Let them try to keep *me* out," he said and burst into a neighing laugh.

Miss Hamilton slightly opened her mouth, hardened her upper lip, and with the closest attention painted it a purplish red. "Really," she said briskly, "you'd much better behave prettily, you know. You'll end by having her on your hands with a nervous breakdown."

"The sooner the better if it's a good one."

"Honestly, John, you are the rock *bottom* when you get like this. If you didn't write the plays you do write—if you weren't the greatest dramatist since—"

"Spare me the raptures," he said, "and give me some actors. And while we're on the subject, I may as well tell you that I don't like the way Ben is shaping in the big scene. If Adam doesn't watch him he'll be up to some bloody leading-man hocus-pocus, and by God if he tries that on I'll wring his neck for him."

She turned and faced him. "John, he *won't*. I'm sure he won't."

"No, you're not. You can't be sure. Nor can I. But if there's any sign of it to-night, and Adam doesn't tackle him, I will. I'll tickle his catastrophe, by God I will. As for that Mongolian monstrosity, that discard from the waxworks, Mr. Parry Percival, what devil—will you answer me—what inverted sadist foisted it on my play?"

"Now, look here, John—" Miss Hamilton began with some warmth, and was shouted down.

"Have I not stipulated from the beginning of my disastrous association with this ill-fated playhouse that I would have none of these abortions in my works? These Things. These foetid Growths. These Queers."

"Parry isn't one."

"Yah! He shrieks it. I have an instinct, my girl. I nose them as I go into the lobby."

She made a gesture of despair. "I give up," she said.

He helped himself to another pinch of snuff. "Hooey!" he snorted. "You don't do anything of the sort, my sweetie-pie. You're going to rock 'em, you and Adam. Think of that and preen yourself. And leave all the rest—to *me*."

"Don't quote from *Macbeth*. If Gay Gainsford heard you doing that she really would go off at the deep end."

"Which is precisely where I'd like to push her."

"Oh, go away," she cried out impatiently but with an air of good nature. "I've had enough of you. You're wonderful and you're hopeless. Go away."

"The audience is concluded?" He scraped the parody of a Regency bow.

"The audience is concluded. The door, Martyn."

Martyn opened the door. Until then, feeling wretchedly in the way, she had busied herself with the stack of suitcases in the corner of the room and now, for the first time, came absolutely face to face with the visitor. He eyed her with an extraordinary air of astonishment.

"Here!" he said. "Hi!"

"No, John," Miss Hamilton said with great determination. "No!"

"*Eureka!*"

"Nothing of the sort. Good morning."

He gave a shrill whistle and swaggered out. Martyn turned back to find her employer staring into the glass. Her hands trembled and she clasped them together. "Martyn," she said, "I'm going to call you Martyn because it's such a nice name. You know, a dresser is rather a particular sort of person. She has to be as deaf as a post and as blind as a bat to almost everything that goes on under her very nose. Dr. Rutherford is, as I expect you know, a most distinguished and brilliant person. Our Greatest English Playwright. But like many brilliant people," Miss Hamilton continued, in what Martyn couldn't help thinking a rather too special voice, "he is *eccentric*. We all understand and we expect you to do so too. Do you know?"

Martyn said she did.

"Good. Now, put me into that pink thing and let us know the worst about it, shall we?"

When she was dressed she stood before the cheval-glass and looked with cold intensity at her image. "My God," she said, "the lighting had better be good."

Martyn said: "Isn't it right? It looks lovely to me."

"My poor girl!" she muttered. "You run to my husband and ask him for cigarettes. He's got my case. I need a stimulant."

Martyn hurried into the passage and tapped at the next door. "So they are married," she thought. "He must be ten years younger than she is but they're married and he still sends her orchids in the morning."

The deep voice shouted impatiently: "Come!" and she opened the door and went in.

The little dresser was putting Poole into a dinner jacket. Their backs were turned to Martyn. "Yes?" Poole said.

"Miss Hamilton would like her cigarette case, if you please."

"I haven't got it," he said and shouted: "Helena!"

"Hullo, darling?"

"I haven't got your case."

There was a considerable pause. The voice beyond the wall called: "No, no. Ben's got it. Mr. Bennington, Martyn."

"I'm so sorry," Martyn said, and made for the door, conscious of the little dresser's embarrassment and of Poole's annoyance.

Mr. Clark Bennington's room was on the opposite side of the passage and next the Greenroom. On her entrance Martyn was abruptly and most unpleasantly transported into the immediate past—into yesterday with its exhaustion, muddle and panic, to the moment of extreme humiliation when

Fred Badger had smelt brandy on her breath. Mr. Bennington's flask was open on his dressing-shelf and he was in the act of entertaining a thick-set gentleman with beautifully groomed white hair, wearing a monocle in a strikingly handsome face. This person set down his tumbler and gazed in a startled fashion at Martyn.

"It's not," he said, evidently picking up with some difficulty the conversation she had interrupted, "it's not that I would for the world interfere, Ben, dear boy. Nor do I enjoy raising what is no doubt a delicate subject in these particular circumstances. But I feel for the child damnably, you know. Damnably. Moreover, it does rather appear that the Doctor never loses an opportunity to upset her."

"I couldn't agree more, old boy, and I'm bloody angry about it. Yes, dear, wait a moment, will you?" Mr. Bennington rejoined, running his speeches together and addressing them to no one in particular. "This is my wife's new dresser, J.G."

"Really?" Mr. J. G. Darcey responded and bowed politely to Martyn. "Good morning, child. See you later, Ben, my boy. Thousand thanks."

He rose, looked kindly at Martyn, dropped his monocle, passed his hand over his hair and went out, breaking into operatic song in the passage.

Mr. Bennington made a half-hearted attempt to put his flask out of sight and addressed himself to Martyn.

"And what," he asked, "can I do for the new dresser?"

Martyn delivered her message. "Cigarette case? Have I got my wife's cigarette case? God, I don't know. Try my overcoat, dear, will you? Behind the door. Inside pocket. No secrets," he added obscurely. "Forgive my asking you. I'm busy."

But he didn't seem particularly busy. He twisted round in his chair and watched Martyn as she made a fruitless search of his overcoat pockets. "This your first job?" he asked. She said it was not and he added: "As a dresser, I mean."

"I've worked in the theatre before."

"And where was that?"

"In New Zealand."

"*Really?*" he said, as if she had answered some vitally important question. "I'm afraid," Martyn went on quickly, "it's not in the overcoat."

"God, what a bore! Give me my jacket then, would you? The grey flannel." She handed it to him and he fumbled through the pockets. A pocket-book dropped on the floor, spilling its contents. Martyn gathered them together and he made such a clumsy business of taking them from her that she was obliged to put them on the shelf. Among them was an envelope bearing a foreign stamp and postmark. He snatched it up and it fluttered in his fingers. "Mustn't lose track of that one, must we?" he said and laughed. "All the way from Uncle Tito." He thrust it at Martyn. "Look," he said and steadied his hand against the edge of the shelf. "What d'you think of *that?* Take it."

Troubled at once by the delay and by the oddness of his manner Martyn took the envelope and saw that it was addressed to Bennington.

"Do you collect autographs," Bennington asked with ridiculous intensity—"or signed letters?"

"No, I'm afraid I don't," she said and put the letter face-down on the shelf.

"There's someone," he said with a jab of his finger at the envelope, "who'd give a hell of a lot for *that* one in there. A hell of a lot."

He burst out laughing, pulled a cigarette case out of the jacket and handed it to her with a flourish. "Purest gold," he said. "Birthday present but not from me. I'm her husband, you know. What the hell! Are you leaving me? Don't go."

Martyn made her escape and ran back to Miss Hamilton's room, where she found her in conference with Adam Poole and a young man of romantic appearance whom she recognized as the original of the last of the photographs in the foyer—Mr. Parry Percival. The instinct that makes us aware of a conversation in which we ourselves have in our absence been involved warned Martyn that they had been talking about her and had broken off on her entrance. After a moment's silence, Mr. Percival, with far too elaborate a nonchalance, said: "Yes. Well, there you have it," and it was obvious that there was a kind of double significance in this remark. Miss Hamilton said: "My poor Martyn, where *have* you been?" with a lightness that was not quite cordial.

"I'm sorry," Martyn said. "Mr. Bennington had trouble in finding the case." She hesitated for a moment and added, "Madam."

"That," Miss Hamilton rejoined, looking at Adam Poole, "rings dismally true. Would you believe it, darling, I became so furious with him for taking it that, most reluctantly, I gave him one for himself. He lost it instantly, of course, and now swears he didn't and mine is his. If you follow me."

"With considerable difficulty," Poole said, "I do."

Parry Percival laughed gracefully. He had a winning, if not altogether authentic, air of ingenuousness, and at the moment seemed to be hovering on the edge of some indiscretion. "I am afraid," he said ruefully to Miss Hamilton, "I'm rather in disgrace myself."

"With me, or with Adam?"

"I hope not with either of you. With Ben." He glanced apologetically at Poole, who did not look at him. "Because of the part, I mean. I suppose I spoke out of turn, but I really did think I could play it—still do for a matter of that, but there it is."

It was obvious that he was speaking at Poole. Martyn saw Miss Hamilton look from one man to the other before she said lightly, "I think you could too, Parry, but as you say, there it is. Ben *has* got a flair, you know."

Percival laughed. "He has indeed," he said. "He has had it for twenty years. Sorry. I shouldn't have said that. Honestly, I *am* sorry."

Poole said: "I dislike post mortems on casting, Parry."

"I know, I *do* apologize." Percival turned ingratiatingly, and the strong light caught his face sideways. Martyn saw with astonishment that under the thin film of greasepaint there was a system of incipient lines, and she realized that he was not, after all, a young man. "I know," he repeated, "I'm being naughty."

Poole said: "We open on Thursday. The whole thing was thrashed out weeks ago. Any discussion now is completely fruitless."

"That," said Miss Hamilton, "is what I have been trying to tell the Doctor."

"John? I heard him bellowing in here," Poole said. "Where's he gone? I want a word with him. And with you, Parry, by the way. It's about that scene at the window in the second act. You're not making your exit line. You must top Ben there. It's most important."

"Look, old boy," Mr. Percival said with agonized intensity, "I *know*. It's just another of those things. Have you *seen* what Ben does? Have you seen that business with my handkerchief? He won't take his hands off me. The whole exit gets messed up."

"I'll see what can be done."

"John," said Miss Hamilton, "is worried about it too, Adam."

Poole said: "Then he should talk to me."

"You know what the Doctor is."

"We all do," said Parry Percival, "and the public, I fear, is beginning to find out. God, there I go again."

Poole looked at him. "You'll get along better, I think, Parry, if you deny yourself these cracks against the rest of the company. Rutherford has written a serious play. It'd be a pity if any of us should lose faith in it."

Percival reddened and made towards the door. "I'm just being a nuisance," he said. "I'll take myself off and be photographed like a good boy." He made an insinuating movement of his shoulders towards Miss Hamilton, and fluttered his hand at her dress. "Marvellous," he said—"a triumph, if the bit-part actor may be allowed to say so."

The door shut crisply behind him, and Miss Hamilton said: "Darling, aren't you rather high and grand with poor Parry?"

"I don't think so. He's behaving like an ass. He couldn't play the part. He was born to be a feed."

"He'd *look* it."

"If all goes well Ben will *be* it."

"If all goes well! Adam, I'm terrified. He's—"

"Are you dressed, Helena? The cameras are ready."

"Shoes, please, Martyn," said Miss Hamilton. "Yes, darling. I'm right."

Martyn fastened her shoes and then opened the door. Miss Hamilton swept out, lifting her skirts with great elegance. Martyn waited for Poole to follow, but he said: "You're meant to be on-stage. Take make-up and a glass and whatever Miss Hamilton may need for her hair."

She thanked him and in a flurry gathered the things together. Poole took the Persian lamb coat and stood by the door. She hesitated, expecting him to precede her, but found that he was looking at the cheval-glass. When she followed his gaze it was to be confronted by their images, side by side in the mirror.

"Extraordinary," he said abruptly, "isn't it?" and motioned her to go out.

iii

When Martyn went out on the stage, she was able for the first time to see the company assembled together, and found it consisted, as far as the players were concerned, of no more than the six persons she had already encountered: first in their fixed professional poses in the show-frame at the front of the house, and later in their dressing-rooms. She had attached mental tags to them and found herself thinking of Helena Hamilton as the Leading Lady, of Gay Gainsford as the Ingenue, of J. G. Darcey as the Character Actor, of Parry Percival as the Juvenile, of Clark Bennington regrettably, perhaps unjustly, as the Drunken Actor, and of Adam Poole—but as yet she had found no label for Poole, unless it was the old-fashioned one of "Governor," which pleased her by its vicarious association with the days of the Victorian actor-managers.

To this actual cast of six she must add a number of satellite figures—the author, Dr. John Rutherford, whose eccentricities seemed to surpass those of his legend, with which she was already acquainted; the man in the red sweater, who was the stage-manager, and was called Clem Smith; his assistant, a morose lurking figure; and the crew of stage-hands, who went about their business or contemplated the actors with equal detachment.

The actors were forming themselves now into a stage "picture," moving in a workman-like manner under the direction of Adam Poole, and watched with restless attentiveness by an elderly, slack-jointed man, carrying a paint pot and brushes. This man, the last of all the figures to appear upon the stage that morning, seemed to have no recognizable jobs but to be concerned in all of them. He was dressed in overalls and a tartan shirt, from which his long neck emerged, bird-like and crepe-y, to terminate in a head that wobbled slightly as if its articulation with the top of the spine had loosened with age. He was constantly addressed with exasperated affection as Jacko. Under his direction, bunches of lights were wheeled into position, camera men peered and muttered, and at his given signal the players, by an easy transition in behaviour and appearance, became larger than life. A gap was left in the middle of the group, and into this when all was ready floated Helena Hamilton, ruffling her plumage, and becoming at once the focal point of the picture.

"Darling," she said, "it's not going to be a flash, is it, with all of you looking like village idiots, and me like the Third Witch on the morning after the cauldron scene?"

"If you can hold it for three seconds," Adam Poole said, "it needn't be a flash."

"I can hold anything, if you come in and help me."

He moved in beside her. "All right," he said, "let's try it. The end of the first act"; and at once she turned upon him a look of tragic and burning intensity. The elderly man wandered across and tweaked at her skirts. Without changing pose or expression, she said: "Isn't it shameful the way Jacko can't keep his hands off me." He grinned and ambled away. Adam Poole said "Right"; the group froze in postures of urgency that led the eye towards the two central figures and the cameras clicked.

Martyn tried, as the morning wore on, to get some idea of the content of the play, but was unable to do so. Occasionally the players would speak snatches of dialogue leading up to the moment when a photograph was to be taken, and from these she gathered that the major conflict of the theme was between the characters played by Adam Poole and Clark Bennington and that this conflict was one of ideas. About a particular shot there was a great deal of difficulty. In this Poole and Gay Gainsford confronted each other, and it was necessary that her posture, the arrested gesture of her hand, and even her expression should be an exact reflection of his.

To Martyn, Poole had seemed to be a short-tempered man, but with Gay Gainsford he showed exemplary patience. "It's the old story, Gay," he said. "You're over-anxious. It's not enough for you to look like me. Let's face it—" he hesitated for a moment and said quickly: "We've had all this, haven't we—but it's worth repeating—you can't look strikingly like me, although Jacko's done wonders. What you've got to do is to *be* me. At this moment, don't you see, you're my heredity, confronting me like a threat. As far as the photograph is concerned, we can cheat—the shot can be taken over your shoulder, but in the performance there can be no cheating, and that is why I'm making such a thing of it. Now let's take it with the line. Your head's on your arms, you raise it slowly to face me. Ready now. Right, up you come."

Miss Gainsford raised her face to his as he leaned across the writing desk and whispered: "Don't you like what you see?" At the same moment there was a cascade of laughter from Miss Hamilton. Poole's voice cracked like a whip-lash: "Helena, please," and she turned from Parry Percival to say: "Darling, I'm so sorry," and in the same breath spoke her line of dialogue: "But it's you, don't you see? You can't escape from it. It's you." Gay Gainsford made a hopeless little gesture and Poole said: "Too late, of course. Try again."

They tried several times, in an atmosphere of increasing tension. The amiable Jacko was called in to make an infinitesimal change in Gay's make-up, and Martyn saw him blot away a tear. At this juncture a disembodied voice roared from the back of the circle:

"Madam, have comfort: all of us have cause
To wail the dimming of our shining star!"

Poole glanced into the auditorium. "Do shut up like a good chap, John," he said.

> "Pour all your tears! I am your sorrow's nurse,
> And I will pamper it with la-men-ta-ti-ons."

The man called Jacko burst out laughing and was instantly dismissed to the dressing-rooms by Poole.

There followed a quarter of an hour of mounting hysteria on the part of Gay Gainsford and of implacable persistence from Adam Poole. He said suddenly: "All right, we'll cheat. Shift the camera."

The remaining photographs were taken without a great deal of trouble. Miss Gainsford, looking utterly miserable, went off to her dressing-room. The man called Jacko reappeared and ambled across to Miss Hamilton. There was an adjustment in make-up while Martyn held up the mirror.

"Maybe it's lucky," he said, "you don't have to look like somebody else."

"Are you being nice or beastly, Jacko?"

He put a cigarette between her lips and lit it. "The dresses are good," he said. He had a very slight foreign accent.

"You think so, do you?"

"Naturally. I design them for *you*."

"Next time," she said grimly, "you'd better write the play as well."

He was a phenomenally ugly man, but a smile of extraordinary sweetness broke across his face.

"All these agonies!" he murmured. "And on Thursday night everyone will be kissing everyone else and at the Combined Arts Ball we are in triumph and on Friday morning you will be purring over your notices. And you must not be unkind about the play. It is a good play." He grinned again, more broadly. His teeth were enormous and uneven. "Even the little niece of the great husband cannot entirely destroy it."

"Jacko!"

"You may say what you like, it is not intelligent casting."

"Please, Jacko."

"All right, all right. I remind you instead of the Combined Arts Ball, and that no one has decided in what costume we go."

"Nobody has any ideas. Jacko, you must invent something marvellous."

"And in two days I must also create out of air eight marvellous costumes."

"Darling Jacko, how beastly we are to you. But you know you love performing your little wonders."

"I suggest then, that we are characters from Tchekhov as they would be in Hollywood. You absurdly gorgeous, and the little niece still grimly ingenue. Adam perhaps as Vanya if he were played by Boris Karloff. And so on."

"Where shall I get my absurdly gorgeous dress?"

"I paint the design on canvas and cut it out and if I were introduced to your dresser I would persuade her to sew it up." He took the glass from Martyn and said: "No one makes any introductions in this theatre, so we introduce ourselves to each other. I am Jacques Doré, and you are the little chick whom the stork has brought too late, or dropped into the wrong nest. Really," he said, rolling his eyes at Miss Hamilton, "it is the most remarkable coincidence, if it is a coincidence. I am dropping bricks," he added. "I am a very privileged person but one day I drop an outsize brick, and away I go." He made a circle of his thumb and forefinger and looked through it, as though it were a quizzing-glass, at Martyn. "All the same," he said, "it is a pity you are a little dresser and not a little actress."

iv

Between the photograph call and the dress rehearsal, which was timed for seven o'clock, a state of uneven ferment prevailed at the Vulcan. During the rare occasions on which she had time to reflect, Martyn anticipated a sort of personal zero hour, a moment when she would have to take stock, to come to a decision. She had two and fourpence and no place of abode, and she had no idea when she would be paid, or how much she would get. This moment of reckoning, however, she continually postponed. The problem of food was answered for the moment by the announcement that it would be provided for everyone whose work kept them in the theatre throughout the day. As Miss Hamilton had discovered a number of minor alterations to be made in her dresses, Martyn was of this company. Having by this time realized the position of extraordinary ubiquity held by Jacko, she was not surprised to find him cooking a mysterious but savoury mess over the gas ring in Fred Badger's sink-room.

This concoction was served in enamel mugs, at odd intervals, to anyone who asked for it, and Martyn found herself eating her share in company with Bob Cringle, Mr. Poole's dresser. From him she learnt more about Mr. Jacques Doré. He was responsible for the décor and dressing of all Poole's productions. His official status was that of assistant to Mr. Poole, but in actual fact he seemed to be a kind of superior odd-job man.

"General dogsbody," Cringle gossiped, "that's what Mr. Jacko is. 'Poole's Luck,' people call him, and if the Guv'nor was superstitious about anything, which 'e is *not*, it would be about Mr. Jacko. The lady's the same. Can't do without 'im. As a matter of fact it's on 'er account 'e sticks it out. You might say 'e's 'er property, a kind of pet, if you like to put it that way. Joined up with 'er and 'is nibs when they was in Canada and the Guv'nor still doing the child-wonder at 'is posh college. 'E's a Canadian-Frenchy, Mr. Jacko is. Twenty years ago that must 'ave been, only don't say I said so. It's what they call dog-like devotion, and that's no error. To 'er, *not* to 'is nibs."

"Do you mean Mr. Bennington?" Martyn ventured.

"Clark Bennington, the distinguished character actor, that's right," said Cringle dryly. Evidently he was not inclined to elaborate this theme. He entertained Martyn, instead, with a lively account of the eccentricities of

Dr. John Rutherford. "My oaff," he said, "what a daisy! Did you 'ear 'im chi-iking from the front this morning? Typical! We done three of 'is pieces up to date and never a dull moment. Rows and ructions, ructions and rows from the word go. The Guv'nor puts up with it on account he likes the pieces and what a time 'e 'as with 'im, oh dear! It's something shocking the way Doctor cuts up. Dynamite! This time it's the little lady and 'is nibs and Mr. Parry Profile Percival 'e's got it in for. Can't do nothing to please 'im. You should 'ear 'im at rehearsals. 'You're bastardizing my play,' 'e 'owls. 'Get the 'ell aht of it,' 'e shrieks. You never see such an exhibition. Shocking! Then the Guv'nor shuts 'im up and 'e 'as an attack of the willies or what-have-you and keeps aht of the theaytre for a couple of days. Never longer, though, which is very unfortunate for all concerned."

Martyn tried to find out from Cringle what the play was about. He was not very illuminating. "It's 'igh-brow," he said. "Intellectually, it's clarse. 'A Modern Morality' he calls it, the Doctor does. It's all about whether you're brought up right makes any difference to what your old pot 'ands on to you. ''Eredity versus environment' they call it. The Guv'nor's environment, and all the rest of 'em's 'eredity. And like it always is in clarse plays, the answer's a lemon. Well, I must go on me way rejoicing."

To Martyn, held as she was in a sort of emotional suspension, the lives and events enclosed within the stage walls and curtain of the Vulcan Theatre assumed a greater reality than her own immediate problem. Her existence since five o'clock the previous afternoon, when she had walked into the theatre, had much of the character and substance of a dream with all the shifting values, the passages of confusion and extreme clarity, which make up the texture of a dream. She was in a state of semi-trauma and found it vaguely agreeable. Her jobs would keep her busy all the afternoon and to-night there was the first dress rehearsal.

She could, she thought, tread water indefinitely, half in and half out of her dream, as long as she didn't come face to face with Mr. Adam Poole in any more looking-glasses.

CHAPTER III

First Dress Rehearsal

Martyn's official jobs were all finished by about three o'clock, but by some curious process of which she herself was scarcely aware she had by that time turned into a sort of odd-job girl, particularly where Jacko was concerned.

He was engaged in re-painting a piece of very modern decoration above the main and central entrance of the second act set.

"It was lousy in the design," he said, "and it was therefore twelve times lousier when it was twelve times bigger, so now I make it a little worse. Before the first dress rehearsal it is a good thing to be at one's wits' ends, or else one would lose them altogether. When there is not a job, I invent it, because after all there must be someone sane to watch the dress rehearsal. Now if you pass me up the pot of pink, I make a very civilized little flourish in the mode of the second act, and we take time off for you to tell me how clever I am, and why you are such a simpleton as to turn yourself into a dresser."

"I wish," Martyn said, "I knew what the play was about. Is it really a modern morality and do you think it good?"

"All good plays are moralities," said Jacko sententiously, and he leant so far back on the top of his step-ladder that Martyn hurriedly grasped it. "And this is a good play with a very old theme." He hesitated for a moment and she wondered if she only imagined that he looked worried. "Here is a selected man with new ideas in conflict with people who have very old ones. Adam is the selected man. He has been brought up on an island by a community of idealists; he represents the value of environment. By his own wish he returns to his original habitat, and there he is confronted by his heredity, in the persons of his great-uncle, who is played by J. G. Darcey, his brilliant but unstable cousin, who is played by Clark Bennington, this cousin's wife, who is Helena, and with whom he falls in love, and their daughter, who is freakishly like him, but vicious, and who represents therefore his inescapable heredity. This wretched girl," Jacko continued with great relish, looking at Martyn out of the corner of his eyes, "is engaged to a nonentity but finds herself drawn by a terrrible attraction to Adam himself. She is played by Gay Gainsford. Receive again from me the pink pot, and bestow upon me the brown. As I have recited it to you so baldly, without nuance and without detail, you will say perhaps if Ibsen or Kafka or Brecht or even Sartre had written this play it would be a good one."

Inexplicably, he again seemed to be in some sort of distress. "It has, in fact," he said, "a continental flavour. But for those who have ears to hear and eyes to see, it has a wider implication than I have suggested. It is a tale, in point of fact, about the struggle of the human being in the detestable situation in which from the beginning he has found himself. Now I descend." He climbed down his step-ladder, groaning lamentably. "And now," he said, "we have some light, and we see if what I have done is good. Go out into the front of the house and in a moment I join you."

By the time Martyn reached the sixth row of the stalls the stage was fully illuminated, and for the first time she saw the set for Act II as Jacko had intended it.

It was an interior, simple in design and execution, but with an air of being over-civilized and stale. "They are," Jacko explained, slumping into a seat beside her, "bad people who live in it. They are not bad of their own volition, but because they have been set down in this place by their heredity and cannot escape. And now you say, all this is pretentious nonsense, and nobody will notice my set except perhaps a few oddities who come to first nights and in any case will get it all wrong. And now we wash ourselves and go out to a place where I am known, and we eat a little, and you tell me why you look like a puppy who has found his tail but dare not wag it. Come."

The restaurant where Jacko was known turned out to be hard by the theatre, and situated in a basement. He insisted on paying for a surprisingly good meal, and Martyn's two and fourpence remained in her pocket. Whereas the curiosity of Fred Badger and Bob Cringle, and in some degree of the actors, had been covert and indirect, Jacko's was unblushing and persistent.

"Now," he said, over their coffee, "I ask you my questions. If there is a secret you tell me so, and with difficulty I shut myself up. If not, you confide in me, because everybody in the Vulcan makes me their confidant and I am greatly flattered by this. In any case we remain friends, no bones broken, and we repeat our little outings. How old do you think I am?"

With some embarrassment, Martyn looked at his scrawny neck, at the thin lichen-like growth of fuzz on his head, and at his heavily scored and indented face. "Fifty-seven," she ventured.

"Sixty-two," said Jacko complacently. "I am sixty-two years old, and a bit of a character. I have not the talent to make a character of myself for the people who sit in front, so instead I play to actors. A wheel within wheels. For twenty years I have built up my role of confidant, and now if I wanted to I couldn't leave off. For example, I can speak perfect English, but my accent is a feature of the role of Papa Jacko and must be sustained. Everybody knows it is a game and, amiably, everyone pretends with me. It is all rather ham and jejune, but I hope that you are going to play too."

Martyn thought: "It would be pleasant to tell him: I'm sure he's very nice and so why don't I do it? I suppose it's because he looks so very odd." And whether with uncanny intuition or else by a queer coincidence he said: "I'm not nearly as peculiar as I look."

Martyn said tentatively: "But I honestly don't know what you want me to tell you."

On the opposite wall of the restaurant there was a tarnished looking-glass, upon the surface of which someone had half-heartedly painted a number of water-lilies and leaves. Among this growth, as if drowned in Edwardiana, Jacko's and Martyn's faces were reflected. He pointed to hers.

"See," he said. "We rehearse a play for which it is necessary a secondary-part actress should resemble, strikingly, the leading man. We have auditions, and from the hundreds of anxious ingenues we select the one who is least unlike him, but she is still very unlike him. Incidentally," Jacko continued, looking Martyn very hard in the eye, "she is the niece of Clark Bennington. She is not very like him, either, which is neither here nor there and perhaps fortunate for her. It is her unlikeness to Adam that we must deplore. Moreover, although I am a genius with make-up, there is very little I can do about it. So we depend instead on reflected emotions and echoed mannerisms. But although she is a nice little actress with a nice small talent, she cannot do this very well either. In the meantime our author, who is a person of unbridled passion where his art is in question, becomes incensed with her performance and makes scenes and everybody except her Uncle Bennington retires into corners and tears pieces of their hair out. The little actress also retires into corners and weeps and is comforted by her Uncle Bennington, who nevertheless knows she is not good.

"Upon this scene there enters, in the guise of a dresser—" he jabbed his finger at the fly-blown mirror—"this. Look at it. If I set out to draw the daughter or the young sister of the leading man, that is what I should draw. Everybody has a look at her and retires again into corners to ask what it is about. Because obviously, she is not a dresser. Is she perhaps—and there are many excited speculations. 'A niece for a niece?' we ask ourselves, and there is some mention of Adam's extreme youth—you must excuse me—and the wrong side of the rose-bush, and everybody says it cannot be an accident and waits to see, except Papa Jacko, whose curiosity will not permit him to wait."

Martyn cried out: "I've never seen him before, except in films in New Zealand. He knows nothing about me at all. Nothing. I came here from New Zealand a fortnight ago and I've been looking for a job ever since. I came to the Vulcan looking for a job, that's all there is about it."

"Did you come looking for the job of dresser to Miss Hamilton?"

"For any job," she said desperately. "I heard by accident about the dresser."

"But it was not to be a dresser that you came all the way from New Zealand, and yet it was to work in the theatre, and so perhaps after all you hoped to be an actress."

"Yes," Martyn said, throwing up her hands, "all right, I hoped to be an actress. But please let's forget all about it. You can't imagine how thankful I am to be a dresser, and if you think I'm secretly hoping Miss Gainsford will get laryngitis or break her leg, you couldn't be more mistaken. I don't believe in fairy-tales."

"What humbugs you all are."

"Who?" she demanded indignantly.

"All you Anglo-Saxons. You humbug even yourselves. Conceive for the moment the *mise-en-scène*, the situation, the coincidence, and have you the cheek to tell me again that you came thirteen thousand miles to be an actress and yet do not wish to play this part? Are you a good actress?"

"Don't," Martyn said, "don't. I've got a job and I'm in a sort of a trance. It makes everything very simple and I don't want to come out of it."

Jacko grinned fiendishly. "Just a little touch of laryngitis?" he suggested.

Martyn got up. "Thank you very much for my nice dinner," she said. "I ought to be getting on with my job."

"Little hypocrite. Or perhaps after all you know already you are a very bad actress."

Without answering she walked out ahead of him, and they returned in silence to the Vulcan.

ii

Timed to begin at seven, the dress rehearsal actually started at ten past eight. They were waiting, it appeared, for the author. Miss Hamilton had no changes in the first act, and told Martyn she might watch from the front. She went out and sat at the back of the stalls near the other dressers. There was a sprinkling of onlookers, two of whom were understudies, in the auditorium. About half-way down the centre-aisle Adam Poole, made up and wearing a dressing-gown, sat between Jacko and a young man whom Martyn supposed to be a secretary. Jacko had told her that Poole's first entrance came at the end of the act. The atmosphere that hangs over all dress rehearsals seeped out into the auditorium. The delay seemed interminable. Poole turned from time to time and peered up towards the circle. At last a door slammed upstairs, somebody floundered noisily down the circle steps, a seat banged and a voice—Dr. John James Rutherford's—shouted:

"Hung be the heavens with black, yield day to night!
Comets, importing change of times and states,
Brandish your crystal tresses in the sky,
And with them scourge the bad revolting stars—

Repeat," Dr. Rutherford bawled, leaning over the balustrade, "repeat: *bad revolting stars*. I'm here, my hearties. Take it away and burn it."

Martyn saw Poole grin. "You behave yourself, up there," he said. "Have you got your paper and pencil?"

"I am provided in that kind."

"Good."

The lights went up along the fringe of the curtain. Martyn's flesh began to creep. Poole called "All right," and lit a cigarette. Throughout the auditorium other little flames sprang up, illuminating from below, like miniature footlights, the faces of the watchers in front. A remote voice said: "O.K. Take it away"; a band of gold appeared below the fringe of the curtain, widened and grew to a lighted stage. Parry Percival spoke the opening line of Dr. Rutherford's new play.

Martyn liked the first act. It concerned itself with the group of figures Jacko had already described—the old man, his son, his son's wife, their daughter and her fiancé. They were creatures of convention, the wife alone possessed of some inclination to reach out beyond her enclosed and aimless existence. In his production Adam Poole, with Jacko's décor to help him, delicately underlined the playwright's symbolic treatment of his theme. It was, as all

first acts should be, anticipatory in character. The group awaited the
arrival of the islander, the man from outside. Their behaviour suggested that
of caged creatures who were completely resigned to their confinement, and
in his arrival already saw a threat to their tranquillity. Again Helena Hamilton, as the wife, alone suggested, and she did so with great artistry, a kind of
awareness of their sterility and decadence. Bennington, as her hard-drinking,
brilliant and completely defeated husband, was giving an exciting performance, though at times Martyn wondered if he was not playing against his
author's intention. Was he not, with facile bits of business and clever, unexpected inflections, superimposing upon the part a false quality? Wouldn't
the audience, against the tenor of the play, find themselves liking this man,
and become increasingly tolerant of the very traits with which the author
sought to disgust them? As his father, J. G. Darcey seemed to Martyn to
follow adequately the somewhat conventional die-hard the author had intended. As the completely colourless, almost puppet-like juvenile, Parry
Percival with his magazine-cover looks was exactly right in what actors call a
most ungrateful part. She could understand his dislike of it.

Gay Gainsford's entry as the daughter was a delayed one, and try as she
might not to anticipate it, Martyn felt a sinking in her midriff when at last
towards the end of the act Miss Gainsford came on. It was quite a small
part but one of immense importance. Of the entire group, the girl represented
the third generation, the most completely lost, and in the writing of her part
Rutherford displayed the influence of Existentialism. It was clear that with
few lines to carry her she must make her mark, and clever production was
written over everything she did. Agitated as she was by Jacko's direct attack,
Martyn wondered if she only imagined that there was nothing more than
production there, and if Miss Gainsford was really as ill at ease as she
herself supposed. A specific gesture had been introduced and was evidently
important, a sudden thrust of her fingers through her short hair, and she
twice used a phrase—"That was not what I meant"—where in the context
it was evidently intended to plant a barb of attention in the minds of the
audience. When this moment came, Martyn sensed uneasiness among the
actors. She glanced at Poole and saw him make the specific gesture he had
given Miss Gainsford, a quick thrust of his fingers through his hair.

At this juncture the voice in the circle ejaculated: "Boo!"

"Quiet!" said Poole.

Miss Gainsford hesitated, looked wretchedly into the auditorium, and lost
her words. She was twice prompted before she went on again. Bennington
crossed the stage, put his arm about her shoulders and glared into the circle.
The prompter once more threw out a line, Miss Gainsford repeated it and
they were off again. Poole got up and went back-stage through the pass-door.
The secretary leant forward and shakily lit one cigarette from the butt of
another. For the life of her, Martyn couldn't resist glancing at Jacko. He
was slumped back in his stall with his arms folded—deliberately imperturb-
able, she felt—putting on an act. The light from the stage caught his emu-

like head and, as if conscious of her attention, he rolled his eyes round at her. She hastily looked back at the stage.

With Gay Gainsford's exit, Martyn could have sworn a wave of relaxation blessed the actors. The dialogue began to move forward compactly with a firm upward curve towards some well-designed climax. There was an increase in tempo corresponding with the rising suspense. Martyn's blood tingled and her heart thumped. Through which door would the entrance be made? The players began a complex circling movement accompanied by a sharp crescendo in the dialogue. Up and up it soared. "Now," she thought, "now!" The action of the play was held in suspense, poised and adjusted, and into the prepared silence, with judgement and precision, at the head of Jacko's twisted flight of steps, came Adam Poole.

"Is that an entrance," thought Martyn, pressing her hands together, "or is it an entrance?"

The curtain came down almost immediately. The secretary gathered his notes together and went back-stage. Dr. Rutherford shouted: "Hold your horses," thundered out of the circle, reappeared in the stalls, and plunged through the pass-door to back-stage where he could be heard cruelly apostrophizing the Almighty and the actors. Jacko stretched elaborately and slouched down the centre-aisle, saying into the air as he passed Martyn: "You had better get round for the change."

Horrified, Martyn bolted like a rabbit. When she arrived in the dressing-room she found her employer, with a set face, attempting to unhook an elaborate back fastening. Martyn bleated an apology which was cut short.

"I hope," said Miss Hamilton, "you haven't mistaken the nature of your job, Martyn. You are my dresser and as such are expected to be here, in this dressing-room, whenever I return to it. Do you understand?"

Martyn, feeling very sick, said that she did, and with trembling fingers effected the complicated change. Miss Hamilton was completely silent, and to Martyn, humiliated and miserable, the necessary intimacies of her work were particularly mortifying.

A boy's voice in the passage chanted: "Second act, please. Second act," and Miss Hamilton said: "Have you got everything on-stage for the quick change?"

"I think so, madam."

"Very well." She looked at herself coldly and searchingly in the long glass and added: "I will go out."

Martyn opened the door. Her employer glanced critically at her. "You're as white as a sheet," she said. "What's the matter?"

Martyn stammered: "Am I? I'm sorry, madam. It must have been the first act."

"Did you like it?"

"*Like* it?" Martyn repeated. "Oh yes, I liked it."

"As much as that?" As easily as if she had passed from one room into another, Miss Hamilton re-entered her mood of enchantment. "What a ridiculous child you are," she said. "It's only actresses who are allowed to have temperaments."

She went out to the stage, and as Martyn followed her she was surprised to feel in herself a kind of resistance to this woman who could so easily command her own happiness or misery.

An improvised dressing-room had been built on the stage for the quick change, and in or near it Martyn spent the whole of the second act. She was not sure when the quick change came, and didn't like to ask anybody. She therefore spent the first quarter of an hour on tenterhooks, hearing the dialogue, but not seeing anything of the play.

After a short introductory passage the act opened with a long scene between Helena Hamilton and Adam Poole in which their attraction to each other was introduced and established, and her instinctive struggle against her environment made clear and developed. The scene was admirably played by both of them, and carried the play strongly forward. When Miss Hamilton came off she found her dresser bright-eyed and excited. Martyn managed the change without any blunders and in good time. Miss Hamilton's attention seemed to be divided between her clothes and the scene which was now being played between J. G. Darcey, Poole and her husband. This scene built up into a quarrel between Poole and Bennington which at its climax was broken by Poole saying in his normal voice, "I dislike interrupting dress rehearsals, Ben, but we've had this point over and over again. Please take the line as we rehearsed it."

There was complete silence, perhaps for five seconds, and then, unseen, so that Martyn formed no picture of what he was doing or how he looked, Bennington began to giggle. The sound wavered and bubbled into a laugh. Helena Hamilton whispered: "Oh, my God!" and went out toward the stage. Martyn heard the stage-hands who had been moving round the set stop dead as if in suspended animation. She saw Parry Percival, waiting off-stage, turn with a look of elaborate concern toward Miss Hamilton and mime bewilderment.

Bennington's laughter broke down into ungainly speech. "I always say," he said, "there is no future in being an actor-manager unless you arrange things your own way. I want to make this chap a human being. You and John say he's to be a monster. All right, all right, dear boy, I won't offend again. He shall be less human than Caliban, and far less sympathetic."

Evidently Poole was standing inside the entrance nearest to the dressing-room, because Martyn heard Bennington cross the stage and when he spoke again he was quite close to her, and had lowered his voice. "You're grabbing everything, aren't you?" the voice wavered. "On and off stage, as you might say—domestically and professionally. The piratical Mr. Poole."

Poole muttered: "If you are not too drunk to think, we'll go on," and pitching his voice threw out a line of dialogue: "If you knew what you wanted, if there was any object, however silly, behind anything you say or do, I could find some excuse for you—"

Martyn heard Helena Hamilton catch her breath in a sob. The next moment she had flung open the door and had made her entrance.

iii

Through the good offices of Jacko, Martyn was able to watch the rest of the act from the side. Evidently he was determined she should see as much as possible of the play. He sent her round a list, scribbled in an elaborate hand, of the warnings and cues for Miss Hamilton's entrances and exits and times when she changed her dress. *Stand in the O.P. corner,* he had written across the paper, *and think of your sins.* She wouldn't have dared to follow his advice if Miss Hamilton, on her first exit, had not said with a sort of irritated good nature: "You needn't wait in the dressing-room perpetually. Just be ready for me, that's all."

So she stood in the shadows of the O.P. corner and saw the one big scene between Adam Poole and Gay Gainsford. The author's intention was clear enough. In this girl, the impure flower of her heredity, the most hopelessly lost of all the group, he sought to show the obverse side of the character Poole presented. She was his twisted shadow, a spiritual incubus. In everything she said and did the audience must see a distortion of Poole himself, until at the end they faced each other across the desk, as in the scene that had been photographed, and Helena Hamilton re-entered to speak the line of climax: *"But it's you, don't you see? You can't escape from it. It's you,"* and the curtain came down.

Gay Gainsford was not good enough. It was not only that she didn't resemble Poole closely: her performance was too anxious, too careful a reproduction of mannerisms without a flame to light them. Martyn burnt in her shadowy corner. The transparent covering in which, like a sea-creature, she had spent her twenty-four hours respite now shrivelled away and she was exposed to the inexorable hunger of an unsatisfied player.

She didn't see Bennington until he put his hand on her arm as the curtain came down, and he startled her so much that she cried out and backed away from him.

"So you think you could do it, dear, do you?" he said.

Martyn stammered: "I'm sorry. Miss Hamilton will want me," and dodged past him towards the improvised dressing-room. He followed, and with a conventionally showy movement barred her entrance.

"Wait a minute, *wait* a minute," he said. "I want to talk to you."

She stood there, afraid of him, conscious of his smell of greasepaint and alcohol, and thinking him a ridiculous as well as an alarming person.

"I'm *so* angry," he said conversationally, "just literally *so* angry that I'm afraid you're going to find me quite a difficult man. And now we've got that ironed out perhaps you'll tell me who the bloody hell you are."

"You know who I am," Martyn said desperately. "Please let me go in."

"M'wife's dresser?"

He took her chin in his hand and twisted her face to the light. Poole came round the back of the set. Martyn thought: "He'll be sick of the sight of me. Always getting myself into stupid little scenes." Bennington's hand felt wet and hot round her chin.

"M'wife's dresser," he repeated. "And m'wife's lover's little by-blow. That the story?"

Poole's hand dropped on his arm. "In you go," he said to Martyn, and twisted Bennington away from the door. Martyn slipped through and he shut it behind her. She heard him say: "You're an offensive fellow in your cups, Ben. We'll have this out after rehearsal. Get along and change for the third act."

There was a moment's pause. The door opened and he looked in.

"Are you all right?" he asked.

"Perfectly, thank you," Martyn said, and in an agony of embarrassment added: "I'm sorry to be a nuisance, sir."

"Oh, don't be an ass," he said with great ill humour. The next moment he had gone.

Miss Hamilton, looking desperately worried, came in to change for the third act.

iv

The dress rehearsal ended at midnight in an atmosphere of acute tension. Because she had not yet been paid, Martyn proposed to sleep again in the Greenroom. So easily do our standards adjust themselves to our circumstances that whereas on her first night at the Vulcan the Greenroom had seemed a blessed haven, her hours of precarious security had bred a longing for a bed and ordered cleanliness, and she began to dread the night.

In groups and singly, the actors and stage-staff drifted away. Their voices died out in the alley and passages, and she saw, with dismay, that Fred Badger had emerged from the door of his cubby-hole and now eyed her speculatively. Desolation and fear possessed Martyn. With a show of pre-occupation, she hurried away to Miss Hamilton's dressing-room, which she had already set in order. Here she would find a moment's respite. Perhaps in a few minutes she would creep down the passage and lock herself in the empty room and wait there until Fred Badger had gone his rounds. He would think she had found a lodging somewhere and left the theatre. She opened the door of Miss Hamilton's room and went in.

Adam Poole was sitting in front of the gas fire.

Martyn stammered: "I'm sorry," and made for the door.

"Come in," he said and stood up. "I want to see you for a moment."

"Well," Martyn thought sickly, "this is it. I'm to go."

He twisted the chair round and ordered rather than invited her to sit in it.

As she did so she thought: "I won't be able to sleep here to-night. When he's sacked me I'll get my suitcase and ask my way to the nearest women's hostel. I'll walk alone through the streets and when I get there the hostel will be shut."

He had turned his back to her and seemed to be examining something on the dressing-shelf.

"I would very much rather have disregarded this business," he said irritably, "but I suppose I can't. For one thing, someone should apologize to you for Bennington's behaviour. He's not likely to do it for himself."

"It really didn't matter."

"Of course it mattered," he said sharply. "It was insufferable. For both of us."

She was too distressed to recognize as one of pleasure the small shock this last phrase gave her.

"You realize, of course, how this nonsense started," he was saying. "You've seen something of the play. You've seen me. It's not a matter for congratulation, I dare say, but you're like enough to be my daughter. You're a New Zealander, I understand. How old are you?"

"Nineteen, sir."

"You needn't bother to pepper your replies with this 'sir' business. It's not in character and it's entirely unconvincing. I'm thirty-eight. I toured New Zealand in my first job twenty years ago, and Bennington was in the company. That, apparently, is good enough for him. Under the circumstances, I hope you won't mind my asking you who your parents are and where you were born."

"I've no objection whatever," said Martyn with spirit. "My father was Martin Tarne. He was the son and grandson of a high-country run-holder— a sheep-farmer—in the South Island. He was killed on Crete."

He turned and looked directly at her for the first time since she had come into the room.

"I see. And your mother?"

"She's the daughter of a run-holder in the same district."

"Do you mind telling me her maiden name, if you please?"

Martyn said: "I don't see what good this will do."

"Don't you, indeed? Don't you, after all, resent the sort of conjecture that's brewing among these people?"

"I certainly haven't the smallest desire to be thought your daughter."

"And I couldn't agree more. Good Lord!" he said. "This is a fatheaded way for us to talk. Why don't you want to tell me your mother's maiden name? What was the matter with it?"

"She always thought it sounded silly. It was Paula Poole Passington."

He brought the palm of his hand down crisply on the back of her chair. "And why in the world," he asked, "couldn't you say so at once?" Martyn was silent. "Paula Poole Passington," he repeated. "All right. An old cousin of my father's—Cousin Paula—married someone called Passington and dis-

appeared. I suppose to New Zealand. Why didn't she look me up when I
went out there?"

"I believe she didn't care for theatricals," said Martyn. "She was my grand-
mother. The connection is really quite distant."

"You might at least have mentioned it."

"I preferred not to."

"Too proud?"

"If you like," she said desperately.

"Why did you come to England?"

"To earn my living."

"As a dresser?" She was silent. "Well?" he said.

"As best I could."

"As an actress? Oh, for God's sake," he added, "it's damnably late and I'll
be obliged if you'll behave reasonably. I may tell you I've spoken to Jacko.
Don't you think you're making an ass of yourself? All this mystery act!"

Martyn got up and faced him. "I'm sorry," she said. "It's a silly business
but it's not an act. I didn't want to make a thing of it. I joined an English
touring company in New Zealand a year ago and they took me on with them
to Australia."

"What company was this? What parts did you play?"

She told him.

"I heard about the tour," he said. "They were a reasonably good company."

"They paid quite well and I did broadcasting too. I saved up enough to
keep me in England for six months and got a job as assistant children's
minder on a ship coming here. Perhaps I should explain that my father lost
pretty well everything in the slump, and we are poor people. I had my money
in traveller's cheques and the day we landed they were stolen out of my
bag, together with my letters of introduction. The bank will probably be
able to stop them and let me have it back, but until they decide, I'm hard
up. That's all."

"How long have you been here?"

"A fortnight."

"Where have you tried?"

"Agencies. All the London theatres, I think."

"This one last? Why?"

"One of them had to be last."

"Did you know of this—connection—as you call it?"

"Yes. My mother knew of it."

"And the resemblance?"

"I—we saw your pictures—people sometimes said—"

They looked at each other, warily, with guarded interest.

"And you deliberately fought shy of this theatre because you knew I was
playing here?"

"Yes."

"Did you know about this piece? The girl's part?"

Martyn was beginning to be very tired. A weariness of spirit and body seeped up through her being in a sluggish tide. She was near to tears and thrust her hand nervously through her short hair. He made some kind of ejaculation and she said at once: "I didn't mean to do that."

"But you knew about the part when you came here?"

"There's a lot of gossip at the agencies when you're waiting. A girl I stood next to in the queue at Garnet Marks's told me they wanted someone at the Vulcan who could be made up to look like you. She'd got it all muddled up with yesterday's auditions for the touring company in another piece."

"So you thought you'd try?"

"Yes. I was a bit desperate by then. I thought I'd try."

"Without, I suppose, mentioning this famous 'connection'?"

"Yes."

"And finding there was nothing for you in the piece you applied for the job of dresser?"

"Yes."

"Well," he said, "it's fantastic, but at least it's less fantastic than pure coincidence would have been. One rather respects you by the way, if it's not impertinent in a second cousin once removed to say so."

"Thank you," she said vaguely.

"The question is, what are we going to do about it?"

Martyn turned away to the ranks of dresses, and with business-like movements of her trembling hands tweaked at the sheets that covered them. She said briskly: "I realize of course that I'll have to go. Perhaps Miss Hamilton—"

"You think you ought to go?" his voice said behind her. "I suppose you're right. It's an awkward business."

"I'm sorry."

"But I'd like to—it's difficult to suggest—"

"I'll be perfectly all right," she said with savage brightness. "Please don't give it another thought."

"Why, by the way, are you still in the theatre?"

"I was going to sleep here," Martyn said loudly. "I did last night. The night-watchman knows."

"You would be paid on Friday."

"Like the actors?"

"Certainly. How much is there in the exchequer between now and Friday?" Martyn was silent and he said with a complete change of voice: "My manners, you will already have been told, are notoriously offensive, but I don't believe I was going to say anything that would have offended you."

"I've got two and fourpence."

He opened the door and shouted "Jacko!" into the echoing darkness. She heard the Greenroom door creak and in a moment or two Jacko came in. He carried a board with a half-finished drawing pinned to it. This he exhibited to Poole. "Crazy, isn't it?" he said. "Helena's costume for the ball. What must I do but waste my beauty-sleep concocting it. Everybody will have to work very hard if it is to be made. I see you are in need of my counsel. What goes on?"

"Against my better judgement," Poole said, "I'm going to follow your advice. You always think you're indispensable at auditions. Give me some light out there and then sit in front."

"It is past midnight. This child has worked and worried herself into a complete *bouleversement*. She is as pale as a Pierrot."

Poole looked at her. "Are you all right?" he asked her. "It won't take ten minutes."

"I don't understand, but I'm all right."

"There you are, Jacko," Poole said and sounded pleased. "It's over to you."

Jacko took her by the shoulders and gently pushed her down on the chair. "*Attention,*" he said. "We make a bargain. I live not so far from here in an apartment house kept by a well-disposed French couple. An entirely respectable house, you understand, with no funny business. At the top one finds an attic room as it might be in a tale for children, and so small, it is but twice the size of its nice little bed. The rental is low, within the compass of a silly girl who gets herself into equivocal situations. At my recommendation she will be accommodated in the attic, which is included in my portion of the house, and will pay me the rent at the end of a week. But in exchange for my good offices she does for us a little service. Again, no funny business."

"Oh, dear!" Martyn said. She leant towards the dressing-shelf and propped her face in her hands. "It sounds so wonderful," she said and tried to steady her voice, "a nice little bed."

"All right, Jacko," Poole said. She heard the door open and shut. "I want you to relax for a few minutes," his voice went on. "Relax all over like a cat. Don't think of anything in particular. You're going to sleep sound to-night. All will be well."

The gas fire hummed, the smell of roses and cosmetics filled the warm room. "Do you smoke?" Poole asked.

"Sometimes."

"Here you are."

She drew in the smoke gratefully. He went into the passage and she watched him light his own cigarette. Her thoughts drifted aimlessly about the bony structure of his head and face. Presently a stronger light streamed down the passage. Jacko's voice called something from a great distance.

Poole turned to her. "Come along," he said.

On the stage, dust-thickened rays from pageant-lamps settled in a pool of light about a desk and two chairs. It was like an island in a vague region of blueness. She found herself seated there at the desk, facing him across it. In response to a gesture of Poole's she rested her arms on the desk and her face on her arms.

"Listen," he said, "and don't move. You are in the hall of an old house, beautiful but decaying. You are the girl with the bad heredity. You are the creature who goes round and round in her great empty cage like a stoat filled with a wicked little desire. The object of your desire is the man on the other side of the desk, who is joined to you in blood and of whose face and mind you are the ill reflection. In a moment you will raise your face to his. He will make a gesture and you will make the same gesture. Then you will say: 'Don't you like what you see?' It must be horrible and real. Don't move. Think it. Then raise your head and speak."

There was a kind of voluptuousness in Martyn's fatigue. Only the chair she sat on and the desk that propped her arms and head prevented her, she felt, from slipping to the floor. Into this defencelessness Poole's suggestions entered like those of a mesmerist, and that perfection of duality for which actors pray and which they are so rarely granted now fully invested her. She was herself and she was the girl in the play. She guided the girl and was aware of her and she governed the possession of the girl by the obverse of the man in the play. When at last she raised her face and looked at him and repeated his gesture it seemed to her that she looked into a glass and saw her own reflection and spoke to it.

"Don't you like what you see?" Martyn said.

In the pause that followed, the sound of her own breathing and Poole's returned. She could hear her heart beat.

"Can you do it again?" he said.

"I don't know," she said helplessly. "I don't know at all." She turned away and with a childish gesture hid her face in the crook of her arm. In dismay and shame she let loose the tears she had so long denied herself.

"There, now!" he said, not so much as if to comfort her as to proclaim some private triumph of his own. Out in the dark auditorium Jacko struck his hands together once.

Poole touched her shoulder. "It's nothing," he said. "These are growing pains. They will pass." From the door in the set he said: "You can have the understudy. We'll make terms to-morrow. If you prefer it, the relationship can be forgotten. Good night."

He left her alone and presently Jacko returned to the stage carrying her suitcase.

"Now," he said, "we go home."

CHAPTER IV

Second Dress Rehearsal

When Martyn opened her eyes on the second morning of her adventure it was with the sensation of having come to rest after a painful journey. At first the events of the previous night seemed to be incorporated in the sleep that had followed them, and her happiness had something of the precarious and transitory quality of a remembered dream. It was difficult to believe that nine hours ago she had faced Adam Poole across a table on the stage of the Vulcan Theatre and had done so, for the moment at least, as an actress. The subsequent drive in a taxi with the unusually silent Jacko, their entrance into a sleeping house, creaking tiptoe up the stairs, the rapture of a hot bath and her subsequent oblivion—all these events flowed together in her memory and she felt she was as yet neither asleep nor fully wakened.

She lay quiet and looked about her. It was a bright morning and the sun came in at the attic window above her bed. The room had an air of great cleanliness and freshness. She remembered now that Jacko had told her he occasionally made use of it and indeed, tiny as it was, it bore his eccentric imprint. A set of designs for *Twelfth Night* was pinned to a wall-board. Ranged along the shelf were a number of figures dressed in paper as the persons in the play and on the wall facing her bed hung a mask of the fool, Feste, looking very like Jacko himself.

"There never was such a little room," Martyn sighed, and began to plan how she would collect and stow away her modest belongings. She was filled with gratitude and with astonished humility.

The bathroom was on the next floor and as she went downstairs she smelt coffee and fresh bread. A door on the landing opened and Jacko's clownish head looked out.

"Breakfast in ten minutes," he said. "Speed is essential."

Of all the amenities, it seemed to Martyn, a hot bath was the most beneficent, and after that a shower under which one could wash one's hair quickly. "Lucky it's short," she thought, and rubbed it dry with her towel.

She was out again in eight minutes to find Jacko on the landing.

"Good," he said. "In your woollen gown you are entirely respectable. A clean school-child. In."

He marshalled her into a largish room set out in an orderly manner as a workshop. Martyn wondered why Jacko, who showed such exquisite neatness in his work, should in his person present such a wild front to the world. He was dressed now in faded cotton trousers, a paint-stained undervest and a tattered dressing-gown. He was unshaven and uncombed and his prominent eyes were slightly bloodshot. His manner, however, was as usual amiable and disarming.

"I propose," he said, "that we breakfast together as a general rule. A light breakfast and supper are included in the arrangement. You will hand me your ration book and I shall shop with discretion. Undoubtedly I am a better cook than you and will therefore make myself responsible for supper. For luncheon you may return if you wish and forage ineffectually for yourself or make what other arrangement seems good to you. Approved?"

Martyn said carefully: "If you please, Jacko, I'm so grateful and so muddled I can't think at all sensibly. You see, I don't know what I shall be earning."

"For your dual and unusual role of understudy and dresser, I imagine about eight pounds a week. Your rental, *demi-pension*, here is two."

"It seems so little," Martyn said timidly. "The rent, I mean."

Jacko tapped the side of the coffee-pot with a spoon.

"*Attention*," he said. "How often must I repeat. You will have the goodness to understand I am not a dirty old man. It is true that I am virile," he continued with some complacency, "but you are not my type. I prefer the more mature, the more *mondaine*, the—" He stopped short, the spoon with which he had been gesticulating still held aloft. His eyes were fixed on the wall behind Martyn. She turned her head to see a sketch in water-colour of Helena Hamilton. When she faced Jacko again, he was grinning desperately.

"Believe me," he said, "you are in no danger of discomfort from the smallest whisper of scandal. I am notoriously pure. This morning there are eggs and therefore an omelette. Let us observe silence while I make it."

He was gay, in his outlandish fashion, from then onwards. When they had finished their admirable breakfast she helped him wash up and he gave her what he called her orders for the day. She was to go down to the theatre with him, set about her work as a dresser, and at three o'clock she would be given a formal rehearsal as understudy. At night, for the second dress rehearsal, she would again take up her duties as Miss Hamilton's dresser.

"An eccentric arrangement," Jacko said. He groped in the bosom of his undervest and produced a somewhat tattered actor's "part," typewritten and bound in paper. "Only thirteen sides," he said. "A bit-part. You will study the lines while you press and stitch and by this afternoon you are word-perfect, isn't it? You are, of course, delighted?"

"Delighted," Martyn said, "is not exactly the word. I'm flabbergasted and excited and grateful for everything and I just can't believe it's true. But it is a bit worrying to feel I've sort of got in on a fluke and that everybody's wondering what it's all about. They are, you know."

"All that," Jacko said with an ungainly sweep of his arm, "is of no importance. Gay Gainsford is still to play the part. She will not play it well but she is the niece of the leading lady's husband and she is therefore in a favourable position."

"Yes, but her uncle—"

He said quickly: "Clark Bennington was once a good actor. He is now a stencil. He drinks too much and when he is drunk he is offensive. Forget him." He turned away and with less than his usual deftness began to set out his work-table. Finally, from an adjoining room he said indistinctly: "I advise that which I find difficult to perform. Do not allow yourself to become hag-ridden by this man. It is a great mistake. I myself—" His voice was lost in the spurt of running water. Martyn heard him shout: "Run off and learn your lines. I have a job in hand."

With a feeling of unease she returned to her room. But when she opened her part and began to read the lines, this feeling retreated until it hung like a very small cloud over the hinterland of her mind. The foreground was occupied entirely by the exercise of memorizing and in a few minutes she had almost, but not quite, forgotten her anxiety.

ii

She was given her moves that afternoon by the stage-manager, and at three o'clock rehearsed her scenes with the other two understudies. The remaining parts were read from the script. Jacko pottered about back-stage intent on one of his odd jobs: otherwise the theatre seemed to be deserted. Martyn had memorized her lines but inevitably lost them from time to time in her effort to associate them with physical movement. The uncompromising half-light of a working-stage, the mechanical pacing to-and-fro of understudies, the half-muted lines raised to concert-pitch only for cues, and the dead sound of voices in an empty house—all these workaday circumstances, though she was familiar enough with them, after all, laid a weight upon her: she lost her belief in the magic of the previous night. She was oppressed by this anti-climax, and could scarcely summon up the resources of her young experience to meet it.

The positions and moves had been planned with a vivid understanding of the text and seemed to spring out of it. She learnt them readily enough. Rather to her surprise, and, she thought, that of the other understudies, they were finally taken through her scenes at concert-pitch, so that by the end of the rehearsal the visual and aural aspects of her part had fused into a whole. She had got her routine. But it was no more than a routine: she spoke and paused and moved and spoke and there was no reality at all, she felt, in anything she did. Clem Smith, the stage-manager, said nothing about interpretation but, huddled in his overcoat, merely set the moves and then crouched over the script. She was not even a failure, she was just another colourless understudy and nothing had happened.

When it was over, Clem Smith shut the book and said: "Thank you, ladies and gentlemen. Eleven in the morning, if you please." He lit a cigarette and went down into the auditorium and out through the front of the house.

Left alone on the stage, Martyn struggled with an acute attack of deflation. She tried to call herself to order. This in itself was a humiliating, if salutary, exercise. If, she thought savagely, she had been a Victorian young lady, she would at this juncture have locked herself away with a plush-bound journal and, after shedding some mortified tears, forced a confession out of herself. As it was, she set her jaw and worked it out there and then. The truth was, she told herself, she'd been at her old tricks again: she'd indulged in the most blatant kind of day-dream. She'd thought up a success-story and dumped herself down in the middle of it with half a dozen pageant-lamps bathing her girlish form. Because she looked like Poole and because last night she'd had a mild success with one line by playing it off her nerves she'd actually had the gall to imagine— Here Martyn felt her scalp creep and her face burn. "Come on," she thought, "out with it."

Very well, then. She'd dreamt up a further rehearsal with Poole. She'd seen herself responding eagerly to his production, she'd heard him say regretfully that if things had been different— She had even— At this point, overtaken with self-loathing, Martyn performed the childish exercise of throwing her part across the stage, stamping violently and thrusting her fingers through her hair.

"*Damn and blast and hell*," said Martyn, pitching her voice to the back row of the gallery.

"Not quite as bad as all that."

Adam Poole came out of the shadowed pit and down the centre-aisle of the stalls. He rested his hands on the rail of the orchestral well. Martyn gaped at him.

"You've got the mechanics," he said. "Walk through it again by yourself before to-morrow. Then you can begin to think about the girl. Get the layout of the house into your head. Know your environment. What has she been doing all day before the play opens? What has she been thinking about? Why does she say the things she says and do the things she does? Listen to the other chaps' lines. Come down here for five minutes and we'll see what you think about acting."

Martyn went down into the house. Of all her experiences during these three days at the Vulcan Theatre, she was to remember this most vividly. It was a curious interview. They sat side by side as if waiting for the rise-of-curtain. Their voices were deadened by the plush stalls. Jacko could be heard moving about behind the set and in some distant room back-stage, somebody in desultory fashion hammered and sawed. At first Martyn was ill at ease, unable to dismiss or to reconcile the jumble of distracted notions that beset her. But Poole was talking about theatre and about problems of the actor. He talked well, without particular emphasis but with penetration and authority. Soon she listened with single hearing and with all her attention to what he had to say. Her nervousness and uncertainty were gone, and presently she was able to speak of matters that had exercised her in her own brief experience of the stage. Their conversation was adult and fruitful. It didn't even occur to her that they were getting on rather well together.

Jacko came out on the stage. He shielded his eyes with his hand and peered into the auditorium.

"Adam?" he said.

"Hullo? What is it?"

"It is Helena on the telephone to inquire why have you not rung her at four, the time being now five-thirty. Will you take it in the office?"

"Good Lord!" he ejaculated and got up. Martyn moved into the aisle to let him out.

He said: "All right, Miss Tarne. Work along the lines we've been talking about and you should be able to cope with the job. We take our understudies seriously at the Vulcan and like to feel they're an integral part of the company. You'll rehearse again to-morrow morning and—" He stopped unaccountably, and after a moment said hurriedly: "You're all right, aren't you? I mean you feel quite happy about this arrangement?"

"Yes," she said. "Very happy."

"Good." He hesitated again for a second and then said: "I must go," and was off down the aisle to the front of the house. He called out: "I'll be in the office for some time, Jacko, if anyone wants me."

A door banged. There was a long silence.

Jacko advanced to the footlights. "Where are you?" he asked.

"Here," said Martyn.

"I see you. Or a piece of you. Where is the rest? Reassemble yourself. There is work to be done."

The work turned out to be the sewing together of a fantastic garment created and tacked up by Jacko himself. It had a flamboyant design, stencilled in black and yellow, of double-headed eagles, and was made in part of scenic canvas. There was an electric sewing machine in the wardrobe-room, which was next to Mr. J. G. Darcey's at the end of the passage. Here Jacko sat Martyn down, and here for the next hour she laboured under his exacting direction while he himself crawled about the floor cutting out further garments for the Combined Arts Ball. At half past six he went out, saying he would return with food.

Martyn laboured on. Sometimes she repeated the lines of the part, her voice drowned by the clatter of the machine. Sometimes, when engaged in hand-work, it would seem in the silent room that she had entered into a new existence, as if she had at that moment been born and was a stranger to her former self. And since this was rather a frightening sensation, though not new to Martyn, she must rouse herself and make a conscious effort to dispel it. On one of these occasions, when she had just switched off the machine, she felt something of the impulse that had guided her first attempt at the scene with Poole. Wishing to retain and strengthen this experience, she set aside her work and rested her head on her arms as the scene required. She waited in this posture, summoning her resources, and when she was ready raised her head to confront her opposite.

Gay Gainsford stood on the other side of the table, watching her.

iii

Martyn's flesh leapt on her bones. She cried out and made a sweeping gesture with her arms. A pair of scissors clattered to the floor.

"I'm sorry I startled you," said Miss Gainsford. "I came in quietly. I thought you were asleep but I realize now—you were doing that scene. Weren't you?"

"I've been given the understudy," Martyn said.

"You've had an audition and a rehearsal, haven't you?"

"Yes. I was so frightful at rehearsal, I thought I'd have another shot by myself."

"You needn't," Miss Gainsford said, "try to make it easy for me."

Martyn, still shaken and bewildered, looked at her visitor. She saw a pretty face that under its make-up was sodden with tears. Even as she looked, the large photogenic eyes flooded and the small mouth quivered.

"I suppose," Miss Gainsford said, "you know what you're doing to me."

"Good Lord!" Martyn ejaculated. "What *is* all this? What have I done? I've got your understudy. I'm damn thankful to have it and so far I've made a pretty poor showing."

"It's no good taking that line with me. I know what's happening."

"Nothing's happening. Oh, *please*," Martyn implored, torn between pity and a rising fear, "*please* don't cry. I'm nothing. I'm just any old understudy."

"That's pretty hot, I must say," Miss Gainsford said. Her voice wavered grotesquely between two registers like an adolescent boy's. "To talk about 'any old understudy' when you've got that appearance. What's everyone saying about you when they think I'm not about? 'She's got the appearance!' It doesn't matter to them that I've had to dye my hair because they don't like wigs. I still haven't got the appearance. I'm a shoulder-length natural ash-blonde, and I've had to have an urchin cut and go black and all I get is insults. In any other management," she continued wildly, "the author wouldn't be allowed to speak to the artists like that man speaks to me. In any other management an artist would be protected against that kind of treatment. Adam's worse, if anything. He's so bloody patient and persistent and half the time you don't know what he's talking about."

She drew breath, sobbed and hunted in her bag for her handkerchief.

Martyn said: "I'm so terribly sorry. It's awful when things go badly at rehearsals. But the worst kind of rehearsals *do* have a way of turning into the best kind of performances. And it's a grand play, isn't it?"

"I loathe the play. To me it's a lot of high-brow hokum and I don't care who knows it. Why the hell couldn't Uncle Ben leave me where I was, playing leads and second leads in fortnightly rep? We were a happy family in fortnightly rep; everyone had fun and games and there wasn't this ghastly graveyard atmosphere. I was miserable enough, God knows, before you came but now it's just *more* than I can stand."

"But I'm not going to play the part," Martyn said desperately. "You'll be all right. It's just got you down for the moment. I'd be no good, I expect, anyway."

"It's what they're all saying and thinking. It's a pity, they're saying, that you came too late."

"Nonsense. You only imagine that because of the likeness."

"Do I? Let me tell you I'm not imagining *all* the things they're saying about you. And about Adam. How you *can* stay here and take it! Unless it's true. *Is* it true?"

Martyn closed her hands on the material she had been sewing. "I don't want to know what they're saying. There's nothing unkind that's true for them to say."

"So the likeness is purely an accident? There's no relationship?"

Martyn said: "It seems that we are very distantly related, so distantly that the likeness is a freak. I didn't want to tell anyone about it. It's of no significance at all. I haven't used it to get into the theatre."

"I don't know how and why you got in but I wish to God you'd get out. How you *can* hang on, knowing what they think, if it isn't true! You can't have any pride or decency. It's so cruel. It's so *damnably* cruel."

Martyn looked at the pretty tear-blubbered face and thought in terror that if it had been that of Atropos it could scarcely have offered a more dangerous threat. "Don't!" she cried out. "Please don't say that; I need this job so desperately. Honestly, *honestly* you're making a thing of all this. I'm not hurting you."

"Yes, you are. You're driving me completely frantic. I'm nervously and emotionally exhausted," Miss Gainsford sobbed, with an air of quoting somebody else. "It just needed you to send me over the border-line. Uncle Ben keeps on and on and on about it until I think I'll go mad. This is a beastly unlucky theatre anyway. Everyone knows there's something wrong about it and then you come in like a Jonah and it's the rock *bottom*. If," Miss Gainsford went on, developing a command of histrionic climax of which Martyn would scarcely have suspected her capable, "if you have *any* pity at all, *any* humanity, you'll spare me this awful ordeal."

"But this is all nonsense. You're making a song about nothing. I won't be taken in by it," Martyn said and recognized defeat in her own voice.

Miss Gainsford stared at her with watery indignation and through trembling lips uttered her final cliché. "You can't," she said, "do this thing to me," and broke down completely.

It seemed to Martyn that beyond a façade of stock emotionalism she recognized a real and a profound distress. She thought confusedly that if they had met on some common and reasonable ground she would have been able to put up a better defence. As it was they merely floundered in a welter of unreason. It was intolerably distressing to her. Her precarious happiness died, she wanted to escape, she was lost. With a feeling of nightmarish detachment she heard herself say: "All right. I'll speak to Mr. Poole. I'll say I can't do the understudy."

Miss Gainsford had turned away. She held her handkerchief to her face. Her shoulders and head had been quivering but now they were still. There was a considerable pause. She blew her nose fussily, cleared her throat, and looked up at Martyn.

"But if you're Helena's dresser," she said, "you'll still be *about*."

"You can't mean you want to turn me out of the theatre altogether."

"There's no need," Miss Gainsford mumbled, "to put it like that."

Martyn heard a voice and footsteps in the passage. She didn't want to be confronted with Jacko. She said: "I'll see if Mr. Poole's still in the theatre. I'll speak to him now if he is."

As she made for the door Miss Gainsford snatched at her arm. "Please!" she said. "I *am* grateful. But you will be really generous won't you? Really big? You won't bring me into it, will you? With Adam I mean. Adam wouldn't underst—"

Her face set as if she had been held in suspension, like a motion picture freezing into a still. She didn't even release her hold on Martyn's arm.

Martyn spun round and saw Poole, with Jacko behind him, in the passage. To her own astonishment she burst out laughing.

"No, really!" she stammered. "It's too much! This is the third time. Like the demon-king in pantomime."

"What the devil do you mean?"

"I'm sorry. It's just your flair for popping up in crises. Other people's crises. Mine, in fact."

He grimaced as if he gave her up as a bad job. "What's the present crisis?" he said and looked at Miss Gainsford, who had turned aside and was uneasily painting her mouth. "What is it, Gay?"

"Please!" she choked. "Please let me go. I'm all right, really. Quite all right. I just rather want to be alone."

She achieved a tearful smile at Poole and an imploring glance at Martyn. Poole stood away from the door and watched her go out with her chin up and with courageous suffering neatly portrayed in every inch of her body.

She disappeared into the passage and a moment later the door of the Greenroom was heard to shut.

"It is a case of mis-casting," said Jacko, coming into the room. "She should be in Hollywood. She has what it takes in Hollywood. What an exit! We have misjudged her."

"Go and see what's the matter."

"She wants," said Jacko, making a dolorous face, "to be alone."

"No, she doesn't. She wants an audience. You're it. Get along and do your stuff."

Jacko put several parcels on the table. "I am the dogsbody," he said, "to end all dogsbodies," and went out.

"Now, then," Poole said.

Martyn gathered up her work and was silent.

"What's the matter? You're as white as a sheet. Sit down. What is all this?"

She sat behind the machine.

"Come on," he said.

"I'm sorry if it's inconvenient for you but I'm afraid I've got to give notice."

"Indeed? As a dresser or as understudy?"

"As both."

"It's extremely inconvenient and I don't accept it."

"But you must. Honestly, you must. I can't go on like this: it isn't fair."

"Do you mean because of that girl?"

"Because of her and because of everything. She'll have a breakdown. There'll be some disaster."

"She doesn't imagine you're going to be given the part over her head, does she?"

"No, no, of course not. It's just that she's finding it hard anyway and the—the sight of me sort of panics her."

"The likeness?"

"Yes."

"She needn't look at you. I'm afraid she's the most complete ass, that girl," he muttered. He picked up a fold of the material Martyn had been sewing, looked absently at it and pushed the whole thing across the table. "Understand," he said, "I won't for a second entertain the idea of your going. For one thing Helena can't do without you, and for another I will not be dictated to by a minor actress in my own company. Nor," he added with a change of tone, "by anyone else."

"I'm so terribly sorry for her," Martyn said. "She feels there's some sort of underground movement against her. She really feels it."

"And you?"

"I must admit I don't much enjoy the sensation of being in the theatre on sufferance. But I was so thankful—" She caught her breath and stopped.

"Who makes you feel you're on sufferance? Gay? Bennington? Percival?"

"I used a silly phrase. Naturally, they all must think it a bit queer, my turning up. It *looks* queer."

"It'd look a damn sight queerer if you faded out again. I can't think," he said impatiently, "how you could let yourself be bamboozled by that girl."

"But it's *not* all bamboozle. She really is at the end of her tether."

Martyn waited for a moment. She thought inconsequently how strange it was that she should talk like this to Adam Poole, who two days ago had been a celebrated name, a remote legend, seen and heard and felt through a veil of characterization in his films.

"Oh, well," she thought and said aloud: "I'm thinking of the show. It's such a good play. She mustn't be allowed to fail. I'm thinking about that."

He came nearer and looked at her with a sort of incredulity. "Good Lord," he said, "I believe you are! Do you mean to say you haven't considered your own chance if she did crack up? Where's your wishful thinking?"

Martyn slapped her palm down on the table. "But of course I have. Of course I've done my bit of wishful thinking. But don't you see—"

He reached across the table and for a brief moment his hand closed over hers. "I think I do," he said. "I'm beginning, it seems, to get a taste of your quality. How do you suppose the show would get on if you had to play?"

"That's unfair," Martyn cried.

"Well," he said, "don't run out on me. That'd be unfair, if you like. No dresser. No understudy. A damn shabby trick. As for this background music, I know where it arises. It's a more complex business than you may suppose.

I shall attend to it." He moved behind her chair, and rested his hands on its back. "Well," he said, "shall we clap hands and a bargain? How say you?" Martyn said slowly: "I don't see how I can do anything but say yes." "There's my girl!" His hand brushed across her head and he moved away. "Though I must say," Martyn added, "you do well to quote Petruchio. And Henry the Fifth, if it comes to that."

"A brace of autocratic male animals? Therefore it must follow you are 'Kate' in two places. And—shrewd Kate, French Kate, kind Kate, but never curst Kate—you will rehearse at eleven to-morrow, hold or cut bow-strings. Agreed?"

"I am content."

"Damned if you look it, however. All right. I'll have a word with that girl. Good day to you, Kate."

"Good day, sir," said Martyn.

iv

That night the second dress rehearsal went through as for performance, without, as far as Martyn knew, any interruption during the action.

She stayed throughout in one or the other of Miss Hamilton's dressing-rooms and, on the occasions when she was in transit, contrived to be out of the way of any of the players. In the second act, her duties kept her in the improvised dressing-room on the stage and she heard a good deal of the dialogue.

There is perhaps nothing that gives one so strong a sense of theatre from the inside as the sound of invisible players in action. The disembodied and remote voices, projected at an unseen mark, the uncanny quiet off-stage, the smells and the feeling that the walls and the dust listen, the sense of a simmering expectancy; all these together make a corporate life so that the theatre itself seems to breathe and pulse and give out a warmth. This warmth communicated itself to Martyn and, in spite of all her misgivings, she glowed and thought to herself, "This is my place. This is where I belong."

Much of the effect of the girl's part in this act depended not so much on what she said, which was little, but on mime and on that integrity of approach which is made manifest in the smallest gesture, the least movement. Listening to Miss Gainsford's slight uncoloured voice, Martyn thought: "But perhaps if one watched her it would be better. Perhaps something is happening that cannot be heard, only seen."

Miss Hamilton, when she came off for her changes, spoke of nothing but the business in hand and said little enough about that. She was indrawn and formal in her dealings with her dresser. Martyn wondered uneasily how much Poole had told her of their interviews, whether she had any strong views or prejudices about her husband's niece, or shared his resentment that Martyn herself had been cast as an understudy.

The heat radiated by the stong lights of the dressing-rooms intensified their characteristic smells. With business-like precision Miss Hamilton would aim an atomizer at her person and spray herself rhythmically with scent while Martyn, standing on a chair, waited to slip a dress over her head. After the end of the second act, when she was about this business in the star-room, Poole came in. "That went very nicely, Helena," he said.

Martyn paused with the dress in her hands. Miss Hamilton extended her whitened arms, and with a very beautiful movement turned to him.

"Oh, darling," she said. "Did it? Did it really?"

Martyn thought she had never seen anyone more lovely than her employer was then. Hers was the kind of beauty that declared itself when most simply arrayed. The white cloth that protected her hair added a Holbein-like emphasis to the bones and subtly turning planes of her face. There was a sort of naïveté and warmth in her posture: a touching intimacy. Martyn saw Poole take the hands that were extended to him and she turned her head away, not liking, with the voluminous dress in her arms, to climb down from her station on the chair. She felt suddenly desolate and shrunken within herself.

"Was it *really* right?" Miss Hamilton said.

"You were, at least."

"But—otherwise?"

"Much as one would expect."

"Where's John?"

"In the circle, under oath not to come down until I say so."

"Pray God, he keep his oath!" she quoted sombrely.

"Hullo, Kate," Poole said.

"Kate?" Miss Hamilton asked. "Why Kate?"

"I suspect her," said Poole, "of being a shrew. Get on with your job, Kate. What are you doing up there?"

Miss Hamilton said: "Really, darling!" and moved away to the chair. Martyn slipped the dress over her head, jumped down and began to fasten it. She did this to a running accompaniment from Poole. He whispered to himself anxiously as if he were Martyn, muttered and grunted as if Miss Hamilton complained that the dress was tight, and thus kept up a preposterous duologue, matching his words to their actions. This was done so quaintly and with so little effort that Martyn had much ado to keep a straight face and Miss Hamilton was moved to exasperated laughter. When she was dressed she took him by the arms. "Since when, my sweet, have you become a dressing-room comedian?"

"Oh God, your only jig-maker."

"Last act, please, last act," said the call-boy in the passage.

"Come on," she said, and they went out together.

When the curtain was up, Martyn returned to the improvised dressing-room on the stage and there, having for the moment no duties, she listened to the invisible play and tried to discipline her most unruly heart.

Bennington's last exit was followed in the play by his suicide, off-stage. Jacko, who had, it seemed, a passion for even the simplest of off-stage stunts, had come round from the front of the house to supervise the gunshot. He stood near the entry into the dressing-room passage with a stage-hand who carried an effects-gun. This was fired at the appropriate moment and, as they were stationed not far from Martyn in her canvas room, she leapt at the report, which was nerve-shatteringly successful. The acrid smell of the discharge drifted into her roofless shelter.

Evidently Bennington was standing near by. His voice, carefully lowered to a murmur, sounded just beyond the canvas wall. "And that," he said, "takes me *right* off, thank God. Give me a cigarette, Jacko, will you?" There was a pause. The stage-hand moved away. A match scraped and Bennington said: "Come to my room and have a drink."

"Thank you, Ben, not now," Jacko whispered. "The curtain comes down in five minutes."

"Followed by a delicious post mortem conducted by the Great Producer and the Talented Author. Entrancing prospect! How did I go, Jacko?"

"No actor," Jacko returned, "cares to be told how he goes in anything but terms of extravagant praise. You know how clever you always are. You are quite as clever to-night as you have always been. Moreover, you showed some discretion."

Martyn heard Bennington chuckle. "There's still to-morrow," he said. "I reserve my fire, old boy. I bide my time."

There was a pause. Martyn heard one of them fetch a long sigh—Jacko, evidently, because Bennington, as if in answer to it, said: "Oh, nonsense." After a moment he added: "The kid's all right," and when Jacko didn't answer: "Don't you think so?"

"Why, yes," said Jacko.

On the stage the voices of Helena Hamilton and Adam Poole built towards a climax. The call-boy came round behind the set and went down the passage chanting: "All on for the curtain, please. All on."

Martyn shifted the chair in the dressing-room and moved noisily. There was a brief silence.

"I don't give a damn if she can hear," Bennington said more loudly. "Wait a moment. Stay where you are. I was asking you what you thought of Gay's performance. She's all right. Isn't she?"

"Yes, yes. I must go."

"Wait a bit. If the fools left her alone she'd go tremendously. I tell you what, old boy. If our Eccentric Author exercises his talent for wisecracking on that kid to-night I'll damn well take a hand."

"You will precipitate a further scene, and that is to be avoided."

"I'm not going to stand by and hear her bullied. By God, I'm not. I understand you've given harbourage, by the way, to the Mystery Maiden."

"I must get round to the side. By your leave, Ben."

"Plenty of time."

And Martyn knew that Bennington stood in the entry to the passage, barring the way.

"I'm talking," he said, "about this understudy-cum-dresser. Miss X."

"You are prolific in cryptic titles."

"Call her what you like, it's a peculiar business. What is she? You may as well tell me, you know. Some ancient indiscretion of Adam's adolescence come home to roost?"

"Be quiet, Ben."

"For tuppence I'd ask Adam himself. And that's not the only question I'd like to ask him. Do you think I relish my position?"

"They are getting near the tag. It is almost over."

"Why do you suppose I drink a bit? What would you do in my place?"

"Think before I speak," said Jacko, "for one thing."

A buzzer sounded. "There's the curtain," said Jacko. "Look out."

Martyn heard a kind of scuffle followed by an oath from Bennington. There were steps in the passage. The curtain fell with a giant whisper. A gust of air swept through the region back-stage.

"All on," said the stage-manager distantly. Martyn heard the players go on and the curtain rise and fall again.

Poole, on the stage, said: "And that's all of that. All right, everyone. Settle down and I'll take the notes. John will be round in a moment. I'll wait for you, Helena."

Miss Hamilton came into the improvised room. Martyn removed her dress and put her into her gown.

"I'll take my make-up off out there," she said. "Bring the things, Martyn, will you? Grease, towels and my cigarettes?"

Martyn had them ready. She followed Miss Hamilton out and for the first time that night went onto the set.

Poole, wearing a dark dressing-gown, stood with his back to the curtain. The other five members of the cast sat, relaxed but attentive, about the stage. Jacko and Clem Smith waited by the Prompt corner with papers and pencils. Martyn held a looking-glass before Miss Hamilton, who said: "Adam, darling, you don't mind, do you? I mustn't miss a word but I *do* rather want to get on," and began to remove her make-up.

Upon this scene Dr. John James Rutherford erupted. His arrival was prefaced in his usual manner by slammed doors, blundering footsteps and loud ejaculations. He then appeared in the central entrance, flame-headed, unshaven, overcoated, and grasping a sheaf of papers.

"Roast me," he said, "in sulphur! Wash me in steep-down gulfs of liquid fire! 'Ere I again endure the loathy torment of a dress rehearsal! What have I done, ye gods, that I should—"

"All right, John," Poole said. "Not yet. Sit down. On some heavy piece of furniture and carefully."

Clem Smith shouted: "Alf! The Doctor's chair."

A large chair with broken springs was brought on and placed with its back to the curtain. Dr. Rutherford hurled himself into it and produced his snuff-box. "I am a child to chiding," he said. "What goes on, chums?"

Poole said: "I'm going to take my stuff. If anything I have to say repeats exactly any of your own notes you might leave it out for the sake of saving time. If you've any objections, be a good chap and save them till I've finished. Agreed?"

"Can't we cut the flummery and get down to business?"

"That's just what I'm suggesting."

"Is it? I wasn't listening. Press on, then, my dear fellow. Press on."

They settled down. Jacko gave Poole a block of notes and he began to work through them. "Nothing much in Act I," he said, "until we get to—" His voice went on evenly. He spoke of details in timing, of orchestration and occasionally of stage-management. Sometimes a player would ask a question and there would be a brief discussion. Sometimes Clem Smith would make a note. For the scenes where Poole had been on, Jacko, it appeared, had taken separate notes. Martyn suddenly remembered that Jacko's official status was that of assistant to Poole, and thought it characteristic of him that he made so little of his authority.

From where she stood, holding the glass for Helena Hamilton, she could see all the players. In the foreground was the alert and beautiful face of her employer, a little older now with its make-up gone, turning at times to the looking-glass and at times, when something in his notes concerned her, towards Poole. Beyond Miss Hamilton sat J. G. Darcey, alone and thoughtfully filling his pipe. He glanced occasionally, with an air of anxious solicitude, at Miss Gainsford. At the far side Parry Percival lay in an armchair looking fretful. Bennington stood near the centre with a towel in his hands. At one moment he came behind his wife. Putting a hand on her shoulder, he reached over it, helped himself to a dollop of grease from a jar in her case and slapped it on his face. She made a slight movement of distaste and immediately afterwards a little secret grimace, as if she had caught herself out in a blunder. For a moment he retained his hold of her shoulder. Then he looked down at her, dragged his clean fingers across her neck and, smearing the grease over his face, returned to his former position and began to clean away his make-up.

Martyn didn't want to look at Gay Gainsford but was unable altogether to avoid doing so. Miss Gainsford sat, at first alone, on a smallish sofa. She seemed to have herself tolerably well in hand, but her eyes were restless and her fingers plaited and replaited the folds of her dress. Bennington watched her from a distance until he had done with his towel. Then he crossed the stage and sat beside her, taking one of the restless hands in his. He looked hard at Martyn, who was visited painfully by a feeling of great compassion for both of them and by a sensation of remorse. She had a notion, which she tried to dismiss as fantastic, that Poole sensed this reaction. His glance rested for a moment on her and she thought: "This is getting too complicated. It's

going to be too much for me." She made an involuntary movement and at
once Miss Hamilton put out a hand to the glass.

When Poole had dealt with the first act he turned to Dr. Rutherford, who
had sat throughout with his legs extended and his chin on his chest, directing
from under his brows a glare of extreme malevolence at the entire cast.

"Anything to add to that, John?" Poole asked.

"Apart from a passing observation that I regard the whole thing as a *tour
de force* of understatement and with reservations that I keep to myself"—
here Dr. Rutherford looked fixedly at Parry Percival—"I am mum. I reserve
my fire."

"Act II, then," said Poole, and began again.

Martyn became aware after a few minutes that Dr. Rutherford, like Bennington, was staring at her. She was as horridly fascinated as a bird is said to
be by the unwinking gaze of a snake. Do what she could to look elsewhere
about the stage, she must after a time steal a glance at him, only to meet
again his speculative and bloodshot regard. This alarmed her profoundly.
She was persuaded that a feeling of tension had been communicated to the
others, and that they too were aware of some kind of impending crisis. This
feeling grew in intensity as Poole's voice went steadily on with his notes.
He had got about half-way through the second act when Dr. Rutherford
ejaculated: "Hi! Wait a bit!" and began a frenzied search through his own
notes, which seemed to be in complete disorder. Finally he pounced on a
sheet of paper, dragged out a pair of spectacles and, with a hand raised to
enjoin silence, read it to himself with strange noises in his breathing. Having
scattered the rest of his notes over his person and the floor, he now folded
this particular sheet and sat on it.

"Proceed," he said. The cast stirred uneasily. Poole continued. He had
come to the scene between himself and Miss Gainsford, and beyond a minor
adjustment of position said nothing about it. Miss Hamilton, who had arrived
at the final stage of her street make-up, dusted her face with powder, nodded
good-humouredly at Martyn and turned to face Poole. Martyn thankfully
shut the dressing-case and made for the nearest exit.

At the same moment Poole reached the end of his notes for the second
act and Dr. Rutherford shouted: "Hold on! Stop that wench!"

Martyn, with a sensation of falling into chaos, turned in the doorway.

She saw nine faces lifted towards her own. They made a pattern against
the smoke-thickened air. Her eyes travelled from one to the other and rested
finally on Poole's.

"It's all right," he said. "Go home."

"No, you don't," Dr. Rutherford shouted excitedly.

"Indeed she does," said Poole. "Run away home, Kate. Good night to you."

Martyn heard the storm break as she fled down the passage.

CHAPTER V

Opening Night

From noon until half past six on the opening night of Dr. Rutherford's new play, the persons most concerned in its birth were absent from their theatre. Left to itself, the Vulcan was possessed only by an immense expectancy. It waited. In the auditorium rows of seats, stripped of their dust-cloths, stared at the curtain. The curtain itself presented its reverse side to Jacko's set, closing it in with a stuffy air of secrecy. The stage was dark. Battalions of dead lamps, focussed at crazy angles, overhung it with the promise of light. Cue-sheets, fixed to the switchboard, awaited the electrician, the prompt-script was on its shelf, the properties were ranged on trestle-tables. Everything bided its time in the dark theatre.

To enter into this silent house was to feel as if one surprised a poised and expectant presence. This air of suspense made itself felt to the occasional intruders: to the boy who from time to time came through from the office with telegrams for the dressing-rooms, to the girl from Florian's and the young man from the wig-makers, and to the piano-tuner who for an hour twanged and hammered in the covered well. And to Martyn Tarne who, alone in the ironing-room, set about the final pressing of the dresses under her care.

The offices were already active and behind their sand-blasted glass walls typewriters clattered and telephone bells rang incessantly. The blacked-out box-plan lay across Bob Grantley's desk, and stacked along the wall were rectangular parcels of programmes, fresh from the printer.

And at two o'clock the queues for the early doors began to form in Carpet Street.

ii

It was at two o'clock that Helena Hamilton, after an hour's massage, went to bed. Her husband had telephoned, with a certain air of opulence which she had learnt to dread, that he would lunch at his club and return to their flat during the afternoon to rest.

In her darkened room she followed a practised routine and, relaxing one set of muscles after another, awaited sleep. This time, however, her self-discipline was unsuccessful. If only she could hear him come in, it would be better; if only she could see into what sort of state he'd got himself. She used all her formulae for repose but none of them worked. At three o'clock she was still awake and still miserably anxious.

It was no good trying to cheer herself up by telling over her rosary of romantic memories. Usually this was a successful exercise. She had conducted her affairs of the heart, she knew, with grace and civility. She had almost always managed to keep them on a level of enchantment. She had simply allowed them to occur with the inconsequence and charm of self-sown larkspurs in an otherwise correctly ordered border. They had hung out their gay little banners for a season and then been painlessly tweaked up. Except, perhaps, for Adam. With Adam, she remembered uneasily, it had been different. With Adam, so much her junior, it had been a more deeply rooted affair. It had put an end, finally, to her living with Ben as his wife. It had made an enemy of Ben. And at once her thoughts were infested with worries about the contemporary scene at the theatre. "It's such a muddle," she thought, "and I hate muddles." They'd had nothing but trouble all through rehearsals. Ben fighting with everybody and jealous of Adam. The Doctor bawling everybody out. And that wretchedly unhappy child Gay (who, God knew, would never be an actress as long as she lived) first pitchforked into the part by Ben and now almost bullied out of it by the Doctor. And, last of all, Martyn Tarne.

She had touched the raw centre of her anxiety. Under any other conditions, she told herself, she would have welcomed the appearance out of a clear sky and—one had to face it—under very odd circumstances, of this little antipodean: this throw-back to some forebear that she and Adam were supposed to have in common. She would have been inclined to like Martyn for the resemblance instead of feeling so uncomfortably disturbed by it. Of course she accepted Adam's explanation, but at the same time she thought it rather naïve of him to believe that the girl had actually kept away from the theatre because she didn't want to make capital out of the relationship. That, Helena thought, turning restlessly on her bed, was really too simple of Adam. Moreover, he'd stirred up the already exacerbated nerves of the company by giving this girl the understudy without, until last night, making public the relationship.

There she went, thinking about last night's scene: John Rutherford demanding that even at this stage Martyn should play the part, Gay imploring Adam to release her, Ben saying he'd walk out on the show if Gay went, and Adam—Adam had done the right thing of course. He'd come down strongly with one of his rare thrusts of anger and reduced them to complete silence. He had then described the circumstances of Martyn's arrival at the theatre, and had added in a voice of ice that there was and could be no question of any change in the cast. He finished his notes and left the theatre, followed by Jacko.

This had been the signal for an extremely messy row in which everybody seemed to bring to light some deep-seated grudge. Ben had quarrelled almost simultaneously with Parry Percival (on the score of technique), with Dr. Rutherford (on the score of casting), with his niece (on the score of humanity) and, unexpectedly, with J. G. Darcey (on the score of Ben bullying

Gay). Percival had responded to a witticism of the Doctor's by a stream of shrill invective which astonished everybody, himself included, and Gay had knitted the whole scene into a major climax by having a fit of hysterics from which she was restored with brutal efficiency by Dr. Rutherford himself.

The party had been broken up. J.G. sustained his new role of knightly concern by taking Gay home. Parry Percival left in a recrudescence of fury occasioned by the Doctor flinging after him a composite Shakesperian epithet: "Get you gone, you dwarf; you minimus, of hindering knot-grass made; you bead, you acorn." She herself had retired into the wings. The stage-staff had already disappeared. The Doctor and Ben, finding themselves in undisputed possession of the stage, had squared up to each other with the resolution of all-in wrestlers, and she, being desperately tired, had taken the car home and asked their man to return to the theatre for her husband. When she had awakened late in the morning she was told he had already gone out.

"I wish," a voice cried out in her mind, "I wish to God he'd never come back."

And at that moment she heard him stumble heavily upstairs.

She expected him to go straight to his room and was dismayed when he came to a halt outside her door and, with a clumsy sound that might have been intended for a knock, opened it and came in. The smell of brandy and cigars came in with him and invaded the whole room. It was more than a year since that had happened.

He walked uncertainly to the foot of the bed and leant on it—and she was frightened of him.

"Hullo," he said.

"What is it, Ben? I'm resting."

"I thought you might be interested. There'll be no more nonsense from John about Gay."

"Good," she said.

"He's calmed down. I got him to see reason."

"He's not so bad, really—old John."

"He's had some good news from abroad. About the play."

"Translation rights?"

"Something like that." He was smiling at her, uncertainly. "You look comfy," he said. "All tucked up."

"Why don't you try and get some rest yourself?" He leant over the foot of the bed and said something under his breath. "What?" she said anxiously. "What did you say?"

"I said it's a pity Adam didn't appear a bit sooner, isn't it? I'm so extraneous."

Her heart thumped like a fist inside her ribs. "Ben, *please*," she said.

"And another thing. Do you both imagine I don't see through this dresser-cum-understudy racket? Darling, I don't much enjoy playing the cuckold in your Restoration comedy, but I'm just bloody well furious when you so grossly under-estimate my intelligence. When was it? On the New Zealand tour in 1930?"

"What is this nonsense!" she said breathlessly.

"Sorry. How are you managing to-night? You and Adam?"

"My dear Ben!"

"I'll tell you. You're making shift with me for once in a blue moon. And I'm not talking about to-night."

She recognized this scene. She had dreamt it many times. His face had advanced upon her while she lay inert with terror, as one does in a nightmare. For an infinitesimal moment she was visited by the hope that perhaps after all she had slept and, if she could only scream, would awaken. But she couldn't scream. She was quite helpless.

iii

Adam Poole's telephone rang at half past four. He had gone late to rest and was wakened from a deep sleep. For a second or two he didn't recognize her voice, and she spoke so disjointedly that even when he was broad awake he couldn't make out what she was saying.

"What is it?" he said. "Helena, what's the matter? I can't hear you."

Then she spoke more clearly and he understood.

iv

At six o'clock the persons in the play began to move towards the theatre. In their lodgings and flats they bestirred themselves after their several fashions: to drink tea or black coffee, choke down pieces of bread and butter that tasted like sawdust, or swallow aspirin and alcohol. This was their zero hour: the hour of low vitality when the stimulus of the theatre and the last assault of nerves was yet to come. By a quarter past six they were all on their way. Their dressers were already in their rooms and Jacko prowled restlessly about the darkened stage. Dr. John James Rutherford, clad in an evening suit and a boiled shirt garnished with snuff, both of which dated from some distant period when he still attended the annual dinners of the B.M.A., plunged into the office and made such a nuisance of himself that Bob Grantley implored him to go away.

At twenty past six the taxi carrying Gay Gainsford and J. G. Darcey turned into Carpet Street. Darcey sat with his legs crossed elegantly and his hat perched on them. In the half-light his head and profile looked like those of a much younger man.

"It *was* sweet of you to call for me, J.G.," Gay said unevenly.

He smiled, without looking at her, and patted her hand. "I'm always petrified myself," he said, "on first nights."

"Are you? I suppose a true artist must be."

"Ah, youth, youth!" sighed J.G.—a little stagily perhaps, but, if she hadn't been too preoccupied to notice it, with a certain overtone of genuine nostalgia.

"It's worse than the usual first-night horrors for *me*," she said. "I'm just boxing on in a private hell of my own."

"My poor child."

She turned a little towards him and leant her head into his shoulder. "Nice!" she murmured and after a moment: "I'm so frightened of him, J.G."

With the practised ease of a good actor, he slipped his arm round her. "I won't have it," he said. "By God, I won't! If he worries you again, author or no author—"

"It's not *him*," she said. "Not the Doctor. Oh, I know he's simply filthy to work with and he does fuss me dreadfully, but it's not the Doctor *really* who's responsible for all my misery."

"No? Who is then?"

"Uncle Ben!" She made a small wailing noise that was muffled by his coat. He bent his head attentively to listen. "J.G., I'm just plain *terrified* of Uncle Ben."

v

Parry Percival always enjoyed his arrival at the theatre when there was a gallery queue to be penetrated. One raised one's hat and said: "Pardon me. Thanks so much," to the gratified ladies. One heard them murmur one's name. It was a heartening little fillip to one's self-esteem.

On this occasion the stimulant didn't work with its normal magic. He was too worried to relish it wholeheartedly. For one thing his row with Dr. Rutherford still lingered like an unpleasant taste in his memory. Apart from the altogether unforgiveable insults the Doctor had levelled at his art, there was one in particular which had been directed at himself as a man and this troubled him deeply. It had almost brought him to the pitch of doing something that he dreaded to do—take stock of himself. Until now he had lived in an indeterminate hinterland, drifting first towards one frontier, then the other, unsure of his impulses and not strongly propelled by them in any one direction. He would, he thought, perhaps have turned out a happier being if he had been born a woman. "Let's face it," he thought uneasily, "I'm interested in their kind of things. I'm intuitive and sensitive in their way." It helped a little to think how intuitive and how sensitive he was. But he was not in any sense a fair target for the sort of veiled insults the Doctor had levelled at him. And as if this weren't enough of a worry, there was the immediate menace of Clark Bennington. Ben, he thought hotly, was insufferable. Every device by which a second-leading man could make a bit-part actor look foolish had been brought into play during rehearsals. Ben had up-staged him, had flurried him by introducing new business, had topped his lines and, even while he was seething with impotent fury, had reduced him to nervous giggles by looking sideways at him. It was the technique with which a schoolmaster could torture a small boy, and it revived in Parry hideous memories of his childhood.

Only partially restored by the evidence of prestige afforded by the gallery queue, he walked down the stage-door alley and into the theatre. He was at once engulfed in its warmth and expectancy.

He passed into the dressing-room passage. Helena Hamilton's door was half-open and the lights were on. He tapped, looked in and was greeted by the smell of greasepaint, powder, wet-white and flowers. The gas fire groaned comfortably. Martyn, who was spreading out towels, turned and found herself confronted by his deceptively boyish face.

"Early at work?" he fluted.

Martyn wished him good evening.

"Helena not down yet?"

"Not yet."

He hung about the dressing-room, fingering photographs and eyeing Martyn.

"I hear you come from Down Under," he said. "I nearly accepted an engagement to go out there last year, but I didn't really like the people so I turned it down. Adam played it in the year dot, I believe. Well, more years ago than he would care to remember, I dare say. Twenty, if we're going to let our back-hair down. Before you were born, I dare say."

"Yes," Martyn agreed. "Just before."

Her answer appeared to give him extraordinary satisfaction. "Just before?" he repeated. "Really?" and Martyn thought: "I mustn't let myself be worried by this."

He seemed to hover on the edge of some further observation and pottered about the dressing-room examining the great mass of flowers. "I'll swear," he said crossly, "those aren't the roses I chose at Florian's. Honestly, that female's an absolute menace."

Martyn, seeing how miserable he looked, felt sorry for him. He muttered: "I do so *abominate* first nights," and she rejoined: "They are pretty ghastly, aren't they?" Because he seemed unable to take himself off, she added with an air of finality: "Anyway, may I wish you luck for this one?"

"Sweet of you," he said. "I'll need it. I'm the stooge of this piece. Well, thanks, anyway."

He drifted into the passage, halted outside the open door of Poole's dressing-room and greeted Bob Cringle. "Governor not down yet?"

"We're on our way, Mr. Percival."

Parry inclined his head and strolled into the room. He stood close to Bob, leaning his back against the dressing-shelf, his legs elegantly crossed.

"Our little stranger," he murmured, "seems to be new-brooming away next door."

"That's right, sir," said Bob. "Settled in very nice."

"Strong resemblance," Parry said invitingly.

"To the Guv'nor, sir?" Bob rejoined cheerfully. "That's right. Quite a coincidence."

"A coincidence!" Parry echoed. "Well, not precisely, Bob. I understand there's a distant relationship. It was mentioned for the first time last night. Which accounts for the set-up, one supposes. Tell me, Bob, have you ever before heard of a dresser doubling as understudy?"

"Worked out very convenient, hasn't it, sir?"

"Oh, very," said Parry discontentedly. "Look, Bob. You were with the Governor on his New Zealand tour in 'thirty, weren't you?"

Bob said woodenly: "That's correct, sir. 'E was just a boy in them days. Might I trouble you to move, Mr. Percival? I got my table to lay out."

"Oh, sorry. I'm in the way. As usual. Quite! Quite!" he waved his hand and walked jauntily into the passage.

"Good luck for to-night, sir," said Bob and shut the door after him.

In the room opposite to Poole's and next to the Greenroom, Parry could hear Bennington's dresser moving about whistling softly through his teeth. There is a superstition in the theatre that it's unlucky to whistle in a dressing-room and Parry knew that the man wouldn't do it if Ben had arrived. He didn't much like the sound of it himself, and moved on to J. G. Darcey's room. He tapped, was answered, and went in. J.G. was already embarked on his make-up.

"Bob," said Parry, "refuses to be drawn."

"Good evening, dear boy. About what?"

"Oh, you know. The New Zealand tour and so on."

"Quite right," said J.G. firmly, and added: "He was the merest stripling."

"Well—eighteen," Parry began and then broke off. "I know, I know. I couldn't care less, actually." He dropped into the only other chair in the room and buried his face in his hands. "Oh, dear," he said, "I'm so bored with it all. By-blow or not, what does it matter!"

"It only matters," said J.G., laying down a stick of No. 5, "in so far as it's driving Gay Gainsford pretty close to a nervous breakdown, and to that I do most strongly object."

"Really?" Parry raised his head and stared at him. "How altruistic of you, J.G. Well, I mean, I'm sorry for her, poor child. Naturally. And one trembles for the performance, of course."

"The performance would be all right if people left her alone. Ben, in particular."

"Yes," said Parry with great satisfaction. "The situation appears to be getting under the skin of the great character actor. There is that."

"I'm told," said J.G., "there was a midnight audition. Jacko professes ecstasy."

"My dear J.G., there have been two more-or-less public auditions. The object, no doubt, being to make everything look as clean as a whistle. The second affair was this morning."

"Did you see her?"

"I happened to look in."

"What's she like?"

Parry lit a cigarette. "As you have seen," he said, "she's fantastically like *him*. Which is really the point at issue. But *fantastically* like."

"Can she give a show?"

"Oh, yes," said Parry. He leant forward and hugged his knees boyishly. "Oh, yes indeed. Indeed she can, my dear J.G. You'd be surprised."

J.G. made a non-committal sound and went on with his make-up.

"This morning," Parry continued, "the Doctor was there. And Ben. Ben, quite obviously devoured with chagrin. I confess I couldn't help rather gloating. As I remarked, it's getting under his skin. Together, no doubt, with vast potations of brandy and soda."

"I hope to God he's all right to-night."

"It appears Gay was in the back of the house, poor thing, while it was going on."

"She didn't tell me that," J.G. said anxiously and, catching Parry's sharp-ened glance, he added: "I didn't really hear anything about it."

"It was a repetition of last night. Really, one feels quite dizzy. Gay rushed weeping to Adam and again implored him to let her throw in the part. The Doctor, of course, was all for it. Adam was charming, but Uncle Ben pro-duced another temperament. He and the Doctor left simultaneously in a silence more ominous, I assure you, than last night's dog-fight. Ben's not down yet."

"Not yet," J.G. said and repeated: "I hope to God he's all right."

For a moment the two men were united in a common anxiety. J.G. said: "Christ, I wish I didn't get nervous on first nights."

"You, at least, have something to be nervous about. Whereas I half kill myself over the dimmest bit in the West End. When I first saw the part I nearly screamed the place down. I said to Adam if it wasn't that he and Helena had always been very sweet to me—"

J.G. paid this routine plaint the compliment of looking gloomily acquies-cent, but he barely listened to it.

"—and anyway," Parry was saying, "what chance has any of us as long as this *fantastic* set-up continues? In Poole-Hamilton pieces the second leads go automatically to the star's husband. I suppose Adam thinks it's the least he can do. Actually, I *know* I'm too young for the part but—"

"I wouldn't say you were," J.G. said, absently. Parry shot an indignant glance at him but he was pressing powder into the sides of his nose.

"If he tries any of his up-stage fun-and-games on me to-night," Parry said, furiously hissing his sibilants, "I'll just simply bitch up his big exit for him. I could, you know. It'd be no trouble at all."

"I wouldn't, dear boy," J.G. said good-naturedly. "It never does one any good, you know. One can't afford these little luxuries, however tempting. Well, that's taken the polish off the knocker on the old front door." He took his nose delicately between his thumb and forefinger. "The play stinks," he said thoughtfully. "In my considered opinion, it stinks."

"Well, I must say you *are* a comfort to us."

"Pay no attention. I always feel like that at about half-hour time."

"Half-hour! God, have they called it?"

"They will in five minutes."

"I must dart to my paints and powders." Parry went out, but re-opened the door to admit his head. "In case I don't see you again, dear J.G., all the very best."

J.G. turned and raised his hand. "And to you the best, of course, dear boy."

Left alone, he sighed rather heavily, looked closely at his carefully made-up face and, with a rueful air, shook his head at himself.

v i

Clark Bennington's dresser, a thin melancholy man, put him into his gown and hovered, expressionless, behind him.

"I shan't need you before the change," said Bennington. "See if you can help Mr. Darcey."

The man went out. Bennington knew he'd guessed the reason for his dismissal. He wondered why he could never bring himself to have a drink in front of his dresser. After all, there was nothing in taking a nip before the show. Adam, of course, chose to make a great thing of never touching it. And at the thought of Adam Poole he felt resentment and fear stir at the back of his mind. He got his flask out of his overcoat pocket and poured a stiff shot of brandy.

"The thing to do," he told himself, "is to wipe this afternoon clean out. Forget it. Forget everything except my work." But he remembered, unexpectedly, the way, fifteen years ago, he used to prepare himself for a first night. He used to make a difficult and intensive approach to his initial entrance so that when he walked out on the stage he was already possessed by a life that had been created in the dressing-room. Took a lot of concentration: Stanislavsky and all that. Hard going, but in those days it had seemed worth the effort. Helena had encouraged him. He had a notion she and Adam still went in for it. But now he'd mastered the easier way—the repeated mannerism, the trick of pause and the unexpected flattening of the voice—the technical box of tricks.

He finished his drink quickly and began to grease his face. He noticed how the flesh had dropped into sad folds under the eyes, had blurred the jawline and had sunk into grooves about the nostrils and the corners of the mouth. All right for this part, of course, where he had to make a sight of himself, but he'd been a fine-looking man. Helena had fallen for him in a big way until Adam cut him out. At the thought of Adam he experienced a sort of regurgitation of misery and anger. "I'm a haunted man," he thought suddenly.

He'd let himself get into a state, he knew, because of this afternoon. Helena's face, gaping with terror, like a fish almost, kept rising up in his mind and wouldn't be dismissed. Things always worked like that with him: remorse always turned into nightmare.

It had been a bad week altogether. Rows with everybody; with John Rutherford in particular and with Adam over that blasted little dresser. He felt he was the victim of some elaborate plot. He was fond of Gay; she was a nice friendly little thing—his own flesh and blood. Until he had brought her into this piece she had seemed to like him. Not a bad little artist either, and good enough, by God, for the artsy-craftsy part they'd thrown at her. He thought of her scene with Poole and of her unhappiness in her failure and how, in some damned cockeyed way, they all, including Gay, seemed to blame him for it. He supposed she thought he'd bullied her into hanging on. Perhaps in a way he had, but he felt so much that he was the victim of a combined assault. "Alone," he thought, "I'm so desperately *alone*," and he could almost hear the word as one would say it on the stage, making it echo, forlorn and hopeless and extremely effective.

"I'm giving myself the jim-jams," he thought. He wondered if Helena had told Adam about this afternoon. By God, that'd rock Adam, if she had. And at once a picture rose up to torture him, a picture of Helena weeping in Adam's arms and taking solace there. He saw his forehead grow red in the looking-glass and told himself he'd better steady-up. No good getting into one of his tempers with a first performance ahead of him and everything so tricky with young Gay. There he was, coming back to that girl, that phoney dresser. He poured out another drink and began his make-up.

He recognized with satisfaction a familiar change of mood, and he now indulged himself with a sort of treat. He brought out a little piece of secret knowledge he had stored away. Among this company of enemies there was one over whom he exercised almost complete power. Over one, at least, he had overwhelmingly the whip-hand, and the knowledge of his sovereignty warmed him almost as comfortably as the brandy. He began to think about his part. Ideas, brand new and as clever as paint, crowded each other in his imagination. He anticipated his coming mastery.

His left hand slid towards the flask. "One more," he said, "and I'll be fine."

vii

In her room across the passage, Gay Gainsford faced her own reflection and watched Jacko's hands pass across it. He dabbed with his finger-tips under the cheek-bones and made a droning sound behind his closed lips. He was a very good make-up; it was one of his many talents. At the dress rehearsals the touch of his fingers had soothed rather than exacerbated her nerves, but to-night evidently she found it almost intolerable.

"Haven't you finished?" she asked.

"Patience, patience. We do not catch a train. Have you never observed the triangular shadows under Adam's cheek-bones? They are yet to be created."

"Poor Jacko," Gay said breathlessly, "this must be such a bore for you! Considering everything."

"Quiet, now. How can I work?"

"No, but I mean it must be so exasperating to think that two doors away there's somebody who wouldn't need your help. Just a straight make-up, wouldn't it be? No trouble."

"I adore making up. It is my most brilliant gift."

"But she's your find in a way, isn't she? You'd like her to have the part, wouldn't you?"

He rested his hands on her shoulders. "*Ne vous dérangez pas*," he said. "Shut up, in fact. Tranquillize yourself, idiot girl."

"But I want you to tell me."

"Then I tell you. Yes, I would like to see this little freak play your part because she is in fact a little freak. She has dropped into this theatre like an accident in somebody else's dress and the effect is fantastic. But she is well content to remain off-stage and it is you who play, and we have faith in you and wish you well with all our hearts."

"That's very nice of you," Gay said.

"What a sour voice! It is true. And now reflect. Reflect upon the minuteness of Edmund Kean, upon Sarah's one leg and upon Irving's two, upon ugly actresses who convince their audiences they are beautiful and old actors who persuade them they are young. It is all in the mind, the spirit and the preparation. What does Adam say? Think in, and then play out. Do so."

"I can't," Gay said between her teeth. "I can't." She twisted in her chair. He lifted his fingers away from her face quickly, with a wide gesture. "Jacko," she said, "there's a jinx on this night. Jacko, did you know? It was on the night of the Combined Arts Ball that it happened."

"What is this foolishness?"

"You know. Five years ago. The stage-hands were talking about it. I heard them. The gas fire case. The night that man was murdered. Everyone knows."

"Be silent!" Jacko said loudly. "This is idiocy. I forbid you to speak of it. The chatter of morons. The Combined Arts Ball has no fixed date and, if it had, shall an assembly of British bourgeoisie in bad fancy dress control our destiny? I am ashamed of you. You are altogether too stupid. Master yourself."

"It's not only that. It's everything. I can't face it."

His fingers closed down on her shoulders. "Master yourself," he said. "You must. If you cry I shall beat you and wipe your make-up across your face. I defy you to cry."

He cleaned his hands, tipped her head forward and began to massage the nape of her neck. "There are all sorts of things," he said, "that you must remember and as many more to forget. Forget the little freak and the troubles of to-day. Remember to relax all your muscles and also your nerves and your thoughts. Remember the girl in the play and the faith I have in you, and Adam and also your Uncle Bennington."

"Spare me my Uncle Bennington, Jacko. If my Uncle Bennington had left me where I belong, in fortnightly rep, I wouldn't be facing this hell. I know what everyone thinks of Uncle Ben and I agree with them. I never want to see him again. I hate him. He's made me go on with this. I wanted to throw the part in. It's not my part. I loathe it. No, I don't loathe it, that's not true. I loathe myself for letting everybody down. Oh, God, Jacko, what am I going to do?"

Across the bowed head Jacko looked at his own reflection and poked a face at it. "You shall play this part," he said through his teeth. "Mouse-heart, skunk-girl. You shall play. Think of nothing. Unbridle your infinite capacity for inertia and be dumb."

Watching himself, he arranged his face in an unconvincing glower and fetched up a Shakesperian belly-voice.

"*The devil damn thee black, thou cream-faced loon! Where got'st thou that goose look?*"

He caught his breath. Beneath his fingers, Gay's neck stiffened. He began to swear elaborately, in French and in a whisper.

"Jacko. *Jacko.* Where does that line come from?"

"I invented it."

"You didn't. You *didn't.* It's *Macbeth*," she wailed. "*You've quoted from Macbeth!*" and burst into a flurry of terrified weeping.

"Great suffering and all-enduring Saints of God," apostrophized Jacko, "give me some patience with this Quaking Thing."

But Gay's cries mounted in a sharp crescendo. She flung out her arms and beat with her fists on the dressing-table. A bottle of wet-white rocked to and fro, overbalanced, rapped smartly against the looking-glass and fell over. A neatly splintered star frosted the surface of the glass.

Gay pointed to it with an air of crazy triumph, snatched up her towel and scrubbed it across her make-up. She thrust her face, blotched and streaked with black cosmetic, at Jacko.

"*Don't you like what you see?*" she quoted, and rocketed into genuine hysteria.

Five minutes later Jacko walked down the passage towards Adam Poole's room, leaving J.G., who had rushed to the rescue in his shirt-sleeves, in helpless contemplation of the screaming Gay. Jacko disregarded the open doors and the anxious painted faces that looked out at him.

Bennington shouted from his room: "What the hell goes on? Who *is* that?"

"Listen," Jacko began, thrusting his head in at the door. He looked at

Bennington and stopped short. "Stay where you are," he said and crossed the passage to Poole's room.

Poole had swung round in his chair to face the door. Bob Cringle stood beside him, twisting a towel in his hands.

"Well?" Poole said. "What is it? Is it Gay?"

"She's gone up. Sky-high. I can't do anything nor can J.G., and I don't believe anyone can. She refuses to go on."

"Where's John? Is this his doing?"

"God knows. I don't think so. He came in an hour ago and said he'd be back at five to seven."

"Has Ben tried?"

"She does nothing but scream that she never wants to see him again. In my opinion, Ben would be fatal."

"He must be able to hear all this."

"I told him to stay where he is."

Poole looked sharply at Jacko and went out. Gay's laughter had broken down in a storm of irregular sobbing that could be heard quite clearly. Helena Hamilton called out, "Adam, shall I go to her?" and he answered from the passage: "Better not, I think."

He was some time with Gay. They heard her shouting: "No! No! I won't go on! No!" over and over again like an automaton.

When he came out he went to Helena Hamilton's room. She was dressed and made up. Martyn, with an ashen face, stood inside the doorway.

"I'm sorry, darling," Poole said, "but you'll have to do without a dresser."

The call-boy came down the passage chanting: "Half-hour. Half-hour, please."

Poole and Martyn looked at each other.

"You'll be all right," he said.

CHAPTER VI

Performance

At ten to eight Martyn stood by the entrance.

She was dressed in Gay's clothes and Jacko had made her up very lightly. They had all wished her luck: J.G., Parry Percival, Helena Hamilton, Adam Poole, Clem Smith and even the dressers and stage-hands.

There had been something real and touching in their way of doing this, so that even in her terror she had felt they were good and very kind. Bennington alone had not wished her well but he had kept right away, and this abstention, she thought, showed a certain generosity.

She no longer felt sick but the lining of her mouth and throat was harsh as if, in fact, she had actually vomited. She thought her sense of hearing must have become distorted. The actors' voices on the other side of the canvas wall had the remote quality of voices in a nightmare, whereas the hammer-blows of her heart and the rustle of her dress that accompanied them sounded exceeding loud.

She saw the frames of the set, their lashings and painted legends—ACT I, P.2—and the door which she was to open. She could look into the Prompt corner where the A.S.M. followed the lighted script with his finger, and where, high above him, the electrician leaned over his perch, watching the play. The stage lights were reflected in his face. Everything was monstrous in its preoccupation. Martyn was alone.

She tried to command the upsurge of panic in her heart, to practise an approach to her ordeal, to create, in place of these implacable realities, the reality of the house in the play and that part of it in which now, out of sight of the audience, she must already have her being. This attempt went down before the clamour of her nerves. "I'm going to fail," she thought.

Jacko came round the set. She hoped he wouldn't speak to her and, as if he sensed this wish, he stopped at a distance and waited.

"I must listen," she thought. "I'm not listening. I don't know where they've got to. I've forgotten which way the door opens. I've missed my cue." Her inside deflated and despair griped it like a colic.

She turned and found Poole beside her.

"You're all right," he said. "The door opens on. You can do it. Now, my girl. On you go."

Martyn didn't hear the round of applause with which a London audience greets a player who appears at short notice.

She was on. She had made her entry and was engulfed in the play.

ii

Dr. Rutherford sat in the O.P. box with his massive shoulder turned to the house and his gloved hands folded together on the balustrade. His face was in shadow but the stage lights just touched the bulging curve of his old-fashioned shirt-front. He was monumentally still. One of the critics, an elderly man, said in an aside to a colleague that Rutherford reminded him of Watts's picture of the Minotaur.

For the greater part of the first act he was alone, having, as he had explained in the office, no masochistic itch to invite a guest to a Roman holiday where he himself was the major sacrifice. Towards the end of the act, however, Bob Grantley came into the box and stood behind him. Grantley's attention was divided. Sometimes he looked down through beams of spotlights at the stalls, cobbled with heads, sometimes at the stage and sometimes, sideways and with caution, at the Doctor himself. Really, Grantley thought, he was quite uncomfortably motionless. One couldn't tell what he was thinking and one hesitated, the Lord knew, to ask him.

Down on the stage Clark Bennington, Parry Percival and J. G. Darcey had opened the long crescendo leading to Helena's entrance. Grantley thought suddenly how vividly an actor's nature could be exposed on the stage: there was, for instance, a kind of bed-rock niceness about old J.G., a youthfulness of spirit that declaimed itself through the superimposed make-up, the characterization and J.G.'s indisputable middle age. And Bennington? And Percival? Grantley had begun to consider them in these terms when Percival, speaking one of his colourless lines, turned down-stage. Bennington moved centre, looked at Darcey and neatly sketched a parody of Percival's somewhat finicking movement. The theatre was filled with laughter. Percival turned quickly; Bennington smiled innocently at him, prolonging the laugh.

Grantley looked apprehensively at the Doctor.

"Is that new?" he ventured in a whisper. "That business?"

The Doctor didn't answer, and Grantley wondered if he only imagined that the great hands on the balustrade had closed more tightly over each other.

Helena Hamilton came on to a storm of applause, and with her entrance the action was roused to a new excitement and was intensified with every word she uttered. The theatre grew warm with her presence and with a sense of heightened suspense.

"Now they're all on," Grantley thought, "except Adam and the girl."

He drew a chair forward stealthily and sat behind Rutherford.

"It's going enormously," he murmured to the massive shoulder. "Terrific, old boy." And because he was nervous he added: "This brings the girl on, doesn't it?"

For the first time the Doctor spoke. His lips scarcely moved. A submerged voice uttered within him. "Hence," it said, "heap of wrath, foul indigested lump."

"Sorry, old boy," whispered Grantley, and began to wonder what hope in hell there was of persuading the distinguished author to have a drink in the office during the interval with a hand-picked number of important persons.

He was still preoccupied with this problem when a side door in the set opened and a dark girl with short hair walked out on the stage.

Grantley joined in the kindly applause. The Doctor remained immovable.

The players swept up to their major climax, Adam came on, and five minutes later the curtain fell on the first act. The hands of the audience filled the house with a storm of rain. The storm swelled prodigiously and persisted even after the lights had come up.

"Ah, good girl," Bob Grantley stammered, filled with the sudden and excessive emotion of the theatre. "Good old Adam. Jolly good show!"

Greatly daring, he clapped the Doctor on the shoulder.

The Doctor remained immovable.

Grantly edged away to the back of the box. "I must get back," he said. "Look, John, there are one or two people coming to the office for a drink who would be—"

The Doctor turned massively in his seat and faced him.

"No," he said, "thank you."

"Well, but look, dear boy, it's just one of those things. You know how it is, John, you know how—"

"Shut up," said the Doctor without any particular malice. "I'm going backstage," he added. He rose and turned away from the audience. "I have no desire to swill tepid spirits with minor celebrities among the backsides of sand-blasted gods. Thank you, however. See you later."

He opened the pass-door at the back of the box.

"You're pleased, aren't you?" Grantley said. "You *must* be pleased."

"Must I? Must I indeed?"

"With the girl, at least? So far?"

"The wench is a good wench. So far. I go to tell her so. By your leave, Robert."

He lumbered through the pass-door and Grantley heard him plunge dangerously down the narrow stairway to the stage.

iii

Dr. Rutherford emerged in a kaleidoscopic world: a world where walls fell softly apart, landscapes ascended into darkness and stairways turned and moved aside. A blue haze rose from the stage, which was itself in motion. Jacko's first set revolved bodily, giving way to a new and more distorted version of itself, which came to rest facing the curtain. Masking pieces were run forward to frame it in. The Doctor started off for the dressing-room passage and was at once involved with moving flats. "If you please, sir." "Stand aside there, *please*." "Clear stage, *by* your leave." His bulky shape was screened and exposed again and again as he plunged forward confusedly. Warning bells rang, the call-boy began to chant: "Second act beginners, please, Second act."

"Lights," Clem Smith said.

The shifting world stood still. Circuit by circuit, the lights came on and bore down on the acting area. The last toggle-line slapped home and was made fast and the sweating stage-hands walked disinterestedly off the set. Clem Smith, with his back to the curtain, made a final check. "Clear stage," he said and looked at his watch. The curtain-hand climbed an iron ladder.

"Six minutes," said the A.S.M. He wrote it on his chart. Clem moved into the Prompt corner. "Right," he said. "Actors, please."

J. G. Darcey and Parry Percival walked onto the set and took up their positions. Helena Hamilton came out of her dressing-room. She stood with her hands clasped lightly at her waist at a little distance from the door by which she must enter. A figure emerged from the shadows near the passage and went up to her.

"Miss Hamilton," Martyn said nervously, "I'm not on for your quick change. I can do it."

Helena turned. She looked at Martyn for a moment with an odd fixedness. Then a smile of extraordinary charm broke across her face and she took Martyn's head lightly between her hands.

"My dear child," she murmured, "my ridiculous child." She hesitated for a moment and then said briskly: "I've got a new dresser."

"A new dresser?"

"Jacko. He's most efficient."

Poole came down the passage. She turned to him and linked her arm through his. "She's going to be splendid in her scene," she said. "Isn't she?"

Poole said: "Keep it up, Kate. All's well." And in the look he gave Helena Hamilton there was something of comradeship, something of compassion and something, perhaps, of gratitude.

Dr. Rutherford emerged from the passage and addressed himself to Martyn. "Here!" he said. "I've been looking for you, my pretty. You might be a lot worse, considering, but you haven't done anything yet. When you play this next scene, my poppet, these few precepts in thy—"

"No, John," Poole and Helena Hamilton said together. "Not now."

He glowered at them. Poole nodded to Martyn, who began to move away but had not got far before she heard Rutherford say: "Have you tackled that fellow? Did you see it? Where is he? By God, when I get at him—"

"Stand by," said Clem Smith.

"Quiet, John," said Poole imperatively. "Back to your box, sir."

The curtain rose on the second act.

For the rest of her life the physical events that were encompassed by the actual performance of the play were to be almost lost for Martyn. That is to say, she was to forget all but a few desultory and quite insignificant details, such as the fact of Jacko kissing her after she came off in the second act (he smelt of toothpaste and nicotine), and of Poole, when the curtain came down, giving her his handkerchief, which surprised her until she found her face was wet with her own tears. He had said something to her, then, with a manner so unlike anything she had found in him before that it had filled her with immense surprise, but she couldn't remember his words and thought: "I shall never know what he said." She knew that when she was not playing and during the intervals, she had stood near the entry to the passage and that people had spoken to her while she was there. But these recollections had no more substance than a dream. Still more unreal was her actual performance: she thought she remembered a sense of security and command that had astonishingly blessed her, but it was as if these things had happened to someone else. Indeed, she could not be perfectly certain that they had happened at all. She might have been under hypnosis or some partial anaesthesia for all the reality they afterwards retained.

This odd condition, which was perhaps the result of some kind of physical compensation for the extreme assault on her nerves and emotions, persisted until she made her final exit in the last act. It happened some time before the curtain. The character she played was the first to relinquish its hold and to fade out of the picture. She came off and returned to her corner near the entry into the passage. The others were all on; the dressers and stage-staff, drawn by the hazards of a first night, watched from the side and Jacko was near the Prompt corner. The passage and dressing-rooms seemed deserted and Martyn was quite alone. She began to emerge from her trance-like suspension. Parry Percival came off and spoke to her.

"Darling," he said incoherently, "you were perfectly splendid. I'm just *so* angry at the moment I can't *speak*, but I do congratulate you!"

Martyn saw that he actually trembled with an emotion that was, she must suppose, fury. Out of the dream from which she was not yet fully awakened there came a memory of Gargantuan laughter and she thought she associated it with Bennington and with Percival. He said: "This settles it. I'm taking action. God, this settles it!" and darted down the passage.

Martyn thought, still confusedly, that she should go to the dressing-room and tidy her make-up for the curtain-call. But it was not her dressing-room, it was Gay's and she felt uneasy about it. While she hesitated J. G. Darcey, who had come off, put his hand on her shoulder. "Well done, child," he said. "A very creditable performance."

Martyn thanked him and, on an impulse, added: "Mr. Darcey, is Gay still here? Should I say something to her? I'd like to, but I know how she must feel and I don't want to be clumsy."

He waited for a moment, looking at her. "She's in the Greenroom," he said. "Perhaps later. Not now, I think. Nice of you."

"I won't unless you say so, then."

He made her a little bow. "I am at your service," he said and followed Percival down the passage.

Jacko came round the set with the stage-hand who was to fire the effects-gun. When he saw Martyn his whole face split in a grin. He took her hands in his and kissed them and she was overwhelmed with shyness.

"But your face," he said, wrinkling his own into a monkey's grimace. "It shines like a good deed in a naughty world. Do not touch it yourself. To your dressing-room. I come in two minutes. Away, before your ears are blasted."

He moved down-stage, applied his eye to a secret hole in the set through which he could watch the action, and held out his arm in warning to the stage-hand, who then lifted the effects-gun. Martyn went down the passage as Bennington came off. He caught her up: "Miss Tarne. Wait a moment, will you?"

Dreading another intolerable encounter, Martyn faced him. His make-up had been designed to exhibit the brutality of the character and did so all too successfully. The lips were painted a florid red, the pouches under the eyes and the sensual drag from the nostrils to the mouth had been carefully emphasized. He was sweating heavily through the greasepaint and his face glistened in the dull light of the passage.

"I just wanted to say—" he began, and at that moment the gun was fired and Martyn gave an involuntary cry. He went on talking. "—when I see it," he was saying. "I suppose you aren't to be blamed for that. You saw your chance and took it. Gay and Adam tell me you offered to get out and were not allowed to go. That may be fair enough, I wouldn't know. But I'm not worrying about that." He spoke disjointedly. It was as if his thoughts were too disordered for any coherent expression. "I just wanted to tell you that you needn't suppose what I'm going to do—you needn't think—I mean—"

He touched his shining face with the palm of his hand. Jacko came down the passage and took Martyn by the elbow. "Quick," he said. "Into your room! You want powdering, Ben. Excuse me."

Bennington went into his own room. Jacko thrust Martyn into hers, and leaving the door open followed Bennington. She heard him say: "Take care with your upper lip. It is dripping with sweat." He darted back to Martyn, stood her near the dressing-shelf and, with an expression of the most ardent concentration, effected a number of what he called running repairs to her make-up and her hair. They heard Percival and Darcey go past on their way to the stage. A humming noise caused by some distant dynamo made itself heard, the tap in the wash-basin dripped, the voices on the stage sounded intermittently. Martyn looked at Gay's make-up box, at her dressing-gown and at the array of mascots on the shelf and wished very heartily that Jacko would have done. Presently the call-boy came down the passage with his summons for the final curtain. "Come," said Jacko.

He took her round to the Prompt side.

Here she found a group already waiting: Darcey and Percival, Clem Smith, the two dressers and, at a distance, one or two stage-hands. They all watched the final scene between Helena Hamilton and Adam Poole. In this scene Rutherford tied up and stated finally the whole thesis of his play. The man was faced with his ultimate decision. Would he stay and attempt, with the woman, to establish a sane and enlightened formula for living in place of the one he himself had destroyed, or would he go back to his island community and attempt a further development within himself and in a less complex environment? As throughout the play, the conflict was set out in terms of human and personal relationships. It could be played like many another love-scene, purely on those terms. Or it could be so handled that the wider implications could be felt by the audience, and in the hands of these two players that was what happened. The play ended with them pledging themselves to each other and to an incredible task. As Poole spoke the last lines, the electrician, with one eye on Clem below, played madly over his switchboard. The entire set changed its aspect, seemed to dissolve, turned threadbare, a skeleton, a wraith, while beyond it a wide stylized landscape was flooded

...nd became, as Poole spoke the tag, the background upon which ...I fell.

...as well be back in panto," said the electrician, leaning on his dim-... We got the transformation scene. All we want's the bloody fairy ..."

It was at this moment—when the applause seemed to surge forward and beat against the curtain, when Clem shouted "All on!" and Dr. Rutherford plunged out of the O.P. pass-door, when the players walked on and linked hands—that Poole, looking hurriedly along the line, said: "Where's Ben?"

One of those panic-stricken crises peculiar to the theatre boiled up on the instant. From her position between Darcey and Percival on the stage, Martyn saw the call-boy make some kind of protest to Clem Smith and disappear. Above the applause they heard him hare down the passage yelling: "Mr. Bennington! Mr. Bennington! Please! You're on!"

"We can't wait," Poole shouted. "Take it up, Clem."

The curtain rose and Martyn looked into a sea of faces and hands. She felt herself led forward into the roaring swell, bowed with the others, felt Darcey's and Percival's hands tighten on hers, bowed again and with them retreated a few steps up-stage as the first curtain fell.

"Well?" Poole shouted into the wings. The call-boy could be heard beating on the dressing-room door.

Percival said: "What's the betting he comes on for a star call?"

"He's passed out," said Darcey. "Had one or two more since he came off."

"By God, I wouldn't cry if he never came to."

"Go on, Clem," said Poole.

The curtain rose and fell again, twice. Percival and Darcey took Martyn off and it went up again on Poole and Helena Hamilton, this time to those cries of "Bravo!" that reach the actors as a long open sound like the voice of a singing wind. In the wings Clem Smith, with his eyes on the stage, was saying repeatedly: "He doesn't answer. He's locked in. The b—— doesn't answer."

Martyn saw Poole coming towards her and stood aside. He seemed to tower over her as he took her hand. "Come along," he said. Darcey and Percival and the group off-stage began to clap.

Poole led her on. She felt herself resisting and heard him say: "Yes, it's all right."

So bereft was Martyn of her normal stage-wiseness that he had to tell her to bow. She did so, and wondered why there was a warm sound of laughter in the applause. She looked at Poole, found he was bowing to her and bent her head under his smile. He returned her to the wings.

They were all on again. Dr. Rutherford came out from the O.P. corner. The cast joined in the applause. Martyn's heart had begun to sing so loudly that it was like to deafen every emotion but a universal gratitude. She thought Rutherford looked like an old lion standing there in his out-of-date evening clothes, his hair ruffled, his gloved hand touching his bulging shirt, bowing

in an unwieldy manner to the audience and to the cast. He moved forwa
and the theatre was abruptly silent—silent, but for an obscure and intermittent thudding in the dressing-room passage. Clem Smith said something to the
A.S.M. and rushed away, jingling keys.

"Hah," said Dr. Rutherford with a preliminary bellow. "Hah—thankee. I'm
much obliged to you, ladies and gentlemen, and to the actors. The actors are
much obliged, no doubt, to you, but not necessarily to me." Here the audience laughed and the actors smiled. "I am not able to judge," the Doctor
continued with a rich roll in his voice, "whether you have extracted from this
play the substance of its argument. If you have done so, we may all felicitate
each other with the indiscriminate enthusiasm characteristic of these occasions: if you have not, I for my part am not prepared to say where the blame
should rest."

A solitary man laughed in the audience. The Doctor rolled an eye at him
and, with this clownish trick, brought the house down. "The prettiest epilogue to a play that I am acquainted with," he went on, "is (as I need perhaps
hardly mention to so intelligent an audience) that written for a boy actor
by William Shakespere. I am neither a boy nor an actor, but I beg leave to
end by quoting it to you. 'If it be true that good wine needs no bush—'"

"Gas!" Parry Percival said under his breath. Martyn, who thought the
Doctor was going well, glanced indignantly at Parry and was astonished to see
that he looked frightened. " '—therefore,' " the Doctor was saying arrogantly,
" 'to beg will not become me—' "

"Gas!" said an imperative voice off-stage and someone else ran noisily round
the back of the set.

And then Martyn smelt it. Gas.

iv

To the actors, it seemed afterwards as if they had been fantastically slow
to understand that disaster had come upon the theatre. The curtain went
down on Dr. Rutherford's last word. There was a further outbreak of applause. Someone off-stage shouted: "The King, for God's sake!" and at once
the anthem rolled out disinterestedly in the well. Poole ran off the stage and
was met by Clem Smith, who had a bunch of keys in his hand. The rest
followed him.

The area back-stage reeked of gas.

It was extraordinary how little was said. The players stood together and
looked about them with the question in their faces that they were unable
to ask.

Poole said: "Keep all visitors out, Clem. Send them to the foyer." And
at once the A.S.M. spoke into the Prompt telephone. Bob Grantley burst
through the pass-door, beaming from ear to ear.

he shouted. "John! Helena! Adam! My God, chaps, you've

stock-still, his arms extended, the smile drying on his face.

, Bob," Poole said. "Cope with the people. Ask our guests to go

t wait for us. Ben's ill. Clem, get all available doors open. We

Grantley said: "Gas?"

"Quick," Poole said. "Take them with you. Settle them down and explain. He's ill. Then ring me here. But quickly, Bob. Quickly."

Grantley went out without another word.

"Where is he?" Dr. Rutherford demanded.

Helena Hamilton suddenly said: "Adam?"

"Go on to the stage, Helena. It's better you shouldn't be here, believe me. Kate will stay with you. I'll come in a moment."

"Here you are, Doctor," said Clem Smith.

There was a blundering sound in the direction of the passage. Rutherford said, "Open the dock-doors," and went behind the set.

Poole thrust Helena through the Prompt entry and shut the door behind her. Draughts of cold air came through the side entrances.

"Kate," Poole said, "go in and keep her there if you can. Will you? And, Kate—"

Rutherford reappeared and with him four stage-hands, bearing with difficulty the inert body of Clark Bennington. The head hung swinging upside down between the two leaders, its mouth wide open.

Poole moved quickly, but he was too late to shield Martyn.

"Never mind," he said. "Go in with Helena."

"Anyone here done respiration for gassed cases?" Dr. Rutherford demanded. "I can start but I'm not good for long."

"I can," said the A.S.M. "I was a warden."

"I can," said Jacko.

"And I," said Poole.

"In the dock, then. Shut these doors and open the outer ones."

Kneeling by Helena Hamilton and holding her hand, Martyn heard the doors roll back and the shambling steps go into the dock. The doors crashed behind them.

Martyn said: "They're giving him respiration. Dr. Rutherford's there."

Helena nodded with an air of sagacity. Her face was quite without expression and she was shivering.

"I'll get your coat," Martyn said. It was in the improvised dressing-room on the O.P. side. She was back in a moment and put Helena into it as if she were a child, guiding her arms and wrapping the fur about her.

A voice off-stage—J. G. Darcey's—said: "Where's Gay? Is Gay still in the Greenroom?"

Martyn was astonished when Helena, behind that mask that had become her face, said loudly: "Yes. She's there. In the Greenroom."

There was a moment's silence and then J.G. said: "She mustn't stay there. Good God—"

They heard him go away.

Parry Percival's voice announced abruptly that he was going to be sick. "But where?" he cried distractedly. "Where?"

"In your dressing-room, for Pete's sake," Clem Smith said.

"It'll be full of gas. Oh, *really!*" There was an agonized and not quite silent interval. "I couldn't be more sorry," Percival said weakly.

"I want," Helena said, "to know what happened. I want to see Adam. Ask him to come, please."

Martyn made for the door, but before she reached it Dr. Rutherford came in, followed by Poole. Rutherford had taken off his coat and was a fantastic sight in boiled shirt, black trousers and red braces.

"Well, Helena," he said, "this is not a nice business. We're doing everything that can be done. I'm getting a new oxygen thing in as quickly as possible. There have been some remarkable saves in these cases. But I think you ought to know it's a thinnish chance. There's no pulse and so on."

"I want," she said, holding out her hand to Poole, "to know what happened."

Poole said gently: "All right, Helena, you shall. It looks as if Ben locked himself in after his exit, and then turned the gas fire off—and on again. When Clem unlocked the door and went in he found Ben on the floor. His head was near the fire and a coat over both. He could only have been like that for quite a short time."

"This theatre," she said. "This awful theatre."

Poole looked as if he would make some kind of protest, but after a moment's hesitation he said: "All right, Helena. Perhaps it did suggest the means, but if he had made up his mind he would, in any case, have found the means."

"Why?" she said. "Why has he done it?"

Dr. Rutherford growled inarticulately and went out. They heard him open and shut the dock-doors. Poole sat down by Helena and took her hands in his. Martyn was going, but he looked up at her and said: "No, don't. Don't go, Kate," and she waited near the door.

"This is no time," Poole said, "to speculate. He may be saved. If he isn't, then we shall of course ask ourselves just why. But he was in a bad way, Helena. He'd gone to pieces and he knew it."

"I wasn't much help," she said, "was I? Though it's true to say I did try for quite a long time."

"Indeed you did. There's one thing you must be told. If it's no go with Ben, we'll have to inform the police."

She put her hand to her forehead as if puzzled. "The police?" she repeated, and stared at him. "No, darling, no!" she cried, and after a moment whispered: "They might think—oh, darling, darling, darling, the Lord knows what they might think!"

The door up-stage opened and Gay Gainsford came in, followed by Darcey.

She was in her street-clothes, and at some time during the evening had made extensive repairs to her face, which wore, at the moment, an expression oddly compounded of triumph and distraction. Before she could speak she was seized with a paroxysm of coughing.

Darcey said: "Is it all right for Gay to wait here?"

"Yes, of course," said Helena.

He went out and Poole followed him, saying he would return.

"Darling," Miss Gainsford gasped, "I knew. I knew as soon as I smelt it. There's a Thing in this theatre. Everything pointed to it. I just sat there and *knew*." She coughed again. "*Oh*, I do feel so sick," she said.

"Gay, for pity's sake, what are you talking about?" Helena said.

"It was Fate, I felt. I wasn't a bit surprised. I just knew something had to happen to-night."

"Do you mean to say," Helena murmured, and the wraith of her gift for irony was on her mouth, "that you just sat in the Greenroom with your finger raised, telling yourself it was Fate?"

"Darling Aunty—I'm sorry. I forgot. Darling Helena, wasn't it amazing?"

Helena made a little gesture of defeat. Miss Gainsford looked at her for a moment and then, with the prettiest air of compassion, knelt at her feet. "Sweet," she said, "I'm so terribly, terribly sorry. We're together in this, aren't we? He was my uncle and your husband."

"True enough," said Helena. She looked at Martyn over the head bent in devoted commiseration, and shook her own helplessly. Gay Gainsford sank into a sitting posture and leant her cheek against Helena's hand. The hand, after a courteous interval, was withdrawn.

There followed a very long silence. Martyn sat at a distance and wondered if there was anything in the world she could do to help. There was an intermittent murmur of voices somewhere off-stage. Gay Gainsford, feeling perhaps that she had sustained her position long enough, moved by gradual degrees away from her aunt by marriage, rose and, sighing heavily, transferred herself to the sofa.

Time dragged on, mostly in silence. Helena lit one cigarette from the butt of another, Gay sighed with infuriating punctuality and Martyn's thoughts drifted sadly about the evaporation of her small triumph.

Presently there were sounds of arrival. One or two persons walked round the set from the outside entry to the dock and were evidently admitted into it.

"Who can that, be, I wonder?" Helena Hamilton asked idly, and after a moment: "Is Jacko about?"

"I'll see," said Martyn.

She found Jacko off-stage with Darcey and Parry Percival. Percival was saying: "Well, naturally, nobody wants to go to the party, but I must say that as one is quite evidently useless here, I don't see why one can't go home."

Jacko said: "You would be recalled by the police, I dare say, if you went."

He caught sight of Martyn, who went up to him. His face was beaded with sweat. "What is it, my small?" he asked. "This is a sad epilogue to your success story. Never mind. What is it?"

"I think Miss Hamilton would like to see you."

"Then I come. It is time, in any case."

He took her by the elbow and they went in together. When Helena saw him she seemed to rouse herself. "Jacko?" she said.

He didn't answer and she got up quickly and went to him. "Jacko? What is it? Has it happened?"

Jacko's hands, so refined and delicate that they seemed like those of another woman, touched her hair and her face.

"It has happened," he said. "We have tried very hard but nothing is any good at all, and there is no more to be done. He has taken wing."

Gay Gainsford broke into a fit of sobbing, but Helena stooped her head to Jacko's shoulder and when his arms had closed about her said: "Help me to feel something, Jacko. I'm quite empty of feeling. Help me to be sorry."

Above her head Jacko's face, glistening with sweat, grotesque and primitive, had the fixed inscrutability of a classic mask.

CHAPTER VII

Disaster

The fact of Bennington's death had the effect of changing the values of other circumstances in the theatre. One after another the members of the company had said what they could to Helena Hamilton, and she had thanked them. She was very tremulous and uncertain of her voice, but she did not break down at any time and seemed, Martyn thought, to be in a kind of trance. At first they were all uncomfortably silent but, as the minutes slipped by, they fell into muted conversation. Most of what they said was singularly aimless. Matters of normal consequence were forgotten, details of behaviour became ridiculously important.

The question, for instance, of where they should assemble exercised the whole company. It was almost eleven o'clock and the stage was beginning to grow cold.

Clem Smith had rung up the police as soon as Dr. Rutherford said that Bennington was beyond recovery, and within five minutes a constable and sergeant had appeared at the stage-door. They went into the dock with Rutherford and then to Bennington's dressing-room, where they remained alone for some time. During this period an aimless discussion developed among the members of the company about where they should go. Clem

Smith suggested the Greenroom as the warmest place, and added tactlessly that the fumes had probably dispersed and if so there was no reason why they shouldn't light the fire. Both Parry Percival and Gay Gainsford had made an outcry against this suggestion on the grounds of delicacy and susceptibility. Darcey supported Gay, the A.S.M. suggested the offices and Jacko the auditorium. Dr. Rutherford, who appeared to be less upset than anyone else, merely remarked that "All places that the eye of heaven visits are to a wise man ports and happy havens," which, as Percival said acidly, got them nowhere.

Finally, Poole asked if the central-heating couldn't be stoked up and a stage-hand was dispatched to the underworld to find out. Evidently he met with success as presently the air became less chilled.

They waited in the last-act set, much as they had waited when Poole summed up at the dress rehearsal. In this final scene, which was painted on gauze, Jacko had, by the use of grotesque perspective and exaggerated emphases, achieved a distortion of the second set, which itself was a distortion of the first. The walls and staircase seemed to lean over the actors, crushing them into too small a compass. Martyn became very much aware of this and disliked it.

The resemblance to the dress rehearsal was heightened by Jacko, who had fetched Helena's dressing-case from her room. Again she removed her make-up on the stage, but this time it was Jacko who held the glass for her. He had brought powder and her bag for Martyn and a towel for each of them. With only a spatter of desultory conversation, the players sat about the stage and cleaned their faces. And they listened.

They heard the two men come back along the passage and separate. Then the central door opened and the young constable came in.

He was a tall, good-looking youth with a charming smile.

"The sergeant," he said, "has asked me to explain that he's telephoning Scotland Yard. He couldn't be more sorry, but he's afraid he'll have to ask everybody to wait until he gets his instructions. He's sure you'll understand that it's just a matter of routine."

He might have been apologizing for his mother's late arrival at her own dinner-party.

He was about to withdraw when Dr. Rutherford said: "Hi! Sonny!"

"Yes, sir?" said the young constable obligingly.

"You intrigue me. You talk, as they say, like a book. *Non sine dis animosus infans.* You swear with a good grace and wear your boots very smooth, do you not?"

The young constable was, it seemed, only momentarily taken aback. He said: "Well, sir, for my boots, they are after the Dogberry fashion, and for my swearing, sir, it goes by the book."

The Doctor, who until now had seemed to share the general feeling of oppression and shock, appeared to cheer up with indecent haste. He was, in fact, clearly enchanted. "Define, define, well educated infant," he quoted exultantly.

"I mean that in court, sir, we swear by the book. But I'm afraid, sir," added the young constable apologetically, "that I'm not much of a hand at 'Bardinage.' My purse is empty already. If you'll excuse me," he concluded, with a civil glance round the company, "I'll just—"

He was again about to withdraw when his sergeant came in at the O.P. entrance.

"Good evening, ladies and gentlemen," the sergeant said, in what Martyn, for one, felt was the regulation manner. "Very sorry to keep you, I'm sure. Sad business. In these cases we have to do a routine check-up, as you might say. My superior officers will be here in a moment and then, I hope, we shan't be long. Thank you."

He tramped across the stage, said something inaudible to the constable and was heard to go into the dock. The constable took a chair from the Prompt corner, placed it in the proscenium entrance and, with a modest air, sat on it. His glance fell upon Martyn and he smiled at her. They were the youngest persons there and it was as if they signalled in a friendly manner to each other. In turning away from this pleasant exchange, Martyn found that Poole was watching her with fixed and, it seemed, angry glare. To her fury she found that she was very much disturbed by this circumstance.

They had by this time all cleaned their faces. Helena Hamilton with an unsteady hand put on a light street make-up. The men looked ghastly in the cold working-lights that bleakly illuminated the stage.

Parry Percival said fretfully: "Well, I must say I do *not* see the smallest point in our hanging about like this."

The constable was about to answer when they all heard sounds of arrival at the stage-door. He said: "This will be the party from the Yard, sir," and crossed to the far exit. The sergeant was heard to join him there.

There was a brief conversation off-stage. A voice said: "You two go round with Gibson then, will you? I'll join you in a moment."

The young constable reappeared to usher in a tall man in plain clothes.

"Chief Detective-Inspector Alleyn," he said.

ii

Martyn, in her weary pilgrimage round the West End, had seen men of whom Alleyn at first reminded her. In the neighbourhood of the St. James's Theatre they had emerged from clubs, from restaurants and from enchanting and preposterous shops. There had been something in their bearing and their clothes that gave them a precise definition. But when she looked more closely at Inspector Alleyn's face, this association became modified. It was a spare and scholarly face with a monkish look about it.

Martyn had formed the habit of thinking of people's voices in terms of colour. Helena Hamilton's voice, for instance, was for Martyn golden, Gay Gainsford's pink, Darcey's brown and Adam Poole's violet. When Alleyn spoke she decided that his voice was a royal blue of the clearest sort.

Reminding herself that this was no time to indulge this freakish habit of classification, she gave him her full attention.

"You will, I'm sure," he was saying, "realize that in these cases our job is simply to determine that they are, on the face of it, what they appear to be. In order to do this effectively we are obliged to make a fairly thorough examination of the scene as we find it. This takes a little time always, but if everything's quite straightforward, as I expect it will be, we won't keep you very long. Is that clear?"

He looked round his small audience. Poole said at once: "Yes, of course. We all understand. At the same time, if it's a matter of taking statements, I'd be grateful if you'd see Miss Hamilton first."

"Miss Hamilton?" Alleyn said, and after a moment's hesitation looked at her.

"I'm his wife," she said. "I'm Helena Bennington."

"I'm so sorry. I didn't know. Yes, I'm sure that can be managed. Probably the best way will be for me to see you all together. If everything seems quite clear there may be no need for further interviews. And now, if you'll excuse me, I'll have a look round and then rejoin you. There is a doctor among you, isn't there? Dr. Rutherford?" Dr. Rutherford cleared his throat portentously. "Are you he, sir? Perhaps you'll join us."

"Indubitably," said the Doctor. "I had so concluded."

"Good," Alleyn said and looked faintly amused. "Will you lead the way?"

They were at the door when Jacko suddenly said: "A moment, if you please, Chief Inspector."

"Yes?"

"I would like permission to make soup. There is a filthy small kitchen-place inhabited only by the night-watchman, where I have waiting a can of prepared soup. Everyone is very cold and fatigued and entirely empty. My name is Jacques Doré, I am dogsbody-in-waiting in this theatre and there is much virtue in my soup."

Alleyn said: "By all means. Is the kitchen-place that small sink-room near the dock with the gas jet in it?"

"But you haven't looked at the place yet!" Parry Percival ejaculated.

"I've been here before," said Alleyn. "I remember the theatre. Shall we get on, Dr. Rutherford?"

They went out. Gay Gainsford, whose particular talent from now onwards was to lie in the voicing of disquieting thoughts which her companions shared but decided to leave unspoken, said in a distracted manner: "*When* was he here before?" And when nobody answered, she said dramatically: "I can see it all! He must be the man they sent that other time." She paused and collected their reluctant attention. She laid her hand on J.G.'s arm and raised her voice. "That's why he's come again," she announced.

"Come now, dear," J.G. murmured inadequately, and Poole said quickly: "My *dear* Gay!"

"But I'm right!" she persisted. "I'm sure I'm right. Why else should he know about the sink-room?" She looked about her with an air of terrified complacency.

"*And last time,*" she pointed out, "*it was Murder.*"

"Climax," said Jacko. "Picture and Slow Curtain! Put your hands together, ladies and gentlemen, for this clever little artist."

He went out with his eyes turned up.

"Jacko's terribly hard, isn't he?" Gay said to Darcey. "After all, Uncle Ben *was* my uncle." She caught sight of Helena Hamilton. "And your husband," she said hurriedly, "of course, darling."

iii

The stage-hands had set up in the dock one of the trestle-tables used for properties. They had laid Clark Bennington's body on it and had covered it with a sheet from the wardrobe-room. The dock was a tall echoing place, concrete-floored, with stacks of old flats leaning against the walls. A solitary unprotected lamp bulb, dust-encrusted, hung above the table.

A group of four men in dark overcoats and hats stood beside this improvised bier, and it so chanced they had taken up their places at the four corners and looked therefore as if they kept guard over it. Their hats shadowed their faces and they stood in pools of shadow. A fifth man, bareheaded, stood at the foot of the bier and a little removed from it. When the tallest of the men reached out to the margin of the sheet, his arm cast a black bar over its white and eloquent form. His gloved hand dragged down the sheet and exposed a rigid gaping face encrusted with greasepaint. He uncovered his head and the other three, a little awkwardly, followed his example.

"Well, Curtis?" he said.

Dr. Curtis, the police surgeon, bent over the head, blotting it out with his shadow. He took a flash lamp from his pocket and the face, in this changed light, stared out with an altered look as if it had secretly rearranged its expression.

"God!" Curtis muttered. "He looks pretty ghastly, doesn't he? What an atrocious make-up!"

From his removed position Dr. Rutherford said loudly: "My dear man, the make-up was required by My Play. It should, in point of fact, be a damn sight more repellent. But—*vanitas vanitatum.* Also: *Mit der Dummheit kämpfen Götter selbst vergebens.* I didn't let them fix him up at all. Thought you'd prefer not." His voice echoed coldly round the dock.

"Quite so," Curtis murmured. "Much better not."

"Smell very noticeable still," a thick-set, grizzled man observed. "Always hangs about in these cases," rejoined the sergeant, "doesn't it, Mr. Fox?"

"We worked damn hard on him," Dr. Rutherford said. "It never looked like it from the start. Not a hope."

"Well," said Curtis, drawing back, "it all seems straightforward enough, Alleyn. It doesn't call for a very extensive autopsy, but of course we'll do the usual things."

"Lend me your torch a moment," Alleyn said, and after a moment: "Very heavy make-up, isn't it? He's so thickly powdered."

"He needed it. He sweated," Dr. Rutherford said, "like a pig. Alcohol and a dicky heart."

"Did you look after him, sir?"

"Not I. I don't practise nowadays. The alcohol declared itself and he used to talk about a heart condition. Valvular trouble, I should imagine. I don't know who his medical man was. His wife can tell you."

Dr. Curtis replaced the sheet. "That," he said to Rutherford, "might account for him going quickly."

"Certainly."

"There's a mark on the jaw," Alleyn said. "Did either of you notice it? The make-up is thinner there. Is it a bruise?"

Curtis said: "I saw it, yes. It might be a bruise. We'll see better when we clean him up."

"Right. I'll look at the room," Alleyn said. "Who found him?"

"The stage-manager," said Rutherford.

"Then perhaps you wouldn't mind asking him to come along when you rejoin the others. Thank you so much, Dr. Rutherford. We're glad to have had your report. You'll be called for the inquest, I'm afraid."

"Hell's teeth, I suppose I shall. So be it." He moved to the doors. The sergeant obligingly rolled them open and he muttered "Thankee," and with an air of dissatisfaction went out.

Dr. Curtis said: "I'd better go and make professional noises at him."

"Yes, do," Alleyn said.

On their way to Bennington's room they passed Jacko and a stage-hand bearing a fragrant steaming can and a number of cups to the stage. In his cubby-hole, Fred Badger was entertaining a group of stage-hands and dressers. They had steaming pannikins in their hands and they eyed the police party in silence.

"Smells very tasty, doesn't it?" Detective-Inspector Fox observed rather wistfully.

The young constable, who was stationed by the door through which Martyn had made her entrance, opened it for the soup party and shut it after them.

Fox growled: "Keep your wits about you."

"Yes, sir," said the young constable and exhibited his note-book.

Clem Smith was waiting for them in Bennington's room. The lights were full on and a white glare beat on the dressing-shelf and walls. Bennington's street-clothes and his suit for the first act hung on coat-hangers along the wall. His make-up was laid out on a towel, and the shelf was littered with small objects that in their casual air of usage suggested that he had merely left the room for a moment and would return to take them up again. On the floor, hard by the dead gas fire, lay an overcoat from which the reek of gas, which still hung about the room, seemed to arise. The worn rug was drawn up into wrinkles.

Clem Smith's face was white and anxious under his shock of dark hair. He shook hands jerkily with Alleyn and then looked as if he wondered if he ought to have done so. "This is a pretty ghastly sort of party," he muttered, "isn't it?"

Alleyn said: "It seems that you came in for the worst part of it. Do you mind telling us what happened?"

Fox moved behind Clem and produced his note-book. Sergeant Gibson began to make a list of the objects in the room. Clem watched him with an air of distaste.

"Easy enough to tell you," he said. "He came off about eight minutes before the final curtain and I suppose went straight to this room. When the boy came round for the curtain-call, Ben didn't appear with the others. I didn't notice. There's an important light-cue at the end and I was watching for it. Then, when they all went on, he just wasn't there. We couldn't hold the curtain for long. I sent it up for the first call and the boy went back and hammered on this door. It was locked. He smelt gas and began to yell for Ben and then ran back to tell me what was wrong. I'd got the Doctor on for his speech by that time. I left my A.S.M. in charge, took the bunch of extra keys from the Prompt corner and tore round here."

He wetted his lips and fumbled in his pocket. "Is it safe to smoke?" he asked.

"I'm afraid we'd better wait a little longer," Alleyn said. "Sorry."

"O.K. Well, I unlocked the door. As soon as it opened the stink hit me in the face. I don't know why, but I expected him to be sitting at the shelf. I don't suppose, really, it was long before I saw him, but it seemed fantastically long. He was lying there by the heater. I could only see his legs and the lower half of his body. The rest was hidden by that coat. It was tucked in behind the heater, and over his head and shoulders. It looked like a tent. I heard the hiss going on underneath it." Clem rubbed his mouth. "I don't think," he said, "I was as idiotically slow as all this makes me out to be. I don't think, honestly, it was more than seconds before I went in. Honestly, I don't think so."

"I expect you're right about that. Time goes all relative in a crisis."

"Does it? Good. Well, then: I ran in and hauled the coat away. He was on his left side—his mouth—it was— The lead-in had been disconnected and it was by his mouth, hissing. I turned it off and dragged him by the heels. He sort of stuck on the carpet. Jacko—Jacques Doré bolted in and helped."

"One moment," Alleyn said. "Did you knock over that box of powder on the dressing-table? Either of you?"

Clem Smith stared at it. "That? No, I didn't go near it and I'd got him half-way to the door when Jacko came in. He must have done it himself."

"Right. Sorry. Go on."

"We lifted Ben into the passage and shut his door. At the far end of the passage there's a window, the only one near. We got it open and carried him to it. I think he was dead even then. I'm sure he was. I've seen gassed cases before, in the blitz."

Alleyn said: "You seem to have tackled this one like an old hand, at all events."

"I'm damn glad you think so," said Clem, and sounded it.

Alleyn looked at the Yale lock on the door. "This seems in good enough shape," he said absently.

"It's new," Clem said. "There were pretty extensive renovations and a sort of general clean-up when Mr. Poole took the theatre over. It's useful for the artists to be able to lock up valuables in their rooms and the old locks were clumsy and rusted up. In any case—" He stopped and then said uncomfortably: "The whole place has been repainted and modernized."

"Including the gas installations?"

"Yes," said Clem, not looking at Alleyn. "That's all new, too."

"Two of the old dressing-rooms have been knocked together to form the Greenroom?"

"Yes."

"And there are new dividing walls? And ventilators, now, in the dressing-rooms?"

"Yes," said Clem unhappily and added, "I suppose that's why he used his coat."

"It does look," Alleyn said without stressing it, "as if the general idea was to speed things up, doesn't it? All right, Mr. Smith, thank you. Would you explain to the people on the stage that I'll come as soon as we've finished our job here? It won't be very long. We'll probably ask you to sign a statement of the actual discovery as you've described it to us. You'll be glad to get away from this room, I expect."

Inspector Fox had secreted his note-book and now ushered Clem Smith out. Clem appeared to go thankfully.

"Plain sailing, wouldn't you say, Mr. Alleyn," said Fox, looking along the passage. "Nobody about," he added. "I'll leave the door open."

Alleyn rubbed his nose. "It looks like plain sailing, Fox, certainly. But in view of the other blasted affair we can't take a damn thing for granted. You weren't on the Jupiter case, were you, Gibson?"

"No, sir," said Gibson, looking up from his note-book. "Homicide dressed up to look like suicide, wasn't it?"

"It was, indeed. The place has been pretty extensively chopped up and rehashed, but the victim was on this side of the passage and in what must have been the room now taken in to make the Greenroom. Next door there was a gas fire backing on to his own. The job was done by blowing down the tube next door. This put out the fire in this room and left the gas on, of course. The one next door was then re-lit. The victim was pretty well dead-drunk and the trick worked. We got the bloke on the traces of crepe hair and greasepaint he left on the tube."

"Very careless," Fox said. "Silly chap, really."

"The theatre," Alleyn said, "was shut up for a long time. Three or four years at least. Then Adam Poole took it, renamed it the Vulcan and got a permit for renovation. I fancy this is only his second production here."

"Perhaps," Fox speculated, "the past history of the place played on deceased's mind and led him to do away with himself after the same fashion."

"Sort of superstitious?" Gibson ventured.

"Not precisely," said Fox majestically. "And yet something after that style of thing. They're a very superstitious mob, actors, Fred. Very. And if he had reason, in any case, to entertain the notion of suicide—"

"He must," Alleyn interjected, "have also entertained the very very nasty notion of throwing suspicion of foul play on his fellow-actors. If there's a gas fire back-to-back with this—"

"And there is," Fox said.

"The devil there is! So what does Bennington do? He re-creates as far as possible the whole set-up, leaves no note, no indication, as far as we can see, of his intention to gas himself, and—who's next door, Fox?"

"A Mr. Parry Percival."

"All right. Bennington pushes off, leaving Mr. Parry Percival ostensibly in the position of the Jupiter murderer. Rotten sort of suicide that'd be, Br'er Fox."

"We don't know anything yet, of course," said Fox.

"We don't, and the crashing hellish bore about the whole business lies in the all-too-obvious fact that we'll have to find out. What's on your inventory, Gibson?"

Sergeant Gibson opened his note-book and adopted his official manner.

"Dressing-table or shelf," he said. "One standing mirror. One cardboard box containing false hair, rouge, substance labelled 'nose-paste,' seven fragments of greasepaint and one unopened box of powder. Shelf. Towel spread out to serve as table-cloth. On towel, one tray containing six sticks of greasepaint. To right of tray, bottle of spirit-adhesive. Bottle containing what appears to be substance known as liquid powder. Open box of powder overturned. Behind box of powder, pile of six pieces of cotton-wool and a roll from which these pieces have been removed." He looked up at Alleyn. "Intended to be used for powdering purposes, Mr. Alleyn."

"That's it," Alleyn said. He was doubled up, peering at the floor under the dressing-shelf. "Nothing there," he grunted. "Go on."

"To left of tray, cigarette case with three cigarettes and open box of fifty. Box of matches. Ash-tray. Towel, stained with greasepaint. Behind mirror, flask—one-sixth full—and used tumbler smelling of spirits."

Alleyn looked behind the standing glass. "Furtive sort of cache," he said. "Go on."

"Considerable quantity of powder spilt on shelf and on adjacent floor area. Considerable quantity of ash. Left wall, clothes. I haven't been through the pockets yet, Mr. Alleyn. There's nothing on the floor but powder and some paper ash, original form undistinguishable. Stain as of something burnt on hearth."

"Go ahead with it then. I wanted," Alleyn said with a discontented air, "to *hear* whether I was wrong."

Fox and Gibson looked placidly at him. "All right," he said, "don't mind me. I'm broody."

He squatted down by the overcoat. "It really is the most obscene smell, gas," he muttered. "How anybody *can* always passes my comprehension." He poked in a gingerly manner at the coat. "Powder over everything," he grumbled. "Where had this coat been? On the empty hanger near the door, presumably. That's damned rum. Check it with his dresser. We'll have to get Bailey along, Fox. And Thompson. Blast!"

"I'll ring the Yard," said Fox and went out.

Alleyn squinted through a lens at the wing-taps of the gas fire. "I can see prints clearly enough," he said, "on both. We can check with Bennington's. There's even a speck or two of powder settled on the taps."

"In the air, sir, I dare say," said Gibson.

"I dare say it *was*. Like the gas. We can't go any further here until the dabs and flash party has done its stuff. Finished, Gibson?"

"Finished, Mr. Alleyn. Nothing much in the pockets. Bills. Old racing card. Cheque-book and so on. Nothing on the body, by the way, but a handkerchief."

"Come on, then. I've had my belly-full of gas."

But he stood in the doorway eyeing the room and whistling softly.

"I wish I could believe in you," he apostrophized it, "but split me and sink me if I can. No, by all that's phoney, not for one credulous second. Come on, Gibson. Let's talk to these experts."

iv

They all felt a little better for Jacko's soup, which had been laced with something that, as J. G. Darcey said (and looked uncomfortable as soon as he'd said it), went straight to the spot marked X.

Whether it was this potent soup, or whether extreme emotional and physical fatigue had induced in Martyn its familiar complement, an uncanny sharpening of the mind, she began to consider for the first time the general reaction of the company to Bennington's death. She thought: "I don't believe there's one of us who really minds very much. How lonely for him! Perhaps he guessed that was how it would be. Perhaps he felt the awful isolation of a child that knows itself unwanted and thought he'd put himself out of the way of caring."

It was a shock to Martyn when Helena Hamilton suddenly gave voice to her own thoughts. Helena had sat with her chin in her hand, looking at the floor. There was an unerring grace about her and this fireside posture had the beauty of complete relaxation. Without raising her eyes she said: "My dears, my dears, for pity's sake don't let's pretend. Don't let me pretend. I didn't love him. Isn't that sad? We all know and we try to patch up a decorous scene but it won't do. We're shocked and uneasy and dreadfully tired. Don't let's put ourselves to the trouble of pretending. It's so useless."

Gay said. "But I *did* love him!" and J.G. put his arm about her.

"Did you?" Helena murmured. "Perhaps you did, darling. Then you must hug your sorrow to yourself. Because I'm afraid nobody really shares it."

Poole said: "We understand, Helena."

With that familiar gesture, not looking at him, she reached out her hand. When he had taken it in his, she said: "When one is dreadfully tired, one talks. I do, at all events. I talk much too easily. Perhaps that's a sign of a shallow woman. You know, my dears, I begin to think I'm only capable of affection. I have a great capacity for affection, but as for my loves, they have no real permanency. None."

Jacko said gently: "Perhaps your talent for affection is equal to other women's knack of loving."

Gay and Parry Percival looked at him in astonishment, but Poole said: "That may well be."

"What I meant to say," Helena went on, "only I do sidetrack myself so awfully, is this. Hadn't we better stop being muted and mournful and talk about what may happen and what we ought to do? Adam, darling, I thought perhaps they might all be respecting my sorrow or something. What should we be talking about? What's the situation?"

Poole moved one of the chairs with its back to the curtain and sat in it. Dr. Rutherford returned and lumped himself down in the corner. "They're talking," he said, "to Clem Smith in the—they're talking to Clem. I've seen the police surgeon, a subfusc exhibit, but one that can tell a hawk from a handsaw if they're held under his nose. He agrees that there was nothing else I could have done, which is no doubt immensely gratifying to me. What are you all talking about? You look like a dress rehearsal."

"We were about to discuss the whole situation," said Poole. "Helena feels it should be discussed and I think we all agree with her."

"What situation pray? Ben's? Or ours? There is no more to be said about Ben's situation. As far as we know, my dear Helena, he has administered to himself a not too uncomfortable and effective anaesthetic, which, after he had become entirely unconscious, brought about the end he had in mind. For a man who had decided to shuffle off this mortal coil he behaved very sensibly."

"Oh, *please*," Gay whispered. "*Please!*"

Dr. Rutherford contemplated her in silence for a moment and then said: "What's up, Misery?" Helena, Darcey and Parry Percival made expostulatory noises. Poole said: "See here, John, you'll either pipe down or preserve the decencies."

Gay, fortified perhaps by this common reaction, said loudly: "You might at least have the grace to remember he was my uncle."

"Grace me no grace," Dr. Rutherford quoted inevitably, "and uncle me no uncles." After a moment's reflection, he added: "All right, Thalia, have a good cry. But you must know, if the rudiments of reasoned thinking are within your command, that your Uncle Ben did you a damn shabby turn. A scurvy trick, by God. However, I digress. Get on with the post mortem, Chorus. I am dumb."

"You'll be good enough to remain so," said Poole warmly. "Very well, then. It seems to me, Helena, that Ben took this—this way out—for a number of reasons. I know you want me to speak plainly and I'm going to speak very plainly indeed, my dear."

"Oh, yes," she said. "Please, but—" For a moment they looked at each other. Martyn wondered if she imagined that Poole's head moved in the faintest possible negative. "Yes," Helena said, "very plainly, please."

"Well, then," Poole said, "we know that for the last year Ben, never a very temperate man, has been a desperately intemperate one. We know his habits undermined his health, his character and his integrity as an actor. I think he realized this very thoroughly. He was an unhappy man, who looked back at what he had once been and was appalled. We all know he did things in performance to-night that, from an actor of his standing, were quite beyond the pale."

Parry Percival ejaculated: "Well, I mean to say—oh, well. Never mind."

"Exactly," Poole said. "He had reached a sort of chronic state of instability. We all know he was subject to fits of depression. I believe he did what he did when he was at a low ebb. I believe he would have done it sooner or later by one means or another. And in my view, for what it's worth, that's the whole story. Tragic enough, God knows, but, in its tragedy, simple. I don't know if you agree."

Darcey said: "If there's nothing else. I mean," he said diffidently, glancing at Helena, "if nothing has happened that would seem like a further motive."

Helena's gaze rested for a moment on Poole and then on Darcey. "I think Adam's right," she said. "I'm afraid he was appalled by a sudden realization of himself. I'm afraid he was insufferably lonely."

"Oh, my God!" Gay ejaculated, and having by this means collected their unwilling attention she added: "I shall never forgive myself. Never."

Dr. Rutherford groaned loudly.

"I failed him," Gay announced. "I was a bitter, bitter disappointment to him. I dare say I turned the scale."

"Now in the name of all the gods at once," Dr. Rutherford began, and was brought to a stop by the entry of Clem Smith.

Clem looked uneasily at Helena Hamilton and said: "They're in the dressing-room. He says they won't keep you waiting much longer."

"It's all right, then?" Parry Percival blurted out and added in a flurry: "I mean there won't be a whole lot of formalities. I mean we'll be able to get away. I mean—"

"I've no idea about that," Clem said. "Alleyn just said they'd be here soon." He had brought a cup of soup with him and he withdrew into a corner and began to drink it. The others watched him anxiously but said nothing.

"What did he ask you about?" Jacko demanded suddenly.

"About what we did at the time."

"Anything else?"

"Well, yes. He—well, in point of fact, he seemed to be interested in the alterations to the theatre."

"To the dressing-rooms in particular?" Poole asked quickly.

"Yes," Clem said unhappily. "To them."

There was a long silence, broken by Jacko.

"I find nothing remarkable in this," he said. "Helena has shown us the way with great courage and Adam has spoken his mind. Let us all speak ours. I may resemble an ostrich but I do not propose to imitate its behaviour. Of what do we all think? There is the unpleasing little circumstance of the Jupiter case and we think of that. When Gay mentions it she does so with the air of one who opens a closet and out tumbles a skeleton. But why? It is inevitable that these gentlemen, who also remember the Jupiter case, should wish to inspect the dressing-rooms. They wish, in fact, to make very sure indeed that this is a case of suicide and not of murder. And since we are all quite certain that it is suicide we should not disturb ourselves that they do their duty."

"Exactly," Poole said.

"It's going," Darcey muttered, "to be damn bad publicity."

"Merciful Heavens!" Parry Percival exclaimed. "The Publicity! None of us thought of that!"

"Did we not!" said Poole.

"I must say," Parry complained, "I *would* like to know what's going to happen, Adam. I mean—darling Helena, I know you'll understand—but I mean, about the piece. Do we go on? Or what?"

"Yes," Helena said. "We go on. Please, Adam."

"Helena, I've got to think. There are so many—"

"We go on. Indeed, indeed we do."

Martyn felt rather than saw the sense of relief in Darcey and Percival.

Darcey said: "I'm the understudy, Lord help me," and Percival made a tiny ambiguous sound that might have been one of satisfaction or of chagrin.

"How are you for it, J.G.?" Helena asked.

"I *know* it," he said heavily.

"I'll work whenever you like. We've got the week-end."

"Thank you, Helena."

"Your own understudy's all right," said Clem.

"Good."

It was clear to Martyn that this retreat into professionalism was a great relief to them, and it was clear also that Poole didn't share in their comfort. Watching him, she was reminded of his portrait in the Greenroom: he looked withdrawn and troubled.

A lively and almost cosy discussion about re-casting had developed. Clem Smith, Jacko and Percival were all talking at once when, with her infallible talent for scenes, Gay exclaimed passionately:

"I can't bear it! I think you're all awful!"

They broke off. Having collected their attention, she built rapidly to her climax. "To sit round and talk about the show as if nothing had happened! How you can! When beyond those doors, he's lying there, forgotten. Cold and forgotten! It's the most brutal thing I've ever heard of, and if you think I'm coming near this horrible, fated, *haunted* place again, I'm telling you here and now that wild horses wouldn't drag me inside the theatre once I'm away from it. I suppose someone will find time to tell me when the funeral is going to be. I happen to be just about his only relation."

They all began to expostulate at once, but she topped their lines with the determination of a robust star. "You needn't bother to explain," she shouted. "I understand only too well, thank you." She caught sight of Martyn and pointed wildly at her. "You've angled for this miserable part, and now you've got it. I think it's extremely likely you're responsible for what's happened."

Poole said: "You'll stop at once, Gay. Stop."

"I won't! I won't be gagged! It drove my Uncle Ben to despair and I don't care who knows it."

It was upon this line that Alleyn, as if he had mastered one of the major points of stage technique, made his entrance up-stage and centre.

v

Although he must have heard every word of Gay's final outburst, Alleyn gave no sign of having done so. He and the young constable came in and, as if he had walked into somebody's flat, he took off his hat and put it on a table near the door. The young constable looked round and then went off-stage, returning with two chairs which he placed, one in a central position for Alleyn, and one in the O.P. corner for himself. To Martyn he had fantastically the air of an A.D.C. As he settled himself he gave her another of his friendly smiles.

Clem and Parry had got uncomfortably to their feet and now sat down again in a faintly huffy manner. With the exception of Dr. Rutherford, the company reorientated itself, unobtrusively, on Alleyn.

"Well, now," he said, "I'm afraid the first thing I have to say to you all won't be very pleasant news. We don't look like getting through with our side of this unhappy business as quickly as I hoped. I know you are all desperately tired and very shocked and I'm sorry. But the general circumstances aren't quite as straightforward as, on the face of it, you have probably supposed them to be."

A trickle of ice moved under Martyn's diaphragm. She thought: "No, it's not fair. I can't be made to have two goes of the jim-jams in one night."

Alleyn addressed himself specifically to Helena Hamilton.

"You'll have guessed—or course you will—that one can't overlook the other case of gas poisoning that is associated with this theatre. It must have jumped to everybody's mind, almost at once."

"Yes, of course," she said. "We've been talking about it."

The men looked uneasily at her but Alleyn said at once: "I'm sure you have. So have we. And I expect you've wondered, as we have, if the memory of that former case could have influenced your husband."

"I'm certain it did," she said quickly. "We all are."

The others made small affirmative noises. Only Dr. Rutherford was silent. Martyn saw with amazement that his chin had sunk on his rhythmically heaving bosom, his eyes were shut and his lips pursed in the manner of a sleeper who is just not snoring. He was at the back of the group and, she hoped, concealed from Alleyn.

"Have you," Alleyn asked, "any specific argument to support this theory?"

"No *specific* reason. But I know he thought a lot of that other dreadful business. He didn't *like* this theatre. Mr. Alleyn, actors are sensitive to atmosphere. We talk a lot about the theatres we play in and we get very vivid— you would probably think absurdly vivid—impressions of their 'personalities.' My husband felt there was a—an unpleasant atmosphere in this place. He often said so. In a way I think it had a rather horrible fascination for him. We'd a sort of tacit understanding in the Vulcan that its past history wouldn't be discussed among us, but I know he did talk about it. Not to us, but to people who had been concerned in the other affair."

"Yes, I see." Alleyn waited for a moment. The young constable completed a note. His back was now turned to the company. "Did anyone else notice this preoccupation of Mr. Bennington's?"

"Oh, yes!" Gay said with mournful emphasis. "I did. He talked to me about it, but when he saw how much it upset me—because I'm so stupidly sensitive to atmosphere—I just can't help it—it's one of those things—but I *am* —because when I first came into the theatre I just knew—you may laugh at me but these things can't be denied—"

"When," Alleyn prompted, "he saw that it upset you?"

"He stopped. I was his niece. It was rather a marvellous relationship."

"He stopped," Alleyn said. "Right." He had a programme in his hand and now glanced at it. "You must be Miss Gainsford, I think. Is that right?"

"Yes, I am. But my name's really Bennington. I'm his only brother's daughter. My father died in the war and Uncle Ben really felt we were awfully *near* to each other, do you know? That's why it's so devastating for me, because I sensed how wretchedly unhappy he was."

"Do you mind telling us why you thought him so unhappy?"

J. G. Darcey interposed quickly: "I don't think it was more than a general intuitive sort of thing, was it, Gay? Nothing special."

"Well—" Gay said reluctantly, and Helena intervened.

"I don't think any of us have any doubt about my husband's unhappiness, Mr. Alleyn. Before you came in I was saying how most, *most* anxious I am that we should be very frank with each other and of course with you. My husband drank so heavily that he had ruined his health and his work quite completely. I wasn't able to help him and we were not—" The colour died out of her face and she hesitated. "Our life together wasn't true," she said. "It had no reality at all. To-night he behaved very badly on the stage. He coloured his part at the expense of the other actors and I think he was horrified at what he'd done. He was very drunk indeed to-night. I feel he suddenly looked at himself and couldn't face what he saw. I feel that very strongly."

"One *does* sense these things," Gay interjected eagerly, "or I do at any rate."

"I'm sure you do," Alleyn agreed politely. Gay drew breath and was about to go on when he said: "Of course, if any of you can tell us any happenings or remarks or so on that seem to prove that he had this thing in mind, it will be a very great help."

Martyn heard her voice—acting, it seemed, of its own volition. "I think, perhaps—"

Alleyn turned to her and his smile reassured her. "Yes?" he said. "Forgive me, but I don't yet know all your names." He looked again at his programme and then at her. Gay gave a small laugh. Darcey put his hand over hers and said something undistinguishable.

Poole said quickly: "Miss Martyn Tarne. She is, or should be, our heroine to-night. Miss Gainsford was ill and Miss Tarne, who was the understudy, took her part at half-an-hour's notice. We'd all be extremely proud of her if we had the wits to be anything but worried and exhausted."

Martyn's heart seemed to perform some eccentric gyration in the direction of her throat and she thought: "That's done it. Now my voice is going to be ungainly with emotion."

Alleyn said: "That must have been a most terrifying and exciting adventure," and she gulped and nodded. "What had you remembered," he went on after a moment, "that might help us?"

"It was something he said when he came off in the last act."

"For his final exit in the play?"

"Yes."

"I'll be very glad to hear it."

"I'll try to remember exactly what it was," Martyn said carefully. "I was in the dressing-room passage on my way to my—to Miss Gainsford's room and he caught me up. He spoke very disjointedly and strangely, not finishing his sentences. But one thing he said—I think it was the last—I do remember quite distinctly because it puzzled me very much. He said: 'I just wanted to tell you that you needn't suppose what I'm going to do—' and then he stopped as if he was confused and added, I think: 'You needn't suppose—' and broke off again. And then Jacko—Mr. Doré—came and told me to go into the dressing-room to have my make-up attended to and, I think, said something to Mr. Bennington about his."

"I told him he was shining with sweat," said Jacko. "And he went into his room."

"Alone?" Alleyn asked.

"I just looked in to make sure he had heard me. I told him again he needed powder and then went at once to this Infant."

"Miss Tarne, can you remember anything else Mr. Bennington said?"

"Not really. I'm afraid I was rather in a haze myself just then."

"The great adventure?"

"Yes," said Martyn gratefully. "I've an idea he said something about my performance. Perhaps I should explain that I knew he must be very disappointed and upset about my going on instead of Miss Gainsford, but his manner was not unfriendly and I have the impression that he meant to say he didn't bear for me, personally, any kind of resentment. But that's putting it too definitely. I'm not at all sure what he said, except for that one sentence. Of that I'm quite positive."

"Good," Alleyn said. "Thank you. Did you hear this remark, Mr. Doré?"

Jacko said promptly: "But certainly. I was already in the passage and he spoke loudly as I came up."

"Did you form any opinion as to what he meant?"

"I was busy and very pleased with this Infant and I did not concern myself. If I thought at all it was to wonder if he was going to make a scene because the niece had not played. He had a talent for scenes. It appears to be a family trait. I thought perhaps he meant that this Infant would not be included in some scene he planned to make or be scolded for her success."

"Did he seem to you to be upset?"

"Oh, yes. Yes. Upset. Yes."

"Very much distressed, would you say?"

"All his visage wann'd?" inquired a voice in the background. "Tears in his eyes, distraction in's aspect?"

Alleyn moved his position until he could look past Gay and Darcey at the recumbent Doctor. "Or even," he said, "his whole function suiting with forms to his conceit?"

"Hah!" The Doctor ejaculated and sat up. "Upon my soul, the whirligig of time brings in his revenges. Even to the point where dull detection apes at artifice, inspectors echo with informed breath their pasteboard prototypes of fancy wrought. I am amazed and know not what to say." He helped himself to snuff and fell back into a recumbent position.

"Please don't mind him," Helena said, smiling at Alleyn. "He is a very foolish vain old man and has read somewhere that it's clever to quote in a muddled sort of way from the better known bits of the Bard."

"We encourage him too much," Jacko added gloomily.

"We have become too friendly with him," said Poole.

"And figo for thy friendship," said Dr. Rutherford.

Parry Percival sighed ostentatiously and Darcey said: "Couldn't we get on?" Alleyn looked good-humouredly at Jacko and said: "Yes, Mr. Doré?"

"I would agree," Jacko said, "that Ben was very much upset, but that was an almost chronic condition of late with poor Ben. I believe now with Miss Hamilton that he had decided there was little further enjoyment to be found in observing the dissolution of his own character and was about to take the foolproof way of ending it. He wished to assure Martyn that the decision had nothing to do with chagrin over Martyn's success or the failure of his niece. And that, if I am right, was nice of Ben."

"I don't think we need use the word 'failure,'" J.G. objected. "Gay was quite unable to go on."

"I hope you are better now, Miss Gainsford," Alleyn said.

Gay made an eloquent gesture with both hands and let them fall in her lap. "What does it matter?" she said. "Better? Oh, yes, I'm better." And with the closest possible imitation of Helena Hamilton's familiar gesture she extended her hand, without looking at him, to J. G. Darcey. He took it anxiously. "Much better," he said, patting it.

Martyn thought: "Oh, dear, he *is* in love with her. *Poor* J.G.!"

Alleyn looked thoughtfully at them for a moment and then turned to the others.

"There's a general suggestion," he said, "that none of you was very surprised by this event. May I just—sort of tally-up the general opinion as far as I've heard it? It helps to keep things tidy, I find. Miss Hamilton, you tell us that your husband had a curious, an almost morbid interest in the Jupiter case. You and Mr. Doré agree that Mr. Bennington had decided to take his life because he couldn't face the 'dissolution of his character.' Miss Gainsford, if I understand her, believes he was deeply disturbed by the *mise-en-scène* and also by her inability to go on to-night for this part. Miss Tarne's account of what was probably the last statement he made suggests that he wanted her to understand that some action he had in mind had nothing to do with her. Mr. Doré supports this interpretation and confirms the actual words that were used. This, as far as it goes, is the only tangible bit of evidence as to intention that we have."

Poole lifted his head. His face was very white and a lock of black hair had fallen over his forehead, turning him momentarily into the likeness, Martyn thought inconsequently, of Michelangelo's Adam. He said: "There's the fact itself, Alleyn. There's what he did."

Alleyn said carefully: "There's an interval of perhaps eight minutes between what he said and when he was found."

"Look here—" Parry Percival began, and then relapsed. "Let it pass," he said. "*I* wouldn't know."

"Pipe up, Narcissus," Dr. Rutherford adjured him, "the Inspector won't bite you."

"Oh, shut up!" Parry shouted, and was awarded a complete and astonished silence. He rose and addressed himself to the players. "You're all being *so* bloody frank and sensible about this suicide," he said. "You're *so* anxious to show everybody how honest you are. The Doctor's *so* unconcerned he can even spare a moment to indulge in his favourite pastime of me-baiting. I know what the Doctor thinks about me and it doesn't say much for his talents as a diagnostician. But if it's queer to feel desperately sorry for a man who was miserable enough to choke himself to death at a gas jet, if it's queer to be physically and mentally sick at the thought of it, then, by God, I'd rather be queer than normal. Now!"

There followed a silence broken only by the faint whisper of the young constable's pencil.

Dr. Rutherford struggled to his feet and lumbered down to Parry.

"Your argument, my young coxcomb," he said thoughtfully, "is as sea-worthy as a sieve. As for my diagnosis, if you're the normal man you'd have me believe, why the hell don't you show like one? You exhibit the stigmata of that water-fly whom it is a vice to know, and fly into a fit when the inevitable conclusion is drawn." He took Parry by the elbow and addressed himself to the company in the manner of a lecturer. "A phenomenon," he said, "that is not without its dim interest. I invite your attention. Here is an alleged actor who, an hour or two since, was made a public and egregious figure of fun by the deceased. Who was roasted by the deceased before an audience of a thousand whinnying nincompoops. Who allowed his performance to be prostituted by the deceased before this audience. Who before his final and most welcome exit suffered himself to be tripped up contemptuously by the deceased, and who fell on his painted face before this audience. Here is this phenomenon, ladies and gents, who now proposes himself as Exhibit A in the Compassion Stakes. I invite your—"

Poole said "*Quiet!*" and when Dr. Rutherford grinned at him added: "I meant it, John. You will be quiet if you please."

Parry wrenched himself free from the Doctor and turned on Alleyn. "You're supposed to be in charge here—" he began, and Poole said quickly: "Yes, Alleyn, I really do think that this discussion is getting quite fantastically out of hand. If we're all satisfied that this is a case of suicide—"

"Which," Alleyn said, "we are not."

They were all talking at once: Helena, the Doctor, Parry, Gay and Darcey. They were like a disorderly chorus in a verse-play. Martyn, who had been watching Alleyn, was terrified. She saw him glance at the constable. Then he stood up.

"One moment," he said. The chorus broke off as inconsequently as it had begun.

"We've reached a point," Alleyn said, "where it's my duty to tell you I'm by no means satisfied that this is, in fact, a case of suicide."

Martyn was actually conscious, in some kind, of a sense of relief. She could find no look either of surprise or of anger in any of her fellow-players. Their faces were so many white discs and they were motionless and silent. At last Clem Smith said with an indecent lack of conviction: "He was horribly careless about things like that—taps, I mean—" His voice sank to a murmur. They heard the word "accident."

"Is it not strange," Jacko said loudly, "how loath one is to pronounce the word that is in all our minds. And truth to tell, it has a soft and ugly character." His lips closed over his fantastic teeth. He used the exaggerated articulation of an old actor. "Murder," he said. "So beastly, isn't it?"

It was at this point that one of the stage-hands, following, no doubt, his routine for the night, pulled up the curtain and exhibited the scene of climax to the deserted auditorium.

CHAPTER VIII

Afterpiece

From this time onward, through the watches of that night, it seemed to Martyn that a second play was acted out in the Vulcan: a play that wrote itself as it went along, with many excursions into irrelevance, with countless *longueurs* and with occasional unanticipated scenes of climax. She was unable to dismiss the sense of an audience that watched in the shrouded seats, or the notion that the theatre itself was attentive to the action on its stage.

This illusion was in some sort created by the players, for it seemed to Martyn that each of them was acting a part. She was not on this account repelled by any of them, but rather felt drawn towards them all as one is to people with whom one shares a common danger. They were of one guild. Even Gay Gainsford's excesses were at first a cause only of resigned irritation, and Parry Percival's outburst, Martyn felt, was understandable. On the whole she thought the better of him for it.

When she considered them all as they sat about their own working-stage, bruised by anxiety and fatigue, Jacko's ugly word sounded not so much frightening as preposterous. It was unthinkable that it could kindle even a batlight of fear in any of their hearts. "And yet," thought Martyn, "it has done so. There are little points of terror burning in all of us like match-flames."

After Jacko had spoken there was a long silence, broken at last by Adam Poole, who asked temperately: "Are we to understand, Alleyn, that you have quite ruled out the possibility of suicide?"

"By no means," Alleyn rejoined. "I still hope you may be able, among you, to show that there is at least a clear enough probability of suicide for us to leave the case as it stands until the inquest. But where there are strong indications that it may *not* be suicide we can't risk waiting as long as that without a pretty exhaustive look round."

"And there are such indications?"

"There are indeed."

"Strong?"

Alleyn waited a moment. "Sufficiently strong," he said.

"What are they?" Dr. Rutherford demanded.

"It must suffice," Alleyn quibbled politely, "that they are sufficient."

"An elegant sufficiency, by God!"

"But, Mr. Alleyn," Helena cried out, "what can we tell you? Except that we all most sincerely believe that Ben did this himself. Because we know him to have been bitterly unhappy. What else is there for us to say?"

"It will help, you know, when we get a clear picture of what you were all doing and where you were between the time he left the stage and the time he was found. Inspector Fox is checking now with the stage-staff. I propose to do so with the players."

"I see," she said. She leant forward and her air of reasonableness and attention was beautifully executed. "You want to find out which of us had the opportunity to murder Ben."

Gay Gainsford and Parry began an outcry, but Helena raised her hand and they were quiet. "That's it, isn't it?" she said.

"Yes," Alleyn said, "that really is it. I fancy you would rather be spared the stock evasions about routine enquiries and all the rest of it."

"Much rather."

"I was sure of it," Alleyn said. "Then shall we start with you, if you please?"

"I was on the stage for the whole of that time, Mr. Alleyn. There's a scene, before Ben's exit, between J.G.—that's Mr. Darcey over there—Parry, Adam, Ben and myself. First Parry and then J.G. goes off and Ben follows a moment later. Adam and I finish the play."

"So you, too," Alleyn said to Poole, "were here, on the stage, for the whole of this period?"

"I go off for a moment after his exit. It's a strange, rather horridly strange, coincidence that in the play he—the character he played, I mean—does commit suicide off-stage. He shoots himself. When I hear the shot I go off. The other two men have already made their exits. They remain off but I come on again almost immediately. I wait outside the door on the left from a position where I can watch Miss Hamilton, and I re-enter on a 'business' cue from her."

"How long would this take?"

"Shall we show you?" Helena suggested. She got up and moved to the centre of the stage. She raised her clasped hands to her mouth and stood motionless. She was another woman.

As if Clem had called "Clear stage"—and indeed he looked about him with an air of authority—Martyn, Jacko and Gay moved into the wings. Parry and J.G. went to the foot of the stairs and Poole crossed to above Helena. They placed themselves thus in the business-like manner of a rehearsal. The Doctor, however, remained prone on his sofa, breathing deeply and completely disregarded by everybody. Helena glanced at Clem Smith, who went to the book.

"From Ben's exit, Clem," Poole said, and after a moment Helena turned and addressed herself to the empty stage on her left.

"I've only one thing to say, but it's between the three of us." She turned to Parry and Darcey. "Do you mind?" she asked them.

Parry said: "I don't understand and I'm past minding."

Darcey said: "My head is buzzing with a sense of my own inadequacy. I shall be glad to be alone."

They went out, each on his own line, leaving Helena, Adam, and the ghost of Bennington on the stage.

Helena spoke again to vacancy. "It must be clear to you, now. It's the end, isn't it?"

"Yes," Clem's voice said. "I understand you perfectly. Good-bye, my dear."

They watched the door on the left. Alleyn took out his watch. Helena made a quick movement as if to prevent the departure of an unseen person and Poole laid his hand on her arm. They brought dead Ben back to the stage by their mime and dismissed him as vividly. It seemed that the door must open and shut for him as he went out.

Poole said: "And now I must speak to you alone." There followed a short passage of dialogue which he and Helena played *a tempo* but with muted voices. Jacko, in the wings, clapped his hands and the report was as startling as a gun-shot. Poole ran out through the left-hand door.

Helena traced a series of movements about the stage. Her gestures were made in the manner of an exercise but the shadow of their significance was reflected in her face. Finally she moved into the window and seemed to compel herself to look out. Poole re-entered.

"Thank you," Alleyn said, shutting his watch. "Fifty seconds. Will you all come on again, if you please?"

When they had assembled in their old positions, he said: "Did anyone notice Mr. Poole as he waited by the door for his re-entry?"

"The door's recessed," Poole said. "I was more or less screened."

"Someone off-stage may have noticed, however." He looked from Darcey to Percival.

"We went straight to our rooms," said Parry.

"Together?"

"I was first. Miss Tarne was in the entrance to the passage and I spoke to her for a moment. J.G. followed me, I think."

"Do you remember this, Miss Tarne?"

It had been at the time when Martyn had begun to come back to earth. It was like a recollection from a dream. "Yes," she said. "I remember. They both spoke to me."

"And went on down the passage?"

"Yes."

"To be followed in a short time by yourself and Mr. Bennington?"

"Yes."

"And then Mr. Doré joined you and you went to your rooms?"

"Yes."

"So that after Mr. Bennington had gone to his room, you, Mr. Percival, were in your dressing-room, which is next door to his, Mr. Darcey was in his room which is on the far side of Mr. Percival's, and Miss Tarne was in her room—or more correctly, perhaps, Miss Gainsford's—with Mr. Doré, who joined her there after looking in on Mr. Bennington. Right?"

They murmured an uneasy assent.

"How long were you all in these rooms?"

Jacko said: "I believe I have said I adjusted this Infant's make-up and returned with her to the stage."

"I think," said Martyn, "that the other two went out to the stage before we did. I remember hearing them go up the passage together. That was before the call for the final curtain. We went out after the call, didn't we, Jacko?"

"Certainly, my Infant. And by that time you were a little more awake, isn't it? The pink clouds had receded a certain distance?"

Martyn nodded, feeling foolish. Poole came behind her and rested his hands on her shoulders. "So there would appear at least to be an alibi for the Infant Phenomenon," he said. It was the most natural and inevitable thing in the world for her to lean back. His hands moved to her arms and he held her to him for an uncharted second while a spring of well-being broke over her astounded heart.

Alleyn looked from her face to Poole's and she guessed that he wondered about their likeness to each other. Poole, answering her thoughts and Alleyn's unspoken question, said: "We are remotely related, but I am not allowed to mention it. She's ashamed of the connection."

"That's unlucky," Alleyn said with a smile, "since it declares itself so unequivocally."

Gay Gainsford said loudly to Darcey: "Do you suppose, darling, they'd let me get my cigarettes?"

Helena said: "Here you are, Gay." Darcey had already opened his case and held it out to her in his right hand. His left hand was in his trousers pocket. His posture was elegant and modish, out of keeping with his look of anxiety and watchfulness.

"Where are your cigarettes?" Alleyn asked and Gay said quickly: "It doesn't matter, thank you. I've got one. I won't bother. I'm sorry I interrupted."

"But where are they?"

"I don't really know what I've done with them."

"Where were you during the performance?"

She said impatiently: "It *really* doesn't matter. I'll look for them later or something."

"Gay," said Jacko, "was in the Greenroom throughout the show."

"Lamprey will see if he can find them."

The young constable said: "Yes, of course, sir," and went out.

"In the Greenroom?" Alleyn said. "Were you there all the time, Miss Gainsford?"

Standing in front of her with his back to Alleyn, Darcey held a light to her cigarette. She inhaled and coughed violently. He said: "Gay didn't feel fit enough to move. She curled up in a chair in the Greenroom. I was to take her home after the show."

"When did you leave the Greenroom, Miss Gainsford?"

But it seemed that Gay had half-asphyxiated herself with her cigarette. She handed it wildly to Darcey, buried her face in her handkerchief and was madly convulsed. P. C. Lamprey returned with a packet of cigarettes, was waved away with vehemence, gave them to Darcey and on his own initiative fetched a cup of water.

"If the face is congested," Dr. Rutherford advised from the sofa, "hold her up by the heels." His eyes remained closed.

Whether it was the possibility of being subjected to this treatment or the sip of water that Darcey persuaded her to take or the generous thumps on her back, administered by Jacko, that effected a cure, the paroxysm abated. Alleyn, who had watched this scene thoughtfully, said: "If you are quite yourself again, Miss Gainsford, will you try to remember when you left the Greenroom?"

She shook her head weakly and said in an invalid's voice: "Please, I honestly don't remember. Is it very important?"

"Oh, for pity's sake, Gay!" cried Helena, with every sign of the liveliest irritation. "Do stop being such an unmitigated ass. You're not choking: if you were your eyes would water and you'd probably dribble. Of course it's important. You were in the Greenroom and next door to Ben. Think!"

"But you can't imagine—" Gay said wildly. "Oh, Aunty—I'm sorry, I mean Helena—I do think that's a frightful thing to suggest."

"My dear Gay," Poole said, "I don't suppose Helena or Mr. Alleyn or any of us imagines you went into Ben's room, knocked him senseless with a straight left to the jaw and then turned the gas on. We merely want to know what you did do."

J.G., who had given a sharp ejaculation and half risen from his chair, now sank back.

Alleyn said: "It would also be interesting, Mr. Poole, to hear how you knew about the straight left to the jaw."

ii

Poole was behind Martyn and a little removed from her. She felt his stillness in her own bones. When he spoke it was a shock rather than a relief to hear how easy and relaxed his voice sounded.

"Do you realize, Alleyn," he said, "you've given me an opportunity to use, in reverse, a really smashing detective's cliché: 'I didn't know. You have just told me!'"

"And that," Alleyn said with some relish, "as I believe you would say in the profession, takes me off with a hollow laugh and a faint hiss. So you merely guessed at the straight left?"

"If Ben was killed, and I don't believe he was, it seemed to me to be the only way this murder could be brought about."

"Surely not," Alleyn said without emphasis. "There is the method that was used before in this theatre with complete success."

"I don't know that I would describe as completely successful a method that ended with the arrest of its employer."

"Oh," Alleyn said lightly, "that's another story. He underestimated our methods."

"A good enough warning to anyone else not to follow his plan of action."

"Or perhaps merely a hint that it could be improved upon," Alleyn said. "What do you think, Mr. Darcey?"

"I?" J.G. sounded bewildered. "I don't know. I'm afraid I haven't followed the argument."

"You were still thinking about the straight-left theory, perhaps?"

"I believe with the others that it was suicide," said J.G. He had sat down again beside Gay. His legs were stretched out before him and crossed at the ankles, his hands were in his trousers pockets and his chin on his chest. It was the attitude of a distinguished M.P. during a damaging speech from the opposite side of the House.

Alleyn said: "And we still don't know when Miss Gainsford left the Greenroom."

"Oh, *lawks!*" Parry ejaculated. "This is *too* tiresome. J.G., you looked in at the Greenroom door when we came back for the curtain-call, don't you remember? Was she there then? Were you there then, Gay darling?"

Gay opened her mouth to speak but J.G. said quickly: "Yes, of course I did. Stupid of me to forget. Gay was sound asleep in the armchair, Mr. Alleyn. I didn't disturb her." He passed his right hand over his beautifully groomed head. "It's a most extraordinary thing," he said vexedly, "that I should have forgotten this. Of course she was asleep. Because later, when—well, when, in point of fact, the discovery had been made—I asked where Gay was and someone said she was still in the Greenroom, and I was naturally worried and went to fetch her. She was still asleep and the Greenroom, by that time, reeking with gas. I brought her back here."

"Have you any idea, Miss Gainsford," Alleyn asked, "about when you dropped off?"

"I was exhausted, Mr. Alleyn. Physically and emotionally exhausted. I still am."

"Was it, for instance, before the beginning of the last act?"

"N—n—no. No. Because J.G. came in to see how I was in the second interval. Didn't you, darling? And I was exhausted, wasn't I?"

"Yes, dear."

"And he gave me some aspirins and I took two. And I suppose, in that state of utter exhaustion, they worked. So I fell into a sleep—an exhausted sleep, it was."

"Naturally," Helena murmured with a glance at Alleyn, "it would be exhausted."

"Undoubtedly," said Jacko, "it was exhausted."

"Well, it was," said Gay crossly. "Because I was. Utterly."

"Did anyone else beside Mr. Darcey go into the Greenroom during the second interval?"

Gay looked quickly at J.G. "Honestly," she said, "I'm so muddled about times it really isn't safe to ask me. I'm sure to be wrong."

"Mr. Darcey?"

"No," J.G. said.

"Well, my dearest J.G.," Parry said, "I couldn't be more reluctant to keep popping in like one of the Eumenides in that utterly incomprehensible play, but I do assure you that you're at fault here. Ben went into the Greenroom in the second interval."

"Dear Heaven!" Helena said, on a note of desperation. "What has happened to us all!"

"I'm terribly sorry, Helena darling," Parry said, and sounded it.

"But why should you be sorry? Why shouldn't Ben go and see his niece in the interval? He played the whole of the third act afterwards. Of course you should say so, Parry, if you know what you're talking about. Shouldn't he, Adam? Shouldn't he, Mr. Alleyn?"

Poole was looking with a sort of incredulous astonishment at Darcey. "I think he should," he said slowly.

"And you, Mr. Darcey?" asked Alleyn.

"All right, Parry," said J.G., "go on."

"There's not much more to be said, and anyway I don't suppose it matters. It was before they'd called the third act. Helena and Adam and Martyn had gone out. They begin the act. I come on a bit later and Ben after me and J.G. later still. I wanted to see how the show was going and I was on my way in the passage when Ben came out of his room and went into the Greenroom next door. The act was called soon after that."

"Did you speak to him?" Alleyn asked.

"I did not," said Parry with some emphasis. "I merely went out to the stage and joined Jacko and the two dressers and the call-boy, who were watching from the Prompt side, and Clem."

"That's right," Clem Smith said. "I remember telling you all to keep away from the bunches. The boy called J.G. and Ben about five minutes later."

"Were you still in the Greenroom when you were called, Mr. Darcey?"

"Yes."

"With Mr. Bennington?"

"He'd gone to his room."

"Not for the life of me," Helena said wearily, "can I see why you had to be so mysterious, J.G."

"Perhaps," Alleyn said, "the reason is in your left trousers pocket, Mr. Darcey."

J.G. didn't take his hand out of his pocket. He stood up and addressed himself directly to Alleyn.

"May I speak to you privately?" he asked.

"Of course," Alleyn said. "Shall we go to the Greenroom?"

iii

In the Greenroom and in the presence of Alleyn and of Fox, who had joined them there, J. G. Darcey took his left hand out of his trousers pocket and extended it palm downwards for their inspection. It was a well-shaped and well-kept hand but the knuckles were grazed. A trace of blood had seeped out round the greasepaint and powder which had been daubed over the raw skin.

"I suppose I've behaved very stupidly," he said. "But I hoped there would be no need for this to come out. It has no bearing whatever on his death."

"In that case," Alleyn said, "it will not be brought out. But you'll do well to be frank."

"I dare say," said J.G. wryly.

"There's a bruise on the deceased's jaw on the right side that could well have been caused by that straight left Mr. Poole talked about. Now, we can of course determine whether make-up from your left fist is mixed with Bennington's own make-up over this bruise. If you tell me you didn't let drive at him we'll make this experiment."

"I assure you that you don't need to do any such thing. I'll willingly admit that I hit him," J.G. said with a shudder.

"And also why you hit him?"

"Oh, yes, if I can. If I can," he repeated and pressed his hand to his eyes. "D'you mind if we sit down, Alleyn? I'm a bit tired."

"Do."

J.G. sat in the leather armchair where Martyn, and, in her turn, Gay Gainsford had slept. In the dim light of the Greenroom his face looked wan and shadowed. "Not the chicken I was," he said, and it was an admission actors do not love to make.

Alleyn faced him. Fox sat down behind him, flattened his note-book on the table and placed his spectacles across his nose. There was something cosy about Fox when he took notes. Alleyn remembered absently that his wife had once observed that Mr. Fox was a cross between a bear and a baby and exhibited the most pleasing traits of both creatures.

The masked light above Jacko's sketch of Adam Poole shone down upon it, and it thus was given considerable emphasis in an otherwise shadowed room.

"If you want a short statement," J.G. said, "I can give it to you in a sentence. I hit Ben on the jaw in this room during the second act wait. I didn't knock him out but he was so astonished he took himself off. I was a handy amateur welter-weight in my young days but it must be twenty years or more since I put up my hands. I must say I rather enjoyed it."

"What sort of condition was he in?"

"Damned unpleasant. Oh, you mean drunk or sober? I should say ugly-drunk. Ben was a soak. I've never seen him incapacitated, but really I've hardly ever seen him stone-cold either. He was in his second degree of drunkenness: offensive, outrageous and incalculable. He'd behaved atrociously throughout the first and second acts."

"In what way?"

"As only a clever actor with too much drink in him can behave. Scoring off other people. Playing for cheap laughs. Doing unrehearsed bits of business that made nonsense of the production. Upon my word," said J.G. thoughtfully, "I wonder Adam or the Doctor or poor little Parry, if he'd had the guts, didn't get in first and give him what he deserved. A perfectly bloody fellow."

"Was it because of his performance that you hit him?"

J.G. looked at his finger-nails and seemed to ponder. "No," he said at last. "Or not directly. If I thought you'd believe me I'd say yes, but no doubt you'll talk to her and she's so upset anyway—"

"You mean Miss Gainsford?"

"Yes," said J.G. with the oddest air of pride and embarrassment. "I mean Gay."

"Was it on her account you dotted him one?"

"It was. He was damned offensive."

"I'm sorry," Alleyn said, "but you'll realize that we do want to be told a little more than that about it."

"I suppose so." He clasped his hands and examined his bruised knuckles. "Although I find it extremely difficult and unpleasant to go into the wretched business. It's only because I hope you'll let Gay off, as far as possible, if you know the whole story. That's why I asked to see you alone." He slewed round and looked discontentedly at Fox.

"Inspector Fox," Alleyn said, "is almost pathologically discreet."

"Glad to hear it. Well, as you've heard, I'd managed to get hold of a bottle of aspirins and I brought them to her, here, in the second interval. Gay was sitting in this chair. She was still terribly upset. Crying. I don't know if you've realized why she didn't go on for the part?"

"No. I'd be glad to have the whole story."

J.G. embarked on it, with obvious reluctance, but as he talked his hesitancy lessened and he even seemed to find some kind of ease in speaking. He described Gay's part and her struggle at rehearsals. It was clear that, however unwillingly, he shared the general opinion of her limited talent. "She'd have given a reasonable show," he said, "if she'd been given a reasonable chance but from the beginning the part got her down. She's a natural ingenue and this thing's really 'character.' It was bad casting. Adam kept the Doctor at bay as much as possible but she knew what he thought. She didn't *want* the part. She was happy where she was in repertory but Ben dragged her in. He saw himself as a sort of fairy-godfather-uncle and when she found the part difficult he turned obstinate and wouldn't let her throw it in. Out of vanity really. He was very vain. She's a frail little thing, you know, all heart and sensitivity, and between them they've brought her to the edge of a breakdown. It didn't help matters when Miss Martyn Tarne appeared out of a clear sky, first as Helena Hamilton's dresser and then as Gay's understudy and then—mysteriously, as some of the cast, Ben in particular, thought—as Adam's distant cousin. You noticed the uncanny resemblance but you may not know the part in the play requires it. That was the last straw for Gay. She'd been ill with nerves and fright and to-night she cracked up completely and wouldn't—couldn't go on. When I saw her in the first interval she was a bit quieter but in the second act little Miss Tarne did very well indeed. Quite startling, it was. Incidentally, I suppose her success infuriated Ben. And Gay heard everybody raving about her as they came off. Naturally that upset her again. So she was in tears when I came in."

He leant forward and rested his head in his hands. His voice was less distinct. "I'm fond of her," he said. "She's got used to me being about. When I came in she ran to me and— I needn't go into the way I felt. There's no explaining these things. She was sobbing in my arms, poor bird, and God knows my heart had turned over. Ben came in. He went for her like a pickpocket. He was crazy. I tried to shut him up. He didn't make a noise—I don't mean that—matter of fact what he said streamed out of him in a whisper. He was quite off his head and began talking about Helena—about his wife. He used straight-out obscenities. There'd been an episode in the afternoon and— well, he used the sort of generalization that Lear and Othello and Leontes use, if you remember your Shakespere."

"Yes."

"Gay was still clinging to me and he began to talk the same sort of stuff about her. I'm not going into details. I put her away from me and quite deliberately gave him what was coming to him. I don't remember what I said. I don't think any of us said anything. So he went out nursing his jaw and they called me for the last act and I went out too. During this last act, when we were on together, I could see the bruise coming out under his make-up."

"What was his general behaviour like during the final act?"

"As far as I was concerned he behaved in the way people do when they play opposite someone they've had a row with off-stage. He didn't look me in the eye. He looked at my forehead or ears. It doesn't show from the front. He played fairly soundly until poor Parry got out of position. Parry is his butt in the piece, but of course what Ben did was outrageous. He stuck out his foot as Parry moved and brought him down. That was not long before his own exit. I never saw him again after that until he was carried out. That's all. I don't know if you've believed me but I hope you'll let Gay off any more of this stuff."

Alleyn didn't answer. He looked at the young-old actor for a moment. J.G. was lighting a cigarette with that trained economy and grace of movement that were part of his stock-in-trade. His head was stooped, and Alleyn saw how carefully the silver hair had been distributed over the scalp. The hands were slightly tremulous. How old was J.G.? Fifty? Fifty-five? Sixty? Was he the victim of that Indian Summer that can so unmercifully visit an ageing man?

"It's the very devil, in these cases," Alleyn said, "how one has to plug away at everyone in turn. Not that it helps to say so. There's one more question that I'm afraid you won't enjoy at all. Can you tell me more specifically what Bennington said about—I think you called it an episode—of the afternoon, in which his wife was concerned?"

"No, by God, I can't," said J.G. hotly.

"He spoke about it in front of Miss Gainsford, didn't he?"

"You can't possibly ask Gay about it. It's out of the question."

"Not, I'm afraid, for an investigating officer," said Alleyn, who thought that J.G.'s delicacy, if delicacy were in question, was possibly a good deal more sensitive than Miss Gainsford's. "Do you suppose Bennington talked about this episode to other people?"

"In the condition he was in I should think it possible."

"Well," Alleyn said, "we shall have to find out."

"See here, Alleyn. What happened, if he spoke the truth, was something entirely between himself and his wife and it's on her account that I can't repeat what he said. You know she and Poole were on-stage at the crucial time and that there's no sense in thinking of motive, if that's what you're after, where they are concerned."

Alleyn said: "This episode might constitute a motive for suicide, however."

J.G. looked up quickly. "Suicide? But—why?"

"Shame?" Alleyn suggested. "Self-loathing if he sobered up after you hit him and took stock of himself? I imagine they've been virtually separated for some time."

"I see you have a talent," said J.G., "for reading between the lines."

"Let us rather call it an ugly little knack. Thank you, Mr. Darcey, I don't think I need bother you any more for the moment."

J.G. went slowly to the door. He hesitated for a moment and then said: "If you're looking for motive, Alleyn, you'll find it in a sort of way all over the place. He wasn't a likeable chap and he'd antagonized everyone. Even poor little Parry came off breathing revenge after the way he'd been handled, but, my God, actors do that kind of thing only too often. Feeling runs high, you know, on first nights."

"So it would seem."

"Can I take that child home?"

"I'm sorry," Alleyn said, "not yet. Not just yet."

iv

"Well," Alleyn said when J.G. had gone, "what have you got at your end of the table, Br'er Fox?"

Fox turned back the pages of his note-book.

"What you might call negative evidence, on the whole, Mr. Alleyn. Clearance for the understudies, who watched the show from the back of the circle and then went home. Clearance for the two dressers (male), the stage-manager and his assistant, the stage-hands and the night-watchman. They were all watching the play or on their jobs. On statements taken independently, they clear each other."

"That's something."

"No female dresser," Mr. Fox observed. "Which seems odd."

"Miss Tarne was the sole female dresser and she's been promoted over-night to what I believe I should call starletdom. Which in itself seems to me to be a rum go. I've always imagined female dressers to be cups-of-tea in alpaca aprons and not embryo actresses. I don't think Miss Tarne could have done the job, but she comes into the picture as the supplanter of Uncle Ben's dear little niece, whom I find an extremely irritating ass with a certain amount of low cunning. Miss Tarne, on the other hand, seems pleasant and intelligent and looks nice. You must allow me my prejudices, Br'er Fox."

"She's Mr. Poole's third cousin or something."

"The case reeks with obscure relationships—blood, marital and illicit, as far as one can see. Did you get anything from Bennington's dresser?"

"Nothing much," said Fox, sighing. "It seems the deceased didn't like him to hang about on account of being a secret drinker. He was in the dressing-room up to about seven and was then told to go and see if he could be of any use to the other gentlemen, and not to come back till the first interval when the deceased changed his clothes. I must say that chap earns his wages pretty easily. As far as I could make out the rest of his duties for the night consisted in tearing off chunks of cotton-wool for the deceased to do up his face with. I checked his visits to the dressing-room by that. The last time he looked in was after the deceased went on the stage in the third act. He cleared away the used cotton-wool and powdered a clean bit. In the normal course of events I suppose he'd have put Mr. Bennington into the fancy dress he was going to wear to the ball and then gone home quite worn out."

"Was he at all talkative?"

"Not got enough energy, Mr. Alleyn. Nothing to say for himself barring the opinion that deceased was almost on the D.T. mark. The other dresser, Cringle, seems a bright little chap. He just works for Mr. Poole."

"Have you let them go?"

"Yes, sir, I have. And the stage-hands. We can look them out again if we want them, but for the moment I think we've just about cleaned them up. I've let the assistant stage-manager—A.S.M. they call him—get away, too. Wife's expecting any time and he never left the prompting book."

"That reduces the mixed bag a bit. You've been through all the rooms, of course, but before we do anything else, Br'er Fox, let's have a prowl."

They went into the passage. Fox jerked his thumb at Bennington's room. "Gibson's doing a fly-crawl in there," he said. "If there's anything, he'll find it. That dresser-chap didn't clear anything up except his used powder-puffs."

They passed Bennington's room and went into Parry Percival's, next door. Here they found Detective-Sergeants Thompson and Bailey, the one a photographic and the other a finger-print expert. They were packing up their gear.

"Well, Bailey?" Alleyn asked.

Bailey looked morosely at his superior. "It's there all right, sir," he said grudgingly. "Complete prints, very near, and a check-up all over the shop."

"What about next door?"

"Deceased's room, sir? His prints on the wing-tap and the tube. Trace of red greasepaint on the rubber connection at the end of the tube. Matches paint on deceased's lips."

"Very painstaking," said Alleyn. "Have you tried the experiment?"

"Seeing the fires are back-to-back, sir," Fox said, "we have. Sergeant Gibson blew down this tube and deceased's fire went out. As in former case."

"Well," Alleyn said, "there you are. Personally I don't believe a word of it, either way." He looked, without interest, at the telegrams stuck round the frame of Parry's looking-glass and at his costume for the ball. "*Very* fancy," he muttered. "Who's in the next room?"

"Mr. J. G. Darcey," said Thompson.

They went into J.G.'s room, which was neat and impersonal in character and contained nothing, it seemed, of interest, unless a photograph of Miss Gainsford looking *insouciante* could be so regarded.

In the last room on this side of the passage they saw the electric sewing-machine, some rough sketches, scraps of material and other evidences of Martyn's sewing-party for Jacko. Alleyn glanced round it, crossed the passage and looked into the empty room opposite. "Dismal little cells when they're unoccupied, aren't they?" he said, and moved on to Gay Gainsford's room.

He stood there, his hands in his pockets, with Fox at his elbow. "This one suffers from the fashionable complaint, Fox," he said. "Schizophrenia. It's got a split personality. On my left a rather too-smart overcoat, a frisky hat, chi-chi gloves, a pansy purse-bag, a large bottle of one of the less reputable scents, a gaggle of mascots, a bouquet from the management and orchids from—who do you suppose?" He turned over the card. "Yes. Alas, yes, with love and a thousand good wishes from her devoted J.G. On my right a well-worn and modest little topcoat, a pair of carefully tended shoes and gloves that remind one of the White Rabbit, a grey skirt and beret and a yellow jumper. A hand-bag that contains, I'm sure, one of those rather heartrending little purses and—what else?" He explored the bag. "A New Zealand passport issued this year in which one finds Miss Tarne is nineteen years old and an actress. So the dresser's job was—what? The result of an appeal to the celebrated third cousin? But why not give her the understudy at once? She's fantastically like him and I'll be sworn he's mightily catched with her. What's more, even old Darcey says she's a damn good actress." He turned the leaves of the passport. "She only arrived in England seventeen days ago. Can that account for the oddness of the set-up? Anyway, I don't suppose it matters. Let's go next door, shall we?"

Cringle had left Poole's room in exquisite order. Telegrams were pinned in rows on the walls. A towel was spread over the make-up. A cigarette had been half-extracted from a packet and a match left ready on the top of its box. A framed photograph of Helena Hamilton stood near the glass. Beside it a tiny clock with a gay face ticked feverishly. It stood on a card. Alleyn moved it delicately and read the inscription. *From Helena. To-night and to-morrow and always—bless you.*

"The standard for first-night keepsakes seems to be set at a high level," Alleyn muttered. "This is a French clock, Fox, with a Sèvres face encircled with garnets. What do you suppose the gentleman gave the lady?"

"Would a tiara be common?" asked Fox.

"Let's go next door and see."

Helena's room smelt and looked like a conservatory. A table had been brought in to carry the flowers. Jacko had set out the inevitable telegrams and had hung up the dresses under their dust sheets.

"Here we are," Alleyn said. "A sort of jeroboam of the most expensive scent on the market. Price, I should say, round about thirty pounds. 'From Adam.' Why don't you give me presents when we solve a petty larceny, Foxkin? Now, I may be fanciful, but this looks to me like the gift of a man who's at his wit's end and plumps for the expensive, the easy and the obvious. Here's something entirely different. Look at this, Fox."

It was a necklace of six wooden medallions strung between jade rings. Each plaque was most delicately carved in the likeness of a head in profile and each head was a portrait of one of the company of players. The card bore the date and the inscription: *From J.*

"Must have taken a long time to do," observed Fox. "That'll be the foreign gentleman's work, no doubt. Mr. Doré."

"No doubt. I wonder if love's labour has been altogether lost," said Alleyn. "I hope she appreciates it."

He took up the leather case with its two photographs of Poole. "He's a remarkable looking chap," he said. "If there's anything to be made of faces in terms of character, and I still like to pretend there is, what's to be made of this one? It's what they call a heart-shaped face, broad across the eyes with a firmly moulded chin and a generous but delicate mouth. Reminds one of a Holbein drawing. Doré's sketch in the Greenroom is damn good. Doré crops up all over the place, doesn't he? Designs their fancy dresses. Paints their faces, in a double sense. Does their décor and, with complete self-effacement, loves their leading lady."

"Do you reckon?"

"I do indeed, Br'er Fox," Alleyn said and rubbed his nose vexedly. "However. Gibson's done all the usual things in these rooms, I suppose?"

"Yes, Mr. Alleyn. Pockets, suitcases and boxes. Nothing to show for it."

"We can let them come home to roost fairly soon, then. We'll start now to see them separately. Blast! I suppose I'll have to begin with checking Darcey's statement with the Gainsford. She gives me the horrors, that young woman."

"Shall I see her, Mr. Alleyn?"

"You can stay and take your notes. I'll see her in the Greenroom. No, wait a bit. You stay with the others, Fox, and send young Lamprey along with her. And you might try again if you can dig up anything that sounds at all off-key with Bennington over the last few days. Anything that distressed or excited him."

"He seems to have been rather easily excited."

"He does, doesn't he, but you never know. I don't believe it was suicide, Fox, and I'm not yet satisfied that we've unearthed anything that's good enough for a motive for murder. Trip away, Foxkin. Ply your craft."

Fox went out sedately. Alleyn crossed the passage and opened the door of Bennington's room. Sergeant Gibson was discovered, squatting on his haunches before the dead gas fire.

"Anything?" Alleyn asked.

"There's this bit of a stain that looks like a scorch on the hearth, sir."

"Yes, I saw that. Any deposit?"

"We-ll—"

"We may have to try."

"The powder pads deceased's dresser cleared away were in the rubbish bin on the stage where he said he put them. Nothing else in the bin. There's this burnt paper on the floor, but it's in small flakes—powder almost."

"All right. Seal the room when you've finished. And Gibson, don't let the mortuary van go without telling me."

"Very good, sir."

Alleyn returned to the Greenroom. He heard Miss Gainsford approaching under the wing of P. C. Lamprey. She spoke in a high grand voice that seemed to come out of a drawing-room comedy of the twenties.

"I think you're *too* intrepid," she was saying, "to start from rock bottom like this. It must be so devastatingly boring for you, though I will say it's rather a comfort to think one is in the hands of, to coin a phrase, a gent. Two gents, in fact."

"Chief Inspector Alleyn," said P. C. Lamprey, "is in the Greenroom I think, Miss."

"My dear, you do it quite marvellously. You ought, again to coin a phrase, to go on the stage."

Evidently Miss Gainsford lingered in the passage. Alleyn heard his subordinate murmur: "Shall I go first?" His regulation boots clumped firmly to the door, which he now opened.

"Will you see Miss Gainsford, sir?" asked P. C. Lamprey, who was pink in the face.

"All right, Mike," Alleyn said. "Show her in and take notes."

"Will you come this way, Miss?"

Miss Gainsford made her entrance with a Mayfairish gallantry that was singularly dated. Alleyn wondered if she had decided that her first reading of her new role was mistaken. "She's abandoned the brave little woman for the suffering *mondaine* who goes down with an epigram," he thought, and sure enough, Miss Gainsford addressed herself to him with staccato utterance and brittle high-handedness.

"Ought one to be terribly flattered because one is the first to be grilled?" she asked. "Or is it a sinister little hint that one is top of the suspect list?"

"We have to start somewhere," Alleyn said. "I thought it might be convenient to see you first. Will you sit down, Miss Gainsford?"

She did so elaborately, gave herself a cigarette, and turned to P. C. Lamprey. "May one ask The Force for a light," she asked, "or would that be against the rules?"

Alleyn lit her cigarette while his unhappy subordinate retired to the table. She turned in her chair to watch him. "Is he going to take me down and use it all in evidence against me?" she asked. Her nostrils dilated, she raised her chin and added jerkily, "That's what's called the Usual Warning, isn't it?"

"A warning is given in police practice," Alleyn said as woodenly as possible, "if there is any chance that the person under interrogation will make a statement that is damaging to himself. Lamprey will note down this interview and, if it seems advisable, you will be asked later on to give a signed statement."

"If that was meant to be reassuring," said Miss Gainsford, "I can't have heard it properly. Could we get cracking?"

"Certainly. Miss Gainsford, you were in the Greenroom throughout the performance. During the last interval you were visited by Mr. J. G. Darcey and by your uncle. Do you agree that as the result of something the deceased said, Mr. Darcey hit him on the jaw?"

She said: "Wasn't it too embarrassing! I mean the Gorgeous Primitive

504   THREE-ACT SPECIAL

Beast is one thing, but one old gentleman banging another about is so utterly another. I'm afraid I didn't put that very clearly."

"You agree that Mr. Darcey hit Mr. Bennington?"

"But madly. Like a sledge-hammer. I found it so difficult to know what to say. There just seemed to be no clue to further conversation."

"It is the conversation before rather than after the blow that I should like to hear about, if you please."

Alleyn had turned away from her and was looking at Jacko's portrait of Poole. He waited for some moments before she said sharply: "I suppose you think because I talk like this about it I've got no feeling. You couldn't be more at fault." It was as if she called his attention to her performance.

He said, without turning: "I assure you I hadn't given it a thought. What did your uncle say that angered Mr. Darcey?"

"He was upset," she said sulkily, "because I was ill and couldn't play."

"Hardly an occasion for hitting him."

"J.G. is very sensitive about me. He treats me like a piece of china."

"Which is more than he did for your uncle, it seems."

"Uncle Ben talked rather wildly." Miss Gainsford seemed to grope for her poise and made a half-hearted return to her brittle manner. "Let's face it," she said, "he was stinking, poor pet."

"You mean he was drunk?"

"Yes, I do."

"And abusive?"

"I didn't care. I understood him."

"Did he talk about Miss Hamilton?"

"Obviously J.G.'s already told you he did, so why ask me?"

"We like to get confirmation of statements."

"Well, you tell me what he said and I'll see about confirming it."

For the first time Alleyn looked at her. She wore an expression of rather frightened impertinence. "I'm afraid," he said, "that won't quite do. I'm sure you're very anxious to get away from the theatre, Miss Gainsford, and we've still a lot of work before us. If you will give me your account of this conversation I shall be glad to hear it; if you prefer not to do so I'll take note of your refusal and keep you no longer."

She gaped slightly, attempted a laugh and seemed to gather up the rags of her impersonation.

"Oh, but I'll tell you," she said. "Why not? It's only that there's so pathetically little to tell. I can't help feeling darling Aunty—she likes me to call her Helena—was *too* Pinero and Galsworthy about it. It appears that poorest Uncle Ben came in from his club and found her in a suitable setting and—well, there you are, and—well, really, even after all these years of segregation, you couldn't call it a seduction. Or could you? Anyway, she chose to treat it as such and raised the most piercing hue-and-cry and he went all primitive and when he came in here he was evidently in the throes of a sort of hangover, and seeing J.G. was being rather sweet to me he put a sinister interpretation on it and described the whole incident and was rather rude about women generally and me and Aunty in particular. And J.G. took a gloomy view of his attitude and hit him. And, I mean, taking it by and large one can't help feeling: *what* a song and dance about nothing in particular. Is that all you wanted to know?"

"Do you think any other members of the company know of all this?"

She looked genuinely surprised. "Oh yes," she said. "Adam and Jacko, anyway. I mean Uncle Ben appeared to have a sort of nation-wide hook-up idea about it but even if *he* didn't mention it, *she'd* naturally tell Adam, wouldn't you think? And Jacko, because everybody tells Jacko everything. And he was doing dresser for her. Yes, I'd certainly think she'd tell Jacko."

"I see. Thank you, Miss Gainsford. That's all."

"Really?" She was on her feet. "I can go home?"

Alleyn answered her as he had answered J.G. "I'm sorry, not yet. Not just yet."

P. C. Lamprey opened the door. Inevitably, she paused on the threshold. "Never tell *me* there's nothing in atmosphere," she said. "I *knew* when I came into this theatre. As if the very walls screamed it at me. I *knew.*"

She went out.

"Tell me, Mike," Alleyn said, "are many young women of your generation like that?"

"Well, no, sir. She's what one might call a composite picture, don't you think?"

"I do, indeed. And I fancy she's got her genres a bit confused."

"She tells me she's been playing in *Private Lives, The Second Mrs. Tanqueray* and *Sleeping Partners* in the provinces."

"That may account for it," said Alleyn.

An agitated voice—Parry Percival's—was raised in the passage, to be answered in a more subdued manner by Sergeant Gibson's.

"Go and see what it is, Mike," Alleyn said.

But before Lamprey could reach the door it was flung open and Parry burst in, slamming it in Gibson's affronted face. He addressed himself instantly and breathlessly to Alleyn.

"I'm sorry," he said, "but I've just remembered something. I've been so *hideously* upset, I just simply never gave it a thought. It was when I smelt gas. When I went back to my room, I smelt gas and I turned off my fire. I ought to have told you. I've just realized."

"I think perhaps what you have just realized," Alleyn said, "is the probability of our testing your gas fire for finger-prints and finding your own."

CHAPTER IX

The Shadow of Otto Brod

Parry stood inside the door and pinched his lips as if he realized they were white and hoped to restore their colour.

"I don't know anything about finger-prints," he said. "I never read about crime. I don't know anything about it. When I came off after my final exit I went to my room. I was just going back for the call when I smelt gas. We're all nervous about gas in this theatre and anyway the room was frightfully hot. I turned the thing off. That's all."

"This was after Bennington tripped you up?"

"I've told you. It was after my last exit and before the call. It wasn't—"

He walked forward very slowly and sat down in front of Alleyn. "You can't think that sort of thing about me," he said, and sounded as if he was moved more by astonishment than by any other emotion. "My God, *look* at me. I'm so hopelessly harmless. I'm not vicious. I'm not even odd. I'm just harmless."

"Why didn't you tell me at once that you noticed the smell of gas?"

"Because, as I've tried to suggest, I'm no good at this sort of thing. The Doctor got me all upset and in any case the whole show was so unspeakable." He stared at Alleyn and, as if that explained everything, said: "I saw him. I saw him when they carried him out. I've never been much good about dead people. In the blitz I sort of managed but I never got used to it."

"Was the smell of gas very strong in your room?"

"No. Not strong at all. But in this theatre—we were all thinking about that other time, and I just thought it was too bad of the management to have anything faulty in the system considering the history of the place. I don't know that I thought anything more than that: I smelt it and remembered, and got a spasm of the horrors. Then I felt angry at being given a shock and then I turned my fire off and went out. It was rather like not looking at the new moon through glass. You don't really believe it can do anything but you avoid it. I forgot all about the gas as soon as I got on-stage. I didn't give it another thought until I smelt it again during the Doctor's speech."

"Yes, I see."

"You do, really, don't you? After all, suppose I—suppose I had thought I'd copy that other awful thing—well, I'd scarcely be fool enough to leave my finger-prints on the tap, would I?"

"But you tell me," Alleyn said, not making too much of it, "that you don't know anything about finger-prints."

"God!" Parry whispered, staring at him. "You do frighten me. It's not fair. You frighten me."

"Believe me, there's no need for an innocent man to be frightened."

"How can you be so sure of yourselves? Do you never make mistakes?"

"We do indeed. But not," Alleyn said, "in the end. Not nowadays on these sorts of cases."

"What do you mean these sorts of cases!"

"Why, I mean on what may turn out to be a capital charge."

"I can't believe it!" Parry cried out. "I shall never believe it. We're not like that. We're kind, rather simple people. We wear our hearts on our sleeves. We're not complicated enough to kill each other."

Alleyn said with a smile: "You're quite complicated enough for us at the moment. Is there anything else you've remembered that you think perhaps you ought to tell me about?"

Parry shook his head and dragged himself to his feet. Alleyn saw, as Martyn had seen before him, that he was not an exceedingly young man. "No," he said. "There's nothing I can think of."

"You may go to your dressing-room now, if you'd like to change into— what should I say?—into plain clothes?"

"Thank you. I simply loathe the thought of my room after all this but I shall be glad to change."

"Do you mind if Lamprey does a routine search before you go? We'll ask this of all of you."

Parry showed the whites of his eyes but said at once: "Why should I mind?"

Alleyn nodded to young Lamprey, who advanced upon Parry with an apologetic smile.

"It's a painless extraction, sir," he said.

Parry raised his arms in a curve with his white hands held like a dancer's above his head. There was a silence and a swift, efficient exploration. "Thank you so much, sir," said Mike Lamprey. "Cigarette case, lighter and handkerchief, Mr. Alleyn."

"Right. Take Mr. Percival along to his room, will you?"

Parry said: "There couldn't be a more fruitless question, but it would be nice to know, one way or the other, if you have believed me."

"There couldn't be a more unorthodox answer," Alleyn rejoined, "but at the moment I see no reason to disbelieve you, Mr. Percival."

When Lamprey came back he found his senior officer looking wistfully at his pipe and whistling under his breath.

"Mike," Alleyn said, "the nastiest cases in our game are very often the simplest. There's something sticking out under my nose in this theatre and I can't see it. I know it's there because of another thing that, Lord pity us all, Fox and I *can* see."

"Really, sir? Am I allowed to ask what it is?"

"You're getting on in the service, now. What have you spotted on your own account?"

"Is it something to do with Bennington's behaviour, sir?"

"It is indeed. If a man's going to commit suicide, Mike, and his face is made up to look loathsome, what does he do about it? If he's a vain man (and Bennington appears to have had his share of professional vanity), if he minds about the appearance of his own corpse, he cleans off the grease-paint. If he doesn't give a damn, he leaves it as it is. But with time running short, he does *not* carefully and heavily powder his unbecoming make-up for all the world as if he meant to go on and take his curtain-call with the rest of them. Now, does he?"

"Well, no sir," said Mike. "If you put it like that, I don't believe he does."

ii

By half past twelve most of the company on the stage seemed to be asleep or dozing. Dr. Rutherford on his couch occasionally lapsed into bouts of snoring from which he would rouse a little, groan, take snuff and then settle down again. Helena lay in a deep chair with her feet on a stool. Her eyes were closed but Martyn thought that if she slept it was but lightly. Clem had made himself a bed of some old curtains and was curled up on it be-yond the twisting stairway. Jacko, having tucked Helena up in her fur coat, settled himself on the stage beside her, dozing, Martyn thought, like some eccentric watch-dog at his post. After J.G. silently returned from the Green-room, Gay Gainsford was summoned and in her turn came back—not silently, but with some attempt at conversation. In the presence of the watchful Mr. Fox this soon petered out. Presently she, too, fell to nodding. Immediately after her return Parry Percival suddenly made an inarticulate ejaculation and, before Fox could move, darted off the stage. Sergeant Gibson was heard to accost him in the passage. Fox remained where he was and there was another long silence.

Adam Poole and Martyn looked into each other's faces. He crossed the stage to where she sat, on the left side, which was the farthest removed from Fox. He pulled up a small chair and sat facing her.

"Kate," he muttered, "I'm so sorry about all this. There are hare's-foot shadows under your eyes, your mouth droops, your hands are anxious and your hair is limp, though not at all unbecoming. You should be sound asleep in Jacko's garret under the stars and there should be the sound of applause in your dreams. Really, it's too bad."

Martyn said: "It's nice of you to think so but you have other things to consider."

"I'm glad to have my thoughts interrupted."

"Then I still have my uses."

"You can see that chunk of a man over there. Is he watching us?"

"Yes. With an air of absent-mindedness which I'm not at all inclined to misunderstand."

"I don't think he can hear us, though it's a pity my diction is so good. If I take your hand perhaps he'll suppose I'm making love to you and feel some slight constabular delicacy."

"I hardly think so," Martyn whispered, and tried to make nothing of his lips against her palm.

"Will you believe, Kate, that I am not in the habit of making passes at young ladies in my company?"

Martyn found herself looking at the back of Helena's chair.

"Oh yes," Poole said. "There's that, too. I make no bones about that. It's another and a long and a fading story. On both parts. Fading on both parts, Kate. I have been very much honoured."

"I can't help feeling this scene is being played at the wrong time, in the wrong place and before the wrong audience. And I doubt," Martyn said, not looking at him, "if it should be played at all."

"But I can't be mistaken. It has happened for us, Martyn. Hasn't it? Suddenly, preposterously, almost at first sight we blinked and looked again and there we were. Tell me it's happened. The bird under your wrist is so wildly agitated. Is that only because you are frightened?"

"I am frightened. I wanted to ask your advice and now you make it impossible."

"I'll give you my advice. There. Now you are alone again. But for the sake of the law's peace of mind as well as my own you must take a firm line about your blushing."

"It was something he said to me that morning," she murmured in the lowest voice she could command.

"Do you mean the morning when I first saw you?"

"I mean," Martyn said desperately, "the morning the photographs were taken. I had to go to his dressing-room."

"I remember very well. You came to mine too."

"He said something, then. He was very odd in his manner. They've asked us to try and remember anything at all unusual."

"Are you going to tell me what it was?"

In a few words and under her breath she did so.

Poole said: "Perhaps you should tell them. Yes, I think you should. In a moment I'll do something about it, but there's one thing more I must say to you. Do you know I'm glad this scene has been played so awkwardly— inaudible, huddled up, inauspicious and uneffective. Technically altogether bad. It gives it a kind of authority, I hope. Martyn, are you very much surprised? Please look at me."

She did as he asked and discovered an expression of such doubt and anxiety in his face that to her own astonishment she put her hand against his cheek and he held it there for a second. "God," he said, "what a thing to happen!" He got up abruptly and crossed the stage.

"Inspector," he said, "Miss Tarne has remembered an incident three days

old which we both think might possibly be of some help. What should we
do about it?"

The others stirred a little. J.G. opened his eyes.

Fox got up. "Thank you very much, sir," he said. "When Mr. Alleyn is
disengaged I'm sure he'll— Yes? What is it?"

P. C. Lamprey had come in. He delivered a message that the dressing-
rooms were now open for the use of their occupants. At the sound of his
brisk and loudish voice they all stirred. Helena and Darcey got to their feet.
Jacko sat up. Clem, Gay and Dr. Rutherford opened their eyes, listened to
the announcement and went to sleep again.

Fox said: "You can take this young lady along to the Chief in three minutes, Lamprey. Now, ladies and gentlemen, if you'd care to go to your rooms."

He shepherded Helena and Darcey through the door and looked back at
Poole. "What about you, sir?"

Poole, with his eyes on Martyn, said: "Yes, I'm coming." Fox waited
stolidly at the door for him and, after a moment's hesitation, Poole followed
the others. Fox went with them.

Mike Lamprey said: "We'll let them get settled, Miss Tarne, and then I'll
take you along to Mr. Alleyn. You must be getting very bored with all this
hanging about."

Martyn, whose emotional processes were in a state of chaos, replied with
a vague smile. She wondered disjointedly if constables of P. C. Lamprey's
class were a commonplace in the English Force. He glanced good-humouredly
at Gay and the three dozing men and evidently felt obliged to make further
conversation.

"I heard someone say," he began, "that you are a New Zealander. I was out
there as a small boy."

"Were you, really?" Martyn said, and wondered confusedly if he could
have been the son of a former governor-general.

"We had a place out there on a mountain. Mount Silver, it was. Would
that be anywhere near your part of the world?"

Something clicked in Martyn's memory. "Oh yes!" she said. "I've heard
about the Lampreys of Mount Silver, I'm sure, and—" Her recollection
clarified a little. "Yes, indeed," she added lamely.

"No doubt," said Mike with a cheerful laugh, "a legend of lunacy has
survived us. We came Home when I was about eight, and soon afterwards
my uncle happened to get murdered in our flat and Mr. Alleyn handled the
case. I thought at the time I'd like to go into the Force and the idea sort of
persisted. And there you are, you know. Potted autobiography. Shall we go
along and see if he's free?"

He escorted her down the passage to the Greenroom door, past Sergeant
Gibson, who seemed to be on guard there. Mike chatted freely as they went,
rather as if he were taking her into supper after a successful dance. The
star-bemused Martyn found herself brightly chatting back at him.

This social atmosphere was not entirely dispelled, she felt, by Alleyn himself, who received her rather as a distinguished surgeon might greet a patient.

"Come in, Miss Tarne," he said cordially. "I hear you've thought of something to tell us about this wretched business. Do sit down."

She sat in her old chair, facing the gas fire and with her back to the table. Only when she looked up involuntarily at the sketch of Adam Poole did she realize that young Lamprey had settled himself at the table and taken out a note-book. She could see his image reflected in the glass.

Inspector Fox came in and went quietly to the far end of the room, where he sat in a shadowed corner and appeared to consult his own note-book.

"Well," Alleyn said, "what's it all about?"

"You'll probably think it's about nothing," Martyn began, "and if you do I shall be sorry I've bothered you with it. But I thought—just in case—"

"You were perfectly right. Believe me, we are 'conditioned,' if that's the beastly word, to blind alleys. Let's have it."

"On my first morning in this theatre," Martyn said, "which was the day before yesterday . . . no, if it's past midnight, the day before that."

"Tuesday?"

"Yes. On that morning I went to Mr. Bennington's room to fetch Miss Hamilton's cigarette case. He was rather strange in his manner, but at first I thought that was because—I thought he'd noticed my likeness to Mr. Poole. He couldn't find the case and in hunting through the pockets of a jacket, he dropped a letter to the floor. I picked it up and he drew my attention to it in the oddest sort of way. I'd describe his manner almost as triumphant. He said something about autographs. I think he asked me if I collected autographs or autographed letters. He pointed to the envelope, which I still had in my hand, and said there was somebody who'd give a hell of a lot for that one. Those, I'm almost sure, were his exact words."

"Did you look at the letter?"

"Yes, I did, because of what he said. It was addressed to him and it had a foreign stamp on it. The writing was very bold and it seemed to me foreign-looking. I put it on the shelf face downwards and he drew my attention to it again by stabbing at it with his finger. The name of the sender was written on the back."

"Do you remember it?"

"Yes, I do, because of his insistence."

"Good girl," said Alleyn quietly.

"It was Otto Brod and the address was a theatre in Prague. I'm afraid I don't remember the name of the theatre or the street. I *ought* to remember the theatre. It was a French name, Théâtre de—something. Why can't I remember!"

"You haven't done badly. Was there something in the envelope?"

"Yes. It wasn't anything fat. One sheet of paper, I should think."

"And his manner was triumphant?"

"I thought so. He was just rather odd about it. He'd been drinking—brandy,

I thought—the tumbler was on the dressing-shelf and he made as if to put the flask behind his looking-glass."

"Did you think he was at all the worse for wear?"

"I wondered if it accounted for his queer behaviour."

"Can you tell me anything else he said? The whole conversation if you remember it."

Martyn thought back, and it seemed she had journeyed half a lifetime in three days. There was the room. There was J.G. going out and leaving her with Bennington, and there was Bennington staring at her and talking about the cigarette case. There was also something else, buried away behind her thoughts, of which the memory now returned. She was made miserable by it.

"He said, I think, something about the cigarette case. That he himself hadn't given it to Miss Hamilton."

"Did he say who gave it to her?"

"No," Martyn said, "I don't think he said that. Just that *he* didn't."

"And was his manner of saying this strange?"

"I thought his manner throughout was—uncomfortable and odd. He seemed to me to be a very unhappy man."

"Yet you used the word 'triumphant'?"

"There can be unhappy victories."

"True for you. There can, indeed. Tell me one thing more. Do you connect the two conversations? I mean, do you think what he said about the cigarette case had anything to do with what he said about the letter?"

"I should say nothing. Nothing at all."

"Oh Lord!" Alleyn said resignedly and called out: "Have you got all that, Mike?"

"Coming up the straight, sir."

"Put it into longhand, now, will you, and we'll ask Miss Tarne to have a look at it and see if she's been misrepresented. Do you mind waiting a minute or two, Miss Tarne? It'll save you coming back."

"No, of course not," said Martyn, whose ideas of police investigation were undergoing a private revolution. Alleyn offered her a cigarette and lit it for her. The consultation, she felt, was over, and the famous surgeon was putting his patient at her ease.

"I gather from Lamprey's far-reaching conversation that you are a New Zealander," he said. "If I may say so, you seem to have dropped out of a clear sky into your own success-story. Have you been long at the Vulcan, Miss Tarne?"

"A little over three days."

"Good Lord! And in that time you've migrated from dresser to what sounds like minor stardom. Success-story, indeed!"

"Yes, but—" Martyn hesitated. For the first time since she walked into the Vulcan she felt able to talk about herself. It didn't occur to her that it was odd for her confidant to be a police officer.

"It's all been very eccentric," she said. "I only reached England a little over a fortnight ago and my money was stolen in the ship, so I had to get some sort of job rather quickly."

"Did you report the theft to the police?"

"No. The purser said he didn't think it would do any good."

"So much," said Alleyn with a wry look, "for the police!"

"I'm sorry—" Martyn began and he said: "Never mind. It's not an uncommon attitude, I'm afraid. So you had a rather unhappy arrival. Lucky there was your cousin to come to your rescue."

"But—no—I mean—" Martyn felt herself blushing and plunged on. "That's just what I didn't want to do. I mean I didn't want to go to him at all. He didn't know of my existence. You see—"

It was part of Alleyn's professional equipment that something in his make-up invited confidence. Mr. Fox once said of his superior that he would be able to get himself worked up over the life-story of a mollusc, provided the narrative was obtained first-hand. He heard Martyn's story with the liveliest interest up to the point where she entered the theatre. He didn't seem to think it queer that she should have been anxious to conceal her relationship to Poole, or that she was stupid to avoid the Vulcan in her search for a job. She was describing her interview with Bob Grantley on Monday night when Sergeant Gibson's voice sounded in the passage. He tapped on the door and came in.

"Excuse me, sir," he said, "but could you see the night-watchman? He seems to think it's important."

He'd got as far as this when he was elbowed aside by Fred Badger, who came angrily into the room.

" 'Ere!" he said. "Are you the guv'nor of this 'owd'yerdo?"

"Yes," said Alleyn.

"Well, look. You can lay orf this young lady, see? No call to get nosey on account of what she done, see? I don't know nothink abaht the law, see, but I'm in charge 'ere of a night and what she done she done wiv my permission. Nah!"

"Just a moment—" Alleyn began and was roared down.

"Suppose it was an offence! What abaht it! She never done no 'arm. No offence taken where none was intended, that's correct, ain't it! Nah ven!"

"What," Alleyn said turning to Martyn, "is this about?"

"I'm afraid it's about me sleeping in the theatre that first night. I'd nowhere to go and it was very late. Mr. Badger very kindly—didn't turn me out."

"I see. Where did you sleep?"

"Here. In this chair."

"Like a charld," Fred Badger interposed. "Slep' like a charld all night. I looked in on me rahnds and seen 'er laying safe in the arms of Morpus. Innercent. And if anyone tells you different you can refer 'im to me. Badger's the name."

"All right, Badger."

"If you put me pot on with the management fer what I done, leaving 'er to lay—all right. Aht! Finish! There's better jobs rahnd the corner."

"Yes. All right. I don't think we'll take it up."

"Awright. Fair enough." He addressed himself to Martyn. "And what was mentioned between you and me in a friendly manner needn't be mentioned no more. Let bygones be bygones." He returned to Alleyn. "She's as innercent as a babe. Arst 'is nibs."

Alleyn waited for a moment and then said: "Thank you." Gibson succeeded in removing Fred Badger, but not before he had directed at Martyn that peculiar clicking sound of approval which is accompanied by a significant jerk of the head.

When he had gone Alleyn said: "I think I'd better ask you to interpret. What *was* his exquisite meaning?"

Martyn felt a dryness in her mouth. "I think," she said, "he's afraid he'll get into trouble for letting me sleep in here that night and I think he's afraid I'll get into trouble if I tell you that he showed me how the murder in the Jupiter case was accomplished."

"That seems a little far-fetched."

Martyn said rapidly: "I suppose it's idiotic of me to say this, but I'd rather say it. Mr. Bennington very naturally resented my luck in this theatre. He tackled me about it and he was pretty truculent. I expect the stage-hands have gossiped to Badger and he thinks you might—might—"

"Smell a motive?"

"Yes," said Martyn.

"Did Bennington threaten you?"

"I don't remember exactly what he said. His manner was threatening. He frightened me."

"Where did this happen?"

"Off-stage, during the first dress rehearsal."

"Was anyone present when he tackled you?"

The image of Poole rose in Martyn's memory. She saw him take Bennington by the arm and twist him away from her.

"There were people about," she said. "They were changing the set. I should think it very likely—I mean it was a very public sort of encounter."

He looked thoughtfully at her and she wondered if she had changed colour. "This," he said, "was before it was decided you were to play the part?"

"Oh, yes. That was only decided half an hour before the show went on."

"So it was. Did he do anything about this decision? Go for you again?"

"He didn't come near me until I'd finished. And knowing how much he must mind, I was grateful for that."

Alleyn said: "You've been very sensible to tell me this, Miss Tarne."

Martyn swallowed hard. "I don't know," she said, "that I would have told you if it hadn't been for Fred Badger."

"Ah, well," Alleyn said, "one mustn't expect too much. How about that statement, Mike?"

"Here we are, sir. I hope you can read my writing, Miss Tarne."

When she took the paper, Martyn found her hands were not steady. Alleyn moved away to the table with his subordinate. She sat down again and read the large schoolboyish writing. It was a short and accurate résumé of the incident of the letter from Prague.

"It's quite right," she said. "Am I to sign it?"

"If you please. There will be statements for most of the others to sign later on, but yours is so short I thought we might as well get it over now."

He gave her his pen and she went to the table and signed. P. C. Lamprey smiled reassuringly at her and escorted her to the door.

Alleyn said: "Thank you so much, Miss Tarne. Do you live far from here?"

"Not very far. A quarter of an hour's walk."

"I wish I could let you go home now but I don't quite like to do that. Something might crop up that we'd want to refer to you."

"Might it?"

"You never know," he said. "Anyway, you can change now." Lamprey opened the door and she went to the dressing-room.

When she had gone, Alleyn said: "What did you make of her, Mike?"

"I thought she was rather a sweetie-pie, sir," said P. C. Lamprey. Fox, in his disregarded corner, snorted loudly.

"That was all too obvious," said Alleyn. "Sweetness apart, did you find her truthful?"

"I'd have said so, sir, yes."

"What about you, Br'er Fox? Come out of cover and declare yourself."

Fox rose, removed his spectacles and advanced upon them. "There was something," he observed, "about that business of when deceased went for her."

"There was indeed. Not exactly lying, wouldn't you think, so much as leaving something out?"

"Particularly in respect of whether there was a witness."

"She had her back to you but she looked at this portrait of Adam Poole. I'd make a long bet Poole found Bennington slanging that child and ordered him off."

"Very possibly, Mr. Alleyn. He's sweet on the young lady. That's plain to see. *And* she on him."

"Good Lord!" Mike Lamprey ejaculated. "He must be forty! I'm sorry, sir."

Mr. Fox began a stately reproof but Alleyn said: "Go away, Mike. Go back to the stage. Wake Dr. Rutherford and ask him to come here. I want a change from actors."

iii

Dr. Rutherford, on his entry into the Greenroom, was a figure of high fantasy. For his greater ease in sleeping he had pulled his boiled shirt from its confinement and it dangled fore and aft like a crumpled tabard. Restrained only by his slackened braces, it formed a mask, Alleyn conjectured, for a free adjustment of the Doctor's trouser buttoning. He had removed his jacket and assumed an overcoat. His collar was released and his tie dangled on his bosom. His head was tousled and his face blotched.

He paused in the doorway while Lamprey announced him and then, with a dismissive gesture, addressed himself to Alleyn and Fox.

"Calling my officers about me in my branched velvet gown," he shouted, "having come from a day-bed where I left Miss Gainsford sleeping, I present myself as a brand for the constabular burning. What's cooking, my hearties?"

He stood there, puffing and blowing, and eyed them with an expression of extreme impertinence. If he had been an actor, Alleyn thought, he would have been cast, and cast ideally, for Falstaff. He fished under his shirt-tail, produced his snuff-box, and helped himself, with a parody of Regency deportment, to a generous pinch. "Speak!" he said. "Pronounce! Propound! I am all ears."

"I have nothing, I'm afraid, to propound," Alleyn said cheerfully, "and am therefore unable to pronounce. As for speaking, I hope you'll do most of that yourself, Dr. Rutherford. Will you sit down?"

Dr. Rutherford, with his usual precipitancy, hurled himself into the nearest armchair. As an afterthought he spread his shirt-tail with ridiculous finicking movements across his lap. "I am a thought down-gyved," he observed. "My points are untrussed. Forgive me."

"Tell me," Alleyn said. "Do you think Bennington was murdered?"

The Doctor opened his eyes very wide, folded his hands on his stomach, revolved his thumbs and said "No."

"No?"

"No."

"We do."

"Why?"

"I'll come to that when I'm quite sure you may be put into the impossible class."

"Am I a suspect, by all that's pettifogging?"

"Not if you can prove yourself otherwise."

"By God," said Dr. Rutherford deeply, "if I'd thought I could get away with it, be damned if I wouldn't have had a shot. He was an unconscionable rogue, was Ben."

"In what way?"

"In every way, by Janus. A drunkard. A wife-terrorist. An exhibitionist. And what's more," he went on with rising intensity, "a damned wrecker of plays. A yea-forsooth knavish pander, by Heaven! I tell you this, and I tell you plainly, if I, sitting in my O.P. box, could have persuaded the Lord to stoop out of the firmament and drop a tidy thunderbolt on Ben, I would have done it with bells on. Joyously!"

"A thunderbolt," Alleyn said, "is one of a few means of dispatch that we have not seriously considered. Would you mind telling me where you were between the time when he made his last exit and the time when you appeared before the audience?"

"Brief let me be. In my box. On the stairs. Off-stage. On the stage."

"Can you tell me exactly when you left your box?"

"While they were making their initial mops and mows at the audience."

"Did you meet anyone or notice anything at all remarkable during this period?"

"Nothing, and nobody whatever."

"From which side did you enter for your own call?"

"The O.P., which is actors' right."

"So you merely emerged from the stairs that lead from the box to the stage and found yourself hard by the entrance?"

"Precisely."

"Have you any witness to all this, sir?"

"To my knowledge," said the Doctor, "none whatever. There may have been a rude mechanical or so."

"As far as your presence in the box is concerned, there was the audience. Nine hundred of them."

"In spite of its mangling at the hands of two of the actors, I believe the attention of the audience to have been upon My Play. In any case," the Doctor added, helping himself to a particularly large pinch of snuff and holding it poised before his face, "I had shrunk in modest confusion behind the curtain."

"Perhaps someone visited you?"

"Not after the first act. I locked myself in," he added, taking his snuff with uncouth noises, "as a precautionary measure. I loathe company."

"Did you come back-stage at any other time during the performance?"

"I did. I came back in both intervals. Primarily to see the little wench."

"Miss Tarne?" Alleyn ventured.

"She. A tidy little wench it is and will make a good player. If she doesn't allow herself to be debauched by the sissies that rule the roost in our lamentable theatre."

"Did you, during either of these intervals, visit the dressing-rooms?"

"I went to the Usual Office at the end of the passage, if you call that a dressing-room."

"And returned to your box—when?"

"As soon as the curtain went up."

"I see." Alleyn thought for a moment and then said: "Dr. Rutherford, do you know anything about a man called Otto Brod?"

The Doctor gave a formidable gasp. His eyes bulged, his nostrils wrinkled and his jaw dropped. This grimace turned out to be the preliminary spasm to a Gargantuan sneeze. A handkerchief not being at his disposal, he snatched up the tail of his shirt, clapped it to his face and revealed a state of astonishing disorder below the waist.

"Otto Brod?" he repeated, looking at Alleyn over his shirt-tail as if it were an improvised yashmak. "Never heard of him."

"His correspondence seems to be of some value," Alleyn said vaguely but the Doctor merely gaped at him. "I don't," he said flatly, "know what you're talking about."

Alleyn gave up Otto Brod. "You'll have guessed," he said, "that I've already heard a good deal about the events of the last few days: I mean as they concerned the final rehearsals and the change in casting."

"Indeed? Then you will have heard that Ben and I had one flaming row after another. If you're looking for motive," said Dr. Rutherford with an expansive gesture, "I'm lousy with it. We hated each other's guts, Ben and I. Of the two I should say, however, that he was the more murderously inclined."

"Was this feeling chiefly on account of the part his niece was to have played?"

"Fundamentally it was the fine flower of a natural antipathy. The contributive elements were his behaviour as an actor in My Play and the obvious and immediate necessity to return his niece to her squalid little *métier* and replace her by the wench. We had at each other on that issue," said Dr. Rutherford with relish, "after both auditions and on every other occasion that presented itself."

"And in the end, it seems, you won?"

"Pah!" said the Doctor with a dismissive wave of his hand. "Cat's meat!"

Alleyn looked a little dubiously at the chaotic disarray of his garments. "Have you any objection," he asked, "to being searched?"

"Not I," cried the Doctor and hauled himself up from his chair. Fox approached him.

"By the way," Alleyn said, "as a medical man, would you say that a punch on the jaw such as Bennington was given could have been the cause of his fainting some time afterwards? Remembering his general condition?"

"Who says he had a punch on the jaw? It's probably a hypostatic discolouration. What do *you* want?" Dr. Rutherford demanded of Fox.

"If you wouldn't mind taking your hands out of your pockets, sir," Fox suggested.

The Doctor said: "Let not us that are squires of the night's body be called thieves of the day's beauty," and obligingly withdrew his hands from his trousers pockets. Unfortunately he pulled the linings out of them.

A number of objects fell about his feet—pencils, his snuff-box, scraps of paper, a pill-box, a programme, a note-book and a half-eaten cake of chocolate. A small cloud of snuff floated above this collection. Fox bent down and made a clucking sound of disapproval. He began to collect the scattered objects, inhaled snuff and was seized with a paroxysm of sneezing. The Doctor broke into a fit of uncouth laughter and floundered damagingly among the exhibits.

"Dr. Rutherford," Alleyn said with an air of the liveliest exasperation, "I

would be immensely obliged to you if you'd have the goodness to stop behaving like a Pantaloon. Get off those things, if you please."

The Doctor backed away into his chair and examined an unlovely mess of
chocolate and cardboard on the sole of his boot. "But, blast your lights, my
good ass," he said, "there goes my spare ration. An ounce of the best rappee,
by Heaven!" Fox began to pick the fragments of the pill-box from his boot.
Having collected and laid aside the dropped possessions, he scraped up a
heap of snuff. "It's no good now, Dogberry," said the Doctor with an air of
intense disapproval. Fox tipped the scrapings into an envelope.

Alleyn stood over the Doctor. "I think," he said, "you had better give this
up, you know."

The Doctor favoured him with an antic grimace but said nothing. "You're
putting on an act, Dr. Rutherford, and I do assure you it's not at all convincing. As a red herring it stinks to high Heaven. Let me tell you this. We
now know that Bennington was hit over the jaw. We know when it happened. We know that the bruise was afterwards camouflaged with make-up.
I want you to come with me while I remove this make-up. Where's your
jacket?"

"Give me my robe; put on my crown; I have immortal longings in me . . ."

Fox went out and returned with a tail-coat that was in great disorder.
"Nothing in the pockets, Mr. Alleyn," he said briefly. Alleyn nodded and he
handed it to Dr. Rutherford, who slung it over his shoulder.

Alleyn led the way down the passage, where Gibson was still on guard,
and round the back of the stage to the dock. P. C. Lamprey came off the set
and rolled the doors back.

Bennington had stiffened a little since they last looked at him. His face
bore the expression of knowledgeable acquiescence that is so often seen in
the dead. Using the back of a knife-blade, Alleyn scraped away the greasepaint fom the right jaw. Fox held a piece of card for him and he laid
smears of greasepaint on it in the manner of a painter setting his palette.
The discoloured mark on the jaw showed clearly.

"There it is," Alleyn said, and stood aside for Dr. Rutherford.

"A tidy buffet, if buffet it was. Who gave it him?"

Alleyn didn't answer. He moved round to the other side and went on cleaning the face.

"The notion that it could have contributed to his death," the Doctor said,
"is preposterous. If, as you say, there was an interval between the blow and
the supposed collapse. Preposterous!"

Fox had brought cream and a towel, with which Alleyn now completed
his task. The Doctor watched him with an air of impatience and unease.
"Damned if I know why you keep me hanging about," he grumbled at last.

"I wanted your opinion on the bruise. That's all, Fox. Is the mortuary van
here?"

"On its way, sir," said Fox, who was wrapping his piece of card in paper.

Alleyn looked at the Doctor. "Do you think," he said, "that his wife will want to see him?"

"She won't want to. She may think she ought to. Humbug, in my opinion. Distress herself for nothing. What good does it do anybody?"

"I think, however, I should at least ask her."

"Why the blazes you can't let her go home passes my comprehension. And where do *I* go, now? I'm getting damn bored with Ben's company."

"You may wait either on the stage or, if you'd rather, in the unoccupied dressing-room. Or the office, I think, is open."

"Can I have my snuff back?" Dr. Rutherford asked with something of the shamefaced air of a small boy wanting a favour.

"I think we might let you do that," Alleyn said. "Fox, will you give Dr. Rutherford his snuff-box?"

Dr. Rutherford lumbered uncertainly to the door. He stood there with his chin on his chest and his hands in his pockets.

"See here, Alleyn," he said, looking from under his eyebrows at him. "Suppose I told you it was I who gave Ben that wallop on his mug. What then?"

"Why," Alleyn said, "I shouldn't believe you, you know."

CHAPTER X

Summing Up

Alleyn saw Helena Hamilton in her dressing-room. It was an oddly exotic setting. The scent of banked flowers, of tobacco smoke and of cosmetics was exceedingly heavy, the air hot and exhausted. She had changed into her street-clothes and sat in an armchair that had been turned with its back to the door, so that when he entered he saw nothing of her but her right hand trailing near the floor with a cigarette between her fingers. She called: "Come in, Mr. Alleyn," in a warm voice as if he were an especially welcome visitor. He would not have guessed from this greeting that when he faced her he would find her looking so desperately tired.

As if she read his thoughts she put her hands to her eyes and said: "My goodness, this is a long night, isn't it?"

"I hope that for you, at least, it is nearing its end," he said. "I've come to tell you that we are ready to take him away."

"Does that mean I ought to—to look at him?"

"Only if you feel you want to. I can see no absolute need at all, if I may say so."

"I don't want to," she whispered and added in a stronger voice: "It would be a pretence. I have no real sorrow and I have never seen the dead. I should only be frightened and confused."

Alleyn went to the door and looked into the passage, where Fox waited with Gibson. He shook his head and Fox went away. When Alleyn came back to her she looked up at him and said: "What else?"

"A question or two. Have you ever known or heard of a man called Otto Brod?"

Her eyes widened. "But what a strange question!" she said. "Otto Brod? Yes. He's a Czech or an Austrian, I don't remember which. An intellectual. We met him three years ago when we did a tour of the continent. He had written a play and asked my husband to read it. It was in German and Ben's German wasn't up to it. The idea was that he should get someone over here to look at it, but he was dreadfully bad at keeping those sorts of promises and I don't think he ever did anything about it."

"Have they kept in touch, do you know?"

"Oddly enough, Ben said a few days ago that he'd heard from Otto. I think he'd written from time to time for news of his play but I don't suppose Ben answered." She pressed her thumb and fingers on her eyes. "If you want to see the letter," she said, "it's in his coat."

Alleyn said carefully: "You mean the jacket he wore to the theatre? Or his overcoat?"

"The jacket. He was always taking my cigarette case in mistake for his own. He took it out of his breast-pocket when he was leaving for the theatre and the letter was with it." She waited for a moment and then said: "He was rather odd about it."

"In what way?" Alleyn asked. She had used Martyn's very phrase, and now when she spoke again it was with the uncanny precision of a delayed echo: "He was rather strange in his manner. He held the letter out with the cigarette case and drew my attention to it. He said, I think: 'That's my trump card.' He seemed to be pleased in a not very attractive way. I took my case. He put the letter back in his pocket and went straight out."

"Did you get the impression he meant it was a trump card he could use against somebody?"

"Yes. I think I did."

"And did you form any idea who that person could be?"

She leant forward and cupped her face in her hands. "Oh yes," she said. "It seemed to me that it was I myself he meant. Or Adam. Or both of us. It sounded like a threat." She looked up at Alleyn. "We've both got alibis, haven't we? If it was murder."

"*You* have, undoubtedly," Alleyn said, and she looked frightened.

He asked her why she thought her husband had meant that the letter was a threat to herself or to Poole but she evaded this question, saying vaguely that she had felt it to be so.

"You didn't come down to the theatre with your husband?" Alleyn said.

"No. He was ready before I was. And in any case—" She made a slight expressive gesture and didn't complete her sentence. Alleyn said: "I think I must tell you that I know something of what happened during the afternoon."

The colour that flooded her face ebbed painfully and left it very white. She said: "How do you know that? You can't know." She stopped and seemed to listen. They could just hear Poole in the next room. He sounded as if he was moving about irresolutely. She caught her breath and after a moment she said loudly: "Was it Jacko? No, no, it was never Jacko."

"Your husband himself—" Alleyn began and she caught him up quickly. "Ben? Ah, I can believe that. I can believe he would boast of it. To one of the men. To J.G.? Was it J.G.? Or perhaps even to Gay?"

Alleyn said gently: "You must know I can't answer questions like these."

"It was never Jacko," she repeated positively and he said: "I haven't interviewed Mr. Doré yet."

"Haven't you? Good."

"Did you like Otto Brod?"

She smiled slightly and lifted herself in her chair. Her face became secret and brilliant. "For a little while," she said, "he was a fortunate man."

"Fortunate?"

"For a little while I loved him."

"Fortunate indeed," said Alleyn.

"You put that very civilly, Mr. Alleyn."

"Do you think there was some connection here? I mean between your relationship with Brod and the apparent threat when your husband showed you the letter?"

She shook her head. "I don't know. I don't think Ben realized. It was as brief as summer lightning, our affair."

"On both parts?"

"Oh no," she said, as if he had asked a foolish question. "Otto was very young, rather violent and dreadfully faithful, poor sweet. You are looking at me in an equivocal manner, Mr. Alleyn. Do you disapprove?"

Alleyn said formally: "Let us say that I am quite out of my depth with—"

"Why do you hesitate? With what?"

"I was going to say with a *femme fatale*," said Alleyn.

"Have I been complimented again?"

He didn't answer and after a moment she turned away as if she suddenly lost heart in some unguessed-at object she had had in mind.

"I suppose," she said, "I may not ask you why you believe Ben was murdered?"

"I think you may. For one reason: his last act in the dressing-room was not consistent with suicide. He refurbished his make-up."

"That's penetrating of you," she said. "It was an unsympathetic make-up. But I still believe he killed himself. He had much to regret and nothing in the wide world to look forward to. Except discomfiture."

"The performance to-night, among other things, to regret?"

"Among all the other things. The change in casting, for one. It must have upset him very much. Because yesterday he thought he'd stopped what he called John's nonsense about Gay. And there was his own behaviour, his hopeless, *hopeless* degradation. He had given up, Mr. Alleyn. Believe me, he had quite given up. You will find I'm right, I promise you."

"I wish I may," Alleyn said. "And I think that's all at the moment. If you'll excuse me, I'll get on with my job."

"Get on with it, then," she said and looked amused. She watched him go and he wondered after he'd shut the door if her expression had changed.

ii

Adam Poole greeted Alleyn with a sort of controlled impatience. He had changed and was on his feet. Apparently Alleyn had interrupted an aimless promenade about the room.

"Well?" he said. "Are you any further on? Or am I not supposed to ask?"

"A good deal further, I think," Alleyn said. "I want a word with you, if I may have it, and then with Mr. Doré. I shall then have something to say to all of you. After that I think we shall know where we are."

"And you're convinced, are you, that Bennington was murdered?"

"Yes, I'm quite convinced of that."

"I wish to God I knew why."

"I'll tell you," Alleyn said, "before the night is out."

Poole faced him. "I can't believe it," he said, "of any of us. It's quite incredible." He looked at the wall between his own room and Helena's. "I could hear your voices in there," he said. "Is she all right?"

"She's perfectly composed."

"I don't know why you wanted to talk to her at all."

"I had three things to say to Miss Hamilton. I asked her if she wanted to see her husband before he was taken away. She didn't want to do so. Then I told her that I knew about an event of yesterday afternoon."

"What event?" Poole demanded sharply.

"I mean an encounter between her husband and herself."

"How the hell did you hear about that?"

"You knew of it yourself, evidently."

Poole said: "Yes, all right. I knew," and then, as if the notion had just come to him and filled him with astonishment, he exclaimed: "Good God, I believe you think it's a motive for *me!*" He thrust his hand through his hair. "That's about as ironical an idea as one could possibly imagine." He stared at Alleyn. An onlooker coming into the room at that moment would have thought that the two men had something in common and a liking for each other. "You can't imagine," Poole said, "how inappropriate *that* idea is."

"I haven't yet said I entertain it, you know."

"It's not surprising if you do. After all, I suppose I could, fantastically, have galloped from the stage to Ben's room, laid him out, turned the gas on and doubled back in time to re-enter! Do you know what my line of re-entry is in the play?"

"No."

"I come in, shut the door, go up to Helena, and say: 'You've guessed, haven't you? He's taken the only way out. I suppose we must be said to be free.' It all seems to fit so very neatly, doesn't it? Except that for us it's a year or more out of date." He looked at Alleyn. "I really don't know," he added, "why I'm talking like this. It's probably most injudicious. But I've had a good deal to think about the last two days and Ben's death has more or less put the crown on it. What am I to do about this theatre? What are we to do about the show? What's going to happen about—" He broke off and looked at the wall that separated his room from Martyn's. "Look here, Alleyn," he said. "You've no doubt heard all there is to hear, and more, about my private life. And Helena's. It's the curse of this job that one is perpetually in the spotlight."

He seemed to expect some comment on this. Alleyn said lightly: "The curse of greatness?"

"Nothing like it, I'm afraid. See here, Alleyn. There are some women who just can't be fitted into any kind of ethical or sociological pigeon-hole. Ellen Terry was one of them. It's not that they are above reproach in the sense most people mean by the phrase, but that they are outside it. They behave naturally in an artificial set-up. When an attachment comes to an end, it does so without any regrets or recrimination. Often, with an abiding affection on both sides. Do you agree?"

"That there are such women? Yes."

"Helena is one. I'm not doing this very well but I do want you to believe that she's right outside this beastly thing. It won't get you any further and it may hurt her profoundly if you try to establish some link between her relationship with her husband or anyone else and the circumstances of his death. I don't know what you said to each other, but I do know it would never occur to her to be on guard for her own sake."

"I asked her to tell me about Otto Brod."

Poole's reaction to this was surprising. He looked exasperated. "There you are!" he said. "That's exactly what I mean. Otto Brod! A fantastic irresponsible affair that floated out of some midsummer notion of Vienna and Strauss waltzes. How the devil you heard of it I don't know, though I've no doubt that at the time she fluttered him like a plume in her bonnet for all to see. I never met him but I understand he was some young intellectual with a pale face, no money and an over-developed faculty for symbolic tragedy. Why bring him in?"

Alleyn told him that Bennington, when he came down to the theatre, had had a letter from Brod in his pocket and Poole said angrily: "Why the hell shouldn't he? What of it?"

"The letter is not to be found."

"My dear chap, I suppose he chucked it out or burnt it or something."

"I hardly think so," said Alleyn. "He told Miss Hamilton it was his trump card."

Poole was completely still for some moments. Then he turned away to the dressing-shelf and looked for his cigarettes.

"Now what in the wide world," he said with his back to Alleyn, "could he have meant by a trump card?"

"That," said Alleyn, "is what, above everything else, I should very much like to know."

"I don't suppose it means a damn thing, after all. It certainly doesn't to me."

He turned to offer his cigarettes but found that Alleyn had his own case open in his hands. "I'd ask you to have a drink," Poole said, "but I don't keep it in the dressing-room during the show. If you'd come to the office—"

"Nothing I'd like more but we don't have it in the working hours either."

"Of course not. Stupid of me." Poole glanced at his dress for the ball and then at his watch. "I hope," he said, "that my business manager is enjoying himself with my guests at my party."

"He rang up some time ago to enquire. There was no message for you."

"Thank you." Poole leant against the dressing-shelf and lit his cigarette.

"It seems to me," Alleyn said, "that there is something you want to say to me. I've not brought a witness in here. If what you say is likely to be wanted as evidence I'll ask you to repeat it formally. If not, it will have no official significance."

"You're very perceptive. I'm damned if I know why I should want to tell you this, but I do. Just out of earshot behind these two walls are two women. Of my relation with the one, you seem to have heard. I imagine it's pretty generally known. I've tried to suggest that it has come to its end as simply, if that's not too fancy a way of putting it, as a flower relinquishes its petals. For a time I've pretended their colour had not faded and I've watched them fall with regret. But from the beginning we both knew it was that sort of affair. She didn't pretend at all. She's quite above any of the usual subterfuges and it's some weeks ago that she let me know it was almost over for her. I think we both kept it up out of politeness more than anything else. When she told me of Ben's unspeakable behaviour yesterday, I felt as one must feel about an outrage to a woman whom one knows very well and likes very much. I was appalled to discover in myself no stronger emotion than this. It was precisely this discovery that told me the last petal had indeed fallen and now—" He lifted his hands. "Now Ben gets himself murdered, you say, and I've run out of the appropriate emotions."

Alleyn said: "We are creatures of convention and like our tragedies to take a recognizable form."

"I'm afraid this is not even a tragedy. Unless—" He turned his head and looked at the other wall. "I haven't seen Martyn," he said, "since you spoke to her. She's all right, isn't she?" Before Alleyn could answer he went on:

"I suppose she's told you about herself—her arrival out of a clear sky and all the rest of it?"

"Everything, I think."

"I hope to God— I want to see her, Alleyn. She's alone in there. She may be frightened. I don't suppose you understand."

"She's told me of the relationship between you."

"The *relationship!*" he said quickly. "You mean—"

"She's told me you are related. It's natural that you should be concerned about her."

Poole stared at him. "My good ass," he said, "I'm nineteen years her senior and I love her like a boy of her own age."

"In that case," Alleyn remarked, "you can *not* be said to have run out of the appropriate emotions."

He grinned at Poole in a friendly manner and, accompanied by Fox, went to his final interview—with Jacques Doré.

iii

It took place on the stage. Dr. Rutherford had elected to retire into the office to effect, he had told Fox, a few paltry adjustments of his costume. The players, too, were all in their several rooms and Clem Smith had been wakened, re-examined by Fox, and allowed to go home.

So Jacko was alone in the tortured scene he had himself designed.

He looked a frightful scarecrow in his working clothes, with grey stubble on his chin, grey bags under his eyes and grey fuzz standing up on his head. His long crepe-y neck stuck out of the open collar of his tartan shirt. His eyes were bloodshot and his delicate hands were filthy.

"I have slept," he announced, rising from the heap of old curtains which Clem had transformed into a bed, "like the Holy Innocents, though it is possible that I do not resemble any of them. However deceptive the outward man may be, gentlemen, the inner is entirely at your service." He smiled ingratiatingly at them. His lips curled back and exposed teeth like a row of yellow pegs in a dice box. "What do we talk about?" he asked, and began to roll himself a cigarette.

"First of all," Alleyn said, "I must tell you that I am asking for a general search through the clothes that have been worn in the theatre. We have no warrant at this stage but so far no one has objected."

"Then who am I to do so?"

Fox went through his pockets and found a number of curious objects—chalk, pencils, a rubber, a surgeon's scalpel which Jacko said he used for wood carving, and which was protected by a sheath, a pocket-book with money, a photograph of Helena Hamilton, various scraps of paper with drawings on them, pieces of cotton-wool and an empty bottle smelling strongly of ether. This, he told Alleyn, had contained a fluid used for cleaning purposes. "Always they are messing themselves and always I am removing the mess. My overcoat is in the junk room. It contains merely a filthy handkerchief, I believe."

Alleyn thanked him and returned the scalpel, the pocket-book and drawing materials. Fox laid the other things aside, sat down and opened his note-book.

"Next," Alleyn said, "I think I'd better ask you what your official job is in this theatre. I see by the programme—"

"The programme," Jacko said, "is euphemistic. 'Assistant to Adam Poole,' is it not? Let us rather say: Dogsbody in Ordinary to the Vulcan Theatre. Henchman Extraordinary to Mr. Adam Poole. At the moment, dresser to Miss Helena Hamilton. Confidant to all and sundry. Johannes Factotum and not without bells on. *Le Vulcan, c'est moi*, in a shabby manner of speaking. Also: *j'y suis, j'y reste*. I hope."

"Judging by this scenery," Alleyn rejoined, "and by an enchanting necklace which I think is your work, there shouldn't be much doubt about that. But your association with the management goes farther back than the Vulcan, doesn't it?"

"Twenty years," Jacko said, licking his cigarette paper. "For twenty years I improvise my role of Pantaloon for them. Foolishness, but such is my deplorable type. The eternal doormat. What can I do for you?"

Alleyn said: "You can tell me if you still think Bennington committed suicide."

Jacko lit his cigarette. "Certainly," he said. "You are wasting your time."

"Was he a vain man?"

"Immensely. And he knew he was artistically sunk."

"Vain in his looks?"

"But yes, *yes!*" Jacko said with great emphasis, and then looked very sharply at Alleyn. "Why, of his looks?"

"Did he object to his make-up in this play? It seemed to me a particularly repulsive one."

"He disliked it, yes. He exhibited the vanity of the failing actor in this. Always, always he must be sympathetic. Fortunately Adam insisted on the make-up."

"I think you told me that you noticed his face was shining with sweat before he went for the last time to his room?"

"I did."

"And you advised him to remedy this? You even looked into his room to make sure?"

"Yes," Jacko agreed after a pause, "I did."

"So when you had gone he sat at his dressing-table and carefully furbished up his repellent make-up as if for the curtain-call. And then gassed himself?"

"The impulse perhaps came very suddenly." Jacko half-closed his eyes and looked through their sandy lashes at his cigarette smoke. "Ah, yes," he said softly. "Listen. He repairs his face. He has a last look at himself. He is about to get up when his attention sharpens. He continues to stare. He sees the ruin of his face. He was once a coarsely handsome fellow, was Ben, with a bold rakehelly air. The coarseness has increased, but where, he asks himself, are the looks? Pouches, grooves, veins, yellow eyeballs—and all emphasized most hideously by the make-up. This is what he has become, he thinks, he has become the man he has been playing. And his heart descends into his belly. He knows despair and he makes up his mind. There is hardly time to do it. In a minute or two he will be called. So quickly, quickly he lies on the floor, with trembling hands he pulls his coat over his head and puts the end of the gas tube in his mouth."

"You knew how he was found, then?"

"Clem told me. I envisage everything. He enters a world of whirling dreams. And in a little while he is dead. I see it very clearly."

"Almost as if you'd been there," Alleyn said lightly. "Is this, do you argue, his sole motive? What about the quarrels that had been going on? The change of cast at the last moment? The handing over of Miss Gainsford's part to Miss Tarne? He was very much upset by that, wasn't he?"

Jacko doubled himself up like an ungainly animal and squatted on a stool. "Too much has been made of the change of casting," he said. "He accepted it in the end. He made a friendly gesture. On thinking it over I have decided we were all wrong to lay so much emphasis on this controversy." He peered sideways at Alleyn. "It was the disintegration of his artistic integrity that did it," he said. "I now consider the change of casting to be of no significance."

Alleyn looked him very hard in the eye. "And that," he said, "is where we disagree. I consider it to be of the most complete significance: the key, in fact, to the whole puzzle of his death."

"I cannot agree," said Jacko. "I am sorry."

Alleyn waited for a moment and then—and for the last time—asked the now familiar question.

"Do you know anything about a man called Otto Brod?"

There was a long silence. Jacko's back was bent and his head almost between his knees.

"I have heard of him," he said at last.

"Did you know him?"

"I have never met him. Never."

"Perhaps you have seen some of his work?"

Jacko was silent.

"*Können Sie Deutsch lesen?*"

Fox looked up from his notes with an expression of blank surprise. They heard a car turn in from Carpet Street and come up the side lane with a chime of bells. It stopped and a door slammed.

"*Jawohl,*" Jacko whispered.

The outside doors of the dock were rolled back. The sound resembled stage-thunder. Then the inner and nearer doors opened heavily and someone walked round the back of the set. Young Lamprey came through the Prompt entrance. "The mortuary van, sir," he said.

"All right. They can go ahead."

He went out again. There was a sound of voices and of boots on concrete. A cold draught of night air blew in from the dock and set the borders creaking. A rope tapped against canvas and a sighing breath wandered about the grid. The doors were rolled together. The engine started up and, to another chime of bells, Bennington made his final exit from the Vulcan. The theatre settled back into its night-watch.

Jacko's cigarette had burnt his lip. He spat it out and got slowly to his feet.

"You have been very clever," he said. He spoke as if his lips were stiff with cold.

"Did Bennington tell you how he would, if necessary, play his trump card?"

"Not until after he had decided to play it."

"But you had recognized the possibility?"

"Yes."

Alleyn nodded to Fox, who shut his note-book, removed his spectacles and went out.

"What now?" Jacko asked.

"All on," Alleyn said. "A company call. This is the curtain speech, Mr. Doré."

iv

Lamprey had called them and then retired. They found an empty stage awaiting them. It was from force of habit, Martyn supposed, that they took up, for the last time, their after-rehearsal positions on the stage. Helena lay back in her deep chair with Jacko on the floor at her feet. When he settled himself there, she touched his cheek and he turned his lips to her hand. Martyn wondered if he was ill. He saw that she looked at him and made his clown's grimace. She supposed that, like everybody else, he was merely exhausted. Darcey and Gay Gainsford sat together on the small settee and Parry Percival on his upright chair behind them. At the back, Dr. Rutherford lay on the sofa with a newspaper spread over his face. Martyn had returned to her old seat near the Prompt corner and Poole to his central chair facing the group. "We have come out of our rooms," Martyn thought, "like rabbits from their burrows." Through the Prompt entrance she could see Fred Badger, lurking anxiously in the shadows.

Alleyn and his subordinates stood in a group near the dock-doors. On the wall close by them was the baize rack with criss-crossed tapes in which two receipts and a number of commercial cards were exhibited. Fox had read them all. He now replaced the last and looked through the Prompt corner to the stage.

"Are they all on?" Alleyn asked.

"All present and correct, sir."

"Do you think I'm taking a very risky line, Br'er Fox?"

"Well, sir," said Fox uneasily, "it's a very unusual sort of procedure, isn't it?"

"It's a very unusual case," Alleyn rejoined, and after a moment's reflection he took Fox by the arm. "Come on, old trooper," he said. "Let's get it over."

He walked onto the stage almost as if, like Poole, he were going to sum up a rehearsal. Fox went to his old chair near the back entrance. Martyn heard the other men move round behind the set. They took up positions, she thought, outside the entrances and it was unpleasant to think of them waiting there, unseen.

Alleyn stood with his back to the curtain and Poole at once slewed his chair round to face him. With the exception of Jacko, who was rolling a cigarette, they all watched Alleyn. Even the Doctor removed his newspaper, sat up, stared, groaned and returned ostentatiously to his former position.

For a moment Alleyn looked round the group, and to Martyn he seemed to have an air of compassion. When he began to speak his manner was informal but extremely deliberate.

"In asking you to come here together," he said, "I've taken an unorthodox line. I don't myself know whether I am justified in taking it, and I shan't know until those of you who are free to do so have gone home. That will be in a few minutes, I think.

"I have to tell you that your fellow-player has been murdered. All of you must know that we've formed this opinion, and I think most of you know that I was first inclined to it by the circumstance of his behaviour on returning to his dressing-room. His last conscious act was to repair his stage make-up. While that seemed to me to be inconsistent with suicide, it was, on the other hand, much too slender a thread to tie up a case for homicide. But there is more conclusive evidence and I'm going to put it before you. He powdered his face. His dresser had already removed the pieces of cotton-wool that had been used earlier in the evening and put out a fresh pad. Yet after his death there was no used pad of cotton-wool anywhere in the room. There is, on the other hand, a fresh stain near the gas fire which may, on analysis, turn out to have been caused by such a pad having been burnt on the hearth. The box of powder has been overturned on the shelf and there is a deposit of powder all over that corner of the room. As you know, his head and shoulders were covered, tent-wise, with his overcoat. There was powder on this coat and over his finger-prints on the top of the gas fire. The coat had hung near the door and would, while it was there, have been out of range of any powder flying about. The powder, it is clear, had been scattered after and not before he was gassed. If he was, in fact, gassed."

Poole and Darcey made simultaneous ejaculations. Helena and Gay looked bewildered, and Percival incredulous. Jacko stared at the floor and the Doctor groaned under his newspaper.

"The post mortem," Alleyn said, "will of course settle this one way or the other. It will be exhaustive. Now, it's quite certain that the dresser didn't go into the room after Mr. Bennington entered it this last time, and it is equally certain that the dresser left it in good order—the powder-pad prepared, the clothes hung up, the fire burning and the door unlocked. It is also certain that the powder was not overturned by the men who carried Mr. Bennington out. It was spilt by someone who was in the room after he was on the floor with the coat over his head. This person, the police will maintain, was his murderer. Now the question arises, doesn't it, how it came about that he was in such a condition—comatose or unconscious—that it was possible to get him down on the floor, put out the gas fire, and then disengage the connecting tube, put the rubber end in his mouth and turn the gas on again, get his finger-prints on the wing-tap and cover him with his own overcoat. There is still about one-sixth of brandy left in his flask. He was not too drunk to make up his own face and he was more or less his own man, though not completely so, when he spoke to Miss Tarne just before he went into his room. During the second interval Mr. Darcey hit him on the jaw and raised a bruise. I suppose it is possible that his murderer hit him again on the same spot—there is no other bruise—and knocked him out. A closer examination of the bruise may show if this was so. In that case the murderer would need to pay only one visit to the room: he would simply walk in a few minutes before the final curtain, knock his victim out and set the stage for apparent suicide.

"On the other hand, it's possible that he was drugged."

He waited for a moment. Helena Hamilton said: "I don't believe in all this. I don't mean, Mr. Alleyn, that I think you're wrong: I mean it just sounds unreal and rather commonplace like a case reported in a newspaper. One knows that probably it's all happened but one doesn't actively believe it. I'm sorry. I interrupted."

"I hope," Alleyn said, "you will all feel perfectly free to interrupt at any point. About this possibility of drugging. If the brandy was drugged, then of course we shall find out. Moreover, it must have been tinkered with after he went on for his final scene. Indeed, any use of a drug, and one cannot disregard the possibility of even the most fantastic methods, must surely have been prepared while he was on the stage during the last act. We shall, of course, have a chemical analysis made of everything he used—the brandy, his tumbler, his cigarettes, his make-ups and even the greasepaint on his face. I tell you, quite frankly, that I've no idea at all whether this will get us any further."

Fox cleared his throat. This modest sound drew the attention of the company upon him but he merely looked gravely preoccupied and they turned back to Alleyn.

"Following out this line of thought, it seems clear," he said, "that two visits would have to be made to the dressing-room. The first, during his scene in the last act, and the second, after he had come off and before the smell of gas was first noticed—by Mr. Parry Percival."

Percival said in a high voice: "I knew this was coming." Gay Gainsford turned and looked at him with an expression of the liveliest horror. He caught her eye and said: "Oh, don't be fantastic, Gay darling. *Honestly!*"

"Mr. Percival," Alleyn said, "whose room is next to Mr. Bennington's and whose fire backs on his, noticed a smell of gas when he was about to go out for the curtain-call. He tells us he is particularly sensitive to the smell because of its associations in this theatre and that he turned his own fire off and went out. Thus his finger-prints were found on the tap."

"Well, naturally they were," Parry said angrily. "Really, Gay!"

"This, of course," Alleyn went on, "was reminiscent of the Jupiter case, but in that case the tube was not disconnected because the murderer never entered the room. He blew down the next-door tube and the fire went out. In that instance the victim was comatose from alcohol. Now, it seems quite clear to us that while this thing was planned with one eye on the Jupiter case, there was no intention to throw the blame upon anyone else and that Mr. Percival's reaction to the smell was not foreseen by the planner. What the planner hoped to emphasize was Mr. Bennington's absorption in the former case. We were to suppose that when he decided to take his own life he used the method by which he was obsessed. Suppose this to have been so. Wouldn't we, remembering the former case, suspect that it was not suicide at all and look for what my colleague likes to call funny business? On the other hand . . ." Alleyn paused. Percival, who was obviously lost in his sense of release, and Gay Gainsford, who equally obviously was in a high state of confusion, both seemed to pull themselves together.

"On the other hand," Alleyn repeated, "suppose this hypothetical planner was none other than Bennington himself?"

v

Their response to this statement had a delayed action. They behaved as actors do when they make what is technically known as a "double take." There were a few seconds of blank witlessness followed by a sudden and violent reaction. Darcey and Percival shouted together that it would be exactly like Ben, Helena cried out inarticulately and Poole gave a violent ejaculation. The Doctor crackled his newspaper and Martyn's thoughts tumbled about in her head like dice. Jacko alone stared incredulously at Alleyn.

"Do you mean," Jacko asked, "that we are to understand that Ben killed himself in such a way as to throw suspicion of murder upon one of us? Is that your meaning?"

"No. For a time we wondered if this might be so, but the state of the dressing-room, as I'd hoped I'd made clear, flatly contradicts any such theory. No. I believe the planner based the method on Bennington's preoccupation with the other case and hoped we would be led to some such conclusion. If powder had not been spilt on the overcoat we might well have done so."

"So we are still—in the dark," Helena said, and gave the commonplace phrase a most sombre colour.

"Not altogether. I needn't go over the collection of near-motives that have cropped up in the course of our interviews. Some of them sound far-fetched, others at least possible. It's not generally recognized that, given a certain temperament, the motive for homicide can be astonishingly unconvincing. Men have been killed from petty covetousness, out of fright, vanity, jealousy, boredom or sheer hatred. One or other of these motives lies at the back of this case. You all, I think, had cause to dislike this man. In one of you the cause was wedded to that particular kink which distinguishes murderers from the rest of mankind. With such beings there is usually some, shall I say, explosive agency—a sort of fuse—which, if it is touched off, sets them going as murder-machines. In this case I believe the fuse to have been a letter written by Otto Brod to Clark Bennington. This letter has disappeared and was probably burnt in his dressing-room. As the powder-pad may have been burnt. By his murderer."

Poole said: "I can't begin to see the sense of all this," and Helena said drearily: "Dark. In the dark."

Alleyn seemed to be lost in thought. Martyn, alone of all the company, looked at him. She thought she had never seen a face as withdrawn and—incongruously the word flashed up again—compassionate. She wondered if he had come to some crucial point and she watched anxiously for the sign of a decision. But at this moment she felt Poole's eyes upon her, and when she looked at him they exchanged the delighted smiles of lovers. "How *can* we," she thought, and tried to feel guilty. But she hadn't heard Alleyn speak and he was half-way through his first sentence before she gave him her attention.

"—so far about opportunity," he was saying. "If there were two visits to the dressing-room during the last act I think probably all of you except Miss Hamilton could have made the earlier one. But for the second visit there is a more restricted field. Shall I take you in the order in which you are sitting? Miss Tarne, in that case, comes first."

Martyn thought: "I ought to feel frightened again."

"Miss Tarne has told us that after she left the stage, and she was the first to leave it, she stood at the entry to the dressing-room passage. She was in a rather bemused state of mind and doesn't remember much about it until Mr. Percival, Mr. Darcey and Mr. Bennington himself came past. All three spoke to her in turn and went on down the passage. It is now that the crucial period begins. Mr. Doré was near by, and after directing the gun-shot took her to her dressing-room. On the way he looked in for a few seconds on Mr. Bennington, who had just gone to his own room. After Miss Tarne and Mr. Doré had both heard Mr. Darcey and Mr. Percival return to the stage, they followed them out. They give each other near-alibis up to this point and the stage-hands extend Miss Tarne's alibi to beyond the crucial time. She is, I think, out of the picture."

Gay Gainsford stared at Martyn. "That," she said, "must be quite a change for you."

"Miss Gainsford comes next," Alleyn said as if he had not heard her. "She was in the Greenroom throughout the crucial period and tells us she was asleep. There is no witness to this."

"George!" said Gay Gainsford wildly and turned to Darcey, thus revealing for the first time his Christian name. "It's all right, dear," he said. "Don't be frightened. It's all right."

"Mr. Darcey and Mr. Percival are also in the list of persons without alibis. They left the stage and returned to it, together, or nearly so. But they went of course to separate rooms. Mr. Percival is the only one who noticed the smell of gas. Dr. Rutherford," Alleyn went on, moving slightly in order to see the Doctor, "could certainly have visited the room during this period, as at any other stage of the performance. He could have come down from his box, passed unobserved round the back of the scenery, taken cover and gone in after these four persons were in their own rooms."

He waited politely, but the Doctor's newspaper rose and fell rhythmically. Alleyn raised his voice slightly. "He could have returned to his O.P. stairs when the rest of you were collected on the Prompt side and he could have made an official entry in the character of Author." He waited for a moment. The others looked in a scandalized manner at the recumbent Doctor but said nothing.

"Mr. Poole has himself pointed out that he could have darted to the room during his brief period off-stage. He could not, in my opinion, have effected all that had to be done, and if he had missed his re-entry he would have drawn immediate attention to himself.

"Mr. Doré is in a somewhat different category from the rest," Alleyn continued. "We know he came away from her dressing-room with Miss Tarne, but although he was seen with the others on the Prompt side, he was at the back of the group and in the shadows. Everyone's attention at this period was riveted on the stage. The call-boy checked over the players for the curtain-call and noticed Mr. Bennington had not yet appeared. Neither he nor anyone else had reason to check Mr. Doré's movements."

Jacko said: "I remind you that Parry said he smelt gas while I was still with Miss Tarne in her room."

"I have remembered," Alleyn answered, "what Mr. Percival said." He looked at Helena Hamilton. "And while all this was happening," he concluded, "Miss Hamilton was on the stage holding the attention of a great cloud of witnesses in what I think must have been a most remarkable play."

There was a long silence.

"That's all I have to say." Alleyn's voice changed its colour a little. "I'm going to ask you to return to your rooms. You'll want to do so in any case to collect your coats and so on. If you would like to talk things over among yourselves you are quite free to do so. We shall be in the Greenroom. If each of you will come in and leave us an address and telephone number

I'll be grateful." He looked round them for a moment. Perhaps deliberately he repeated the stage-manager's customary dismissal: "Thank you, ladies and gentlemen. That will be all."

CHAPTER XI

Last Act

Alleyn stood in front of Adam Poole's portrait and looked at his little group of fellow-policemen.

"Well," he said, "I've done it."

"Very unusual," said Fox.

Bailey and Thompson stared at the floor.

Gibson blew out a long breath and wiped his forehead.

P. C. Lamprey looked as if he would like to speak but knew his place too well. Alleyn caught his eye. "That, Mike," he said, "was an almost flawless example of how an investigating officer is not meant to behave. You will be good enough to forget it."

"Certainly, sir."

"What do you reckon, Mr. Alleyn?" Fox asked. "A confession? Brazen it out? Attempt to escape? Or what?"

"There'll be no escape, Mr. Fox," Gibson said. "We've got the place plastered outside. No cars without supervision within a quarter of a mile and a full description."

"I said 'attempt,' Fred," Mr. Fox pointed out majestically.

"If I've bungled," Alleyn muttered, "I've at least bungled in a big way. A monumental mess."

They looked uneasily at him. Bailey astonished everybody by saying to his boots, with all his customary moroseness: "That'll be the day."

"Don't talk Australian," Mr. Fox chided immediately, but he looked upon Bailey with approval.

A door in the passage opened and shut.

"Here we go," said Alleyn.

A moment later there was a tap at the Greenroom door and Parry Parcival came in. He wore a dark overcoat, a brilliant scarf, yellow gloves and a green hat.

"If I'm still under suspicion," he said, "I'd like to know but I suppose no one will tell me."

Fox said heartily: "I shouldn't worry about that if I were you, sir. If you'd just give me your address and 'phone number. Purely as a reference."

Parry gave them and Lamprey wrote them down.

"Thank you, Mr. Percival," Alleyn said. "Good night." Parry walked to the door. "They all seem to be going home in twos except me," he said. "Which is rather dreary. I hope no one gets coshed for his pains. Considering one of them seems to be a murderer it's not too fantastic a notion, though I suppose you know your own business. Oh well. Good night."

Evidently he collided with Gay Gainsford in the passage. They heard her ejaculation and his fretful apology. She came in followed by Darcey.

"I couldn't face this alone," she said and looked genuinely frightened. "So George brought me."

"Perfectly in order, Miss Gainsford," Fox assured her.

Darcey, whose face was drawn and white, stood near the door. She looked appealingly at him and he came forward and gave their addresses and telephone numbers. His voice sounded old. "I should like to see this lady home," he said and was at once given leave to do so. Alleyn opened the door for them and they went out, arm in arm.

Poole came next. He gave a quick look round the room and addressed himself to Alleyn. "I don't understand all this," he said, "but if any member of my company is to be arrested, I'd rather stay here. I'd like to see Martyn Tarne home—she lives only a few minutes away—but if it's all right with you, I'll come back." He hesitated and then said quickly: "I've spoken to Jacques Doré."

Alleyn waited for a moment. "Yes," he said at last, "I'd be glad if you'd come back."

"Will you see Helena now? She's had about all she can take."

"Yes, of course."

"I'll get her," Poole said and crossed the passage. They heard him call: "Helena?" and in a moment he re-opened the door for her.

She had put a velvet beret on her head and had pulled the fullness forward so that her eyes were shadowed. Her mouth drooped with fatigue but it had been carefully painted. Fox took her address and number.

"Is the car here?" she asked, and Fox said: "Yes, madam, in the yard. The constable will show you out."

"I'll take you, Helena," Poole said. "Or would you rather be alone?"

She turned to Alleyn. "I thought," she said, "that if I'm allowed, I'd rather like to take Jacko. If he's still about. Would you mind telling him? I'll wait in the car."

"There's no one," Alleyn asked, "that you'd like us to send for? Or ring up?"

"No, thank you," she said. "I'd just rather like to have old Jacko."

She gave him her hand. "I believe," she said, "that when I can think at all sensibly about all this, I'll know you've been kind and considerate."

Poole went out with her and Lamprey followed them.

A moment later, Martyn came in.

As she stood at the table and watched Fox write out her address she felt how little she believed in herself here, in this quietly fantastic setting. Fox and his two silent and soberly dressed associates were so incredibly what she had always pictured plain-clothes detectives to be, and Alleyn, on the contrary, so completely unlike. She was much occupied with this notion and almost forgot to give him her message.

"Jacko," she said, "asked me to say his address is the same as mine. I have a room in the house where he lodges." She felt there might be some ambiguity in this statement and was about to amend it when Alleyn asked: "Has Mr. Doré gone?"

"I think he's waiting for Miss Hamilton in her car."

"I see," Alleyn said. "And I believe Mr. Poole is waiting for you. Good-bye, Miss Tarne, and good luck."

Her face broke into a smile. "Thank you *very* much," said Martyn.

Poole's voice called in the passage: "Where are you, Kate?"

She said good night and went out.

Their steps died away down the passage and across the stage. A door slammed and the theatre was silent.

"Come on," said Alleyn.

He led the way round the back of Jacko's set to the Prompt corner.

Only the off-stage working-lights were alive. The stage itself was almost as shadowy as it was when Martyn first set foot on it. A dust-begrimed lamp above the letter-rack cast a yellow light over its surface.

In the centre, conspicuous in its fresh whiteness, was an envelope that had not been there before.

It was addressed in a spidery hand to Chief Detective-Inspector Alleyn.

He took it from the rack. "So he did it this way," he said, and without another word led them onto the stage.

Jacko's twisted stairway rose out of the shadows like a crazy ejaculation. At its base, untenanted chairs faced each other in silent communion. The sofa was in the darkest place of all.

Young Lamprey began to climb the iron steps to the switchboard. The rest used their flash-lamps. Five pencils of light interlaced, hovered and met at their tips on a crumpled newspaper. They advanced upon the sofa as if it housed an enemy, but when Alleyn lifted the newspaper and the five lights enlarged themselves on Dr. Rutherford's face, it was clearly to be seen that he was dead.

ii

The little group of men stood together in the now fully lit stage while Alleyn read the letter. It was written on official theatre paper and headed: "The Office. 1:45 A.M."

DEAR ALLEYN,

I cry you patience if this letter is but disjointedly patched together.

Time presses and I seem to hear the clink of constabular bracelets.

Otto Brod wrote a play which he asked Clark Bennington to read and help him improve. Ben showed it to the two persons of his acquaintance who could read German and had some judgement. I refer to Doré and myself. The play we presented last night was my own free adaptation of Brod's piece made without his consent or knowledge. Base is the slave that pays. In every way mine is an improvement. Was it George Moore who said that the difference between his quotations and those of the next man was that he left out the inverted commas? I am in full agreement with this attitude and so, by the way, was Will Shakespere. Doré, however, is a bourgeois where the arts are in question. He recognized the source, disapproved, but had the grace to remain mum. The British critics, like Doré, would take the uncivilized view and Ben knew it. He suspected the original authorship, wrote to Brod and three days ago got an answer confirming his suspicions. This letter he proposed to use as an instrument of blackmail. I told Ben, which was no more than the truth, that I intended to make things right with Brod, who, if he's not a popinjay, would be well content with the honour done him and the arrangement proposed. Ben would have none of this. He threatened to publish Brod's letter if a certain change was made in the casting. The day before yesterday, under duress, I submitted and no longer pressed for this change. However, owing to Miss G.'s highstrikes, it was, after all, effected. Five minutes before the curtain went up on the first act, Ben informed me, with, ho! such bugs and goblins in my life, that at the final curtain he intended to advance to the footlights and tell the audience I'd pinched the play. Knowing Ben meant business, I acted: in a manner which, it appears, you have rumbled and which will be fully revealed by your analysis of the greasepaint on his unlovely mug.

He powdered his face with pethidine-hydrochloride, an effective analgesic drug now in fashion, of which the maximum therapeutic dose is 100 milligrams. Ben got about 2 grams on his sweaty upper lip. I loaded his prepared powder-pad with pethidine (forgive the nauseating alliteration) while he was on in the last act and burnt the pad when I returned, immediately before the curtain-call. He was then comatose and I doubt if the gassing was necessary. However, I wished to suggest suicide. I overturned his powder-box in opening out his overcoat. My own vestment being habitually besprinkled with snuff was none the worse, but the powder must have settled on his coat after I had covered his head. Unfortunate. I fancy that with unexpected penetration you have in all respects hit on the *modus operandi*. Pity we couldn't share the curtain-call.

It may interest you to know that I have formed the habit of pepping up my snuff with this admirable drug and had provided myself with a princely quantity in the powder form used for dispensing purposes. One never knew which way the cat would jump with Ben. I have been equipped for action since he threatened to use his precious letter. By the way, it would amuse me to know if you first dropped to it when I trampled on my pethidine box in the Greenroom. Dogberry, I perceived, collected the pieces.

My other spare part is secreted in the groove of the sofa. I shall now return to the sofa, listen to your oration and if, as I suspect, it comes close to the facts, will take the necessary and final step. I shall instruct the moronic and repellent Badger to place this letter in the rack if I am still asleep when the party breaks up. Pray do not attempt artificial respiration. I assure you I shall be as dead as a doornail. While I could triumphantly justify my use of Brod's play, I decline the mortification of the inevitable publicity, more particularly as it would reflect upon persons other than myself. If you wish to hang a motive on my closed file you may make it vanity.

Let me conclude with a final quotation from my fellow-plagiarist.

> *And sometimes we are devils to ourselves,*
> *When we will tempt the frailty of our powers,*
> *Presuming on their changeful potency.*

I hear the summons to return. *Moriturus*—to coin, as Miss G. would say, a phrase—*te saluto, Caesar.*

Yours, etc., on the edge of the viewless winds.

JOHN JAMES RUTHERFORD

iii

Alleyn folded the letter and gave it to Fox. He walked back to the sofa and stood looking down at its burden for some time.

"Well, Fox," he said at last, "he diddled us in the end, didn't he?"

"Did he, Mr. Alleyn?" asked Fox woodenly.

Bailey and Thompson moved tactfully off-stage. Young Lamprey came on with a sheet from one of the dressing-rooms. Fox took it and dismissed him with a jerk of his head. When the sheet was decently bestowed, Alleyn and Fox looked at each other.

"Oh, let us yet be merciful!" Alleyn said, and it is uncertain whether this quotation from the Doctor's favourite source was intended as an epitaph or an observation upon police procedure.

Poole switched off his engine outside Jacko's house. Martyn stirred and
he said: "Do you want to go in at once? We haven't said a word to each
other. Are you deadly tired?"

"No more than everybody else but—yes. Aren't you? You must," she said
drowsily, "be so dreadfully puzzled and worried."

"I suppose so. No. Not really. Not now. But you must sleep, Martyn.
Martyn. There, now I've used your Christian name again. Do you know that
I called you Kate because I felt it wasn't time yet, for the other? That
astonished me. In the theatre we be-darling and be-Christian-name each
other at the drop of a hat. But it wouldn't do with you."

He looked down at her. She thought: "I really must rouse myself," but
bodily inertia, linked with a sort of purification of the spirit, flooded
through her and she was still.

"It isn't fair," Poole said, "when your eyelids are so heavy, to ask you if
I've made a mistake. Perhaps to-morrow you will think you dreamed this,
but Martyn, before many more days are out, I shall ask you to marry me. I
do love you so very much."

To Martyn his voice seemed to come from an immensely long way away
but it brought her a feeling of great content and refreshment. It was as if
her spirit burgeoned and flowered into complete happiness. She tried to express something of this but her voice stumbled over a few disjointed words
and she gave it up. She heard him laugh and felt him move away. In a moment he was standing with the door open. He took her keys from her hand.

"Shall I carry you in? I must go back to the theatre."

The cold night air joined with this reminder of their ordeal to awaken her
completely. She got out and waited anxiously beside him while he opened
the house door.

"Is it awful to feel so happy?" she asked. "With such a terror waiting?
Why must you go to the theatre?" And after a moment. "Do you *know*?"

"It's not awful. The terrors are over. Alleyn said I might return. And I
think I do know. There. Good night. Quickly, quickly, my darling heart, good
night and good morning."

He waited until the door shut behind her and then drove back to the
theatre.

The pass-door into the foyer was open and the young policeman stood
beside it.

"Mr. Alleyn is in here, sir," he said.

Poole went in and found Alleyn with his hands in his pockets in front of
the great frame of photographs on their easel.

"I'm afraid I've got news," he said, "that may be a shock to you."

"I don't think so," Poole said. "Jacko spoke to me before I left. He knew about the play: I didn't. And we both thought John's sleep was much too sound."

They stood side by side and looked at the legend over the photographs.

Opening at this theatre
on
THURSDAY, MAY 11TH
THUS TO REVISIT
A New Play
by
JOHN JAMES RUTHERFORD